Charles had no previous knowledge of seduction, nor plan for it now; yet he noted that Meg's nervousness had left her as the port warmed her veins, that her brown eyes grew brilliant, and soft red appeared on her cheekbones. She leaned back against his arm and sighed happily. He began to kiss her. After a moment of shrinking she returned his kisses. Her breath was sweet as violets, her little body yielded to his increasing ardor. Though once she cried out in protest, when he whispered hoarsely, "Don't, Meg, don't, sweetheart, I won't hurt you." She gave a little sob and shut her eyes, then, clasping his neck tight with her arms, she let him do as instinct bade him.

Fawcett Crest Books
by Anya Seton:

AVALON

DEVIL WATER

DRAGONWYCK

FOXFIRE

GREEN DARKNESS

KATHERINE

MY THEODOSIA

THE TURQUOISE

THE WINTHROP WOMAN

Anya Seton

DEVIL WATER

FAWCETT CREST • NEW YORK

DEVIL WATER

Published by Fawcett Crest Books, a unit of CBS Publications,
the Consumer Publishing Division of CBS Inc.,
by arrangement with Houghton Mifflin Company.

ISBN: 0-449-23633-1

Selection of the Literary Guild
Selection of the Reader's Digest Condensed Books

Printed in the United States of America

14   13   12   11   10   9   8   7   6   5

Contents

Maps

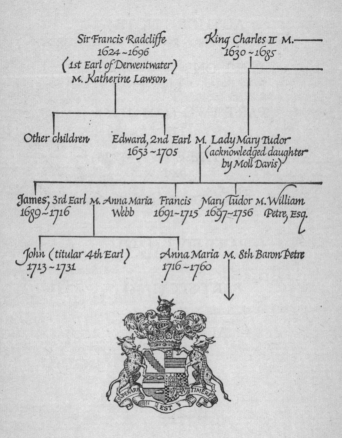

Sir Francis Radcliffe
1624~1696
(1st Earl of Derwentwater)
M. Katherine Lawson

King Charles II M.————
1630~1685

Other children   Edward, 2nd Earl M. Lady Mary Tudor
1653~1705   (acknowledged daughter
by Moll Davis)

James, 3rd Earl M. Anna Maria   Francis   Mary Tudor M. William
1689~1716   Webb   1691~1715   1697~1756   Petre, Esq.

John (titular 4th Earl)   Anna Maria M. 8th Baron Petre
1713~1731   1716~1760

SUPERARE TIMERE EST

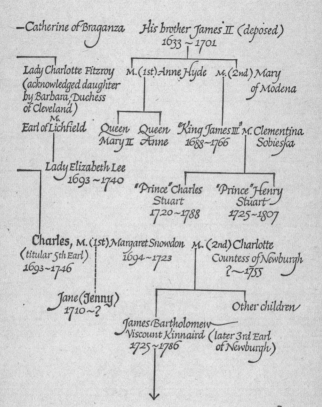

—Catherine of Braganza   His brother James II (deposed)
1633~1701

Lady Charlotte Fitzroy   M. (1st) Anne Hyde   M. (2nd) Mary
(acknowledged daughter   of Modena
by Barbara, Duchess
of Cleveland)
M.
Earl of Lichfield   Queen   Queen   "King James III" M. Clementina
              Mary II   Anne   1688~1766   Sobieska

Lady Elizabeth Lee
1693~1740   "Prince"Charles   "Prince"Henry
                      Stuart   Stuart
                     1720~1788   1725~1807

Charles, M. (1st) Margaret Snowdon   M. (2nd) Charlotte
(titular 5th Earl)   1694~1723   Countess of Newburgh
1693~1746   ?~1755

Jane (Jenny)   Other children
1710~?

James Bartholomew
Viscount Kinnaird (later 3rd Earl
1725~1786   of Newburgh)

AUTHOR'S NOTE

In this biographical novel about England and Virginia in the early eighteenth century, about the two Jacobite rebellions, the Radcliffe family and that of William Byrd of Westover, I have adhered scrupulously to facts, when they can be found. A great deal is known about some of these people at dramatic moments in their lives, and yet a great deal has been lost too. What records there are frequently conflict.

In my "Afterword" I have given my acknowledgments, some of my sources, a limited bibliography, and my reasons for drawing certain conclusions. Several people have suggested that I put this material at the *end* of the book, for the information of those who like such data. Many, however, read only for story—and I hope that they won't be disappointed.

This book developed out of my love for Northumberland, from Tyneside (where my father was born) to the Scottish Border, whence many of my ancestors came. I know the country well, and have many friends and cousins there. I have struggled to indicate the flavor of the varying dialects, without swamping the reader, and may the Northumbrians forgive me for lapses!

My interest in this subject deepened when I found the story included the wild North Country dales, and Tyneside coal pits, as well as London life amongst members of British royalty and society. I was further gripped when the subject led me to Virginia, not only to William Byrd's household and Williamsburg but on to the Piedmont wilderness.

It has taken me four years to do the writing and research

on this book, though the wish to write it has, I think, always been latent—ever since my first years in England as a small child, when I heard the romantic tales current in my father's family. These included our descent from George Seton, the last Earl of Winton. I've found scant proof of that, but in genealogical delvings on the spot I encountered the equally picturesque—and far more convincing—Snowdon story, and its interrelation with Charles Radcliffe. I was fired to try to write about these people, to try, with the help of all the documentation I could discover, to re-create their lives, and it seemed to me that their story included not only dramatic conflicts, but the themes of loyalty, and a "lost cause" as poignant as any of the lost causes with which history is studded.

The lovely burn which still flows by the pathetic ruins of Dilston Castle in Hexhamshire (Northumberland) is today called "Devil's Water." On eighteenth-century maps the possessive is dropped, as it is in my title. The "Devil's Water" is an old simile for fear.

L'eau bénite du diable c'est la peur was a medieval French saying. The Radcliffes were perforce much occupied with various ways of transmuting the "Devil Water" into courage, as their family motto also indicates.

Genealogical charts are provided on pages 6 and 7. Also, there are maps of Northumberland and early Virginia, which accompany the text at appropriate places.

PART ONE

1709—1710

SCOTLAND

Berwick

River Tweed

Berwick upon Tweed

Roxburgh

The Border

CHEVIOT HILLS

Simonside Hills

Tosson

Rothbury

River Aln

Bamburgh

River Coquet

North Sea

Cumberland

Hexham

Corbridge

Dilston

Devil Water

Blanchland

Allenheads

Newcastle

Gateshead

River Tyne

Northumberland

Scale of Miles

0 ——————— 20

IRELAND

SCOTLAND

Berwick

Northumberland

Durham

Lancaster

Preston

North Sea

WALES

ENGLAND

London

Dover

Cornwall

Calais

ENGLAND *and* Northumberland

0   100 Miles

ONE

There was the sound of bitter weeping in the heavy air. Young Charles Radcliffe heard it as he rode down the hill from Dilston Castle towards the Devil Water. Those wild despairing sobs came only from a kitchen wench whose lover —a scurvy Hexham beggar—had four days since stolen a cow from the Dilston byre. The rogue had soon been caught with the cow, hidden in a copse. The castle steward said the thief had protested that his mother was starving—some such tale. But the thief was very properly hanged forthwith. The kitchen wench might think herself lucky that no more had happened to *her* than a good tongue-lashing from Mrs. Busby, the castle housekeeper. And yet the stupid girl, half crazed, they said, wept on and on. "Greeting," they idiotically called weeping up here in their barbarous tongue, which was partly Scottish and partly the English of five hundred years ago, or so said Mr. Brown, the chaplain.

The unseen girl gave a louder wail and the noise aggravated all Charles's pent-up boredom. The dripping mists lifted at last, and he rode aimlessly off in search of amusement.

The stream called Devil Water roared over cascades at the foot of the castle hill. It was in spate this September morning. There had been heavy rain on the moors to swell the burns with rushing brown water. Charles yanked at his mare's bridle when they ambled across the stone bridge. He dismounted and peered down into the torrent wondering if there might be any salmon running—fighting from the Tyne up the rushing stream. If not salmon there would certainly

13

be trout in the black pool beneath the Linnel Rocks.

Charles thought of shouting for a servant to bring his fishing gear, but then decided that the feckless knaves would not hear him up at the castle. Or if they did, would not bother to come. Undisciplined and sullen they were—these Northumbrians—silent when commanded, or muttering among themselves in their gobble-mouthed dialect.

It would be different when James came home from France. He'd beat manners into his servants and tenants. They'd have to obey their feudal lord, albeit they'd never yet seen him. Aye, thought Charles, sighing, nor have I seen him since I was nine. He turned abruptly and mounted his mare, having lost interest in fishing. The mare trotted across the bridge, and downstream towards the mill where the miller's children often fed her apples. Charles let her pick her own way while wondering, not for the first time, nor without uneasiness, about the brother who was soon coming home.

Brother James. The Heir. The most noble Earl of Derwentwater, Viscount Radcliffe and Langley, Baron Tyndale. All that and yet but twenty. Owner too of estates in Northumberland, Cumberland, and other counties, a landed heritage so vast that Sir Marmaduke said there was no other nobleman in England's North could surpass it. James'll be proud as Lucifer, Charles thought, and play the master over me—the frenchified popinjay!

At once Charles felt familiar stabs of envy and guilt. James had not been in France these seven years for trivial reasons. He had been sent there in 1702 to companion his cousin, James Stuart, in exile. "James the Third of England," this cousin should have been now, had not that fat old frump of a Queen Anne proved an unnatural daughter, and allowed the scurvy Protestants to hoist her on the throne. May she rot! Charles thought, but without much heat. During his childhood in London he had never seen Queen Anne. Nor were the long-ago wrongs suffered by the deposed James the Second very real to Charles, despite the occasional harpings of Sir Marmaduke and Cousin Maud. Charles clicked his tongue impatiently as he thought of these two good people who had taken him into their Yorkshire home when his father died four years since. Sir Marmaduke Constable was a wispy, earnest man, cousin to the Radcliffes through his mother. When the second Earl died Sir Marmaduke had been appointed Charles's guardian. Cousin Maud was his faded spinsterish wife, who often lamented the loss of the vocation she had felt as a girl, when many of her friends had professed as nuns in Belgium. But she was a conscientious woman, and anxiously performed all her duties—except the production of an heir to Sir Marmaduke. They were both up at the castle now, fussing over the shabby dusty rooms, empty so many years, worrying over the dilapidations James would find when he came home to claim his patrimony. And doubtless they were irritably asking the housekeeper and the new priest they'd just taken as chaplain, *where* Master Charles could have gone off to in such damp unhealthy weather?

Charles's young face tightened. He rubbed his dirty forefinger tenderly over his chin, feeling the golden prickles which had lately begun to sprout. He straightened his shoulders. They were broad enough for a man's. He felt manhood surging in him, manhood and the need for mastery. But Cousin Maud clucked over him as though he were a child, never letting him forget that he was scarce sixteen and a younger brother. The *youngest* brother—for there was Francis, too, coming back with James from the exiled Court at St. Germain.

Charles slapped his horse's rump and turning the startled mare spurred her to a gallop. Back over the bridge they clattered, up the castle hill and past Dilston village, along the muddy road which led northward to the Tyne. As they entered a gloomy wood the mare snorted and shied.

"Saint Mary! You jade, what ails you!" Charles cried angrily, for he almost lost his seat. Then he saw. From the stout limb of a beech tree there hung a gibbet—an iron cage slowly turning in the wind. In the cage was the chained and bloated corpse of a naked man. The tongue lolled from a black mouth hole, the cut rope still dangled from the livid neck down the matted black curls on the chest. The stench, which the trembling mare had first caught, made Charles retch.

It was the corpse of the thief for whom the kitchen wench was wailing. As the custom was, he had been hanged here where he had been caught.

Charles swallowed and made the sign of the cross. He had seen no dead man before. The chained thing that hung there in the iron gibbet frightened and shamed him. It had been only a lad by the look of the twisted body. And to end like this—inhuman, evil, hanging with no shred of decent covering while the ravens tore off gobbets of flesh and the bones rotted and crumbled throughout the years.

A peculiar feeling came over Charles as he tried to look away and could not, and he thought of the kitchen wench.

He did not recognize the sensation as pity, but he muttered, "I'll make them cut it down. She can bury it properly."

In voicing this resolve he lost it, knowing what Sir Marmaduke and the steward would say. These were wild lawless parts up near the Border. Thievery must be punished at once. The thing in the gibbet hung there as a deterrent. And the lad—not a Catholic of course—had been damned anyway. To brood over the disgusting sight had in it something of the mollycoddle, the chickenhearted.

Charles shook himself, and backing the mare up the road guided her through the woods far around the gibbet.

When he reached the bridge over the Tyne he paused. He had meant to cross to Corbridge, an ancient market town first settled by the Romans. It offered modest entertainment, which Charles had managed to sample during his month at Dilston. The "Angel" served good arrack punch, and the barmaid was not averse to a bit of cuddling behind the taproom door.

Today the Angel did not appeal. Charles decided to ride into Newcastle by the south bank of the Tyne, which he had never explored. As he cantered along the riverbank his mood lightened. Action and new sights were ever a cure for megrims. He did not slacken pace for the village of Riding Mill, where two giggling girls jumped off the road to safety as he galloped by. Charles heard one of them cry out, "I' fakins, 'tis young Radcliffe o' Dilston! Oh, but he seems a canny-looking lad!"

Charles tossed his head and gave the girls a grin over his shoulder. Up here "canny" was a compliment, already he had learned that.

Charles had no interest in his appearance. His straight fair hair was clubbed back with a greasy black ribbon, his blue plush coat had once been fashionable, but he had outgrown it; his broad shoulders strained the seams, his young bony wrists protruded. The reddened hands were slender, long-fingered, and according to Cousin Maud proclaimed his Stuart blood, as did the thin nose set between large heavy-lidded gray eyes. His grandfather, Charles the Second, had been a swarthy Stuart; Charles was a fair Stuart, but the resemblance was unmistakable, they said. Always, however, managing to ignore the other side, about which Charles had once dared to twit Sir Marmaduke. "Yes, sir, to be sure I'm proud of royal blood—but what of my grandmother? Tell me of her, a play actress was she not, like Nell Gwynn?"

This had irritated his cousin, who assured him sharply that there was no resemblance between Nell Gwynn and Moll Davis, that the *latter* came of noble stock. "Albeit from the wrong side of the blanket, too!" Charles had brashly murmured, and incurred a beating from Sir Marmaduke, and the command to hold his tongue about matters of which he knew nothing.

But Charles did know about his ancestry. A gossipy London nurse had seen to that long ago. The Radcliffes were of ancient North Country lineage and they had always kept to the old faith, despite the tribulations they sometimes suffered for it. The Radcliffes had also been shrewd and acquisitive. Fortunate too, since each generation had found a Roman Catholic heiress to marry, one who brought yet more manors and castles into the family. The Radcliffes had been knighted and made baronets. but they were neither noble nor of the great London world until Charles's other grandfather, Sir Francis Radcliffe, turned out to be the shrewdest, most acquisitive, and by far the luckiest of them all. He had profited by the brief return of Catholicism to England under James the Second, and angled successfully both for marriage to a Stuart and a peerage. The Stuart marriage was that of his son Edward to Lady Mary Tudor, youngest of the many children by many mistresses Charles the Second recognized. Lady Mary was the daughter of Moll Davis, whose sweet singing and graceful dancing at the Duke's Playhouse had one evening caught the King's ever-roving and desirous eye. Moll's mother had been a milkmaid, but her father was Lord Berkshire, and both Nell Gwynn and Lady Castlemaine had been furious at this unexpected rival. Nell had even managed to lace little Moll's chocolate with jalap one night when the new favorite was to receive the King in the smart London house he had given her. Whether it was the resulting embarrassment for Moll— caused by this powerful purgative—which cooled the King's ardor, or whether it was the lovely Louise de Kéroualle's charms, nobody knew. At any rate, Moll Davis soon fell from favor, though the King ennobled their daughter, little Mary Tudor, casually bestowing on her the most exalted royal surname of them all. Thus by his son's marriage to this child—who was thirteen in 1687—Sir Francis Radcliffe achieved connection with royalty and the peerage for which he yearned. King James created Sir Francis the Earl of Derwentwater in March of the following year, just before the revolution which deposed the Catholic king and enthroned William and Mary.

Charles Radcliffe had always found the Moll Davis tale entertaining but remote. He had known none of his grandparents. His mother, the second Countess of Derwentwater, who had been that little Mary Tudor—*she* was another matter. For her Charles felt the baffled bitterness of the deserted child. He had not seen his mother since he was six, on the day she abandoned them all—James, Francis, Charles himself, and the baby Mary. Charles remembered the pungent scent of his mother's curls as she kissed him coldly on the forehead, saying "Farewell, child. Render obedience to your father, though I no longer intend to."

Charles had not then understood these words. He did not quite now. They might have referred to her Protestantism and the Radcliffes' Papacy, or far more likely to her infatuation with another man. She had married twice since her husband's death and gone to live abroad. I wonder if *she's* dead, Charles thought. The Constables never spoke of her, but then there were many uncomfortable topics which they never mentioned.

And much good my Stuart blood does me, thought Charles, stuck as I am either on a Yorkshire moor or in this dingy hole. The mare had now carried him along the Tyne into the coal country. The green riverbank was stippled with black piles, scaffoldings, and great yawning pits. The acrid smell of coal dust and smoke thickened the air. Soon, at the edge of Gateshead, the road was lined with mean little miners' hovels, roofed with turf. Suddenly Charles was blocked by a Galloway pony and cart full of coals which cut straight across his path. The cart came from the Bensham colliery a mile away and was bound for the Tyne. The wagon wheels ran on an oaken track the like of which Charles had never seen. A ragged ten-year-old urchin at the pony's head was softly whistling a plaintive tune while he tugged at the reluctant pony. Charles knew nothing of coal mining but these signs of activity caught his interest. He turned the mare and followed the cart as it trundled along the track until they reached the river where there was a wharf, called a staith. The sultry sun burnished the leaden waters of the Tyne. On the opposite bank in Newcastle, chimneys, roofs, Guild Hall, and the great quay all floated in a smoky haze.

Charles rode onto the staith and watched while the cart was dumped into a waiting keelboat. "Oof," he said, backing hastily from the choking cloud of coal dust.

The small boy at the pony's head chuckled rudely at the stranger's discomfiture. Charles was annoyed and, frowning, examined the boy attentively. He was a skinny child with coarse dark hair and alert hazel eyes in a sooty, square Northumbrian face. There was a cockiness about him and total lack of the deference Charles was accustomed to from the lower classes. The boy's nose was bleeding slightly.

"Been fighting, I see," Charles said, shrugging.

"Wuns!" said the boy wiping the blood off with the back of his hand. "Dost call it a fight wen the pit-overman bangs out wi' a clout?"

"What for?" said Charles. He didn't quite like the boy, and yet he felt strong curiosity about him.

"Fur that I slipped wile dumping a chaldron i' the cart, that's wot."

"Oh," said Charles. "Aren't you very young for dumping coals?"

"Leuk man!" said the boy with an impudent grin. "Ye ask a lot o' questions, an' I'll fend off the rest. M'name's Rob Wilson, I'm ten I guess. I been warking the pits one way or t'other five year, me big brother's doon there i' the keelboat, the overman's waiting at Bensham pithead, an' if I divven't gan back there soon I'll get another punch, d'ye twig?"

Charles nodded reluctantly, amused by what was essentially an expert snubbing. He watched the sturdy independent set of Rob's shoulders as the boy backed the pony up the staith and trudged away towards the pithead for another load. As he trudged Rob began to whistle again—the plaintive minor tune, which even Charles recognized as being both musical and unchildlike.

An odd little knave, Charles thought, and the air being now clear of coal dust he rode down the staith and peered into the keelboat, which was squat and broad. It had oars, one small furled sail, and a tiny cabin. The rest of the boat contained two keelmen busily spreading the dumped coals.

The keelmen each had red rags around their foreheads to keep sweat from their eyes, their grimy hair was plastered down save for a lovelock at each temple. The locks were twisted up in paper like horns. The men wore short, tight breeches and were naked to the waist. And they were black, a glistening black compounded of sweat and coal dust. Near as black as a Negro slave Charles had seen long ago in London. Charles stared and began to laugh.

The larger of the keelmen, a great brawny young man,

jerked up his head. His eyes flashed blue between the sooty lids. "Gan awa'!" he cried to Charles. "Wha's thou think to be, a-nickering an' gawking at us!"

Charles's life had provided few comical sights, and he continued to chuckle at this one, nor did he quite understand the keelman's speech. The young keelman jumped from his boat to the staith, and advanced with his chin out. "Hast niver seen a keelman afore? Art wanting a brawl? Get off that nag, ye toad, and I'll show thee how much there's to laugh at in a keelman's fists!"

Charles controlled his mirth. "No offense," he said pleasantly. "But you do look like a couple of horned beetles heaving away in that coal."

The keelman had been but semiserious, though touchy and eager to fight as were all keelmen. His scowl continued as he listened to Charles's comment, but the fierce blue eyes grew puzzled. "Gentry, begock!" he said. "An' a Southron by the sound o' him!" He turned to his workmate, who was resting on his shovel and watching the two on the staith. "What sayst thou, Neddy? Shall we learn him not to call us 'beadles'?"

"Hoot, Dick," answered Ned from the keelboat, "'tis only a lad. Leave be! Here's the next load a-coming an' this one not spread. If Black Will cotch us, he'll make ould Creeper dock our pay."

"Then we'll go on steek again!" said Dick. "We niver got the pawky shilling we axed for last time. They needna think they can starve us out. The keelmen'll mutiny 'til justice is done. We're not afeard o' pit-owners, nor hostmen, nor yet shipmasters neither!"

Despite these brave words, Dick clambered down to the boat and picked up his shovel. Charles, who had been listening intently, hastily pulled the mare back as another cartload of coal guided by a different boy came down the track onto the staith and was dumped. The black cloud subsided, and Charles approached the boat. "D'you mean you'd really strike against your masters?" he asked with reproof.

Dick hunched his back and did not answer, but Ned, who was more easygoing, said, "Aye, young sir, when they squat i' their mansions glutting meat an' swilling fancy wine, yet cry 'Poor mouth, poor mouth' whilst we crack our bones to load their coals for Lunnon town an' some pay nights get naught at all."

Charles considered this without belief. Servants and laborers always got paid, or at least they got their board and lodging, and they certainly should not be allowed to mutiny for any reason. "Who's Black Will and old Creeper?" he asked curiously, whereupon Dick whirled round and shouted, "For the matter o' that, who art *thou*? A spy mebbe—with all thy nosy questions!"

"I'm not a spy. I'm a Radcliffe of Dilston. I've only been up here a month and I don't know a thing about your stupid coal pits."

Dick elevated his brows until they touched the red rag. He elaborately laid down his shovel and executed a deep mocking bow across the coals. "A *Radcliffe!*" he said to Ned. "D'ye hear that? Not mere gentry, Neddy, marra—but a lord. We s'ld be honored by his lordship's questions."

"I'm not a lord," said Charles stiffly. "My brother is. The Earl of Derwentwater. He'll soon be home from France."

Dick gave Charles a long sardonic look. " 'Umble as we be, we still knaw that," he said. "Iverybody Tyneside knaws that, an' quite a few wonders how it'll be when his lordship gets hyem. Him being Papist and kin to that prince o'er the water."

"Whist—Dicky," said Ned uneasily. "Hould yor gob, divven't gabble so free!" Dick shrugged and both keelmen went on spreading the coal in silence. As Charles had no idea how anything would be when James came home, and had heard little Jacobite talk in the secluded Yorkshire manor where he had spent his last years, he found nothing more to say. A cart reappeared on the track, and Charles turned reluctantly to leave. Dick interested him despite his truculence. And now that Charles was used to the horned lovelocks and the sweaty blackness, he saw how admirable were the physiques of the two young men; their thick strength and rippling muscles were bred from years of shoveling the chaldrons of coal up into the holds of the ships which waited downriver.

He murmured "Farewell," but the men paid no attention. He turned the mare, then pulled her up as a girl came running down the path by the track. "Dickie! Dickie!" she called, her voice high with frightened urgency.

Dick looked up, then jumped again to the staith. "What's ado, lass? Meg, hinny, what ails thee?" His voice was suddenly gentle, and Charles had the impression that the big keelman would have hugged the girl had he not been so sooty.

The girl was panting, half crying, as she tried to speak.

" 'Tis Nan—been i' the straw since daybreak—the howdy says she'll not last through it—she's calling for Geordie."

Dick licked his lips, staring at the girl. He understood, as Charles did not, that her sister Nan was in labor and that the midwife thought she would die. Charles understood only grave emergency, and he saw that the girl was very young. A brown little thing, with tangled nut-brown hair, round eyes brown as peat water, rumpled russet bodice and skirt, and dusty bare feet.

"Canst not fetch Geordie?" said Dick frowning.

She shook her head. "I tried. Squire William himsel' was there at the pithead. He wouldna let them send word down. He said—" she gave a sharp sob and twisted her hands, "said I was crazed to dare to summons a pitman from wark, only because a brat was a-birthing. I told him Nanny was dying, and he said 'Let her then.' "

Dick's fists clenched. "Damn Black William's guts! Damn him! Oh, *I'll* get Geordie from the pit."

"I pray so," she whispered. "But how *can* thee?"

Dick grabbed a homespun shirt from the staith rail, pulled it over his head. "I've means," he said. "Ned, do the best ye can, if ould Creeper comes tell him I'm took wi' sudden gripes." He turned to the girl. "I'll bring Geordie. Hurry back to Nan. Canst make it, lass? Ye're shaking."

"Could I take her on the mare?" offered Charles. The girl started. She had not noticed Charles. Dick had forgotten him, but he nodded quickly. " 'Tis a welcome offer if ye'll be so kind," and he began to run up the track towards the highway and the Park colliery to find his eldest brother Geordie.

Charles helped the girl clamber up behind him on the mare, where she perched lightly, her arms around Charles's waist. She did not speak except to give muffled directions.

They passed the bridge to Newcastle, turned south a bit, and came to another row of squalid stone hovels all alike. "There," said the girl, pointing, "thank'ee," and slipping off the horse she ran toward the center cottage. In front of it there was a group of pit-women. They made way for the girl, gaped at Charles, and then, peering in through the door and shaking their heads, resumed a dreary murmuring.

Charles had no reason to linger, but he was anxious to know if Dick would manage to get Geordie here in time. And he hoped to see the girl again. The modest delicate touch of her arms around his waist had been pleasant.

After a bit, as nothing happened, Charles rode down the road towards a smoking wooden structure he saw looming against the sky. He suspected that it might be the colliery where Geordie worked, and soon had confirmation, when he rode through an open gate and was hailed by a lanky man on a bay stallion. "Halt! What's the meaning o' this, fellow! Don't ye know you're trespassing?"

The man had very sharp black eyes, set near together in a purple-veined flabby face. He wore a cocked hat trimmed with braid over his own coarse grizzled hair, and a sober brown coat with pewter buttons.

"Forgive me, sir. I've no wish to intrude," said Charles in his politest manner. "I saw the gate open and was curious to see a colliery. It is one, isn't it?"

"This is the Park Pit, and I'm the owner o' it, Esquire William Cotesworth. Ah, I see ye've heard of me."

Charles had given a blink. So this was Black Will, and how could Dick possibly get Geordie out from under this long bulbous nose?

"And I've seen *your* face before," added Cotesworth, whose driving brain was ever vigilant of smallest details. "Or one like it. Well, speak up, knave, who are ye?"

"Charles Radcliffe of Dilston," said Charles, resenting Cotesworth's tone and beginning to dislike him as much as Dick did.

"Ah, the Honorable Charles Radcliffe, to be sure," said Cotesworth with a sudden twisted smile which did not affect the cold stare. "That's who ye look like, a Radcliffe. Matter o' twenty years since I had some dealings wi' his lordship your father. He bilked me out o' six guineas for tallow and wine he ordered."

"What!" cried Charles. "You're mad, sir! My father never cheated anyone in his life, and I assure you earls do not concern themselves with household provisioning."

"All the same I niver got m' six guineas. I'm a plain North Country man and I speak plain. I hear the new Earl's coming home, and ye may tell him I expect the account to be settled."

"No doubt my brother's steward will see you're paid," said Charles with all the condescension he could muster above an impulse to punch that knobby tight-lipped face. "So you deal in tallow and wine as well as coals," he added bitingly. "A Jack-of-all-trades."

The muscles flickered around Cotesworth's eyes, but he ignored Charles's tone. "I've many trades," Cotesworth agreed blandly. "But ye may also tell your noble brother white roses aren't one of 'em."

Charles blinked again. He knew that the white rose was

the Jacobite emblem, and he was annoyed into saying, "So you'd not hope to see the rightful king on the throne when Queen Anne dies!"

"The rightful king'll never be a *Papist*," said Cotesworth. "Good day. In future keep off m'land!" He sat motionless while Charles rode back through the gate onto the roadway. Then Cotesworth shut the gate and trotted off to his pithead.

Insufferable boor, Charles thought. I hope James never gives him his miserable six guineas! But he felt that there was something more sinister about Squire Cotesworth than a long memory for a trivial debt.

Charles presently got back to the row of miners' hovels, and saw Dick standing on the street, watching him come. Charles spurred the mare and galloped up. "You *got* here! Did you bring Geordie?"

"Oh aye," said Dick. "He's in wi' poor Nanny."

"But how did you ever do it? I've just been to the pit, I met Black Will, you never got past *him!*"

Dick grinned. A streak of white in the dirty face. "The Park's an ould pit, laddie. Our grandfaither hewed in it. There's passages to the outside Cotesworth divven't knaw, but Geordie an' me do. Now I'm off to join m'marra in the keelboat. Gan thou hyem to thy castle. Gatsheed pits're no place for quality." He gave a mocking, not unfriendly wave, and hastened back towards the Bensham staith where Ned was working.

Charles did not take Dick's advice. He dismounted instead and knocked timidly at the Wilson door, which was now shut. The girl opened it, and looked astonished, but her eyes were shining and a clear rose color had come into her cheeks. "She's better," she whispered. "Nanny's better, the moment Geordie came she took heart."

"Is the baby—" said Charles awkwardly, and stopped.

"Aye—'tis born. A fine boy. I guess 'twill be another pitman some day, poor bairnie. It seems to me a fearful life." She turned as someone spoke in the house, and answered, "Aye, I will so." She came out of the hovel and shut the door. "I'm to get ale frae the Lion in case Nanny fancies some."

Charles tethered the mare and walked along beside the girl, whose brown head barely reached to his shoulder. "I didn't know a pitman's lass would think this a fearful life, if you're used to it," he offered diffidently.

"But I'm not!" she cried flashing up at him like an indignant kitten. "Did you think me a Tynesider? I'm from

Coquetdale—from the North on the Border," she emended as she saw him look puzzled. "Can ye not hear-r it in m'speech? They tease me enough."

All the speech he had heard today had sounded strange to Charles, but now he noticed that she made her *r*'s with a throaty little burr, and yet he found her easier to understand than Dick's broad Tyneside. As they went to the Lion and waited for ale and walked back again, Charles learned something about the girl.

Her name was Margaret Snowdon, but everyone called her Meg. She was fifteen. She had been born near a remote village called Tosson on the Coquet river, as had her big brothers and her sister Nan. Their mother had died last January and then Meg had been sent to her sister in Gateshead. The father, John Snowdon, was one of a large clan of Snowdons who lived in Coquetdale. John Snowdon was a farmer, but he was also something of a scholar. In the long winter nights he read many books, mostly sermons, and he had taught all his children to read and write. He lived in an isolated peel tower and saw little of his kinsmen, for he was a Dissenter—a Calvinistic form of Protestantism Charles barely knew existed. Charles was familiar only with Protestants who belonged to the Established Church of England. Meg's father held with the Scottish church, which was frowned on in England.

"But are you Scots then?" Charles asked, not greatly interested, but anxious to keep Meg talking, for without questions she fell shyly silent.

"Lord save us, but no!" cried the girl with so much horror that Charles laughed.

"We're Northumbr-r-ians," said Meg tilting her chin. "M'faither and brothers'd not thank ye for thinking us part o' those thieving shifting Scots across the Border!"

Charles had heard of Border raids, and received the impression that the English gave as good as they got when it came to sudden forays, pillage, and cattle-stealing, but he made no comment, for it suddenly occurred to him that Meg was pretty, and that he would like to kiss her. They had returned to the Wilson doorstep, and the girl clutching her jug of ale was about to disappear inside.

"Meg—" he said putting his hand on her smooth brown arm, "will you come out again? I'll give you a ride over to Newcastle—there might be a cockfight or such." He was not sure what diversion the town could offer.

Meg's little face brightened. "I heard the Faws're camping

by Jesmond," she said eagerly. "They'll ha' a piper. I hanker fur the pipes."

"The Faws?" asked Charles still holding her arm.

"Egyptians and tinklers," said the girl. "We call them Faws. They wander England but live on the Border." The need for explanation reminded her of the gulf between herself and this tall good-looking lad who was staring down at her so winningly. She turned and releasing her arm put her hand on the door latch. "Nanny might need me," she said. "—and Dick wouldna like that I go wi' ye."

"Why not?" said Charles frowning. "Has he the say over you?"

She lowered her lashes, staring at the doorstep. "He has a mind to court me," she answered slowly. "If he can put by a few shilling, but 'tis mortal hard."

"Well, you're not bound to him *now*," said Charles whose ardor was increased by this opposition. As she still hesitated his face changed and lost its boyish diffidence. "Come along, Meg!" he said sharply. "You know you want to and I think it unseemly that you should argue with me."

Unseemly to gainsay the son of an earl, the grandson of a king—his thought needed no voicing for Meg to understand it. Dick, while in the hovel, had explained just who the lad was, and she swallowed nervously, half flattered and half frightened. "I'll see what Nanny says." She turned and slipped through the door, leaving Charles to stand on the road, his spurt of haughtiness evaporated.

Inside the pitman's cottage, Geordie had gone and Nan was asleep, so Meg put the jug of ale on the only table and consulted the midwife.

Mrs. Dodd was town-bred and a great respecter of rank, unlike Meg's kinfolk. Up in the dales on the Border, there was neither servility nor feudal spirit. Each family was pretty much a law unto itself, and did as it pleased regardless of earls or dukes or even the Queen.

Mrs. Dodd, never backward with advice, settled the matter of Meg's invitation at once. "Ye obey your betters, m'lass—and do as the young gent wants. If he's took a fancy to ye, ye might wheedle from him a pound or two which'd not come amiss here as *I* can see." The midwife gave a disdainful sniff towards the frowzy straw pallet where Nan slept with the baby. "No need to mention it to your sister or that Dick Wilson neither. I'll bide till ye get back."

Meg's heart beat fast as she washed her face in the pail,

tidied her hair with Nan's comb, put on her one pair of shoes, and going outside said shyly to Charles, "I'll come, sir."

Charles and Meg had a glorious afternoon. They rode the mare across the Tyne Bridge and then explored Newcastle. They gaped at the Blackgate and St. Nicholas' Church. They went to the squalid quarter near Sandgate where Dick and many of the keelmen lived, they explored the dark alleys Meg said were called "chares," they walked out on the great quay and admired the line of barges with foreign flags, ships from Sweden, Holland, and even Turkey. Sailors were unloading bales of damask, barrels of figs and indigo, while the outgoing cargoes of tallow and candles lay ready on the wharf. "Must be Squire Cotesworth's," said Meg pointing to the bales. " 'Tis his chandlery's mark. And some of those colliers down river're his too."

Charles glanced at the great ships lying at anchor, and said, "Black William's done well for himself."

"Aye," said the girl. "Naught but a poor yeoman to start with, but the de'il's taught him all his tricks."

"And the devil may have him," said Charles absently. "Where are those Faws you spoke of?" He was tiring of sights and wishful of getting Meg to a more secluded spot. Once, on the quay, he had put his arm around her, but she had slipped away.

They remounted the mare and went along Pilgrim Street, where there were many fine shops, but the young people scarcely glanced at the silks and furbelows to be glimpsed through the twinkling-paned windows. Charles had no taste for shopping and Meg no acquisitiveness at all. They passed through the city wall at Pilgrim Street Gate and presently came to the town moor. Soon they saw an encampment of brightly painted wagons around a fire and heard the skirling of the small Northumbrian pipes.

"Ah—" whispered Meg on a deep breath. "The bonny sound! Why 'tis the very band o' Faws who were camped near our burn yesteryear. Mother had them do tinkering fur us. The piper's called Jem Bailey. Hark! He's playing 'On Cheviot side the wind bla-aws wide—' Is't not beautiful?"

Charles did not think it beautiful at all, he distinguished no melody in the shrill squealing of the pipes, but he saw that Meg's face had melted into a look of yearning and exaltation.

"You're homesick?" he asked, startled.

"Aye, hinny," she answered without thinking, using to him the Tyneside pet name, which Dick often used to her. "Homesick fur the winds and the moors and the hills, fur the sound of the pipes through the mist on Ravensheugh."

Charles slid off the mare and helped her down. "Don't think of all that now!" he said with sudden petulance. "You're here with me. Can't you think about *me?*"

She was startled. It was true that she had forgotten him while the pipes evoked her father's stern face, the rough-hewn ones of her brothers, and the aching memory of her mother's smile as they had once all gathered around the hearth by the flickering light of the peat fire. If only the bitterness of exile in the stifling pit-hovels of Gateshead could be over. If only she might go home. Meg was overcome with hopelessness. Dick would not let her go. And her father would not let her come back either, for he had decided that she must stay south three years. To better herself—by which John Snowdon meant going into good service at Newcastle. There was a secretly dissenting minister there, Mr. Smithson. Snowdon had heard of him through Mr. Dean, the Presbyterian minister on the Border at Falstone. They had exchanged letters. Mr. Smithson had agreed to take Meg into his home after Christmas to teach her the Gospel, while his wife taught her sewing, brewing, and cookery, of a refinement unknown in Coquetdale. It was all arranged, and John Snowdon never changed his mind.

"Well—" said Charles, who had been watching her face darken and the pink mouth droop at the corners. "Cat got your tongue, Meg?"

"No, sir." She tried to smile up at him. "I'm sorry. 'Tis only that m'heart is heavy because I can't be hame."

"You mean you're going to wed Dick Wilson?"

She sighed. "I'll have to—or into service as m'faither wants."

They had begun to walk towards the Faw wagons, but the pipes had stopped. Charles put his arm around Meg's shoulders, and squeezing her to him said, "You don't love Dick, or you wouldn't talk like that."

"I divven't knaw," she said after a moment, but she did not draw away. The tingle of closeness, and the pleasure it gave her caught her unaware. She began to breathe faster. Charles heard it and, bending, gave her a quick awkward kiss on the cheek. At once they both blushed, and moved apart. "Look at that old crone," said Charles hastily at random.

A skinny woman in a dirty pink skirt and brass earrings

made beckoning gestures in their direction, while she sat on a three-legged stool by the campfire. Jem Bailey, the piper, stood watchfully behind her. He wore a large black felt hat with a sprig of heather stuck in the buckle. The small Northumbrian pipes dangled from their red plush bag, the bellows were fastened around his waist and right elbow.

"The Faws tell a body's fate," said Meg doubtfully. "She wants ye to gi' her silver."

"Why not?" Charles cried. "I'd like to hear my future!" He walked up to the Faw woman. "Here's sixpence for you. Tell me something fine."

The old woman took the sixpence, bit it between her two remaining teeth, then dropped it down her dirty bodice. She peered up at the tall youth, and stiffening spoke quickly in Romany to the piper, who gave an exclamation. A dozen swarthy men who had been currying their horses and donkeys behind the wagons, now glided up to the campfire. They said nothing. They stood silent and watched.

The sun had set, gloaming stole across the heath, and Charles had an uneasy pang as he saw the piper eying his mare avidly.

The Faw woman's beady eyes remained fixed on Charles. She said something unintelligible in a soft hissing voice. The piper stopped gazing at the mare and translated what was obviously a command. "Maria says we'll not harm thee, or thine. She sees the white rose on thy brow. We Faws follow the white rose."

The old woman nodded and suddenly grabbed Charles's hand. She squinted at it, poked along one of the lines with her cracked fingernail, then dropped the hand. She folded her arms and looked again at Charles with what seemed to be pity and fear.

"What does she see?" asked Charles uncomfortably. "What does the old hag see?"

The piper himself appeared astonished and questioned Maria rapidly. She shook her head, and finally said a few reluctant words. The piper translated with the same reluctance. "She sees the white rose wither and turn black. She sees a sword. She'll not say more, she's afraid."

"What of?" said Charles tossing his head. "All flowers fade, and as for swords, I expect to do some fighting in my time, 'tis a gentleman's calling. Can't she do better than that? What about love?" He squeezed Meg's waist.

The woman understood him, and was annoyed by his tone. She spoke again, and the piper drew a quick breath. He stared at Meg, then turned to Charles. "The royal blood in thy veins is accursed. True love cannot flow in it. No sweetheart need hope for true love from thee." He glanced again at Meg and shrugged. "Also Maria says that in thy palm she saw an axe—a red axe."

Meg gasped and tugged at Charles's arm. "Come awa', sir. They're out to frighten ye."

"Bah!" said Charles. "Not with that folderol!" though he had barely prevented himself from making the sign of the cross. He turned on his heel, the girl with him, and they mounted the mare.

The Faws watched them go. After a few paces the piper squeezed the bellows with his elbow and a mournful wailing pierced the twilight. Meg shuddered. It was "The Lament for a Dying Chieftain" that the piper played; her heart was full of fear, and another feeling, which centered on the boy who rode in front of her. But she said nothing.

Charles spurred the mare to a canter, and they soon left the heath and passed again through Pilgrim Street Gate, where they slowed down.

"I dislike your Faws," said Charles angrily. He had recovered from his momentary disquiet, and dismissed the crone's vaporings. Yet the tender mood had vanished, and he saw no means of regaining it.

Candles now gleamed in the city windows, the streets were dark. Meg would be in trouble if he did not get her home. For that matter, so would he. It was many miles back to Dilston, and long before this Sir Marmaduke would be pacing the courtyard, and Cousin Maud likely as not ringing the alarm bell and sending out grooms to find him. "I wish I was of age," he said through his teeth, "and my own master."

He had not spoken to Meg, but she heard and laid her cheek quickly on his shoulder in sympathy. The little gesture touched him, who had never known simple affection, and he said, "Meg sweet, you'll meet me again, won't you? When can you be free?"

She did not answer at once, and thought of all the reasons why she should not meet him again. When she spoke it felt to her as though someone else were speaking. "Sunday I might get out. Dick, Geordie, and wee Rob all go to their bed-fast mother at Shields. Nanny won't question my leaving."

Charles gave a happy laugh and they made plans in whispers. When the Newcastle bells pealed for services she would come to the riverbank west of the Bensham staith. This would shorten his ride a trifle, and she would wait until he came. Rain or shine.

When Charles put Meg down before the Wilson hovel, he took her chapped grimy little hand and gave it a fumbling kiss. Then he rode back to Dilston, his mind so full of Meg and the delightful though formless emotion she inspired that he was impervious to the exasperation of his guardians.

"This sort of vagabonding simply *will not do!*" cried Sir Marmaduke, his periwig askew with indignation. "Where have you been, sir, since early morn? Answer me at once!"

"Yes, where have you been, Charles?" echoed Cousin Maud. Her nose was red, her pale eyes even waterier than usual, for she had been much alarmed.

"Oh, I rode into Newcastle," said Charles airily. "Nothing to make such a pother about. You *said* it was a good thing for me to get to know the country up here, and I'm not the child you think me. I can take care of myself!"

Sir Marmaduke continued to argue and threaten above a sense of growing helplessness. Short of locking Charles permanently in his room there seemed no way of making him promise to stay on the estate. Charles had changed of late. He was no longer a biddable lad, who only indulged in little pranks which a thrashing soon checked.

Finally in desperation the Constables called in their new chaplain. George Brown was a hard-working and scholarly Jesuit who had been attached to the Durham missions until his superior decided that he would be a suitable priest for the Earl of Derwentwater's reopened chapel at Dilston. Mr. Brown, therefore, had known the Constables and Charles but a month, and was impartial. When a servant had summoned him, he walked into the Hall with his breviary in his hand, his sober black suit loose on his gaunt body. Like all priests during these uncomfortable times he neither wore a cassock nor was addressed publicly as "Father." He listened to Sir Marmaduke's account of Charles's insubordination, then turned to the culprit, who looked decidedly impenitent. "Well, my son, I regret to hear that you refuse to obey the commands of the good people God has put in authority over you!"

To Charles's astonishment there was a twinkle in the priestly eye. Charles said quickly, "I don't, sir, at least nothing reasonable, but it's dull here at Dilston, and I don't see why I can't ride out when and where I like."

Nor did the priest. He glanced from the tall stubborn lad to the two fussing elders, saw with an inward sigh the eternal battle of the generations in progress, and said mildly, "But you are very late, my son. Lady Constable feared you had been set on by footpads."

"Oh fiddle," said Charles. "Nobody'd dare, they all seem to know the Radcliffes. Besides I can defend myself."

"So everyone knows your high birth," put in Sir Marmaduke with fresh grievance. "And dressed like a filthy plowboy, unattended, without even a sword, do you think people consider you do *justice* to your birth—and your brother's rank?"

"I'll dress better in future," said Charles to Mr. Brown, whom he perceived to be an ally.

"I think," said the priest to the Constables, "that if Master Charles will promise to watch his attire and not be out so late, he might be allowed a little freedom. Exercise is beneficial."

Sir Marmaduke gave an angry grunt, his wife fluttered and dabbed her eyes, but neither dared dispute their chaplain's decision. Cousin Maud, however, had the last word, and she flung it in Charles's triumphant face. "How glad I shall be when dear James comes home, *he* will know how to control a forward boy who is barely out of the nursery!"

A chill dampened Charles. He bowed silently to his cousins and the priest, then escaped to the kitchen, where the cook glumly fed him cold meat pasty and a mug of ale.

This episode, while it secured Charles's immediate freedom, also emphasized the need of making the most of it while there was time.

Two days after Charles's ride to Gateshead a messenger arrived with a letter from the Earl to the Constables. It was written in a disconcerting mixture of French and English, and Sir Marmaduke had to call in the chaplain for help in deciphering the sprawling hand.

Then the purport was clear enough. On the twenty-fifth of July, Queen Anne had finally granted permission for her noble kinsman and his party to return home. The party included the Earl's next youngest brother, Francis Radcliffe, his elderly bachelor uncle, Colonel Thomas Radcliffe, a priest-tutor, Father Benjamin Petre, and a Newcastle attorney, Roger Fenwick, who had crossed over to Holland to acquaint the young Earl with his Northumbrian affairs. All these people, and their servants, were gathered at Rotterdam awaiting suitable passage to London. They proposed, when they finally arrived in London, to stay with a distant cousin, Dr. John Radcliffe, who was a court physician and thought it well that the Earl should see something of his native city before proceeding North. The Earl finished by sending greeting to

le petit Charles, mes hommages to my kindsmen, Sir Marmed: & her Ldyship, whoume I estime profondement,

Yr humble & obedient servant
DERWENTWATER

"And so," said Lady Constable anxiously when they had all heard the letter, "it won't be long before he comes, but I wonder *when!* Will it be for Christmas? Dear, oh dear, I'm sure I don't know how to plan. All those people—the bedrooms in a shocking state too, and I must find another cook, the only thing this one can properly make is that disgusting mess of entrails they call haggis."

The men quickly vanished, Sir Marmaduke to worried consultation with the steward, the priest to his austere little room in the gatehouse, Charles in quest of his mare, while passionately wishing that it were Sunday and he could see Meg. He had dreamed of her each night, startling virile dreams of a kind he had not had before, and from which he awoke sweating, excited, and somewhat ashamed.

On Sunday morning Charles arose before five and slipped out of the castle before anyone awoke. He would miss Mass and there would be a fearful hullabaloo, but no matter. Later he would gracefully accept whatever penance Mr. Brown gave him. He avoided the wood where the thief hung in the gibbet, and cantered fifteen miles along tracks and muddy lanes towards the trysting place. He crossed the Derwent River, then began to look for the abandoned windmill Meg had told him of. He found it easily. It had been abandoned because of its situation next to a way-leave on which ran tracks from Sir Henry Liddell's colliery near Ravensworth to his staith three miles away on the Tyne. The farmer had exacted enough rent for the way-leave across his property to enable him to buy a new farm he coveted.

On weekdays the clear morning air would have been acrid with smoke from a dozen nearby pits, a line of coal wagons would have been trundling by to the waiting keelboats. But today there was no danger of being seen. It was quiet around the crumbling mill, except for a blackbird singing in the branches of a scarlet-berried rowan tree which had escaped the hatchet.

Charles had barely time to tether the mare and begin to worry as to whether Meg had changed her mind before he saw her coming. She sped across a field in her bare feet, having left her shoes home. They would have hampered her for the two miles of running from the Wilsons' cottage. Otherwise she wore her Sunday clothes—faded blue wool and a fresh-laundered white kerchief. Her brown hair was tied back with a bit of tape, for she owned no ribbons.

Charles went to meet her and then they both stopped dead, struck with embarrassment. " 'Tis a fine day, sir," said Meg. "I thought it might be yestere'en—the sun so red, I'm early, mebbe, the bells havena rung yet, Nanny thinks I'm off to see the minister in town, I divven't lie though, she just thought it. Dick, Geordie, an' Robbie went to their ould mother—" She knew she was gabbling, but Charles, of whom she too had dreamed, now seemed a stranger. He wore fawn-colored breeches, there were silver buttons on his riding coat, white ruffles at his throat and wrists, his black cocked hat was gold-laced, and a small sword dangled from his hip. He resembled the gallants she had seen riding haughtily through the Newcastle streets, and tears came into her eyes as she realized her wicked folly in coming. "I wouldna've knawn ye—" she faltered, in answer to his look of concern.

"Oh," said Charles, not displeased. He had dressed up to impress her. His shyness passed as he saw hers; he put his arm around her waist and, laughing, pulled her to the mill. It was dark and quiet inside beneath the huge millstones. And there was a pile of old sacks on the rotting floor. "Let's sit and talk," Charles said, drawing her down onto the sacks beside him. "Have you breakfasted?"

She shook her head and Charles pulled a flask of port and some marchpane cakes from his pocket. He had found both in the dining hall on his way out, since he dared not go to the larders.

Meg was entranced by the sticky sweetness of Charles's provisions, which were unknown to her, and the two eagerly consumed every drop and crumb. Charles had no previous knowledge of seduction, nor plan for it now; yet he noted that Meg's nervousness had left her as the port warmed her veins, that her brown eyes grew brilliant, and soft red appeared on her cheekbones. She leaned back against his arm and sighed happily. He flung his hat to the corner of the

34

mill and began to kiss her. After a moment of shrinking she returned his kisses. Her breath was sweet as violets, her little body yielded to his increasing ardor. Though once she cried out in protest, when he whispered hoarsely, "Don't, Meg, don't, sweetheart, I won't hurt you." She gave a little sob and shut her eyes, then clasping his neck tight with her arms, she let him do as instinct bade him.

But later when the sun slanted through the mill door, and aroused Charles from a delicious languor their thoughts were very different. Charles's were exultant. He was a man now! No one could gainsay his manhood any more. He turned with a smile to kiss again the partner of so delightful an experience, and found Meg's chest heaving, and tears dripping off her cheeks onto the sacking.

"Why come, poppet," he said, half exasperated. "There's no cause for weeping. What's amiss?"

She pulled away from him and buried her face in her arms. He barely heard her choking voice. "I divven't knaw *that* was going to happen. I divven't guess 'twould be like that. I've brought shame to m'family."

"They'll never know," said Charles confidently. "Silly girl, this happens every day 'twixt two young folk who take joy in each other."

"Not wi'out a wedding first," she cried, and sobbed harder. "I've done very wrong, but I love ye, sir. Mebbe the Faw woman cast a spell on me fur I began to love ye then."

"Love is sweet," said Charles abstractedly kissing the top of her head.

She twisted around to look up at him. "But there's naught ahead fur us," she said with dreary finality. "We may *not* love outside our class. 'Tis very wrong."

Inexperienced as he was, it occurred to Charles that that particular wrong was widespread, but arguments wearied him, and he pulled her onto his lap, saying, "Smile, Meg! Smile the way you did before! You're pretty as a posy when you smile."

"Am I then?" she said striving to obey. In a while he had kissed and cozzened her back to a happier mood. When at last they parted, she had promised to meet him here the following Sunday.

On five Sundays, Charles and Meg kept their trysts in the old windmill. Nobody suspected them, though there had been such a fuss over the neglected Mass that Charles did not dare repeat his sin. He rearranged his meetings with Meg so that before leaving Dilston he might first attend the family

Mass at eight. He avoided confession, in which he had been most irregular anyway, and he told a few shrewd lies to Sir Marmaduke, who had washed his hands of the rebellious boy.

On the last Sunday in October Charles set out as usual, though it was pouring with cold rain. For the first time he found himself reluctant to go. He felt tenderness for the girl, and gratitude for the pleasure she gave him, yet the first rapture had dwindled. He knew now all the secrets of her small body, and he knew precisely how she would act. She would be initially reluctant, even sullen, she would weep a while and worry about her wrongdoing, presently she would let him kiss her into surrender again. And despite the freezing rain, she would be waiting docilely inside the mill. Of all these things Charles was certain. Great then was his astonishment when he arrived sodden and quite late to find that Meg was not there. He frowned and peered around the dark building until he spied a piece of torn paper folded on the sacks. He carried it to the light and deciphered the childish scrawl: "Fareweel, sir. I'll not forget thee but 'tis beter we meet na more."

Charles gave a startled grunt. A hot flush stained his face. He felt betrayed, and after a stunned moment he solaced himself by kicking over the pile of sacks. So this was all her vows of love amounted to! The false trollop! Then it occurred to him that not only had she apparently had the effrontery to tire of him first, but that she had probably gone to Dick, whom he had ceased to consider as a rival long ago. In thinking back to their last tryst, Charles now remembered that Meg had fallen into heavy silences, had seemed about to speak and then stopped. That when they kissed at parting, she had clung to him and whispered, "I'll pray for thy happiness!" She had then meant it as farewell?

She'd not get away so easily! Charles, smarting and suffering more than he let himself realize, mounted the mare and rode through Gateshead to the Wilson cottage. He had no idea what he was going to say, but he expected to find Meg there. He hammered on the door. It was opened by a taller, paler edition of Meg who had an infant at the breast and cried "Lawks a me!" as she stared at the thunderous young gentleman in the dripping greatcoat. "What can I do for ye, sir?"

"Where's Meg?" cried Charles beyond discretion. "Is Meg here?"

Nan Wilson's eyes narrowed and she drew back. "What's

it to thee, where Meg is? Who are ye?"

Charles did not answer. He could see into the tiny bare room behind, and there was nobody there. Nan put her hand on the latch to close the door. She had known that lately something was very wrong with Meg, and the world being what it was, had wondered if a man would likely be the cause. But the girl had never said anything. She had worked hard in the cottage, helping with the baby and the eternal filthy wash a pitman made, and she had been remarkably glum. Even when Dick came courting of a Saturday night, Meg had shown no lightening of spirit. She'd cling to her sister, and then tell poor Dick she had the headache when he wanted to take her to a jig in Sandgate, or to watch football on the fell. Meg was such a good, honest girl that Nan had not questioned her. Besides, they were proud, the Snowdons, and kept their troubles to themselves.

Yet now, as she looked again at the youth on her doorstep, her hand fell from the latch, and she said, "Would ye be the Mr. Radcliffe my husband tould me was here the day I birthed the babby?"

"Yes," said Charles. "Where's Meg?"

Nan opened the door and motioned him inside. "Come to the fire, an' warm yoursel'—'tis bitter."

Charles came in and stood beside the tiny grate, where a shovelful of coals burned sulkily. "Thank you," he said with more grace, "and I pray you tell me where Meg is."

"I cannot," said Nan, putting the baby on the bed and fastening her bodice. "The lass is gone, I knaw not whither."

"She—she is always out of a Sunday morning, isn't she?" asked Charles, trying to be offhand. "To see a Dissenting minister in Newcastle?"

"Aye," said Nan with a sharp look. "'Tis what I thought. But she's not there, nor has been this month o' Sundays. Maybe *you* know where she's been instead these Sundays?"

Charles flushed and stared down at the bare grease-stained hearth. "I se ye do," said Nan. She sighed and shook her head. "I'd niver've believed it o' Meg, nor that she'd leave me as she did yestermorn, afore I waked, wi' all her gear in a kerchief, and a note to say—" Nan stopped. The note had said, "I'm sick for home. I mun get back to the Coquet or die. My Sister, tell nobody this." Nan had not told, though Dick had stormed and pleaded at her, and now this lad— Nan had a sudden fear. "Mr. Radcliffe," she said, "ye've not got m'wee Meg in trouble, have ye?"

"In trouble," repeated Charles blankly. "What trouble?"

Nan started and peered up into his face. "How ould are ye?" she snapped.

Charles answered resentfully. "Sixteen."

"Oh lawks," cried Nan, collapsing on the stool with an unwilling laugh. "I had thought ye full grown! Weel, sir, 'twon't be long afore ye learn what trouble means 'twixt lad and lass, but niver mind that now."

She was ashamed of her suspicion, which did Meg scant justice besides. A bit of love-making there had certainly been, a kiss or two and the poor girl's heart sorely touched, but Meg, no doubt seeing with her usual good sense that any mingling with a gentleman was dangerous, had certainly put the most decisive end to it she could. So Nan reasoned, and she looked on Charles more kindly. " 'Tis best to forget her, sir, she wishes it, and ye soon will. Why, when his lordship comes, fur sure he'll bring a bevy o' fair young ladies alang wi' him. Ye'll not hanker then for a simple lass like Meg."

Part of Charles knew this to be true, and he wondered if there were a chance that James would bring any gay company to Dilston. Yet the sense of loss continued, and he said, "Mrs. Wilson, I *pray* you, tell me where Meg's gone! It's not to your brother-in-law, Dick, is it?"

Nan shook her head. "Nay, Dickie's as 'wildered as you —an' far more stricken," she added with a rueful smile. Dick truly loved the foolish girl, and had made a shocking scene when he found her gone. So much so that Nan had nearly told him where to look, which would be the road north from Newcastle to Morpeth. But she had not.

Charles finally left Gateshead and started sadly back to Dilston. He passed the windmill and searched again inside. There was nothing there but field mice. As he sloshed through puddles on the riverbank, he tried to hold on to his anger at Meg, yet there was a lump in his chest, and unmanly prickling around his eyes. He did not speculate any more as to why or where Meg had gone, that was not his nature. When a thing was done it was done. But he found the days more tedious than ever now, and the sense of emptiness could only be assuaged by hard dangerous riding, by training the apathetic stable dogs to rat-catching, or by wandering back across the bridge to the Angel at Corbridge, where the giggling barmaid no longer seemed so attractive.

TWO

The Earl of Derwentwater and his party landed in London
by the end of November. A few days later a letter arrived
at Dilston which dissipated all Charles's lonely boredom,
for James summoned his young brother to London for Christmas, and the invitation did not include the Constables. The
Earl wrote that he presumed the winter journey would be too
rigorous for Cousin Maud, and that since he expected to
be North shortly such hardship was unnecessary, and Charles
might travel in the care of Mr. Thomas Errington of Beaufront, who was also coming South.

Charles was wild with excitement, nor was he even much
annoyed by the requirement that he should travel in anybody's care. At least he would be free from the bleak,
gloomy old castle, and from lingering discomfort when
anything reminded him of Meg.

On the morrow after the arrival of the Earl's letter,
Charles bade his cousins and the priest a lighthearted
adieu, rode across the Tyne through Corbridge, and presented himself at Beaufront Hall—as he had been directed.
This stately Tudor mansion was the seat of the Erringtons,
and Mr. William Errington, its owner, was locally known
as the "Chief." He came stamping out to the courtyard as
Charles appeared and shouted at him genially. "So young
Radcliffe, here ye be! Come in for a stirrup cup, afore ye
start. Tom's about ready, and ye two've a lang way to go.
Some neighbors're here to see ye off!"

Charles dismounted and bowed, a trifle startled by the

Chief's appearance. The old man, who did not believe in chopping and changing, was dressed in patched red plush breeches and the long coat of his ancestors. This costume was topped by a ragged Northumbrian plaid and a black felt bonnet which flopped over his hairy left ear.

Charles followed his host into a smoky wainscoted hall full of people drinking October ale from pewter flagons. They all turned and stared at Charles while the Chief clapped him on the back and boomed out a list of names. Swinburne, Shaftoe, Collingwood, Widdrington, Forster, and others which Charles, confused and trying to bow in all directions, did not hear at all.

That these names belonged to old Northumbrian families, and that they were mostly Roman Catholic he did know, but he had met none of them before, because Cousin Maud from the moment of their arrival at Dilston had discouraged callers. Time enough for that, she said, when the castle was in order and the Earl had come. Besides, how did one know which of these Northerners were suitable? One must be careful not to cause dear James future annoyance.

There were a few ladies among the group; the handsomest of them came up to Charles and, smiling, took his hand. "For shame, sir," she said to Mr. Errington. "The boy's all mazed with so many to greet." She turned to Charles. "I'm Mary Swinburne. This is my husband, Sir William." She indicated a middle-aged man with auburn hair and a pleasant face. "We live at Capheaton Hall, where we hope very soon to welcome you and your brothers. Though indeed," she made a charming little curtsey towards the Chief, "nobody can hope to equal the hospitality of Beaufront!"

"So say we all, my lady!" called young George Collingwood, a handsome man who was clinking mugs with one of the Widdrington youths.

Lady Swinburne smiled again and said, "Mr. Radcliffe, will you tell his lordship, I pray you, how eagerly we all await his coming, and that though we do not know him yet, our hearts already do him great honor."

Charles stammered an assent. He thought the lady agreeable, but he was embarrassed that she still held his hand. "We are kin to his lordship," continued Lady Swinburne, "at least Sir William is. I was but a poor spinster from Berkshire before my heart's delight here—" she waved towards her husband, "carried me off to the splendors of the North."

"Hoot, Mary," interposed her husband laughing. "Enough of your Southern compliments and graces, or young Radcliffe'll take you for a mincing courtier! As a matter o' fact, there are several of his lordship's cousins here today."

"Aye," said the youth, Peregrine Widdrington, putting down his ale flagon. "His lordship is kin to *me*."

"And to me," boomed a fat young man with piggy eyes and snuff stains on his splayed fingers. "Tom Forster of Etherstone, at your service, sir," he said, winking at Charles. "Tell his lordship m'fair sister Dorothy'll be here to greet him when he comes, fairest flower o' Northumberland *she* is! He'll like that I'll warrant!" Forster gave a lewd, slightly drunken chuckle, and inhaling a huge pinch of snuff sneezed luxuriously.

It occurred to Charles that if all these folk were kin to James they were also kin to him, though nobody mentioned it, and he felt the old twinge of being forever neglected and passed over in favor of the magnificent James.

Lady Swinburne was watching him covertly and read some of his thoughts, for she was a discerning gentlehearted woman. She loosed his hand, which had grown very sweaty, and said to the Chief, "But we forget that Mr. Radcliffe has not himself seen his brother in many a year, and must be eager to start. Where is your nephew, sir?"

"Up to his ears in paper and ink, no doubt," said the old man, shrugging, "ever trying to turn our few shillings into pounds, which can't be done." He raised his voice and bellowed, "Thomas! Thomas! Where the devil are ye!"

A stooped, frowning man walked into the hall, saluted the company briefly, and said to his uncle with reproof, "I was putting your bills in order, sir. I *pray* you, endeavor while I'm gone not to lose the rents again, and to pay our most importunate creditors or we'll have the bailiff here."

"Ha!" said the Chief, wagging his head. "Don't fret, m'boy. I'll keep out of a muddle if 'tis only to spite Will Cotesworth and his long-nosed canting Whiggish chums!"

"Aye so," said Tom Forster, sitting up. "Damn the Whigs, damn the Dissenters, and damn poverty! I've had m'belly full of it!" He tilted his hat over his eyes, slumped back, and quite suddenly began to snore.

After that the leave-taking was brief. Charles found himself hustled efficiently out of the hall by his traveling companion. They both mounted, and set out for Newcastle, where they picked up the post from Edinburgh at the Queen's Head.

During the four days which it took them to reach London, Charles's determination to enjoy himself had no help

41

from Thomas Errington. Thomas was twenty-five and looked older. He had done some soldiering in France, but that profession did not attract him. He was pale and earnest, his main topics were the scandalous prices charged at the coaching inns, and the doubtful success of his mission to London. Of this mission Thomas talked frequently and Charles perforce listened either in the coach—while sleet froze on the windowpanes, or in gloomy inn parlors—while Thomas pecked at his food and Charles longed to be out exploring the town—of York, or Newark, or Huntingdon, wherever they happened to be.

It seemed that there was a rich merchant from the North now living in London. His name was Henry Liddell, and he came from Ravensworth in Durham. It seemed also that this wealthy man was an intimate friend of Black Will Cotesworth's. At this Charles pricked his ears, thinking of the day when he had met the keelsmen and Meg. He said, "Oh, *that* scoundrel! What do you want with a friend of *his?*"

"Scoundrels they may all be," said Thomas gloomily, "but that lot control Tyneside collieries and shipping. They've got a monopoly, and we have to do as they say."

"Not your uncle!" said Charles. "The Chief of Beaufront doesn't have to toady, and he hasn't any collieries!"

"No. But he has a ship, the *Hexham*, an old coasting schooner, he won long ago on a wager. The Chief can't afford to fit her, and we hope Liddell will buy her, he's bought in a score of ships."

"Why don't you offer her to Cotesworth, instead of going all the way to London?" asked Charles.

Thomas flushed. "Cotesworth wouldn't touch her. He'd never help out a Papist, besides—well, the *Hexham*'s a poor risk."

Oh, Charles thought. This Liddell was obviously as sharp a businessman as his friend was, and Charles thought the whole project a forlorn one. He was faintly sorry for Thomas and tried to treat him to extra ales or a slice of capon from the skimpy funds Sir Marmaduke had allotted for the journey. Thomas would not accept; he was as proud as he was penny-pinching. Charles was very glad when they changed horses for the last time and presently at five o'clock of a cold December evening saw on the gray horizon the smoking chimneys and myriad church spires of London.

The coach was bound for the City, but it paused to let Charles out near Bloomsbury Square, where he said goodbye to Thomas. Charles stood blankly on the pavement, holding his small cowhide trunk in his arms and staring at the big new stone houses which lined the square. One of these houses belonged to Dr. Radcliffe, and inside it would be James. Candles in house lanterns shed a flickering light on the cobblestones. From several of the great houses there came bursts of singing, the plinking of a harpsichord, though the tall windows were all darkened by shutters.

A sedan chair whisked by as Charles stood there. The chairmen, shouting "Have a care!" pushed Charles roughly off the pavement when he didn't move. He stumbled on the slimy cobbles, then righted himself. A coach and four came thundering by and drew up before one of the mansions. A bevy of young ladies tumbled from the coach when a footman opened the door. Charles saw the jewels in their hair, heard the rustling of silks, and gay high voices sharpened by careless laughter. They swept through a door into a brilliant hall. The door closed, and still Charles stood on the curb.

Then, angered by his own timidity, he plunged up the nearest steps and pounded the knocker. A red- and silver-liveried footman opened, and seeing a youth of no apparent consequence, snapped, "Whatjerwant?"

Charles said he wanted Dr. Radcliffe's house and the footman said, " 'Tis here. Go to the back door. We've company. His Lordship of Derwentwater's visiting us."

"I know," said Charles. "And I am his brother from the North."

He walked into the hall.

The footman stared uncertainly at the old trunk, at the shabby travel-stained young man. "Wait here then." He did not quite dare shove Charles outside, and he disappeared down the passage to consult higher authority.

Charles put down his trunk and stood on the gleaming parquet. His heart was pounding. He had done no wrong but he felt guilt. It changed to fear as he heard the wailing of a man's voice, which seemed to come from somewhere upstairs. It was a muffled, tormented sound. Charles could at first not make out the words, though they seemed to be of anguished protest; then the voice rose to a scream. "He's here! 'Tis the fiend! He's come for me! Help me! Help!"

Charles started instinctively for the stairs, then stopped as a door to the right flew open and a girl came running out so fast she didn't see Charles and bumped into him. 'Oh la! I'm sorry," she cried, laughing. She examined Charles by the wavering light of the candle sconces. "Why,

I know who you are! You're Charles Radcliffe, aren't you? They've been waiting for you."

"Who makes that sound?" said Charles, pointing upstairs, and scarcely aware of the girl. The voice had now dropped to a confused sobbing and muttering.

"Why 'tis poor old Colonel Radcliffe—your uncle, I suppose he'd be. He had a fever in the Netherlands and has been a little mad ever since. But why do you hang about here like a stray dog, sir? Ah, to be sure—you don't *know* any of them, do you! I'd forgot. Lud, what a romp!" She clapped her hands, laughing again.

Charles stared at her. She was very young and not pretty. Both her snub-nosed face and her body—clothed in yellow brocade—looked round as dumplings. Moreover she had a large mouth, and freckles imperfectly concealed by a drift of powder. But there was a zest about her, a sparkle in the pile of reddish-curls, and her bright sherry-brown eyes were full of mischief. "Have a peep at them, before they see *you!*" she cried. " 'Tis ever good sport to glimpse others in secret —like a masquerade."

"I don't know—" began Charles, bewildered.

"Shall I announce the gentleman, your ladyship?" barked the footman, who had returned and was standing frozen-faced behind them.

"No," said the girl. "Go away!" The footman bowed and vanished.

She clutched Charles's sleeve and pushed him down the hall, towards a great door which she drew carefully ajar to disclose a slit of brilliance. This was the Doctor's drawing room, wainscoted in white and lit by fifty wax tapers. Charles had a good view of the dozen or so people within. "There," whispered the girl. "Your brother Francis in the alcove at the gaming table. The one who squints."

There were four men sitting intently around an inlaid table where the cards were laid out for basset. But Charles had no trouble recognizing his brother; despite the squint which gave an oblique unfocused look to the heavy-lidded eyes, despite an elaborate brown periwig, and hollow cheeks pitted by smallpox, and air of elegant languor, Charles saw that Francis was, physically at least, an older version of himself. Nor was this recognition pleasant. In that first glimpse Charles felt something secret and unhealthy in Francis.

"Yonder by the fire," whispered his guide pressing Charles's arm. "See the little maids prattling to Dr. Radcliffe?"

Charles saw two dark-haired children of eleven or twelve standing at the knees of a fat old gentleman in black silk who had a white peruke, and a nose purple and bulbous as a plum.

Charles grunted assent.

"The shortest one in the blue gown is your sister Mary—the other is a friend of hers, Anna Webb. They're both at the convent school in Hammersmith."

"Indeed," said Charles, who had almost forgotten that he had a sister, and was becoming more nervous, and impatient of this game. "But where is my brother James—the Earl?"

"Ah—" said the girl, drawing him back from the door. "Not in there. He often leaves the company. Listen." She moved with Charles towards another closed door farther down the hall. They both heard the plaintive chords of a guitar and a tenor voice singing softly in French.

James? thought Charles, embarrassed and astounded. James must be singing French love songs to someone, and yet the tune was sad.

"Don't!" Charles said to stop his impetuous guide, but she had already opened the door to the music room.

There was nobody inside except the Earl, who stood by the window looking out into the garden, a guitar slung around his neck. His head with the full-bottomed wig of cascading flaxen curls was turned from them.

But this was a woman! Charles thought for a horrified second. So small was the figure in the rose-embroidered satin suit, so small the gilt leather shoe which was raised on a chair rung to support the guitar.

The Earl turned and stared at the two intruders. "Lady Betty," he said with a blend of courtesy and coldness, "you and your gallant wish to join in making music?"

Charles gave a long sigh. It was a completely male voice which spoke, a rich pleasant voice with a slightly foreign intonation.

The girl flushed, seeing that, as so often, her pranks had bordered on rudeness. "Forgive me, my lord," she said curtseying. "But I bring you your brother Charles."

"My brother?" said the Earl. He put down the guitar, and walked slowly over to Charles. "*Mon dieu*," he said peering up at the tall gangling lad in the shabby suit, "and I had thought of you as my *little* brother!" His pale grave face broke into a singularly sweet smile. "Embrace me, *petit Charles*," he said. "I'm glad to see you."

The boy bent awkwardly, and James kissed him on either cheek. "I'm glad to see *you*, m-my lord," Charles stammered, trying to rearrange his ideas.

"You've already met Lady Elizabeth Lee, I observe," said the Earl.

"Not precisely, my lord," said Betty giggling. "I bumped into him in the hall when I was running away from our uncle of Richmond, who is ever trying to pinch me when Mama's not looking. He reeks of cognac too," she added tossing her head.

James ceased smiling. The Duke of Richmond was the relative through King Charles whom he liked the least, a libertine, adventurer, and turncoat, whose politics were as variable as were the morals of his mother, who had once been the beautiful Louise de Kéroualle, sent to England by France for the express purpose of seducing King Charles. Far worse in James's opinion was Richmond's religious behavior. He had been born a Roman Catholic, but had long since decided that in England Protestantism was more comfortable. Which it undoubtedly was.

"Were this my house," said James gravely, "I would not receive His Grace of Richmond. Cousin Betty, I suggest that you stay closer under your lady mother's kindly eye, she may be worried at your absence." He softened the dismissal with his gentle smile, and Betty immediately took the hint and disappeared.

"Is *she* a cousin *too!*" Charles cried looking after the girl. "Where does she come in, my lord?"

"She is a grandchild of King Charles, as we are," said James. "Though a Protestant, of course. I've been amazed myself at meeting so many new relatives since my arrival. But 'tis not of that I wish to speak. Sit down, Charles."

The boy obeyed, and his brother sat opposite him and spoke earnestly. "I'm sorry you should find me singing a French song when you came in. There'll be no more of that, nor of harking to the melancholy past at Saint Germain. I am an Englishman, and will so live in every way. How is it in the North, Charles? How is it at Dilston, which will be my dear home—as it was my forefathers'?"

Charles felt the wistfulness in the questions, and he tried to answer them, though he made a lame job of it, and ran down completely when it came to describing Sir Marmaduke and Cousin Maud.

James nodded a little and said, "I see. We've none of us had happy boyhoods." He stood up and, walking again to the garden window, gazed out into the darkness. He looked back at the years in France. There had been gaiety at times, picnics and hunting parties, the companionship of other young Jacobite exiles. There had been glittering ceremonies at Versailles where Louis XIV, *le roi soleil*, and Madame de Maintenon shed their benevolent but patronizing rays over the rightful King of England and his sorrowing, anxious mother. Yet now as James looked back at those years he saw them all bordered in black, the black of disappointment, of humiliations, and of homesickness. Not all the exiles felt that way; certainly Francis did not. Francis had not wanted to come home. Yet wherever Francis might find a gaming table or a horse to wager on he would be as content as his sardonic nature would allow.

To James, it seemed now that every night of those years he had dreamed of home. Of London sometimes, more often of the surrounding English countryside where he had once snared rabbits, and ridden his pony, or played by the flowering hedge rows, or collected robins' eggs in the happy years before his father died. Lately he had dreamed much of the North which he had never seen, and yet the moors and the wild mountains up there were in his blood, as they were his inheritance.

Last year all the exiles had thought they would be going home. King James—so wickedly called the "Pretender" by his enemies—had at last persuaded King Louis to give him French ships for the invasion of England. The attempt had failed miserably. There had been bungling of orders, and stupidities, and then the young King had got the measles in Dunkirk and been too ill for action. More heartsickness then, at St. Germain, more anguish for the widowed Queen, who retired as usual to her frenzied prayers at the Convent of Chaillot.

The whispers had begun again, whispers that there was a curse on all those of Stuart blood. That moaning ghosts were seen in the shadowy couloirs of St. Germain, that Satan was heard to laugh from under the shabby gilt chair which served as "throne" to the exiled King. Superstitions these were, of course. James had refused to listen to them; yet in the sickly atmosphere of that pathetic sham court he had himself suffered forebodings, and once thought to have seen the ghost of the old deposed King James.

These ghosts had now ben left behind, James thought, staring with relief into Dr. Radcliffe's neat new garden, where the shrubs were as yet so small they could scarcely have hidden a cat.

James sighed and, turning, said to Charles, "I shall be grateful as long as I live to Dr. Radcliffe. It was he, you know, through his great friend, the Duke of Ormond, who prevailed upon Queen Anne to give us permission to come home."

"I didn't know," said Charles. He added tentatively after a moment, "Did the Pretender—that is, the king-over-the-water—mind your leaving?"

The Earl shook his head. "No. He is content to wait until Queen Anne dies, when he will certainly be called back here to reign peacefully. 'Tis the wisest course and in God's hands. We'll say Masses of Intention for it. Charles, I trust you pray for our most wronged and Catholic majesty daily?"

Charles looked blank. "I—I haven't, my lord."

"Ah well," said James with his quick, warm smile. "You will. And don't look so gloomy! I hope we'll all be merrier than we have been—now that I'm home again."

For Charles the next fortnight was indeed merry. There were festivities of many kinds. Musicals and balls, supper parties and theaters; there was a masquerade at the Duchess of Cleveland's. Through Dr. Radcliffe's hospitable drawing rooms there flowed a stream of the illustrious, mostly Tories and frequently Jacobites, for such were the wealthy old Doctor's own convictions. Since the arrival of the young Earl and his family, Roman Catholics were also invited. Dr. Radcliffe was a dedicated Anglican, but he was also a man of the world, and willing to abey his prejudices to please Lord Derwentwater, for he was very proud of the kinship. Besides, he was rapidly growing fond of James.

So was Charles. In all his anxious, resentful imaginings about his elder brother, he had never suspected that he might find James admirable, that he might feel love for him. Yet so it proved. James was kind; despite his small stature he had a strong, composed dignity. And James was exceedingly generous.

A fashionable green velvet suit and brocaded waistcoat were made for Charles. He was given a small flaxen tie wig—not, naturally, a long full-bottomed one like James's, which would have been suitable neither to his age nor rank. Charles was given a sword with gilt scabbard and hilt. He was given fine linen shirts with lace ruffles, and he even took to washing himself occasionally, so delighted was he with the gallant he now saw in the mirror.

Two women also contributed to Charles's new interest in his appearance. One was the beautiful Duchess of Bolton and the other was Lady Betty Lee, who became a frequent companion at balls or in a theater box, or at Dr. Radcliffe's gatherings.

Betty Lee was nearly as unused to fashionable life as Charles. She was also sixteen, and this was her first winter in London, for she had been raised quietly in the country at Ditchley Park, Oxfordshire, where her father, the Earl of Lichfield, had retired from public life after refusing to take oaths of allegiance to William III.

"As for Mama," said Betty one day to Charles in the Radcliffe drawing room, "she had a baby every year or so for eighteen years—and no time for gadding. But now all the older ones are settled, so Mama's come here to see what the London marriage mart'll offer *me!*"

"How perplexing," said Charles laughing at her. She always rattled on and it was hard to take her seriously.

This was on a snowy twilight two days before Christmas, and Dr. Radcliffe had asked several friends to drop in for a collation—coffee or chocolate, cakes and madeira. Lady Lichfield had arrived early with Betty. She bestowed an absent-minded frown on Charles but allowed him to lead the girl to a sofa by the windows. The Countess herself drifted towards another matron, Lady Stamford. The middle-aged ladies each accepted a cup of chocolate from a footman, then settled near the fire to gossip.

Francis Radcliffe was at the gaming table in the alcove playing ombre with two Catholic barons. The elder, Lord Widdrington, was a Northumbrian, a spindling paunchy man of thirty with chronic indigestion and a touch of gout in his left foot. He played irritably, slapping down the cards and cursing when they were trumped. The other baron was little Lord Petre, who was only nineteen, undersized, and somewhat like a whippet. His round eyes darted anxious looks at Francis, who played languidly, never seemed to glance at his cards but always won.

Dr. Radcliffe had not yet returned, having been called out to treat the Duke of Beaufort, a friend so close and influential that the Doctor had for once accepted an inconvenient summons. The old physician was famous for his brusque treatment of patients, and for the offense he had once given Queen Anne, though his reputation was not thereby affected, and he commanded immense fees.

Nor was James present in the drawing room. He was closeted in the library with the Northumbrian lawyer Roger Fenwick and with Thomas Errington who had dropped by to pay his respects. The Earl was eager to understand all he could about his Northern estates before he went to Dilston.

Charles was unused to sitting in warm scented rooms, he longed to be out walking in the snow, sampling the giddy life of the great city, but it would be rude to leave Betty and, besides, Henrietta, Duchess of Bolton, would soon be arriving. Charles was fascinated by that practiced and seductive lady. That the Duchess was over thirty, and that Dr. Radcliffe was infatuated with her too, did not decrease Charles's interest. She aroused in him a voluptuous excitement, and he had dreamed of lying in her arms.

"Charlie!" said Betty giggling, and pinching his knee. "Say something, you great booby. I dislike being ignored."

Charles jumped and said gaily, "Oh, I was trying to picture you married, my pet, and I can't—no more than me. Has your lady mother found some likely takers?"

"Not yet. I've a fair dowry, but I haven't the looks my mother and grandmother had. 'Tis a pity," she added flatly. Lady Lichfield, still a handsome woman, had been Lady Charlotte Fitzroy, King Charles's favorite daughter, and a great beauty, while *her* mother had been the Duchess of Cleveland, best known to the world as the "incomparable Barbara Castlemaine."

"But I think you comely," said Charles awkwardly. He had not yet learned the easy bandying of compliments, nor did Betty invite them. Still she *was* comely—despite red hair, big mouth, and freckles. Charles liked her, he was comfortable with her, and he found her smooth plumpness appealing enough, though he had no wish to fondle her as did various elderly noblemen, who were always stroking Betty's round arms or chucking her under the chin as if she were a dairymaid. "And I hope," he said grinning, "her ladyship finds you a rich titled husband who'll dote on you and let you romp at every masquerade!"

Betty laughed, showing all her strong white teeth. "She had her eye on Derwentwater, and I wouldn't mind much though he's shorter than me."

"*James?*" cried Charles, startled. "Has he offered for you?"

"Oh no. I said *Mama* had her eye on him, but she's giving up hope. She didn't realize how devout a Papist he is. He's such a grand match that my father'd overlook that, but my Lord Derwentwater wouldn't."

50

"No," said Charles. He could not imagine James marrying out of the Church, nor imagine him marrying at all, for that matter. James was agreeable to everyone, he made graceful speeches to the pretty ladies who fluttered around him, yet there was something untouchable and solitary about him. Still, marry he would, of course. The name, the title, the estates must all be carried on, and already Charles knew that his brother would never let selfish inclination stand in the way of family duty.

The drawing room door opened, the supercilious footman stalked in and announced, "Her Grace the Duchess of Bolton" to the ceiling, then stalked out again.

"Oh gemini!" cried Betty with a flounce. "Here's her high and mightiness and you'll have no eyes for *me*—what you can see in that painted old doxy—"

"She isn't!" said Charles indignantly. "Sh-h." He stood up, preparing to bow. Betty stood up and sank into a curtsey. At the gaming table Francis quietly pulled towards him the ten guineas he had just won from the others, then stood up, his narrow face expressionless. Little Lord Petre rose eagerly, craning to see the Beauty. Lord Widdrington muttered something, belched, and hauled himself up onto his good leg. By the fireplace the Ladies Lichfield and Stamford rose in a sedate, reluctant manner and exchanged a look of exasperation. The Duchess was no favorite with her own sex, and though by marriage she far outranked these ladies they considered that, in view of her dubious parentage, her superior airs were ridiculous. To be sure, Henrietta Crofts was an acknowledged Stuart, but a tarnished one since she was only the natural daughter of the illegitimate Duke of Monmouth, who had been beheaded after his rebellion.

The Duchess entered, pausing a moment in the doorway, a vision in a new French gown of flowing violet taffeta garnished with brilliants. Two long blank curls hung forward over naked white shoulders and down to her slender tight-corseted waist. She waited regally for the customary tribute of the indrawn breath, which duly came from Charles and Lord Petre, then she undulated into the drawing room on a wave of musk and sweet tinkling laughter. She was followed by two admirers, for Henrietta never moved without an entourage. Today these were a red-faced country baronet, Sir Coplestone Bamfylde, and a cadet of her husband's house, a simpering coxcombe called Mr. Paulet who made himself generally useful in return for lodging and an allowance. There was also a small turbaned blackamoor page

51

who carried the Duchess' fan and pomander ball.

The Duchess inclined her graceful head in recognition of the various bows and curtsies which greeted her, and her sapphire eyes roamed lightly over the assembled faces. "The worthy Doctor is not present?" she asked with a delicious pout of her rouged lips. Her blue gaze rested on Francis because she had found him bafflingly unresponsive to her charms.

Francis bowed again. "*Il est sorti, madame*," he replied. "*Il va revenir tout à l'heure*." Francis spoke French because he preferred it to English, and also because he knew it embarrassed the Duchess, who understood little of the language. His squint gave the effect of his looking past her, and she turned away with a petulant shrug.

"Well," she said, "then someone must amuse me until my dear Doctor appears—not you gentlemen who have put yourselves to such endless trouble in my behalf already." She gave Sir Coplestone and Paulet an enchanting smile and a dismissing wave of her white beringed hand, "But *you*, sir!" She turned the smile full upon Charles, who crimsoned to his eartips. "If," went on the Duchess smoothly, "Lady Elizabeth will be so good as to yield her place on the sofa?"

"Old strumpet!" murmured Betty as loud as she dared, but there was nothing for it but to curtsey and move away, leaving the dazzled Charles to the Duchess.

Henrietta settled herself gracefully, spreading her violet skirts, arranging the silver-lace ruffles at her bosom to disclose the tops of her breasts, which were pushed up by the stays to a rounded firmness they did not actually possess. Nor was her face as oval as it once was, though the slight slackness of throat, and the fine lines near her mouth were well concealed by an enameling of paint and powder. On her temple a black beauty patch like a crescent moon drew attention to her best features—the sensuous blue eyes and the dark curls which clustered above them, and she knew from his expression that Charles found her very seductive.

It was pique which had first roused her interest in the young Radcliffe lad, pique that both his brothers seemed indifferent to her. The Earl politely so, Francis with a silky insolence she could never quite fathom. Also, Charles was handsome in a callow rawboned way, and it occurred to the Duchess that it had been several years since she had taken a very young lover. There would be a fillip to it.

As Charles continued to gape at her wordlessly, she laughed and gestured to her Negro page, who handed her a painted gauze fan. She flicked the fan open and lowering her long darkened lashes said, "You will put me out of countenance, sir, if you stare at me like that. Do you think me such a fright?"

"You know I d-don't, your grace," said Charles. "I don't know what to say, except I-I wish I could kiss you," he went on in a desperate rush.

"Oh la, sir, you go *monstrous* fast!" cried Henrietta, feigning anger so well that Charles was fooled.

"Forgive me, madam," he said miserably. "I don't know what made me speak so. Forgive me." And to cover his confusion, he added at random, "Your blackamoor, he has a silver collar with a crest on it."

"Why, 'tis my crest, to be sure," said the Duchess, seeing that she had frightened Charles and must let him recover. "Juba is my slave. Dr. Radcliffe gave him to me, and Juba was sent him by some Colonial planter in the Virginias— William Byrd was, I believe, the name of the planter, wasn't it, poppet?" She turned indulgently to the Negro boy, who bowed solemnly.

"Yuss, mistiss. I'uz born in the Quarters o' Master Byrd's plantation in Virginny, then Master he sold me 'cross that big ocean to Dr. Radcliffe."

"And you like it better here, don't you!" said the Duchess, patting the turbaned head. Juba's intelligent brown face creased in an ingenuous grin. He rolled his eyes ecstatically, and made the expected answer.

"Sho do, mistiss. Jest like heaven with you, no beatings, have ale an' white bread ev'ry day. A pure angel you is, mistiss."

The Duchess laughed complacently. Not all her servants evinced such devotion, and she enjoyed seeing herself in this flattering light.

"*Sure* you're not homesick, Juba?" teased the Duchess. "Shall I send you back to Virginia with a Mr. Spotswood who's going out as Governor?"

"No, no, mistiss!" cried Juba kneeling and nuzzling a portion of the violet skirt. "Don't make me leave you, never! I'd die ef I couldn't see your beautiful sweet angel face a-smiling at me."

"Well, well," said the Duchess. "It's a good little black dog it is, and shall stay with me." She waved Juba aside, and the page instantly sprang to his post behind the sofa, where he folded his arms and stood motionless.

"How delightful," said Henrietta, glancing sideways at

53

Charles, "to be certain of *one* person's affection in this miserable world."

"Your husband, madam," answered Charles nervously after a moment. "For sure the Duke must dote upon you."

This piece of naïveté startled Henrietta, but it intrigued her too. She proceeded to explain with many sighs and flutterings of her lashes that the Duke was an old man, with no thoughts for her, that they seldom met, and in any case that doting affection was woefully vulgar in an aristocratic marriage. During this conversation, she moved gently nearer to Charles, so that he felt the warmth and pressure of her body against his side. His head began to spin and presently he found himself making amorous speeches which the Duchess no longer rebuffed.

Betty, after one disgusted look at this scene, drank a cup of chocolate and allowed herself to be ogled by Sir Coplestone and Mr. Paulet, a pastime which annoyed her mother since the baronet was married to somebody in Devon and Paulet was a nobody.

In fact, thought Lady Lichfield, there was no one here of any eligibility at all, just Roman Catholics and hangers-on. A situation not improved when the footman curtly announced, "Mr. Pope."

"Merciful heaven!" murmured Lady Lichfield as a tiny young man with a crooked back most obvious under a plain black suit, hunched into the room. "Another Papist! And a dwarfed linen-draper's son to boot. I must say Dr. Radcliffe has a singular taste in friends."

The two ladies watched Alexander Pope wander towards the gaming table, where nobody welcomed him, so he took a cup of coffee and sitting down surveyed the company alertly. He had come because he was a protégé and past patient of the Doctor's, and because he was, as yet, much flattered by inclusion among the nobility.

"He looks very odd," said Lady Stamford, "though I've heard he's written some pretty pastorals, and is quite the thing at Will's Coffeehouse these days."

"Oh, those *Whigs* have no discrimination at all!" said the Countess acidly. "Pack of warmongers and place-seekers, running after the Marlboroughs, toadying that dreadful Duchess—don't speak to me of Whigs!"

Lady Stamford quite agreed, but felt it only fair to remark that the Duke of Marlborough had won some glorious victories for England against France, and that one might even hope the war would soon be over. Her friend retorted that it never would be, unless the Tories got in, though there seemed to be a dawning hope of that, and forgetting for the moment her disappointment in Dr. Radcliffe's guests, she leaned forward whispering, "Have you head that Her Majesty will not speak to the Duchess of Marlborough any more—is casting her off? And high time too. Such insolence that woman has!"

Lady Stamford nodded. They pieced together the court gossip they had heard. Queen Anne's long domination by Sarah, Duchess of Marlborough was ended. The quiet, insinuating chamberwoman Abigail Masham was the new favorite, an excellent thing, since Mrs. Masham intrigued for the Tories as ably as the Duchess had intrigued for the Whigs. The Duchess had even managed to place all members of her family in the highest state positions. Now there was hope of overthrowing the whole lot of Marlboroughs. The Queen might vacillate for years, as she had, but once her mind was settled, or she allowed a stronger mind to settle it, she could be as stubborn as a tortoise. "Like she is in naming her successor," said Lady Stamford, who was a secret Jacobite. "*Nobody* can make her speak."

"But surely the succession's all settled on Hanover!" cried the Countess. "Willy-nilly we must have those Germans in, I fear. And 'tis perhaps better than a Papist king."

Lady Stamford did not think so, but she smiled and said pleasantly, "I wonder to hear *you*, my lady, who are a Stuart say that, and many believe that if Her Majesty actually names her brother as her successor he might go Protestant, and if he did not, he would certainly guarantee freedom of worship to his subjects."

"True, true," said Lady Lichfield vaguely. Queen Anne might live for years and her successor was not of great importance to a harassed mother just then. She had just noticed that Betty was almost sitting on the arm of Mr. Pope's chair and was laughing down at him in a saucy provocative fashion. The Countess rose, intent on putting a stop to such behavior, but was checked by the arrival at last of their host.

Dr. Radcliffe stamped in, flourishing his gold-headed cane and crying, "Welcome, welcome, my good friends! A thousand apologies for my unavoidable absence!" There was snow on his boots, snow on the collar of his cape, from which a servant was disentangling him, snow mingled with the silver-gray of his peruke. His great nose flamed red from the cold as well as from the brandy which the Duke of

Beaufort had given him. "Ecod!" he cried. " 'Twill be a good old-fashioned Christmas, and we must all make merry! Bring a bowl of punch!" he said to the footman. The Doctor's shrewd little eyes twinkled as he greeted each of his guests, and then he turned towards the Duchess of Bolton, who had drawn away from Charles and was smiling tenderly at her host.

"Ah my darling Duchess," cried the Doctor lumbering over to her. He seized her hand and kissed it with lingering gusto. "Did you miss me, hey, m'dear? Has young Radcliffe been diverting you? Get up, you puppy, and let me sit here!"

Charles was already up, and glad enough to yield his place, for matters had moved fast indeed on the sofa. He was choked with excitement, his head was hot, his hands were cold, and he wanted to collect himself. Henrietta had invited him to her mansion tomorrow night at ten, "When we will be quite safe from intrusion since it is Christmas Eve." There was no mistaking what she meant, and Charles was torn between desire and apprehension. He wanted to be alone, and wandered into a small anteroom where a coal fire was burning. He rested his hand on the carved mantel and stared down, unseeing, at the fire. But Betty followed him.

"What are you and the Duchess up to?" Betty asked with deadly feminine precision. "You look peculiar, Charlie—are you really going to let that woman seduce you?"

Charles stiffened, his eyes narrowed. "Lady Elizabeth, I find your remark offensive, and I fail to see what sanction you have for making it."

"Hoity-toity!" said Betty reddening. She drew back and her teasing smile faded. "I'm sorry, sir. I thought we were good enough friends for a jest. It seems I'm at fault."

Charles received the girl's apology with a slight bow, and might have spoken something civil had not a lackey come into the room with a scuttleful of coals, which he dumped on the fire. The rattle of the coals and the tiny cloud of dust they raised brought instant memory to Charles. He was standing on Tyneside by the keelboat on that September morning when he had met Meg. These very coals might be some of those he had seen then, a bizarre speculation which he clung to, so as not to go deeper into memories, for they were painful. And though certain of the sensations aroused by the Duchess were like those he had felt for Meg, others were not. The result was a confusion of shame and discomfort.

Betty saw that he had forgotten all about her, and was dismayed to feel her eyes sting with tears. Head high, she walked back into the drawing room.

Lord Derwentwater had now joined the company, and Dr. Radcliffe was imparting great news in his booming voice.

"What d'ye think, my lord? Imagine what my friend His Grace of Ormond has arranged!"

James smiled. "Something good, I vow, my dear host, since all your arrangements are surpassing kind."

The Doctor chuckled. "Oh, this is none of my doing. The Queen can't abide me, never could unless one of her miserable brats was a-dying and then I was always called too late. But it *is* an audience with Her Majesty I mean. She wants to see you and your brothers—alone. You're to go to her private apartments at the Palace. What d'ye think o' that?"

"That we are much honored," said James quietly.

The company had all turned to listen. Though the peeresses had long ago been presented at Court, none of them had had much contact with the Queen, who since the death of her husband, Prince George of Denmark, had almost entirely withdrawn from public life. This summons was an extraordinary mark of favor.

"Now what can *that* mean?" murmured Lady Lichfield. She surveyed Lord Derwentwater with new attention. He was kin to the Queen, and if Her Majesty was really wavering towards the Jacobites this Earl might become of tremendous importance—and even the younger brothers might also, thought the Countess, who was too realistic for any great hopes of inflaming Derwentwater with Betty. But the younger brothers were evidently not such devout Papists, and mixed marriages were common. Besides one heard that both youths were amply provided for by their father's will. Lady Lichfield glanced at Francis, then looked away. One did not get sentimental about marriage, yet she was fond of her daughter, and that pock-marked squint-eyed macaroni, permanently glued to a gaming table, would not make a pleasant husband. The youngest then—he was a promising lad, and the Queen's favor might produce all sorts of peripheral benefits even, some day, a title. Moreover, the young people seemed to like each other. The Countess looked around for Charles, who had come to the drawing room door and heard Dr. Radcliffe's announcement. Charles was staring at the Duchess, and waiting to hear, as she was, the date of the royal summons.

If it were tomorrow night, then their rendezvous would have to be canceled. But it was not.

The Queen's summons was for the Thursday after Christmas. The Duchess gave Charles one lightning glance of relief. Charles turned away, and beckoned for some punch.

The three brothers went to St. James's Palace on the following Thursday noon. They rode in Dr. Radcliffe's enormous new gilded coach, which was drawn by six horses. Eventually the Earl would keep his own London coach, and would repossess the mansion in Arlington Street where he had been born. But these things took time, and the Doctor's generosity continued to be most welcome.

In the coach the elegantly dressed young men were silent, each with his own preoccupation. James had had many political talks with the Doctor, who saw the royal audience as a splendid chance to further the Jacobite cause, and also, if possible, to sound out the Queen on the fate of Henry Sacheverell. Dr. Sacheverell was a violently Anglican and Tory clergyman who had delivered a couple of inflammatory sermons demanding that all Nonconformists be suppressed. The Whigs were furious. Dr. Sacheverell had been arrested and thrown in the Tower to await trial. All England was roused, and in the coffeehouses they talked of nothing else. James had scant interest in Protestant squabbles, though he respected Dr. Radcliffe's opinions. He did, naturally, have an interest in discovering whether the Queen had softened towards his cousin, her half brother, and intended to name him her successor. Yet, James thought comfortably, it didn't matter much. When Queen Anne died this rigmarole of Hanoverian succession would be forgotten and England demand the return of the rightful ruler. Everybody at St. Germain was certain of that. And James was weary of political intrigue, weary even of London. He wanted to get home up North.

Francis was subdued because his brother had given him a stern lecture on his want of manners, had forbidden him to speak French publicly, and suggested that he employ his time on something other than hazard, ombre, and basset. Study the Classics, for instance—or English history. A ridiculous suggestion. Francis had no intention of going north and was brooding about the best way of handling James.

Charles was silent because his head ached, and he was already sick of his affair with Henrietta. He had spent part of three nights with her. Nights of surfeit. He thought of the

Shadowy firelit hours in the huge soft bed. Smothering white-ness and softness. The scent of musk gone fetid and mingling with sweat. The white softness of her body, *too* soft beneath its concealing wisps of rosy gauze. The sourness of wine on her breath. Her clinging avid insatiability, and the tricks she knew to reinspire lust. He thought of how she had looked when he left her at dawn today and lit a candle so that he might dress. She had shrunk from the light, but he had seen the raddled face, the slack mouth, drooping in lewdness as were the breasts, and even the half-closed black-shadowed eyes. He had escaped without promising the time of his re-turn despite her pleadings. And outside the bedroom door, Juba, the Negro page who always stood on guard, had moved aside to let him pass, while the black face wore a look of knowing lasciviousness.

Charles leaned forward and grabbing the strap threw the coach window down. He inhaled deeply of the cold winter air. James looked around in surprise and Francis said in his languid drawl, "Damme, my dear Charles, I'm sorry you suffer for your interesting excesses, but I don't see why *I* should." He began to cough, raised blood-flecked spittle, which he examined on his handkerchief. Then he shrugged. "*Merde!* Shut that window!"

Charles obeyed. James said nothing, though he was dis-tressed by both his brothers. Francis coughed often of late, and was growing thinner, yet he flatly refused to take Dr. Radcliffe's prescriptions. As for Charles, one guessed of course that there was some sort of dissipation in progress, a whore, no doubt, somewhere—natural enough later but at sixteen neither vigor nor common sense was well established. It would be necessary to caution Charles about the dangers of gleet or pox, or even blackmail. A prospect James found distasteful.

The coach passed the Palace guards, who saluted when the postilion had stated the Radcliffe business. In the court-yard they drew up before the entrance to the Royal Apart-ments. The Queen's vice-chamberlain met them on the steps, and, ushering them up to a small tapestry-hung salon, said that Her Majesty would receive them presently.

There were two magnificent ladies already waiting in the salon. They had been conversing in low tones, but as the Radcliffes entered they both turned and stared at the broth-ers with open hostility. The elder lady was a stout hand-some woman of fifty with graying hair, and golden keys dangling at her ample waist. She glared at the newcomers, then turned her back with a sharp rustle of taffeta. The younger woman—fair-haired, with bright probing eyes—seemed to hesitate, then walked forward. "The Earl of Derwentwater?" she said, accurately picking James, who bowed. "I am Lady Cowper, wife to the Lord Chancellor," she continued. "We—that is the Duchess of Marlborough and I—have been discussing your arrival today."

"Indeed?" said James gently, now understanding the hostility, for nobody in the land was more Whig and anti-Jacobite than the Duchess of Marlborough. He bowed again. "My brothers and I are most flattered to be topic of conversation between two such illustrious ladies."

The Duchess gave a snort, and whirled around. "What does she *want* of you, that's what I'd like to know! And who arranged this private audience, which sort of thing has always been *my* privilege. That serpent of a Masham, I presume, for there's no limit to her insolence!"

"Madam, madam," said Lady Cowper, anxiously. Everyone knew that the Duchess of Marlborough in a temper would say anything she felt like, even—and apparently once too often—to her royal mistress. The Whig cause was shaky these days, and tact would not come amiss with this young Earl who was cousin to the Queen.

"Bah!" said the Duchess. "What's the use of beating round the bush. Let's find out what my lord here wants, and then we can tell him that he'll never get it from that guzzling, witless sack of meal in there."

Charles stared, jolted out of his own broodings into shocked amusement. It had taken all of them a moment to realize that it was the Queen to whom the Duchess thus referred.

"Her Grace is not herself today," apologized Lady Cowper quickly. "A touch of fever. My Lord Derwentwater, perhaps you didn't know that I come from the North as your family does?"

"Why, no," said James, who had never heard of Lady Cowper until now, though her husband, the Lord Chancellor, was a familiar and enemy name at St. Germain. "What part of the North?"

"Chopwell in Durham. I was Mary Clavering, and am kin to my Lord Widdrington, whom I hear you already know. You must understand however that I share neither Widdrington's politics nor his religion."

"Nor mine then," said James. "We must agree to disagree, my lady."

That was pretty cool of him, Charles thought, admiringly. Lady Cowper bit her lips. Even the formidable Duchess looked baffled. The small Earl in his lavish flaxen periwig, his blue embroidered satin suit, his amber gold-tipped cane, his shoes with high red heels in the French manner gave a first impression of effeteness. The Duchess, in fact, had just decided that he might be bullied, or possibly bribed into submission. The tone of James's voice, and the expression of his gray eyes now made this seem unlikely. The Duchess lifted her chin and jingled her golden keys— the keys Anne had once lovingly bestowed on her as Mistress of the Robes, Groom of the Stole, Keeper of the Privy Purse. Symbols of power, commensurate with the power Marlborough had won for himself at Blenheim, Oudenarde, and Malplaquet. Impossible that this power, so well deserved, might be threatened by a meaching chamberwoman. Abigail Masham! That viper whom the Duchess herself had put near the Queen as spy, and who now rewarded her benefactor with treachery. "What did you pay her, my lord, for this favor today?" said the Duchess through her teeth.

"Pay whom, your grace?" said James. "And I confess the reasons for your choler and insinuations quite escape me. We have no ulterior purpose here. We simply wish to present our respects to Her Majesty as she has requested. I believe our conversation need not be prolonged?" He walked over to the windows and gazed down at St. James's Park, where Christmas mummers were gyrating in the snow before a few passing noblemen. Charles and Francis joined him at the window.

"Bravo!" said Charles.

"*Quelle horreur que ces dames!*" remarked Francis, with a malicious chuckle. Lady Cowper heard in part, and she sent the Duchess, who was preparing to do further battle, a look of warning. French was the language of conspiracy, and the Radcliffes' behavior appeared threatening.

The vice-chamberlain came in and said that Her Majesty was now prepared to receive His Lordship of Derwentwater and the Honorable Mr. Francis and Mr. Charles Radcliffe.

"Then I am coming too!" announced the Duchess, gathering up her skirts.

"Pardon, your grace," said the vice-chamberlain. "Her Majesty said nobody else would be received, and she named you in particular."

"God's death!" the Duchess cried, color flaming up her

cheeks. "What have I done to deserve such treatment—monstrous ingratitude after a lifetime of faithful service! Oh, she shall hear what I think of this! Fetch ink, pen, and paper!"

As the brothers left the salon the angry Duchess was already sitting at a small desk, and Lady Cowper hung over her with soothing anxious sounds.

Queen Anne lay propped up in her gilt-canopied bed when the brothers were ushered in, and she was an appalling sight, so swollen with dropsy that the embroidered crown on the coverlet did not hide the enormous mound of her belly, and her features beneath a brown wig were blurred in fat. The weak eyes teared constantly, and the hand she extended, though still white and beautifully kept, was knotted at the joints from the rheumatism which had crippled her whole body.

James, Francis, and then Charles knelt and kissed the hand, while the Queen struggled higher on the pillows and peered at them through the dim light. She motioned to a quiet little woman in brown silk, who was the invidious Abigail Masham. "Open the blinds, that I may see better!"

The chamberwoman silently obeyed. Snowy daylight flooded the room and the Queen, blinking, stared from one to the other of the brothers.

"Indeed, Masham—there *is* a likeness, as we heard!" she whispered, dismissing Charles and Francis and turning back to James. "*You*, my lord, are very like him." She sank back on the pillows and shut her eyes, while the chamberwoman closed the blinds. The Queen gave a shuddering half sob.

"There, there, ma'am," said Mrs. Masham, gently patting the swollen hand which trembled on the bed. "Pray calm yourself. Here is your potion." She gave the Queen a china teacup which contained straight brandy. The Queen gulped greedily, not from natural intemperance, as many a sly lampoon had suggested, but because it was the only thing which eased the continual pains of her wracked body.

In a moment she sighed with relief and opened her eyes. "Your pardon, my lord," she said looking at James. "The resemblance upset me." Her voice, no longer gasping, was clear and pleasant, even sweet in tone, and James, seeing that he was expected to answer though not certain of his ground, said, "Indeed, Your Majesty, I know I somewhat resemble my cousin the King—" He broke off, as he saw Anne start, and emended hastily, "The Chevalier Saint George, that is, of course."

The Queen sat up. She spoke with a flash of regal indignation. "Surely you could not think me so moved by any likeness you may have to—to him they call *the Pretender!* And whom I have never seen."

"I crave your pardon, ma'am," James said, quite at a loss.

"'Tis my little William, that I speak of," said the Queen reproachfully. "The Duke of Gloucester! The erstwhile hope of England, and the only one of my poor children to live past infancy. Ah—he would have been your age now. Though taller, I warrant, as your brother is." She gestured towards Charles. "Bring the picture, Masham," she added.

The chamberwoman took a red velvet case from a drawer and opening it gave the Queen a miniature bordered with diamonds. The Queen held it close between her quivering hands. "See," she whispered, tracing each feature with her finger, "the large gray eyes, the roundness of the chin—yet more than that—there is an expression which you share that the painter has not caught."

James bending respectfully over the miniature, saw a general Stuart look about the eleven-year-old boy but no startling resemblance to himself. He murmured in sympathy, "'Twas the Will of God, to be sure, that Your Majesty lost this poor child; yet everyone must feel for your bereavement."

"Seventeen times," said the Queen in a flat, weary voice, "have I quickened with child, and not one has lived. 'Tis the Will of God—but I wonder—if it is the punishment of God as well." Her voice trailed off, she pressed the miniature to her mountainous breasts, and shut again her inflamed eyes.

James thought that the Queen's illnesses and tragedies might indeed be a judgment on one who had supplanted her father, and had so far refused to recognize the rights of her brother. His heartbeat quickened as he said, "When wrong is done, punishment follows. But wrongs may be repented of, and rectified. There is still time for that, Your Majesty."

For a moment Charles, who was watching from a little distance beside Francis, thought that James's grave sincerity had succeeded. That the Queen would speak some hopeful word about the future of the exiled King. A tremor passed over the swollen face, a look of yearning and uncertainty, then it was gone. The weak mouth closed to a stubborn line, and she spoke in querulous displeasure. "So, you too, my lord, must badger me, and remind me of how short a time you think I have to reign. Ah, that they'd let me be—these dogs and foxes ever yapping and snarling at each other. All that

I want, or have ever wanted, is the true good of England."

"I've no doubt of that, ma'am," said James gently. "I love England too. And I thank you from my heart for the permission to return you gave me."

"Yes, yes," said the Queen. " 'Twas because they told me you were like my poor little Gloucester, and that you were no intriguer, and would be content to live peaceably upon your great estates up North."

"I shall, Your Majesty," said James with utmost conviction.

The Queen stared at him hard for a second. "Were you not Papist I might wish to keep you near my person. There are so few I can trust. Many other peers have turned Anglican—which is the *true* church. Will you consider it?"

"No, Your Majesty," said James.

The Queen slumped back again, with a sigh. "Then you may go. Masham, my potion! My knee is aching so. Will you rub it for me? Oh, Abigail, what should I do without your kindness, when all the world else is pain!"

Dr. Radcliffe was greatly disappointed in the account of James's interview with the Queen. "So you found out nothing at all, except she fancies you look like that hydrocephalic little prince she once had! I might have known 'twas for some such dim-witted reason she wanted to see you. The woman's got a mind like a hen—flutter here, flutter there, never settle anywhere."

"Her Majesty is ill," said James with reproof. "Physically unable, I believe, to cope at present with the jangling factions around her."

The Doctor had the grace to look slightly ashamed. "Oh, no doubt. I kept her well enough in the days when I was her physician, wouldn't let her gourmandize and swill spirits all the time, though I couldn't keep her litter of little weaklings alive. 'Tis a tainted stock. But never mind that. Did she offer you any place or preferment?"

"Only on condition I turn Protestant."

The Doctor gave a derisive snort. "And I needn't ask your answer. Stiff-necked, misguided bunch you Papists are! Look at the old King James, traded three kingdoms for a Mass. Will his son do the same?"

James gave the peppery Doctor a quiet smile. "I'm sure he would, but I pray and believe no such trade will be asked of him. Is it not possible for all religions to live in amity in England?"

The Doctor shook his head. "My lord, you're wise beyond your years, but not yet wise enough to know how few people share your charitable temperament."

THREE

The Thursday following the visit to the Queen was Epiphany, and Dr. Radcliffe always celebrated the Twelfth Night of Christmas with rich observance of the ancient customs. He had decided on a small intimate gathering at his home, before the revelry continued at a ball given by the Duke and Duchess of Ormond. These festivities were also to constitute a London farewell for the Earl, who was heading north on the next Monday.

Charles viewed Dr. Radcliffe's Twelfth Night party with alarm, since both the Duchess of Bolton and Lady Betty Lee had been invited, and he saw no means of being comfortable near either of them. With the Duchess he had been playing a belated Joseph. Twice she had sent Juba to the Radcliffes bearing surreptitious letters for Charles, one beseeching him and the other haughtily commanding him to appear at Bolton House as before. Charles had sent back terse, misspelled notes saying that he had an ague and dared not go out. He felt an utter fool, especially as he could no longer remember what her early fascination for him had been. And he resented being forced into deceit. His uneasiness had been apparent to James, who entered Charles's bedroom one day and in the course of their interview evoked the fresh embarrassment which had to do with Betty Lee.

Charles was crouching by the fire and actually leafing through his Missal when James entered—an occupation so unusual that James stared, then said, "Why, Brother, I'm glad to see you so well employed. You're going to confession tonight?"

Charles nodded gloomily. "I hope Mr. Petre won't be too hard on me."

James lifted his eyebrows. Father Benjamin Petre was a stout, worldly priest who had spent these last years at St. Germain as tutor to James and Francis. Since their return to London the priest had been visiting his Petre relatives in Essex, but was now back at his post as family chaplain. "Mr. Petre'll be no harder on you than you deserve," said James noncommittally. "I don't want to pry, but I know you've something on your conscience, and it may be I could help. 'Tis a woman, I presume?"

Charles nodded again, and looking up into his brother's kind, composed face he blurted out the whole story of his miserable affair with the Duchess. Then, as James made no comment but listened gravely, Charles suddenly found himself speaking—though in a casual way—of a girl up North.

James was startled and inwardly amused. A pitman's lass and a duchess already, though the boy had only turned sixteen in September!

"I see," said James. "We all have our particular sins to struggle against, and yours I am beginning to think is lechery. Mr. Petre will concern himself with your spiritual direction, but I've been thinking of a material remedy too. An early marriage, my dear Charles, will help you."

"*Marriage!*" Charles repeated in so horrified a voice that James touched him affectionately on the hand.

"Not at once, of course, and you'll get used to the idea. Besides I know you like the lady, and she seems very fond of you."

"Who?" whispered Charles, recoiling.

"Why, our cousin, Betty Lee. Lady Lichfield had already approached me on the subject, and though at first I was dismayed because Betty is Protestant, I began to see the advantages for you. And we can pray that, as so often happens to a wife, Betty will convert."

"But, good lord!" cried Charles. "The Lichfields wanted *you!* And I—why I've never thought of Betty that way. Nor she *me!*"

"I take leave to doubt the latter," said James smiling, "if what her mother says is true. As for *your* feelings, Charles, I wonder if you know them? No one will force you, naturally. I just want you to think about it."

James ignored Charles's outburst that the Lichfields had

first thought of himself for Betty, because he did not wish to explain that his ideal wife would be someone quite different. She would be quiet and, convent-bred, well schooled to the responsibilities incumbent on the head of a great Catholic family. The rattling, heedless Betty did not answer James's needs though he thought she might suit Charles very well. Nor was Charles apt to have so good a chance again. Younger brothers seldom did. In fact, not having had the benefit of Lady Lichfield's private musings on the night when Dr. Radcliffe announced the coming audience with the Queen, and being himself without guile, James had been astonished at the offer. He had put it down to parental fondness, swayed by the girl's feelings, and he was quite sure that Charles would in time find the marriage desirable.

James was right, and Charles's capitulation came much sooner than he had expected.

Dr. Radcliffe spared no pains to insure his guests' pleasure on Twelfth Night. His spacious rooms had all been decorated with fresh garlands of holly and ivy. Nearly a thousand wax candles sparkled on the crystal of sconces and candelabra; the main fires were stoked with sweet-smelling applewood. He had also hired musicians, and placed them in the drawing room alcove. When Charles walked in trying to look unconcerned, flute, fiddles, and guitar were playing a lively rendition of "The Gloucestershire Carol."

Charles saw with acute relief that it was still only a family party; outside guests had not yet arrived. Dr. Radcliffe sat in his great walnut chair by the fire, beaming like a Father Christmas and waving a silver cup full of brandy punch while he sang with the music, "Wassail, Wassail all over the town, Our bread it is white and our ale it is brown . . ." though nothing so unsophisticated as bread and ale would be served tonight. "Ha, Charles!" he cried. "Go talk to your little sister, before a more interesting young lady arrives!" He gave a prodigious wink, by which Charles understood that the Doctor must have heard something of negotiations with the Lichfields, though nobody but James and Father Petre knew of the entanglement with the Duchess, whom Dr. Radcliffe continued to dote on.

Charles bowed unsmiling and joined James, who was sitting on the sofa with their sister, Lady Mary, and her friend Anna Maria Webb on either side of him. Both little girls had been released from the convent for the occasion. Charles had seen his sister but once, and didn't know what to say to her, though she greeted him prettily and held out a wax doll for his inspection. "Thee my baby, Brother Charleth," she said with a lisp, which made her seem younger than her twelve years. "I embroidered her gown mythelf, the nuns taught me." Charles murmured something and patted the doll, while James said, "They've taught you well, Molly." He turned to the other girl. "I'm sure you embroider too, Miss Webb?"

"Yes, my lord," said Anna. "I'm working on an altar cloth. Sister Hilda says I am too old for toys." She sighed, her large dark eyes looked wistful. She was a tiny little thing who gave promise of beauty someday, though she did not look even as old as Mary, so James asked smiling, "You cannot be so very aged, I think?"

"Fourteen, my lord," she answered solemnly. "Mama agrees with the sisters that I must now spend my time in serious study for a year. I dislike arithmetic," she added shaking her sleek dark head.

"Do you indeed?" James laughed. "And what do you like? Music, for instance?" He nodded towards the alcove, where the fiddlers were playing a gay number from Purcell's *Fairy Queen*.

"Oh yes, my lord!" Her little pink mouth widened in a smile. "I can play the virginals, and sing parts."

"Ah," said James courteously. "You have tastes like mine." His own words startled him, and he thought quickly of what he knew about the girl. She was the eldest daughter of a baronet, Sir John Webb, who was a wealthy Catholic land owner in Dorset. James, upon his arrival in London, had investigated the background of Mary's great friend and found her a suitable companion for his sister. The Mother Superior spoke highly of Anna's breeding and intelligence. It would be interesting to see what she was like in a couple of years. James put the thought aside and, turning to Mary, included both girls in his questions about their convent life, thus releasing Charles, who was far too preoccupied to pay proper attention to his little sister.

He glanced at Francis, who was standing in a corner speaking French with Father Petre. Francis looked sulky, because there would be no gaming here tonight, and the priest was endeavoring to divert him with an anecdote he had heard about a duel recently fought at St. Germain. The priest was the only person in the world who had any real influence on Francis, and that influence had waned of late.

Charles walked restlessly past the two and settled near his uncle, Colonel Thomas Radcliffe. The elderly man, dressed in his scarlet regimentals, had been brought down-stairs tonight and sat in a corner behind the fire screen, where Dr. Radcliffe could keep an eye on him. The bouts of madness had lessened owing to the laudanum and hen-bane the Doctor had been giving him, but the Colonel's behavior was unpredictable. He greeted Charles with trem-bling eagerness and said, "Nephew, nephew, ye won't let 'em put me in Bedlam, will ye? That's what *he* wants to do. I heard him whispering."

"Oh no, Uncle," said Charles kindly. "Neither the Doctor nor James would dream of such a thing."

"Not *them!* I don't mean *them!*" The thin blue-veined hands waved in agitation, he leaned towards Charles whis-pering. " 'Tis old Scrat, ye know who I mean, he's hiding now behind yon door, I can see his cloven hoof, can't you?"

Charles shook his head. "The dev—that is, Old Scrat—wouldn't dare come here on Twelfth Night. Why 'tis Epiphany and we've all been to Mass!"

This seemed to satisfy the Colonel, who crossed himself, said "*Ave Maria!*" and, resting his head on his hand, went to sleep. At that moment Lady Lichfield and Betty were an-nounced. They had brought a gentleman with them, a cousin of Lord Lichfield's called Francis Lee. He seemed an agree-able, stout, ruddy-faced man, but he made no impression on Charles, who was busy bowing and trying to avoid Betty's eye. It took Charles a while to realize that Betty was equally anxious to avoid his. In fact she was barely civil, and kept her back turned to him as she carried on an interrupted conversation with her cousin, whom she called "Dear Frank" in a determined, breathless voice. Betty wore a new green gown which became her. The auburn hair, freshly coiffed, was piled high on her head, and this lengthened her round face. She wore a pearl necklace and earrings and was alto-gether more elegant than Charles had ever seen her. He stole thoughtful glances at her. So did Dr. Radcliffe, who was puzzled at her obvious avoidance of Charles. The bache-lor Doctor enjoyed matchmaking, and had thought this one settled, but he now perceived there was something wrong between the young people. He left the drawing room and went to the kitchens, where he gave certain directions.

Upon his return the Duchess of Bolton and Mr. Paulet were announced. Henrietta swept in with her usual assur-ance, while her cavalier minced after her, a willowy, chinless sprig from the ducal tree whose hard pale eyes belied his general appearance of fawning effeminacy. Henrietta, dressed for the Ormond ball later, was resplendent in red velvet and as many of the Bolton jewels as she could arrange about her person. There was no denying her beauty, and the Doctor was in ecstasies; but for Charles there was no lessening of disgust. He now knew too well the corruption of soul and body which lay beneath this glittering surface, and he prayed that the Duchess had found someone else to satisfy her lusts and would ignore him—a hope quite inconsistent with Henrietta's character. She attacked at once, as soon as he had kissed the air above the hand she held out to him.

"Ah—Mr. Radcliffe," she said with great solicitude. "Have you *quite* recovered from the ague which I heard has confined you to the house all week?"

"Ague? Ague?" put in the Doctor laughing, before Charles could speak. "Why, my darling Duchess, you've been misinformed. This is the healthiest young dog that ever *I* saw, and not a day's passed but he's been out sampling our city's pleasures. Make hay while the sun shines—eh, Charles? For it won't shine much in Northumberland, I'll wager."

"Indeed," said the Duchess. There was a pause. "How relieved I am that I was misinformed." Her lids drooped over the sapphire eyes, but not before Charles had seen in them a glint of pure malignancy. James too caught the glint, and was not surprised, having observed in France the fury of a fading woman scorned. Still, there was no particular mischief she could do, James thought. He leapt in to divert her from Charles, who stood tongue-tied.

"What a magnificent brooch you are wearing, your grace! I'm sure it has a history, though none of its former owners can have been as lovely as this one!"

Angry though she was, Henrietta could not resist a tribute, and she allowed James to draw from her the history of the Bolton brooch. While she talked she glanced several times at Mr. Paulet, who was lolling against the mantel, and once at Juba, who stood by the door holding her fan and pomander ball.

Betty had watched the contretemps, and was first pleased by Charles's embarrassment, then sorry for him, then relieved as the meaning of it came to her. Charles, the idiot, had certainly philandered with the Duchess, and as certainly tired of it and fobbed the great lady off with excuses, thus alleviating one part of Betty's own discomfort with Charles. Jealousy. She had faced this in herself since their last meeting, and further faced the undeniable fact that one wasn't jealous unless another emotion was also present. This discovery had cost her many tears. Tears which had not escaped her mother, who commanded to know the cause of them and seemed not ill pleased when she found out. Betty had then passionately exacted a promise that Lady Lichfield would never breathe a word of this to anyone. "For Charles doesn't love me, and I'm not sure I care for him, and anyway I'd die if he came to know anything."

Lady Lichfield soothingly promised, and broke the promise at once by hurrying off to find Lord Derwentwater, with the first tentative offer of Betty's hand. She did not confide in her daughter, partly to shield Betty from possible disappointment, and partly because the child's further emotions had now no bearing on the matter at all, though Charles's had; and Lady Lichfield had tonight shrewdly brought along their cousin Frank Lee and instructed Betty to flirt with him, so that the situation might not look too pointed.

At stven Dr. Radcliffe rose. The time had come for the feast. Mr. Lee hastily made his excuses and told Betty he would see her later at the ball. Mr. Petre gathered up Colonel Radcliffe, who was still drowsy, and said that he would make sure the poor man was safely consigned to his valet before his own retirement for private devotions.

That left a party of ten, who proceeded to the dining room followed by the musicians. In the hall the Duchess created a slight diversion by relinquishing Dr. Radcliffe's arm as she cried, "Oh, Paulet! I have forgot a message to you from the Duke! I vow my memory worsens daily! 'Tis of rather a private nature—" she lowered her voice in an aside to Dr. Radcliffe, "to do with the governorship, you know—and I really must speak to the man a minute, if I may?"

"Of course, dear madam," said the Doctor. "In the anteroom there?" Henrietta gave him her dazzling smile and walked into the anteroom, followed by Paulet and Juba. She shut the door.

The company waited, and Dr. Radcliffe said importantly, " 'Tis not generally known that the Duke of Bolton may resign his governorship on the Isle of Wight in favor of Ireland, some such thing is in the wind. I believe Mr. Paulet is often used as confidential agent."

"Useful man, I expect," Francis drawled suddenly, " 'ld do anything his masters pay him to, I'm sure. We should have one like that in *our* family, James."

"I see no particular need for such," said the Earl pleasantly. And they continued to wait until Henrietta reappeared with Paulet and Juba trotted to the kitchens. The Duchess preceded the others to the dining room. She seated herself at Dr. Radcliffe's right, James beside her, little Anna Webb next, and then Mr. Paulet, whose vacuous expression was quite unchanged by whatever news the Duchess had given him. Since the child, Lady Mary, was on his right, he felt no need to exert himself, and the entire meal passed without his uttering a word. Lady Lichfield sat on the Doctor's left and Betty found herself between Francis and Charles.

There was a silence, then Betty burst out, "The moon was rising as we came in the coach but I wonder if it might snow again."

Charles said, "Well, 'tis the season for it." Francis coughed and did not bother to say anything. There was another silence, which Dr. Radcliffe broke. "Look, what's coming in the door! We must greet our Twelfth Night cake!"

Everyone turned to see two footmen bearing an enormous creation on a silver platter. It was a tiered cake, frosted with marchpane figures—a gold crown on top and sugared sculptures of the Three Kings and their camels around the bottom layer. The footmen solemnly deposited the cake in front of the host.

They all exclaimed, the girls clapped their hands, and the Doctor, with a gesture to the musicians, began to sing.

"Now, now the mirth comes, with cake full of plums
Where bean's the king of the sport here;
Besides we must know, the pea also
Must revel as queen in the court here."

"How delightful!" cried the Duchess. "What a truly splendid cake! Hasten, sir, and let us find out who are to be our rulers tonight!" She seemed as full of youthful merriment and anticipation as the children were, there was no sign of ill humor about her. The Doctor cut the cake and carefully portioned out the slices with a knowing smile. Everyone duly hunted for the mystic bean and pea which would turn them into temporary royalty, according to a custom observed since the Romans had brought it to the island with Julius Caesar.

Betty crumbled listlessly through her slice, for the Duchess would certainly be Queen. Those matters were usually arranged beforehand. Great was her surprise, therefore, to find the hard green pea at the same moment that Charles sheepishly held out the bean. Everyone clapped again, even the Duchess, whose gaiety did not diminish. "We salute Your Majesties!" she cried, getting up and curtseying to Charles and Betty.

The servants brought purple velveteen robes trimmed with false ermine and gilded brass crowns which were encrusted with paste brilliants, as were the two scepters. A small dais was carried in and the young couple's chairs placed upon it. The Doctor conducted the coronation, and made a speech which slyly hinted that perhaps this was not the only occasion in which the "King and Queen" would be seated side by side as the principal figures in a ceremony. Betty blushed. James smiled. Lady Lichfield beamed. The Duchess gave her most tinkling laugh and said, "La, dear Doctor, you are indeed a consummate master of the revels. Now surely their majesties have a command for us?"

This sudden notice and the Duchess' magnanimous behavior bewildered Charles, but all Betty's constraint had vanished, her head was spinning with excitement and the consciousness that Charles—now linked so publicly with her—looked handsome in his regalia, and she cried, "We command that you amuse us! Do we not, my liege lord? A riddle! Let the Doctor tell a riddle!"

Dr. Radcliffe immediately complied with

"My first's a negation as all will agree,
My second's deep water but not from the sea,
My whole is the season of festivity."

Charles got it first, "Nowell," and began to enjoy himself. The Duchess had obviously decided to forget the past. Betty was a gay co-ruler. The Wassail bowl circulated freely. The port and claret bottles were brought, whereupon the Doctor rose somewhat unsteadily and said, "Before we drink to the Twelfth Night, I propose the health of our true king-over-the-water! To King James!" He raised his glass, drained it, and flung it into the fireplace, where it shattered. The others sipped more delicately, Lady Lichfield after a moment's hesitation, the Duchess with a shrug. "You are courageous, sir," she said to the Doctor. "Many would think such a toast was treason, but to be sure we are all friends here. Dear friends," she repeated, smiling at him through her lashes, and squeezing his thick mottled hand. He had just been telling her of the huge legacy he intended to leave to her young son, Lord Nassau-Paulet. This legacy was not the only benefit Henrietta knew how to extract from the Doctor —and with the minimum of effort on her part.

The feast continued. They had a boar's head and sang "The Boar's Head Carol." They ate eel pie and plum puddings. They told jokes and more riddles. Charles, having found his voice, vied with Betty in issuing commands. The jests grew more bawdy. The young girls were sent to bed. Francis, after the fourth glass of claret, even roused himself and recited a ribald poem in French, which none of them quite understood except James, who laughed.

It was then Betty discovered that Mr. Paulet had disappeared.

"Why, look!" she cried, waving her scepter and frowning. "One of our courtiers has left without our permission. We are *most* displeased."

Charles added, "We are displeased. When he returns he shall be punished by dancing a jig for us."

Betty fancied there was a peculiar look on the Duchess' face, though Henrietta's voice was sweet and mock-apologetic as she said, "Forgive the poor wretch, Your Majesties, he has a weak head; he has doubtless need of air."

"To be sure," said Lady Lichfield, who was finding her stays too tight. "And indeed 'tis time we *all* set off for Ormond House."

The Doctor instantly agreed. One of the footmen went to summon the coaches, and reported that Lady Lichfield's coach had not returned, that there was a message from the coachman saying it had broken an axle.

"Ah," cried the Duchess gaily. "But 'tis of no consequence! Our King and Queen shall ride in *my* coach, and there's ample room for the rest of us in the Doctor's. Yes, yes, I insist! The royal couple must ride beneath a ducal coronet at least. 'Tis only fitting."

Henrietta was irresistible, since she appeared to be making a benevolent effort to give the young couple a ride alone with each other. Betty had a qualm. Surely the Duchess had never before shown like willingness to relinquish any of the trappings of her rank, or to squeeze herself into an inferior conveyance. But nobody else saw anything peculiar, and her mother was actually nodding approval.

Betty and Charles laid aside their robes and crowns, donned their cloaks, and entered the gilded coach, which was manned by four servants—the coachman, a footman on the box beside him, another on the step behind, and a postillion on the near lead horse.

In the darkness of the great coach, constraint returned to Charles and Betty, and they sat primly far apart upon the satin cushions. They listened to the rumbling of the wheels on the cobblestones, the clatter of hoofs from six horses, the crack of the coachman's whip, and the warning shouts of the postillion. Neither spoke for some time until Charles, peering out the window, said with some surprise, "Why, I don't see any lights, and there seem to be trees around us."

Betty looked through her window. "Ormond House is in St. James's Square, isn't it? I should've thought we'd stay in town to get there, but perhaps the coachman thinks the streets will be too crowded on Twelfth Night."

"It may be," said Charles, but he frowned as they passed the dim outline of a tiny thatched building which looked like a village tavern, and then plunged into the darkness of a tree-lined road, while beneath the wheels the bumping of cobbles had given way to the crackling of frozen dirt.

Charles reached up and knocked on the sliding panel which communicated with the footman behind. His knocks produced no response, nor did the panel budge. "Jesus!" said Charles. "What's the matter with that knave back there!" and he banged on the glass dividing them from the coachman. By the flickering coach lamps they could dimly see his rump on the box, and that of the footman beside him. This effort produced no result, either, except that the long whip snapped and the horses went faster.

"'Tis odd," Charles muttered. He did not wish to make a fool of himself by opening the door and shouting for attention, in case this were a customary byroad between Bloomsbury and St. James's Squares. Betty had no such reflection. "How *dare* they ignore us!" she cried, and jumping forward she grabbed the ponderous door handle, shouting, "Halt, I say, halt! Open the door!"

Tht coach stopped and the door opened, though it was not because of Betty's shouts, as they soon learned. The rear footman, a great burly fellow, thrust his head inside and said in a hurried voice, "We're in trouble, milady, there's a 'ighwayman outside. Now keep quiet and ye won't get 'urt." The footman reached in the coach, scooped Betty up in his arms, stood her on the ground, and held her pinioned with his huge arms before the astounded Charles could move.

Then Charles drew his sword and was out of the coach at a bound. Directly in front of him in the wan moonlight there was a shadowy masked figure on horseback; the figure held a large shiny pistol which pointed at Charles's head. "Give me your purse," said the masked figure to Charles in a muffled falsetto.

"By God, I *won't!*" cried Charles. "And what's the matter with you scoundrels up there?' he shouted turning to the Duchess' motionless servants. "There's only one of *him!*"

"We wouldn't want to get shot, sir," said the coachman calmly. "Best do as 'e says, if ye value your own life."

Betty gave a shrill cry, which was at once stifled by the hand of the footman who held her.

The highwayman brandished his pistol and said to Charles, "So you'll not obey me—then I must shoot."

It was not so much courage that caused Charles's next move as blind fury consequent upon the sudden perception of a plot. He knew that this was no real highwayman, and that the whole scene was as sham as any play-acting the stage could offer. That there might be real enough danger as well, he did not think. With all his agile young strength he lunged sideways for the horse's head, and whacked it across the nose with his sword. The horse snorted and reared, the pistol went off and smashed the coach window, whereupon the coachman and his mate and the postillion had their hands full calming the six frightened horses.

Charles grabbed the highwayman's leg and yanked the man from his saddle. Charles jumped on him and began to flail with his fists.

Betty, who had ceased struggling as she watched, felt the restraining arms around her begin to loosen. And she heard the footman begin to chuckle. "Go it, young sir," he whispered. "Bash 'im in!" Charles neither heard nor heeded the advice. The man beneath him hit back as best he could, but Charles delivered a violent punch on the nose and the man went limp.

"'Ave ye killed 'im, sir?' asked the footman who held Betty. Charles heard that and slowly drew back, staring down at the face from which the mask had long since fallen off. Despite the bleeding lip and mud smears, the narrow pimply face was recognizable.

"It's Paulet!" said Charles blankly, his head spinning. The footman released Betty, walked over to the man on the ground, and felt him. "No, ye've not killed 'im, sir, I see. Mr. Paulet'll live to do 'er grace's dirty biddings yet another day."

"Shut up, Will!" called the coachman angrily. "Dump Mr. Paulet in the coach, and get back where ye belong. That free tongue o' yours'll get ye 'anged at Tyburn yet."

The footman shrugged. "What abaht them?" he said gesturing towards Charles and Betty.

"Leave 'em 'ere," said the coachman. "We'll know wot ter sye to any story *they* tell."

The footman shrugged and, picking up Paulet, flung him into the coach, slammed the door, and climbed up to his perch.

"Wait!" cried Betty. "You can't leave us here like this!"

"Aye but we can, milady," said the coachman. "Ye may be sure our orders wasn't to coddle ye, *or* the young gentleman, an' I obey me orders." He cracked his whip and the horses started.

Charles and Betty watched the coach trundle off between the trees.

"Blessed Mary and the saints," said Charles on a long breath. "I can't think yet." He jerked his head several times, and fingered a lump behind his left ear. "I'm something addled."

"Oh, Charles," Betty cried, throwing her arms around him. "He *hurt* you! What a fearful thing this has been. Oh, what are we going to do?" And she began to cry.

"Don't," said Charles, the dizziness waning. "Don't weep, Betty. We're safe enough now. Just a matter of a long walk back to town."

"But *can* you?" she whispered. "Charlie, you were so *brave!* To think how you routed that villain!"

Charles was aware that his victory had been caused by rage, good luck, and the feebleness of his opponent, but her praise was sweet. He pulled her arm through his and they began to walk back along the country road. In a few minutes they reached the tiny tavern Charles had noticed earlier. There was a candle in the window, and Betty said, "Could we go in and rest for a while—get warm?" Her voice shook, and Charles forgot his own misery.

"Poor little coz," he said. "You must be frozen, and in those satin shoes." Betty's feet were, indeed, soaked from the icy puddles.

A slatternly landlady at length answered their knock. She listened sceptically to the tale of a highwayman, while scowling at the bedraggled young couple, then Charles showed his purse and she finally installed them by a fire in the empty taproom. She brought in some mulled ale. The warm liquor revived them both. They sat side by side on the settle, and began to talk.

" 'Tis clear enough now," said Betty. "That bitch gave her

orders to Paulet and the blackamoor page when she called them aside before supper, pretending there was a message from the Duke."

"Yes," said Charles slowly. "Juba had ample time to arrange all her connivings, to alert her servants—and the broken axle on your mother's coach—a lie! We fell headlong into her schemes. My only wonder is what punishment Paulet had orders to deal me. Would he have killed me, do you think?"

Betty shuddered. "I doubt that even the Duchess would put murder on her soul."

Charles nodded. "Maybe not. I was to be wounded, no doubt, and you left stranded alone in the dark. And whatever we said later, the Duchess could deny, saying that an encounter with a highwayman had so befuddled our memories that we knew not what happened."

"This she can *still* say—and will." Betty shook her head. "Who'd believe our tale against that of the Duchess of Bolton? Oh—she concocted a pretty revenge."

"And so can I!" cried Charles violently. "I'll find a way to make her smart, I'll—"

"Charles!" Betty interrupted, putting her hand on his. "I pray you, please don't. You'd run into more danger, and you're leaving for the North on Monday, anyway. Forget this outrageous attack, in which you—you were not, in the beginning, quite guiltless." Her voice thickened, and she averted her head. She extracted a lace handkerchief from her bosom and wiped her eyes.

Charles stared at her. Until tonight he had never thought of her as anything but a sharp-tongued, lively girl, with a passion for teasing and pranks. He was startled by this shaky disheveled Betty, obviously much concerned for his safety. And there was the strong, new bond of danger shared and surmounted.

"Betty," he said after a moment. "You're sorry I'm going North?"

"Of course, you great booby, except you'll be safe from the Duchess, and any other angry ladies you may have insulted here." Betty blew her nose, and turned to Charles with something of her usual briskness. "You've lost your peruke," she said, "and that cravat'll never again be fit for society."

Charles paid no attention to this. He took another drink of ale. "Would you mind being betrothed to me?" he asked on one quick breath, staring elaborately into the fire. "I—I've reason to think James and your parents wouldn't object. I mean—I don't either if you want to. I think we'd get along."

"La!" said Betty, the color flaming up under her freckles. Her heart began to beat as hard as it had when she struggled with the footman. "Truly, sir, you confuse me. I don't know what to say."

Charles did not either, being somewhat horrified at what he had already said. He took her plump little hand and kissed it. The hand trembled, and he saw that Betty's lips were trembling too. So he kissed them. The kiss was pleasant, though it inspired none of the sensations he had felt with Meg and, initially, with the Duchess. The kiss was safe, warm, companionable. There was respect too, an element notably absent in the other kisses he had given. "So now we're betrothed?" he asked shyly.

She swallowed. "I suppose so, Charles. I'm fond of you, I must confess." Fonder than he was of her, she knew, but time might remedy that, and in any case one did not expect wild romance in marriage.

"Are you warm enough now?" he asked with solicitude, enjoying a new proprietorial feeling. "Do you think you can walk back to London?"

Charles and Betty arrived in Bloomsbury Square at about four in the morning. They found the house ablaze with candles, James pacing up and down the hall, and Dr. Radcliffe ministering to Lady Lichfield, who was in hysterics.

Both youngsters were too cold and weary to correct the story the Duchess had already given. Her coach had returned to Ormond House just before the ball finished. It had been waylaid, it appeared, by a ferocious gang of highwaymen; the servants had been overpowered, Charles and Betty abducted for ransom, no doubt. The bullet-smashed window-pane lent credence to the tale. Which was not unique. Lord Dorchester's coach had been held up last week, and Lady Salisbury's a month ago. The news-sheets had been full of the scandalous laxity of the Watch.

Charles satisfied his distraught elders by some confused account of their escape, and changed the tenor of Lady Lichfield's cries by adding that he and Betty had plighted troth to each other, and hoped this met with approval. It did. James shook his brother's hand, Lady Lichfield kissed him and her daughter, Dr. Radcliffe brought madeira in which to drink a toast. The young couple finally went to bed, in a haze of rejoicing and congratulations.

Charles told James the true story of the highwayman next day, and found that his brother agreed with Betty. "It is wiser to forget this despicable matter since no real harm was done. I need not point out that this'll be a lesson to you, Charles. You played the fool and got burnt. But good has come of evil, since the adventure precipitated an understanding between you and our cousin Betty. She's a fine girl."

"She is," Charles agreed humbly. "And I find I'm very loath to leave her. I fear for her in this wicked town."

James smiled. "You needn't. She's going back to Ditchley Park with her mother. Mr. Petre can marry you there by special dispensation in the summer. But I want you with me in Northumberland first." He sighed. "Frank won't go, and I'm bound to admit a northern winter wouldn't help his chest. He and Uncle Tom will stay in the good Doctor's care. But I'd not like to go home without either of my brothers."

"Nor shall you, my lord," cried Charles. "You can ever count on me. And I swear I'll never give you cause for disquiet again."

On Sunday Betty and Charles were formally betrothed. James produced a cabochon ruby ring and Charles put it on Betty's finger. The young couple were then sent to the music room to amuse themselves, while Lady Lichfield and her lawyer, James and *his* lawyer, Roger Fenwick, all conferred in the library over the initial proposals for the marriage settlements. Betty was to have a jointure of £800 a year, and a manor in Berkshire. James offered to give Charles some of his Cumberland estates in addition to the £3000 left Charles by their father's will. Lady Lichfield's lawyer and Mr. Fenwick haggled a bit, as in duty bound, but the interview was harmonious. James was generous, and Lady Lichfield delighted that the the strain of husband-hunting was over and she could retire to the peace of the country.

There was also harmony in the music room. Happiness had beautified Betty. She sparkled and laughed and flirted with Charles, who warmly responded. When Lady Lichfield came to summon her daughter she found the two playing a hideous jangling duet on the harpsichord, while Charles nuzzled Betty's ear and she giggled and ducked her head.

"Foolish children," said Lady Lichfield smiling. "I can see that Betty will need every minute of your separation to learn proper decorum. I shall hope to give you a model of wifely dignity, Charles."

"Thank you, my lady," he said grinning. "Betty pleases

me as she is, and I long for the day in which I may claim her."

James and his French valet, Mr. Petre, Roger Fenwick, and Charles all set off on Monday in a hired post chaise. Often during the long uncomfortable ride north Charles thought about Betty. At York he even wrote to her, a laborious blotted effort which started with a catalogue of the sights he had seen. James, unlike Thomas Errington, encouraged sightseeing. Then Charles finished his letter with a shameless copy of one of his father's courtly poems, which was supplied by James.

> *My Goddess Lydia, heav'nly Fair*
> *As Lilies sweet, as soft as Air;*
> *Let loose thy Tresses, spread thy Charms,*
> *And to my love give fresh Alarms.*

Charles did not think it made much sense, but James assured him that young ladies expected love poetry, and Charles was anxious to please Betty, and increasingly willing to be guided by James.

The brothers stopped a few days in Durham to visit their elderly aunt, Lady Mary Radcliffe, and she took them to call on Lord Crewe, the powerful Bishop of Durham, whose wife's father was distantly related to the Radcliffes. There was hardly a great family in the North which was not related in some degree, it seemed. James was pleased. It confirmed the feeling of roots for which he longed.

Finally on a cold, cloudy January morning their chaise reached Gateshead,

The foggy air was yellow and acrid with smoke from the collieries. The Durham Road passed near the Park Pit, where Charles had met Black William Cotesworth on that far-off September day. If he continued to look he would soon see the row of pitmen's hovels where Meg had lived. Charles did not look. He was as unwilling to be reminded of his affair with Meg as he was of that with the Duchess. Both seemed incredible and shamed the many good resolutions he had made. From now on he would be a worthy and noble Radcliffe as James was. He would perfect his sketchy education by studying the Classics with Mr. Petre. He would fulfill his religious duties, and help James with the estate responsibilities. He would make himself into a dependable upright husband for Betty. Tenderly he thought of her laughing face, her plump wholesome body, of her voice and the little airs she had which showed her high breeding. Both she and he had royal blood in their veins, though Betty's ancestry was of longer noble lineage than his, Charles thought with humility. And she'll turn Catholic for me. I know she will, Charles thought with an added glow. Betty had as much as said so, during their last intimate moments of farewell.

Charles was so delighted with these happy reflections that he did not notice the crossing of Tyne Bridge into Newcastle. "Here's the town, my lord," said Roger Fenwick on an apologetic note. "Not much of one after Paris or London, I fear."

"It certainly seems extraordinarily dark and smoky," remarked Mr. Petre with a sharp sigh. His high-beaked nose twitched and he sneezed. What a pity that the young Earl's inheritance should lie in these freezing gray northlands. Nor could one hope for civilized welcome today in the shape of good food, wine, or beds. The last nights on the road had taught him that. The priest savored his comforts and was beginning to think that his agreeable chaplaincy might soon develop into a penance. He frowned at the nearly deserted streets, the huddled smoke-grimed houses and said, "*C'est morne.*"

James spoke quickly. "It *won't* seem dreary, sir, when we're used to it up here. In any case it's home, and in one's home, I'm sure one sees few imperfections. Where's my town house, Fenwick?"

"On Newgate Street, my lord," answered the young lawyer. "Not worth looking at today since it's been untenanted for years, of course."

"To be sure," said the Earl. "And we must hurry on to Dilston." He spoke the name of his castle as some speak the name of a lover, the priest noted bleakly. A curious name, said to be a contraction of Devilston, and located on the Devil Water. Bizarre fancies the ancient Radcliffes must have had, in fact all these Northerners, the priest amended to himself as Roger Fenwick, usually taciturn during all the months he had been of the Earl's entourage, suddenly cried, "There's Denton Hall, my lord, on the right. It was haunted by a ghost named Silky! She always kept an eye on her family there—the Rogers—and also on the pits nearby. She warned time and again the colliers o' danger, but some years ago Silky got offended; she's gone further north to Belsay Castle. Since she left there's been naught but trouble at

Denton. The old squire's turned lunatic, and the colliery caught fire. 'Tis still bur-rning, you can see the glow yonder."

They all looked through the window and saw a black cloud and sullen wisps of flame on a great desert of turf.

"What a taradiddle, Mr. Fenwick," snapped the priest. "I never thought to find you superstitious."

" 'Tis not superstition but tr-ruth," said Roger resentfully. "Not being of our blood *you* may meet none of the 'presences' up her-re, but I'll be bound his lordship will."

James stared at the young lawyer, who had hitherto been eminently sensible. Even Fenwick's speech had changed during this tale of Silky. It had broadened, the Northumbrian burr had crept in.

"I've no wish to met a ghost," said James smiling, "unless 'tis part of my duties. Is there one attached to Dilston?"

"Aye, my lord. Some say 'tis of a nun who was murdered by the Scots. There was a nunnery nearby in olden days. Some say 'tis the ghost of a Radcliffe who was slaughtered for defending his king at the Battle of Hexham Levels, which happened on your estate. King Henry Sixth, that was, during the Wars of the Roses."

"Well," said James lightly. "I believe I could make shift to welcome either a pitiable nun or a brave man who died for his rightful king."

"Nonsense!" said Mr. Petre, sneezing again and blowing his nose irritably. "I grieve to hear you speak thus, my lord. Though the Church holds with exorcism on occasion, I do not believe there is ever the slightest need for it, save in the minds of self-deluded simpletons."

"A lot *you* know," muttered Roger. He was Protestant and he didn't like priests, particularly stout arrogant ones.

"Can we see aught of the Roman Wall, Fenwick?" James interposed tactfully. "Even at Saint Germain I've heard of that, though little else was known about Northumberland."

" 'Tis here, my lord," Roger gestured from side to side. "This road runs along it. There's the *vallum* to the left, and here you can see the mounds that cover the stones. Further west, the wall shows plainer."

Charles looked up with interest, though he had scarcely listened to the ghostly controversy. "I've ridden along the Wall," he said. "Once it was manned by Roman soldiers, centurions, Sir Marmaduke told me. They were great fighters. I'd like to have lived in those times."

James laughed. "You find life too tame now? Well, we'll try to furnish you some excitement anyway. Fox-hunting for instance. I long to learn this sport myself."

"There'll be plenty to teach you, my lord," said Roger. "Not a squire in the county but dotes on hunting and shooting. Though 'tis tough sport. Not like in France."

"Good," James said. They were silent until at one o'clock the chaise reached Corbridge and drew up at the Angel. There was a crowd of townspeople assembled in the little square by the inn. As soon as the Earl stepped out on the cobbles he was greeted by a mighty cheer, and a babble of voices crying, "Darntwater! Darntwater! God bless his lordship!"

"Why, they expect me?" said James, taken aback. "Is it for *me* they're cheering?"

The landlord of the Angel had rushed out when he heard the chaise arrive. "We've been expecting ye all day, my lord," he cried, bowing. "Iver since Mr. Thomas Errington o' Beaufront come an' tould us when ye might be arriving. Please to step in the parlor whilst we sends over to warn 'em at Dilston. There's gents inside t'meet ye too."

James nodded. He turned again to look at the eager welcoming faces in the square. Tears came into his eyes and he raised his arm in greeting, tried to say something, then walked hastily into the Angel.

In the parlor the old Chief of Beaufront and Sir William Swinburne were waiting. They rose uncertainly as they saw the Earl, so small, so erect, and so gorgeously dressed in plum-colored satin and velvet cape, a gold-braided tricorne on his flaxen periwig.

"Y're exceedingly welcome, my Lord Derwentwater," said Sir William, bowing with great ceremony and mindful of his lady's warnings that Northumbrian heartiness and familiarity would not do. "We are gathered to pay you honor and to offer our most humble services in any accommodation we—"

"Why, you must be my cousin, Will Swinburne," cried James cutting through the speech and staring at the red hair. "And you, sir," he turned to the old man, "the Chief of Beaufront! Come, you 'can't treat me like a stranger, for I know all about you and have dreamed of you many a night."

"By God then—you're *not* a stranger!" cried the Chief suddenly rushing forward, hugging the Earl and slapping his back. "Ye've the look of a Radcliffe and ye're home at last, where ye belong, and I vow this is the happiest day o' me life!"

It was the happiest day of James's life. His own Dilston

horses soon were brought over the bridge to the inn. They all mounted. The horses were decorated with rosettes, their tails braided with ribbons. The cortege rode towards Dilston and the cheering crowd grew each moment, as word of the Earl's arrival got abroad. When James rode off the bridge onto his own land he saw that the riverbank was dense with people, all dressed in Sunday best. The men were bowing and tugging their forelocks, the women curtseying. They were his own people, a thousand of them—his tenants and servants, and pitworkers too from his lead mines as far away as Alston. Busby, the steward, had gathered them in readiness at dawn this morning.

As James came among them, an old crofter from Slaley began to play the Northumbrian pipes and the crowd began to sing in their wild throaty voices. Not one word did James understand, yet he could not mistake the warmth of their welcome. When they entered the wood which led to the castle two lads ran forward with a banner on which someone had painted the Radcliffe arms. James saw the two black bulls as supporters, the familiar quarterings, which included the royal arms of Britain, and even the motto worked out in uncertain lettering, *Sperare est timere*. An odd motto, he thought—"To hope is to fear." But his father had once explained it. Hope in a way meant apprehension, and the lack of faith. And this I'll never lack, James thought, so God will help me always to care for my loyal people here. Once more tears came to his eyes as he waved and smiled and thanked them.

James did not see the caged skeleton hanging on the gibbet as they passed through the castle grove, for a small girl had darted up with a large bouquet of pine cones—the only offering which could be garnered from the January woods. She thrust it at the Earl, stammered something, and retired in confusion. Charles, who followed his brother at some paces, saw the gibbet without emotion. The contents were no longer human at all. The horses did not even turn their heads, and Charles wondered that he had felt so much revulsion last September. He had been a child then—no doubt of that. Afraid of a gibbet, afraid even of James! Sir Marmaduke and Cousin Maud, who were now dithering a welcome on the castle steps, they no longer counted. There was no cloud ahead, no prospect more dire than a winter of sport and at the end of it—Betty. They would come here on their wedding journey, and ride the moors together and dance the night through. Together, as they had been whilst King and Queen of Twelfth Night, they would shake up the staid Northumbrian gentry. The old castle would ring with laughter and music, and then at times alone, there would be the dear companionship in the great new bed which James had said he would buy for them. Soon, but not too soon, there would be children. Charles saw them as shadowy little figures with no characteristics except the ones he had lately come to admire—the pride of high birth and suitability. Doubly royal these children would be, bearers of a great name and lineage, raised too in the Catholic faith which would doubtless be the faith of most Englishmen, when Queen Anne died and James Stuart crossed the water to his rightful throne.

"Move on, move on, Radcliffe!" Mr. Petre's irritable voice jarred Charles out of his thoughts. "How long d'you expect me to stand here in the cold?"

Charles had been blocking the castle doorway, and he jumped aside. "Forgive me, sir. I was thinking how well content I am—as James is." He indicated his brother, who stood smiling in the hall and soothing Cousin Maud's spate of apologies for the condition of the castle.

"Humph," said the priest casting a disgusted eye at the stained plaster of the Great Hall, at the rush-strewn floor, where two hounds were snarling over a bone, at the pewter flagon of small beer which Lady Constable was offering the Earl and which was apparently the only drink which *would* be offered. "So you're content! *De gustibus non est disputandum*. And since nobody seems to have succeeded in teaching you Latin in this barbarous country, I will add that it means I don't agree with you at all."

FOUR

From the day of his arrival home, James lost the brooding melancholy he had sometimes shown. He became alert and vigorous, full of enthusiastic plans for the improvement of Dilston. On the morrow of his arrival, James summoned Busby and commenced a tour of the property. Busby was a quiet, spare Northumbrian who had been born in the castle fifty years ago and had received his education from the resident chaplain of that time. He was proud of the black silk suit and official gold chain which proclaimed his stewardship. He was proud that he and his wife, the housekeeper, managed to regulate some thirty-three servants, despite the recent handicap of Lady Constable's twitterings.

Busby showed the Earl Dilston's natural beauties first—the avenue of magnificent chestnuts, the cascade in the Devil Water, the view, somewhat overgrown, of Corbridge across the Tyne. They went to the breweries, the dairies, and the stables. "Ah," said the Earl, "I see we need more mounts. And I must breed a pack of beagles too."

They walked to the adjacent village, and the Earl knocked at every door, greeted the inmates personally, and kept a sharp eye out for needed improvements. At the cottage of John Selby, the blacksmith, Mrs. Selby tried to hide her idiot son Jackie from the Earl, thinking that he might order the lad sent to the lunatic asylum at Newcastle as Sir Marmaduke had threatened.

But the Earl did no such thing. He took the boy's flaccid hand, smiled into the vacant eyes, and said, "Perhaps, Mrs.

Selby, a new suit will cheer the poor innocent. See to it, Busby, I pray."

Nellie Selby burst into tears. She was something of a ballad-maker, and that night, while spooning crowdy into Jackie's gaping mouth, she expressed her gratitude in a song, which all the village soon learned.

> *"O Derwentwater's a bonny earl,*
> *He wears gowld in his hair*
> *And glenting is his hawking eye*
> *Wi' kind love dwelling there."*

Last of all, James went over his castle, which had only twenty-four rooms, besides the attics and offices. He began in the stone tower, which had stood here since the fifteenth century, when Sir Edward Radcliffe married the heiress of Cartington and moved from Cumberland to Dilston. The old ivy-covered tower contained the disused nurseries and the stewards' suite; beneath there was a dungeon vastly older than the tower itself. "There's said to be a tunnel from here to the Tyne, my lord," said the steward, "but I canna be sure. 'Tis only the Lord o' Dilston is permitted to know Dilston's secrets."

"Permitted by whom?" asked James, glancing with distaste at the dingy vaults of the dungeon.

"Why by the 'presences'!" said Busby, somewhat surprised. "The ould Radcliffes went to all the trouble to make hidy-holes and escapes. They'd not like anybody but the owner to know of 'em. An' if everybody knew them, what good'd these escapes be in time o' danger?"

"Ah, the times of danger are past, Busby. And now since the Union we needn't even fear the Scots any more."

The steward waggled his head. "I wouldna trust 'em *neither*. But 'tisn't only the Scots—there was need o' priests' holes here last century. Your great-great-grandsir, Sir Francis, that was—the first baronet—he made a priest hole when he built the new wing time o' Queen Bess. And used it too, I've heard."

"No doubt," said James, and he thought of the many Catholic persecutions there had been since Henry the Eighth took religion into his own hands. There were no persecutions any more, but there were galling restrictions—a Catholic might not hold public office, or a commission, he might not attend the universities or run for Parliament. On sufferance we are in our own land, James thought, yet would not let his joy be dampened. Someday there'd be a change for the better, and in the meantime give thanks for being home.

"Do you know where the priest's hole *is*, Busby?" he asked as they walked from the old tower into the wing the first baronet had built. "Near one of these fireplaces, I suppose?"

"I don't know, my lord," said Busby. "Ye'll find all Dilston's secrets in the ironbound coffer in the chapel. I've gi'en ye the key."

James nodded absently. "I'll read the papers soon, for I must hire a good builder. I want to enlarge this house."

Dilston should be made modern and airy with spacious wings around a marble courtyard. There would be fountains, vistas, formal gardens. The old tower might be left for sentiment's sake but it should be disguised and incorporated into a harmonious whole. This would be a costly project, yet it would be of benefit to all the countryside and eventually employ many workmen. James did not lag in ordering immediate benefits for his people, either. Long overdue repairs were made to each cottage in every hamlet on his vast estates; near his Alston lead mines he built new dwellings for the miners, while from now on, bread and beer were always to be had for the asking at the Dilston kitchens.

The Earl's tenants were jubilant. There had been many fears before he came. Fears of a Catholic landlord who might compel his people to attend the popish Masses in Dilston chapel. Not by law, of course, but a lord of the manor had no need of law to enforce his views. There were subtle ways. Land might be suddenly confiscated, rents might be trebled, roads might be barred so that access to markets became difficult. Some of the village gaffers had prophesied just such distresses when they heard that a second priest was to be quartered at Dilston and saw that the chapel was refurbished with a crucifix, candles, and images of saints.

But the young Earl pressed his beliefs on nobody, and it turned out that the new priest, Mr. Petre, was no trouble at all. Mr. Brown continued to minister to the scattered Catholics on the estate, and continued to offer most of the Masses, while Mr. Petre was scarcely seen. The castle servants averred that he spent all his time by his bedroom fire, huddled in a fur-lined cape, sipping hot sack, jabbering to the Earl's French valet, Pierre, and writing interminable letters to France. He did not even accompany the Earl and Charles and Sir Marmaduke on their hunting expeditions or on the initial round of visits to great Northumbrian Catholic houses. Mr. Petre said that his constitution would not stand freezing in the dankness of old Border keeps, or stand a diet of burned mutton. Anyway, since the Earl seemed forgetful of France and the plight of their rightful king, someone must keep in close touch with St. Germain.

James did not deserve the rebuke. He prayed constantly for his cousin, James Stuart; nightly he toasted him. Once, in response to a ciphered letter which the priest decoded, he had sent a hundred pounds to James Stuart's mother, Queen Mary of Modena. But James was too honest not to admit to himself how much he preferred this way of life to the anxious intrigues at the exiled Court, and preferred as companions these staunch Northumbrians, many of whom were his kin, and all of whom made him feel welcome.

He visited the Erringtons at Beaufront, and then the Swinburnes at Capheaton Hall. He was charmed with the gay Lady Swinburne, played his guitar for her, and even sang French madrigals at her request. Every day he was in the saddle, and whenever there was a thaw during the winter snows he went fox-hunting. He was thrown several times, he injured his leg, his small hands reddened, then cracked and oozed with chilblains, but he never flinched.

"Wey now," cried the old Chief of Beaufront, " 'tis a canny laddie wi' a lion's heart, a tr-rue Northman we've got for Ear-rl!" And nobody gainsaid him.

James, Charles, and their entourage visited the Thorntons at Netherwitton and then rode to Morpeth, where on Saturday, February 18, they turned North for Widdrington. Lord Widdrington had invited them to spend the Shrovetide at his castle. It was the culminating visit, and Mr. Petre had dislodged himself from Dilston for the occasion. He joined the Earl's party in Morpeth. The priest was glum, sneezing, and red-nosed yet determined to do his duty. The Earl of Derwentwater was Northumberland's first Catholic peer, but Lord Widdrington was the second, and the priest had received instructions from St. Germain. His Majesty wished to know all about Lord Widdrington—the size of his estates, the number of men at arms he might command in case of need, the strength of his loyalty to the Stuart cause. Particularly since the Lord Chancellor's wife, Lady Cowper, was related to Widdrington, and one wondered if so strong a Whig influence had unsettled the Baron's allegiance. These matters were known and brooded over at St. Germain.

Neither the Earl nor Charles shared Mr. Petre's speculations. Both young men were in high spirits, and eagerly anticipating the Shrove Tuesday ball which Lord Widdrington had promised them.

"Twill hardly be like Mardi Gras in France," said James laughing, "but I'm curious to see how Northumberland holds carnival. Ah," he added as they saw a forbidding gray stone pile looming up on a hill so as to command a view of the coast as far south as Tynemouth, "a splendid stronghold, I see, though a trifle old-fashioned."

Mr. Petre snorted. "If it's had so much as a new window since the time of the Conqueror I'll eat my cassock."

Charles stared with some interest at the stark crenelated fortress, noting the tiny slit windows. Behind them many a bowman had doubtless sheltered in the troubled days when the Scots menaced from the north or there was constant danger of invasion from the sea by whatever enemies England had at the moment—Saxons, Danes, Frenchmen.

James, following the same thoughts, said, "They were a brave race—the Widdringtons. D'you remember 'The Ballad of Chevy Chase'?"

> *"For Widderington my heart is woe,*
> *That ever he slain should be;*
> *For when his legs were hewn in two,*
> *Yet he kneeled and fought on his knee."*

"I trust," said the priest dryly, "that *this* representative of the family would be as zealous in a good cause."

Charles, remembering the peevish gouty baron who had played ombre with Francis at Dr. Radcliffe's, wondered too.

Widdrington greeted his guests in the great castle Hall. He was flanked by his two young brothers, Peregrine and Charles, and was trailed by his wife—a faded little woman who cast anxious, spaniel looks at her lord—and by some of his children, all dressed in new scarlet clothes for the occasion.

Lord Widdrington still had gout, he leaned on a stick, and he had other ailments which kept his wife and a resident apothecary busy brewing a succession of potions and liniments, but his pinched face was as amiable as his dyspepsia would allow it to be, and though he was already wishing the visit ended he was resigned to the demands of hospitality.

There were great wood fires burning at either end of the Hall, there were hearth rugs, and velvet chairs, and tapestries over the draughty little windows. There was a tremendous bowl of usquebaugh punch, with toast and scones to accompany it. There was an ample supply of snuff and tobacco in canisters, and Mr. Petre, stuffing his clay pipe, gave a sigh of relief. Not so uncivilized after all, and many signs of the wealth he had heard imputed to Widdrington. Now to sound out his loyalty.

Lord Widdrington lowered himself into his armchair, waited irritably until his wife had placed a stool under his gouty foot, shoved her away with a sweep of his hand, then said to James, "Well, my lord, we've a great company invited to do you honor at the ball. Everyone of merit in the North Country, saving of course such as the Percys and Greys who wouldn't come if I asked 'em."

Mr. Petre seized his chance. "Why not,. my lord?" he asked. "Are they Whigs? Anti-Papists? Or anti-Jacobites?"

Widdrington jerked his head. His swimming eyes glared at the priest. "Let's say they don't see as we do!" he snapped. "And, Petre, a word of advice. *Discretion*, sir! No awkward questions. Least said soonest mended on—on any topic which might offend some of our neighbors. You know what I mean?"

"Certainly, my lord," answered Mr. Petre with an angry flush. "I doubt anyone has ever thought me a troublemaker, but in *this* household I thought—"

"Don't think," said Widdrington. "Lent'll come on Wednesday and you can think for six weeks. Derwentwater," he turned his back on the priest and addressed James, "I trust it won't distress you, but we've a couple of Scottish noblemen visiting here."

"Why, no," said James smiling. He had been amused at his chaplain's discomfiture and quite agreed with Widdrington's obvious wish to avoid political discussion. "I've known many fine Scots in France."

"Well," said the Baron, "we don't like 'em much in Northumberland, but they turned up here last night on the way to Scotland and I couldn't very well refuse hospitality. Lord Kenmure's all right—a gentle old laird, spends most of his time pottering around his place in Galloway, but I'm not so sure of the other one."

"Oh?" said James politely, noting that Charles and young Peregrine Widdrington were having a wrestling match in the corner of the Hall and regretting that both his dignity and his size prevented him from joining them.

"The other Scot's a Seton," said the Baron. "A very odd

fish, seems to have spent his life lurking on the Continent, living like a peasant, even took up blacksmithing, I believe. But he's just been served Earl of Winton after considerable fuss. Has a woman with him too, he calls his Countess, though old Kenmure say Winton's not bothered to marry her, unless it's by one of those flimsy Scotch rites—Protestant folderol of some kind. Damn it, m'lady," cried the Baron suddenly turning on his wife, "where's my posset? There's the castle clock striking six, and I've not had my posset yet!"

Lady Widdrington gulped nervously and flew towards the kitchen.

James perceived that his interview with his host was over, and he went to join the other young men who were now playing with a litter of hound pups.

The Shrovetide passed agreeably for everyone except Lord Widdrington, who retired to his chamber to nurse a new discomfort in his belly, and for Mr. Petre, who was annoyed at his failure to discover the precise state of his host's Jacobite sentiments. Lukewarm, the priest thought angrily. Even Derwentwater. As for the Scottish lords, they were both Protestants, and tended to avoid the priest altogether. Petre had no opportunity to question them, and he decided that the visit was a failure and there would be nothing of any importance to report to St. Germain.

He was, however, too pessimistic, and the Shrovetide ball produced developments, one of which changed the whole course of Charles Radcliffe's life, though it had little to do with the Jacobite cause.

Shrove Tuesday morning dawned fine and clear. At six all the Catholics went to the Widdrington chapel to be shriven, as was the old custom, and after Mass the "pan-cake" bells began to ring. While the company assembled in the Hall to eat the ritual flapjacks and drink spiced ale, guests began arriving. All day long they came by horseback, in carts, or in heavy lumbering coaches. They came from all over Northumberland; Charltons and Herons from Tynedale, the eccentric Jack Hall from Otterburn, Swinburnes and Middletons and Fenwicks, Shaftoes, Collingwoods, and Claverings. The Forsters came too from Bamburgh—Thomas Forster, the fat hobbledehoy Protestant squire whom Charles had met in December before setting out for London. Forster brought his beautiful sister, Dorothy, with him and all the young men were enchanted. She had chestnut curls, great wide brown eyes and the prettiest roseleaf complexion in Northumberland. Dorothy was something of a coquette, and when the young people trouped to the village green to watch the rustics play their Shrove Tuesday football game, and then burn a straw effigy called "Jack-o'-Lent," she was surrounded by a crowd of admirers. Peregrine Widdrington and George Collingwood fought for a place beside her on the bench. James sat on her right and smiled at her with a softness Charles was astonished to see in his rather ascetic brother. Charles, spurred by all this rivalry, was only deterred from trying his own wiles on Dorothy by the fact that his elders had the field. It was only later as he dressed for the ball that he remembered Betty.

He thought of his betrothed with compunction. Mr. Petre had brought a gay, ardent letter from Betty which had arrived at Dilston. Each day Charles had meant to write her, but the busy moments slipped by. He might start a letter now—if he could find a writing desk and implements. He turned his head and looked towards the little window, distracted by a noise from outside. A piercing, squealing racket which at first he didn't recognize. He went to the window, which opened towards the North Sea, but the sound came from the field below the castle. He peered down and saw the light of fires, the shadowy outlines of tents, and figures moving among a herd of donkeys. The Faws, he thought. And one of them was playing the pipes. They all had pipers or fiddlers. He and James had encountered several bands of these wandering tinkers in the last weeks of travel. The first time this happened he had naturally been reminded of Meg and their expedition to see the Faws on Newcastle town moor. But as he disliked reminders of Meg, the impression soon passed, and he did not think of her now while he hurried to prepare himself for the pleasures of the ball.

This ball at Widdrington Castle was actually a "hopping," in which the young people romped through country dances or jigged together to the boisterous music of fiddles and cymbals and drums. Charles enjoyed it far more than the decorous minuets he had stumbled through in London, and when he grabbed Dorothy Forster's hands and bounced her through a lively hay he laughed with exultation. He did not see a swarthy tinker come to the door of the Great Hall and stand quietly watching the dancers. Charles would not have recognized Jem Bailey if he *had* seen him. It had been dark on the Newcastle moor; Bailey then had worn a large felt hat, and anyway most of the Faws looked alike. But Jem Bailey recognized Charles. His shiny black eyes stared at the boy's laughing face.

Lord Widdrington was sitting in his chair, chatting with the Scottish Earl of Winton, a rugged middle-sized man with the pointed face of an otter. Winton's Seton relations considered him eccentric to the point of lunacy, and were ashamed alike of the tales he told of his wandering life as a laborer and of the mysterious young woman he had suddenly produced as his countess. Magdalen, her name was, and many thought it apt. Lord Winton cared not a fig what anyone thought. He had always done as he pleased, and now in new possesion of his title he could jeer at the world when it suited him. "Ye've invited a tinkler to your dance, my lord?" he asked in his dry ironic voice, indicating Jem Bailey. "I congratulate ye; they're better company than most of the gentry."

Lord Widdrington turned in his chair, saw Bailey, and rapped sharply with his cane. "Come here you! What're you doing here?"

The Faw walked over to the Baron. "Wouldst have me play the pipes, master? I've brought m'pipes."

"I would *not*," cried Widdrington. "Get out! You and all your dirty tribe. I didn't give you leave to come here."

Bailey's thin lips curved. He went on as though the Baron hadn't spoken. "M'pipes play bonny tunes, master, that ye might like to hear—'Walton-le-Dale,' now, is a fine tune."

The Baron's prominent eyes flickered, and he stiffened. "I never heard of any such tune," he said after a moment.

"But ye must've, master," pursued Jem softly, "since 'tis such a favorite o' your own Townley kin in Lancashire. 'Twas there I learned it!"

Mr. Petre had been smoking by the fireside, but he had been watching, and he saw that there was something going on. He edged up close to the scowling Baron, the unperturbable Faw, and to the Earl of Winton, who was himself studying the scene with amusement.

"Yet after all 'tis not so much to *thee*, master, I would play 'Walton-le-Dale,' " continued Bailey. " 'Tis commanded I play it for the Earl of Derwentwater. Be so kind as to point him out."

"That I won't!" cried the Baron. "Be off wi' you and your mischief-making!" He brandished his stick.

"There's Lord Derwentwater yonder—dancing with my Lady Winton," said the priest suddenly, for he had every intention of getting to the bottom of this. "I'll summon him for you, tinker." And he went straight to James and tapped him on the shoulder. Widdrington gave an angry grunt, shrugged, and turned to Lord Winton. "That nest of hotheads down in Lancashire, always brewing up new mysteries. Damn-fool rites and ceremonies they have, too. Most of 'em not even Catholics, bloody Anglicans—begging your pardon, my lord. I forgot you were one."

Lord Winton laughed. "No offense. I take it that Walton-le-Dale refers to some Jacobite fraternity? With which my sympathies are supposed to be engaged, since Setons always *have* fought for Stuarts. Yet I'm no follower of tradition as yet and, like you, my lord, turn a lackluster eye on plottings. Ah, I see that Derwentwater's been lured away from my charming Countess; with your permission, I'll claim her for a dance." The Scottish earl stalked over to his lady, who was a blowzy blonde so furbished with paste brilliants and tags of laces and tawdry ribbons that she seemed to have dressed from a scrapbag.

Mr. Petre drew James into the service hall, where the Faw was waiting and idly fingering his pipes.

"Master—" said Bailey, regarding the small, resolute, and very young Earl with some astonishment. "I mun talk wi' thee. Not here." He glanced at the passage, where servants were running to and fro.

"In the old guard room then," said the priest eagerly, and he hustled Bailey and the bewildered James into an empty room made in the thickness of the walls, and furnished only with rusty muskets, some moldering crossbows and a pike or two.

"What *is* all this?" said James, when the door banged behind them. "What are you doing with this tinker, Mr. Petre?"

The priest shrugged, and said, "I've sharp eyes. I believe I see a tiny *J* stitched on his shirtsleeve."

"Oh," said the Earl on a long sigh. One of the secret Jacobite marks, like a white rose petal or like the famous limp that some of the agents used for identification and which stood for the four royal names—Louis, James, Mary of Modena, and the Prince. Many agents had turned up for orders at St. Germain, and here was apparently also one in the wilds of Northumberland. "Well," said James, "what is it? You've a message from France?"

"Not from France, master. From Lancashire, from Walton-le-Dale. They've sent for thee."

It took James some minutes to understand that there was a zealous society in Walton-le-Dale, a tiny village outside Preston; that the Duke of Norfolk was the president, and the members, both Protestant and Catholic, were all Tories and fierce Jacobites. They wished James to visit them as soon as possible, since there was something new afoot. News that could not be written, nor indeed confided to any of their messengers. The important thing was that James must obey the summons as quickly as he could.

"To be sure he will," said the priest, when Bailey had finished his story. "Lord Derwentwater'll start straight away."

"No," said James. "I will not travel about in Lent, nor travel to Lancashire until I've seen my estates in Cumberland. Later I will go to Walton-le-Dale. You may tell them that, tinker, and here's something for your pains." He tendered Bailey a sovereign. "I can think of no urgency that won't wait a few weeks," he added firmly to the simmering priest. "*You* may go if you wish."

The priest compressed his lips, torn as usual between a possible duty and the intense discomforts he foresaw on the journey.

"I thank thee for the gold, master," said Bailey with dignity, dismissing the whole subject, which was no longer his concern. "And I'll play the pipes for thee in return." He began to work the bellows with his arm, and James, always interested in music and always courteous, smiled indulgently, as the melodious dronings began. Petre gave an exclamation and darted out the door, leaving it ajar.

It was thus that Charles, who had been puzzled by James's disappearance from the dance, heard the sound of the pipes and followed it to the guard room. "God's bones, Brother!" he cried as he burst in. "Have you lost your mind? Here's Dolly Forster wanting to dance with you, and you skulk in here with this infernal racket, which I vow is like starving rats trapped in a drain!" Being half tipsy Charles burst into a guffaw and gave the piper a rough playful shove which pinched the bag into a truly ludicrous squeal. Even James bit his lip to keep from laughing before he said, "Charles! Behave yourself. I'm sure the tinker pipes well."

Bailey knew himself to be the best piper in the North, and had been playing for James the very difficult "Keening on the Moors." He let the pipes dangle, and raising his head stepped back. He gave James a look of contempt and Charles a look of pure hatred. Then he bowed.

"I'll bother thee no more wi' the noise o' starving rats trapped in a drain," he said. His heavy-lidded black eyes rested a moment on Charles's grinning face. The piper walked out of the guard room and disappeared down the passage.

"You've made no friend of him!" said James, "and you've drunk quite enough, my lad, but never mind. Let's enjoy ourselves, there's only two hours left before Lent comes in."

After Easter, James set out on his trip to Cumberland for the inspection of his lands near Keswick and on Lake Derwentwater. From there he proceeded into Lancashire and duly met all the members of the secret society of Walton-le-Dale, in which he was at once enrolled. He had been right that there was no great urgency about his coming. News of a Stuart landing in Devon proved untrue. Now the members simply wanted to welcome Derwentwater, and to hear all they could of conditions at St. Germain. They wanted the reassurance that King Louis of France, as well as their exiled King James, was alert and ready to act fast when Queen Anne died. But the Queen's health was said to be better now. And the society's proceedings consisted mostly of drinking loyal toasts, electing officers, and laying plans for the happy future.

Mr. Petre and Sir Marmaduke accompanied James on his expedition. Charles too would naturally have gone, and was infuriated that he couldn't. On Easter Monday he had come down with a bad case of measles. So ill was he that for several days he did not mind the ministrations of Lady Constable and Mrs. Busby, who took over the sickroom. Then after his spots faded he continued to ail for some time with earaches and continued weakness. The two women, backed by Mr. Brown, kept him confined to his room until after May Day, and as the first part of that month brought chilling rains, Charles was made to stay in the castle and was very much bored, so that he wrote several tender letters to Betty, and even waded through a volume of Robert Herrick's love poems in search of verses to copy for her. In return she sent him her miniature and he spent many moments admiring the pert laughing face in its frame of auburn curls. June and their marriage would soon come. Then what merry times they would have together, Charles thought.

On the first warm day Charles was at last permitted to go out. He went to the stable to see his mare, who greeted him with whickers of delight, while Charles rubbed her nose and fed her a sugarplum.

"Saddle her for me," he said to one of the grooms. "I can see she wants exercise, and so by God do I!" As the man touched his forehead, Charles saw a small boy come staggering between the stalls with buckets of water for James's new hunter, a dappled gray stallion named Monarch. There was something familiar about the boy, who had a shock of dark hair and a cocky tilt to his head.

"Who's that?" said Charles to the groom. "Have I seen him before?"

"Shouldn't think so, sir. Mr. Busby took him on while ye was sick. We needed another stable lad, 'n' this one claimed he'd worked wi' pit ponies on Tyneside."

Pit ponies. Tyneside. But surely it couldn't be *that* one! Charles said nothing. He watched until the boy came out of the stallion's stall, then he cried, "*You* there—come here!" The boy had been going in the other direction, but he stopped and came slowly up to Charles. "Aye?"

Charles stared at the bright hazel eyes, the square face, no longer sooty, the mouth which quirked at the corners with an effect of impudence. "Aren't you Rob Wilson from the Bensham colliery?" asked Charles, finding that his heart was beating hard.

"I am," said the lad, staring straight back at Charles. "An wot's that ter *thee?*"

"Rob!" cried the groom sharply. "This is Mr. Radcliffe, his lordship's brother!"

"I knaw that," said the boy with a peculiar emphasis, which brought the blood to Charles's cheeks. Rob seemed to recollect himself; he stopped staring boldly at Charles and looked at the haystrewn floor. "Bensham pit blew up, sir," he said in a more respectful voice. "There was eighty killed i' the blast. Not being wan o' 'em, I thought I'd look fur some other wark, an' found it here."

"He's a good lad, sir," put in the groom, seeing Charles frown. "Deft wi' the horses."

"Were any of the rest of your family hurt in the pits?" Charles asked unwillingly. He resented the boy's appearance at Dilston, resented reminder of Dick and Geordie Wilson and those callow weeks of shameful folly with Meg.

Rob raised his head and stared again at Charles, the hazel eyes calm and surprisingly mature. "None hurt i' the *pits*," he said. At once he added in a brisk voice, "Shall I saddle the mare? Will ye be riding out, sir?"

Charles nodded, and the groom said importantly, "To be sure, Mr. Charles'll be riding out every day, now he's well." Rob disappeared at once towards the saddle room, while the groom led the mare from her stall. Charles did not see the boy again.

While Charles rode down towards the Devil Water Bridge, he spent some minutes brooding over Rob Wilson's presence at Dilston, and wondering why it made him uneasy. Yet in truth there was nothing strange about it, and in justice no complaint that he could make about the lad except want of manners. I've grown fanciful through my sickness, Charles thought impatiently, and soon forgot everything but the joy of a brisk gallop towards the Linnel Rocks.

On the next two days he rode into Corbridge, as he had used to do, sampling the Angel's punch and bandying jests with a new barmaid whose saucy looks and reddish hair reminded him a little of Betty. On the third day, the weather still held and he set off again towards Corbridge, rejoicing over two things. One, that James would be home tomorrow for Whitsun, which was the next Sunday, and the other, the discovery that Rob Wilson had unaccountably disappeared. "Run off, sir, he did," said the angry groom, "the very day ye spoke wi' him. Serves Mr. Busby right for taking on pit trash. They'll allus do ye dirty."

Charles shrugged, feeling relief. "You can find plenty of other stable lads," he said, and rode lightheartedly past the castle, down the hill towards the Tyne. As he entered Corbridge and turned towards the Angel, he suddenly changed his mind. It was a beautiful day for a gallop across the moors near the Roman Wall—not too hot, yet a flood of liquid gold streaming from behind the dark clouds. In fact it would be a fine day for shooting wildfowl on the loughs beyond the wall. I should have brought my fowling piece, Charles thought, and drew rein near St. Andrew's Church while he considered going back for it.

From behind a pier below the bridge, bright hazel eyes had watched Charles, saw him pause and then continue on through Corbridge. Charles had decided against going back for his gun. It was too late for shooting today since Cousin Maud had delayed him with tiresome questions about the exact number of small clothes and night gear which the seamstress should make him for his wedding. His new suits were naturally being tailored in London. Such a pother, Charles thought, as he drew the mare off the highway to let a wagon train full of market stuff go past.

Behind him in Corbridge, Rob Wilson was running towards the abandoned loft of a house in Water Row. He swarmed up a ladder and addressed the three men who stood waiting inside. "He's no' gan t' the Angel terday! He's heading north fur Stagshaw.

The three men stared at Rob. There were two young ones and one of nearly sixty with long grizzled hair and beard. They were wearing black bonnets and plaids. All three were powerful, sinewy Borderers, with harsh weather-beaten faces. All three were Snowdons from Coquetdale—Meg's brothers and her father. It was the father, John Snowdon, who answered instantly. "All the better. He'll be up by the moors sune. Off wi' us. Hasten!"

They hurried down to the lane, where their mounts were tethered. Good sturdy horseflesh for the Snowdons, and a little Galloway for Rob.

In ten minutes Rob saw the outline of Charles's figure on the road ahead of them. There was no mistaking the long back in its buff velvet coat, the clubbed fair hair under a gentleman's tricorne, the easy swagger with which Charles sat on the trotting mare.

" 'Tis him," said Rob pulling up his pony.

John Snowdon bowed his head. He had the beaked and bearded face of a patriarch, the fanatical eyes of a prophet, and it was as a prophet he spoke. "The Lord hath delivered him unto us, as I knew 'twould be. We'll follow and watch our chance, which God'll gi' us anon."

Roger Snowdon fell back behind his father. Will Snowdon gave a grunt and fingered his pistol, which his father noted. "Mind!" he said sharply. "Ye're not to shoot that Satan's spawn! Ye'll do as I say!"

"Aye, Faither," murmured the young man, sighing.

John Snowdon turned to Rob. "Gan ye back to Gateshead, laddie. Ye've done ye're part. No need to further mix in this."

The boy's face darkened, he looked up at the stern old man. "Divven't send me awa', Mr. Snowdon. I've a reet ter be here—wi' him murdering our Dickie." The boy's hands clenched fiercely on the pony's mane.

Snowdon shook his head. "Your brother wasna murdered, Rob. Ye munna tell falsehoods."

"Same *as* then," retorted Rob stubbornly, and kept on riding with the others, while Charles's figure moved ahead of them, just in sight.

The lines deepened around John Snowdon's mouth, but he did not speak. There was no actual murder about Dick Wilson's drowning—drunk he was and fell off his keelboat just where the current swirled fiercest by the Black Middens. But Dick Wilson hadn't taken to the drink until after he came to Coquetdale and found Meg, and saw how it was with her. After that, as Nanny wrote, he pined and dwindled. All the spirit drained out of him. He lost pride in his work. From morning till midnight he'd huddle in his boat with a jug of whisky at his mouth. He'd not even had the satisfaction of knowing who was the man had done this to Meg. Because the lass had lied. Had lied like a Jezebel, saying she had been raped one dark night in Newcastle by someone she couldn't see. And in Coquetdale they'd believed her and pitied her disgrace and her misery. Until the Faws came back to Tosson, and Jem Bailey, the piper, with them. Bailey got the truth out of Meg at last. When he mentioned meeting Charles Radcliffe at Widdrington, a blind man could have seen Meg blench, and when Bailey went on to tell of the scoundrel's coming marriage to some great lady, Meg had finally broken down and confessed her many vicious deeds of fornication. That Sabbath they had forced her to go the twenty miles to Falstone kirk, had made her sit three hours in sackcloth on the repentance stool enduring the jeers and sneers of the other Covenanters, until she swooned. And later he, her father, had beaten her. Beaten her until Roger grabbed the arm which plied the blackthorn stick, saying, "Halt, Faither—we've other matters to do for Meg." And Roger was right. That was why they were here, after Rob Wilson had galloped all the way to Coquetdale and summoned them.

Charles neared the Roman Wall, along which ran the main road between Newcastle and Carlisle. There were occasional passersby—market wagons, peddlers, a shepherd with his flock, chance travelers. Charles was tired of the road and seized with an urge to strike west across the moors towards a Roman ruin Mr. Brown had told him of. A ruin where they said one might find an old coin or even the statue of a heathen god. He flicked the mare and plunged into the waste of rough hummocks and little hills, covered with grass and patches of heather.

"Ah-h—" said John Snowdon with a majestic nod. "He's off into the moss, we've got him!" He signaled to his sons, who obeyed silently, watching their quarry and yet keeping themselves hidden behind bushes and hummocks. This was a game they knew well in the dales. Nor had the Union with Scotland three years ago lessened their skill in tracking Border thieves. Rob had no such skill, and it was his small distant form on the Galloway that Charles noticed with annoyance, since he was not eager to have some urchin's company. Charles quickened his pace down the great grassy outcropping of the Whinsill. The mare plunged her hoof in a rabbit hole and stumbled. John Snowdon, seeing this and noting that they were well out of sight of the highway, raised his arm in signal and began to gallop, his sons converging with him.

Charles, who had pulled up the mare and was relieved to find she had not hurt herself, stared in surprise. He saw the three gaunt figures on raw-boned horses, saw that they wore bonnets like the Scots', that their plaids were streaming behind them. And an unearthly battle cry came from their throats: "Yet! Yet! Yet! A-Snawdon! A-Snawdon!"

What in Mary's name are they doing? Charles thought, convinced he had stumbled into some sort of sport. The two young men were off their horses and had yanked Charles off his before he knew enough to struggle. He felt his arms jerked behind his back, saw a flash of stout cord in somebody's hand, and tried to fight then, though still bewildered. Charles had strength and courage, but these adversaries were not like the ridiculous Paulet, whom Charles had bested on Twelfth Night. These men were as rugged and grim as their own mountains. Charles's twistings and writhings produced only a violent pain in his arm as Roger Snowdon tied his wrists behind his back.

"Gin ye kick like that, I'll break your leg fur ye," said Will Snowdon, clutching Charles's ankles in a vicious grip. "An' they'll be no use yalping," he added as Charles tried to shout for help. He dealt Charles a great blow across the mouth with his open hand.

"Hist him up on his nag," said the father, who had been watching quietly. "Then lead on!" His sons obeyed. They threw Charles onto his horse and lashed the stirrups to his boots. Will pulled the reins over the mare's head and began to lead her. Charles swayed in the saddle, blood trickled down his chin from the blow. The cavalcade set out over the bleak and trackless moors. "What do you *want* of me?" mumbled Charles when he could speak over the pain in his teeth. "I've no money on me."

Nobody answered him. John Snowdon and Will, leading the mare, rode silently on ahead, Roger Snowdon behind. And now a little way to the left Charles saw the urchin on the pony, and recognized him. It was the sight of Rob Wilson that penetrated Charles's daze and washed him in fear. A blind animal panic, while he strained at the bonds which held his wrists, then hammered with his lashed feet against the mare's flanks. She started and reared and tried to bolt, and Charles fell off sideways, though his feet were not free of the stirrups and the saddle turned under him. He hit his right cheek against a sharp rock. The gash spurted red from his ear to his jawbone, while he was dragged a few feet half on half off the mare.

"Ye blarsted young fule!" cried John Snowdon, as Will quieted the mare and hoisted Charles back on the regirthed saddle. "A bonny face ye've gi'en yoursel'! The lasses'll not favor ye so much now. Here." He threw a dirty brown kerchief to his son. "Stanch his wound. We'd not ha' him bleed to deeth yet."

Will mopped at the gash on Charles's cheek with a handful of grass, then bound the kerchief tight around his head and chin. "Na mair o' your tricks," he growled. "We've a lang way t'get hame as 'tis."

Charles slumped down in the saddle. The procession started off again. They went on for an hour over moors and through copses, splashing along burns, sometimes trotting on a disused cart road. Twice they passed a farmhouse at a distance. Once a man with a gun and dog shaded his eyes to peer at them from a nearby hillock. Will Snowdon waved in a friendly way, the man waved back and disappeared.

The fitful sun had vanished for good behind a black cloudbank when they reached the lake called Sweethope Lough, and saw the high sandstone Wanny Crags behind it. The country grew wilder, ravens circled over the crags, and a curlew shrilled three times through the heavy air.

"Sune we'll be i' the forest," said John Snowdon with satisfaction. "Hurry on, lads."

"Aye," said Will tugging the mare's bridle. "I'd not wish to meet the bogle o' Fallowlees after dark, nor yet the wee folk who dwell i' Selby's Cove." He gave an uneasy laugh. Rothbury Forest was well known to be haunted.

"Who *are* you men?" said Charles speaking at last. "Where're you taking me? What have I done to you?"

John Snowdon did not hear. Will and little Rob did not answer, but Roger, who had in him a trace of his dead mother's softness, was impressed by the numb desperation in their captive's voice. He came up beside the mare, and said, "Is it truth ye dinna ken who we are? Did ye think the wicked ruin o' a poor lass'ld gan unavenged fur aye?"

"You *are* Snowdons then," whispered Charles after a moment. "But what I did with Meg is over long ago, and is no more than happens every day in London!" He didn't understand, and the pain in his wrists and ankles and the throbbing of his cheek wound confused his thinking.

"We ken naught o' your mucky Papist ways, nor what they do i' Lunnon!" cried Roger with sudden anger. "We live by the Good Book, an' the Covenant o' God, and we don't suffer sin amangst us!"

"Aye," said John Snowdon, hearing this and turning in his saddle. "Weel spoke, Roger. Will, are ye sure Master Dean'll be waiting?"

"Aye, Faither," said Will. "Tam went to Falstone fur him yestere'en." Again there was silence, except for the dry thuds of the horses' hoofs on the young bracken and the heather.

They're mad, Charles thought. Mad. Are they going to kill me? I must keep my wits somehow. When we get where we're going, they'll have to take me off the mare. They won't butcher me in cold blood, or they'd have done it sooner. I must keep my wits and watch my chance. Holy Mother of God, help me to think! But his mind was leaden and when he saw the country grow yet wilder and more desolate, fear rose tight in his throat. At gloaming the Simonside Hills loomed up ahead. The ancient bare-topped crags had an air of brooding mystery. Eagles nested in these cliffs. The wastes of heather became darkened at times by streaks of brown peat. They passed a ring of stones and ancient earthworks which had been made by the little folk of the North long before the Romans came. John Snowdon led them on a track around the foot of Dove's Crag, then struck sharply upwards over a spur of gritty sandstone, where the horses slipped and scuffled. They had passed no dwellings for hours, but now for a moment Charles saw a few scattered candles glimmering out of windows down in the Coquet valley. He looked towards them with sudden hope, which the old man extinguished. "Roger," he said to his son. "We'll not go nigh Tosson. Can ye guide us hame, by Wolvershiels? Ye're een're better than mine i' this gloaming. But mind the bog!"

"Aye, Faither,' said Roger moving up ahead. The interminable ride continued. Charles's tired mare stumbled more often and Will jerked her head up. When they disturbed three sheep, which went scurrying and bleating into the darkness, the mare shied and Charles, very nearly thrown again, felt with new dismay that the numbness of his arms had spread to his thighs. I won't swoon, he said to himself. Blessed Virgin, help me. I must keep my wits. But they seemed as numb as the rest of him.

The long May twilight had nearly vanished when they came suddenly on a tiny burn, and beside it, solitary, tucked away and hidden beneath Ravensheugh crag, stood a small high peel. It was made entirely of stone except for the thatching, and it was built like an upended roofed box. It consisted of a cattle-byre below and one room above for humans. It had stood there for centuries, and sheltered many a family with their precious sheep and cattle against sudden thieving raids by Scots or by Redesdalers, who were also hereditary enemies of the Coquet dalesmen.

Two dogs rushed up barking as the horses approached and were silenced at once by their master's voice. The Snowdons and Rob dismounted. Roger unlashed Charles's feet and wrists, then pushed him from the saddle. "Ye'll na get awa' from us now, laddie!" he said not unkindly, and added a grunt of laughter as Charles, whose legs would not support him, collapsed on a patch of grass and tried to rub his throbbing wrists. An outside flight of narrow stone steps was the only approach to the Snowdon living quarters. At the top of them, halfway up the building, the door opened and in a slit of yellow light there showed a woman's tall stout figure. "Did ye get him?" she called down. "We did," snapped John Snowdon. "Is Master Dean here?"

"Aye, since noon. Meg's took worse. Greeting and moaning most pitiful. Ye shouldna ha' beat her so, Jock Snawdon, but Snawdons're a harsh breed as I s'ld knaw who married one."

" 'Tis atwixt me an' the Lord what I do wi' my datter, Belle," retorted the old man. "She'll sune stop greeting when she sees what we've brought her." He leaned over and jerked Charles to his feet by the coat collar. "Get up, ye wretch! We didna fetch ye here to loll on the sward." He and the young men shoved Charles up the stone steps and through the door into a square smoky room which smelled of dung from the byre beneath. A peat fire burned in the crude fireplace. There was no furniture but a table and stools. The woman, Belle Snowdon, held the candle high. She had been Isabel Jack from Hepple and long married to John Snowdon's brother, Edward. Of all the Snowdons who lived hereabouts only she had come to be with Meg, for John Snowdon did not like his other kin, who were none of them Dissenters.

Belle stared hard at Charles. "Ah, he's verra young," she said quickly. "An' what ha' ye done to his face?" The blood from the gash had oozed through the kerchief and caked in dark splotches. Meg had been huddled on a stool near the

107

fire moaning to herself; when her Aunt Belle spoke she raised her head and gave a cry. She staggered to her feet and walked heavily across the stone floor to Charles. "Ye're hurt!" she cried. "Oh, sir, for-r-give me, I didna want this. I ne'er meant them to knaw. I didna tell them, 'twas the Faw who told!"

Charles wet his lips and gaped down at her. He saw that her brown eyes were filled with anguish. He saw that there was a lump on her forehead and bruises on her arms. Then he saw her great swollen belly under the homespun apron. "You're with child," he whispered. "Did I get you with child, Meg?"

"I didna mean ye to knaw," she repeated. " 'Twas all *my* sin."

" 'Twas foul sin in both!" shouted John Snowdon. "An' they'll be no bastards in *my* family! Master Dean, are ye ready?"

A man in a shabby homespun suit had been standing in the shadows by the small shelfful of sermons which were John Snowdon's constant reading. He was John Dean, the Dissenting minister from the Border church at Falstone. He adjusted his wrinkled cotton falling bands, and strode towards the table, where he laid the big Snowdon Bible in the precise center. "Aye, ready," he said in measured tones. "Stand here, you two!" And he pointed from Meg to Charles and indicated the front of the table.

"No, no!" cried Meg, wringing her hands and looking wildly from one to another of the implacable Snowdon faces. "Mr. Radcliffe can't wed *me!* I told ye that, Faither. 'Tis not seemly, and he's betrothed to a great lady in London. He doesna want me, he niver did!"

"Hush thy clatter, lass," said John Snowdon. "The babe mun ha' a name, and he'll wed thee, willy-nilly, gin he values his life." The old man glanced towards his huge blackthorn cudgel which stood by the hearth. Will Snowdon put his hand on his pistol, and watched Charles, who stood rooted by the door, staring at Meg and at her great belly. It is *my* child in there, he thought. Mine, and for it Meg has suffered greatly. A spasm of wondering pity gripped him. Around him the other figures seemed to recede. They grew unreal as the actors in plays he had seen in London. Their menace seemed unreal. He did not feel the menace. Once, at the theater with Betty, a scene had grown tiresome and they had got up and left. Charles felt the same way now, that he might leave this smoky room, these mouthing actors. Meg alone was real. The piteous little face which he had once so eagerly kissed was real—and real too was the fruit of the love-makings which she so incredibly carried within her.

"I will wed you, Meg," he said, walking over beside her.

Belle Snowdon exhaled a great sigh. The Snowdon men and little Rob, who were peering from behind, all slackened their tense muscles, and Will Snowdon said with a curt laugh, "Better a wife than a shroud."

The minister held up his hand. "We will proceed without more ado. Margaret Snowdon, hold the Book of God's Holy Word and swear that this is the father of the child with which you are quick—and will you take him for your wedded husband? . . . Charles Radcliffe . . ." Charles heard neither Meg's tremulous whispers nor his own voice answering "I do" and "I will."

He heard instead the restless stamping of the cattle beneath them, heard the feeble bleating of a sick lamb. How strange, he thought, to have cattle crammed in the house with one. And I wonder if the mare has been properly watered and fed down there. I must see to her. He did not hear when the minister said, "I now pronounce you man and wife." But he was startled when John Snowdon came up to him and shook his hand. " 'Tis the last time I'll do this, Radcliffe," said the old man solemnly. "I like neither your ways nor your religion, nor your name. Yet it *is* a name that now my datter bears, and can hold her head up again wi' God-fearing folk. Come, we mun all sign the paper." Snowdon had provided a marriage certificate in case anyone might question a Nonconformist marriage performed within Rothbury's Church of England parish. So they signed. And when Meg had finished she gave a sharp cry and put her hand to her back. Then she went to the stool and doubled over, her arms across her belly.

"Alack," said her Aunt Belle. "I misdoubted this'ld happen. 'Tis the bairn seeking to be born, and fully airly. Poor Meg's had too much to bear. Into the straw wi' ye, lass!" She gestured towards a plank partition which screened off a few feet at the back of the room. It was in there that Meg slept, while the men lay on heather-stuffed sacks in the open loft.

The girl lurched up from her seat, and began dragging her heavy body towards the partition. "Tend Mr. Radcliffe's wound, Auntie," she pleaded. "There's lamb's wool i' the coffer." Her voice cracked in a stifled scream, and she ran into her cubbyhole.

"*Go* to her!" said Charles, who had turned white as his shirt. "Hurry to her—don't leave her alone!"

"Now—now—" said Belle Snowdon smiling. "Dinna dither so, lad. Meg'll not need me yet awhile. Let me see this cheek." Her stout, deft fingers pulled off the dirty kerchief. "Dear, dear," she added shaking her head. "Ye'll carry *this* mark to your grave. Set down so I can reach ye." She pushed him down on the stool Meg had vacated. "Roger, hold the candle nigh!"

The men had been shuffling uneasily. John Snowdon cast a look of anxiety towards the cubbyhole where Meg's labored breathing could be heard. "Come, lads, an' Master Dean," he said. "This be no place for us. We'll see to the cattle. Roger, ye'll follow?" His younger son nodded, while the others trooped out, slamming the door behind them. Roger held the candle while Belle bathed Charles's gash with water from the kettle on the fire, then took from her apron pocket a needleful of homespun thread. Charles neither winced nor moved as she sewed together the jagged gaping edges of his wound, then bound it with lamb's wool and a clean kerchief of her own.

"Ye've the pluck o' a dalesman, for all ye come from the South," she said as she finished.

"Aye," agreed Roger quietly. He climbed the ladder to the loft and came down with a brown jug. "Here's a drap fur ye," he said giving it to Charles. "We needna tell Faither, but 'twould be a sorry wedding indeed, wi'out a drap.' '

"Thank you," said Charles, and drank the fiery whisky as best he could. The wound had torn his cheek muscles. Then he started as Meg gave a low animal cry. "For the love of God, Mrs. Snowdon. Help her!"

"I will," said Belle. "Though 'twill be a lang time yet. Gan ye off ye two, but Roger, ye've birthed many a calf and lamb, I may need thee, so stay belaw."

Meg's baby was born just as the sun's first rays struggled over the distant Cheviots and brightened the narrow ravine where the Snowdon peel stood. Charles heard the wailing of the newborn as he stood below in the byre, pressed close to his mare. During the long hours he had curried and tended the mare, shuddering each time one of Meg's screams shrilled down through the ceiling, yet unable to leave. The other men came and went as soon as there was light, and

Rob Wilson had gone off to Tosson mill for a sack of flour. They had eaten oatcakes and mutton stew which Belle had sent to them by Roger, who had made several trips upstairs at her request.

When Roger came down finally he walked, grinning, to Charles, "Weel, lad—ye've a datter. 'Tis not much o' one, but the wee lassie's alive, an' so is Meg."

Charles gave a great gulp and stood up straight. "I want to see it."

"And so ye shall. Faither, 'tis over," Roger announced to John Snowdon, who came into the byre dragging a struggling wether by the horns. The old man nodded majestically. "Fetch the minister. He's reading the Book by the burn.'

Mr. Dean had been unable to ride back to Falstone in the darkness and so had acceded to John Snowdon's further request that he wait and baptize the baby when it came. For this service Snowdon had added the promise of a pail of honey to the slaughtered lamb fixed as fee for the wedding. Mr. Dean's lonely little manse on the Border was always in want of provisions and his few church members so scattered and mostly impoverished, themselves, that he often went hungry.

Meg was in exhausted sleep when the men had climbed the stone steps to the big room. Belle sat smiling by the fire, with a bundle on her lap. " 'Tis a pairfect wee lassie," she said to Charles, "An'll be fair-haired like you, lad— someday. Will ye hold her?" Charles mutely put out his arms, and Belle laid the tiny plaid-wrapped bundle in them. The baby gave a funny chirrup and sigh, then looked up at her father, unwinking. Her head was covered with flaxen fuzz, her face was red, but there was a cleft like Charles's in the minute chin. A thrill went through Charles as he looked down at his baby. A thrill of pride and sweetness such as he had never known from any of the things which had given him pleasure. And deeper than the thrill was a certainty of communication and significance. That it was pure love, which he had never felt before, nor would ever feel for anything else—this he could not guess. But his eyes misted, and his arms began to tremble, and John Snowdon said, "Now, now—Radcliffe, dinna drap the bairn afore it's a Christian. Gi'e it to me!" Charles unwillingly obeyed.

Belle brought a cupful of water from the kettle and put it on the table beside the minister, who said, "What name is this child to have?"

"Jane," announced John Snowdon. "Fur its gran'mawther."

Belle stared at the old man. Since the day of the funeral at Falstone, Snowdon had not mentioned the name of his dead wife.

"So 'tis Jenny!" cried Belle. "An' a sweet bonny name!"

Snowdon sternly interrupted this irrelevancy. "And I shall be its sponsor, see to its rearing in all things both Godly an' worldly, and see that it lives by the Covenant."

"Very good," said the minister. "We are all sealed by the Covenant here, except—" He gestured at Charles. "Kindly step aside, sir."

"I won't," said Charles. "It's *my* baby."

"Let him be," said Belle sharply. The minister shrugged, and began the Covenanter's rite of baptism, which he finished with a sprinkle of water on the baby's face, "Jane Radcliffe, child of the Covenant, I baptize thee in the name of the Father, and of the Son, and of the Holy Ghost, Amen. Let us pray." The Snowdon men and Belle fell to their knees, John Snowdon as easily as his sons, though he was hampered by the baby, which he held with the practiced arms of a man who had tended many a small helpless animal.

Throughout the long prayer Charles stood and watched his child. Jenny Radcliffe, he thought. When will she be old enough to walk and talk? I'll teach her to ride with me. She shall have a little blue velvet riding habit, and a wax doll, from Paris. What else did little girls like? He would find out from his sister Mary; perhaps James would know. James, who would be back at Dilston today.

The thought of James startled Charles from his daydream. When the prayer was ended the baby, whimpering a little, was carried back to Meg. She tucked it in the crook of her arm and looked up at Charles with a languid detachment, very different from the pleading frenzied love she had heretofore given him. Her brown eyes showed faint pity as she contemplated the tall gangling boy and the bandage around his head.

"Ye may furget us now," she said. "I'm sorry fur what happened, but ye needna think o' it more. We'll niver trouble ye, any o' us. Ye mun gan awa'. Faither's waiting to guide ye back to Dilston."

"But, Meg—" said Charles. "We're married. And there's her. As soon as you can you must come to Dilston with—with Jenny."

Her mouth tightened and she looked something like John Snowdon as she watched the light in Charles's eyes when

112

he looked down at the little head on her arm. "And what sort o' welcome would *we* get at Dilston?" she asked. "And what kind o' happiness would the bairn and me find there?"

Charles was silent. He could not look ahead, and he knew that he didn't want Meg at Dilston; there was only the peculiar unreasoning desire to be near the baby.

"Hark!" said Meg suddenly. "D'ye hear the singing o' the burn that tumbles down off Ravensheugh? D'ye hear the cry o' the waup? D'ye smell the peat smoke an' the dew-wet heather?"

"What are you trying to say?" Charles asked slowly.

"That I canna live wi'out these things. Nor even wi'out the sternness of m'faither, and the roughness of m'brothers. Nor do ye truly love me, though ye pitied me yestere'en. So we'll bide here. Me an' the bairn. And ye'll go back where ye belang, to the castles an' the lords an' ladies."

There was no more to be said. The Snowdons were finished with him, Meg didn't want him, the baby did not need him, and he had no plan, no arguments to put up against them. They had drawn together, all of them, as stark and solitary as their own peel tower. Even Belle, who had seemed softer than the others, gave him only a brief nod of farewell and said she hoped his wound wouldn't fester.

In the full morning light, John Snowdon and Charles set out on the long way back to Dilston. In silence they plodded around the Simonside crags and through Rothbury Forest. Again they reached the Sweethope Lough and the moors north of the Roman Wall. Their progress was much faster than it had been in the other direction, since Charles now had the free guidance of his mare, and also they need not avoid what roads there were. By five o'clock they had covered the forty-odd miles between Coquetdale and Corbridge. And there by the Tyne Bridge they found one of James's servants stationed. He gave a cry when he saw Charles. "Oh, sir! We've thought ye dead. Or a leg broke at least. There's a hundred out beating the moors and byways for ye. His lordship's been a-fretted since he came home ter find ye missing!"

"Where is Lord Darntwatter?" said John Snowdon.

The servant stared at the bearded old man in the black bonnet and dirty plaid, but he answered, "Mebbe at the castle by now. He's been hunting young master through Dipton Wood, and thereabouts."

When they rode up to the castle, James was standing on

113

the steps ready to mount again, and search for Charles in a different direction.

"Praises to God and the Blessed Virgin," he whispered when he saw his brother, but he saw too not only from the bandage on the boy's head and the haggard look of his face but from the expression of the old bearded man that there was something still very wrong. He asked no questions while he urged the two of them inside, and told a lackey to bring food and drink.

"I'll tak' a bite later, my lord," said John Snowdon, "gin ye still offer it, but first I want a word wi' ye alone." His fierce unswerving gaze rested on Lady Constable, who was embracing Charles, and uttering cries of curiosity, lamentation, and relief, then it passed to Mr. Petre, who stood watchful and suspicious by the mantelpiece.

James nodded and took Snowdon to the library.

Two hours later the old man had gone. He had drunk nothing but water, eaten nothing but bread, and he would not stay the night though the light was beginning to fail. And James, still in the library, had been telling the appalling news to his chaplain. Charles had been interviewed and sent to bed, since he was running a fever and was half dead from exhaustion.

"Poor Charles. Poor boy," said James in a leaden voice, resting his head on his hands, " 'tis near as bad a blow as I can think of. How sorely he has paid for his youthful sin."

The priest made an impatient gesture. "The circumstance is awkward, my lord, but we must not exaggerate it nor give it undue importance."

"I tell you," said James sharply, "the boy is *married!* Married by a minister, with witnesses. Snowdon showed me the marriage lines. And Charles admits it."

"Bah!" said the priest. "You can't call that a marriage—performed by a Dissenter—not even in the Church of England. And Charles only sixteen and forced to submit at the point of a pistol! This is no marriage at all, and certainly not a Catholic one!"

James winced. He picked up the inkpot and laid it down again. "Nevertheless," he said, "it is a *legal* marriage, by the law of the land. And Charles says he did it of his own free will when he saw the girl's condition."

"Nonsense! The whole thing is a farce. Give those people some money, then we'll get it annulled—I'll write to Rome. If only those villains up there on the Border will keep their mouths shut."

James looked at his chaplain with sad disapproval. "The Snowdons will take no money, not even support for the child. I offered it. They were concerned only with having the baby born in wedlock. Which it was. They wish nothing more to do with Charles or us ever."

"Then," said the priest, "*we* need never mention this."

"Perhaps not," said James. "Except to Lady Betty. She can give out what reasons she likes for her match with Charles being broken off."

The priest bit his lips. He had forgotten Lady Betty. "It's all excessively awkward," he said.

"It's tragic, Mr. Petre," said James quietly.

PART TWO

1715—1716

FIVE

In 1715 on Lammas Sunday, August 7, Dilston villagers celebrated the Feast of St. Wilfrid, as their forefathers had done for a thousand years. The Earl of Derwentwater was delighted to honor the old custom, and much pleased to learn about the fiery Northumbrian saint, who, though educated by the monks on Lindisfarne, had introduced Roman church usage into the North of England. Also, Wilfrid in the seventh century had built the first abbey at Hexham—the nearby market town, which had been, under Wilfrid's regime and later, a most famous Catholic shrine and sanctuary.

After Mass in Dilston chapel the Earl, his wife, and aunt, all dressed in mourning, walked to the marble summerhouse, or pavilion, which had just been finished on the edge of the new lawns, overlooking the Devil Water cascade. The pavilion was luxuriously furnished with armchairs, benches, and an inlaid table. Its shade was welcome on this hot August day, and so was the bowl of chilled syllabub which the servants had left.

"Sit down, my love," said James to his young wife, solicitously arranging cushions for her. "I trust you're not tired?"

The Countess shook her dark head with a grave smile, then she turned at once to her husband's aunt—old Lady Mary Radcliffe, who had come yesterday from Durham for an extended visit. "Are you quite comfortable, my lady? I see you have your fan—shall I fan you? 'Tis so warm."

How like my Ann, James thought, watching his wife's pretty courtesy and seeing that his aunt, who had looked

118

cross, as she often did, responded with a softening of her craggy face, though she said, "I'm still able to fan myself, thank you."

James sipped the cool frothy drink and leaned back in his chair, allowing himself a moment of utter contentment. Never for an instant in their three years of marriage had he regretted choosing little Anna Maria Webb from all the available Catholic heiresses. She had developed as he had foreseen on that night at Dr. Radcliffe's. The convent, and her dominating mother, had turned out an earnest, devout, and accomplished young girl, keenly aware of responsibilities; her rather serious character lightened by a love of music, and a wifely pleasure in whatever interested James. They had spent the first two years of their marriage at Hatherope, a manor in Gloucestershire which was lent to the young couple by her parents. This arrangement was at Lady Webb's request since she could not yet bear to part with her daughter, and it also gave James time for the rebuilding of Dilston.

He glanced through the marble pillars of the summerhouse towards his elegant new mansion. It was now nearly completed—a nobleman's seat as modern and magnificent as any in the county. The old Radcliffe tower was still there, but had been so shrewdly incorporated in the new fabric that one scarcely guessed where it stood. And its upper rooms served their earlier purpose as nurseries. Yes, that was another of the joys Ann had brought him. An heir. And she was pregnant again, so she had confided yesterday. The nurseries would soon be filled, as he had always prayed. James turned and searched the expanse of grass and flower beds until he spied his son playing near the Italian fountain. The two-year-old John was tripping and tumbling after a puppy, while the head nurse followed her charge closely.

"I do hope Janet won't let Johnny get near the peacocks," said Ann, also watching her son. "And I wonder if all that noise and excitement is too much for him," she added, frowning towards the commotion at the far end of the garden near the village, where tables were being set up for St. Wilfrid's feast, and two roving jugglers were practicing their skill with yellow balls.

"Pish!" said Lady Mary, fanning herself briskly. "You mustn't coddle the child, Ann. A bit of rough and tumble's good for 'em, and while I think of it, I've noted you feed him too much porridge. Red meat's what he wants, the bloodier the better. Meat and a gill of ale now and then."

Lady Mary gave a nod so decisive that the lappets jiggled on her lace cap. Like many a spinster, she had decided views on the rearing of children.

Ann's dark eyes looked resistant, but she was too polite to argue, and James interposed tactfully, "Anyway, Janet's carrying the child into the house for his nap, my dear—and look; there's a horseman coming up the avenue. I wonder if it could possibly be Charles."

It wasn't Charles, who had ridden to Newcastle two days ago to buy himself a new fowling piece though there were several excellent ones in the gun room already. James sighed and the precarious moment of contentment vanished. Charles was a man now. He'd be twenty-two next month. But he couldn't marry, and he wouldn't settle down. In these last years he had grown wild and extravagant. He had made a name for himself as a rake, even in London, where he kept a succession of actresses. He'd set them up in Bond Street houses, lavish clothes, jewels, and parties on them, then tire of them and have to buy them off. Young Radcliffe takes after his grandfather, the "Merry Monarch," wags snickered in the coffeehouses, a parallel which distressed James. Charles's own income was certainly insufficient for this way of life; so he gamed, and he ran into debt, and, finally repentant, would be forced to come to James, who eventually rescued him—each time hoping that the promises of reform were true.

If Charles could only have married Betty Lee, James thought for the hundredth time. True, this lechery which had been his downfall might have cropped up even then, yet there would have been scant temptation at Ditchley Park and, besides, Betty might have had spirit enough to hold him. She had loved Charles.

James shrank from remembering the dreadful scene with the Lichfields when they were told of Charles's incredible marriage. There had been rage, tears, recrimination, and disgust. None of which James felt poor Charles *quite* deserved. Lady Lichfield, furious with disappointment, had demanded that nobody should know that her daughter had been so flouted, and not long afterward Betty married her staid cousin, Frank Lee. So nobody outside the family did know of Charles's tie to the strange young woman on the Border. There was mild curiosity in some London circles that young Radcliffe should be jilted by Lady Betty, but it soon died away. And Charles began his dissipations.

"I am quite eager to see my nephew Charles," said Lady

Mary acidly. "Since he never bothers to call on me in Durham, and now——" her voice lowered, the ivory fan ceased swishing, "with our recent losses—so few left of the family." She crossed herself. Ann and James also crossed themselves. James said, "God rest their souls." His chair grated on the tiles, and he set down his cup of syllabub. He tried not to brood over the deaths that had come to them the past year. Old Dr. Radcliffe went first, his affection for the Derwentwaters unfortunately dimmed, because he had offered to leave the baby John a fortune if the child were reared as a Protestant. James had written an indignant letter of refusal. And so most of the Doctor's money had gone to Oxford University. The next death was that of Lady Constable, who had returned with Sir Marmaduke to Yorkshire; and then shortly afterward Francis—a sardonic gambler to the end—had coughed away his life in London.

James's mind grew as somber as the black clothes they all wore. These family deaths were harrowing but they were God's Will, and they were done. They left no threats, no disturbances behind them, which was not true of another death. That had happened just a year ago. Queen Anne.

James still felt the shock, like a blow in the stomach, when he learned that the Queen, feebly indecisive to the end, had not named her successor. And George of Hanover was immediately proclaimed King. Half the nation had been as horrified as James was. They had waited daily for King James to cross the water and claim at once his rightful throne. There had been excited demonstrations everywhere. People wore the white rose openly, they wore the Stuart oak leaves, they sang Jacobite songs, and wrote vicious lampoons against the Hanoverians. But nothing happened. Except that a fat German princeling stolidly—even reluctantly—landed at Greenwich, entered London, and was crowned in Westminster Abbey. All so quickly that the Jacobite party seemed to be paralyzed with unbelief. It could not be that England would accept a foreigner who spoke no word of English, who openly disliked the country he had been summoned to rule, who had imprisoned his wife and dragged with him to England rapacious German mistresses, one so fat she was known as the "Elephant," the other so tall and thin she was called the "Maypole." It could not be that England would crown a foreigner whose right to reign was so remote that it was said the Whig ministry had used a telescope to find it.

But barring a few riots, England *had* accepted all this. Here was a King at hand, and he was Protestant. That was the real crux of the matter. Justice, loyalty, practicality, even, had all been jettisoned for fear of a Roman Catholic king.

Personal distress for James had been severe during those first weeks when the news reached them at Dilston. He and Ann wept and prayed together, they had tried to believe that this bitter blow was, in some way, God's Will or a testing. And then they had ceased to talk about it. Secure at Dilston, they lived their own lives among tenants and close friends. Often London seemed as far off as Cathay.

Though recently there had been an annoyance. A rumor reached Dilston that the Government was about to revive an old law that no Catholic might own a horse worth more than five pounds. James, used to these fluctuating anti-Papist nuisances, had made light of the rumor; but Ann was frightened, so the best horses and the valuable gray stallion, Monarch, were sent to a Protestant neighbor's for safekeeping until, as James wrote, "We see what will be done in relating to horses." Miserable times, James thought, but I'll not dwell on them today.

"Look, my ladies." He smiled, pointing to the group of villagers who were laughing and shouting around a colossal effigy made of painted canvas stuffed with straw and crowned with a bishop's mitre. "They've set Saint Wilfrid on his throne! And I see they brought that dancing bear from Hexham. I hear the beast is comical."

Ann, always responsive to her husband's mood, leaned forward to look. "They're happy," she said, watching their excited people, who were forming the procession which would presently pass the summerhouse.

"And why wouldn't they be!" snapped Lady Mary. "You do enough for them. And all those kegs of beer! They'll be drunk by noon. I never heard of a manor lord so liberal as you, James."

"I want them to be content," said her nephew. "And this is Dilston's particular Gaudy Day. 'Foul care begone! Let the golden sun charm every heart to mirth!' "

Lady Mary shrugged and tightened her lips. Soon unexpected guests arrived. Thomas Forster and his pretty sister Dorothy were en route to the little village of Blanchland ten miles south of Dilston. Blanchland had once belonged to Tom Forster, but financial straits had forced him to sell it to his uncle, Lord Crewe. The Forsters were easily persuaded to stop over and see the procession. "Blanchland'll wait," said Tom, loosening his waistcoat buttons as he settled back with a grunt. " 'Tis a poky old hole, not a soul worth passing the time o' day with. If 'twasn't for collecting the Lammas rents for me uncle, I'd not go near it." He scowled and reached out for the punch Ann had ordered when she saw Tom Forster coming. Even among the hard-drinking Northumbrians Tom was conspicuous for consumption. And he looked it, with his big belly, his broken-veined nose, his bloodshot little eyes. Tom was only in his mid-thirties, yet seemed older, particularly since he had become M.P. for Northumberland, and taken on a pompous air.

"Do you always accompany your brother down from Bamburgh, Miss Forster?" asked Ann turning politely to Dorothy, and wondering why the attractive girl of twenty-five had not married.

"Aye, my lady," said Dorothy with her charming smile. "I try to keep Tom from mischief if I can." She spoke lightly but her eyes were on the second cup of punch which Tom was downing. Like as not, she thought, he'd soon be so fuddled they'd never get to Blanchland at all. And they needed their portion of the rents. There were three pennies and a farthing left in Tom's purse. A chronic state which the loyal Dorothy tried to impute to bad luck, never admitting the possibility of mismanagement and stupidity. Tom was all she had to love, or indeed seemed likely to have. Popularity with men was pleasant, though it had waned a trifle since her first girlhood, but it didn't bring husbands suitable for marriage with a Forster whose aunt was the great Lady Crewe and who was besides kin to Lord Derwentwater. And Tom was unable to scrape together enough money for his debts, let alone a sister's dowry. Besides, most of the lads who used to dangle about her were Catholics, and therefore quite ineligible. Dorothy smoothed the skirt of her shabby velveteen riding habit, and looked with momentary envy at Lord and Lady Derwentwater while the young couple murmured something private to each other. They were so exactly suited, both small, neatly made, young, and full of the dignified yet warm courtesy which is the essence of good breeding. Both so rich.

"Miss Forster," said Lady Mary suddenly, "there was talk in Durham that your aunt, Lady Crewe, was unwell—oppressed, they say, by the wretched state of our country. Is it true?"

"I don't know, my lady," said Dorothy. "We've not been to Durham in some while. She has certainly suffered as we all have from this blow to our hopes for the rightful king."

"*Suffered*," repeated the older woman with exasperation. "What's the use of suffering! Why don't they *do* something, hey? That's what I keep telling James here. Though 'tis not so easy for Catholics to act in these shocking times, but what are they doing in France? Tell me that. And *you*, sir," Lady Mary suddenly rapped Tom Forster's fat thigh with her fan, "you're a Protestant, and a Tory, you represent the county— why are you sitting here on your backside swilling spirits, while your nation's going to perdition?"

Tom blinked, while James said, "Auntie, Auntie, I pray you! We agreed not to speak of this subject today; and I must ask you not to chide a guest. The good Lord will lead us aright in His own good time."

"That's true," said Tom with a thick laugh, moving away from the reach of Lady Mary's fan. "Don't see what we c'n do now. Ol' George Porgie's on the throne, an' how're we going to get him down! What?" Tom chuckled and repeated this, which struck him as a fine bit of verse.

"Hush, Tom," said his sister, for the villagers had finally mustered their straggling line and the procession headed by the wobbly effigy of St. Wilfrid was approaching along the graveled path. James and Ann descended from the summerhouse and stood together smiling their welcomes.

For the next two hours even Lady Mary responded to the laughter around her. The village girls wore wreaths of cornflowers and daisies on their heads, and some also had aprons full of flowers, which they tossed at the feet of the Derwentwaters crying, "Saint Wilfrid's luck to ye, dear lord and lady!" The lads had flowers stuck behind their ears, and bells tied to their knees. They pranced by, jingling in time to the music of their band. Selby, the blacksmith, played the fiddle, while his idiot son shambled after him giggling. A carpenter played the flute, two old shepherds from Allendale played the Northumbrian pipes, the local tavernkeeper played the drum, and they all waved and shouted "Long live Darntwatter" as they filed by. Even Busby, the immensely dignified steward, had allowed bells to be tied around his knees and flowers on his hat brim, and later cut deft capers in the Morris dances, at which James laughed and applauded heartily, while Ann smiled and praised the children, who danced an intricate "Ring around a Rosy" for her special admiration.

Then there was the performing bear, and the jugglers, and a fine team of wrestlers who tumbled each other about in Cumberland style, and aroused Tom Forster's interest sufficiently for him to shout out hoarse wagers, quite forgetting that he had nothing with which to pay if he lost.

When time came for the feast, the Derwentwaters, with the Forsters and Lady Mary, sat in the open under the trees and ate among the crowd at a long trestle table. They passed a loving cup from mouth to mouth until the spiced claret was all drained, then James himself filled the cup again.

Mr. Brown, the chaplain, came to join them at the feast, and sang songs with the rest of them, as Mr. Petre never would have done. That priest had refused to come north again. He had gone to stay with his Petre relations in Essex, where Mary—James's young sister—was also visiting. It was a relief to be rid of Mr. Petre and his Jacobite plottings.

The sun shone all that joyful August afternoon, yet a delicious breeze off the moors cooled the air. It was comfortable in the shade of the great trees, and St. Wilfrid's effigy peered down benignly from the huge chestnut affectionately called the "Earl's tree." When little Johnny's nurse brought him back to sit on his mother's lap and suck a marchpane sweet, James looked from his wife and child to the hundreds of affectionate faces around him, and his heart swelled. This is as near to paradise as I can get on earth, he thought. Ann, watching him, nodded and put her hand on his. "Hark!" she said after a moment, turning her head. "I hear horses, I think. Down by the Devil Water."

"What an odd name is Devil Water," said Dorothy. "There could be no devil in this beautiful place."

"It does not refer to *him*," said Mr. Brown, always ready to enlighten, "at least they say it came from the D'eyvilstone family as Dilston does. And yet—" added the priest, "some do think the glen is haunted, perhaps Old Scrat has been there once."

"Nonsense!" said James with such sharpness that his wife stared at him. "I wonder that you can jest about evil, sir!"

The priest was also startled by the young Earl's vehemence. "I'm sorry, my lord," he said. "I spoke idly."

James nodded, ashamed of and not understanding his outburst. How had it been that Dorothy's chance reference to a name they used daily had shattered his happy mood like a discordant crash of cymbals? That he had felt a sudden chill on his scalp and along his spine, and heard the words "Devil Water" not as they applied to a lovely cascading

125

burn but as to some mysterious substance both sinister and dangerous.

"Why 'tis Charles coming, and another gentleman with him," said Ann in a pleased voice, as horsemen appeared on the drive. "Glad I am there's still food left." She hurried to greet her brother-in-law. Like most women, Ann was fond of Charles. And I am too, the rogue, James thought, his equanimity restored.

Charles looked flushed as he dismounted, his gray eyes shone with elation. His long body had thickened and matured. The gangling uncertainty of his boyhood, and the untidiness too, had vanished. He was now a well-groomed man who carried his head high under the blond periwig and gold-edged tricorne. The jagged white scar across his tanned right cheek did not detract from his debonair good looks, and his smile as he kissed Ann's hand and then Lady Mary's had a pleasing assurance. The smile broadened as he saw Dorothy Forster. "Why, Mistress Dolly! What pleasure to see here the toast of Northumbria!" Dorothy blushed and lowered her lashes, wishing that she was wearing something more becoming than her shabby riding habit.

"You did not bring the new fowling piece, Charles?" asked James.

Charles shook his head. "I've brought you something far more important!" He turned to the silent stranger who waited a little apart. "Let me present Colonel Oxburgh, my lord!" he cried triumphantly.

James had never heard of any Colonel Oxburgh, and was at a loss to understand his brother's excitement. Oxburgh had grave eyes, and a long-lipped Irish face. He spoke with an Irish accent as he made courteous rejoinders to the Earl's welcome. He was not dressed like an officer, but wore sober gentleman's clothes, though he had a sword and a pistol. He greeted the priest with particular warmth, saying, "By Saint Michael, I'm glad to see you, Father. I'm in sore need of shriving and a Mass."

The priest smiled. "You've been traveling where such were unavailable, sir?"

"That I have," said Oxburgh with grimness, "ever since I left France."

France, James thought. So that's what it is. His hands clenched against a violent impulse to breach every law of hospitality and bid the man leave. But Charles was saying urgently, "The Colonel must talk with you, James. At once. Shall we go in the house? You too, Tom," he added, giving the somnolent Forster a poke in the belly. "Wake up, there's great news!"

James silently led the way into his mansion. They went to the new library, where the Earl had lovingly accumulated hundreds of books. The four men sat down in an alcove by the sunny west window; a fly buzzed against the glittering new panes.

"Tell them, Oxburgh!" said Charles. "Tell them!"

The Colonel drew a deep breath, and fixed his eyes intently on James. "It has begun at last, my lord," he said solemnly. "The Earl of Mar this day landed in Newcastle from London —as I did. Lord Mar is riding posthaste into Scotland. Soon King James will be proclaimed across the Scottish nation."

"By God, ye don't mean it," said Forster sitting up straight. "Or what *do* ye mean?" He scowled, trying to clear his wits.

"I mean that our rightful king is coming to us, sir," said the Colonel. "He'll land in Scotland. King Louis of France has at last promised him an army at his back."

"Isn't it glorious!" Charles cried, amazed that his brother sat without speaking, his eyes tracing a pattern in the Turkey carpet. "King Jemmie'll come into his own again!"

James lifted his head. "Revolution," he said in a flat voice. "It means civil war."

"Well, of course, there'll be some fighting!" said Charles. "Can't make an omelet without breaking eggs."

James turned from his eager brother to Oxburgh. "Will you explain the situation in detail, sir. And what positive assurance is there that King James will land this time, who has so often failed?"

Henry Oxbough hastened to speak. He was passionately dedicated to the restoration of a Catholic king in Great Britain. He was one of the Jacobites' best secret agents, and had during the last months slipped back and forth between London and Bar-le-Duc, where James Stuart awaited his chance. Lord Bolingbroke was at Bar-le-Duc, and the Duke of Ormond too, arranging the last details of the Expeditionary Force. While in London, and in fact throughout England, the Jacobite leaders were ready. The countryside was being steadily alerted by agents, many of them Irish who posed as simple travelers. "Like me, my lord," said Oxburgh with his quiet smile. "The rising will start in the west of England, under Sir William Wyndham, while Lord Mar is rousing Scotland. Our party at Walton-le-Dale will see to Lancashire, and, surely, here in the North we can count on thousands to rally for us."

127

"Who are they?" said James after a moment.

Oxburgh stiffened. He had not expected such restraint from this Earl, who was not only the premier Catholic up here but cousin to King James as well. Especially as Charles Radcliffe had shown instant enthusiasm. Oxburgh reached inside his waistcoat and brought out a paper on which were listed over a hundred names. "This was confided to me in London," he said, putting the paper in James's hands. "These are the heads of Northern families on which we shall rely."

James glanced down at the paper. "I see that my name tops the list," he said after a long pause.

"I' faith to be sure it does!" cried Oxburgh. "Who else? Though they think in London 'twould be best to make Mr. Forster, here, the General—him being Protestant. So the Whigs can't say 'tis only Catholics who want the rightful king. For it isn't. We can count on all the Tories and High Churchmen too."

"I'm to be a general?" sputtered Tom, his little eyes brightening. "Gen'ral Forster, o-ho! We must have a drink on that, m'lord! What d'ye say!"

Nobody answered him. Charles and Oxburgh were staring at James, who had turned his head and was gazing out of the window where he could see his villagers still dancing and singing on the lawns. Oxburgh followed the Earl's glance and said, "Your people love you, my lord. You could easily raise a thousand men here yourself!"

"Probably," said James. "Yet they are content as they are, and have no fault to find with King George. They'd follow me, but has God given me the right to wrench them from their homes and force them into war? Into revolution against the laws of their country—into treason?"

"I can*not* understand you, James!" Charles burst out. "Isn't this what we've always prayed and hoped for? How can you be so wavering and tepid? You, who know our cousin, you who were raised with him?"

James's lips tightened. Aye, he thought, and it is *because* I know my cousin that I seem tepid. Because there is a heaviness about him, because his life has been passed in shadows and sour indecisions, because he is forever oppressed by the Stuart doom—as I find I do not wish to be. "If I refuse to go out in this rebellion," he said slowly to Oxburgh, "what then?"

The Colonel was dismayed. "Why—I—I'll go to Lord Widdrington. I believe the Earl of Mar has already stopped there on his way north."

"I doubt," said James quietly, "that Widdrington will be much more eager than I am."

"By God, m'lord," cried Tom Forster, lumbering to his feet, "I'm with Charles. I canna fathom this shilly-shally. Why, I'll be in action at once. I'll get men together, put 'em under arms. I'll rally 'em to the cause wi' never a backward thought." He thumped his chest, glaring down at the Earl, whose gray eyes were masked as he contemplated the fat county squire who had frittered away all his patrimony. "*You* have nothing to lose, Tom," he said. "As for me, I can make no decision now, I must pray on it."

Later on Charles could never remember the happenings of the next few weeks, so clouded were they by uncertainty and bewildered disappointment in his brother. Colonel Oxburgh had had to leave Dilston without securing James's promise of support. Oxburgh rode off into Northumberland to alert other known Jacobites, but he went gloomily, knowing that without Derwentwater's leadership many would refuse to join.

During those weeks James plunged into one of the melancholies which had long been foreign to him. Sometimes he disappeared for hours, and once Ann found him in the dungeon below the old wing tapping with a chisel. At other times he had the chest of Radcliffe papers brought to him and kept it in his apartments, locking his door even against Ann. Pale and distraught, she slipped about the castle and tried to avoid the furious questions Lady Mary bombarded her with.

On September 15 Charles rode over to Corbridge seeking, as he had when a boy, some amusement. And in the taproom of the Angel, he heard news so cataclysmic that he rushed back to Dilston, and straight to his brother.

James was sitting at a desk in the morning room glancing over his bailiff's accountings of the harvest, which had been excellent. He had other papers underneath the accounts, and these papers he hid from Ann. She sat near him embroidering a baby cap, and casting anxious glances at her husband. He looked haggard and he kept his hand to his head as though it ached.

When Charles burst in, James looked up with a frown. "What is it? I thought your London years had taught you quieter manners."

"They've raised the standard in Scotland!" Charles cried.

"Our King has been proclaimed at Braemar, at Aberdeen and Inverness, everywhere!"

Ann drew a sharp breath, and turned her dark eyes hopefully to James, but he only compressed his lips, and said, "Well, it's what we've been expecting, isn't it? Has the King landed, then?"

"They say not yet," said Charles reluctantly. "There's been a blow to his plans. King Louis of France is dead."

There was a silence. James picked up his goose quill, and made with it small meaningless marks on the top papers.

"That's not all," said Charles on a quieter note. "Will Shaftoe was at the Angel. He's had a letter from his brother in London, who says there may be some warrant out against *you*."

James's head jerked up. "Against me? I don't believe it. If there's any such rumor Mr. Bacon will know of it—excellent Whig magistrate that he is!" James got up and pulled the bell rope.

"What are you going to do, dear?" Ann whispered. The baby cap slipped from her fingers to the floor.

"I'm going to Mr. Bacon to find out what, if any, charges there may be against me. Saddle some nag, bring my hat and cloak," he added to the servant who answered the bell pull.

"James!" cried Charles in despair. "*Why* do you do this?"

"Because England is my country and I wish to obey its laws."

"But don't you understand that Scotland's won over!" Charles shouted. "That England soon will be. *King James* will now make the laws!"

"That will be difficult unless he is here to make them." The gray eyes flashed with sudden anger. "You young fool! Don't you realize what King Louis's death means? Do you think that France will *now* give the Jacobites her backing?" James turned on his heel and stalked out the door, leaving Charles aghast.

"'The Jacobites'!" he said to Ann. "My God, he speaks as though he wasn't one of us. What's happened to him? Holy Blessed Virgin, I don't understand him at all."

"Leave him alone," said Ann, her eyes full of tears. "He has been wrestling with his conscience. He's had headaches and monstrous dreams. I believe he's had a warning from one of the 'presences' Busby says do show themselves to Radcliffes. James will not speak of it, but as we left the nurseries t'other night he went down the tower stairs ahead of me, and I heard him cry out as though in horror."

"But he should fight!" cried Charles scarcely listening. "How can he stand by like this, while the Rising we always hoped for has started! I must leave him and join. God forfend there should be bad blood between us, yet—"

"Wait!" said Ann putting her hand out with a groping gesture. "He needs your loyalty, and Charles, you think only of fighting. He sees many things clearer than you do. Wait, I beg you."

"Bah!" cried Charles angrily. Then he heard her give a strangled sob, and he heard a choking whisper, "Holy Mother, I cannot understand James either."

It was nearing dusk when James rode back from Hexham. It had been a sultry day, and there was thunder in the air, but James had no thought of the weather. The interview with Mr. Bacon had been reassuring. The magistrate made scandalized denial of any possible charges against the great Earl of Derwentwater. Why should there be? Oh there was the temporary inconvenience about the horses, of course, and—said Mr. Bacon shrugging—one must expect muddled restrictions and misunderstandings from a new ministry, mustn't one! And one must not credit the perpetual rumors of unrest, which moreover nobody could possibly connect with Lord Derwentwater, whose beneficence, popularity, and loyalty were known from the Tweed to the Tyne—and farther.

James had made suitable rejoinders and taken a courteous leave of the magistrate, but his mood had not lightened nor had his headache gone. Outside Hexham he passed a tavern and on impulse went in and ordered a brandy. He had no wish to talk and had hoped to be unnoticed. A ridiculous hope. The innkeeper was so awed by the honor of serving the Earl that his hand shook. The taproom drinkers all stood up bowing and God-blessing him. Most of these were his own tenants, and James had to force himself to respond easily to their greetings. Then he must buy them all drinks. He escaped after the third brandy. His head was spinning slightly. His thoughts shimmered and blurred, yet were no longer stamping on the ceaseless treadmill which had clattered in his brain for weeks.

When he reached the bridge over Devil Water, he hesitated, aware of a great reluctance to return to Dilston Hall and its reproachful inmates. He turned the horse instead and followed the rough path up the burn. For years he had loved riding through the wild glen, with its steep mossy rocks speared by ferns and bordered with alders and willows, while the bright brown waters tumbled in musical cascades beneath. The glen darkened as he climbed through a copse of ancient beeches and lost sight of the burn. There were fallow deer bounding among these trees, it had been the Dilston Deer Park for how long? For centuries. These trees had seen his ancestors—Radcliffes, Claxtons, Cartingtons—ancestors who never doubted themselves, who had been as ready with their swords as with their prayers. With half-closed eyes James let the horse pick its way through the wood, and seemed to feel them near him, the multitude who had once loved and owned this place as he did. But they weren't *Stuarts*, he thought. And what have I to do with Stuarts except through a King's chance light o' love! "Yet what of your cousin?" came the inexorable question again. However it came, you share the same faith and blood. You swore fealty to James Stuart long ago. Long ago—too long ago . . . The wind caught up the echoing words and sighed them through the fir trees on the bank.

The old nag stumbled along the path out of the wood, and down to the burn again, where the ground spread out in a grassy level nearly surrounded by a horseshoe of rushing water. A few trees grew on this open space, a couple of willows, an oak. There was also the remnant of a crumbling wall, some fallen stones, and a rude cross lying on its side against the oak. Here had been the nunnery in the olden days. Here in this gentle shadowy place had been a cloister. James dismounted and stood near the broken cross, watching the stream as it swirled by. He lifted his head and gazed unthinking at the oak tree, dim green in the failing light.

There was one rusty spot in that mass of green, one leaf that had obeyed the commands of autumn before its brothers. As James noticed it the leaf quivered, it detached itself and floated, balancing and swaying, until it rested on the grass at James's feet. He recoiled, staring down at the little ruddy spot. Sweat broke out on his forehead. His heart hammered and seemed to stop. He fell to his knees and crossed himself while the verse he had read in the Radcliffe papers, and then forgotten, jangled in his mind:

When a green oakleaf shall turn red
The last earl shall die in his gory bed.
The fox and the owl shall inhabit his halls,

132

The bat and the spider shall cling to his walls.
His lands from his house the strong arm shall sever
And the name of his race be extinguished forever.

"*Kyrie eleison,*" he whispered, "Lord have mercy on me."
He covered his face with his hands, and crouched on the grass. The minutes passed, shadows deepened under the oak tree. Then mingling with the sound of the burn he thought he heard another voice. It spoke gently the words of the Mass. "*Misereatur tui omnipotens Deus, et dimissis peccatis tuis, perducat te ad vitam aeternam.*"

James lifted his head in wonder, for the voice seemed not inside him as had been the cruel prophecy. A nebulous gray shape shimmered by the fallen cross. Its flowing robes were nunlike, its face misty against the wavering leaves, and from the figure with its uplifted face James felt an outflowing of peace. He moved, his arms stretched in supplication.

He implored in his heart, "Speak to me again!" and heard the far echo of the gentle voice repeating "May Almighty God have mercy on thee, forgive thy sins, and bring thee to life everlasting."

"Aye, but what do you mean?" he whispered, his eyes straining to see. There was nothing standing beside the cross. Nothing but the tree trunks and the flat grassy little plain. After a while he got to his feet, trembling. He bent over, picked up the red leaf, and held it in his palm for a moment, then he walked to the brink of the water, and stood looking down. He tossed the leaf in and watched it carried swiftly away by the tumbling ripples. He knew then what the Devil Water had come to mean to him, why it referred not to this beautiful burn but to the black waves which had been swamping him. The devil's water was uncertainty. No. The devil's water was fear.

At Dilston Hall the family were gathered uneasily in the smaller drawing room, waiting for the Earl's return. Ann was on the cushioned seat in the bay window so that she might watch the drive. Charles paced the floor, except when he paused occasionally to take a reviving pinch of snuff—a fashionable habit he had acquired in London. Lady Mary sat ramrod stiff by the empty fireplace, and fanned herself with rhythmic clicks. It was still hot, the threatened storm had not broken. The old lady's vast displeasure with James had quite unfairly transferred itself to Ann and Charles, since her inborn reverence for the head of the family had as yet curbed her tongue where the Earl was concerned. So she had ceased speaking to anyone but Mr. Brown, who hovered near her chair and racked his brains for topics which might not lead to the thoughts in all their minds.

"I believe I've a new convert," said the priest brightly. "Will Purdy, my lord's coachman, has been coming for instruction."

"Humph," said Lady Mary. "Pity there aren't more of 'em, though I expect you try. By the way, I think, Father, you should know of Peggy, the baker's wife's scandalous—"

Whatever Peggy's sins, the priest was not destined to hear them. Alec Armstrong, Charles's valet, suddenly appeared in the doorway and said, "By your leave, sir!"

Charles turned in astonishment. Alec was originally a Dilston lad, but he had spent these London years with Charles, and being quick, shrewd, and adaptable had become the perfect valet, and knew his place—which was not the drawing room.

"What's ado?" said Charles, staring at the sandy-haired freckled young man whose wide mouth had a humorous quirk to it.

"A young woman ter see ye, sir," said Alec with the suggestion of a wink. He had assisted at several of Charles's amours, and knew how to have a bit of fun himself. "Very urgent she is. Won't tell her business, she's panting wi' haste—*must* see ye, sir!"

Ann was so anxiously watching the driveway that she paid no attention, but Lady Mary snorted. "I sincerely trust, nephew, that you've not been indulging your deplorable whims up here."

"If you mean women, Aunt, I have not," Charles snapped. These troubled weeks at Dilston had provided neither the mood nor the opportunities for dalliance. He preceded Alec into the passage. "Who is she?"

"Haven't a notion, sir. But she would speak to ye private, so I put her in the brewery."

There was one candle lit among the great kegs and fermenting vats in the brewery; the light flickered over a woman in a black shawl and patched dress. She gave a cry when she saw Charles, and whispered, "Where's his lordship? Ye mun warn him! They're after him, no more'n an hour behind me. I've galloped all the way fra Gatsheed."

"What are you talking about?" said Charles sternly. Then her shawl slipped down and he recognized her. "Nan

134

Wilson?" he said, taken completely aback. "Is it Nan Wilson, Meg's sister?"

"Aye, and divven't stand there gawking. Warn his lordship. There's three deputies from Lunnon, and that foul blackguard's own bailiffs coming wi' 'em to arrest the Earl."

"He's not here yet," said Charles frowning. "And, Mrs. Wilson, how do you know this so positively?"

"Because I wark as servant for Squire Cotesworth, damn his black heart, but I need the pittance, now Geordie's been sick sae lang wi' the lung rot. Those Lunnon deputies was at table terday wi' the Squire and I heard 'em plotting."

"Sir!" interrupted Alec urgently, turning from the window where he had had his nose pressed to the panes. "His lordship's here now!"

"Come with me then," said Charles to Nan. "Tell *him* your story!" For he was not quite convinced by this warning, and he had scant reason to trust the Snowdons, or indeed the Wilsons. He remembered how little Rob had spied on him for days before the Snowdon men abducted him.

Nan nodded desperately. She knew what Charles was thinking.

When they got up to the drawing room, James looked even grimmer than when he had started out for Hexham, but he was patiently answering his wife's nervous questions. "No, my dear. There was nothing to the rumor, Mr. Bacon assured me . . ."

"I don't know about that," said Charles, pushing Nan forward. "Here's Mrs. Wilson with a different tale."

"They're after ye, m'lord," cried Nan twisting her fingers. "A whole posse o' 'em, Squire William Cotesworth's sending wi' the London deputies. They've a warrant wi' 'em. They'll put ye in jail."

Ann gave a gasp and ran to her husband, who stood frowning on the hearth rug. Before he could speak Lady Mary rose up to her full height and cried in a great voice, "No doubt my lord would *rather* be safe in a quiet jail than fight for the cause! No doubt that's what he wants! Here, nephew," she shrilled, "give me your sword so I may fight for my King, and take my fan instead, 'tis the only weapon fit for you!" She flung the fan at James's feet.

His pallor deepened, his jaw clenched. He looked at the fan and he looked at his shaking aunt.

"Your little drama, my lady, is unnecessary," he said in a steely tone no one had ever heard from him. "I had already made up my mind to join the Rising. And 'tis no part of my plan to be taken now before I can be of use to it."

"Thank God," said Charles, and gave a nervous laugh of supreme relief. The priest touched his crucifix, and expelled his breath in a long sigh. Ann was murmuring brokenly, "Oh, my dear love, I'm glad and yet—oh, I can't think what 'twill mean!" Lady Mary's withered cheeks reddened, moisture came to her sharp eyes. She leaned over with difficulty and, picking up the fan, retired silently to the window seat.

"Ye mun *hide*, my lord! Hurry! 'Tis why I'm here to warn ye!" cried Nan in anguish, not understanding everyone's behavior.

"*Why* do you warn me?" said James quietly. "I don't even know who you are."

"*He* does," she cried, pointing to Charles. "I'm sister to his wife who's not a wife, I'm aunt to his bonny bairn. Yet not for this do I warn ye, Lord Darntwatter. 'Tis because I hate Black William wi' all my soul, and I wish to balk his clarty tricks."

"She's speaking truth, James," Ann whispered, staring at the woman. "Oh, my dear, what are we to do? Where can you go?"

"I know where to go," said James. "But I'll need some help. Mrs. Wilson, did you hear them speak of arresting anyone else here?"

She shook her head. "Only you, m'lord."

"That's fortunate," said James with his first smile in weeks. "For alas, Mr. Brown, I was stupid enough to close up the priest's hole when I rebuilt. As for you, Charles, I'll need you for a while; then come back here to the others, and receive this posse courteously, telling any lies your fertile brain can invent as to my whereabouts. And you, Mrs. Wilson, I beg you to accept this. I'm deeply grateful." He held out a gold sovereign, but she stepped back. "I'd rather die," she said with a toss of her head. "D'ye think a Snawdon'd tak' money fur a thing like this!"

"Well, no, now I think of it, I don't," said James with another smile. "You must not be found here or on the road, they'll search thoroughly."

"I'll to the kitchen, and play beggar woman till they've gone," said Nan. "But they wouldna knaw me if they saw me. Folk divven't notice sarvants."

"Where are you going?" Ann cried again to her husband. "I must know where you'll be!"

"Not now, dear." James gave her a quick kiss. "Nobody but Charles shall know, you'll hear later. Come," he added to his brother, and they hurried from the drawing room.

There were a dozen fully armed men in the posse which arrived at Dilston twenty minutes later. They used guile in their attempt to capture the Earl. An under-sheriff ascertained at the gatehouse that Lord Derwentwater had recently returned from a ride and was in his Hall. At the great front door, they told the footman that they were a delegation from Newcastle come to solicit the Earl's help in founding a new almshouse. The footman innocently showed them to the drawing room. Here they found a quiet family scene. Two ladies embroidering, the priest and Mr. Charles Radcliffe playing chess in the corner, and no sign of the Earl.

"Why, we haven't seen his lordship since noon. Have we, Mr. Brown?" said Charles blandly. "I expect he's riding somewhere on the moors; he's very fond of exercise."

"*At night! In the rain!*" cried the London messenger who carried the warrant. "Besides, the gateward said 'e'd come 'ome."

"The gateward," said Charles, "is getting old and is mistaken."

" 'Ere's a diddling pack o' lies!" shouted the London messenger. "Get on wi' it, lads, and search the place!"

"You're heartily welcome to," said Charles, neatly checkmating Mr. Brown. "Aren't they, my ladies?"

Ann and Lady Mary both inclined their heads and went on embroidering. The posse tramped throughout every nook and cranny of Dilston Hall. They hunted through the attics and the cellars, they peered under beds and tapped on paneled walls, they clambered up fireplaces looking for the priest's hole tradition had always said existed at Dilston. By two in the morning they gave it up, believing that young Radcliffe must have told the truth when he said the Earl was out.

Charles had the posse provided with beer and they settled down to wait. But by daylight they lost confidence. It became clear to the dullest of the Newcastle bailiffs that the Earl had somehow been warned and escaped. By six o'clock they mounted their horses, and straggled back towards Newcastle, though they left a bailiff at Dilston as spy. Fortunately he was a thick-witted yokel, whose one idea was to sit by the front door and apprehend the Earl when he rode up. Charles found the man no hindrance at all to the carrying out of certain plans. The first of these concerned Nan Wilson, who was eating breakfast in the kitchen, under Alec's sympathetic eye. "Nan," said Charles, "you're safe to leave now. The posse's way ahead of you, and that chucklehead on the steps'll never see you."

She nodded and got up, wiping her mouth. "Aye, I mun haste back and feed poor Geordie."

Charles drew her outside and behind the stables, where her Galloway pony was waiting. "We needn't tell you again our heartfelt gratitude, and I insist that you take this basket of provisions for Geordie, since you won't take the money."

She bit her lips, but she let him strap the hamper to her saddle.

"Tell me," said Charles in a low voice, putting his hand on the pommel, "how is my little girl? My Jenny?"

"D'ye think of her?" asked Nan in astonishment.

"I do. And I've often written Meg asking about the child, but she doesn't answer."

Nan sighed. "Aye, Meg ha' a strange darkling heart, an' she wants ye to forget her an' the bairn."

"I've tried right enough," said Charles grimly, "and succeeded most the time; but you'll admit the circumstances are peculiar, though 'tis never Meg I think of."

"Jenny's weel," said Nan after a moment. "I've not seen her in a year, but Faither writes now an' agyen. She's a canny towheaded mite, bonny an' blithe as a lark. A glint o' sunshine i' that dark old peel tower. They're all fond o' her."

"I'm glad," said Charles. "I've been planning to ride up there, force them to let me see her—but now . . ." He came back with a jolt to the change in all their circumstances, and the thought that James was hidden in the tunnel. "Farewell, Nan, God's blessing on you for what you've done—you're not too Protestant to mind a Catholic's blessing?"

"I'm not," she said, touched his hand quickly, and kicking the Galloway started down the far side of the hill, out of sight of the house.

Charles cautiously skirted the Hall, ascertained that the bailiff was still squatting on the steps, then went in search of old Busby. The steward alone of anyone at Dilston guessed where his master might be hiding and he whispered to Charles, "How did ye get that dungeon wall open, sir?"

"His lordship had already opened it in readiness," Charles answered. Though it was not the wall which led to the underground tunnel. It was a pavingstone in the blackest corner of the dungeon floor. It lifted when a chisel was wedged under it a certain way.

"Would there be enough air for him?" asked Busby

anxiously. "If the tunnel goes all the way to the Tyne?"

"There'll be enough," said Charles. The tunnel did not run to the Tyne, it debouched two hundred yards below in a hidden cave beside the Devil Water. "Busby, I need two farmers' smocks and hats, and one of the farm carts filled with sacks of wheat. Put a stout nag to the cart, too."

The steward nodded and hurried off. In an hour Charles drove the farm cart down the road to the Devil Water Bridge, as though he were going to the mill. He wore big boots, a faded blue smock, and a broad hat. He had greased his hair and pulled it forward around his face where it hung lankly and almost hid the scar. He looked about carefully, before he stopped the horse by the bridge. There was nobody in sight. He jumped down and clambered through nettles and brambles until he found the approximate spot by the burn James had told him of. Then he called cautiously, "James! All clear."

The long ferns parted in a place Charles had not expected them to, and James stuck his head out. " 'Tis snug in here," he said cheerfully. "I've made good use of my time. Done much thinking. Naught went wrong?"

"No. And they've gone. Here's your farmer's gear."

James was soon dressed like Charles except that, since the Earl always wore a periwig, his head was shaven and had to be covered with a kerchief under the hat. "I think you'll do," said Charles eying his brother critically. "Slump down in the sacks behind. I'll drive."

So the two farmers started off for Corbridge, as though they were carrying wheat from Dilston mill. They passed through the little town without the slightest difficulty. Charles answered one or two friendly hails from other farmers with a muffled "Good day to ye." James apparently snored on the sacks in a drunken stupor. They turned left out of Corbridge, and lumbered along to Beaufront, the Errington castle. Charles drew up in the farmyard. "Stay where you are," he whispered to James, while to a curious stable boy who came up to greet them he said in a passable Northumbrian accent, "M'brother's a bit the wor-rse for a stop we made at the Angel. Leave him be, like a good lad, to sleep it off, and fetch the Chief fur me. Here's a load he or-rdered."

The boy nodded and disappeared into the castle kitchen. In a while the old Chief stalked out of his house, shaggy brows beetling. "What's the meaning o' this, man!" he shouted at Charles. "We didna order-r corn! There's some mistake."

"Will ye look at the sacks, master?" said Charles. "Ye'll

see they're meant fur ye, reet enough."

The old man frowned but he went close to the cart, whereupon James pushed up his hat and showed his face for an instant.

The Chief jerked back. "Sainted Peter!" he muttered. He looked from the huddled figure in the cart to Charles. His gnarled hands trembled. "So 'tis come to this at last, has it," he said beneath his breath. He glanced over his shoulder at the hovering stable boy, then shouted at James, "Get up, ye drunken rogue! Get up and come i' the house wi' your mate. I'll not stand here i' the hot sun arguing wi' ye."

James arose and staggered off the cart. The two brothers followed the Chief into his stark old Hall, where Tom Errington was casting accounts at a desk by the window. He gaped at the farmers, and said with disapproval, "Since when do you bring the likes of them into your Hall, sir, send them to the kitchen."

The old man ignored his nephew, and turned to James. "My lord," he said in a sad dragging voice, "are they after ye? Does this mean what I fear it does?"

James threw off his hat and kerchief, and young Errington jumped to his feet. "It means," said the Earl, "that I am going out for King James."

The old man's face crumpled, he drew a difficult breath. "I didn't think ye would, my boy," he said. "And I didn't think ye should. Look!" He pointed to the window. "D'ye see Dilston over there across the Tyne? D'ye see your fair bonny home? D'ye know what ye risk by going out with the Rising?"

"I know," said James. They all stared at him, at the small figure in the farmer's dirty smock and the shaven pate above it. A figure of fun it might have been, but it was not. James's strength and dignity filled the hall, and the old man bowed his head. "So be it. If ye go we must be with ye. What's to be done?"

"I will tell you," said James. "I have made careful plans, and the first ones must be carried out from here since Dilston is under surveillance."

SIX

During the next frantic days Charles marveled often at the speed and decision with which James went into action. While they were sheltered by the old Chief at Beaufront, James set up an organization of secret messengers who rallied all the Jacobite families in Northumberland. For these messengers James selected the most trustworthy among his own servants and tenants. He consigned the list to Charles an hour after the brothers reached Beaufront, since James had made all his plans during that night of hiding at the mouth of the tunnel.

"Is this *all?*" asked Charles dismayed, when James gave him the list. "Why, you could call out hundreds more."

"But I will not," said James quietly. "These men I've chosen because I know them to be Catholics or personally dedicated to King James. And they are young, without families who might suffer. I'll have none of my people jeopardized because of personal loyalty to me alone."

"Ah, ye're a good lad, m'lord!" cried the Chief tremulously. "I wish I could go out wi' ye, but I canna ride hard any more. Tom, you're going!" It was a command, not a question, but his nephew had already decided.

"Aye," he said in his precise way. "If Derwentwater goes, I will." He sat down at the desk and picked up the pen. "At Capheaton," he said thoughtfully, "I doubt Sir William'll come out, but his brothers should. And we can count on Shaftoes, Claverings, Stockoes, my Lord Widdrington, of course . . ."

"Not 'of course,' " said James with a grim smile. "But I

141

shall write him a letter which'll bring him, if he's not decided yet." James glanced at the paper, where Errington was neatly putting down names as they occurred to him. "You've not forgotten Tom Forster, who's to be our general, I believe?"

"No," said Errington. "But he's on the run. There was a warrant for him, too. Fenwick of Bywell knows where he is."

"Find Forster," said James, "and bring him to me!"

"At Dilston?"

"Not at Dilston Hall, that's too risky. I know a place where we can all meet and our enemies'll never think to look."

At dawn on Thursday morning the sixth of October, Charles and thirty-three of the Earl's men waited impatiently on the lawn in front of Dilston Hall while James made his final farewell to Ann, who was sobbing on the doorstep. "Pray for us, darling, and be brave," James said, kissing his wife, then snatching up little John for another hug.

"I'll pray," she whispered, "and each night a lamp'll burn in the tower to guide you home again. Oh, my dear love, the Rising can't fail, can it? Not when our cause is just!"

"We must trust in God, Ann."

"Aye, trust in God," said Mr. Brown from the doorway, where he had given James his benediction.

"Where's your ring?" cried Ann, her distraught eyes suddenly noticing an empty space on her husband's middle finger. He always wore the Stuart diamond ring which King Charles had given to little Moll Davis, his grandmother. James perfectly hid his discomfiture. The ring had unaccountably fallen from his finger while he dressed an hour ago. James had searched as long as he dared yet he could not find it. "I thought it might encumber me," he answered. "Ann, you know what to do with the Radcliffe papers in case there should be ill news."

"Yes, yes," she said crossing herself. "Take them to Capheaton where the Swinburnes'll hide them. But there won't be ill news, why even if—if the Rising should fail they'd dare not touch *you*."

"My lord!" Charles called out urgently, reining in his prancing horse. " 'Tis almost sunup."

James nodded, kissed Ann again, and rapidly mounted his gray stallion, Monarch. James dug in his spurs, but the great horse refused to budge, he stiffened his forelegs and lay back his ears. James felt the gasp of superstitious fear Ann gave, because its counterpart was in his own throat.

"Damme," cried Charles giving the stallion a whack on

the rump. "This beast's grown lazy at pasture. Move along, you scamp!"

Monarch snorted, then bounded forward resentfully. James had so much ado controlling him that he did not see Ann, the child, and the priest waving from the doorstep, nor Lady Mary's handkerchief fluttering in a window. By the time the stallion was trotting quietly at the head of the cavalcade, Dilston was only a fair white blur among the trees.

James did not look back again. While they followed a track south along the burn he constrained himself to think only of the matter at hand. Though some of his men were riding coach horses, on the whole the company was well mounted. There had been a slight difficulty in arranging for the return of the best horses, but the neighbor in whose keeping they were, had overcome his Whiggish scruples when Busby offered him a hundred pounds "as a gift." The men were well armed too, each with a pistol, or musket, and they wore stout leather doublets to protect their vitals. Charles had done well, James thought gratefully, glancing at his brother, who rode a fleet raw-boned gelding. James had issued directions from his hiding places, either in the Queen's Cave up Dipton Burn, or in a ruinous shepherd's cot on the edge of the moor. Here Charles brought for inspection the men James had picked, then went back to Dilston and made necessary arrangements there. One of these was to get rid of the Newcastle bailiff, and of another bailiff who presently arrived.

The two bailiffs were now snugly ensconced in the lightest and airiest of Dilston's dungeons, with Busby as warder. And a mercy it is, James thought, that I didn't destroy the old tower when I rebuilt. A further mercy had been the loyalty of all his people. Word had got around, of course, that the Earl was hiding somewhere on his estates, and there had been many who knew the exact spots yet not a whisper had reached the authorities at Hexham or Newcastle.

Several miles from Dilston but still on Derwentwater land the Earl turned his horse away from the burn and struck out into rough hilly country north of Hexhamshire Common. "Can Forster find Greenriggs, d'you think?" James asked of Charles as they entered a purple waste of heather and began to look for the old farmhouse which was the landmark.

"If he doesn't," said Charles, "his head's even thicker than I think it. I made him a map."

"Brother," James said reining in the stallion, and speaking sternly, "Tom Forster is our general. He's received his commission from our King himself. You must remember this, obey his orders, and from now on speak of him with respect."

"Aye, my lord," said Charles after a moment. "Needs must, since I obey *you*. And there's Forster now, on yonder hill!"

The new General, on a huge black horse, was easy to identify since he had dressed himself in a scarlet coat trimmed with gold braid and wore a general's hat tufted with cock feathers. He carried a large green taffeta standard on which King James's emblem was emblazoned. Forster had about twenty horsemen with him, and the two parties galloped to meet each other. "Thought ye'd never come, m'lord," said Tom somewhat peevishly. "Began to think ye'd got cold feet again. No matter since ye're here," he added hastily, seeing both James and Charles stiffen. "There's some officers for ye to meet. One ye already know—that's Colonel Oxburgh. I've made him me aide-de-camp."

Henry Oxburgh came forward and bowed to James. "It does my heart good to see your lordship again, and Mr. Radcliffe. Our cause is mightily prospering in Scotland, I've much news for you. And may I present two young Irish officers who'll ride with us? Captains Nicholas and Charles Wogan."

The Irish brothers were startlingly young, both in their teens, but were already trained soldiers. They had twinkling eyes and a dashing gallantry.

"Now we'll have a drop all around, afore we plan our march," said Forster, struggling to reach the flask which was wedged between his rump and coattails.

"May I speak with my Lord Derwentwater?" murmured a meek oily voice, at Tom's elbow. "I'd like his lordship to know I've joined the Rising."

"Begock!" said Tom. "I forgot ye, Patten!" He shoved forward a meager man with a knobbly head and a sharp nose, who wore the black suit and round collar of an Episcopal curate. "Robert Patten from Allendale," said Tom carelessly. "Wants to be me chaplain."

"Yes, I know Mr. Patten," said the Earl without enthusiasm. He had met the clergyman a year ago at the Alston lead mines over a matter of arranging burial service for one of the Earl's Protestant miners, and he had then thought Patten both greedy and servile.

Yet King James had directed that they enlist as many Protestants as possible. And a cleric might be useful as spy or messenger.

"Now 'tis time we march to Coquetdale," said Tom

wiping his mouth on the back of his hand. "Oxburgh says there's a moor near Rothbury's to be our next rally ground."

Coquetdale! Charles thought. So he was to go back to that wild Border where lived Meg—and Jenny.

"I suggest," James said, "that we march by way of Beaufront, where Tom Errington awaits us with whatever men he's been able to muster."

"And I quite agree, sir," said Oxburgh to Forster, who was frowning while he mulled over this new idea. In a moment, having nothing better to suggest, Tom nodded graciously. "So be it. We'll march through Corbridge wi' drawn swords, show 'em our mettle, eh? Now we're fifty strong."

"And maybe have a skirmish!" cried Charles, delighted. "Some action at last after all this while of skulking about!"

"I doubt ye're so pleased wi' action when ye get it, m'lad," said Tom repressively. "And don't ye start anything, young buck, d'ye hear!"

"Yes, sir," said Charles, trying to sound properly submissive to a general who had somehow been metamorphosed from Tom Forster, the fat, pompous, turnip-headed country squire.

They certainly saw no action that day, nor for many weeks thereafter. Wherever they marched the people ran from their houses, stared at the Jacobite standard, then drew back murmuring, watchful. But nobody challenged them. Occasionally a cheer was raised for King James—usually in a female voice. Twice they picked up a recruit, but Forster refused several who were not already furnished with arms or horses. "Ye can come out later," he said to these volunteers, "when we've taken Newcastle. Then we'll have gear for foot-soldiers."

At dusk they reached the Coquet River, crossed it at Hepple, and went to Plainfield moor, a lonely heath some miles west of Rothbury. Here there was already a campfire burning and a party of horsemen were waiting as Forster's troops rode up.

Charles listened rather absently to the greetings and information from the Coquetdale contingent, none of whom he knew, with the exception of young George Collingwood of Eslington. Some stonemason called Robson seemed to be spokesman, and assured Forster that the little town of Rothbury was chiefly Jacobite and therefore quite safe to use as headquarters. That enough lodging for all had been commandeered, and it was thus not necessary to camp on this comfortless moor.

While the parley was in progress, Charles kept gazing across the Coquet to the jagged black outline of the Simonside Hills. The highest peak was Tosson. And beneath it— not three miles from here—the Snowdon peel huddled in its narrow glen. I have a wife and child there, Charles thought. An incongruity which moved him to painful amusement. And he stared again across the river.

"Come along, Charlie," said James in surprise, seeing by the firelight an odd expression on his brother's face. "We're off to Rothbury for the night. What ails you, are you weary?"

Charles started to explain, then thought better of it. James had quite enough to worry him without reminder of his brother's predicament. Besides, Charles had just made a decision, and did not wish to provoke a restraining command.

The whole company rode along the Coquet into Rothbury, where the men of rank were quartered at the Three Half Moons next the church. Others went to the Black Bull, and the rest were bedded down in various lodgings.

The Earl had a room to himself up under the inn's thatching, and Charles was relieved when James, after eating and drinking moderately, said that he would retire. "You've a bed with the Swinburne lads, haven't you? Mind you don't get drunk, Charles. We've a hard march to Warkworth tomorrow. And leave the town lasses be!"

"Aye, my lord," said Charles grinning. He glanced into the crowded taproom, where Forster was waving a tankard and singing "Though Geordie Reigns in Jamie's Stead," and "The Wee Wee German Lairdie" at the top of his lungs. Then Charles slipped around to the inn kitchen and asked for Alec Armstrong, his valet.

Alec, with his mouth full of oatcake, ran to his master. "Are ye ready for bed, sir?"

"No. Saddle a horse and fetch me a lantern."

"Shall I come?" asked Alec eagerly, and when Charles shook his head, he added, "Ye'll be prudent, sir? Might be dangerous to ride out."

"Bosh," said Charles. "This junket's like no war I ever heard of. Tame as milk. Don't wait up for me."

Charles rode unnoticed out of Rothbury, where the two inns and many houses were crammed with noisy celebrating Jacobites. He crossed the bridge and turned west for Tosson. The road was good so far, he had fitful moonlight and the lantern to guide him, also his excellent memory of the silent ride along this road with John Snowdon on the way back to Dilston. When he came to a farmhouse at Ryehill, the farmer's wife, though obviously startled, acceded to his courteous insistence and gave him further directions.

In a while he turned south up a cart track and followed a burn until it reached the moors, and he saw ahead the dark boxy shape of the Snowdon peel. Intermingled with the gurgle of a little cascade he heard the droning of the small-pipes and the sound of a boyish voice singing. As Charles's horse clopped up, a big shockhaired lad ran out from the cow-byre in the peel, crying, "Wot the de'il do ye want here, stranger?"

Charles raised his lantern and with some surprise recognized Rob Wilson, but before he could speak, the door above the stone steps opened and Meg called down sharply, "What i'st, Rob? Who's belaw?"

"It's Charles Radcliffe, Meg," said Charles guiding his horse to the foot of the steps. "I've come to see you and the child."

He saw her stiffen, and put her hand to the doorpost. She flung a quick look over her shoulder into the room behind. Then she shut the door behind her and came down the steps. Charles dismounted and waited for her. She seemed much older, almost gaunt. Her brown hair hung in wisps on her shoulders. Her feet were bare, and filthy.

"Gan awa'," she said in a tense breathless voice. "Ye mustna come here. Ye're one o' the Jack rebels, one o' the foul traitors who're o'errunning Coquetdale."

Charles controlled a spurt of anger. "And if I *am* one of those who ride for King James, yet I have a right to see my wife and my child."

She shook her head and interlaced her fingers tight in the way he remembered. "Faither'd kill ye gin he found ye here! He'd kill ye. M'brothers would too. Kill any rebel like a dog."

"Where *are* your menfolk?" asked Charles dryly.

"Up i' the hills bringing down the sheep. Oh gan awa'— and leave us be. We've all forgot ye lang syne."

"I'll leave when I've seen Jenny," said Charles. "Meg, I used to think you gentle and just. You have altered indeed. You've grown harsh like your father."

"That's naught to you." She lifted her chin, and her face was somber in the flickering light.

"Let him see his bairn, Meg," said Rob Wilson suddenly,

147

from the shadows by the byre. "I'll keep watch belaw here, an' warn ye gin I hear the men."

Meg turned on Rob furiously. "Oh, ye're besotted over the bairn! Ye think our life here's not good enow fur her! No doubt ye'd like Jenny to mince around in silks an' satins!"

Charles was startled and glanced at the boy, but this was no time for wonderings. And he spoke in cold determination. "I insist upon my right to see my daughter, and will do so, Meg—whether you wish it or no." He started to push her aside and mount the stairs, but she made a rough sound in her throat, let her hands fall open and led the way silently. They entered the square dark room, which smelled stronger than ever of peat smoke and dung and mutton fat. A tallow dip flickered on the clumsy table. In the corner cubicle boarded off from the room, the five-year-old child slept on a straw-stuffed pallet. Charles held his lantern high and walked into the tiny room. Meg made a quick restraining gesture, then checked it.

Charles knelt down on the stone floor by his child. He saw the fair curly hair clinging in tendrils around a rosy face which was squared at the jaws, a little like Meg's. Nothing else resembled Meg. The dimple in the baby chin would someday be a cleft like his own. And the outspread fingers as they lay on the ragged quilt were long, delicately modeled. Charles gazed at her, feeling all the instinctive poignancy, the yearning love he had felt on the morning of her birth. Jenny stirred and, opening her dark gray eyes, looked up, and smiled. "Gentle-man," she announced contentedly in a clear little voice. "Bonny gentle-man."

"I'm your father, Jenny," said Charles, his voice quivering.

The child smiled again, misted with sleep, then the round eyes grew puzzled. "Faither?" she said tentatively. "I ha' no faither. Less ye mean gran'faither?"

"'Tis what he means," said Meg sharply. "Shut your een, bairnie, an' back to sleep wi' ye! Ye're dreaming! For God's love," added Meg in a whisper to Charles, "come awa' now, she mustna tell she saw ye here, or I darena think—"

The child shut her eyes obediently. Charles leaned over and gave her a kiss on the forehead. Then he got up. "Meg, I've got to talk with you." They walked to the fire in the big room.

"What about?" snapped Meg, her face hardening. "We've naught to say to each other. Ye've seen the bairn. Gan back to your ranting Papist rebels!"

"Damn it, Meg!" cried Charles furiously. He paused to

master himself, and marshal his arguments. "Listen," he said on a softer tone. "You love the child, I know that. Will you not believe I love her too?"

"I see no reason fur it." The brown eyes stared at him like a wary animal's, watchful, uncertain.

"Do you think it right to keep her here for ever, buried like—like a pearl in a raven's nest! Do you think it right for a Radcliffe to go barefoot, sleep on straw, and be reared with rough men who think of nothing but their cattle and sheep and their fanatical creed?"

Meg stared at him, her lips grew thin. "Jenny's a Snawdon. She's mine. Ye'll niver-r get her awa' fra me!"

"Not now," said Charles. "I can't do anything for her, right now, and she's over young. But when King James is on the throne, and the country's settled down, then, Meg, don't you see what I can do for Jenny? She must go to London, be educated, learn her true place as a gentlewoman and a Radcliffe. You *couldn't* be so selfish as to keep her mewed up forever in this crumbling hovel in the wilderness!"

"Ha!" cried Meg. "So ye'd turn her into a Papist, as Faither iver said!"

"No," said Charles, after a moment. "I'd not force her. When she is grown she may decide these matters for herself. I'd place her in a Protestant home, if you like. There are many ladies who'd take her, and rear her gently." Betty, he thought to his own amazement. Would Betty Lee take her?

"Aye," Meg said with a harsh laugh, watching him. "For love o' you, na doubt, many ladies might do much." Charles stared at her. He had by now had many experiences with jealous women, but so different was Meg from any of them, and so long ago were both his brief infatuation for her and then his pity on the night of their marriage that he could not think of her in this light.

"Is it that you might want to go with Jenny to London?" he said slowly, thinking of all the complications and embarrassments this could mean.

"Nay," she cried. "Ye'll niver make a lady o' me. I tould ye that afore. And the Faws said—that night at Newcastle—" For the first time she faltered. The hard look left her eyes and she turned away. She had been about to throw in his face what the Faw woman had said to him. "The royal blood in thy veins is accursed, true love can not flow in it, no sweetheart need hope for true love from thee." But now came memory of the other things the Faw woman had said. That the white rose would wither and turn black, that there was

149

a bloody axe in Charles's fate. She had forgotten this part during the long years of willful bitterness. Was it possible that those dire words could still move her heart to fear for him whose handsome face was turned towards her with coldness and yet a pleading which had nothing to do with her—only with Jenny?

Charles did not remember what the Faws had said in Newcastle, and had no curiosity as to why Meg had stopped speaking, but he saw the change in her expression, and he hastened to press his advantage. "Even Rob Wilson, Meg, seems to think as I do about the child, that she should have the life I can give her—"

"Oh, Robbie's a restless young fule," she said. "Ambitious. He wants to rise i' the world, be a great man, but doesna knaw how." She dismissed Rob and, suddenly turning, cried, "Why've ye not had our marriage cut off? There mun be ways, when for ye 'tis *no* marriage."

Charles was silent. He and James had discussed annulment, but it was a difficult process, there had been nobody Charles wanted to marry, and moreover it might make Jenny's status equivocal.

"It seems that you want the child all to yourself!" he said, scowling. "But you'll not have her, Meg. When the Rising is finished, I'll claim my legal rights by force, since you won't give them."

"So 'tis threats now!" she cried. Then she heard a sound and started. "Hark!"

They both listened to Rob's muffled voice from below. "'Ware! Snawdons!" And they heard the distant bleating of sheep. "They're coming back," Meg gasped. "Run or they'll shoot ye."

"I wonder that you mind!" said Charles with a curt laugh. He snatched the lantern from the table. "Farewell, my good wife!" He saw her face crumple and become more as it had once been. He leaned over and gave her a violent, angry kiss on the mouth. "That's for my Jenny," he said. "Take care of her or you'll rue it."

He sprang through the door and down the stone steps. Rob held the horse in readiness. Charles leapt into the saddle and was galloping along the cart track as the figures of the three Snowdons loomed against the hillside far up the burn.

Charles returned safely to Rothbury. Nobody had noticed his absence. He climbed into bed with the Swinburne youths, but it was a time before he slept. He did not think of Meg, except to curse her unreasoning stubbornness. He thought of the little face on the straw pallet, of the trustful look in the gray eyes which had gazed for a moment into his. His arms hungered to cradle the child, to hold her close with a tenderness and sweetness he had felt for no woman.

Two weeks later Charles and the Northumbrian Jacobite army returned to Rothbury, having marched over most of Northumberland, and proclaimed their King in various towns. They had seen no fighting at all, barring a skirmish or two with some frightened farmers who soon took to their heels. But there should have been fighting at Newcastle. Charles was disgusted, though he did not dare say so even to James. Tom Forster had been so confident of taking Newcastle that he had not bothered to plan a campaign at all. He had counted on welcome from the Tories there, he had counted on earlier word given him by Sir Walter Blackett that there would be no resistance. He had counted on most of the powerful keelmen joining the Jacobites. He had been wrong on all counts. His spies were so inefficient—or untrustworthy—that he had received no information of the real conditions in Newcastle. Johnson, the Whig mayor, and the formidable William Cotesworth had vastly outmaneuvered the Jacobites. The Whigs had had time—while Forster marched from place to place waving banners—to organize the militia, and to muster trainbands and summon help from Yorkshire.

When the Jacobites' vanguard finally reached Newcastle, they found the great gates closed, barricaded, cemented with limestone. And the ancient city walls were themselves impregnable except to cannon, which the rebels did not then have. Worse than that, while Forster's troops milled helplessly on the road, he received word from a secret sympathizer that His Majesty, King George, had already dispatched General Carpenter from London with a large force for the reduction of the Jacobites. To Charles's fury, Forster immediately retreated twenty miles to Hexham, without a blow being struck against Newcastle.

Colonel Oxburgh had also advised caution. He thought it best to get more news from Scotland, to send messages safely to Lancashire. Oxburgh was a cautious man. As for James, he had been able to profit from the three days spent so near Dilston. He had seen Ann again, and his son, though their reunion lasted only an hour. The Government at Newcastle, suspecting that he would return to Dilston, had sent more bailiffs and messengers to catch him, and James had been obliged to escape through the tunnel as he had before. Then Forster received an express summoning them all back to Rothbury to meet the Scottish lowland lords.

And here they were in Rothbury again, Charles thought, and nothing much gained but saddle galls, and the proclaiming of their King in a few market towns—where the Jacobite standard was hastily pulled down as soon as the troops marched on.

Charles had thought longingly of Jenny when he found himself back in Rothbury, but there was no opportunity for stealing across the Coquet this time, even had such an endeavor not been obviously rash and useless. Charles, as co-officer of his brother's troop, was required at the war council in the Three Half Moons.

The little inn was so jammed with lords and officers that most of them would have to sleep on the floor that night. And the modest assembly room in which they were holding their conference was so crowded that Charles, the young Wogan brothers, and Thomas Errington stood along the wall. Charles, indeed, as the tallest, was particularly cramped and kept his head bowed to avoid the blackened ceiling beams. He surveyed his seniors with an eager though somewhat disillusioned interest, especially the newly arrived Scottish lords, two of whom he had already met years ago at Widdrington. George Seton, the Earl of Winton, and William Gordon, Viscount Kenmure. The latter was a plump elderly man with a pleasant, rosy face under his white cockaded bonnet. He had the dignity Tom Forster lacked, but there was no sign here, either, of the fierce determination and leadership Charles had hoped to see in the Scottish general of their forces. Yet Kenmure had been commissioned by the Earl of Mar, who was currently engaged in Scotland's far north, and—one hoped—successfully routing the Duke of Argyle's Whig army.

The two generals, Kenmure and Forster, sat side by side at the head of an ale-stained table. James sat on Forster's right; Lord Widdrington scowling beside him. Lord Widdrington and his brothers had joined the Rising at Warkworth, and since that day Widdrington had not ceased complaining of his gout or his stomach, for which he was at the moment gloomily drinking mutton broth. Ranged on the other side by Kenmure sat the Scots: the Earls of Winton, of Nithsdale, and of Carnwath. Nithsdale was a skinny dark man of forty, a hairy man with stubbly chin and bushy black eyebrows. A humorless man, yet perhaps more passionately dedicated to the Cause than any of the Scots, for he was a Roman Catholic, and had known King James at St. Germain. He did not look like an earl to Charles, who was used to his brother's fastidious and polished dignity. In fact none of the Scottish lords looked like aristocrats. They wore no wigs, their plaids and bonnets were dirty, their hair was unkempt and doubtless lousy; with uncouth slobbering noises they drank the raw whisky, which was all the inn could provide.

Carnwath was small, as small as James, but clumsily made; he had carroty hair and freckles, and a high voice which belied the virility that had made him marry four wives. He was Kenmure's brother-in-law, and agreed to everything the older man said with a rather facile alacrity. "Aye, m'lord, as ye say, m'lord, verra true."

Kenmure was not saying much, Charles soon discovered. Nobody knew whether the King was ready to sail from France yet; nor had they recent news from Mar's army at Perth, but it was assumed that he was preparing to do battle with the Duke of Argyle. In the meantime, it would be wise to march across the border to Kelso. There they would join the Highlanders whom Brigadier General Mackintosh had been able to round up.

"I've no use for Highlanders," said Forster, suddenly coming out of an abstraction. "Cannibals, I hear they are. Bloodthirsty cannibals. And what d'ye want to go to Scotland for, Kenmure? 'Tis in England we belong—marching south to victory. Marching to London."

Lord Kenmure, who was beginning to be dismayed by this co-general of his, started to explain courteously that they would gather many more recruits in Scotland, that Mackintosh's battalion was to meet them there, that the Earl of Mar, who was their commander-in-chief, had advised this course, when Lord Winton cut in with his peculiarly ironic voice, addressing Forster, "If ye don't like Scotland, sir—what about capturing Newcastle *this* time? It does seem a pity to've left it unscathed."

Tom flushed, staring at Winton's alert, otterlike face. "I have *told* ye all," he said resentfully, "why we were disappointed at Newcastle. 'Tis a small matter. In Lancashire there's twenty thousand who'll rise to join us."

"Indeed," said Winton. "Brave news. But I agree wi' Kenmure, 'tis better to be sure o' Scotland before we head south. I've noticed," he cocked his head and grinned impishly, "in my *blacksmithing* days abroad, that not only 'tis better to strike while the iron's hot, which it is in Scotland,

153

but that 'tis better to finish shoeing one nag afore ye start on the next one!"

"Pish!" said Tom, burying his head in his mug. He didn't like the Scots, no true Northumbrians did, and he didn't wish to go to Scotland. He shook his head stubbornly, and said "Pish" again.

James, next to him, felt the sinking of the heart which had often bedeviled him during these weeks of marching. He resolutely ignored the feeling. "We can hardly divide our scanty force, Tom," he whispered in Forster's ear, "and Kenmure has instructions from Mar."

As Forster did not answer, James smiled at the company, and said, "I take it we're agreed? We start for Kelso to-morrow?"

"Aye," cried all the Scots firmly. Lord Widdrington said nothing. His belly rumbled and he belched feebly.

"I propose an English toast," said James, trying to lighten the atmosphere at the council table. "One you Scottish gentlemen may not have heard, though we've used it much and publicly this last year." He raised his mug of small beer—he hated whisky—arose, and said,

> *"God bless the king, I mean the faith's defender*
> *God bless—no harm in blessing—the Pretender*
> *But who Pretender is, or who is king—*
> *God bless us all—that's quite another thing."*

"Very neat," observed the Earl of Winton as they clinked mugs and drank.

"Soon by God's mercy," said Nithsdale earnestly, "there'll be no need for double meanings. When the Stuart's back again. A day sae joyful for us, I tremble to think of it!"

"Aye," said Tom Forster rousing himself and brightening. A peerage for me, he thought. "Lord Bamburgh" would sound well. It was humiliating to sit at a conference like this and be the only commoner. A peerage and a place at Court presented by his grateful king.

"Shing!" He thumped his fist on the table. "Everybody shing!"

> *"When October ale's a-pouring*
> *And lashes—lasses—go a-whoring*
> *Then each man s'all merry merry be*
> *Then we'll all so merry merry be . . ."*

The lords were used to drunkenness and bawdy songs, but nobody was in the mood for joining in except Carnwath. James and Lord Kenmure exchanged a look of worried perplexity. The older man rose and, murmuring something about wanting his bed, walked heavily out of the room. The others got up too. Lord Winton shrugged his narrow shoulders and remarked affably, "I take it this exhilarating conference is over? I'm going to see what my men're doing. Never trust a Scot in England, or a Sassanach in Scotland is another bit o' advice I picked up on m'lowly travels."

Charles followed the Earl downstairs and paused at the taproom door, wondering if it would be possible after all to get a glimpse of Jenny. But there was a freezing drizzle outside, the Snowdon men would certainly be home, and it would hardly be to Jenny's advantage if they shot her father. Damn the Snowdons, he thought, and slumping dejectedly on a stool decided to have a drink. Charles watched the barmaid idly for a while, a stout red-cheeked lass with big round breasts straining at her laced bodice. She might make good bed-sport, he thought, with the first flickering of desire he had felt since they were in Morpeth, where he had found an accommodating Jacobite lady to pass the night with. But his taste had never really run to barmaids, and he decided to leave this one alone. Let Peregrine Widdrington have her, Charles thought, eying that young man's amorous overtures indulgently.

Suddenly Charles's absent glance was caught by a new figure standing uncertainly near the door of the murky, swarming taproom. A lad it was, with a mass of rain-soaked black hair and a leather jacket. He peered this way and that into the careless faces of the carousing officers. Charles got up and pushed his way through to the door. "Rob Wilson!" he said. "What're you doing here? There's naught wrong with Jenny?" he added, a sudden tightness in his throat.

Rob shook his head. "The bairn's weel. 'Twas Meg sent me."

"*Meg!*" repeated Charles astounded. "Sent you to *me?*"

"Aye, wi' a message."

Charles frowned at the noisy taproom. He saw Ned Swinburne weaving towards him obviously wishful to join him. "Come upstairs," he said to Rob. "I can't hear in this din."

They went up to the Assembly Room. The lords had disappeared, but several men lay wrapped in cloaks snoring on the floor. Charles and Rob picked their way over the men and stood by the dying fire. "Now what is it?" said Charles fingering his pistol and wondering if this might be some scurvy Snowdon trick. Had they sent Rob as a spy? Yet what was there to spy on! The whole of Coquetdale knew that six hundred Jacobites were camped at Rothbury tonight.

"Meg, she said to tell ye, that wen ye get to Lunnon, an' send fur Jenny, she'll gi'e the bairn to ye."

"What!" Charles cried so loud that one of the sleepers stirred. "By God, I can't believe it. You're diddling me, as you did once before."

"Naw," said Rob looking steadily into Charles's face. "I can't blame ye fur thinkin' so, I was but a bairn then m'self an' hot wi' anger at me brother's drownding. 'Tis different terday."

"Then what's come over Meg?" said Charles. "She swore I'd never get the child."

Rob was silent, unable to express at once all the things which had altered Meg's mind. The boy knew that in her own bitter defensive way she still loved Mr. Radcliffe. That was one thing. She'd wandered about like a spook, white and wambly for days after he'd been there. And then she must have seen the justice of rearing Jenny like a lady, for she had asked Rob if he thought Jenny was too fine to live with the cattle in a crumbling peel in the moors. He had answered, aye, because he did. Meg had not been angry as before; she had turned away with a dumb stricken look. Then something else had happened, and it was this Rob tried to tell.

"Ould Snawdon," he said, "he's took very queer at times. He rants off stuff from Scriptures'd make a tinkler blush. Dirty talk. Last Sabbath he was yammering an' shoutin' blasphemies. Running about the yard wi' his breeks off, naked as an egg."

"My God," whispered Charles. "I must get Jenny away now!"

Rob shook his head. "Ye cannot, sir. Jenny canna gan to war wi' ye. An' she'll tak' no harm. Meg an' her brothers'll guard her, an' I'll guard her, sir, ye may trust me.'

Charles stared at the boy with sudden attention. Under the mat of hair, the hazel eyes met his steadily; there was something attractive in the rough, square, North Country face.

"How old are you?' said Charles.

"Fifteen, or thereabouts."

"You're an odd lad. Why didn't you go back to Tyneside and your kin there?"

"Because I had me bellyful o' the pits, an' the Snawdons let me bide here as cow-man."

"Is the care of cattle better than the pits?" asked Charles with a half smile.

"Aye, fur a while. Ould Snawdon an' Meg've taught me m'letters. The Faws they taught me to play the pipes. I've made siller wi' m'pipes of late at weddings an' harvest time. But I'll not bide here when Jenny goes to Lunnon. I aim to rise i' the world, same as she will."

Charles frowned, aware of annoyance which it was silly to identify as jealousy. "You will have nothing to do with Jenny, once she's in London! You understand that, of course, though I'm grateful enough for your care of her now, and will reward you properly, when I can."

Rob also frowned. "I'm no fule," he said sharply. "I'll niver pester the bairn once she's being made a lady of. Ye may count on that. An' I'll earn me *own* way up."

Charles shrugged, not entirely satisfied. There was a great deal about this dark, stubborn boy he did not understand. For that matter, he did not understand the Snowdons—or Meg—and it had ben a rueful day when, scarcely older than Rob, he had wandered along Tyneside and forced himself into the lives of people so alien. And yet, from this mismating there was Jenny.

"I'll gan back now," said Rob. "An' ye'll send fur the bairn when ye get to Lunnon an' have a place fur her?"

"Yes," said Charles. "And it can't be long. The whole country's ripe as a plum to fall in our hands. Why, we've not even had a battle yet, for all that fat German Geordie has sent some dragoons after us. I hear they've not the pluck to fight."

Rob did not question this optimism. In Coquetdale with its swarming Jacobites there was no reason to suspect that other parts of England might prefer the Hanoverians, and to Rob the matter was of scanty interest except as it affected his own future, and that of Jenny, for whom he felt a protective fondness.

"Good luck, sir," said Rob, moving towards the door. Charles, on impulse, put out his hand, and the boy after a startled moment shook it.

"I'll see you in London by Christmas!" said Charles, smiling. "You can pipe for our King when he's crowned at the Abbey!"

Rob's face flushed with pleasure, his mouth widened in a startled grin. "Thank ye, sir!"

But Rob Wilson and Charles did not see each other again for many years.

On Wednesday, November 9, the Jacobite army was in Lancashire, and its cavalry rode into the predominantly Jacobite town of Preston. It had been drizzling for days. James and Charles at the head of their mounted troops were sodden, mud-bespattered; water dripped from the angles of their cocked hats, over the lank tie-wigs. Yet their prospects seemed bright, James thought. Brighter than they had appeared to him at any time during these weeks of constant marches—and constant dissension among the leaders.

Just now, north of Preston, they had been acclaimed by a number of Lancashire Catholics, who welcomed them with huzzahs and the assurance that they had nothing to fear from the enemy. That King George's regiments, commanded by General Wills, were forty miles away and on the run, while the main Government army under General Carpenter were milling helplessly in Scotland, being trounced by the Earl of Mar. Great news!

"And so," said Charles, who had been pursuing the same thoughts, "is it *possible* that we'll march all the way to London without ever coming to grips with the enemy at all?"

"Possible, I suppose," answered James yanking his gray stallion out of a mudhole and wondering if it were weather or fatigue which prevented him from joining in the general elation.

They had been on the move for three weeks since quitting Rothbury the second time. They had entered Scotland to join Brigadier Mackintosh and his Highlanders at Kelso. They had proclaimed King James there and in other towns. Yet in Scotland the Jacobites had suffered serious quarrels among themselves. The Earl of Winton had for a time refused point-blank to re-enter England with his men until all Scotland should first be secured to the Jacobites. Lord Kenmure in his gentle way agreed. As did James. And their counsels were given added weight when it developed that half the Highlanders would not cross the Border. They deserted instead.

Yet Tom Forster's arrogant obstinacy had prevailed. Better call it "obstinacy," James thought, not something else surely. There had been an exceedingly uncomfortable moment in Kelso when a breathless Jacobite spy had reported that General Carpenter with regiments of foot and dragoons was in hot pursuit, and nearing Kelso. Forster had paled when he heard the news, his thick lips had quivered, and he had immediately ordered what amounted to a panicky flight to Jedburgh. Charles and the Earl of Winton had protested violently, Charles was all for leading his Northumbrian troops off to fight Carpenter then and there. James, though sympathizing, had been firm in stopping so rash an unauthorized move, which would have split their forces. And no arguments could sway Forster. He did not listen to them. He had made up his mind to lead the army to Lancashire, where he was certain that the entire county would rush to join them. And he carried the day. Lord Winton glumly gave in at last and summoned his men, saying, "It shall ne'er be told in history that a Seton could break off from or desairt the Stuart's interest, yet—" here he had seized his two ears in his hands, "cut these lugs from my head here and now, if we don't all sore repent this!"

And here they were. Though the whole of Lancashire had not swarmed to their standard—and the High Church Tories semed disturbingly limp—still there had been some gratifying demonstrations, and no opposition at all. Incredibly easy, James thought. It must be that the Stuart doom was lifted at last, and God wrought for them a miracle. Why then continue to feel despondent?

They sloshed on through Preston's narrow streets and drew up at the Mitre, where most of the chief officers were quartered.

Tom Forster was already lolling in the best seat by the parlor fire, a steaming mug in his hand. His scarlet and gold coat was unbuttoned, his boots were off, his fat stockinged feet propped on the fender. Colonel Oxburgh and Robert Patten—the Anglican curate from Allendale—both hovered near him.

"Ho there, my lord!" Forster called jovially to James, while he nodded to Charles. "*Now* will ye own what a fine general ye've got! Hey? Lancaster an' Preston in our pockets already. Next we'll have Manchester an' Liverpool. An' never a soul to stop us. Geordie's lads're scuttling away wi' their tails betwen their legs. Like the bloody Scots!" he added loudly with a glance towards the far end of the room.

Charles followed the glance and saw the Lords Winton and Kenmure and young Murray seated at a table near Brigadier Mackintosh of the Highlanders; all eating from a dish of Lancashire hot pot.

The Scots looked up at Forster's remark. Murray flushed and put his hand to his sword hilt. The Earl of Winton tilted his head and raised one sardonic eyebrow. "You deign to compliment us, General?" he called in a thin voice. "Or do ye suggest that we scuttle back to Scotland, leaving the full glory of these many victories to you alone?" There was a dangerous glint in Winton's small eyes, and Oxburgh hastily leaned over Tom Forster with a nervous murmur.

Tom shrugged but heeded his adviser. "I meant only to speak o' the Highland savages who wouldna follow me down here," he said airily.

After a moment Winton bowed. Murray's hand dropped from his sword. Kenmure looked distressed, his gnarled fingers trembled as he spooned up gravy from the hot pot. Brigadier General Mackintosh shook his head sourly. He was a great lanky laird, a fierce fighter with claymore or battle-axe, but here in the hated England he was ill-at-ease, homesick, as bewildered as the sixty Highlanders who had remained loyal to him and were now quartered in Preston. They did not understand this sort of war, which consisted of nothing except long dull marches and never a battle.

"Where are the others?" asked James, relinquishing his greatcoat to his servant. He had scarcely listened to the altercation, so frequent were such bickerings.

Forster, whose mouth was stuffed with black pudding, did not bother to answer, and Patten, the obsequious little curate, stepped forward bowing. "Their lordships Nithsdale, Carnwath, and Nairn are all at the White Bull, my lord, but my lord Widdrington is here and has gone to his chamber. His gout troubles him much."

"Thank you," said James with his usual courtesy. He liked Patten no better than he ever had, but the man was useful. Protected by his cloth he managed to worm his way into many a place where the obvious Jacobites dared not go. Patten had now become their most efficient spy. "Is it true that two companies of dragoons ran from Preston yesterday when they heard we were coming?" pursued James.

"Aye, my lord," said Patten. "I was hiding in a house by the Riddle Bridge and saw them go."

"All fly before us!" said Tom with a sweeping gesture which upset his ale mug. "They all fly, fly, fly away." He gave a thick chuckle and closed his eyes.

Saint Mary, what a sot! Charles thought, staring at their commander-in-chief, while James walked to the fire and warmed his hands. Yet, in justice, one must admit Forster had been right so far.

"What would you say our strength is now, sir?" asked Charles turning to Forster's aide-de-camp, Colonel Oxburgh.

Oxburgh screwed up his long conscientious Irish face and pondered. He looked tired and had grown thin during these weeks of trying to guide Forster. "Maybe two thousand—when the foot get here tomorrow," he said at last.

"Nonsense!" cried Forster explosively, opening his eyes. "Far more'n that! Ye're a gloomy goat, Oxburgh! We'll have five thousand 'neath our standard tomorrow, they're marching in from all the west. Ain't it so—Patten?"

"Yes indeed, sir," answered the curate eagerly. " 'Tis what I hear on all sides. And I hear too that the dragoons're all deserting General Wills to join us."

"To be sure," said Forster shrugging. "Who'd fight for German Geordie when they came out for their rightful king, who is now *landed* no doubt and sweeping through Scotland to victory?"

James crouched over the fire, and hid a fresh wave of dismayed doubt.

"Amen," said Oxburgh very solemnly, and Charles thought that the man had indeed become a gloomy goat of late. Always telling his beads and going to Mass now that they were in Catholic country. And never a smile out of him. Quite unlike the other Irish officers, the Wogan lads, who were gay blades and found amusement even in these dreary provincial towns. "Where are you off to, James?" he asked the Earl, who was walking towards the stairs.

"Up to see poor Widdrington. There never was such a man for aches and pains," James added with an unusual touch of irritation. "Pity he hasn't the stamina of Kenmure." He threw that dignified and uncomplaining old laird an appreciative glance. "Charles, go see to our men. Dick Stockoe had a touch of fever this morn, see that he gets a dry bed."

"Aye, my lord," said Charles smiling. "Then pray, may I go find myself some entertainment?"

"This savors of impudence," said James also smiling. "Since you will anyway. But console yourself for probable disappointment with visions of the imminent joys of London!"

The brothers exchanged a look of affection, and Charles went whistling out into the rain-washed street.

The next morning, the sun shone on Preston when the Jacobite army gathered in the marketplace and proclaimed

James the Third as King of England. This ceremony had now become so familiar to them that no orders were needed to insure proper decorum. The different troops arranged themselves neatly, headed by their mounted officers, and radiating like spokes of a wheel from the central market cross. On the steps stood the herald with his trumpet. Beside him General Forster, in scarlet and gold on his huge black horse. Smiling citizens were jammed in every window of the neat brick mansions, the half-timbered shops. They cheered as the square filled with mounted gentlemen in laced hats all garnished with the white cockades, in full-bottomed wigs, ruffles, and flashing scabbards. They gawked at the company of Highlanders with their sporrans, their gaudy tartan breeches and plaids, their floppy bonnets, the like of which Preston had never seen.

There was a preliminary roll of drums and the skirling of bagpipes, then a hush, as the herald blew his trumpet and began to shout the proclamation. "Whereas George, Elector of Brunswick, has usurped and taken upon him the style of King of these realms . . . and whereas James the Third by reason of the right of the first-born son and the laws of this land, did immediately after his father's decease become our only and lawful liege . . ."

James listened attentively as he always did, and his heart was suddenly lightened, while the herald finished and the Stuart standard was run up on the pole prepared for it. He stared at the great green taffeta flag with its creamy silk fringe and lavishly embroidered emblem of charity—a pelican feeding her young. As James and all the hundred in the crowded square uncovered their heads, brilliant sunlight gilded the flag, which rippled proudly in a breeze from the sea. "God Save the King!" came the thunderous acclaim. It echoed down the crowded streets, and rang from the windows of the surrounding houses. James in that moment felt a vast surge of happiness. He *has* landed, he thought with joyous certainty. I feel it. A messenger will come to tell us so. Today, tomorrow. We have won! Jemmie, we're ready for you, Cousin. From now on I shall renounce all melancholies or forebodings—how dared I so doubt God's goodness.

James turned smiling, to look from Charles's intent young face back over the faces of his own Northumbrians. Tom Errington there leading Widdrington's troops, since that nobleman had stayed in bed. The Widdrington brothers, the Claverings, the Shaftoes, the Swinburne boys, Jack

Thornton of Netherwitton, and George Collingwood, his special friends. But they were all his friends, down to the servants, to the little drummer boy, and how could he have been so laggard once in summoning them to the rightful, the glorious cause!

"You look very merry, James," said Charles astonished, as he waved his sword in signal that their troops might disperse.

"Aye. I feel sure our King has landed, and was thinking how soon I would be seeing Ann. And you, Charlie—ah I see—" said James laughing ruefully. "Yes, that's a handsome wench yonder in the doorway!"

"I was not looking at her," said Charles. "But at the child beside her. It resembles my Jenny."

James was startled. The brothers had never mentioned the Snowdons since the moment weeks ago when Charles confessed to having seen his child while at Rothbury, and his intention of educating her in London. A course which James approved of as a gentlemanly obligation. That Charles might have love for the child never occurred to him; it was plain that he had no love for the mother. "Well," he said, still puzzled by Charles's unwonted gravity, and the almost yearning note in his voice, "you'll soon be in London to find a place for her, and in the meantime I expect we're off to Manchester!"

But it seemed that they were not yet off to Manchester. Forster found Preston much to his liking. The inn was comfortable, the ale and brandy excellent. And the ladies were charming. Lady Anderton and Mrs. Chorley, whose husbands had just presented their services to the cause, wished to give a ball that night. Besides, said Tom, it was wiser to stay here a day or so to await further recruits, especially turncoats from the Government troops. "For they'll all be coming to us," said Tom comfortably. "Patten says so."

James, true to his recent optimistic resolutions, was convinced. The Scottish lords were not consulted and Mackintosh grumbled mightily. He had trouble enough controlling his Highlanders as it was. Still there was nothing he could do. The Jacobite army settled down for two days of carousing, love-making, and general festivity.

James neither caroused nor made love, yet he clung to the mood of joyous certainty which had come to him in the marketplace, and refused to be daunted by several unpalatable questions which were asked by Lord Winton. If it were true that King James had landed in Scotland, why did no messenger come from there? And where were the hundreds of High Church Tories they had been told would flock to the standard in Lancashire? The new recruits were all Papists.

And why, if the Government forces were so anxious to change sides, did no message come from *them*, nor any inkling of their precise whereabouts?

James was inclined to share Forster's annoyance at these questions, and therefore avoided the Scottish earl.

On Saturday morning, November 12, the weather still being fine, James and Charles decided to exercise their troop in a meadow on the far side of the river Ribble. They extricated their men from the various lodgings, bawdy-houses, and taverns with some difficulty, and here Alec Armstrong, Charles's knowing valet, was useful. By ten o'clock Alec had rounded up the last straggler and Charles, galloping back and forth, had got the foot into line and ready to drill when James called, "Hark!"

Charles rode up to him and listened. Faint on the south wind they heard in the distance toward Wigan the tramp of marching feet, and a drum beating. " 'Tis the Government army come to join us!" James cried happily. "We'll go meet them!"

Charles frowned, uncertain, and felt a tug at his boot. He looked down to see Alec standing there. "Don't go, sir," cried the valet vehemently. "Don't let his lordship go!"

"Why not?" asked James sternly, wheeling his horse to face the valet. "What's wrong?"

"I believe they're coming to *attack* us, my lord. There's a whore in the White Bull was boasting this morn that she'd been in Wigan the night before, and General Wills was planning to surprise us. I didn't believe her, but—"

James swallowed. Before he could speak, Charles cried "Wait here!" and was off in a flash, galloping across the meadow and into a sheltering copse. He came back in twenty minutes. "They're *against* us, James!" he cried, his eyes aglow. "I got near enough to see them—the vanguard of the Royal Dragoons near Walton-le-Dale—marching slow but sure, and they saw my white cockade and shot at me."

James swallowed again, then his small erect body stiffened. "Hurry! Flee back to town!" he shouted to their men. "You, Collingwood and Thornton, come here, ride with me to protect the foot. Charles, go on ahead, give the alarm!"

Charles nodded and sped off, across the bridge into town,

and galloped to the Mitre, where he found that Patten had already given Forster the news. Forster was slumped in a dressing gown, his nightcap askew, for he had been dragged out of bed. As Charles ran in, Brigadier Mackintosh was standing rigid, while Patten was shaking Forster's shoulders and crying, "I tell you 'tis true, sir! Wills is marching to attack Preston—another of our messengers just slipped in!"

"Aye, 'tis true!" Charles shouted into Forster's gaping, pop-eyed face. "I've seen 'em. In the name of God send men to the bridge! Block the bridge!"

Forster swayed his head slowly like a bewildered bull. "But ye said they *wouldn't* attack!" he muttered, glaring at Patten. "Everybody said so. They'll not fight for Geordie. We was *told* that."

"They *are* attacking, you fool!" Charles shouted. "Get off your fat bum and give orders. Or I will!"

Tom transferred his bloodshot glare to Charles. "How dare ye speak—" he began, then the meaning of these warnings penetrated. He sat up, beads of sweat dotted his forehead. "Where's Oxburgh?" he cried in a high, squeaking voice. "Get me Oxburgh!"

"Nae time," said Mackintosh grimly. "I've some o' m'Scots outside. I'll to the brig wi' 'em. How fast're they coming?" he said to Charles.

"Slowly," said Charles. "I saw only the vanguard. I suppose they'll wait for Wills. We'll have an hour anyway."

Mackintosh glanced at Forster, who nodded shakily. "Do as ye like," he mumbled. The Brigadier and Charles ran out of the inn together.

In the ensuing desperate confusion, and lacking any orders from their commander-in-chief, it was each officer for himself and his troops, though Mackintosh took charge and directed the tactics as best he could. And they had time, mercifully, for their preparations. The enemy did come slowly. General Wills expected a battle at the Ribble Bridge, which was a mile from Preston, and he waited far from the riverbank until all his mounted and foot dragoons were asembled. Then he formed his troops into a wedge and prepared to assault the bridge. His dragoons fired several shots and ran up to the bridge with bayonets fixed.

The bridge was totally undefended, which greatly puzzled General Wills. Nor was there any sniping from the hedges which lined the narrow lane that led to town. Unopposed, the Government forces marched towards Preston.

Earlier Brigadier Mackintosh had changed his mind about

defending the bridge, saying that his Highlanders were no good at a mass maneuver against heavy horse, also that holding the bridge was futile, since there must be fords, downriver. So, to the anger of Charles and the tight-lipped dismay of James, he ordered the Jacobites to stay in town, where they might barricade the streets and force the Royal Dragoons to dismount for hand-to-hand fighting.

"My God!" Charles cried to James, after they had been told to withdraw into town. "This old Scotchman's as big a fool as Forster! We could've held the bridge."

"Mackintosh at least *is* a fighting man, and may know what he's doing," James answered. "Never mind that now. Here, give me a hand with this stone, and pile that table here! Faster! Faster!" he cried to his men. His Northumbrians were scurrying about in the street below the church, building a barricade of anything they could find in the neighboring houses—tables, chairs, bedsteads, sacks of grain. James had flung off his coat, waistcoat, and peruke. In his frilled white shirt, panting a little, he shoved, pushed and hauled with the rest of them. As did Charles.

While they worked Mackintosh dashed from this barricade to the three others he had ordered built across the streets at different sites. Presently he galloped back to James's barrier. "Guid!" he shouted. "That'll do! Post some o' your men i' the houses, m'lord! They'll shoot frae the windows, when I gi'e the signal. I'll see to *this* barricade m'sel'."

James nodded, and nodded again as Mackintosh told him to go the churchyard, which was on high ground, to build entrenchments there, and to maintain as replacements a force of men not already stationed elsewhere.

In the churchyard they found the Scottish lords Kenmure, Nithsdale, and Winton. "So ye've brought shovels!" cried Winton, when he saw the Northumbrians. "And can use 'em too!" His face broadened in a grin, as he noted the Earl of Derwentwater's dishevelment, his torn white shirt, his dirty sweat-streaked face, his small scratched and bleeding hands, and saw also that Charles Radcliffe—even sweatier and dirtier than his brother—was stripped to the waist.

"Aye, we're to dig fortifications here," said James.

"That *I* can do," said Winton seizing James's shovel. "Having blacksmith's hands. Ye'd do better to encourage the men!"

They were two hours in the churchyard before anything happened, though they heard distant scattered shots. By tacit consent James took command. He went from one trench to the next, praising, cajoling, exhorting the workers as they dug. Once a lad from Hexham turned hysterical and flung down his shovel and gun, blubbering that he wanted none of this, that he wished he was home with his mother.

James clapped him on the shoulder, crying, "Back to work! And when you've dug your stint, I'll give you a sovereign to soothe your mother!" The boy quieted and went to work. There was not one of them in that churchyard, noble or commoner, who did not look to, and derive strength from that small active figure in the torn white shirt. Charles did too, as the tension mounted. The scattered shots came nearer, they watched the Highlanders dragging up a cannon to Mackintosh's barricade. "And much good it'll do 'em," observed Winton grimly. "I'll warrant there's not a soul there knows how to fire it!"

"Look!" cried Charles, pointing. "Strike me dead if it's not our brave General!" They all stared at Tom's stout figure in a steel cuirass astride his huge black horse, the cock plumes waving on his laced hat. Forster had fortified himself with several brandies, dressed, and sallied from the Mitre. From the churchyard they watched as Forster, brandishing his sword, approached Mackintosh and shouted something in obvious fury.

"Go see what's ado, Charles," James said, and his brother ran to obey. He soon came back and reported. "Forster's trying to countermand all Mackintosh's orders. Wants Mackintosh to lead a charge *now*. Mackintosh refused. Says it would be mad. Cut him off from the body of his horsemen in the marketplace. Forster said he'd have him court-martialed when this was over."

Nobody said anything. Silently they watched Forster shake his fist, then gallop back towards the Mitre. James went off again to inspect the earthworks, which were nearly ready. Lord Winton went to join his fellow Scottish peers in the church porch. Old Kenmure's eyes were shut, his lips moving in prayer. Lord Nithsdale was seated with his naked sword across his knees, staring into space. There was a lull.

Charles was carefully inspecting his pistols, when Alec came up to him carrying a large bundle. "Your clothes, sir," said the valet gravely. " 'Tis not meet for a gentleman to look like a scullion."

"I expect you're right," said Charles, allowing Alec to put on his shirt, ruffled cravat, brown braided coat, tie-wig, and hat. "I've his lordship's attire too," said Alec pointing to the remaining contents of the bundle. "Since Wesby couldn't mind them." James's servant, Wesby, had been posted at the window of a house overlooking the barricade.

"You're a good man, Alec," Charles said suddenly feeling the whole worth of the loyalty he usually took for granted. "We've been through many a merry bedroom romp together, but this is different."

"I was born to serve Radcliffes in any way I can, sir," said Alec with a moving sincerity quite unlike his usual blitheness. He walked off to find Lord Derwentwater, who was relieved to be properly dressed, now that the strenuous preparations were over. And they waited.

The dragoons charged Mackintosh's barricade at two o'clock. In the churchyard they could not at first see the onrushing regiment of foot, who were screened by the barrier and the turn of the street, but they heard an outburst of wild battle cries from the Highlanders, and Mackintosh's bloodcurdling shouts in Gaelic. Then there was a volley of shots, and the red-coated dragoons began assaulting the barricade. "There they are!" said Charles under his breath. His heart pounded with a triumphant excitement. He stood up behind the earthwork, and a bullet whizzed past his head to bury itself in the church wall.

"Down, Charles! Get down!" James shouted.

Charles did not hear him, nor remember the orders that those in the churchyard were to stay under cover, until they were summoned by Mackintosh. Charles leapt from the trench, and ran down the slope to the street, his pistols cocked. As he dashed in among the Scots their cannon went off. The ball went wide, as Winton had prophesied. It knocked down a nearby chimney, yet the explosion served to check for a moment the attack. Wills's forces had no cannon. During the pause there was constant gunfire from the windows. A dozen of the dragoons fell sprawling on the cobblestones, which turned slimy red. Their brigadier, Honeywood, then called again for attack. They reformed and charged the barrier. Charles saw a pointed hat and scarlet coat clambering to the top between the sheltering angles of furniture. He aimed his pistol and pulled the trigger. The dragoon gave a high thin scream, and falling forward, crumbled near Charles's feet. The limbs jerked in convulsions, then were still. I killed him! Charles thought in amazement. He's dead. He was aiming the other pistol when Mackintosh saw him.

"Get ye *gone* frae here, Radcliffe!" the Brigadier shouted furiously. "Gang back where I told ye to!"

Charles heard this but he did not heed. A Highlander beside him was engaged with a dragoon who had pushed through the now crumbling barricade. The Scot, grunting and drenched with blood from a chest wound, was weakly flailing his opponent with the claymore, while the dragoon, having spent his gunshot, was waiting for a chance to sink home the bayonet. The Scot gasped and fell to his knees. Charles took aim and killed the dragoon. Then there was a skirmish behind him. Charles, whirling, spitted another dragoon on his sword. At last he heeded the Brigadier's command, since he could not reload here.

As he scrambled up the bank to the churchyard he barely noted a sharp sting in the flesh of his right arm. He jumped down in the trench beside James. "I got three of 'em!" he cried exultantly. "Where's the powder? I'll load again and get more of 'em!" His eyes were wild with battle lust.

"*No*, Charles," said James trying by a voice of angry command to hide the fear he had felt for his brother. "You'll stay *here*, until we're needed—look, you're wounded! You damned reckless young idiot!"

Charles looked down at his arm in surprise. His coatsleeve was shredded, blood was spreading over the dark cloth and dripping on the ground. "Just a nick," said Charles, tossing his head.

"Alec, come here!" called James. The valet was stationed nearby. He came fast, stooping low inside the trench. "Get your master's coat off, stanch the blood, take him inside the church, and keep him there!" said James.

Charles felt a stab of rage. He wanted to defy James, even to knock him down. Then suddenly came weakness, giddiness, and a wave of nausea. He let Alec shove him into the church.

The bullet had gone clean through the muscles of the upper arm, and just grazed the bone, Alec thought. He applied his own kerchief as tourniquet, and the bleeding presently stopped. Alec gave Charles some brandy from a cask they had hidden earlier, and the giddiness passed. But even Charles was forced to admit that his prowess with pistols or sword was seriously lessened. "I can fight with my left arm," he said glumly. "I know I can."

"You'll not fight again, unless his lordship permits it, sir," said Alec. "Nor is it needful. We was watching how it went at the barricade. And the enemy're giving up that spot."

Charles brightened. They listened a moment to the shots outside, which were fewer and growing more distant. At that moment Patten came running down into the nave from the bell tower, where James had sent him to reconnoiter. The curate's bumpy, long-nosed face was beaming above the round collar. He gave a shocked exclamation when he saw Charles's wound, then said, "Take heart, sir. I could see up there that the enemy's retreating from *all* the barricades. Wills has ordered them out of town. He's not got many men, either. Not near as many as we have!" He rushed from the church to report to Lord Derwentwater.

There was little more fighting that day. The wounded were gathered up and conveyed to the White Bull, where there was a surgeon of sorts. The dead were piled behind the churchyard for burial later. The Jacobites were triumphant. They found only fifteen of their men lying dead in the streets, and they found 130 dragoons.

At dusk, having as a last resort set fire to some houses in a spot which would prevent the Jacobites from attacking, Wills encamped his much weakened forces near the Ribble Bridge outside Preston.

In the Mitre taproom there was qualified rejoicing. Mackintosh received warm congratulations from his fellow Scots, and from James; while Forster, at the moment half sober, did nothing but berate him shrilly for not defending the bridge, for not leading a charge against the enemy. "And I'm still your general, I'll have ye know," Tom shouted, banging a rolled parchment on the table. "D'ye need to see again me commission from King James himself?"

"I dinna need to," said the Brigadier sullenly, "but this verra morn ye had nae plans yoursel', ye told me to tak' charge. I've done as I thought fit, an' canna see aught to regret." He stalked out of the room to write a letter to Lord Mar in Scotland reporting the day's victory. The other Scots followed him.

"Insolent knave," remarked Lord Widdrington languidly of Mackintosh. Widdrington had been carried down from his chamber and sat drinking soup, with his gouty foot on a stool. He knew nothing of the day's event, except what Forster had told him. And he had been much annoyed by the noise in the streets; it had made his head ache.

Forster's purple flush faded. His mood suddenly rocketed to elation. "Tomorrow," he said, laughing, his piggy eyes roving happily from Widdrington to Patten and Colonel Oxburgh, "ye'll see *real* generalship! Charge the enemy! Wipe 'em out. That's what we'll do—eh, Oxburgh?"

"No doubt, sir," said the Colonel in a flat muted voice,

which satisfied Forster but clearly conveyed to James the Colonel's hopeless view of their general. Oxburgh had been fighting that afternoon at the windmill barricade, after finding Forster snoring drunkenly in the Mitre at noon.

Still, James thought, they could do without Forster. See, how well the day had gone! Tomorrow, please God, would see their troubles over. "Get some rest, Charles," he said to his brother, who looked a bit feverish. "I'm sure your wound troubles you, though you won't admit it."

"It's nothing," said Charles. Then he gave a deep contented sigh. "D'you think I mind a little thing like this, when we have at last done battle and won? You were right, James, to think the Stuart doom has lifted."

SEVEN

The long black November night gave way to a cold dark morning. Charles and James had dozed fitfully, alert against any untoward move by the enemy, but there was no sound near the Mitre, nothing to be seen except a distant red glow from the burning houses.

The town was still hushed when the brothers went downstairs and found Patten munching on a lump of bacon. The curate looked up as they entered. For a second James fancied he saw a sly look in the near-set eyes, yet as the man jumped to his feet, bowing, his knobbly face showed nothing but welcome. "More good news, my lord!" he said. "I've been out to reconnoiter, got right into the enemy camp on pretense of needing their chaplain. They've lost heart, and are fleeing from us. Must be across the Ribble by now."

"What excellent news indeed," said James, while Charles broke in with heat, "But, Holy Mary—aren't we going *after* 'em?"

The curate gave him an indulgent smile. "Later, perhaps, when we've all breakfasted and aligned our forces—so the General says. Plenty of time."

Charles scowled, then shrugged. His arm throbbed, and though he had been ready for the expected charge he knew he could not have acquitted himself well. He reached for a sausage from the platter the serving maid had banged on the table. James stopped him. "Wait," he said. " 'Tis Sunday, Charlie. And we must go to Mass, take the sacrament. A Mass of thanksgiving it shall be."

"Yes, to be sure, my lord. There's a priest called Little-ton at the White Bull," the curate said helpfully, "has been tending to the wounded Catholics."

"Thank you," said James, chiding himself for his un-reasonable distrust of this man, who had done nothing to warrant it. Charles sighed and relinquished thoughts of breakfast as yet. They went out and down the street to the White Bull. At the inn they found the priest in a small room with two wounded Lancashire men. One had a bayonet gash through his bowels, and the other's leg had been amputated by the surgeon. Both were dying, and Father Littleton was preparing to administer the last rites.

James and Charles withdrew to wait. "Thank God," said the Earl, "that we've lost none of *our* men. I think I couldn't bear to bring mourning to any of my people at Dilston."

"Aye—Lady Luck is with us!" said Charles, who had recovered his usual spirits and amused himself, while they waited, by waving through the window at a girl who scuttled by.

At last the priest was ready, and said that he would like to celebrate Mass in his own chapel, though it was situated on the Ribble side of town, rather near the enemy camp, and to go there would be dangerous. James asured him it wasn't. That there was nothing more to fear from General Wills. The priest's eyes shone with happy tears, his earnest face reddened with relief, while he said, "The Blessed Virgin has then granted all our prayers!"

They walked through back lanes and dark smoky streets to a tiny hidden chapel, where a handful of Mr. Littleton's parishoners were waiting patiently.

An hour later they left the chapel, and James was exalted. The priest had done full justice to the beautiful thanksgiving Mass, and in his sermon he had pointed out that this November 13 was the Feast of St. Didacus, a humble lay-brother who in his own life had shown how God's Divine Providence could choose the weak things of the world to confound the strong. So it had proved for them gathered here now—the Defenders of the True Faith, of the True King—on this day of rejoicing. Even Charles had been powerfully moved, and had taken the sacrament with a contrite and grateful heart.

Once in the street again the brothers walked in contented silence until they heard the clop of hoofs, and Charles, peering ahead towards the rider, said sharply, "Who's that coming?"

"Colonel Oxburgh?" said James squinting. "He must be searching for the chapel."

"I don't think so," said Charles holding his breath as he stared. "What's that he's carrying? What's that white thing on his arm?"

James looked again, and saw what Charles's stronger eyes had already seen. Oxburgh, in his full dress military uniform, his chin sunk on his chest, carried a small white flag, and had a white band tied around his sleeve. James stepped into the street directly in front of Oxburgh's oncoming horse and cried, "Halt!"

The Colonel pulled up his horse, his face remained expressionless. "Good day, my lord," he murmured.

"Where are you going?" James demanded, catching the horse's bridle. "Why do you carry a white flag?"

There was silence in the street, broken only by the switching of the horse's tail and the clatter of a pan from behind a shuttered window. Then Oxburgh spoke in a toneless voice. "I am going, my lord, at General Forster's command, to see what terms I can get."

"Terms?" James repeated. "I don't understand you. Terms from whom?"

"From King George's army, from General Wills and General Carpenter."

"But you're mad!" Charles shouted. "Wills has retreated with all his men, and Carpenter's up in Scotland."

"General Carpenter is *here*, Radcliffe. With near three thousand fresh dragoons, he arrived two hours ago to join Wills, who was waiting for him. We are now surrounded. General Forster has ordered me to ask for surrender terms."

James stood rooted, his hand trembling on the bridle. There was rushing as of water in his ears, while Charles made a gasping noise like a sob. "I'll kill him," Charles whispered. "I'll kill the whoreson buggering coward—but *you* first. Oxburgh!" Frantically, with his good arm, Charles struggled to get at his pistol. He hauled it from the holster and James knocked it out of his hand. "No, Charles!"

Charles turned furiously on his brother. " 'No, Charles. No, Charles.' Damn you, is that all you can say! You'd let this bastard tamely trot off begging for surrender terms? You'd let that bloated farting toad up there at the Mitre bring shame on us, like this? Well, by God, *I* won't!" Charles flung wildly around, picked up the pistol, stumbled,

174

then righting himself began to run towards the Mitre.

"He'll kill Forster, if he can," said James in a voice as toneless as Oxburgh's.

"Others have already tried this morning," answered the Colonel. "But Forster's well guarded. My lord, stand aside, I must continue my mission."

"I forbid it!" James looked up at Oxburgh; his eyes held the cold gray authority born from generations of ruling. Oxburgh's own glance wavered. He turned away, while he said, "Be reasonable, my lord. Leaderless as we are, inexperienced in real war as most of us are, we'd be cut to pieces now, if we fought. You don't want all your men massacred, do you?"

"Then we will barricade ourselves in town and take them on as we did yesterday," James said after a moment in which he tried to think.

"We cannot, my lord. The town isn't provisioned for a siege, and we've only a few more rounds of powder left. They've trapped us. If we surrender now, for sure they'll give us honorable terms, and King George is known to be clement!"

"So it's 'King George' from you now!" James cried, his nostrils dinting, his cheeks going white. "You sang a very different tune in Dilston! What of King *James*? What will *he* say when news of this degraded treachery reaches him in Scotland!"

Oxburgh's shoulders slumped. He shut his eyes for an instant. "King James has not left France," he said very low. "An express came from Lord Mar yestermorn. Just before the battle."

It was at that moment James gave up hope. His small proud face grew masklike; thoughts like jagged rocks plunged down and clogged his soul. All false had been the certainty of Jemmie's landing—a delusion, a chimera. The truth instead was as it had always been. Bungling incompetence. Betrayal. Cowardice. The Devil Water. Why had God allowed the devil to prevail? Why?

James's hand dropped from the bridle. He lifted his head and walked past the horse, not looking at Oxburgh. Very slowly, his steps dragging, he continued down the street.

On December 9 the chief Jacobite prisoners, under heavy guard, neared the village of Barnet in Hertfordshire, eleven miles from London. James rode in a rickety coach with Lord Widdrington, to whom he had scarcely spoken during all the days of their slow marches down from Preston. There was nothing to discuss with Widdrington, who had been the foremost in urging Forster to surrender. Widdrington, Oxburgh, and Patten, these had been their general's sole advisers during the hour of panic in the Mitre, when Forster first received news of General Carpenter's arrival. Forster had consulted nobody else, had skulked in a locked and guarded room, until the moment next day when he had handed his sword to General Wills, and thereupon received Government protection.

Forster had reason to be terrified of his own troops, James thought, staring out the coach window at the soft falling snow. The Highlanders had been ready to kill him when they learned of the betrayal. Young Murray had actually taken a shot at him. And Charles . . .

Through the despair in James's breast came always a fiercer pain when he thought of Charles. Charles was safe enough at present—riding somewhere a quarter of a mile back, his hands loosely pinioned, his horse's halter led by a dragoon. James had glimpsed him often during the marches, and night stops. But Charles would not come near him.

One of the coach horses stumbled in an icy mudhole, the coach careened sharply. James could hear the cursing of the coachman and their four dragoon guards outside, and did not heed any of it. His mind presented to him yet again, as with a sick compulsion, pictures from that fatal Sunday, November 13. The return to the Mitre to find that Charles had disappeared, and Alec in the stableyard, crying, "Oh, what ails my master, my lord? He ran in like a madman, shouting for General Forster's blood, then my lord Winton joined him and they spoke together. Like stags at bay they was—both of 'em—wild-eyed—panting."

James, unable to bring himself to tell Alec all that had made Charles wild, said only, "I fear we are undone," and as he said it saw Ann's tender face—sorrowing, waiting, hoping, at Dilston. "Alec Armstrong," he said solemnly, "if you take Monarch," he gestured to the stall where his stallion was stamping, "d'you think you could somehow get out of town and back to her ladyship at Dilston?"

"Aye, trust me, my lord. Fisher Gate to the north's not blocked, or wasn't an hour ago—oh, your lordship, is't that bad?"

James bowed his head. "Tell her to hide Dilston papers quickly, get them to Capheaton. Tell her—tell her to be brave and that I love her dearest of any earthly thing."

Alec had set off at once on Monarch, and must have either got through or been shot, since he had not returned.

Other pictures of that dreadful day. The bewilderment of half their troops, the relief of others. The twenty frenzied Scots rebelling when they heard of the surrender. Charles and Lord Winton trying to lead these Scots in a charge, and being stopped by Brigadier Mackintosh himself, backed by Forster's men. Charles had been bound and locked up overnight for safety. But this incident angered General Wills, who now contemptuously demanded hostages, until the negotiations should be complete. He demanded Lord Derwentwater, and a Scottish leader. James had gone to pass the night in the enemy camp. For what use now was resistance which would lead to slaughter? The Rebellion in England was finished. They were powerless. All in reason that was left was to get the best terms possible. And fair trials in London. Charles did not agree, James knew. The most hurtful memory of all was of the look in Charles's eyes when the Jacobite officers handed over their swords to General Wills, while General Carpenter looked on, sneering at the defeated.

In Charles's gray eyes when they met James's there had been implacable accusation, bitter reproach. And since then complete avoidance.

The old coach lurched into the village of Barnet, and at once a yelling crowd collected on the road. "Down with the Pretender!" they shouted. "Death to the Jacks!" "Long live King George!" And someone banged a warming pan against the coach window crying, "Look traitors, here's where your fine Pretender popped from!"

James and Widdrington remained imperturbable. This reception they had had in every town since leaving Lancashire. The fools, James thought wearily. If they could see the king who was a Stuart in every feature, and as like his father as two peas, this canard that he'd been smuggled into Queen Mary's childbed in a warming pan would cease forever. If they could but *see* their rightful king!

Spurred by miserable anger, James broke the silence in the coach. "This mob—like every mob we've come through! *Where* are the High Church Tories who promised to join us! And you'd think one cheer on this dreary march might have been raised for King James!"

Widdrington grunted. His peevish, sickly face showed some surprise at being addressed by Derwentwater. "Self-preservation is the first and strongest law of nature," he answered with a shrug.

"Yes," said James. "It has ever been clear that you think so." He turned his back on Widdrington and gazed through the snow at the many-gabled inn, where they were apparently to stop, because their guards were dismounting. On each night of their journey since leaving Preston the seven lords among the prisoners had been given relative comfort in their lodgings. The two English peers—Derwentwater and Widdrington—and the five Scottish ones—Winton, Kenmure, Nithsdale, Carnwath, and Nairn—had been sequestered from the commoners, who were lodged in churches, stables, or any shelter available.

Tonight, the last before London, and the weather being most inclement, Brigadier Panton of the Royal Dragoons did not bother to maintain nice distinctions. Accordingly, James found himself and his fellow peers all herded into the inn's cramped common rooms, where the rest of the prisoners were presently stuffed as they arrived. Tom Forster came soon— with Patten. James did not greet them, though they both bowed to him. James noted that Tom was pasty-faced and shrunken, that Patten's chin was bruised and his clerical suit badly torn. Both men's wrists were bound together, and the guards showed them no special favor. And yet, the suspicions James had felt on the day of surrender were not allayed. Forster might be too stupid and befuddled for actual treachery. But Patten! Had the curate really been honestly mistaken when he announced the withdrawal of General Wills's troops? He had later shrilly and passionately averred so.

Oxburgh was next shoved through the door into the taproom. He looked at nobody. His head was sunk forward on his chest as it had been the morning of surrender. Brigadier Mackintosh came stumbling through the door, and was followed by the Swinburne lads and a dozen others—the Claverings, the Wogans, Jack Thornton, and Tom Errington. With these last, James exchanged across the room a sad half smile of greeting, but was too sick at heart to speak. The inn became so crowded that soon all the commoners must stand, with barely room to lift the mugs of small beer which they were given.

The outer door opened once again, and Charles, prodded by the butt end of a musket, walked in, his handsome young face glowering. James stiffened and rose, with a great thump of his heart. Charles did not glance his way. He pushed over

178

to Ned Swinburne, and stood by him silently, while the dragoons posted themselves at the door.

The lords were offered seats near the fire on settles and stools. Brigadier Panton, their particular guard, stayed among them. He directed a frightened inn servant to bring October ale for his noble charges, then turned courteously to James, whom the King's generals considered by all odds their most important prisoner. "I regret, my lord, that your lodgings tonight should be so incommodious, but I pray you sit down."

James inclined his head. "I've been sitting all day. I prefer to stand." His somber gaze again sought out Charles's tall figure with the tousled fair hair, the old cheek scar showing white on the rigidly averted profile. "Tell me, Brigadier," James said, turning back to Panton, "where we will be lodged *tomorrow* night, in London? That seems to me of interest."

James's clear quiet voice penetrated through the silent room. Everyone had wondered about this, and everyone waited for the answer.

The Brigadier showed some embarrassment. Unlike the Generals Wills and Carpenter, he had no hatred of his prisoners, and found his duties distasteful, but he spoke decisively. "You, my Lord Derwentwater, and your fellow peers," he glanced at Widdrington and the Scots, "will be lodged in the Tower, as befits your rank. The other rebels will be imprisoned at Newgate, at Marshalsea, and the Fleet in accordance with their quality."

They all heard this. Charles too, for he put his hand to his head and looked dazed, suddenly realizing, James knew, that after tonight there would be no chance to talk between them. There was a stir by the bar and Tom Forster lumbered towards the Brigadier.

"What about *me*?" he cried. "I'm for the Tower, ain't I? I was told so. I'm a general, and M.P. for Northumberland, don't forget that! And m'Lord Crewe, Bishop of Durham, is me uncle."

"You will be jailed at Newgate, Mr. Forster," repeated the Brigadier with stony calm.

Forster gasped. " 'Tis a damned outrage! 'Tis an insult!" he shouted, his pendulous unshaven cheeks suffusing. "I've friends in London, *you'll* see! You'll rue your wicked treatment o' me!" He flailed out with his arm, forgetting that it was pinioned to Patten, who was thrown off balance. The guards by the door snickered.

James made a harsh sound in his throat. "There is one sort

of prison which would hold us all comfortably," he remarked.

"What is that, my lord?" asked the Brigadier astonished.

"Bedlam Hospital," said James, and walking to a tiny window he stared out onto the snowy, littered stable yard.

Charles, at those bitter words, felt the hardness loosen a little in his breast. He watched the small erect figure at the window, and for the first time it occurred to him that James might be suffering as much as he was himself. Possibly he had been so blinded by his own rage at the Preston disaster that he had imputed to James many of the craven motives which had ruled Forster and his tribe. In any case, James was his brother, and it looked as though they would not meet again for some time. And Charles perceived that, though the long nightmarish days of marching were over, arrival in London would not end the humiliation and defeat—as he had somehow expected. It would augment them.

Charles tightened his mouth and made his way slowly to the privileged portion of the room. He spoke to the Brigadier. "May I have a word with his lordship of Derwentwater, sir?"

Six weeks later, on the nineteenth of January, in the Tower of London, Ann, Countess of Derwentwater, was in James's prison apartment in the old Beauchamp tower. She was alone there, kneeling on the stained torn rug which the Tower Lieutenant had provided to cover the filthy stone floor which so many imprisoned feet had trod. Ann's eyes were shut as she prayed, her fingers trembled on the Rosary beads. "Holy Blessed Mother," she whispered as she kissed the crucifix. "Help him! Make them listen to his answer! Move King George's heart to clemency. For the sake of Thine own Dear Lord and Son."

Ann, raised her head, hearing a distant flourish of trumpets, and rising clumsily—she was now five months pregnant —went to the barred window. From it she could see beyond the walls of the outer ward and the icy moat, a glimpse of Tower Hill and Tower Street. And she could see, gleaming in the dusk, the state coach which held the seven impeached Jacobite lords who were returning from Westminster Hall. She recognized the coach by the twenty yeomen warders of the Tower—the Beefeaters—who marched with raised halberds on either side the coach, which presently disappeared behind the walls as it approached the outer entrance of the prison. Ann stood a moment staring into the leaden sky. It was bitter cold. The Thames had been frozen over for days. In the King's menageries across the moat, the lions no longer roared, as they had done at Christmas; they huddled in their dens and slept. Would that I could too, Ann thought. It had been a month of nights since she had truly slept. Not since Alec Armstrong had come to her at Dilston —his ears frostbitten, the great stallion Monarch limping and badly saddle-galled. She had been up in Dilston's old turret, lighting the cresset to guide James home, as she had promised. But it was not James who came.

Only Alec and the dreadful news of defeat. Of her hardships after that—the agonizing journey south through snowbound roads with the priest, Mr. Brown, and Alec—she remembered little except brief rejoicing when she saw James and was allowed to share his imprisonment.

Ann turned as she heard footsteps on the hollowed winding stairs. She put her hand to her throat and waited. A Beefeater unlocked the door and ushered James in. Ann dared not speak, until she had scanned his face. It was weary, haggard, but not entirely cheerless. "'Tis done, my love," he said when they had heard the key turn and the bolt shot in place on the door. "'Tis done as you begged me, as the lawyers told me, as your parents and Mr. Brown advised. May God forgive me."

"But dear heart!" Ann cried. "Did they *listen?* Will they now show mercy? James, James—how did Lord Chancellor Cowper look?"

"At the ceiling," said James with a shrug. "I have been as abject as I can be. I have pleaded guilty of treason and thus denied my rightful king. I have apologized for my misguided actions. I told them that as my offense was sudden, so my submission was early. I have pleaded for pardon and thrown myself on the mercy of the Hanoverian—as you besought me to." James drew off his gloves and warmed his hands at the fire. Ann drew a quivering breath. She touched her crucifix. "When is the trial?" she asked.

"In a month, I believe."

"What of the others, James?" she said after a moment. "How did they plead?"

James gave the harsh laugh which still shocked her. "Widdrington was even more cringing than I. He pleaded his gout, his ill health, which had unsettled his wits, he said. The Scots too ate humble pie—except for Winton. Ah, there's a man of courage! The only one amongst us!"

"That's untrue!" she cried sharply. "James, it wounds me that you talk like this."

"The Earl of Winton," James went on as though she had

181

not spoken, "alone amongst us pleaded *not* guilty, saying that he recognized as his king no person called George the Elector of Hanover, and had thus committed no treason. And he sneered at Lord Cowper, the Chancellor."

"Then Winton has signed his own death sentence!" she cried. "And is mad. They say he's mad. 'Tis naught to do with you. Oh, my dearest, you will be saved now for me—for our children!"

James turned and looked at her, at the dark, frightened eyes, the soft brown curls so neatly dressed, the white ruffles at her throat, her entire little body so delicate and cleanly despite the hardships of the prison which she insisted on sharing with him. His eyes softened, he took her hand and kissed it. "Aye, my dear, I've done my best to save my miserable life for you, for our little John, and for the new one in your womb. What that life will be—attainted, stripped of title and estates—I cannot think."

"Nor will it matter," she said quickly. "We can live in Gloucestershire with my parents, we can go abroad—and Jemmie," she added, "have you forgot the word brought by Mr. Brown? Have you forgot that our King is at last in Scotland?"

"I've not forgot," said James trying to smile. Let Ann rejoice if she could. James had no more illusions. If the King *had* finally landed it was the old story of too little and too late. The Battle of Sheriffmuir had proved that. The Sheriffmuir defeat in Scotland occurred on the same fateful November 13 as the surrender at Preston. No, Scotland would not rise again for the Stuarts. The hollow, gleaming bubble had been pricked for ever, and there was nothing to do but admit it, as he had this day in Westminster Hall.

"I wonder how poor Charles does at Newgate," he said abruptly, pouring them each a glass of wine from a flagon on the table. He had frequent and unhappy thoughts of Charles. Their farewell talk at Barnet had been strained. It had not been the perfect reconciliation James hoped for. There was something still withheld in the boy's eyes.

"Why, there's a note from Charles!" Ann said. " 'Twas brought by Alec this morning. The warder sent it up after you left for Westminster." James held out his hand and she gave him Charles's note. It was extremely brief and formal. Charles thanked James for his letter and said he was well enough, though Ned Swinburne had jail fever. That the cost of paying the turnkeys for any comforts was excessive. That he trusted James and Ann were well, and that all the talk in

Newgate was of a pardon for the impeached lords, and he hoped to soon hear of it. He signed himself, "Your dutyfull brother, Ch: Radclyffe." There was also a postscript: "That swine Patten hath turnd king's evidense & been freed from here."

James sighed as he read the letter, but when he finished the postscript, he gave an exclamation and handed the note to Ann. " 'Tis no surprise to me," he said. "Ever did I suspect that foxy curate, and now I understand why Lord Cowper was so well prepared with every damning detail of our Rising. Without Patten they could scarce construct a case."

"Think not of that, love," said Ann softly. "Will you not cease to think of trouble, and take hope? Your music—" she cried, running to open a chest which contained a guitar packed among the Earl's belongings. "We will play and sing together—forget where we are."

Forget where we are, James thought as he accepted the guitar. He glanced at the barred windows, at the damp stone walls. There were names carved on those walls, carved by those who had been here before him—Dudley, Arundel, Peverel, and many others. One of the names was "Radclyffe. 1576." What long forgotten kin was that? Beneath this name, half concealed by an age-blackened stool were rusty iron rings for leg fetters and the stains of long spilled blood. James turned away from the wall, towards Ann. He began tuning the guitar. "What shall I play, my dear?" he asked.

Three weeks later, February 9, Charles lay on his bed in Newgate jail, dispiritedly leafing through Alexander Pope's "The Rape of the Lock." The book belonged to Jem Swinburne, who had loaned it to Charles while quoting from the poem with a silly titter,

> *"The hungry judges soon the sentence sign*
> *And wretches hang that jurymen may dine."*

A quotation Charles found inconsistent with his hope of diversion from the poem, which had a promising title. But Jem Swinburne had grown very odd since his brother Ned died of jail fever. Jem either sat for hours giggling to himself, or he crouched frowning over a table while covering reams of foolscap with illegible symbols. Yesterday poor Jem had behaved so strangely that Mr. Pitts, the Keeper of the jail, had removed him to a solitary cell in the Press Yard.

Outside the prison walls, St. Sepulchre's bell clanged six times. Another dreary day was ending, Charles thought. Soon he would be permitted to join the other prisoners for an hour in the common room.

He propped himself up on his elbow, and tried again to read by the light of his candle. Candles cost two shillings apiece from the turnkey, and few of Charles's fellow prisoners could afford such luxury. Or the luxury of a private cell, furnished with wooden bedstead and straw mattress—however lousy—of a table, chair, and closestool; or the luxury of coals burning in the grate. Charles had other privileges, accorded to his rank, and purse. It was money which had procured his freedom from leg irons, and a further twenty guineas to Pitts secured Alec's daily visits to bring in meals and wine from a tavern in Cock Lane. Charles might also exercise at times in the Press Yard near the debtors' side of Newgate, angrily ignoring Tom Forster and Oxburgh when he did so. For the rest, Charles paced the filthy stone floor of his narrow cell, he tried to read what few books he could get, and he scratched the days off on a calendar he had made.

Charles let his book fall shut. "The Rape of the Lock" could not hold his restless thoughts tonight. It wasn't bawdy, either. Just a foolish tale about the theft of a woman's curl. Lord Petre was reputedly the "thief"—and who cared? Charles had met the mincing little fop and had no interest in him. A Catholic though Petre was, as was also the author of this poetic nonsense, Alexander Pope. Charles thought of the first time he had met the poet in that Christmastide at Dr. Radcliffe's Bloomsbury Square mansion. Six years ago in time, not two miles away from here in space, and yet those eager careless days were as distant now as the Rome of the Caesars.

Charles flung himself off the bed, and stuffed his clay pipe with tobacco from a canister. He was holding a live coal to the pipe with the tongs when he heard outside his iron door the raucous voice of Muggles, the turnkey.

Is it news? Charles thought, his heartbeat quickening. All day he had avoided thinking of James's trial at Westminster Hall. Yet surely it was too early to hear the result. Charles had resigned himself to waiting for Alec's appearance in the morning.

The lock grated as the huge key turned, the door hinges squealed and the turnkey's fat pock-marked face appeared in the crack.

"Naow then, sir," said Muggles scowling, " 'ere's a lydy ter see ye—your sister she vows." Under pouched lids the turnkey's bleary eyes glared at Charles suspiciously. "That's why I let 'er in."

Charles, much astonished, saw a woman's cloaked figure standing behind the turnkey. And she was masked. Sister? But Mary was sequestered in Gloucestershire under the Webbs' anxious guardianship. Ann then? Was she released from the Tower to bring glad tidings? But Ann was not nearly so tall.

"I'm here to see you, dear Brother," said the figure in a quick muffled voice Charles could not recognize. "To bring you word from our sorrowing old father, who prays for your repentance. I fear your wicked conduct has brought him to the grave."

"Shocking," said Muggles, as Charles collected his wits. "I've never 'ad no traitors 'ere before. It turns me stomick."

Charles, though baffled, accepted his cue. "Oh, my dear Sister," he said, "I can hardly bear to have my miseries increased, yet I'm grateful you've come."

The warder glanced sharply from one to the other, then stepped aside. "In ye go," he said to the cloaked figure. "Ye've 'arf an 'our." He locked the door behind the woman, who then ran to Charles, throwing back her hood and snatching off her mask.

"Lady Betty . . ." whispered Charles, gaping at the glossy reddish curls, the face where the freckles had faded to a creamy tint. Her puppy plumpness had gone. At twenty-two she had become an elegant, almost beautiful woman. Charles, much intrigued, began to smile. But her sherry-colored eyes, once so gay, did not respond; they fixed on him with a painful searching look. "Yes, Charles," she said. " 'Tis Betty Lee."

"And most fervently welcome," he said with caressing warmth, making her a bow. "But why, my dear, have you come to me? And for that matter *how?* I see you've not lost your talent for a masquerade!"

Betty glanced at the iron door behind which the turnkey might be listening. "My husband is a Whig," she whispered. "He expects a Court appointment. I must not be recognized. And as to *how* I got here—well, four guineas eased my way. At the gate with the warder, and up here with the turnkey. Four guineas and my sad story of our dying father."

185

"I see," said Charles eagerly, putting his hand on hers. "But why?"

She moved away and sat down abruptly on the bed. Her gloved fingers clenched on a fold of her amber velvet gown as she looked up at him. Charles was a full-grown man now and far more handsome than she remembered him, despite the prison pallor and a white scar on his right cheek. Charles still had that indefinable blend of swagger and strength, still the charming air of mockery and yet admiration in his bold gray eyes. The look which used to make her heart tremble. I've come, she thought, because I've never ceased to love you—not even in the arms of my dear dull Frank, not even when my babe was born. But this she could not tell, and she turned her head aside. "I'm here," she said with difficulty, "because I'm your cousin, and because I would not have you hear from strangers the—the outcome of the trial."

"The trial," he repeated, his smile fading. "James's trial?"

"Yes. The Earl of Peterborough is my friend. He was in there today with the other peers. I waited outside Westminster Hall, in my chair. He told me the result."

"Which is?" asked Charles through stiff lips.

"Condemned," she said staring at the floor. "All of them condemned, except Winton, who'll be tried later."

"But it can't be!" Charles cried. "They threw themselves on King George's mercy. They were promised clemency if they surrendered!"

"They are condemned to be executed on February twenty-fourth, Charles. And the only mercy to be shown them is the headsman's axe, instead of hanging, drawing, and quartering."

Charles sank down on the stool and put his hand to his forehead. "There will be reprieves," he said at last. "There must be."

"For some, perhaps," Betty said. "Widdrington is kin to Lady Cowper, Lord Nairn has friends at Court. The Princess of Wales is said to interest herself in Carnwath. But what friends has James in London?"

Charles moistened his lips. "Our Stuart cousins," he said groping. "The Dukes of Richmond, Cleveland—"

"All suspected Jacobites," she said, sighing. "And do you think that Stuart kinship will recommend itself to His Majesty now?"

"But then you, Betty?" he cried. "Surely you must have some plan for James—or why are you here?"

"Hush! Speak low! I too have Stuart blood. Though 'tis

186

forgot by all because my husband and I are Whigs, and loyal subjects of King George. *Truly* loyal," she repeated with emphasis. "In my home there are no secret toasts to the Pretender. Frank and I would both despair at seeing a feckless Papist on the throne of England."

Charles started back, his face flushed darkly. He looked at her with anger. "This from you, who once promised to turn Catholic for my sake!"

She too flushed. "I was a child then, Charles. Much has happened to us since then. We mustn't quarrel. I only wanted you to know that—that what I do—or try to do—is done only for—for—"

Betty's voice faltered and stopped. She had no hope of trying to help Lord Derwentwater, and, except in mercy for any suffering, no real desire to save him. He had headed the Rebel Rising in the North, he had dragged Charles into it. His fate was no concern of hers. But Charles's fate was. Alas, that a tortured and long denied yearning had brought her here today, against her principles, against all judgment.

"It's *you*," she said, so low that he barely heard. "Don't you know how your own trial will end—after this?" She raised her eyes, and Charles saw them drenched with fear.

"You still love me," Charles whispered in total disbelief. "You hate the cause for which I'd die, and yet you don't want me hanged?"

She would not look at him. He put his hands on either side of her cheeks and raised her head. At last she met his grave questioning eyes, and her own answered him. He bent and kissed her on the mouth, first gently, then as her lips opened under his, desire swept them both. She felt her veins burn as with a honeyed fire, she weakened in his arms, and clung to him in fierce need, while a great sob rose in her throat.

Yet it was she who heard St. Sepulchre's bell tolling outside the walls. "Dear God!" she whispered, pushing him frantically away. "Dear God—I never meant this."

"Nor I," said Charles in a shaking voice. His arms dropped and he stood up. "It seems that I love you too." How strange, he thought, in confusion. How very strange. To feel with Betty Lee, here in a stinking cell in Newgate, a storm of passion and yet restraint, a sort of tenderness which his many amours had not yielded.

"The turnkey," she whispered, pushing distractedly at her hair, searching for her mask. "He'll be here, directly. Oh, Charles—"

He nodded, squaring his shoulders. "Betty, if you love me, do what you can to help James."

"I will," she breathed. "I will."

"And you'll be back here to see me soon—darling?"

She clenched her fingers on the fold of her skirt, they both heard the grating of the key in the lock outside, she pulled her hood over her head. "I will be back," she said in a strangled voice. "God forgive me, I can't help it."

On Thursday evening, February 23, James sat alone in his prison in the Tower. He had placed the writing table by the window, from which he could see the workmen building by torchlight the scaffold on Tower Hill. James looked from the window to a large wooden crucifix on the wall by the fireplace. The crucifix had been permitted him these last days, as had been the constant visits of his chaplain, Father Brown, now known as Mr. Pippard. It was safer that nobody should guess his priest had lived at Dilston, and had been associated with the Rising.

The Father should have been back long ago, James thought, dipping his pen in the ink. There were still many prayers his soul needed, more ghostly comfort that the priest could provide. And the Mass. This had been promised him. The implements of the Mass were waiting in the chest. And yet the hour grew later. The few and precious hours. God strengthen me, James thought, and returned to the farewell letter he was writing to his aunt, Lady Mary Radcliffe in Durham. He wrote, "I recommend my poor brother, Charles, if he come off, to your care. He hath behaved himself nobly . . ."

It was past eight when the priest came, and two Beefeaters with him, nor did they leave as they usually did. In their scarlet Tudor tunics and flat hats they stood impassively, their crossed halberds barring the door.

"What is this?" said James to Father Brown. "Are they so eager for my life they can't leave me alone until the morrow?"

"It is because Lord Nithsdale has escaped, my lord," said the priest. "This afternoon. His wife sneaked him out disguised as a woman. The Tower is now locked throughout. I had great trouble getting in. And—and—" The priest faltered. He looked with anguished pity at the young man before him. So thin, he was—Derwentwater had been fasting for days. And so composed, an exalted light in his hollow eyes.

"Now they will not let my wife see me again? Is that what

you hesitate to say?" asked James softly, and the priest bowed his head.

The Earl rose from the writing table and knelt down before the crucifix. The priest caught some of the beseeching words. "Father Thy will be done. *Fiat! Fiat!* . . . Nail to Thy cross the black and frightful scroll of my sins, there to be canceled by Thy life-giving blood!" The kneeling figure swayed, and Father Brown rushed to him. "My lord. You must take meat, some wine! You must not grow faint now."

"I do not!" James rose, and gave the priest his peculiarly sweet smile. "But why need I be careful of this carcase which will soon be the food of worms? You must comfort Ann, Father. When this is over. Tell her, as I shall by letter tonight, that she is my dearest worldly treasure, my dear great comfort. That she must take courage and call upon God Almighty, to whom I shall deliver up my soul trusting that through the merits of Our Saviour's passion, I shall obtain peace at last."

"In God's Mercy," murmured the priest. He put his hand to his wet eyes, then shook his head violently. "But there's still time, my lord! Still hope of reprieve! The Lords Nairn and Carnwath are reprieved, at least for a while. You must not doubt that you will be! Her ladyship is certain of it!"

Suddenly James's quiet exaltation was pierced. *Was* there yet hope? He thought of all that Ann had done in the past days since she had extricated herself from the Tower by pleading her pregnancy and the fear of smallpox. She had gone to the Duchess of Cleveland. She had rallied all his other Stuart cousins. She had forced another hearing in the House of Lords, in the House of Commons. She had gone, groveling, weeping, to King George himself, clutching at his coat as he would have passed her in the gallery. Ann had not known whether her plea had moved the King, since he gave no sign and spoke only in German. But she reported that he seemed to look on her with pity, and it was after that Baron Waldegrave came to the Tower and saw James. He had brought a proposition in the King's name. "If you will recant, Derwentwater," he said, "if you will only put aside your papistry, then I believe I can assure you of the King's forgiveness."

"And can you also assure me of *God's* forgiveness?" James asked.

The Baron had left with an angry shrug. They had come again yesterday while Ann was with him. This time the proposition was that he should only seem to read a Protestant Book of Sermons, as though he were considering. Even Ann had pled that he should do this; he saw now her piteous tear-stained face as she had begged him, and heard the cry she gave, when he refused. "Would you have me give people any handle to suspect that I doubt my Faith?" he said to her. "Had I a thousand lives I'd sooner part with them than that."

Strong words, and passionately meant. But *was* there hope the King might be moved to mercy without extorting the impossible bargain? Again James looked out of the window, where the scaffold was abuilding on Tower Hill. "Since Nithsdale has escaped, while Nairn and Carnwath are reprieved, there are then but three of us to mount that scaffold on the morrow," he said to the priest, who was on his knees by the chest setting out the sacrament for the Mass. Father Brown looked up quickly. "Widdrington too, I hear, will be reprieved. Lady Cowper herself has demanded her cousin's life." A worthless life compared to yours, the priest thought, and he added softly, "So you see, there's hope, my lord."

"I dare not think so," said James. "Nay, then 'tis to be Lord Kenmure, poor old man, and me. An English Catholic peer and a Scottish Protestant one—as scapegoats. Perhaps 'tis fitting."

"No! No!" cried the priest harshly. " 'Tis not fitting for *you!* You're young, you are but twenty-six. We'll pray again to Our Blessed Lady. She who works miracles!"

James made a weary motion with his hand, as though to stop the other's vehemence. " 'Tis true," he said, "I do not want to die. Yet I fear I shall. I think I knew this long ago, on a day up the Devil Water at Dilston, when a red leaf fluttered to my feet—Father, are you ready to celebrate the Mass?"

The following afternoon, Friday the 24th, Alec Armstrong waited outside Charles's cell in Newgate. The valet's jaunty face was drawn with sorrow, his eyes red-rimmed from tears. Alec paced up and down the damp stone passage, under the sardonic eye of Muggles, the turnkey, who squatted on a stool, picking his teeth, and occasionally swigging from a jug by his feet. "Won't let ye in?" said Muggles. "Wouldn't let the ordinary in neither—said 'e'd fry in 'ell, afore 'e'd see a Protestant chaplain! Tykin' it 'ard, Radcliffe is. Thought 'e'd throttle me, wen I told 'im it was over. Threw me out o' 'is cell, and 'as propped the furniture against the door. We could force in, but 'e's acting like a madman."

"Damn you!" said Alec. "Why couldn't you wait for *me* to tell him! I was there. I know how his lordship died. It was—it was—" Alec's face crumpled as he searched for a word, and could find none except an inadequate one from his Northumbrian homeland. "It was douce," he finished in a whisper.

The turnkey shrugged and took another swig. "Couple a rebel 'eads rolled todye—Darntwater and Kenmure," he said with relish, "an' there'll be plenty o' rebel necks twisted too on a length o' rope. *'Im* in there," he pointed a dirty finger at Charles's door, " 'is turn soon. Naow, naow—'oo's this?" he added, as a man's hurrying figure showed in the passage.

Alec looked and recognized the priest, Father Brown. "Thank God, ye've come, sir," said Alec in the priest's ear. "I'm afeared for my master—that he'll do himself a hurt."

"Ye can't see Mr. Radcliffe," growled the turnkey. "Nobody can wi'out there's orders." He jangled his huge keys, and looked contemptuously at the newcomer's plain black suit and cheap little tiewig. Not even a sword, and no sign of a purse, either. Some starveling clerk.

"I *have* orders, said Father Brown. "From Lord Townshend, *and* Mr. Pitts, your superior." He took a parchment covered with seals from his pocket. Muggles couldn't read, but he recognized the seals with annoyance.

"Well, get in, if ye can," he said, folding his arms. "I've unlocked the door."

Father Brown went to the grating on Charles's door and opened the shutter. In the dark cell he could dimly see a figure lying prone on the floor, and he heard horrible convulsive sounds, like a wounded animal's.

"Charles Radcliffe!" said the priest through the grating. The figure moved on the stone floor. "Let me alone!" cried a high distorted voice. "God blast you, let me be!"

"I have come as from your brother James," said the priest clearly and slowly. "I bear a letter from him to you. Will you refuse to receive it?"

There was no movement inside for a time, then he heard a hoarse murmur, "Who is it?"

"One who's here to bring you comfort," said the priest, praying that Charles would recognize his voice, as he would not the name of Pippard.

Soon he heard the scraping of furniture on the floor, as Charles unbarricaded the door. The priest walked in, and groping for a candle, lit it at the nearly dead fire. "My poor boy," he whispered when he saw Charles. "My, poor, poor lad." He reached up and placed his hand on Charles's head in benediction. "I see you're wild with grief. But you must *not* be! Lord Derwentwater is a saint. He died for his Faith as truly as ever did the early Christian martyrs."

"He is dead," Charles said. "Dead. I can't believe so horrible a thing."

Nor can I, thought the priest, sternly quelling a wave of nausea. One must forget now that flashing of the headsman's axe as his lordship spoke the name of Jesus. And the fountain of blood which spurted on the avid groaning crowd. And the shaven head which rolled off the scaffold. And the shameful squabbling of the Tower warder and the executioner for Derwentwater's clothes and wig. Forget these memories of mortal dissolution.

"Take your letter, sir," said the priest holding out a folded piece of paper. "Except for her ladyship and his son, his last worldly thoughts were of you."

Charles took the letter and broke the Radcliffe seal—their crest of the black bull. How often had he seen James use the ring which made this seal, how often had he seen this generous broad writing. Charles shivered, he leaned near the candle, but his aching eyes were dim, he could not decipher all, though the phrases which he read were like James speaking.

Dear Brother,

You have behaved yourself like a man of true honour and bravery . . . God who has been so good to us both by giving us time to repent . . . I have great confidence in His goodness for a merciful forgiveness for us both.

You know, dear brother, we have sometimes disputed together . . . but . . . I believe few brothers would have done more than I would have done to serve you. I have recommended your life . . . to those I know; it may be they will be more successful on your behalf. Pray behave yourself decently and honourably, without pride; bear my death with patience, forgive my enemies as I do; and if ever you are free, live as devoutly as ever you can . . .

It is now, dear brother, near the time of execution;—

God grant me courage to the last! And that we may meet one day in eternal bliss, is the hearty prayer of
Your constant, loving Brother,
DERWENTWATER
... Dear Brother, adieu!
Feb. 23, 1715–16.

Another shudder gripped Charles. He held the letter to his cheek, then put it inside his shirt next his breast. He crossed himself. "God rest his soul, his wondrous, kind, pure soul!" They were silent for some minutes then Charles turned quickly to the priest. "Father, tell me of what happened this morning. How did he look? What did he say?"

"He was pale, composed, visibly helped by an extraordinary grace, to the admiration of all that beheld him. It was he himself who told Lord Widdrington that he had been reprieved, and rejoiced with him heartily, so that Widdrington cried, "My Lord Derwentwater; were I to live a thousand years I shall never forget you! So much courage and resignation in so much youth!' "

"*I* cannot forgive Widdrington for being alive," said Charles through his teeth.

"And another thing," went on the priest, unheeding, "he took with heavenly resignation, though it must have been a bitter blow. In the coach which drove him to the scaffold, he was told that King James had fled again to France. The Rebellion in Scotland is over. 'I thought as much,' his lordship said with the saddest of smiles. 'But now I've come to see it matters *not*,' which I did not rightly understand, and then he added, 'The cause is ever bigger than the man, and even Our Lord's disciples themselves had weaknesses.' "

" 'Twas like James," said Charles very low. "Did he say nothing later from the—the scaffold?"

"Aye, indeed. As he stood looking over the heads of the vast silent crowd in his black velvet suit, and black plumed hat and long flaxen wig, his golden crucifix hanging plain for all to see, he told them that he bitterly regretted pleading guilty at his trial, having never had any other than King James the Third for rightful sovereign, and he said, 'Though King James had been a different religion from mine, I should have done for him all that lay in my power, as my ancestors have done for his predecessors, being thereunto bound by the laws of God and man.' "

Charles shut his eyes. Dear Brother, he thought. Christ forgive me that I ever doubted you.

"And do you know," the priest continued, speaking with sudden passion, "that four times in all they offered him his life, if he would forswear Catholicism? Four times, and each time he refused with gallantry and a wondering contempt. Ah, is this not the stuff of saints and martyrs!"

"Aye . . ." said Charles. He clenched his fists and, stalking to the fire, turned his back on the priest. "I loved him," Charles said, his voice thick and barely audible. "Yet I hurt him often—even at Barnet when I meant—meant to make up the quarrel we'd had. I loved him—*why* could I never tell him so!"

The priest looked with compassion at the bowed head, the trembling shoulders. "Be sure he knows it now," he said. "You may be sure he knows it now."

Charles fell to his knees, and crossed himself. "I swear," he cried, "by the precious crucified body of Our Lord Jesus Christ that James Radcliffe's death shall not have been in vain, I swear it!"

"Amen," whispered the priest.

EIGHT

Tuesday night, March 6, of that unhappy spring, 1716, was a night of wonder and supernatural fear all over England. It was a night of smoking clouds and globes of pale fire which rolled across the sky, sending forth streams of rainbow colors, while the horizon glowed with a flickering green. The folk of Northumbria had little doubt as to why God had made the heavens open to disclose His awful glories. Father Brown had no doubt, as he murmured prayers beside the hearse which was conveying the Earl of Derwentwater's body home.

The fiery strangeness in the sky began precisely as the hearse entered the real North Country by crossing the river Wear at Sunderland Bridge near Durham, and Lady Mary Radcliffe, weeping, painfully hobbled out upon the Northern Road to meet it.

All of that weird flashing night, the darkness never came. But the people did. They flocked from the countryside for miles to gaze on the crimson velvet coffin. They came from as far as Dilston itself to join the cortege which next day would continue plodding mournfully towards the dear chapel where the Earl had asked that he be laid to rest.

" 'Tis a miracle!" cried Lady Mary of the flames in the sky, after she had kissed the coffin. "A sign of God's Grace for him!"

"Or of God's judgment on those who murdered him," said the priest solemnly. "And, your ladyship, there have been other miracles!"

He told her of the happenings in London. Of two conversions brought about by Lord Derwentwater's death, and of the healings brought about by touching his lordship's precious heart. The heart, said the priest, in its silver urn, though unembalmed, remained whole, and fragrant, as with incense.

Lady Mary crossed herself and wiped her eyes. Her gaunt face quivered. "What is to be done with, with this relic?" she whispered.

"It will go to the Benedictine nuns at Pontoise, when her young ladyship can bear to part with it. They'll say perpetual Masses for his soul there, though," the priest added to himself, "I verily believe he does not need them."

"And Lady Derwentwater? How *is* she?" asked Lady Mary.

"Lamentably," answered the priest sighing. "She cannot cease to mourn, though I told her 'twas unbecoming when the angels and saints rejoice, and he himself is absorbed in joy. She wished to come North with us, but her mother restrained her, since the babe will soon be born."

"Poor thing," said the old woman turning away. "Ah, poor Ann. I feel such pity for her—and pity even for that young scapegrace, Charles. Is there hope he may get off?"

Father Brown bit his lips and frowned. There seemed no hope at all that Charles would not be hanged. "We must pray so," he said.

He glanced reverently at the coffin, while the sky lit up again in a great burst of flickering lights. Lord Derwentwater's Lights, the priest thought, with a thrill of awe.

In London too, on that same night, darkness never came, while the sky was stabbed with arrows of emerald and ruby flame. Then at one in the morning the whole town suddenly grew light as noon, and the citizens were terrified. Some saw two armies fighting in the sky, others saw a monster with shining scales and fiery breath. The Tories cried it was a judgment on the Whigs for beheading Lord Kenmure and Lord Derwentwater. The Whigs said the phenomenon was sent to show Divine displeasure at the Jacobite Rebellion. And there was scarce a soul who did not think that the world might be ending, and make hasty prayers of profound repentance. Lady Betty Lee was not of those who were terrified. In the intervals of soothing her frightened little son and the servants, she watched the lights the whole night through from her bedroom window. No celestial fireworks could affect the suffering which she felt already—the guilt, the fear, the agonized thwarted love.

She had thought to have suffered once before, when they told her Charles had done something monstrous, and that she could not marry him, that she must marry instead her dull cousin, Francis Lee. She had been frantic with rebellion, she had wept and pleaded and tried to run away. But the pain then was nothing like this. And it had dwindled at last into a state of resignation, then affection for the quiet, worthy husband they had given her. Frank was a good man.

Betty glanced back into the bedroom at the richly brocaded tentbed, where behind the curtains Frank snored rhythmically. She knew how he would look, his tasseled nightcap pulled down over his ears, his embroidered nightshirt neatly swathing his stout body beneath the blankets. On his lips the contented smile of a man who prospered in his undertakings, who had no pangs of conscience, and who was happy in his home. And if she went to bed, creeping in no matter how softly, he would stir and grunt and reach for her hand in perfect trust. This she knew, and knew too that she no longer deserved the trust Frank had in her.

To the north over the Marylebone fields the sky dipped and wheeled again, Betty could see the lights beyond the new mansions they were building on Hanover Square, and below her window on George Street she saw the dirty cobblestones grow luminous, and the foul water in the central gutter sparkle with a greenish tinge. A sedan chair sped by as she watched. The chairmen were running, their faces were aghast, the gentleman inside the chair seemed to be shouting frantically. How ridiculous they were, Betty thought, to be afraid of what Frank had earlier explained as a rare but natural occurrence called by some long Latin name. Yet try as she would, she could not keep her mind on the behavior of passersby, or even the beauty of the lighted sky. Her thoughts returned ever to her misery which seemed to be settled in her breast, like a rat gnawing at her heart.

She had seen Charles but once since his brother's execution. An unhappy interview which she continually relived in every part.

It was last Friday that she had gone again to Newgate jail, after waiting to see Frank set out for St. James's Square, where he had business to discuss with the Chancellor of the Exchequer, Robert Walpole. Betty did not dare take her chair again, lest the chairmen should gossip, and she hurried along the streets, shrinking into her furred hood, alone as any common trollop. For which indeed, the warder and the turnkey this time mistook her.

Muggles, at first, refused pointblank to let her enter Charles's cell. "Ye can see 'im, in the Press Yard tomorrow, sweet'eart," said the turnkey, leering. "Many a whore gets in there by 'ook or crook. An' no good a-telling me you're 'is sister agyne. Sisters don't clamor ter see their brothers alone, they don't." She had kept her temper, smiling at the oaf, and opening her purse. In the end it cost five guineas to see Charles. And where was the money for the next bribes to come from? She had nothing but her pocket money, nor had ever needed more. Frank paid all the bills, and knew in his just methodical way where every penny went to.

When the turnkey let her in the cell, Charles frightened her. He greeted her with apathy, as though he hardly knew her. His skin was flushed, his eyes heavy and too glittering. "Oh, my dear," she cried. "You're ill! Oh, I pray 'tis not jail fever!"

"A touch, perhaps," he said dully. "But would you expect me to be merry after what has happened?"

"I know," she whispered, seeing how violently he still suffered from the shock of his brother's death. "Oh, Charles, I *tried* to save him. Believe me, I did what I could. I even went to Lady Cowper."

"Molly Clavering from County Durham," said Charles in a dead voice. "Dear Lady Cowper, she's saving all her worthless Northern cousins, but she wouldn't save James."

"No," said Betty. "The King wouldn't permit it, even had she wanted to. Charles, it's past now. You must rouse yourself, take heart and think of your own defense! Your trial is coming on in May!" This she had found out by guile, asking innocent questions of the unsuspecting Frank. "We must make plans, think of some new plea which will move them!"

Charles turned his head and stared at her. She saw that he scarcely understood her, and he seemed very ill.

She looked distractedly around the cell, and saw on the floor a hamper. She went to it and found inside, a bottle of claret, cold chicken, and bread. "What's this!" she cried. "You haven't eaten, have you? In how long, Charles?"

He sighed. "I don't remember."

She made him eat, feeding him morsels of bread and chicken with her fingers, filling a tin cup with claret and holding it to his lips. She found a small flask of brandy at the bottom of the hamper and made him drink some of that too. In a few minutes he was better. The glaze left his eyes, he straightened his big frame, and took her hand.

"Betty," he murmured. "Dearest Betty—why do you bother with me?"

"You know why!" she said sharply. "More than my honor or my life I want to help you."

He leaned over and put his cheek against hers a moment, though he did not kiss her, for he knew his breath was foul with fever. "Will you do one thing for me, dear?" he said, staring at the tiny slitted window and its two iron bars.

"You need not ask! Oh Charles, have you thought of a plan? Do you see some way of escape?"

"No, no," he shook his head. " 'Tis not that, Betty. Something very different." He paused and went on slowly. "I have a child in Northumberland. A little girl called Jenny."

Betty winced and drew back, feeling as though he had struck her, though he did not notice. "Is it the child of—of that woman you married?" she said carefully.

"Yes. Meg Snowdon's child. But, Betty, it was no marriage. Meg and I have never lain together since, and we are naught to each other. I could have it annulled. Or could if I were free. But to what purpose. Since now *you* are married."

What sweet balm were these words to her, and yet what anguish too! Still, she felt her long pent hatred of the woman who had taken him from her dissolve, and she could say gently, "What *of* this child Jenny?"

"She is a marigold, growing in a dunghill," said Charles in a far-off voice. "If she stays where she is she'll be trampled. I can't bear it, nor bear the thought that her future not be settled before I die."

"You *will* not die!" cried Betty passionately. "Is it the fever that makes you talk like this?"

"Will you take her, Betty?" Charles went on, turning from the window, and looking at her piteously. "Will you take Jenny, and raise her in your home?"

Betty drew a sharp breath and was silent while her thoughts raced in perplexity. To rear that Border lass's brat —but it was Charles's too! She had said she would do whatever he wanted, yet never envisioned anything like this. And what could she tell Frank? How explain the daughter of Charles Radcliffe, whose name and beliefs Frank despised. Yet the look on Charles's face now—humble, beseeching, lost. He who had been always so confident, so debonair.

"This child," said Betty after a while, "whom you can

scarce ever have seen . . . she means so much to you?"

"Yes," he bowed his head. "I'm sorry I asked you, Betty, I see it was wrong. But I thought—we have love for each other, you and I—we have kinship too. I thought that with you, Jenny could—be—nearer to me."

"And she *shall* be!" Betty cried, no longer able to stand the stricken look in the gray eyes, the futile, helpless motions of his hand on his knee. "Oh, my dearest, of course I'll take her. Of course I will since you want it so!"

His gratitude, the brightening of his face, the love words he had given her, all these had been reward enough at the time. They had made hasty plans together before the turnkey bade her leave, and she had gone home in a happy glow which soon faded. For after all, what had been gained? Charles's life was no more secure, and she had saddled herself with a child whose presence could not help but be awkward, and probably dangerous. If Frank knew whose child it was, he would refuse to receive it in his home, of that she was sure. He loathed all Jacobites, and above all he loathed what he had learned of Charles during the latter's dissipated years in London.

What am I going to do? asked Betty of the Northern Lights. What am I going to do?

Alec had left on Saturday morning for the North; he was to bring Jenny down with him. Charles had had enough ready money for this journey. Simpson, a servant of Lord Derwentwater's still in London, would attend Charles in Newgate for the present. The child might be here in a fortnight, and must be provided for. To do this would mean lies. A tissue of lies to hide Jenny's identity. Which lie would best calm any suspicion Frank might have? And he could be not only suspicious but harsh, if a principle were involved. "Your nimble woman's brain will think of something," Charles had said, smiling at her with vague childlike trust, which brought her renewed fear. "Charles, you *must* get well! Eat and drink properly, call a physician, get blooded," she cried, and he promised.

Indeed he was better, so Simpson reported. She met Simpson occasionally near the pile of building stone behind the unfinished St. George's Church, since she did not yet dare go again to Newgate. More subterfuge and lies. Yet her anguished love for Charles grew greater daily, and she found herself as imprisoned by it as ever Charles could be by Newgate walls. If I could pray, she thought, but private prayer was not natural to her. Prayers belonged in church on Sundays, which neither she nor Frank attended any more often than appearances required. So no prayers came, and her thoughts jumbled into a miserable weariness as she watched the flickering sky.

It was the first week in April before Jenny arrived, and by that time Betty had settled on the simplest lie with which to introduce the child into her home. One noon, instead of Simpson, Alec met her behind St. George's Church, and he had a fair-haired child by the hand. " 'Tis she, m'lady," said Alec in a whisper. "A bonny wee lass she is too."

Betty stared down at the five-year-old girl, and saw—with a violent constriction of the heart—Charles's features in delicate miniature. Brilliant gray eyes with long thick lashes, a clefted chin, silver-gilt curls, and full pink lips which looked made for laughter but were now trembling, while the round eyes stared anxiously at the lady. A beautiful child, a fairy child, she seemed to the astonished Betty. A very dirty and tattered child too. The bright hair was matted. Jenny's hands were filthy and chilblained. Her homespun dress was patched, her plaid shawl tattered, her oversize leather shoes were fastened on with thongs.

"Make your curtsey to her ladyship, as I told ye!" commanded Alec. Jenny bobbed her knees, and continued to stare at the gorgeous lady who was but one more of the extraordinary sights she had seen since she had left Coquetdale days and days ago and then gone to sea on a big collier at Newcastle.

"What's your name, my dear?" asked Betty quietly, giving Alec, who started, a look of warning.

"Jenny," said the child after a moment.

"Jenny what?" pursued Betty.

"Jenny Snawdon I'm a-thinking, though R-Robbie says 'tis not, 'tis—Rad—Rad . . ."

"No, Jenny," Betty cut in solemnly. "Now remember this. If anyone asks your name, just say Jenny. Nothing more. And you will say you were lost here by the church and I found you. Do you understand?"

"Aye," said Jenny, puzzled but acquiescent. Her lips quivered harder. "Be I lost, then? Yet I canna be lost because o' Robbie."

"*Who* is Robbie?" said Betty to Alec, casting a nervous glance behind her, though there were no passersby.

"A great gawking lad who shipped with us to London, m'lady. Worked his passage down," said Alec with some amusement. "He *would* come." Alec lowered his voice still further. "He said my master said he might. Moreover the wee lass is fond o' him, and he o' her."

"But that's dangerous!" Betty said frowning. "*Nobody* else must know who she is or connect her with me. Too many know now."

"You may trust Rob Wilson, m'lady," said Alec. "He'll not talk, and'll keep out o' the way. He wants to find work here in London."

"Well, then," she said unhappily, dismissing the unknown youth, "go to your master now, Alec. Tell him I'll manage to get there soon. And for the love of God, bring me news of him when you can."

"Aye, m'lady," said the valet with sympathy, and melted away around the church. Jenny looked after him, and began to cry.

Betty took the child's hand and murmured comfort, yet it was helpful that Jenny should be weeping when she was led up the steps of the Lees' George Street mansion, that big tears were rolling down her cheeks when Betty took her into the study, where Frank was writing a report on taxation for Walpole.

Frank looked up from his desk. Between the black curls of his full-bottomed wig, his smooth heavy face showed annoyance and surprise, for Betty never interrupted him and he disliked noisy children. "What's this, what's this?" he asked in his incisive voice.

Betty wisely did not answer. She pushed Jenny forward, and after a moment of astonished inspection, Frank's eyes softened, as she had expected. "Who in the world is this ragamuffin, Betty?" he said. "And why is she sobbing?"

"The poor little thing is lost. I found her by the church, as I came from the milliner's."

"Oh—" said Frank, pushing his paper aside and taking command. He enjoyed dealing with problems. "Well, we'll soon set that straight. Stop crying, little girl. You've nothing to fear. What's your name?" Betty held her breath and released it when the child said, "Jenny."

"But you've another name too?"

Jenny gave a great gulp. The lady was looking at her steadily, and did not want her to say more; besides, there was confusion about the name, and always had been, for though she was called Snowdon she had always known there was another name which her mother never mentioned. "I divven't reetly knaw," sobbed Jenny. "Oh, gin only R-Robbie

202

was her-re!" She covered her face with her hands, and Betty, stooping down, put an arm around the heaving shoulders.

"What a dialect she has," said Frank. "I can hardly understand her. From the North, of course—or is it Scotland?"

"We're na Scots," wailed Jenny, who had caught the hated word. "We're o' the Dale, fra Tosson."

"Wherever *that* may be!" said Frank. "Poor child, I suppose she *must* be lost." His voice was kind as he questioned Jenny further, and elicited a tale most satisfactory to Betty. Jenny said a man had taken her from "lang lang awa' on a ship" many days and nights ago, that he had run off in the churchyard just now, and the lady had led her here. The only dangerous moment passed unnoticed by Frank, for though Jenny reported that the lady and the man had talked with each other, she used the Northumbrian word "gobbing" which Frank did not understand. Besides he had made up his mind. "I believe she's been kidnaped," he said to Betty. "Doubtless by a gypsy, who meant to sell her in London. So pretty a child would always find a market. Deplorable! That she doesn't know her name would indicate that she's a bastard—the get of some nobleman, I judge, from the fineness of her features. I'll watch the *Gazette* and see if there's notice of her disappearance."

"And in the meantime, Frank?" said Betty quickly. "May I keep her here? There's a cot in the attic she can have, and I'm sure she'd be no trouble, would you, dear?"

Jenny shook her head. She had stopped crying, and was finding the arm around her comforting. Nobody had ever held her close like this. And the lady smelled good; she smelled like the wood violets up the burn at home, while the stuff of the yellow dress against Jenny's cheek was softer than lamb's wool. She felt the lady's heart beat fast as she waited for an answer, and Jenny knew suddenly that her own fate hung in balance. The gentleman in the black wig was frowning, tapping the tips of his fingers together. And the lady was afraid, Jenny knew it. She raised her head and looked full at the gentleman, and she smiled. "Nay, I'd ne'er trouble ye, hinny," she pleaded breathlessly.

Jenny's smile was like sunlight through clouds; it was a magic of direct communion with a hint of wistfulness. It was a smile which strove to charm, but was unconscious of its great power to do so.

Frank stared and forgot the objections he had been about to give Betty. That there were foundling homes for such cases as this, that the child was filthy, and it was unsafe to expose his own child to lice and disease, that there must be time to weigh the situation.

"She may stay a while," he said gruffly. "Make sure she's bathed at once, Betty, and I see she needs decent clothing. Here." He unlocked the petty-cash box on his desk and tendered Betty a guinea. "Get her what she needs."

"Thank you, my dear," said Betty, and thus was Jenny safely settled in the Lee household.

Charles threw off the last remnants of jail fever when he heard from Alec of Jenny's journey and safe arrival. He listened eagerly to every detail about his child, rejoicing that she was well, and regretting that he could not see her, but even had a visit been feasible he would not have subjected Jenny to Newgate and the sight of an imprisoned father. Yet now that the daze of shock over James's death receded, Charles became filled with strong desires. He wanted to avenge James—in this he never wavered. And he wanted to live. These were the first desires, only second to them and of more immediacy was the wish to see Betty. For this he hungered, and saw no reason why it might not be managed soon. Since bribery was the obvious method of arranging prison visits, and he knew that Betty's purse was straitened, he wrote to Ann, asking about the state of his own finances.

The little Countess was in Gloucestershire, and very ill with grief and pregnancy, but she wrote back a pathetic note, assuring him of her constant prayers, and enclosing a draft for one hundred guineas, which would be honored by Dilston's London agent, Mr. Robbourne; "though how to find more, or what my son and I would subsist on, were it not for my dear parents, I know not yet," she added. From which Charles understood that the Government had not decided on the full extent of punishment or how much of the Derwentwater estates would be forfeited. In the meantime here were funds again, and Charles's spirits rose. He conveyed the news to Betty through Alec, and they arranged a meeting for Wednesday evening, April 11. Always on Wednesday evenings Frank Lee went to St. James's Coffee-house to talk politics with the other Whigs who had made this particular coffeehouse their own. Since Lee's habits were invariable, Betty would thus have at least three hours in which to visit Newgate, and Alec, having hired discreet chairmen from the City, would accompany her through the streets. Muggles and the outer warden had already fixed their garnishes for permitting the visit, and Charles foresaw no difficulties.

On the Tuesday evening before this so-longed-for project, Charles decided to take advantage of the recreation permitted to the higher-class prisoners. Recreation which consisted of mounting to a large gloomy dungeon called the "Castle," where there were tables, benches, and a bar which served bad gin and worse beer for exorbitant prices.

The warder on the stairs unlocked the door for Charles, who stood a moment on the threshold, momentarily halted by the stench made by twenty unwashed men, by vomit, and by the stone latrine in a corner niche. Nor at first, in the light of five guttering candles, could he see exactly who was there. They all looked around and saw him: a tall handsome figure in a black mourning suit, his head held proudly, his flaxen wig tied with a black ribbon. There was a hush, then a low murmur of sympathy.

Charles Wogan, the young Irish captain, rushed forward extending his hand. "Ah, Radcliffe, 'tis good to see ye back with us again. And I speak for all. I needn't tell ye how we've sorrowed with ye since—since—" He broke off, unable to mention Lord Derwentwater's fate, while from the others came a chorus of embarrassed aye's and throat-clearings.

Charles said "Thank you" and sat down on a bench by Thomas Errington. He could now distinguish the company, and saw with relief that Tom Forster was not present. There were the Scots, old Mackintosh and three of his clan, sitting with the Irishmen, Wogan, Talbot, and Gascoigne—and Colonel Oxburgh. Oxburgh glanced at Charles, then looked away. He touched the crucifix at his throat, and stared silently again at the stone floor.

Charles next identified the other Jacobite prisoners present. Two Lancastrians whom he barely knew, and "Mad Jack" Hall of Otterburn, an eccentric Northumbrian who had never attracted him, now talking to Will Shaftoe of Bavington. Jem Swinburne sat on a stool watching three prisoners who were not Jacobites, as they cast dice, and cursed fluently in a thieves' cant largely unintelligible. These prisoners were a highwayman and two house robbers, all elegantly dressed in laced coats and ruffles. Young Swinburne was chained by his left ankle to an iron ring on the stone floor—a restraint due rather to his madness than his crime; none of the other privileged prisoners were fettered. Jem crooned to himself as he watched the robbers, and dabbling his fingers in his beer mug, flicked the suds on his sunken cheeks.

"Poor Jem," said Charles to Errington, "when I think of the wit and mirth he used to have at Capheaton—" Charles bit off his words. He had not come here tonight to brood over the past, nor yet, if possible, to worry over the future. He had come for what diversion he could find, and he rapped on the table and called to the frowzy convict drawer to bring him a drink. "Where's the rest of our company?" he asked briskly of Errington. "Where're the Claverings, and the young Widdringtons?"

Errington sighed. His meager conscientious face had sharpened during these weeks of imprisonment, and though he had fortitude and had never permitted himself to regret the moment at Beaufront when he had thrown in his fate with Lord Derwentwater, he had a vivid realization of what would probably be in store for him. "The Claverings are pardoned," he said. "The Widdringtons are withdrawn from here in custody of a messenger—Lady Cowper has much influence with the Lord Chancellor, her husband."

"So it would seem," said Charles grimly. He took a mouthful of the fetid gin the drawer had brought him, and spat it out in disgust.

"I have a record here," continued Errington, "of the disposition of various other prisoners captured at Preston." He took a notebook from his pocket, and read methodically from a list of names. Charles listened in growing dismay. In Chester and Lancaster and Liverpool, many of their original company had been executed already. Including the gentle George Collingwood, whom James had loved. A hundred or so of the wretched Highlanders and some Englishmen had been transported as convicts to Jamaica and Virginia, there to be sold into slavery. Many had died in the various prisons. Here at Newgate, George Gibson and Richard Butler were dead of jail fever, as well as Ned Swinburne. And the rest?

"Awaiting trial, as we are," said Errington, putting away his notebook.

"A pox on all this!" Charles cried violently. He jumped up. "Gentlemen, the drink is vile, but such as it is, you must all have one with me! You too, gentlemen," added Charles to the three robbers, who had turned around hopefully. "If you'll drink to King James and his rights!"

The highwayman stood up and made a bow. "We'll drink to the devil and the Black Mass if it suits your fancy, sir!"

After a half hour of concentrated effort most of the company had become roistering-drunk. Charles led the singing, which passed from Jacobite ditties to the bawdiest catches he could remember. The warder looked on indulgently, having been given a tin cup full of gin for himself. When there was a knock on the door he had some ado to insert the key. A stout figure pushed past him and entered the room.

Charles stopped in the middle of "So Molly's a Whore" and stared at Tom Forster—fatter and flabbier than ever—who stood by the doorway with a tentative expression on his pasty face.

"D'you smell a new stink?" asked Charles of the company at large. "Can it be a polecat has got in with us?"

Mackintosh and his friends roared, while Forster colored. He walked over to Charles and said nervously, "I heard you were in her-re, Radcliffe. I wanted to see ye."

"Well, you've seen me then," said Charles. "Now go back to the Keeper's lodging or whatever fine berth they've given you. Special guest of Newgate *you* are, my fine General!"

"Only suited to me rank," said Tom defensively. "Mr. Pitts treats me as a man o' rank, but that don't prevent—" He swallowed. "M'trial's coming up Saturday." His little piggy eyes grew round with fear, his pudgy hand crept inside his waistcoat and seemed to be fingering something hidden there.

" 'Tis true," said Errington. "He's to be tried the first of us, and isn't likely to get off."

" 'And so another one'll dance on Tyburn Tree, Tyburn Tree, Tyburn Tree,' " sang the highwayman suddenly. " 'Wi' a rope around his neck from Tyburn Tree . . . 'Tis where all good rogues end!' "

Forster shuddered, and leaned nearer Charles. "I don't know what to plead," he said. "What'll I plead in arrest o' judgment?"

"Why, damn you," said Charles. "Plead your belly, man! Plenty've got off that had not so large an excuse!"

Everyone except Oxburgh exploded into shouts of laughter. Old Mackintosh thumped his mug on the table in an ecstasy.

Forster stood silent. His mouth twitched, and then his right eyelid. "You all hate me," he said. " 'Tisn't fair. I couldna help what happened at Preston."

Mackintosh pushed over a bench and, jumping to his feet, shook a fist under Tom's nose. "Don't ye dare speak o' Preston, ye bluidy dastard!" he shouted. Tom stepped back hastily.

"Oh, leave him be!" said Charles, his own anger fading. "It seems he'll pay for Preston like the rest of us." And if so, Charles added to himself, it would prove that there was no actual treachery involved in Tom's surrender—only cowardice and stupidity.

"Will ye not let bygones be bygones, Charles?" Tom said, with some dignity. "Dorothy's here in London. She wanted me t'ask you that?"

"Dorothy?" Charles echoed in surprise. "Your sister, Dorothy? Ah—she's a loyal lass. I might've known she'd be here. Give her my love. Oh, sit down Tom. Have a drink!"

Forster nodded, and sat on the bench. Mackintosh and the Scots at once got up and moved to the far side of the room. Charles ordered a gin for Forster, who scarcely touched it. He seemed very nervous, and found nothing else to say. Ever and again he put his hand in his waistcoat, then snatched it out guiltily. Charles was a trifle puzzled but assumed that the imminence of trial would explain any strange behavior in a Tom Forster.

Just as the warder bawled out "Time, men! Time! Back to your cells!" Forster glanced at his silver watch and lumbered to his feet. "I must be off. Mr. Pitts is to have a night-cap wi' me in m'room." He looked at Charles as though he wished to add something else. His little eyes held a strange expression—of sorrow, of apology, of pleading. But all he said was "Farewell" and Charles noted that his voice was unsteady, though not from drink.

"Oh, no doubt we'll meet again," said Charles kindly enough. "There're some days yet before your trial." And tomorrow, Charles thought, Betty's coming! He went back to his cell, and after Muggles had turned the key, he indulged his excited thoughts, picturing Betty in his arms, her lips opening again under his, the smooth firm warmth of her body.

But Betty did not come on the morrow, because by morning Tom Forster had escaped from Newgate; Mr. Pitts, the Keeper, had been arrested; and the prison was barred, bolted, and guarded so that scarce a mouse could have slipped in.

It was thus for a week, during which time Charles was kept locked in his cell, as they all were. He did not see Alec. He saw nobody but Muggles, who was so frightened that even bribery could not move him to give any information. Then some of the precautions were relaxed. Charles was allowed the freedom of the Press Yard for exercise again, and he soon heard what had happened.

Someone had smuggled a duplicate key in to Forster. And of course it was this hidden key which Forster had been so nervously fingering on the night of his escape. Forster had put on his nightgown as though ready for bed. Then while he and Pitts were drinking in Forster's room, Forster had suddenly expressed urgent need for the latrine. Pitts had continued to drink and wait, while Tom locked him in with the duplicate key, then threw off his nightgown and fully dressed beneath, scurried down the back stairs to the outer door, which the same duplicate key unlocked. The Keeper's lodging opened onto the street. Tom had got off scot-free and, they said, was in France by now.

"And you know who Forster had to thank for *that* plan!" said Charles to Errington. "So simple and so ingenious. Who but Dorothy? *She* had the brains for it!"

"Aye," said Errington gloomily. "Though I warrant there was connivance too! Why'd the Government arrest Pitts, then release him? Why was there no warder outside the door? It may be Lord Crewe's money was more help than Miss Dorothy! It may be that the Crown didn't want to see another Protestant in the dock—which'll not help *us!*"

Charles was silent. His first flush of elation that any of them had escaped—even Forster—soon died. The fate of those left behind at Newgate was worse than ever for a while, and though Alec was presently allowed to come, and gave him news of Betty, no chance visitors were permitted in the criminals' side of the prison. Particularly after there was another escape, on May 4—just before Charles's trial.

Mackintosh engineered this one by cunning and brute strength. The old soldier bided his time, and each day when they were walking in the Press Yard watched for opportunities. He confided in nobody except his own Scots, yet some of the Irishmen got wind of the plan. Wogan was for including Charles, but Mackintosh forbade it. Essentially he trusted no Englishman, and Charles—rash, impetuous, and a Radcliffe, against whom the Crown had special animosity— would be a danger to them all. So it happened that Charles was not even in the Press Yard when the moment came. He had gone to see Jem Swinburne, who had plunged into another violent state and was chained in his cell.

Mackintosh waited until one afternoon when all visitors had left, and the warder on duty was a particularly small man and the sentinels were changing guard. Then he gave his wild Highland war cry, and fourteen men obeyed him in a desperate rush. Before the other prisoners understood what was happening, Mackintosh's clan had knocked out the warder, overpowered the other guards, and unbolting the gates, fled into the street. By the time the other warders came running, and the hue and cry started, Mackintosh, the Scots, and Wogan had got clear away, hiding in the rabbit warren of alleys and skulking-holes which surrounded the prison, and protected, no doubt, by Jacobite sympathizers. But eight of the fugitives were recaptured, hauled back to Newgate one by one, fettered, and thrown into the Condemned Hold. Mr. Pitts was censured for his laxness, the prison was closed up again to outsiders, and Charles chafed mightily.

On May 7, Charles and the remaining Jacobites were taken in closed coaches under heavy guard and arraigned at the Exchequer Bar for High Treason. Charles contemptuously pleaded "Not Guilty," and added a few insolent remarks of his own, as to the "person who is quite wrongly in possession of the British Crown for the nonce." He was returned to his cell in Newgate to await sentence on May 18. Before that, at midnight on Monday eve, Charles heard the jangling of the execution handbell and heard too the bell-man's whining dirge:

> *"All ye that in the condemned hold do lie*
> *Prepare ye for tomorrow ye shall die. . . ."*

Next morning the great death bell tolled from St. Sepulchre's and continued tolling while the execution cart rumbled west to Tyburn, where the prisoners were hanged. Colonel Oxburgh was among these prisoners, as were the elegant highwayman and the two robbers. Oxburgh, first of the Newgate Jacobites to be executed, was hanged and drawn and quartered, a medieval refinement inflicted only in cases of High Treason. He was cut down before he was dead, his bowels were burned before his eyes, his limbs were dismembered, and his head at last was impaled on Temple Bar. Much of London thronged to this show, and enjoyed it immensely. Charles, in his cell, first prayed for Oxburgh's soul, then got very drunk on brandy sent in by Alec.

On the Friday following, Charles was once more conveyed to Westminster Hall. As the coach passed through Temple Bar, he saw Oxburgh's head stuck up there—decaying but still recognizable. Charles's stomach churned; bitter fluid rose in his mouth. He turned to Thomas Errington, who was wedged next him in the coach. "I trust *my* pate will make a prettier sight," he said. "I'd hate to offend the ladies at my finish."

"How can you be so heartless," said Errington, covering his eyes with his hand. "When will they allow us a priest! Oh, Blessed Virgin, they *must* permit us a confessor!"

Charles was silent, uncertain whether they would or not. Then he began to speak very fast, pointing out that it was a fine sunny May day, that new buildings had sprung up along the Strand, the the girl by the coffeehouse had a neat waist and good upstanding bosom. He interrupted himself when their coach suddenly drew over to the curb and stopped. "What's this?" he said to the Newgate guard who sat opposite. The guard peered out.

"Why, 'tis His Majesty the King a-coming," the guard said reverently and took off his hat. Charles did not uncover. In his mourning suit and his black cocked hat he sat rigid, while the guards and the heralds and the outriders went by. Then came King George's two famous Turkish servants, Mohamet and Mustapha. They wore turbans and long skirts and carried scimitars. At last Charles saw the crowned coach, and heard the bystanders all huzzahing. The royal coach passed within two feet of them, and King George looked directly at Charles, who stared back, seeing the fleshy purple-veined face set above a thick neck and squat shoulders, the pop-eyes which gazed in astonishment at the defiant hatted young man. The King said something to the woman who towered beside him. Charles could hear a guttural German question. The woman, who was the King's "Maypole" mistress, the Schulenberg, must have explained who was in the prisoners' coach, for the muddy prominent eyes turned again on Charles with an expression of bland malignancy. The royal coach passed on towards the City.

"So *that*," said Charles, "that vulgar swollen German hog is what is called a king. *That's* what murdered my brother!"

"Mind your speech, sir!" cried the guard angrily. "Or ye'll rue it!"

"Bah!" said Charles. "The rue *I* feel is quite beyond *your* ken!"

And this, as it was later reported by all the news-sheets, was Charles Radcliffe's attitude throughout his extremely brief trial. It was in this spirit of mockery and impenitence that he watched the usher turn the sharp edge of the axe towards him, and that he received his sentence of death—by hanging, drawing, and quartering for High Treason. It was said that he even laughed in the judge's face.

Betty Lee heard of Charles's sentence from her husband the next morning at breakfast. "A foregone conclusion, of course, my dear," said Frank, motioning to the footman to pour him another cup of chocolate. "And they'll execute this final batch of traitors at once, I understand. Get through with it."

Beneath the table Betty twisted her hands in the folds of her skirt. She fixed her blind gaze on a silver dish full of mutton chops, and waited until the giddiness passed and she could control her voice.

"So *many* have been executed already," she said at last.

"To be sure." Frank speared himself a chop. "And too many have escaped. It's shocking. I can tell you Walpole is gravely concerned about it. Our prison system is rotten, corrupt to the core. Why, at my coffeehouse Wednesday I was chatting with a Virginia planter named William Byrd—quite a gentleman by the bye, for all he's a Colonial—and Mr. Byrd said . . ."

Betty did not hear what Mr. Byrd had said. She was desperately trying to think. The only hope was reprieve. Others under sentence of death had been reprieved several times. Like Lord Widdrington and Lord Carnwath, and Lord Winton. They were still in the Tower, but the first two would eventually be pardoned, everyone was sure of it. Not the Earl of Winton, though, for he had pleaded "Not Guilty." As had Charles! Oh, the imbecile. The stubborn, reckless fool! Through Alec she had warned him, she had begged him to be humble at his trial, to admit his guilt, and throw himself on the mercy of the Crown, who might then be satisfied with having killed his brother.

"What ails you, my dear?" said Frank, wiping his mouth and staring at her across the table. "You look very pale. And thin, it seems to me. Why don't you eat your breakfast?"

"I can't," she said. "Not hungry . . ." For a moment she had a violent desire to tell Frank everything, at least to ask him the best way to go about getting Charles reprieved. Frank would know, he had much influence—if she could persuade him—but before she gave way to the impulse, she saw his blue eyes harden, and coldness come into them. It was the look he gave an untrustworthy servant, or their little son when caught in a lie.

"Is it possible," said Frank slowly, "that you still have an undue interest in Charles Radcliffe? Because if so, I feel the sooner that dissolute traitor is out of this world the better—for your own peace of mind."

Betty stiffened, and terror gave her strength. "What a monstrous suggestion!" she cried. "What interest could I have in Mr. Radcliffe! After the way he used me! After the terrible things he's done! Frank, you know better than that!"

Her husband continued to eye her steadily. "I'm glad to hear you say so. But you've been a trifle distraught of late. It has occurred to me that you show strange discomposure when the rebels are mentioned."

"And why not!" she cried, tossing her head. "Can't one feel pity for gentlemen of rank who are dying ignoble deaths?"

She looked lovely as she gazed straight at him, her eyes flashing, her auburn curls quivering beneath the lace morning cap. Frank was suddenly convinced and he smiled. "Ah, you always have a tender heart, my love." He got up, and coming around the table kissed her on the cheek. "But you must *not* allow it to ache for the unworthy. And I'm concerned about your health. A change of air, I think. Take Harry and go to your father at Ditchley Park for a while. He's not well, and would be delighted to see you. Take Jenny too, if you like," he added kindly. "I know you're fond of the little thing."

Betty acknowledged her husband's kiss by a faint smile, and made a play of drinking her chocolate, while her frightened mind tried to cope with this new threat. Of all the times she must not be out of London now. "Why, I don't want to leave you alone here, Frank," she said. "I assume you won't go to Ditchley at present?" She held her breath while she waited for his answer.

"No," he agreed. "It would be unwise. Since the King is off to Hanover, and the Prince is seeking regent's powers in his father's absence. The situation for the Whigs may be ticklish."

Here Betty had a sudden gleam of hope, and her heart beat fast as she nodded intelligently and said, "Ah yes. The Prince and Princess of Wales incline towards the Tories, don't they!"

"The Prince inclines towards anything that will annoy his father!" Frank snapped. "Most unfilial. My dear, this has nothing to do with you. Where your health is in question, I don't hesitate to sacrifice my comfort. I'd miss you but I insist that you go. You look quite ill, dear!"

"I'm *not*," she cried in desperation. "It's just that I believe I'm breeding. You know how nervous women are at these times, and I couldn't bear to be cooped up in the country!"

Frank looked astonished, and then very pleased. It had been three years since his heir, little Charles-Henry, was born. "Why, Betty—" he said tenderly. "What excellent news. I'd no idea. Of course that explains—and you must do precisely as you wish in all things. A Venice treacle is what you should take, treacle with pounded viper flesh to strengthen you. I beg you will send to the apothecary for it at once."

"Oh, I will," said Betty on a sigh of relief, and Frank in high good humor kissed her again and left her alone.

So—more lies, Betty thought. She had this very morning found evidence that she was *not* with child. The situation would have to be explained later, yet in the meantime she had gained at least a month of free action in London.

While the footmen hovered nervously by the sideboard, Betty sat on at the littered breakfast table, her thoughts pounding this way and that in search of some plan for Charles's reprieve.

An hour later Betty was ready, dressed to go calling. She had goaded her waiting woman, Mrs. Clark, into unseemly haste, and rushed through all the elaborate ritual of hair-dressing, painting and powdering, the pulling in of stays, the donning of silk stockings and jeweled red-heeled shoes. Then to Clark's amazement, her mistress had demanded to wear the new embroidered gold paduasoy, the best cap of Mechlin lace, the pearl necklace and drop earrings. She also demanded her two diamond rings, and her French fan with the gold sticks.

Wherever can we be off to? thought Clark with great interest, though her ladyship was so frowning and hurried the waiting woman didn't dare ask. Clark was a stout, comely person of forty who considered life dull in the Lee household, never a bit of flirting or intrigue to liven one up. Not at all the sort of fashionable home other waiting women managed to find. Though the wages were good, and her ladyship usually sweet-tempered.

Betty ran downstairs and was crossing the hall towards the door when she heard a child crying. Betty stopped and looked around, thinking it was little Harry. But it was Jenny whom she finally spied huddled in a nook under the stairs.

"What is it, dear?" said Betty painfully struck anew by the likeness to Charles in the exquisite little face. "Has someone been unkind to you?"

Jenny shook her head, on which the silver-gilt curls were now properly clean and brushed. "No, m'lady. 'Tis just that

I want R-Robbie so, an' he niver-r comes."

Betty felt mingled sympathy and impatience. Of course the poor child was still strange and lonely, and it was a pity that Betty had had little time for her—but there was certainly none now. "Someday, I promise you, you'll see your precious Robbie," she said more sharply than she meant. "Now go to the nursery and you may play with Master Harry!" She hurried through the door into her chair. The child looked after her with round eyes, startled out of her own grief. Clear as spring water, she knew that her ladyship was unhappy and frightened. How odd that it could be so. If Robbie was here he might tell her what it meant. Robbie had always explained things when she asked him, back in that far-off Northern land where lived her silent, dour mother and uncles and her mad old grandfather. She hadn't missed them on the long journey down here, because on the ship she saw Robbie every day when he wasn't running up the mast, or hauling on the sails. But here she missed her family, for there was nobody to talk to. Master Harry was a baby still. And the servants made fun of her speech.

In her luxurious blue-upholstered chair, Betty sat tense while her liveried chairmen carried her towards St. James's Palace. This was the only plan she had found—a bold venture and a supreme gamble. She had explored and discarded all the other possibilities. The elderly Earl of Peterborough, he was a good friend of hers in his worldly bantering way; but Lord Peterborough was at the ebb of one of his periodic fortune changes. He was totally out of favor at Court, and had gone off to the Continent. The new Marquis of Wharton then? His father had been a famous Whig, and a cousin of her own; he had even lived at Ditchley. But no, Philip Wharton was too young, only eighteen, and too unprincipled. Lady Cowper again? Never. The last interview when Betty had pled for Lord Derwentwater had been decisive. Lady Cowper announced that she had already done what she dared for some of the rebels, and was weary of the topic. She also expressed astonishment that the wife of so good a Whig as Colonel Lee should concern herself with such matters. An awkward moment, which Betty had contrived to shrug off, praying that Frank would never hear of it. Fortunately, he had little contact with the Cowpers. His great friends were Robert Walpole, and Walpole's brother-in-law, Lord Townshend, the Secretary of State.

Betty knew nobody else who might have power. She had never moved in Court circles, and beyond a formal presenta-

215

tion to Hanoverian royalty after the Coronation she had never gone to St. James. Frank preferred it so, he deplored the morals and levity of fashionable life.

Betty looked up to see that her chair had stopped at the Prince of Wales's entrance to St. James's Palace, where the Prince shared cramped quarters with his father the King. Her running footman nodded to the guards and accosted the porter. The porter disappeared and presently told her footman that the ladyship might enter. That Her Royal Highness was still holding levee.

Betty entered the Palace and followed a page up the stairs to a small anteroom crammed with people. There were a milliner and a goldsmith, each holding their boxed wares for the Princess' later inspection. There was a starveling poet come to beg for patronage. There was a country squire from Somerset, his accent unmistakable, as he boomed a grievance into the bored ears of a simpering young beau who twirled a muff and pomander ball, and occasionally inhaled snuff. There was a German gentlewoman with a face like a sheep, who kept glancing nervously at the letter of recommendation someone had given her.

Betty gave her name to the vice-chamberlain. "Urgent business," she added, feeling angry looks from the others who all had "urgent business" of their own. Betty's name meant nothing to the vice-chamberlain, though he was impressed by her title and dress. After a slight delay he bowed her into the Bed Chamber, which was large and also filled with people. Three giggling and very pretty maids of honor were playing cards by the window and chattering loudly. A fiddler scraped away at tunes from Handel's *Rinaldo*. There were two waiting maids fussing over a stain on a white brocaded petticoat. A stout florid blonde in a pink silk nightrobe must certainly be the Princess. Her breasts were like pumpkins, her belly round with early pregnancy. She was not as handsome as they said; her skin was rough, but the cascading yellow hair and large sky-blue eyes were pleasing. The Princess sat on the edge of her canopied bed trying on embroidered slippers and smiling absently at the importunate words of a blowzy middle-aged woman with an elaborate headdress of dyed brassy hair. This woman kept pointing towards a handsome foreign-looking youth, who stood awkwardly by the wardrobe, and seemed embarrassed.

For some moments, nobody paid the slightest attention to Betty, and the announcement of her name went unheard in the din of talk and violin. Then the raddled woman with dyed hair looked around, and Betty, with a woeful shock, recognized her. The Duchess of Bolton! Now Betty remembered that the Duchess was one of the Princess' ladies-in-waiting, but as there were seven of these, and they rotated their duties, it was appallingly bad luck to encounter this particular one.

Betty stood stock-still while the Duchess came up to her, and spoke in the remembered cooing voice. "You wish to see her Royal Highness? I did not hear your name, but—but there's something familiar . . ."

There was a strong smell of brandy on the Duchess' breath, the once beautiful sapphire eyes were bloodshot and peered myopically through pouched lids. Betty realized that she—though happily in a different way—had changed as much as the Duchess. That this new disaster might still be averted. Though not if she gave her name, which must be forever associated with Charles in the Duchess' memory, and with the vile trick Henrietta had played on the young people on the night of the sham robbery in the ducal coach.

"Spelsbury," said Betty quickly, using the lowest of her father's titles. "I'm Mrs. Spelsbury from abroad. On my way to London I heard something which would interest Her Royal Highness, I'm sure."

"Vat does she vant, Duchess?" called Princess Caroline, standing up and flexing her big feet in the new slippers. "And how many more uff them are outside vaiting to see me?"

The Duchess was thus distracted from Betty to her own problems, which concerned the handsome young Frenchman, for whom she had a consuming passion, and whom she was persuading the Princess to appoint as Dancing Master. "There's no one of consequence outside, ma'am," she said returning to the Princess. "And if you would only deign to watch Monsieur Alexandre dance, you would see how able and graceful—"

"Oh, go avay, Duchess!" interrupted the Princess with a good-humored laugh. "Alvays with you, there is some *able*, graceful young man to be placed here—*nicht wahr?*" She waved her hand in dismissal. "No doubt you vish to show him the ballroom *yourself?*"

Into the Duchess' flabby face there came a look of lascivious satisfaction. She walked to the young man and put her hand coaxingly on his arm. They went out together, and Betty was spared.

She went resolutely up to the Princess and, seeing that

nobody was very near them, abandoned all pretense. "Your Royal Highness," she whispered curtseying, "I'm in great trouble. Only you can help me!"

The Princess frowned. Day in, day out they came, the place-seekers, the intriguers, the petitioners, and especially of late—now that everyone knew the King was leaving the country and that the Prince would be temporarily in control.

"Vat is it you vant?" said the Princess impatiently. "A position? For you or a friend?"

"No," said Betty. She clenched her hands. "I want a human life—oh madam, madam—" her voice broke, and tears started to her eyes.

The Princess stared, and recognized real suffering, a rare emotion at Court. Moreover, her interest was piqued. "Tell me," she said, "of vat do you speak?"

Betty glanced at the maids of honor, at the fiddler, at the kneeling shoemaker who had brought the slippers, at the waiting women who were smoothing the coverlet on the bed, and watching her curiously. "If I might see you alone—" she whispered. "Dear madam—I'm so afraid . . ."

"Vell," said the Princess after a moment, "come into my dressing room. Ve can be private there!"

The others in the Bed Chamber looked around as Betty followed the Princess. Mary Lepel, the prettiest of the maids of honor, laughed, shrugged her shoulders, then played a card. The Princess had many whims, she took sudden fancies to people, and her German ways were sometimes startling. So nobody in the room thought anything in particular of this signal attention. The Duchess of Bolton would have been instantly suspicious, but she was elsewhere occupied.

In the dressing room while the Princess sat and toyed with a comb, Betty stood by the gold inlaid toilet table and poured out all her story.

Princess Caroline listened carefully, and at the end when the flood of relief at having told someone at last forced a gasping sob from Betty, the Princess produced her own hand-kerchief and offered a whiff of smelling salts. "So—" she said thoughtfully, "I see, my dear. You vish to save this Radcliffe, and your husband must not know it."

Betty bowed her head. "It is so, madam." She knelt down by the embroidered slippers and clasped her hands in the unconscious immemorial gesture. "I beg of you to help me."

"Vy should I help you?" said the Princess watching her narrowly. "So that you may then undermine the throne—as

218

this cousin of yours whom you love has tried to do?"

"No! No!" cried Betty. "I swear it on my soul. I'm as loyal to the Crown as my husband is. But death, madam! Another horrible, shameful death when there have been so many—surely the King has revenged himself enough! Have mercy, now!"

The Princess was silent, while her shrewd mind considered the situation. These continuing Jacobite executions were most unpopular; only the King and his rigidly Whig ministers, Walpole, Townshend, really approved them. Upon entering the qualified regency, which was all his father would permit, the Prince intended to show England how much more sympathetic he was to the people than the King, how much better fitted to rule. Some small gesture like this might be valuable, and would also annoy Walpole, whom the Prince disliked intensely. Moreover, though she was shrewd, Caroline was full of German sentiment, and the predicament of this young woman—an earl's daughter, it seemed—moved her very much.

She put her hand on Betty's shoulder. "But vat can I *do*, Lady Elizabeth? The King vill not listen to me."

"But His Royal Highness *will!*" cried Betty. "Oh dear madam, everyone knows how much influence you have with the Prince!"

Caroline raised her eyebrows and smiled. "Perhaps—" she said. "But there is no hope of pardon, you know that? Especially for *this* young man who vas an English ringleader and is a Catholic Stuart too."

"Reprieve," said Betty faintly, her mouth twisting. "If we could have time—until—"

"Until?" repeated the Princess frowning. "I do not vish to know vat you mean by that, Lady Elizabeth. I vish to hear nothing more about this matter. It is forgotten."

"Forgotten!" Betty cried in a panic. "Then I've failed. Oh madam, you mean I've failed?"

The Princess rose, pulled her nightrobe around her, extended a hand, and raised Betty from her knees. "No, you haff *not* failed," she said quietly.

NINE

During the next weeks several of the Jacobites in Newgate, including Richard Gascoigne and Jack Hall of Otterburn, were hanged, drawn, and quartered. At each official summons to execution, Charles expected to be chained and thrown in the Condemned Hold with the others. Each time his name was not on the list. Muggles was loud and somewhat admiring in his wonder. "Saving ye fer dessert—that's wot they're a-doing, sir! I never thought ye'd be 'ere this long, stroike me dead if I did!"

Charles said that he heartily wished something *would* strike Muggles dead, and himself too, for this damned strain was getting intolerable.

The turnkey took this as a pleasantry. He was getting rather fond of Charles, who still tipped him well, and he said, "Don't ye be getting nervy now, wile there's life there's 'ope, I allus say, an' wot you need is to see that 'sister' o' yours agen— 'andsome figger of a trollop she was!"

Charles flung around in his cell, poured some claret, and did not answer. Muggles touched on a very sore point. Betty had still not been to see him. Some weeks ago, right after his death sentence, she had sent a strange little note by Alec, written in a disguised hand. It said, "My darling, you will be reprieved. Count on it. More of this when I can come. Dear God, let that be soon."

But she hadn't come. Alec said that she had left London, had been summoned to the sickbed of her father, the Earl of Lichfield. That the whole Lee household had left George

Street, except the underservants. And Charles—uncertain what was really going on, ceaselessly brooding and magnifying trifles—felt betrayed and deserted. It might be that Betty had helped him, at least he was still alive, though that might also be chance, since a few other condemned Jacobites had not been summoned. Tom Errington was of those spared so far, and one afternoon in August he met Charles in the dungeon called the "Castle," the only common room where the condemned men were occasionally permitted. They no longer had the freedom of the Press Yard. "Did you see this?" asked Tom, shoving an old dirty news-sheet at Charles. "The Earl of Winton's got out of the Tower!"

"What!" cried Charles gaping. "But I thought he was beheaded! 'Tis past the date for it!"

"Well, look," said Errington. Charles, in the dim guttering candlelight, peered at several lines of print. It appeared that on August 4, George Seton, Earl of Winton, had contrived to saw through his iron window bars with a watch spring, being of a mechanical turn of mind and having pursued low trades like blacksmithing in his youth. Under cover of night he had somehow crept down the walls and swum the moat. Nor had he yet been recaptured.

"Ah-h-h," said Charles on a long breath. The two men stared at each other silently. Charles looked around the dungeon, as he had many times. The stone walls were three feet thick, there were no windows, no ventilation but the fireplace (which was barred at the chimney breast), and a little grilled hole in the wall which gave onto the passage. A turnkey stood always inside the door, which was locked and bolted. Another turnkey was outside in the passage. Between here and the cells were many barred doors, with warders stationed at each of them.

"No use," agreed Errington in a whisper, having followed Charles's thoughts. "Nor in our cells."

Charles tightened his lips and gave a discouraged grunt. Well he knew, from repeated investigation, how escape-proof Newgate cells were. If one did manage to saw the window bars nothing was gained, since no head could force through the five-inch-wide slit. As for the chimney in his cell, it was not only barred, but was too small to admit the tiniest of chimney sweeps.

"If they'd let us in the Press Yard again," muttered Charles.

"They won't. Not after Mackintosh broke out."

"There'd be only one way then," said Charles. He put his

hand in his pocket and jingled the few shillings that were there.

" 'Twould take a fearful lot," said Errington sighing. "And even then 'twouldn't work now. Pitts is scared, and the turnkeys too, they'd not risk it. Anyway I've not *got* it."

"Nor I," said Charles scowling. Ann's hundred guineas had been faithfully brought by Alec in driblets, since it would naturally be dangerous for any large amount to be kept here. The guineas were almost gone. Five months of food, drink, and tips, besides provision for Alec outside, had absorbed them. "I'll have to write Ann again," said Charles. "She can't mean me to rot here on bread and water—or is she waiting for Tyburn Tree to save her the trouble!"

"That's unfair," said Tom in his judicial way. "Her ladyship would send to you if she could. She has nothing but what her parents can give her, and *they* are much embarrassed now."

"I know," said Charles. And besides, Ann had borne her posthumous child—a girl—in May and was still quite ill. Charles rose abruptly and walked to the corner latrine. When he came back he sat down again on the bench beside Tom. "Did you know there's a small iron door, over there?" he asked in an excited whisper. "Hidden in the angle behind the privy. I felt it, though it's too dark to see. Where could it lead?"

Tom frowned in concentration. "Can it be the women's prison? Yet, no, I think not. That's further back beyond the Press Yard. This 'Castle' we're in is the oldest part, though I don't know what it adjoins."

"Uh-m," said Charles thoughtfully. "Move that candle to the edge of the table. Pretend to read. I must have more light in there." Tom obeyed. Charles started back towards the latrine. The turnkey called out sharply, "What ails ye, sir? Got the gripes? For sure it can't be the gleet, since ye've 'ad no chance to pox yourself in many a month!"

This sally was greeted with laughter by the other prisoners, two well-dressed rogues who had been conferring in hoarse whispers.

Charles shrugged and grinned. "You're quite a wit, warder," he said. "But d'you wonder a man should leak a bit after this foul drink you sell us?" And he retreated again to the niche.

The turnkey, whose name was Black, dubiously watched him go. He had been warned to keep a sharp eye on Mr. Radcliffe, who was by far the most important of the state prisoners. A big swaggering young fellow he was too, tricky no doubt, and should be in leg irons, no matter his rank or pocketbook. Black was one of the new turnkeys, hired over Mr. Pitt's head as a result of the escape scandals. He was eager to succeed at his job, ambitious to be Keeper himself someday, likely as not.

Charles came back and joined Errington, though as Black was obviously listening he said nothing until the turnkey was called to the door. Then Charles muttered, "It's no good, of course. I could see a little. The door's all rusted into the wall, bolted fast, I can't budge the bolts, locked too—and I suppose from t'other side—wherever that is."

As Errington did nothing but nod glumly, Charles got up again and walked over to the two ordinary prisoners. They looked up from their beer mugs in surprise. The short pockmarked one—scarcely more than a youth—quirked a sandy eyebrow at Charles. The older man, who was known as "Blueskin," either from the denseness of his ill-shaven black beard or the tattooed anchors on his arms, said, "Damme, if 'ere's not one o' the Jacks deigning to notice us common prigs!"

"Aye," said Charles pleasantly, sitting down. "Why not? We're all in the same boat."

"Not *us*, mate!" said Blueskin tossing his greasy head. "We'll be up at Old Bailey soon, then out o' 'ere, afore ye can sye 'gammon.'"

"How so?" asked Charles, fingering his remaining shillings and deciding to sacrifice one. "Have another beer?"

The offer accepted, and good will being thus engendered, Charles presently learned several facts about his companions. They were professional thieves, "gentlemen prigs," as Blueskin asserted smugly. There wasn't a house in London he couldn't rifle, if he'd a mind to, said Blueskin, nor a watch, ring or snuffbox he couldn't nab. This temporary inconvenience—here Blueskin waved his dirty hand around the dungeon—was the result of a little mishap. But they'd get off at their trial, no doubt of that. At very worst there might be a sentence of transportation to Virginia.

"How can you be so sure?" asked Charles enviously. Blueskin shrugged and winked and said it was a good thing to have a friend outside.

The turnkey, Black, listened to what he could of this conversation, though he was not interested in Blueskin's boastings, which he knew to be true enough. These two prigs were of the gang run by Jonathan Wild, the "Thieftaker." Wild would get them off, as he had so many. By bribery, false witness, and knowledge of loopholes in the law, Wild had built up an elaborate and lucrative machine. And yet he managed to present himself as the champion of the victimized public. Was a nobleman's gold watch stolen? All that was needed was a plea to Jonathan Wild. Some days later the watch would be returned, and the Thieftaker rewarded for his good offices by a fee. Occasionally he produced a culprit to justify his title, but the victim, delighted to have his property back at small cost, seldom wished to prosecute. And if, as in the case of these two, any of Wild's gang landed in jail, the subsequent trial was never in doubt. All of this was no business of Black's. Nor could he see why Mr. Radcliffe should concern himself with members of the underworld. Black mulled it over and hovered near, but heard nothing suspicious. Charles uttered only encouraging grunts, while Blueskin told of his exploits. It was not until the turnkey had wandered to the beer keg to get himself a draught, that Charles casually brought out the question he had come over to ask.

"That wall," he said, indicating the direction with his eyes, "would you know what's on the other side? I take it you gentlemen are well acquainted with Newgate."

"S'truth, mate," agreed Blueskin. "I been in an' out o' the old Whit sence I was a tot. That'll be the debtors' prison, t'other side the wall. Me uncle was in there oncet."

"Oh," said Charles. "The debtors aren't locked up as we are, are they?"

"Naw," said Blueskin. "Lotta coming an' going. Family and friends can visit any time. Like to change over, you sly young cat's meat, eh?" Blueskin slapped Charles's thigh, and chuckled.

"I would," said Charles, and after a few more remarks he left the two alone.

From then on he thought a great deal about the little door. It prevented him from wondering, each time Muggles entered his cell, whether Pitts was surely behind with the summons to execution. It prevented him from brooding over Betty's defection, and the whereabouts of Jenny. It almost prevented him from worrying over the state of his finances. But as Alec, who came every other day to shave him and bring him food, grew each time longer-faced and gloomier, Charles could not long ignore his poverty. They had already pawned Charles's gold watch and silver snuffbox. Yet Charles was still in arrears to Mr. Pitts for payment of his private cell, and Muggles, untipped for a week, was growing surly.

One morning, Alec came in even more frowning and anxious. His woolen suit was shabby, his stockings darned, his dark brown hair tied back with tape. He put a basket of withered peaches on the table. "Got 'em off a barrow in Covent Garden, sir," he said shaking his head. " 'Twas all I'd pence for. I've been to Mr. Rodbourne, and he won't advance anything. Says the Crown's impounded all the estates, and if they *hadn't*, each shilling must be saved for his young lordship—and there's the entail."

Charles frowned. It was natural that Ann and the Webbs should fight for her children's security, that all their concentration should be on the future of little John, now the titular fourth Earl of Derwentwater. Yet did they realize what the lack of cash would reduce Charles to? Leg irons, a handful of straw in a dungeon with some twenty vicious and diseased criminals, a crust of moldy bread from time to time, no drink except a dipperful of tainted slimy water.

Yes, they must realize this, since he had written it to them, but Charles guessed they had given him up for dead anyway. And that no pain this thought could cause them would be important after the pain of James's death.

"Ye must write to Lady Mary Radcliffe, sir," said Alec sighing. " 'Tis the only hope. Mr. Rodbourne says he thinks she still has funds despite they're stripping all the Catholics."

"No use," said Charles. "That old bitch ever hated me."

"But you're her nephew, sir," Alec coaxed. "Her ladyship is strong for family ties. Pray, try it. I saved enough pennies for the post."

"Oh Alec," said Charles faintly, "you're the only friend I've got. I dare not ask how *you* are subsisting now that I've failed to provide for you."

"Never fear for me, sir," said Alec with the ghost of his old jaunty grin. "Matter o' fact, I've bedded in at Wapping wi' Rob Wilson—the lad from Northumberland. He's got a job unloading coal at the docks, and has got me one. 'Twill bring in a few shillings."

Charles was stricken by this new proof of Alec's loyalty. He thought of the old carefree days in London, when Alec dressed in dark satin suits, wore a tie-wig and discreetly laced hat, and was the perfect "gentleman's gentleman"; when his hands were as white, his manner as debonair, and his amusements as sophisticated as his master's.

"It's degrading for you, Alec," said Charles sadly. "How can you bear it!"

"Not hard at all, sir," said Alec. "Rob he's a fine canny lad. Sometimes he plays me the pipes, then we talk o' the North—of Tyneside, and—Dilston." Alec went on quickly as he saw his master wince. "As for the job. Well, Rob, he won't go for a 'prentice, won't bind himself down for all he's so young and able. He wants to make money, and buy himself land on Tyneside, set up for a squire someday and wipe the eye of Black Will Cotesworth."

"Cotesworth?" said Charles wondering, so far past was the time he had met the grim colliery owner, so far past seemed even the arrival of the bailiffs Cotesworth sent to Dilston to catch James last October. "So 'tis Rob Wilson's ambition to be a squire? Heaving coal at London docks scarce seems a step in that direction."

" 'Tis all that we can find just now," said Alec. "Needs must." The valet's eyes twinkled bravely, but his mouth was pinched, drawn into a lopsided smile.

Charles turned and went to the table. "I'll write to Lady Mary," he said. "I'll write to her now."

It was on Charles's twenty-third birthday, Monday, September 3, that the bleakness of his life was lightened, though he awoke to despair. Pitts refused to extend further credit for the private cell, or to admit Alec again. Tomorrow Charles must move to the common dungeon. The privilege of the "Castle" had already been denied him, so he had no further opportunities to inspect the little door. Muggles never came near him except to shove a jug of filthy water into the cell. Charles had lived for two days on the sausage and bread Alec had brought on his last visit. From Lady Mary there had been no answer.

In the morning Charles marked off his calendar, and saw that it was his birthday, also that he had been nine months less six days in Newgate. There was nothing to read except tattered pages from the Bible the prison chaplain had left here long ago. And no light to read by. The last stub of candle burned out while he marked the calendar. Charles took to pacing his cell. Six paces this way, four that way. Every third time around he rewarded himself by pressing his face against the barred slit of window. Way up and beyond the massive stone wall outside he could see an inch of blue sky. Ever and again he interrupted his ritual to listen while St. Sepulchre's bell bonged out the hour. At two o'clock he stopped pacing and lay down on the cot. There he finished the last crumbs of bread and sausage.

Shortly afterward he heard a noise outside his door; the raucous voice of Muggles, and the grating of the bolts. Pitts at last, Charles thought. To announce my execution tomorrow! For a second he was flooded with relief, and a wild desire to laugh; the next instant the relief vanished and Charles was shaken by a heart-pounding animal fear. His muscles locked and he sat rigid on the cot while the key turned and the door opened letting in light.

The turnkey came in with a candle, and gave a great laugh when he saw Charles staring at him. "Naow then, sir," he said in a voice Charles had not heard in weeks. "Perk up! Wot a wye to greet a lydy!"

"Lady?" repeated Charles stupidly, still gazing past Muggles to find the figure of Pitts.

"Your sister!" said Muggles, and he bowed low, as Betty in her cloak, hood, and mask walked by him. "An' a fine generous 'earted lydy she is!"

Charles swallowed and stared at Betty, until the turnkey shut the door, then he said, "I scarce expected to see *you* again!"

She threw off her mask and cloak, and going to him took his hands in hers. "I couldn't write, Charles. It wasn't safe, and I didn't know where Alec was. But, darling, I knew you weren't in danger, and Charles—what is it?" She broke off. "Aren't you glad to see me?"

"For months I longed and waited," said Charles. "And then I ceased to think about you—as you and others have ceased to think about me."

Betty withdrew her hands, stung by the unfairness of this. Then she saw how thin he was, how pallid, and she remembered that he knew nothing of all that she had done for him.

"Lisen, dear," she said gently. "My father's dead. He died July fourteenth, and we've all been in Oxfordshire, at Ditchley Park."

"Jenny too?" asked Charles quickly. At times during the miserable broodings, he decided Betty had gone back on her word and got rid of Jenny.

"Of course, Jenny too," she said beginning to understand. "The child is blooming, she loved the country—oh, Charles, you *couldn't* think I'd really forgot you when I—every moment—I—even at my poor father's funeral—" She broke off. Her golden-brown eyes misted. She put her hand to her mouth.

"Forgive me," said Charles flushing. He took her hand and kissed it. "This world of black shadows—I've lost my way. I've become a boor. My deepest sympathy, Betty, for the loss of your father."

"Thank you," she whispered, so bemused by the touch of his lips on her hand, that it was with effort she went on. "I was his favorite child, and he left me a legacy. Several thousand pounds. Frank will administer most of it, of course, but I've managed to get a thousand now, for myself. George talked Frank into letting me have it."

"George?"

"George-Henry, my eldest brother, who is now the Earl of Lichfield. Charles, he's a friend to you, and he has not forgotten that we are kin and share a royal grandfather. During those weeks while we were at Ditchley, I told him a little about you. He's in love with a Catholic himself—Frances Hales. He'll marry her now that Father's gone. Do you see what a difference this makes?"

"Not entirely," said Charles. "Except that you look much happier, and have come into money, which I've begun to see is an essential commodity."

"But it's for *you*, you idiot!" Betty cried. "What else would I want with a thousand pounds! It's to get you out of here, and if it isn't enough, George will give me more. I know it."

"Holy Saint Mary," Charles whispered, ashamed that he had doubted Betty, and feeling in his vitals the churning of a wild hope. "I don't know—" he murmured. "It might work, yet, my dear girl, when could I pay you back—and your husband—won't he question?"

She shook her head. Frank was easier to manage now. Not only because of this delight at her legacy, but the other thing. During the sequestered days of mourning at Ditchley, she had often wondered if her other lies for Charles were forgiven, since one of them had been so surprisingly made fact. She had not been pregnant in May when she told Frank so, yet she was now. No doubt of it, and Frank had not even questioned her premature revelation. Such womanish discrepancies did not interest him. And he had indulgently acceded to her wish to do as she pleased with a small part of her legacy. "Don't worry about Frank," Betty said quickly. "Think what's to be done here. You must know a way . . ."

"Perhaps," Charles said slowly. "Though it'll take time. They'll hang me first."

"They *won't*," she cried. "Charles, I told you that they won't! Listen." In a few hurried words she recounted her visit to the Princess Caroline. "So, you see, I think you're safe until the King returns," she finished. "They say he may come back for Christmas—and oh, my love, we must plan fast!"

"Yes," said Charles looking at her steadily. "But not right now." He raised his arms and drew her against his chest. Into the kiss he gave her he put all the fervor of his gratitude. Betty yielded her lips, then as she looked into the gray eyes so close to hers, and saw them narrow with passion, she gave a little whimper in her throat. Her bones and sinews seemed to melt in the sweetness which ran through her body. She forgot the dank prison cell, she did not feel the cot's lumpy straw against which her shoulders were pressed. She knew only the beloved weight of his body on hers, and the wild joy of surrender. He had torn open her silken bodice and was kissing her breasts, when suddenly he gave a shuddering groan and sprang away from her. He got off the cot and pounded his clenched fist on the table. "Betty, I cannot!" he cried in a voice as rough as anger. "Cannot take *you* here like this. Like a common whore. I love you too much. I owe you too much."

She lay tense, quivering, looking at him mutely while the blood pulsed in her throat.

For some minutes there was no sound in the cell, except the heavy rasp of his breathing, and the sputtering of the candle. Then she pulled her bodice over her breasts and sat up slowly, while the long auburn curls fell on her shoulders. "You're right, Charles," she said faintly. "More right than you know." The babe, she thought. The new one which was in her womb. On the night of its conception, she had been thinking of Charles. And ever since, in the secret recesses of her soul, she had thought of the babe as belonging to Charles. A pitiable delusion. "Indeed," she said quickly, "my love for you leads me down many a strange and shameful path."

He walked back and sat beside her on the cot. He took her long white hand in his, and turning it over kissed the pink, fragrant palm.

"Someday—Betty," he said, "when I am not a condemned traitor in Newgate's stinking jail, someday if I am free. Ah, dear God, if we might *both* be free—in France perhaps—in the sunshine—in Italy . . ."

She bowed her head against his shoulder, and they sat silent. For each of them the prison wall dissolved and they saw beyond it the deep blue skies, the flooding gold of southern sunlight which they had never seen in reality. Passion had left them both; they sat like two children lost in their dream. Then Betty roused herself, and looked up into his face with a sad little smile.

"Before that day could come, my dear one," she said, trying to speak lightly, "there are certain considerations.

229

Earlier—earlier this afternoon, you said you had some plan for escape. Tell me now what it is."

Muggles, much gratified by all the guineas with which Betty had bribed him, and accurately foreseeing that Mr. Radcliffe would once again be in funds, did not disturb the two in the cell until six o'clock.

By that time they had concocted and discarded several plans, and finally settled on the most likely procedure.

They kissed goodbye, a quick embarrassed kiss, since both were afraid of the urgent flame in their bodies. But they smiled at each other with hope, and, after Betty had left, Charles sat for a long time staring at the purseful of gold she had given him. Then he got up and banged on the iron door until Muggles came and peered through the grating. "Wot's up, gov'nor?"

"Tell Mr. Pitts I wish to see him at once!" said Charles at his most lordly. "And bring me some coal, candles, and meat. Wine too, if you can find any!"

"Aha!" said the turnkey, his bulbous face splitting into a grin. "There's bin a change in the wind, I see!"

During the next weeks, Charles regained all his former privileges, except the freedom of the Press Yard. Though he did not find Pitts as amenable to certain hints, as he had hoped.

The Keeper's eyes shifted uneasily when Charles spoke of the improvement in his fortunes, and explained with perfect truth that an aunt of his had come to the rescue. On the day after Betty's visit, when Alec was permitted to return, the valet brought news from Rodbourne. Lady Mary had sent a draught from Durham to Radcliffe's agent. It was for five hundred pounds. "Not that I dare hope 'twill save C. R.'s worthless neck," wrote Lady Mary, "but that he may pamper himself in prison in a manner fitting to his rank."

So Charles set to feeling Pitts out, as he and Betty had agreed. After two interviews with the Keeper, Charles was forced to give it up. Pitts's eyes gleamed at the sums Charles tossed out negligently, his shiny red lips positively drooled, yet at last he backed away, and staring hard at the ceiling, said, "Mr. Radcliffe, I understand you, but *you* don't understand *me*. There's been some escapes from this jail, which I might've known about or I might not. I get me orders same as everyone else. An' I've got 'em now. If somehow or other *you* was to break out o' here, they'd have *me* swinging at Tyburn in your stead, and wot use would a sackful o' guineas be to me then?"

"But," said Charles, and the Keeper interrupted angrily, "I can't speak plainer. It's no go, sir. Ye can buy yourself as much comfort as possible here, and here ye'll stay until ye're hanged, which won't be long now." Pitts walked out of the cell, banging shut the door.

Charles was not unduly discouraged. He had never dared hope much from Pitts. It must be the other plan then. The long complicated one which centered about the little door in the "Castle" latrine.

Charles went daily now up to the "Castle" and sometimes saw Tom Errington there. Errington, though insolvent, managed to retain this and other privileges by acting as secretary for the Keeper. Still, Tom had lost spirit, Charles discovered. He had grown morose and excessively religious. In some way he had got hold of a Missal, which he read constantly. He refused the drinks Charles offered him, and on the one occasion in which Charles mentioned the hidden door Errington shrugged unpleasantly and said, "Forget it, Radcliffe, you're getting as crazy as poor Jem Swinburne. You'd best be thinking of the state of your soul, instead of privy doors that don't lead anywhere."

So Charles ceased to confide in him; he spoke to Blueskin instead. Blueskin was in high spirits. His chum had already come up for trial at the Old Bailey and been released. Blueskin's own trial was scheduled for next week and he had had indirect assurance from Jonathan Wild that the outcome would be as favorable. "Too bad ye ain't one o' the gang, sir," he said sympathetically while gulping the gin Charles had bought him. "Ye'd be outa 'ere in a jigtrot. 'Tis a sad thing ter be a gent wot the King hisself 'as taken a scunner at."

"Aye," said Charles, glancing cautiously towards the turnkey. Black, though by now less suspicious, and more at ease in his duties, was nevertheless a constant threat. But Black had one night a week off—Thursdays—on which various substitutes appeared. This was one point about which Charles thought deeply. Another he whispered casually to Blueskin. "If I had an enemy—say—some chap I wanted out of the way for a while, how would I manage . . ." Charles hesitated.

Blueskin's small black eyes watched shrewdly. "Ye mean—" he said. "How'd ye get some cove thrown in the old Whit 'ere? Tis easy as winking."

"Not in *here*! Not *this* side!" cried Charles, so sharply that the turnkey looked around and glared. Blueskin immediately went into a noisy fit of coughing, nose-blowing, and spitting, while Charles in pretended disgust got up and walked away. It was some time before he dared question again; then in bits and pieces he got the information he wanted.

And he got Blueskin's hearty cooperation too. The promise of fifty guineas assured that. On the following Monday, Blueskin was duly taken to trial at the Old Bailey, and next morning Alec arrived in Charles's cell and reported the thief's acquittal. No witnesses had appeared against him.

"So—" said Charles on a long breath of relief. "You know what to do now, Alec. Everything depends on you."

The valet nodded solemnly. "You may trust me, sir. Rob's all set too. He'll be here tomorrow in my stead, though a mighty poor valet he'll make, I warrant!" Alec chuckled.

"Did you tell Muggles you felt ill as he let you in?"

"Aye. I said I'd the bloody flux and could scarce walk."

"Good. And does Lady Elizabeth know our exact plans?"

"Yes, sir. I met her in Moor Fields as we'd agreed. Her ladyship was mighty agitated and nervish but she said everything was ready for you. A Thursday she knows it must be. She's not found a ship for you yet, but that can wait, until you're safe hid—and outa here."

"Out of here . . ." repeated Charles. "Oh Alec, d'you think it'll work?"

"Have you prayed, sir?" asked the valet slowly. "I know you're not much of a one for that, yet it might help."

"I will pray," said Charles swallowing. "Pray to Saint Leonard. He's the patron saint of prisoners, Father Brown once said. Go, Alec. Get going! Now that there's some hope, I don't see how I can bear the wait."

"You must have patience, sir," said the valet gently. "To hurry our scheme would mean ruin."

"Aye, *patience!*" Charles repeated. "When now the King will soon be back from Hanover, and that'll be the end of my reprieves. For God's sake, Alec, go, my friend, and God bless you!"

As Muggles unlocked the iron door to let the valet out, Charles began to pace his cell.

During the next three weeks Betty's anxiety was as sharp as Charles's, and all the harder to bear since she must conceal every sign of it. Her only source of information was now Rob Wilson, because Alec was in Newgate prison on the debtors' side. The scheme had worked so far, thanks to Blueskin and the iniquitous law. All that was necessary to get Alec arrested for debt was two plaintiffs who swore to a magistrate that this foul rogue owed them each ten pounds he wouldn't pay. A warrant was issued, a bailiff took Alec in custody, and twenty-four hours later he was in Newgate. Blueskin and his mate had been the plaintiffs, and had performed their parts perfectly.

So far so good, Betty thought, and tried to calm herself as Rob reported progress. In debtors' prison visitors had free access at any time up to ten o'clock at night, and Rob saw Alec often. Alec had bought himself the freedom of the whole debtors' side, and by his third day there had crept upstairs and found a dark stone passage which ended in a bolted and locked iron door—the door he had been seeking. The passage was disused and filled with litter—broken kegs and the cast-off clothing of long forgotten prisoners. Alec had little difficulty in loosening the bolts on the door so that they would slide easily. Securing the key was another matter. He had hoped to find it in the door, since obviously nobody remembered its existence or would wish to get through to the criminal part of the prison anyway, and if they did would find that side bolted. But he didn't locate the key and the anxious days passed while he warily questioned and tipped the warders. Betty in her George Street home and Charles in his cell separately chafed and agonized.

Then on a Monday at dusk, Betty stole out of her house while Frank was taking his afterdinner nap. She walked rapidly a block north to the newly laid-out Hanover Square. A few houses were a-building there and Betty went towards one which had been erected as far as the first story. It was still only a hollow shell of reddish bricks, though the cellars were finished. This new mansion belonged to Betty's brother, the young Earl of Lichfield. As soon as he inherited, he had leased the land and begun building a town house for his prospective bride, and he had given Betty permission to make such use of it as she pleased.

Betty looked cautiously about, in case there should be any lurking workmen, but the square was deserted at this hour. She shivered—it was now December and very cold—then stepped over a pile of rubble into the half-finished house. At once she saw Rob Wilson's big muffled-up figure waiting for her by the stairwell. He had a dark lantern in his hand, and he turned a beam to guide her.

" 'Tis found," he greeted her abruptly as he always did. Rob was not one for chatter, nor even common courtesies.

"You mean the key?" she whispered, dizzy with relief.

"Aye. It had fallen into some mucky cr-rack i' the stones.

Now Alec's got the door unlocked on his side. All's ready for Thursday night. If *he'll* be."

Betty swallowed hard, knowing that the "he" was Charles. "He's making preparations, isn't he?" she asked tremulously.

"That he is," said Rob. "And is cocky—confident. Where's he to go here?" Betty pointed to the temporary wooden stairs which led to the basement offices. "Wine cellar," she said, and started gingerly down the steps. Rob followed with the lantern. They passed huge empty pantries, larders, the kitchen, and near the coalbin found the door to the wine cellar. Betty had the key at her girdle, and unlocked the door. Several dozen of the Earl's choicest ports and clarets were already lying in their cradles. He had sent them here from Ditchley Park, at Betty's request so that the workmen might not think it strange the door was kept locked—though in fact nobody questioned a nobleman's eccentricities.

" 'Twill do," said Rob glancing around. "Airy. We'll get him a brazier, and blankets against the cold. Food too. And when he's thir-r-sty, there's plenty to drink." He put his hand on one of the cradled bottles and gave a curt laugh.

Betty looked at him curiously, forgetting her worries for a moment. Rob was only a big rough Northern lad, of the age Charles had been when she first met him. He had a dark, rather ugly face, square-jawed beneath a truculent mouth. Under the black eyebrows his hazel eyes were intent. There was an air of strength and purpose about him, which disquieted her.

"Rob," she said suddenly alarmed. "Why are you doing this thing?" Why *were* they trusting this great hulking boy? How had it come about? He now had Charles's life in his power, and she knew enough of Rob Wilson to be sure that he was neither Jacobite nor had ever felt loyalty towards Radcliffes. Quite the contrary. Dear heaven, she thought. Have we made a terrible mistake? "Why are you doing this thing for Mr. Radcliffe?" she repeated on a shrill note.

Rob looked steadily at her frightened face, and shrugged. "Because," he said, "I did him a bad tur-rn once, I wish to even the scor-re. And that's the way o' it. I pay m'debts."

Betty was only slightly reassured, though instinct told her this lad was not deceitful. "You'll be rewarded, you know," she said quickly. "How much do you want?"

He made an impatient, almost a rude sound. "Naught for *this*," he said. "I'd not take br-ribes for a man's life. Later on, ye can speak a wor-rd for me amangst the rich lords and ladies o' your ken. It seems the only way to get on in Lunnon is in good sar-r-vice."

"Service?" she repeated blankly. "You'd be a servant, Rob?"

"Aye," he answered. "I'd be anything where I can ear-rn honest money, quick, enough to buy m'*own* land. Ye may be sur-re I'll brook no master o'er me langer-r than I've got to."

"You mean to turn farmer, then, Rob?" she asked still puzzled. This youth seemed lacking in any traits which would make him either a good servant or farmer.

"*Higher* than far-rmer," Rob snapped, frowning. "In time. I've scor-res yet left to pay off i' the North." He clenched his big coal-blackened hands and picked up the lantern. "We'd best gan now."

"If—" said Betty with an uneasy smile, "you wish me to recommend you as a servant, what sort of servant, by the way?"

"Running footman," said Rob promptly. "I can outrun anyone Tyneside or i' Coquetdale, and I can make high wages i' the job."

"Well," said Betty, "then you'll have to mend your manners. You speak to me as though *I* were a serving wench, you know."

Rob stared at her, his heavy brows drawn together, then suddenly he grinned—a surprisingly pleasant flash of square white teeth. " 'Tis true, m'lady," he said. "I'm in sad want o' polishing."

She nodded, and mounted the stairs while he followed. Her mind at once dismissed Rob, and returned to thoughts of the coming Thursday night. They left the unfinished house together after a murmur of agreement that he would meet her here on Wednesday with further news. They were about to part, when they both heard a strange little noise in the shadows by the areaway. Then a child came running forward, stumbling and crying "Robbie! Robbie!"

Betty stood rooted with astonishment, as the child flung herself on Rob, clutching his neck and giving a whimper of joy. The lad lifted and held Jenny tight against his chest for a moment. "There, there, bair-r-nie," he murmured. "There —there—" He put her down and patted her shoulder awkwardly.

"Jenny! What are you *doing* here!" Betty cried.

The child looked up at her, though she clung to Rob's hand. "Whilst and agyen I come out her-re, m'lady," she said.

"There's tr-rees and fields up yonder, an' 'tis so hot i' the house, I canna br-reathe."

"This is very wrong," said Betty. "Dangerous. Did you follow me?"

Jenny shook her head. "But I saw ye enter this house, m'lady. I cr-rept near and thought I hear-rd Robbie's voice. I waited—" She paused, and perceiving even through the starlit dusk that the ladyship was angry, she added sadly, "Ye *told* me I could see Robbie agyen, yet I havena till now."

"She means no har-rm," said Rob. Then he turned to the child. "Now mind this, Jenny! Ye'll say naught iver o' seeing me or her ladyship this night. And fra now on, ye'll bide at hame wher-re ye belang, d'ye under-r-stand?"

The child gave a great gulp, and said, "Aye, Robbie. But wher-refore canna I see ye?"

"Hist!" he commanded, speaking to her in the full Northumbrian brogue which both he and the child were losing. "Cease thy clack! Ye'd no' be a blabbermouth! Ye mun do as ye're tould, some day ye'll knaw the r-reason."

"Aye, Robbie," she said sighing, and squeezed his hand hard. He patted her again on the shoulder, and was off, running towards the fields. Betty and Jenny continued down the square to George Street. The child was crying quietly. And though Betty was further worried by this unfortunate meeting, it actually worked to her advantage, because Frank was up and waiting in the hall when she returned. "Where in the world," he began, scowling, but Betty checked him with a glance at Jenny, whose delicate face was tear-stained and scarlet with cold. "Go up to the nursery, dear," said Betty. "And don't let this happen again!"

The child curtsied, cast a frightened look at Colonel Lee, and ran towards the back stairs.

"Poor mite," said Betty. "She's taken to slipping outdoors, so 'she can breathe'—I found her, and she has been well scolded, I assure you."

"She should be whipped," said Frank. "You're spoiling the child." He spoke without conviction and Betty smiled, knowing that Frank had grown fond of the little thing and was inclined to spoil her himself, when he remembered her existence.

"She's a wild bird yet," said Betty, "though she's learning fast."

"Uhm-m," said Frank, walking towards his study. "Curious there's never been an advertisement for her, and that we know no more about her than when she appeared out of nowhere. Especially as I'm more convinced than ever that she has gentle blood—And I am," Frank continued, opening his study door, "considered, I believe, quite a judge of breeding in man or beast."

"Oh, indeed you *are*, my dear," said Betty warmly. "By the bye, what are your engagements this week? There's a masquerade at the Haymarket Thursday. I'd rather like to go. My sister wishes us to sup with her first," continued Betty in a rush. "She has asked some rather amusing people . . . I believe the Walpoles have accepted, and George-Henry is going."

Frank, who had opened his mouth for outraged protest, closed it again. A Swiss count called Heidegger had recently introduced public masquerades at the Haymarket Opera House. The King sanctioned them and they had become a fashionable craze. Frank thought them a foolish waste of time. Nor did he much approve of Betty's sister, Charlotte, Lady Baltimore, a frivolous widow of thirty-eight, who had been separated from her husband for some years before his death. Still, on the other hand, if the Walpoles were going, and Lord Lichfield! And it might be that Charlotte needed family backing because she had some advantageous new marriage in mind.

"How odd," Frank said temperately, "that you should wish to go masquerading in your condition."

"Not at all," said Betty. "I shall be a Roman matron. Most decorous with all that drapery. We've had no gaiety for a long time. And it would be so pleasant to be out of mourning just one evening. Do say yes, Frank."

She put a pleading hand on his arm, and he succumbed. "Well, well, my dear, if you really wish to go. But remember, I shan't make a fool of myself in a ridiculous costume. A simple mask later—no more!"

"Of course," she said kissing him lightly on the cheek, and left him to the stack of papers he was obviously aching to peruse.

So that problem at least was surmounted. Now there would be no danger that Frank would wish to stroll out Thursday night to Hanover Square, to see how his brother-in-law's great new mansion was progressing, a little jaunt he was very fond of. And if anything went wrong with the escape, and the hue and cry should come in this direction, he would not be here to listen to it.

God help us, Betty thought. And again she tried to pray.

On Thursday night at seven o'clock, Betty and Frank drove in their coach and six through the snowy streets to Lady Baltimore's house, while Betty strove to hide her nervous shakes. Beneath the left breastfolds of her Roman matron's costume, she had tucked a small piece of paper. A note which Rob had brought her from Charles last night. There were only a few words scrawled in muddy ink: "Whatever befalls, know that my heart is yours."

When she was alone, Betty had kissed the note a dozen times, and all night long she had not slept.

"You're cold, my dear," said Frank crossly. "I hope you've not an ague. This outing is folly."

"No! No!" she said laughing, and peering out the coach window, cried, "Look!" Two link boys with torches, and two footmen behind were escorting a strange figure up Lady Baltimore's steps. Despite a mantle, one could see that the figure represented a fiery devil, with red horns and tail and shiny red spangles. They caught a glimpse of a profile, as the devil entered the house, and Frank said, "Ecod! 'Tis young Baltimore himself. That boy has the most uncouth fancies. Needs a strong stepfather over him."

Betty would ordinarily have agreed. She did not like her seventeen-year-old nephew, who had added eccentricities and overweening pride to essential stupidity when he succeeded to the title, but she had no interest in him now, except as a distraction for Frank. Her whole being was aware that Charles —at this moment—must be starting the first maneuvers of his escape.

In the hall her sister Charlotte greeted Betty with a pre-occupied kiss and an appraising stare. "Do sit down, my dear. You look very wan, and really what a tasteless costume—though I know you're breeding, still it doesn't show yet, and I should have thought—and Frank not even costumed at all," added Charlotte with a resigned shrug, glancing at her brother-in-law's ordinary black satin evening suit.

Betty had thought she looked quite handsome and was at once deflated. Charlotte, who inherited all their mother's beauty and was fifteen years older besides, always deflated her. Betty suddenly felt that the Roman matron costume was not only odd but dowdy. Clark, her maid, had run it up, according to her own ideas, since Betty had taken little interest. It consisted of a good many heavy white draperies, and was topped by an elaborately waved and diademed black wig. Her own red hair would have been too easily recognized later when they were all masked and enjoying the anonymity provided at the Haymarket.

Charlotte, on the other hand, was a French shepherdess, or at least the laced blue lutestring bodice, the gilded crook, and the enchanting straw hat would so indicate. Yet fidelity to her role had not prevented an alluring exhibit of bust and white shoulders, or powdered curls or a gold fan or a patch on her cheek, or diamonds in her ear lobes. Well, thought Betty sighing, Charlotte was on the lookout for a new husband, and it was silly to feel the old pang of envious inferiority. Betty sat down near the drawing room fire, accepted a glass of wine, and immediately began to wonder what was happening to Charles.

She was again interrupted by her sister. "Oh, Betty," Charlotte murmured, "I forgot to tell you I asked rather a peculiar gentleman to come tonight. A Virginia planter, named William Byrd. He's in his forties. A new-made widower, has quite a fortune in the Colonies, they say."

Frank, who was hovering near his wife, broke in with some astonishment. "Why yes, I've met him in the coffeehouses. I found him a sound chap, fellow of the Royal Society and all that, well-bred for a Colonial, though to be sure he was educated *here*. Still, my dear Charlotte, I shouldn't think him quite—quite—" he broke off, frowning as a dreadful suspicion seized him. "I trust you wouldn't encourage any attentions from *that* quarter!"

"Oh, la!" laughed Charlotte. "Not for a moment! Bury myself thousands of miles off in the wilderness with an American? Don't be foolish, Frank! No, I'm nice to him, because of Baltimore." She waved her fan towards her son, who leaned against the mantel in his devil's costume, while languidly sniffing up snuff, and eying his mother's guests superciliously. "I suppose the boy'll have to go out to Maryland, someday," continued Charlotte. "After all he owns the province, and should have a glimpse of it. With that in mind, I'm encouraging him to meet some Colonials."

"Oh," said Frank, "I see. Quite a good idea."

Betty had already ceased to listen. Once she put her hand to her breast and felt the faint crackle of Charles's note, and while the rest of the guests arrived, she sat in a kind of suspension, making mechanical responses when necessary.

The drawing room filled with bizarre figures, which Betty saw through a haze. Mrs. Walpole had come as Diana, with quiver and bow and a rather short tunic which on anyone else would have scandalized Frank. Mr. Walpole did not come at all. Urgent Treasury business had prevented him. There was a Miss Dashwood as a milkmaid, Mrs. Somebody-else as a harem slave. Mr. Byrd presently arrived accompanied by a young man called Sir Wilfred Lawson. Mr. Byrd was dressed as a grand mogul, in belted robes and a turban. Betty smiled as he was presented, noting vaguely that the Virginian was dark, quite handsome in a middle-aged way, and that he bowed over her hand with exaggerated courtesy. His companion, Sir Wilfred, was dressed as Robin Hood in hunter's green, which suited him. He was a rather rakish young man, not tall, with a bold merry brown eye and a curly brown wig. When he greeted her she was aware of a trace of Northern accent, which was explained later on, since he had been born and raised in Cumberland.

Betty could not really rouse herself, until her brother appeared, last of all. The young Earl of Lichfield had come as a Franciscan monk. It was clear that Charlotte disapproved of this drab gray habit, though her respect for the new head of their house restrained her usual frankness. It was only Betty who saw real significance in the Earl's choice, and noted the crucifix which hung from the scourge around his waist. Can it be that George will turn *Catholic* when he marries Frances Hales? Betty wondered in dismay. Nothing would more horrify the rest of the Lee family—and especially Frank. As yet, nobody except Betty even knew of Lichfield's love for Frances. How strange it was that she and her brother should both have secret attachments to Catholics—but what a bond it made between them!

They were moving towards the dining room, now that the Earl had arrived, and as they passed through the doorway, he squeezed near to Betty and said low in her ear, "Any progress?"

"It's *tonight*," she whispered with an involuntary gasp.

"Good luck," her brother said. Beneath the cowl a tremor crossed his lean ascetic face. At once they walked away from each other.

At the table, Betty found Mr. Byrd on her left, and because it was necessary to speak, and because she could think of nothing which was not in some way connected with Charles, she asked brightly, "Was it not *you*, Mr. Byrd, who sent over a little Negro called Juba who became page to the Duchess of Bolton?"

"Ah yes, your ladyship," said William Byrd, much gratified. "It delighted me when I heard I had indirectly given pleasure to so distinguished and beautiful a lady as the Duchess."

"Have you met her?" asked Betty on an acid tone.

Byrd shook his head regretfully. "Though when I married my poor late wife—Lucy Parke that was—many kind people compared her beauty to that of the Duchess." He sighed. "Ah, 'tis a heavy stroke to lose the companion of one's bosom, the mother of one's children. The smallpox—and she had but just arrived in London, poor thing."

Betty made murmurs of sympathy, though by the covert glances Mr. Byrd's heavy-lidded sensual eyes sent towards Charlotte, and even towards the pert Miss Dashwood, Betty suspected that the gentleman was not inconsolable. "You've children?" she asked politely while she put down her fork and gave up the pretense of eating. Twinges of nausea had replaced the nervous shivers.

"Two girls, your ladyship," answered Byrd. "Evelyn, who is nine, and Wilhelmina, only a year. Both are still in Virginia, but I design to bring them over here and—"

Betty did not hear the end of the sentence because Charlotte's gilded mantel clock struck nine. Where was Charles *now?* By sheer force of will she tried to produce an image of him, and her hands clenched under the napkin. William Byrd talked on, charmed by the wide-eyed interest Lady Elizabeth accorded him. He did not notice that she was smiling at him fixedly, and that there was a glassy look in the attractive eyes. He was only aware that here was a lady who was that rarest of beings, a perfect listener. That she was also an Earl's daughter and sister made her conduct even more endearing.

Byrd told her about his estates in Virginia, about his 43,000 acres of land, and his 220 Negro slaves, and his house on the James River, called "Westover," which he intended someday to enlarge. So responsive was she that he alluded to his quarrel with Virginia's present Governor, Spotswood, and hinted that there were some kind and prejudiced friends here in England who were so extravagant as to say that Byrd should be appointed Governor *himself.* He mentioned the names of these friends—the Duke of Argyle, the Earl of Orrery, Lord Percival, dear Mrs. Howard, bedchamber woman to Princess Caroline.

Betty continued to smile, and nod at intervals, until suddenly she was forced to yield more real attention, when she found that Mr. Byrd was becoming personal, was addressing her as "Lovely Lucrece, the worthiest Roman lady in history," and was admiring her sable tresses.

"Oh fie, sir!" cried Betty, accepting the proper role. "The sable tresses aren't mine! And I fear you are a flatterer!"

"Ah," said Mr. Byrd. "Indeed I cannot flatter, and to express the esteem one has for a lady as charming as an angel, one needs an angel's tongue, while mine is but a cloddish one."

"I see you've a pretty turn for gallantry, Mr. Byrd," said Betty. "Gallantries which would be more properly received by others perhaps. Forgive me, sir," she added, for the nausea had increased, and parrying with Mr. Byrd seemed suddenly insupportable. "I must retire for a moment." She left the table, and hurried to a little cabinet beneath the stairs.

Frank, at the other end of the table next to Mrs. Walpole, did not notice, because Mrs. Walpole, high-flown with wine, was being indiscreet about her husband's opinions on the proposed treaty with France which would forever banish "James the Pretender" from that country.

Betty's brother noticed her abrupt departure. He had seen the strain that she was under, had caught now and again the note of hysteria in her few remarks to Mr. Byrd. The Earl was very fond of his young sister and fully aware of the dangers she was in. His eyes narrowed thoughtfully as he considered the possibilities of soon ending her suspense one way or the other.

At the precise moment that Betty felt sick at the supper table, Charles in Newgate jail walked through the little door in the latrine, and entered the debtors' side. Behind him in the "Castle" dungeon he left a crowd of roistering prisoners. For Charles had been giving a party there. It had not been hard to persuade Pitts that depressed by a year in prison, and the rumor that his execution could be no longer stayed, Charles had conceived the idea of a celebration. Mr. Pitts had accepted a gift of fifty pounds, and agreed to Charles's request that Muggles might be appointed warder in the "Castle" for that evening. What harm could it do? thought the Keeper, if Mr. Radcliffe had a whim to be guarded that night by the man who had been his personal jailer all this time. Besides, the Christmas season was approaching, and bonhomie filtered even through the grim stone walls of Newgate.

Muggles was delighted, especially as Mr. Radcliffe laid in a cask of the best brandy for the party, and plum puddings and mince pies too. With all this good cheer, it did not take long for Muggles to reach the state where Charles wanted him—drooling, hiccupping, and giggling mightily when Charles suggested that it might be fun if the warder pretended he were a prisoner. Leg fetters, for instance, and to be chained to that ring on the floor!

"Aw no ye don't sir," said Muggles, giggling harder, yet with a remaining spark of caution. "Ye'll not put *me* in no leg hirons!"

"Only in jest," said Charles laughing. "Only for a moment, old friend. Why you'd not deny me a bit o' sport, tonight? And here's something to make it worth your while!" He dangled a gold watch and chain before the warder's blood-shot, gleaming eyes.

The other prisoners, all as drunk as the warder, crowded around, chuckling and cheering. One or two suspected that something was up, but they couldn't imagine what. There was a turnkey stationed in the passage outside and no other way out of the "Castle" dungeon.

Muggles grabbed the watch, and consented. Charles slapped fetters on the warder's leg, chained him to the ring and casually abstracting the key which would unlock the irons, said, "There you are, my man. And another cup of brandy to keep you content. As for me, I must answer nature's call, and then we'll have a round of merry glees!"

Charles stepped into the latrine, shoved a man out who was already there, then, groping in the darkness, slid back the bolts, so carefully prepared, opened the door, went through and bolted it after him. Alec was waiting for him in the dark attic on the debtors' side. The two men gripped hands hard. Alec whispered, "Hurry, sir, they'll soon call 'Time'!" They descended some steps and came to a row of chambers in each of which whole families lived. There was the smell of cooking, and the sound of a baby crying. Through a half-opened door, Charles saw a woman sewing by the fire, while with her foot she rocked a cradle. Charles's throat closed, and his heart gave a lurch. The homely scene excited him more than all the moments which had gone before. Alec hurried him on, and soon they mingled with other departing visitors. "Your hat and cloak, sir," said Alec. "They're m'own," he added apolo-getically, "but they'll do. Mind, sir, if anyone questions, you're me lawyer."

Charles nodded. He was already dressed in a plain dark suit, with plain linen, and brown tie-wig. The hat Alec gave him was plain too, without lace. The clothes were suitable for a petty lawyer, or law clerk. They went down another flight of stairs, into a warren of common rooms, private cells, and little courtyards. They waited near the great gates, talking of the weather in low tones, until the handbells jangled throughout the debtors' prison, and the wardens began to bawl out, "Time! Time! All outsiders to leave!"

"Remember, sir," said Alec. "Rob is waiting near the Saracen's Head."

Charles nodded again. They watched until the crowd of departing visitors was thickest, then Charles slipped into a place in the queue. He held his breath while he stopped to check out with the gateward. Though he knew his escape had not yet been discovered, for the great alarm bells had not rung from the criminals' side.

"Name?" said the gateward, glancing negligently at a scrawled list.

"John Thompson," said Charles.

"Who for?" mumbled the gateward.

"Alec Armstrong. I'm his lawyer."

Some debtor's pretty sweetheart pushed up behind and the gateward, eying her with relish, said "Pass" to Charles, who took several careful steps through the tiny open gate and out onto the street, where he needed all his self-control not to run. As it was he walked very fast, and crouched to minimize his height. It was snowing a little; he felt the cool wet flakes on his face with a kind of ecstasy. He passed St. Sepulchre's, which began to ring ten o'clock. He reached the Saracen's Head beyond. Its multipaned bow windows shed light on the street, and he saw Rob lurking there, done up in muffler and cap, his nose pressed to the window, as though he longed to enter the cozy inn.

Rob saw Charles from the corner of his eye, let him pass, as they had agreed. Then, since there was nobody about, except a beggar and a muffin man, he caught up with him. "Na tr-rouble?" he asked.

"No," said Charles. They crossed the Fleet Bridge, and were accosted by two whining, ragged whores. "Not tonight, my beauties," said Charles with a loud excited laugh. "But here's something to keep the cold out!" and he gave them each a shilling.

"Care-reful!" said Rob sharply, when the whores had gone. "Such as *you* seem, divven't fling awa' siller like that!" While he spoke there was a din far behind them, the frenzied jangling of bells, shrill whistles and the rattle of a huge alarm from Newgate tower.

"Blessed Mary," Charles whispered. "They've found out!" Then he was silent, as Rob steered him through alleys, and tiny cross streets until they reached the Oxford Road. Here to the North it was still open country, and no other pedestrians dared brave the dangers of frozen ruts and footpads on a dark winter's night. Rob, who had superb vision, besides having studied this route often, never hesitated. At last they turned left into Hanover Square, and paused while a coach and four went past them, then they slid into the Earl of Lichfield's half-finished house, where Rob picked up the lantern he had left there earlier. They went down to the basement, and Rob started to unlock the door of the wine cellar. But the door swung open, and a tall gray cowled figure stood inside looking at them. Charles, who was panting, strangled a cry. The hair prickled on his scalp, and he crossed himself.

"You needn't fear," said the figure softly. "You're safe, Radcliffe. I am Lichfield."

"A monk," whispered Charles incredulous, his flesh still creeping.

"No, no," said the Earl. "Only for a masquerade. You've done well, lad," he said to Rob. "Now leave us alone. I'll give you orders later."

At the Haymarket Opera House, Betty sat despondently in a box, resting her chin on her hand and watching the masked dancers gyrating below. Frank had been sitting beside her until just now, when he had left her with Mrs. Walpole and Sir Wilfred Lawson while he went to find a glass of punch. Betty's nausea had passed, but her head ached and she wondered how long before it would be safe to go home, and how she was then to find out what had happened to Charles. She turned to what she thought was Frank returning, and saw that instead it was her brother who slipped into the cushioned chair. "I wondered where you'd got to, George," she said, then added in a whisper, "Have you heard anything? Oh, do you think they are all right?"

Under the cowl the eyes seemed to glitter through the black mask, and the monk, leaning very near her, whispered, "Yes, darling. 'Tis all right."

Betty's head jerked up, she peered closer, saw a cleft chin, and the beginning of a scar pucker on the right cheek. She swayed, and caught at the railing. "Don't you dare swoon!" said the voice in her ear. "Get us out of here quickly."

The whirling kaleidoscope around her steadied and settled down. She took a deep breath, and said in a loud natural voice, "George, it's so warm. I feel faint again. Would you take me home? When my husband returns, you'll tell him I've gone out with Lord Lichfield, won't you?" she said to Mrs. Walpole, who interrupted her flirtation with Sir Wilfred long enough to say, "Yes, Lady Betty. Certainly."

The Roman matron and the tall monk quitted the box and in the corridor they found a throng of masked revelers who were surging to and fro, either towards the dance floor or the refreshment rooms. "The coach is below by the entrance," said Charles holding her arm firmly.

She could not speak again. They descended the theater steps and she preceded him into her brother's coach.

Charles muffled his mouth with his hand and told one of the footmen to direct the coachman to drive slowly along the river for a while.

"Won't they think it strange?" said Betty faintly.

"No," said Charles. "They think I'm the Earl, and that he's drunk. He played his part well, earlier. For which I'll bless him all my life." In the darkness of the coach he put his arm around her. "He knows what love is, Betty, and he's given us this time together because he's found me passage on a sloop which sails from Rye to Boulogne on Saturday."

"Saturday," she repeated. " 'Tis after midnight now. Charles, that's *tomorrow!*" She turned her cheek on his shoulder and began to weep.

"I'll stay if you want me to, Betty," he said in a grave voice.

"No!" she cried. "Not hid in that cellar, not in danger. Of course not—but oh Charles, I love you so. I can't bear—and yet now I have the thing I wanted most in life. You're *free!*"

"Almost," he said, then taking off his mask and hers, he tried to see her face. "Dear heart," he said half laughing, "had Lichfield not warned me, I'd never have known you in that wig." He passed his hand gently over her head and removed the wig. "So now I can see your bright hair even in the darkness." And he bent and kissed it. She raised her face and put her arms around his neck.

An hour later the Lichfield coach drew up at the Lee door. Betty darted out and ran inside. Frank was waiting, full of wrathful bewilderment, and Betty was constrained to invent a story quickly. She said that her brother's coach had thrown a wheel in some rut, and there had been a natural delay. She pled that Frank should help her up to bed at once, and indeed she looked so wild-eyed and disheveled that he was alarmed.

The Earl's coach proceeded to Hanover Square, where the cowled monk entered the unfinished house, murmuring to a footman that he had a fancy to see what the workmen had done that day. "S'truth," said the footman to the coachman,

" 'is lordship must be tipsy as a goat, or mebbe 'tis a young lydy's meeting 'im in there."

"And none o' your business, any'ow," said the coachman crossly. He and his horses were tired, and these whimsies tonight were unlike his lordship's usual consideration.

Yet it wasn't three minutes before the cowled monk came out again, and said he wished to go home.

Charles remained alone in the wine cellar, not yet daring to rejoice over freedom, still in a wretched turmoil at the parting with Betty, unable to think, or indeed feel any more emotions except one. Betty had promised that she would try to send Jenny here on the morrow to see her father once before he left. During the rest of the long night, Charles was obsessed with longing to see his child.

PART THREE

1723—1726

TEN

On the morning of July 16, 1723, Jenny was standing by the harpsichord in the front parlor of the Hackney School for young gentlewomen. Miss Crowe hunched over the instrument playing Italian trills in a singularly British and thumping manner, while Jenny struggled through an aria by Buononcini with only the faintest notion of what she was singing. Now that Italian music was the rage in London, it had naturally been added to the curriculum of this fashionable school. Jenny suffered as she obediently trilled and quavered, while trying to ignore Miss Crowe's frequent blunders.

Jenny had a natural ear, and a true silvery voice which had lately begun to deepen and lose its childishness. She was thirteen, and the exceptional beauty which had been hers as a small child was reappearing in a new form. Her flaxen hair had turned to a pale cowslip gold, her gray eyes had lengthened and were set off by long brown lashes. Nature had endowed her with a vastly becoming black mole on her left cheekbone; it enhanced her transparent white and rose skin. Her lips were voluptuously full. Too full, really vulgar, Jenny thought them, quite unaware of the coquetry they added to the wistfulness of her enchanting smile. Her second teeth had come in perfect, and were a piece of luck she owed to her mother and the generations of plain-living Border farmers from which Meg sprang. This Jenny did not know, nor that the cleft in her square little chin came from her father, as did the long delicate fingers and the proud tilt of her head.

In fact Jenny knew nothing about her parentage. She was called Miss Lee.

She had recently overheard a conversation which clarified many obscure taunts about her birth. She discovered that the school thought her to be a bastard of Colonel Lee's who had been charitably reared by Lady Betty Lee. Jenny was hurt by the discovery of this theory, which she knew to be false, though she had no means of refuting it.

The memory of that eerie visit to a cellar in Hanover Square, more than six years ago, had greatly blurred. But there *had* been a strange man in the cellar, a tall, fair-haired man who kissed her many times, and told her that he was her father, and who gave her a gold ring with a crest on it—a bull's head, Jenny thought the crest had been, though she was not even sure of that now. Lady Betty had put the ring away when she saw it, saying it was too big, and must be kept until Jenny was grown. The man who said he was her father had tears in his eyes when he said farewell, or had he? Much of the memory was mixed up with dreams which came later. Yet Rob certainly had been in the cellar too. It was he, and Lady Betty, who forbade her ever to mention this mysterious visit. Nor had she. Strongest of all the emotions aroused that evening, was fear and the awareness of danger. Danger to do with the strange man whom Rob and Lady Betty were for some reason trying to help.

Jenny now understood, of course, that there must have been an escape, and she had heard of the wicked Jacobite Rebellion, but saw no connection. The Lee household and the school were so entirely Whig and Hanoverian that Jenny was unaware there *could* be any other viewpoint.

"Miss Lee!" said Miss Crowe sharply, banging out a chord. "Pay attention!"

Jenny jumped, and brought her wandering eyes back to her teacher's fat, purplish face. "I'm sorry, ma'am," she said. "I just saw Mr. Byrd's coach draw up," she indicated the window, "and was wondering whether he had brought Evelyn a birthday present."

"I expect you'll find out in due time," Miss Crowe snapped. "Now the trill again, Fa, sol, fa, sol, fa, sol . . ."

Jenny took a breath, opened her mouth, and warbled, but she went on thinking about her friend, Evelyn Byrd, and Evelyn's great secret.

Jenny was flattered by Evelyn's confidence, pleased by the intimacy which had lately developed between them. Evelyn was sixteen this very day, and might well have ignored a child so much her junior. But Evelyn was not like the other girls. She was taller and thinner, and at times beautiful in a moody, intense way they didn't admire, though Jenny did. Also it might be that she was drawn to Jenny because neither of them had a conventional background. In this school, which accepted only the daughters of landed gentry or nobility, the position of both Jenny and Evelyn was somewhat equivocal. Jenny's exact parentage was in doubt, though the Earl of Lichfield and Lady Betty Lee's influence had assured her admission. While Evelyn's widowered father, though reputedly wealthy and well connected, was after all a kind of rustic foreigner—or so the school deemed one actually born in the Colonies.

"Time's up," said Miss Crowe clapping her music shut, "and I trust you do better tomorrow. Now go to your French lesson, then the dancing master, after that two hours of plain sewing. Miss Simpson says you made a frightful botch of the last linen she allotted you."

"Yes, ma'am," said Jenny and swallowed. "Please, ma'am you—you haven't forgotten that I am permitted a half holiday today, with Evelyn?" she asked anxiously. "You know she's going to a musicale at Lord Peterborough's. Mrs. Strudick said I might go."

"Indeed!" Miss Crowe said. "*I* don't feel you've earned any favors." But she did not dare gainsay the headmistress, whom she thought deplorably lax where Jenny Lee was concerned. Mrs. Strudick positively made a favorite of this little baseborn nobody. Miss Crowe cast a baleful glance at the girl, resenting the rose and gilt coloring, the slender budding body inside the white aproned and cuffed brown serge schooldress. "If you go," she said, "you will arise at five tomorrow and finish all your sewing before prayers."

"Yes, ma'am," said Jenny, curtesying and wondering why Miss Crowe never seemed pleased with her. It was her first intimation of feminine jealousy, though it was not to be the last.

After her dancing lesson, Jenny found Evelyn impatiently awaiting her in the bedroom they shared. "Hurry, Jen," said Evelyn. "Father's in a pet."

Jenny was alarmed. "He hasn't found out anything about —about you and Sir Wilfred?"

"Oh, no," said Evelyn. Her huge dark eyes suddenly softened and glowed as they always did when she thought of Wilfred Lawson. "My father's not *that* angry. And we must be so careful this afternoon at Lord Peterborough's, Wilfred and I, lest he guess." Across Evelyn's oval face there ran a tremor of passionate anticipation. "Jenny, hurry!" urged the girl.

Jenny complied, rushing from her school frock into her best one—a sky-blue silk with black velvet bows which Lady Betty had given her last year. It was much too short, and too tight across the bust, but no matter. Jenny was largely unaware of her appearance. "Why then is Mr. Byrd upset?" Jenny asked running a comb through her thick yellow curls and tying them back at the nape of her neck with a blue ribbon.

"Oh, poor Papa," said Evelyn impatiently indulgent. "I suppose that some lady's refused him again, or hasn't as much fortune as he thought. I wonder if he'll *ever* get a wife to his taste who will have him."

Jenny was startled by this speech, which seemed unfilial. Yet Evelyn often talked in that pert way of her father, though she seemed to love and fear him too. It was puzzling, though Jenny knew humbly that she had no way of gauging feelings such as Evelyn's, either for a father, or for a lover—like Sir Wilfred.

William Byrd rose as his daughter entered the reception room with her friend. He was the very model of a fashionable Londoner, in a gold-buttoned plum velvet coat with stiffened skirts, waistcoat of embroidered mauve brocade, a tricorne edged with ostrich feathers perched on the long flowing gray-powdered wig which emphasized the darkness of his skin. His heavy-lidded black eyes were belied by a firmly compressed mouth. It was a haughty face which combined sensuality, pride, and yet a puritanical restraint, and he did not look his forty-nine years, since he was temperate in diet, and his frequent sexual excesses were balanced by a meticulous attention to his health.

Byrd bowed politely over Jenny's hand, and asked without interest how she did. He did not quite disapprove of Evelyn's friendship with Jenny—who was sponsored by an earl—and he felt that the society of a girl so much younger might curb in his daughter some of the willful tendencies of which he had lately become uneasily aware. Still, he dismissed Jenny as negligible, and once they were seated in the coach, and trundling up the Thames towards the Earl of Peterborough's seat at Parson's Green, he began to catechize his daughter sternly. Was she following the diet he had prescribed? Meat only once a day, no chocolate or fruit whatsoever? Was she doing her morning exercises? Had she taken the physic he left last time he called, and how often had it worked? Did she remember her evening prayers?

Evelyn answered yes to everything, and submitted to his rearrangement of the orange velvet rose she had pinned in her dark hair. She exerted herself to please him by reciting one of Horace's odes, and then asking him sweetly if he had lately written any poems which she and Jenny might hear.

At this Byrd finally smiled. He was proud of his rhymed eulogies to various ladies whom he designated by such names as Sempronia, Cleora, Zenobia—an elegant amusement much in vogue.

"I've written none lately," he said patting Evelyn's hand, "but I'll concoct one for your birthday, my dear, if you like. I shall call you Amasia. Do you know what that means?"

"Not exactly, Papa," said Evelyn, lowering her lashes.

"Why, the 'Beloved One,' of course," said Byrd tenderly. "And indeed she is that to me, Miss Jenny," he added turning towards the latter. "For she is my good obedient beautiful daughter, who shall see someday how much I cherish her, and what provision I'll make for her happy future!"

Jenny felt Evelyn stiffen and heard her take a sharp breath.

"What do you mean by *that*, Father?"

"Nothing for you to fret about, child," said Byrd. "You needn't fear I'd part with you for a long time—yet *someday* of course—it must be faced. You'd not wish to be a spinster —now would you!"

"Have you found me a husband?" asked Evelyn in a peculiar, rough voice, staring hard at her father.

"That is not a proper question," said Byrd repressively. "You are far too young, as yet."

His daughter turned her head away, and gazing out of the window at the village of Chelsea fell into one of her dark silent moods, which annoyed Byrd, whose good humor ebbed. Evelyn's question incited several uncomfortable thoughts. He had not begun to search for a husband suitable to Evelyn, because it was first necessary to settle his own matrimonial state. A wife with some fortune was essential, more essential than anyone knew except Micajah Perry, his business agent. Only Perry was aware of the crippling debts Byrd had inherited from his dead wife's father, or knew of the new debts incurred by the necessities of fashionable life in London. Byrd's mouth tightened, and his eyes grew as somber as Evelyn's while he thought of the five times he had proposed marriage in the last years, and of the embarrassments, the humiliations, inflicted by the five ladies of wealth and quality who had first encouraged his gallantries and then callously refused him as a husband. The last was the worst. Minionet, Byrd thought with a pang. Little Mrs. Jeffreys, who was a plump comely widow of good family and independent means. She had a pretty wit too, and in their exchange of amorous letters had called him the "Black Swan" and signed herself his "entranced and fluttering Minionet." He had then sent her a persuasive word picture of himself signed "Inamorato L'Oiseau." At that time he was amused by puns on his name.

Then, despite his frenzied entreaties she had suddenly ceased writing and she had obviously abandoned discretion about their courtship, for at Will's Coffeehouse, Byrd finally discovered what had changed her. Ridicule. His friends were sniggering over a lampoon, which they were passing from hand to hand.

> Sweet Jeffreys netted by a Byrd
> Had better struggle loose
> Or she will find when 'tis too late
> Black Swan is but an old gray goose.

Everyone denied authorship, of course, but Byrd had seen a mocking glint in Wilfred Lawson's merry brown eyes, and his hatred for the young man crystallized. Long past were their days of real companionship or their jaunts together in quest of gambling and debauchery. Two years ago a quarrel had arisen over another woman and their friends had narrowly averted a duel. Since they had mutual acquaintances, and inevitably met, they resumed distant courtesies. Then Sir Wilfred, who was M.P. for his family borough at Cockermouth in Cumberland, had run into debt, and been publicly accused of corruption in the South Sea scandal. Worse than that, he took to voting Tory. Even last November Sir Wilfred had spoken *against* Walpole in a motion of the Grand Committee for the further punishing of all Papists. Byrd, who had known and admired Wilfred's father, felt compelled to remonstrate acidly with the young Baronet, who rudely shrugged off the rebuke. This happened at a small ball to which Byrd had brought Evelyn, and Sir Wilfred had there further infuriated the father by singling out the girl and sitting with her for hours in a hidden alcove.

I soon put a stop to *that!* Byrd thought, glancing at his daughter's averted profile. He had dragged her back to school, and forbade her ever to speak to the Baronet again, should chance throw them together. She had wept and promised, and seemed so abashed by the whole episode that Byrd had been very gentle with her, and ended by sending her a new ivory fan as consolation. She needed a mother's guidance, Byrd thought, and so did little Wilhelmina, who was seven, and still living with his Horsmanden cousins in Essex. Though it was Evelyn who seemed to have inherited the violent willfulness of her mother, and of her maternal grandfather, Daniel Parke, Governor of the Leeward Islands, who had there contrived to get himself most gruesomely murdered.

Byrd moved irritably on the coach seat, dismissing painful memories and considering the wifely possibilities of Maria Taylor, who had neither high birth, beauty, nor large fortune to recommend her, and was moreover encumbered by a veritable gorgon of a mother. Yet, on the other hand Miss Taylor was young, healthy, and well educated, and she dispensed balm to an oft-wounded heart for she showed genuine signs of attachment to himself.

Jenny huddled between the two silent Byrds, and being unable to see over them out of the windows, fell to picturing scenery in her head, as she often did. Sometimes she thought about the sea—tumultuous waves, white-flecked under moonlight, but always she ended by picturing a moor-clad mountain; dark, craggy, and yet for some reason comforting. "I will lift up mine eyes unto the hills, from whence cometh my help." Mrs. Strudick had read this out of the Psalter during morning prayer last month, and the words had caught Jenny's attention. They gave her a delighted shiver of recognition, like certain pieces of music. Jenny began to sing, "Over the hills and far away . . ." in her head, and felt a bitter-sweet pleasure, mixed with a great longing.

She wasn't sure what the longing was for, except that joined to the image of somber lowering hills was a memory of Rob. Rob had left London three years ago, "going back North," he said in a triumphant way which had wounded her, for he scarcely seemed sorry to say goodbye. Lady Betty had been there at this farewell, and very kind to Jenny later, explaining that Rob had made quite a lot of money as running footman to the Duke of Wharton. That he had won a famous footrace for the Duke, all the way from Woodstock to Tyburn. The Duke had rewarded him well, and then invested Rob's money in the South Sea Company, which was making all their fortunes—had said Lady Betty happily. So Rob would be his own master up North, and a landowner too. And Jenny was only a little girl, and mustn't fret for a rough serving-lad who was not a suitable friend for her at all. Jenny had tried to obey, and often forgot about Rob; yet the feeling

256

of being lost and rootless had deepened in her.

The Byrd coach trundled on through the flat Thames-side villages and drew up before the Peterborough mansion at Parson's Green.

Byrd ushered the two girls into the house and towards their host. Charles Mordaunt, Third Earl of Peterborough, a brisk, dapper gentleman of sixty-five, was—after a singularly hectic military and personal career—beginning to enjoy a quieter life. He stood alertly greeting his guests at the door of his ballroom, which was set out for a concert with sofas and rows of gilded chairs.

"Ha, Byrd!" said Lord Peterborough jovially. "You've brought with you *two* beautiful birds, I see!" He chucked Evelyn under the chin and gave a slight start as he examined Jenny. His wrinkled lids opened wider, his eyes lit with a connoisseur's appreciation. "*This* one yours too?" he asked of Byrd. "What a toast she'll make! Would I were forty years younger!"

Byrd disclaimed Jenny, who blushed and curtsied, thinking the old Earl agreeable, for all he looked very much like a cricket. "You know my family?" continued the Earl, indicating two young people who stood behind him. He introduced the Byrd party to his fourteen-year-old grandson and heir, Lord Mordaunt, and then to his niece, Elizabeth Lucy Mordaunt, who was a plain dumpy girl of about twenty. Both young Mordaunts made polite murmurs, then turned away to greet other friends. "And you know Mrs. Robinson?" said the Earl with special emphasis, and unmistakable pride. He reached out his hand to a large sweet-faced lady who had been standing quietly in the doorway. "She has consented to sing for us today."

Byrd did indeed know Anastasia Robinson. She was the reigning prima donna at the Opera House, yet managed to maintain such a formidable respectability, that rumor said Lord Peterborough, balked of his desire, had actually married her in secret. Deplorable weakness, if so, Byrd thought, since the lady was not only a public performer but a Catholic. Still Mrs. Robinson was accepted by high society, many of whom were present today, and Byrd perceived complacently that he himself knew most of them, at least by sight.

Byrd settled his two charges on a sofa in the empty ballroom, told them to stay there, then, seeing that the musicale would not start for some time, he began a leisurely tour around the rooms.

In the withdrawing room he saw the Twickenham group

chatting together animatedly. Alexander Pope, the famous poet—a hunchback with sharp probing little features—was laughing at some sally of John Gay's. This minor poet was considered to be Pope's satellite, and a chubby beaming moon he looked, too. Miss Martha Blount was seated with them, and everybody knew that Pope was as much in love with her as his warped body and mind would permit.

Byrd had met Miss Blount, and considered joining their party, when he suddenly spied the young dissolute Duke of Wharton, sprawling in an armchair and drinking brandy. Over the Duke hovered two of his particular protégés. One was Edward Young, an aspiring middle-aged playwright, who lived on the Duke's bounty, and had lately gone in for writing tragedies. In consequence Young's narrow short-chinned face wore an appropriate air of studied melancholy. The other dependent was Guido Serpini, an Italian musician whom the Duke had picked up somewhere on his travels. The Italian acted as general factotum for his patron—secretary, procurer, and even more private roles, it was said. Serpini was a North Italian and had sandy eyebrows above squinting green eyes; he smiled quickly and incessantly, disclosing pointed yellowish teeth. Byrd considered that he had a vicious look, and was just such a fellow as Wharton *would* pick for an intimate.

Philip, Duke of Wharton, was only twenty-four, and he had a girlishly pretty face beneath the wig of cascading white curls. But he was president of the blasphemous Hell-Fire Club, and he had a reputation for wildly fantastic depravity, second to none in England. He also had a lowborn wife hidden away somewhere, though her existence was disregarded alike by society and the Duke. At the moment he was ignoring his toadies and flirting languidly with Kitty, the lovely Duchess of Queensbury, and he was half tipsy no doubt. The latest lampoon about him in the coffeehouses went:

> *Some folks are drunk in fine, and some in foul weather*
> *And some, like His Grace of W——n, are drunk twelve*
> *   years together.*

Drunk or not, Wharton was no fool. He occasionally made brilliant speeches in the House of Lords, and by judicious switching of sides at the right moment, he had managed to get himself endowed with extraordinary honors, first from the Pretender in France, then from King George here.

Though in May the Duke had spoken eloquently in defense of the Jacobite Bishop Atterbury, Wharton was still considered a Whig, no matter how erratic a one; and Byrd wondered whether there was any help to be got from that quarter in the matter of Virginia's acting governorship. Other influential friends, though full of promises, had achieved nothing.

Last year Governor Spotswood had been quietly replaced by a nonentity called Drysdale. Byrd, overlooked again, had perforce remained content to be Virginia's agent. This bitter disappointment sprang from two things, as Byrd well knew— that he held no English military title, and that he was born a Colonial. Yet bigger obstacles than that had been surmounted when pressure was brought to bear in the right places. And here was a channel not yet explored. Byrd stared thoughtfully at the Duke of Wharton. He abandoned that scheme upon seeing Mrs. Howard entering the room. Henrietta Howard was not only the Prince of Wales's official mistress and had great influence at Court, but she was an old acquaintance of Byrd's and invariably charming to him. He rushed up to her, bowing and smiling.

From the sofa in the ballroom the two girls also examined the company, Jenny with dazzled interest and Evelyn with a nervous urgency. Finally she gave a start, and whispered to Jenny, "Thank God! *There* he is! Look, just behind the screen!"

Jenny looked, saw a young man eying them intently, and knew it must be Sir Wilfred Lawson. He smiled and made a slight beckoning motion to Evelyn, who rose in confusion. "If Father asks, tell him I've gone to the Necessary House, tell him 'tis the physic," she whispered, and darted towards her lover.

Jenny nodded and stared hard at a statue of Juno, praying that Mr. Byrd would not come back and question. Her every sympathy was with Evelyn, though she was puzzled by her glimpse of Sir Wilfred. He was no taller than Evelyn, and rather square; even at this distance she had seen that he was not handsome. Hardly the romantic figure Jenny had pictured on all those nights when she stood guard and Evelyn had stolen down to the school garden-gate and met him. Love must be a very strange thing, Jenny thought, which was followed by a mature inkling. Did Evelyn's passion for Sir Wilfred have something to do with her feeling for Mr. Byrd —was it partly defiance of her father?

Jenny's musings dissolved in panic as someone approached her sofa, and said, "Well!" in an emphatic voice.

It was not Mr. Byrd. It was a magnificent willowy youth, wearing diamond rings, and starry medals on the breast of his rose-brocaded coat. He was gazing down at her, a peculiar expression in his half-shut pale blue eyes, and Jenny jumped up with a frightened apology.

"No. Sit down," said the youth, shoving her on the shoulder so she had to. "I'm Wharton." Then, as Jenny looked blank as well as frightened, he added, "I'm the Duke of Wharton. Who are *you?*" He sat down beside her.

"Jane Lee," said the girl, recovering her courage. She surveyed him almost as steadily as he did her, and discovered with a mixture of fascination and repulsion that he was not a youth but a man, though his face was painted and powdered like a lady's, and he had a black crescent patch on his forehead. Also his breath reeked of something unpleasant she did not recognize, though it was certainly not wine.

"Where did you come from?" said the Duke. He pulled out his quizzing glass, and screwing it into one myopic eye, examined her insolently from the crown of her yellow hair to the undue expanse of silk-stockinged ankle.

"I came from school, with Miss Byrd, your grace," said Jenny, resenting the appraisal. Inexperienced as she was, she knew it to be sexual and almost impersonal.

"*Exceedingly young—*" he said with relish and a high-pitched laugh. He smacked his rouged lips, and ran one well-polished fingernail down her bare arm. "Don't wince, sweetheart," he said. "You're the tastiest piece of girl-flesh I've seen since leaving Paris."

Had Jenny been older, a dozen acid retorts would have occurred to her. As it was she simply voiced her prime amazement, "So you are the Duke of Wharton, Rob was running footman to!"

"What!" Wharton was startled out of his lascivious thoughts. "What do you mean?"

"I once knew a running footman who was in your service," explained Jenny hastily, wondering if she had said too much. Never before had she dared mention Rob to anyone but Lady Betty.

"I've had many footmen," said the Duke, raising a plucked eyebrow. "I shouldn't have thought a young lady would interest herself—but wait! Did you say your name was Lee? Are you Lord Lichfield's niece?"

"No," said Jenny. "I'm just, just a ward of—of the Lees." And she blushed uncomfortably.

"Ah—" The Duke gave a lazy laugh. "Now, I remember.

The little bastard, of course," he added to himself. Bastard either of his distant cousin Betty's or of that paralytic lunkhead of a colonel she'd married. It had greatly amused him when he came back from abroad to find that there existed such an irregularity in the pompous Lee household. And what a byblow one of them had begot, to be sure! She's exquisite, thought the Duke—green fruit, and I would like to ripen it. "I know the footman you mean. I hired him away from Lichfield," he said pleasantly. "Best runner I ever had. Robert Wilson. I grew quite fond of him—fonder as it happened than he was of me—great male hairy brute that he was." The Duke gave a high laugh and a shrug, which Jenny did not understand. "I treated him very well—but he left me, invested his savings in the South Sea Company, thought he was rich—poor devil."

"And isn't he?" asked Jenny anxiously.

The Duke shrugged again. "Not if he was caught when the bubble burst—like most of us."

Jenny bit her lips and was silent. She knew about the South Sea Bubble. The Lees had lost a great deal of money in it, and Colonel Lee had suffered an apoplexy as a result. Valuable paintings had been sold from the mansion on George Street, the staff cut down to four, and Jenny could not have stayed at school without Lord Lichfield's help; since Lady Betty had three children of her own to rear, and an invalid husband to care for.

"Guido!" called the Duke suddenly, and gestured towards his Italian secretary, who had been hovering some feet away. "Bring another brandy!"

"Wiz pleasure, your grace," said the Italian, running over. "Then it is permitted that I begin the accompaniments? His lordship wishes la Signora Robinson to start singing."

"Aye, indeed," said Wharton languidly. "You can do your tweedling and twanging—that's what I brought you here for. Yet stay—" The Italian turned and waited. "What do you think of my discovery?" The Duke put his hand on Jenny's neck, pinched it gently, then wound his fingers through her thick yellow hair, and pulled her head towards him. She shuddered at his touch; rage such as she had never known exploded through her body. She violently slapped the insinuating painted face which was approaching hers.

"*Per Bacco!*" whispered Guido, appalled. One or two people turned to stare curiously, wondering who the pretty girl was who seemed to have discomfited Wharton. The Duke sat immobile on the sofa, pressing his hand to his rapidly reddening cheek.

"I'm s-sorry, your grace," stammered Jenny, collapsing. "I can't b-bear to be touched."

The Duke looked at her without expression. " 'Tis plain to see you've peasant blood in you, my sweet," he said. "I dislike coarseness." He got up and walking away from her, seated himself on the other side of the room, which was rapidly filling up.

Jenny sat stiff-necked on the sofa, fiercely trying not to cry. She knew that by any of the codes she was being taught, she had been unbearably childish and ill-bred. One did not insult a duke who condescended to admire one, and who had not even hinted at what Mrs. Strudick warned all the girls were "dishonorable proposals." Yet she was not contrite. The Duke, and that Guido too, emanated a sort of decay—like rosebuds which never opened and remained hard and glossy but rotted within, giving forth at last an evil smell because of a hidden black worm inside them.

There was a bustle at the end of the ballroom. Guido glided onto the harpsichord bench, Mrs. Robinson stood up in her gentle stately way and waited for the rustlings and chair-creakings to cease.

Though longing to hear the music, Jenny looked around anxiously for Evelyn, and seeing neither her friend nor Mr. Byrd, she slid from the sofa, and got out the door, before the prima donna started the *Griselda* aria which had made her famous.

Jenny found Evelyn in the hall, very flushed, standing with her hand to her forehead, leaning against the wall. Mr. Byrd stood there too, scowling at his daughter.

Jenny came up to them timidly, and Byrd said with a start, "Oh, Miss Jenny, I'd quite forgot you. We're leaving at once, the coach is coming." He walked to the door to see if it was there, and Jenny whispered, "What happened?"

"He saw Wilfred with me in the garden," Evelyn whispered back. "I denied it, but he's pretty sure. He's sending me away to Essex. To my cousins at Purleigh. Jenny, see that Wilfred *knows!*"

Jenny squeezed her friend's hand, and desolately resigned herself to missing the musicale, and to a thunderous drive back to school. But the surprises of the afternoon were not yet over.

Just as Mr. Byrd's coach was announced, a lady came up the steps and, pushing past the footman, rushed into the hall.

"Lady Betty!" cried Jenny in amazement and delight. She ran towards the woman who had been the only mother she had really known, and curtseying, kissed her hand. Betty gave her a quick hug. "I came here to get you, dear," she said. She glanced at Mr. Byrd and Evelyn. "What—leaving already? Surely, I hear Mrs. Robinson singing?"

"My daughter has displeased me, my lady," said Byrd heavily, for once forgetting all his gallantries. "I am sending her to the country, where she may repent of her behavior."

"Dear, dear," said Betty. "I'm sorry to hear this. Well, I'll disembarrass you of Jenny. I'm taking her back to George Street with me. I've already notified the school."

Jenny gave a gasp of pleasure, while Byrd bowed and Evelyn, looking hard at her friend, formed the words "George Street" with her lips. Jenny signaled agreement. She knew that Sir Wilfred lived on George Street, not six doors from the Lees. She could now manage to tell him directly about Evelyn.

The Byrds went out, and Jenny cried, "Oh, my lady. I'm so happy. May we stay and hear the music?"

"I think not," said Betty. "I've come to fetch you, because of a very important matter. It—it can't wait."

Jenny looked up curiously, seeing that her benefactress was different from her usual quiet self. There was a youthful sparkle about her, a suppressed excitement.

"Has something good happened, my lady?" asked Jenny.

Betty's pale, rather drawn face sobered. "In a way," she said, "in a way. At least I'm sure *you'll* think so." She sighed suddenly. "Come, child, my coach is waiting."

The long summer twilight filtered into the coach, and as they started back towards London, Betty turned to look at the girl. "Heaven!" she said. "That frock's much too small for you. You're growing up. I hadn't realized. I'll have one of mine cut down—" She broke off with an exasperated sound. "I *wish* I could buy you a new one."

"I know, my lady," said Jenny. "And you're so good to me." There was an unconscious tremble in the soft voice, and Betty put her hand over Jenny's. "Tell me, dear," she said, "have you ever wondered about yourself—where you came from?"

"Often and often," said the girl after a moment. "And I confess it has—has hurt me to find I'm baseborn."

"*Baseborn!*" repeated Betty sharply. "What do you mean by that?"

"Why, they say so at school—the mistresses—I heard

263

them, and some of the girls have taunted me. And then today the Duke of Wharton, he called me a bastard."

"Philip?" cried Betty in amazement. "Pay no attention to Philip. He's a stewpot of all the vices, and is quite mad. Anyway he knows nothing about you, nor do they at school. Poor Jenny, I had no idea . . . Tell me, whose child do they say you are?"

"The Colonel's," said Jenny miserably. "I don't think that's true, because of that time long ago—in the cellar at my Lord Lichfield's . . ."

"You remember that?"

Jenny bowed her head. "Like a dream, but I remember."

"And you've never spoken of it?"

"Never, my lady. I promised not to."

"Ah, you're a loyal child," said Betty, on a long sigh. "Sometimes I think that loyalty is the only true virtue in the world worth having." She gazed, unseeing, at the moving line of elms outside the coach.

"I've wondered, my lady," said Jenny looking down at her lap. "I've wondered if—" she faltered. "Please forgive me, if I do wrong to ask, but perhaps *you*—" She stopped as Betty turned her head and gazed at the girl's reddening face.

"No, dear," said Betty very gently. "I wish you *were* my child, in a way you should have been—but forget that. You are not. And, Jenny, though alas you may not talk about it, nor explain to anyone, you must know the truth. You are not baseborn, you are not anyone's bastard. You were born in wedlock."

Jenny breathed hard, and Betty saw in the widened eyes the light of incredulous joy, then the shimmer of tears. Her own eyes misted, and she squeezed Jenny's hand tight. Then Betty spoke with a hint of her old gaiety. "That's not to say that there isn't a bit of bastardy further back in both our lines!"

"*What*, my lady!" For a horrified instant Jenny wondered if Lady Betty was making fun of her, and if the precious assurance she had given was only a jest.

Betty went on. "Though a *king's* bastards do not really count as such, especially if they are recognized and ennobled. Your great-grandfather, Jenny, and my grandfather were the same man—King Charles the Second of England!"

"King Charles?" Jenny repeated blankly. King Charles was somebody out of the history book, the "Merry Monarch who never said a foolish thing and never did a wise one." Miss Crowe always hurried over his career and that of his brother

James to land with relief at the "Glorious Revolution." And even that was long ago, before William and Mary, and before Queen Anne.

"It's quite true," said Betty, "though I can see you doubt it. You have royal Stuart blood."

"But I can't," cried Jenny, her mind spinning. "I mean, aren't the Stuarts—*Jacobites?*"

At Jenny's expression Betty laughed outright. "You speak as though a Jacobite was a serpent, or a kind of ghoulish fiend! And so I dare say many people think. I know that you've been taught so, yet very soon I think you'll alter your opinion—at least you'll modify it."

Jenny slumped back on the red plush coach cushions. "I'm very muddled, my lady," she said, "though I see two things which make me happy, or will if I can believe them. I am not baseborn and you and I have kinship. I've ever longed for both those things."

"Then you may stop longing, my dear, and *be* happy!" said Betty with a faint smile. "In truth you don't ask much." Nor had she ever, Betty thought, looking back over the years in which she had cared for Jenny. The child had never made a demand, she had swallowed many a sorrow and uncertainty in silence. Only one wish had Jenny ever expressed, and that was about the big raw North Country lad, Rob Wilson. Yet it was three years since the lad had gone back North, and Jenny must have forgotten all about him, by now.

"My lady," said Jenny, her lovely eyes anxious, "I was rude to the Duke of Wharton. I slapped his face, when he touched my neck."

"*Did* you!" said Betty. "Well, I'm sure he deserved it." And she frowned, though not at Jenny. She knew Philip's depraved tastes and suddenly perceived that Jenny's budding beauty might bring many dangers.

"He said," went on Jenny, relieved that Lady Betty wasn't annoyed, "that I was coarse, and must have peasant blood. Is it true, my lady?"

"No. At least you could never be coarse, on that I'd stake my life. As for 'peasant' blood, perhaps in a way, your mother—" Betty stopped. How ridiculous to still feel a drumming in her ears and a clutch in the throat when she thought of Meg Snowdon. "Your mother," Betty went on, "is a simple Border lass, her folk are farmers. I—don't know much about her."

"There was darkness in the North," said Jenny slowly. "I see a little tower by a black hill and I hear the sound of water. There was a woman who loved me, I think, but hardly ever spoke to me. She had long brown hair, and o' nights would sit in the ingle, and read from a big book of Scriptures. Sometimes I think she wept, 'greeted' we called it, sometimes she was angry with a poor old daft man. My lady, was that my mother?"

"I suppose so, dear."

"And my name—was it not Snowdon?"

"No. Your name is Radcliffe, one of the proudest names in England, and your father's line goes back unbroken through earls and baronets and knights to the time of the Saxons."

"My father's name was Radcliffe?" said Jenny, struggling with a strong sense of unreality.

"It *is* Radcliffe," said Betty emphatically. "He is alive and well, and he is in London. You'll see him soon. They's why I've fetched you today, yes, you may well look startled, and there is more to come!" Betty glanced at the coach roof to be sure the panel which communicated with the footman was shut, and she lowered her voice.

"He is here incognito, Jenny. You know what that means? He should not have risked coming back, for in England he's under sentence of death—oh, rash and impetuous, daredevil as always—" Betty stopped, seeing the gray eyes grow rounder. "Never mind that. He is here under the name of Mr. Jones."

"What had he done, my lady?" the girl asked in a small voice.

"He was out in the 'Fifteen. He fought very bravely to restore the Pretender to the throne. He is in fact an entirely dedicated Jacobite. And another thing, he's a Roman Catholic. I'm sorry to give you so many shocks at once, but it's necessary now."

Jenny was very still, looking down at her knees. The joy of finding she had the right to an honored name, and was kin to Lady Betty was almost completely canceled by discovering that the mysterious father was a Catholic Jacobite in hiding. And under *still* another name!

"Shall I now be Miss *Jones?*" asked Jenny with the faintest edge to her voice. "My lady, I fear I'm not very eager to meet this—this gentleman. And I—I wonder that you—"

She trailed off, checked by politeness, but Betty understood.

"You wonder that I should be party to a deception so against my principles? I've wondered myself, and don't expect you to understand. So, my dear, there's nothing for you to do except obey, and I promise you," Betty smiled ruefully at the girl, "I believe I can assure you, that you'll not find this meeting with your father as distasteful as you seem to fear."

Two hours later, Betty sat at her husband's bedside, reading to him from the last issue of the *Flying Post*. Frank particularly liked the Court news, and the lists of shares on the Exchange. Betty read the items out mechanically while she speculated on the interview between Charles and Jenny which was taking place in Frank's erstwhile study downstairs.

Betty had made no effort to conceal Charles's visit. None of the servants had ever seen him before, and she had explained him as a potential tutor for the children, and given this verisimilitude by sending in her own three, ahead of Jenny—Little Charles-Henry, who was ten and called Harry, then Bess, who was six, and Caroline, named for the Princess, who was four. Charles, playing his part gravely, had immediately set all three some writing tasks appropriate to their various ages. Betty had removed the little ones when she took Jenny to the study, and waited only long enough to see father and daughter staring at each other in embarrassed astonishment.

Jenny's exceptional prettiness might be no great surprise to Charles, who had seen her as a baby, though it must be startling to be confronted with a nearly grown daughter. Charles, however, must inevitably be another shock to Jenny, who had endured a good many of them in the last hour. Charles did not look like any father the girl could have seen. He was twenty-nine, and extremely handsome. The haggardness and prison pallor, of course, had long since gone. His body was filled out with muscle, his skin tanned and ruddy—evidences that in exile he had managed to enjoy the outdoor sports he loved. The simple dark clothes (suitable to a Mr. Jones) became him; so did a more subdued manner. If he had lost all boyishness, and much of his swagger, and if there were faint lines of suffering around his mouth, and a hint of bitterness in his full bright gaze, to Betty at least, his appeal was but increased.

Frank on the bed gave an inarticulate grunt and waved his good hand.

Betty started and said, "I'm sorry, my dear, where was I? Oh, yes, we finished the shares, now would you like the Court news?"

Frank grunted again, and from long habit she interpreted

it as assent. There had been many months of this, ever since the dreadful day when he had been forced to admit that the South Sea Company's bubble had burst, that no amount of holding on and desperately inflating it with yet more cash, was of any avail. A hundred thousand pounds in paper profits—these were gone. His own private fortune was gone, Betty's legacy was gone—all vanished into nothingness.

Throughout England there were myriads in a similar plight, though this was chill comfort to the Lees, especially as Walpole and a few astute ones had sold out in time. What madness was it that had overcome the staid, cautious Frank? He who would never permit the paltriest of social gambling in his home had yet succumbed to the lure of a "sound investment" backed as it was by the Bank of England. Shame and despair and perhaps the feeling that his best friend Walpole had in a way betrayed him—all these had felled poor Frank. In the very act of rushing into the Exchange, he had collapsed on the sidewalk in a twitching, snoring coma.

The miseries of the next weeks Betty had mercifully forgotten. Her brother Lichfield had come to the rescue. He had settled debts, appointed a new land agent for Frank's remaining Buckinghamshire properties, and helped her govern and apportion the little income that was left. And Lichfield paid Sir Hans Sloane, the great physician, under whose constant care and bleedings Frank gradually improved. Instead of a senseless hulk, he had become half a man. He could hear and think, he could respond a little with painful halting speech, but the limbs on his right side were still much impaired.

Betty glanced at him as she read, and found his eyes fixed on her with a dumb beastlike pleading. "Oh, what *is* it?" she said. "Frank, don't look like that! You're getting better. Soon you'll be much better and can take the waters at Tunbridge. Sir Hans says so."

His mouth twitched, there was a brightening of his dull eyes; she saw, that as so often, she was able to give him reassurance.

"Shall we have the children in?" she asked. "They'll amuse you for a bit. And Jenny's here today, too." His lips moved in a question, and she hurried on. "The child had a half holiday, and I brought her home. You'll see her later." Betty pulled the bell rope, and when Frank's valet appeared she told him to send in the children.

Harry came first, holding his new beagle puppy, treading solemnly, and not looking at his father, whose invalidism he never quite got used to. He was a sturdy, serious child, much like Frank.

The little girls, however, are like me, alas, Betty thought. Or as I used to be. They both had red hair and freckles, they were pudgy, and no amount of maternal fondness could call them anything but plain.

"Come over here, Bess," said Betty to her namesake. "Can you say a new piece for Papa?"

"Yes, Mama," said the child, curtseying. "I can say 'Lithe and *list*en gentle*men* that be of *free*-born *blood*, I shall *tell* you of a *good* yeoman, his *name* was Robin *Hood.*' I know all of it. I said it for Mr. Jones in the study."

Betty saw that this allusion passed Frank by, though she thought it wise to say "I've been interviewing a possible tutor. George-Henry thinks it might be a good idea." Which was true. The Earl had suggested that a tutor would cut school expenses.

Frank nodded. His gaze reverted to Bess, and he motioned for her to start reciting. Long past were the days when he concerned himself with every household matter. Time slipped by for him in a blur, where only the immediate event had much importance.

Bess earnestly embarked on the seventy stanzas of "Robin Hood," while Caroline stood listening with her finger in her mouth and Harry played with his puppy. Frank's lids gradually closed. At the thirty-seventh stanza, the door opened and Jenny came in. She curtsied to Betty and said, "The gentleman is waiting in the study, my lady." The girl spoke steadily, but she looked dazed and very pale. "I'll sit by the Colonel," she said, with a pitying glance at the figure on the bed. She took the chair Betty vacated, and the children crowded around her; little Caroline clambered into her lap.

Betty could not help asking, "What is your opinion of Mr. Jones, my dear? Do you think he qualifies?"

Jenny raised her head and answered Betty's look, "Aye," she said, and her mouth curved into its dazzling smile. "Aye, my lady, I think he does."

Before Betty went downstairs she entered her own bedroom, where she rearranged her hair, fluffing it, pulling little curls forward on her temples. Next she tentatively rubbed the new Bavarian red liquor on her cheeks, and was half shamed, half gratified by the improvement. As she dabbed jessamine water on her neck an inner voice jeered at her for a fool, but she quelled the voice aloud. "Why *should* I look older than my years? Why need I be a frump? Bah! 'Tis every woman's duty to look her best, and I've been remiss of late."

She put her pearls in her ear lobes, selected her best lace handkerchief, and walked down to the study. Charles was standing by the open window looking out into the fragrant, sunny garden. He turned as she entered, and coming towards her kissed her on the lips. "At last, dear Betty," he said softly, "we can really talk together." He handed her to a chair, and took another one beside her. "How often in these years, I've wished for this."

The kiss, the caressing voice so disturbed her that she blushed under the rouge, and said brusquely, "Now you've seen Jenny—which is what I think you really wished for all these years! What do you think of her?"

His smile faded, and he spoke with utmost seriousness. "Jenny is everything a man could want in a daughter. She does you enormous credit too. I needn't tell you of my gratitude—sacred gratitude for Jenny's rearing—and for my own life."

Betty was aware of an unreasonable chill. Was it gratitude alone that he now felt for her? Yet if so, why not rejoice, since the old passions were as unseemly today as they had ever been. "Charles," she said quickly, "why have you risked coming back to England? 'Tis not for plotting, I devoutly pray! You've nothing to do with this recent foul conspiracy, Atterbury and that scoundrel Christopher Layer?"

"No," said Charles. "I'd nothing to do with that. Though I do what I can for the Cause, I assure you. But in Brussels, where I live, we're not in the midstream of King James's plans. The time *will* come when I shall fight for my King again. And we'll win, never doubt it! Yet I believe our best hopes now lie with a three-year-old boy—the bonniest boy in Christendom!"

"Oh," said Betty shrugging. If the Jacobites were transferring their ambitions to the Pretender's son, little Charles Edward Stuart, there could be no immediate danger. "Why then are you here?" she repeated. "It is so rash—if we'd *only* waited until the Act of Grace, you'd be pardoned like all the others instead of still being under the death sentence!"

"And do you think," said Charles smiling ruefully, "that your chivalrous, generous, charitable usurper, George, would have allowed me to remain in Newgate until the General Pardon?"

Betty was silent, then she shook her head. "No, you're right. The escape was necessary. Strange—in these nearly seven years, I had almost forgot the terrors, and the anguish of that time." She shuddered.

"And others have quite forgot," said Charles. "That's why I dare come back as Mr. Jones, a lace merchant who makes frequent trips to Belguim. His papers, which I bear, are all in order. Nor shall I stay in London long, I do assure you."

"No?" she said hiding dismay. "Where *are* you staying here?"

"A lodging on Pall-Mall with Alec. Do you remember Alec?"

"Of course. Still you've not answered my question, Charles. You'd not keep secret from me your reason for risking this journey!"

"I've no secrets from you," he answered with a certain embarrassment. "Though I think I must first explain something of my life since we last met. Shall I confine myself to snuff, or may I smoke?"

She nodded, and silently handed him the flint and tinderbox. She sat down again and waited. The smoke wreathed round them and floated out of the window as Charles began to speak.

He told her of his escape that December night on a smuggler's vessel to Boulogne, and of his wanderings until he found King James at Avignon and kneeling kissed his hand and swore allegiance. The King had wept, and raising Charles kissed him on both cheeks, greeted him as cousin and given him a jeweled crucifix in memory of James—the martyred Earl of Derwentwater. "For *him*," the King had said, "I mourned as I have not for any of all those whose blood is shed for me, and yet such are my continuing misfortunes that I can offer nothing to his family but my love and prayers." As Charles solemnly quoted the King he touched the jeweled crucifix which was hidden beneath his waistcoat.

"What sort of man is he?" asked Betty after a moment.

"Grave and silent, bowed by his troubles, yet every inch a king! And if he has faults, what man has not? 'Tis not for me to judge him—he is my sovereign by divine right."

Betty inclined her head and said no more, half envying this certainty and dedication, much as she disapproved it.

Then Charles, on a lighter note, told her of his adventures after leaving Avignon, when the King had been moved on by a nervous France to Rome, where he found asylum under the Pope's protection. There Charles had met again the young Irish captain, Charles Wogan, who had escaped from Newgate with Brigadier Mackintosh. The two young men had renewed their friendship, and enjoyed many an escapade together. Charles had even helped Wogan plan the romantic abduction of the Polish Princess, Clementina Sobieska, from Innsbruck, so that she might become King James's bride. The elopement succeeded. Clementina, pretty, devout and self-willed, became James's Queen, and in 1720 the mother of his son Charles Edward. The Jacobites exulted, they now had a true Prince of Wales and the succession was assured.

"Ah, you may believe, Betty, how we rejoiced in Rome," said Charles. "On the night the Prince was born I heard the King laugh outright! A sound so startling that we all cheered, and Lord Winton and I—yes, he was there too—were so high-flown with joy and wine we rushed from the Palazzo Muti and raced to the Tiber, wherein we plunged and swam, for all it was December!"

"And did you stay in Rome?" asked Betty smiling.

Charles shook his head, his reminiscent mirth died away. It was soon after the Prince's birth that Charles received a letter from Sir John Webb, Ann Derwentwater's father, summoning him to Brussels. Lady Derwentwater and her two children were there already, wrote Sir John. And it was proper that Charles should join them, as protector to his poor brother's widow. It was also financially advisable, added the practical old Baronet, who had been paying Charles an intermittent pittance from his own pocket.

So Charles went to Brussels, and was welcomed by little Ann. She was greatly changed from the girl he had last seen at Dilston on the fatal mourning he and James rode out along the burn to meet Tom Forster and his men at Greenriggs. This Ann was shrunken, she stooped like an old woman. She was listless and abstracted, seldom rousing to respond even to her ten-year-old John, or the posthumous baby, Anna Maria. They were cared for by a nurse, while Ann spent most of her days praying for James's soul in her private chapel. Once a week, as her only outing, she visited their Radcliffe aunts, who were Augustinian nuns at Louvain. It was not a gay life for Charles, though of course he found some distractions in the Belgian capital, particularly after Ann was able to increase his allowance, which was paid now as from little John, the titular Earl.

After years of bitter fighting on Sir John Webb's part, and violent opposition from the Commissioners for Forfeited Estates, the Court of Delegates had decided that in view of the entail, the "infant John Radcliffe" had a legal right to inherit some of the property despite his father's attainder.

This was a great victory and relief to Sir John, who had paid over a thousand pounds to lawyers. But extracting the Derwentwater funds from the Exchequer was a tortuous business, and Walpole, loath to lose for the Crown so juicy a plum, had in the House of Commons promptly proposed a different approach. A special crippling tax on all Catholics, and revival of a voided statute under William the Third which rendered Catholics incapable of inheriting land at all.

"Well, it didn't pass the House, as I expect you know," said Charles angrily. "But, aside from my loyalties, you can see how little reason I have to love your precious Whigs."

"Yes," said Betty. "Is it then for business reasons you have come here, Charles?"

"Partly," said Charles. "I wish to see Tom Errington and Dilston. Ann appointed him her agent in the North, soon after he was released from Newgate in the General Pardon."

"He's not administering the estates well?" she asked, wondering very much where all this was leading. Throughout Charles's recital she had a feeling that he was hesitating, that something was kept back.

"Well enough, in Tom's plodding careful way—'tis not that. I had a letter from him a fortnight ago . . ." Charles put down his pipe, turned around and looking hard at Betty, said in a quick, harsh voice, "Meg is dead. Errington says so but I want to get legal confirmation."

Betty exhaled sharply, while fiery pinwheels whirled in her head. She got up and walking to the window began to twist at the velvet curtain pull. She looked out towards the blurred brightness of the garden as she said carefully over her shoulder, "So Meg Snowdon is dead, and you are free."

"Yes," said Charles frowning at her stiff back. "I cannot pretend it's anything but a piece of marvelous good fortune, at this time."

"At this time," she repeated in a cold flat tone. "You have some woman in mind you wish to marry?"

Charles made a sound in his throat and, jumping up, seized her by the shoulders, "Betty, turn around! Don't act like that! We've had love for each other, we always will have—but—"

"But?" she said. "There is more 'but' than the tenous life of my poor Frank, isn't there!"

Charles's eyelids flickered, his hands dropped from her shoulders. "What are you implying, Betty? That I wait around until your husband's death?"

She started, her head moved in a feeble, helpless gesture,

then she sank down on the chair and covered her face. "You might at least let me think so," she whispered. "For a moment let me think you wanted me—as you once did."

Charles stared down at her. He walked to the empty fireplace, knocked his pipe out against the grate, then came back, and touched her cheek. "Would you live a life of exile and poverty?" he said. "Would you subject your children to it? Would you incur the odium of all your friends and embrace the Jacobites? Do you think, Betty, that for romantic love the world, and all else in it, is well lost?"

She did not answer, her head dropped lower, and she held her handkerchief pressed against her eyes. Charles tightened his lips and said, "I did not know your husband was so very ill, Betty."

And as he spoke her seething single-minded anguish died down a little. Decency returned, bringing a picture of Frank's pleading face as he had looked at her upstairs. "He isn't," she said. "Sir Hans has told me Frank may live for years—he may even almost recover."

"Well, then," said Charles, and there was no mistaking the relief in his voice. "Darling, I *do* love you, how can you doubt it? Yet I think heaven has never meant us to be together. And we are friends, Betty, that we can always be. Isn't that better than lovers whose passions always fade?"

"*Yours* do," she said.

She dabbed her eyes and gave him a thin, bitter smile. "Charles, you have indeed altered, have become so logical and so prudent, and so right. I will endeavor to be likewise. Who is this woman you want to marry? Let me see if—as a friend—I approve your choice."

Charles reddened. This was a Betty he had never seen, and he resented her tone while knowing that he had no right to. Women—he thought, unreasonable, jealous, demanding, even such a one as Betty, to whom he owed so embarrassingly much.

"The lady," he said curtly, "is the Countess of Newburgh in her own right. A Scottish title. She is the widow of a Thomas Clifford. She's about my age."

"I see," said Betty. "Eminently suitable, and she has fortune I presume?"

"She has a comfortable jointure," he snapped.

"Splendid," said Betty, "and where did you meet this paragon?"

"At a ball in Brussels. She lives in Louvain, not being sympathetic to the regime in this fair land."

"Hah!" said Betty. "Her ladyship is a Jacobite? How very fortunate."

"It is," Charles shouted. "And far more than that. She is a Roman Catholic!"

Betty flinched. Her miserable, cutting pride gave way. "I see," she repeated but in a different tone. "And I'm glad for you, Charles. Very glad. Is she pretty?" she added despite herself.

Charles responded to the softening of her face and answered with a gleam of humor, "No, Charlotte is not pretty—not near so handsome as you are, Betty. She's dark-skinned and rather large—her black hair is oily like a Spaniard's."

"Thank you for that crumb," said Betty, with a more natural smile. "And now I need not ask if you love her very much."

"Enough," he said. "I believe we'll be compatible. That is, if she'll have me. She has indicated that she will."

"Oh, she'll have you all right, I'd wager any sum you like on that."

"That's just it!" said Charles. "I have no sums to wager, nor have you. Don't you see what this marriage will mean? Independence for me. No more living off my nephew's bounty, or begging the reluctant Sir John for a loan. If I marry Lady Newburgh I can pay back all I owe you, and I can support Jenny."

Betty was silent, while she fought off the final clutches of jealousy. This marriage apparently was indeed for Charles a tremendous piece of luck, and even were she free there was nothing she could offer him that was commensurate. And because she truly loved him, she was presently able to put her hand on his knee and say sincerely, "I wish you well, and I'll pray it comes to pass."

"Thank you," he said touched. He covered her hand with his and they sat thus for a moment. Then she began to question him further.

The Countess, it seemed, had two small daughters by the defunct Clifford. Charles made light of this, saying they were agreeable children and he would try to be a good stepfather. It occurred to Betty that a countess in her own right, and a widowed heiress to boot, might not be as amenable in regard to *Charles's* daughter, especially such a one as Jenny, and that she might keep a tight hold on her money; but Betty did not disturb Charles's happy plans. She only said gently, "I shall be very sorry to lose Jenny. She has grown into all our hearts."

"Ah—" said Charles, his whole face lighting. "How could she help it!"

Yes, I wonder very much, Betty thought, if the Countess will like the expression of his eyes, the change in his voice when he speaks of his child. Will she see, as I begin to, that no woman on earth will ever hold him close for long—except, perhaps, Jenny.

"You won't lose her yet a while," said Charles sighing. "At least after I've taken her to Northumberland and Essex, I must beg of you to care for her again, until after my marriage."

"Northumberland and Essex! Why so?" said Betty amazed.

"I want her with me every minute that I can. I must make the trip as you know, and as for Essex, my sister Mary Tudor has married one of the Petres and is living there."

"Charles, it's so dangerous! Have you forgot that you must keep in hiding? And Jenny's none so easy to hide."

"Not Essex then—" he said reluctantly after a moment. "But I'll take her north. I want her to see Dilston. I want her to see the homeland of her Radcliffe ancestors—to see—" He stopped, while Betty waited, noting with pain the sudden anguish of his face. "I want Jenny to understand why her father is an exile," Charles continued vehemently, "why he thirsts for revenge, and will never rest till he gets it. I want her to see James's grave."

ELEVEN

The fifth of September, high on the lonely, rugged Durham fells, Jenny at last approached Northumberland, the county of her birth. Charles rode ahead, Jenny in the middle, and Alec, cheerily whistling "Up in the North Countree," came last. It was late afternoon of a warm cloudy day in which bursts of sunlight alternated with sharp showers. Jenny was happy as she had never been before. She took blissful gulps of the wind-swept moorland air, while her dreaming gaze roved from her father's elegant back out over the limitless brown moors and their great drifts of pinkish-purple heather.

She was exhilarated by a sense of freedom and well-being. She had no desire in the world except the wish to find some white heather. The rare white heather meant good luck.

> They that pluck the heather white
> The de'il himself canna smite.

Someone had told her this long ago in Coquetdale. And she had searched then without success. Now as they trudged along the rough stony track which would at last lead them across the Derwent River into the Northumbrian village of Blanchland, Jenny watched for a patch of white among the purple. Once she thought she saw it, but it was only a stray ewe which lumbered to its feet and ran off, bleating angrily. A memory of London flitted through Jenny's mind and she wondered what had happened to Evelyn's love affair, though London seemed as far off as America, and equally unimportant. Ten days of travel by coach and horseback had supervened since she left London and she forgot it again when a golden plover fluttered past them, singing its liquid *Too-ee, too-ee*.

Charles did not notice the plover, he was thinking of the good horseflesh under them, and mulling over the interview with Tom Errington three days ago at York. The new horses were a joy. Jenny's chestnut mare was gentle and fleet. The girl had loved the horse on sight and named it "Coquet," somewhat to Charles's dismay. It was not the wild Borders which Charles wanted Jenny to remember in Northumberland, it was Dilston and the Radcliffe portions of the county which she did not yet know. But he had not protested. He found great pleasure in indulging Jenny. His roan snorted and shied a little as a hare streaked across into a patch of russet bracken. Charles stroked his horse's neck, delighted to have something mettlesome to ride after years of plodding Flemish nags. Even Alec was now mounted on a fine big-boned hunter.

The horses, Jenny's lace collar, gloves, and smart little silver-tipped riding crop, all were the result of an inspired bet Charles had made at the York races. Three guineas had brought him a hundred on the first race, and he had continued to win on the ensuing ones. They had merrily celebrated that night at the Black Swan in York, and next day Charles would have made more lavish purchases if Tom Errington had not arrived at the inn, by written prearrangement.

Errington was lean and serious as ever, and he very soon managed to dampen Charles's exuberance. It might be unfair to think that he was actually sorry to see Charles, but in Tom's conscientious gloomy way he indicated that this clandestine visit might be burdensome, and he expressed astonished disapproval at Jenny's presence. The country was very unsettled, he said. The Whigs on Tyneside, as represented by William Cotesworth and the other big pit-owners were extremely powerful. And there were Government spies everywhere. "I'm not saying," said Tom, "that most of the tenants at Dilston aren't still loyal to Derwentwaters. They worship the Earl's memory, though they hate Lady Derwentwater, whom they think responsible for his going out in the 'Fifteen. Most of them would probably protect you, but that's only at Dilston. You've got to be far more discreet than this as you travel north. Too many enemies'd recognize you up there, especially with that scar!"

Charles put his hand to his cheek, in some surprise. He

seldom remembered the scar. "Well, what do you suggest?" he asked slowly.

"Keep off the main roads," said Errington. "Go west to the Durham fells, then up to Dilston through Blanchland. And by the bye, don't think of visiting your aunt at Durham town." Errington went on to explain at some length that old Lady Mary Radcliffe was having trouble with the Commissioners, who were still trying to impound her estates and inflict the Catholic penal laws. She did not wish to be embarrassed with an attainted exile.

"I certainly will spare Lady Mary," said Charles dryly. He glanced at Jenny, who was sitting by the inn fire mending a rent in her riding cloak and humming to herself. Before they started the journey he had told her of her mother's death, and she had cried a little—though it was evident that she felt no great sense of loss. The relatives she had known in her early childhood seemed of far less importance to her than memories of the Dale itself—of moors and hills and burns.

"You know very well the chief reason for my visit to the North," he said, in a low voice. "I want *official* proof of Meg's death; you didn't send it to me."

"I couldn't get it," said Errington. "She's dead, I'm sure, but those Snowdons—they're wild as wolves and mad as March hares. They're Covenanters, won't go near the parish church, won't tell where she's buried."

"Then what am I going to do?" Charles frowned, unable to keep the anxiety from his voice. "Go up and force a certificate out of them?"

"I don't think that necessary. Rob Wilson is getting it. He's gone to Coquetdale with his widowed sister-in-law—Meg Snowdon's sister—that Nan Wilson who used to work for Cotesworth and warned you of the bailiffs coming to Dilston at the beginning of the 'Fifteen."

"I remember," said Charles flatly, and turned as Jenny gave an exclamation.

The girl put down her mending and leaned forward. "Did you say Robbie Wilson?" she asked, her cheeks very pink, her eyes alight. "Oh, where *is* Rob?"

Errington was startled. "I didn't know you knew him, miss. I presume that he is on his way to Dilston where he will meet your—err—Mr. Radcliffe."

"Then I'll see him!" Jenny cried. "I was so *hoping* that!"

Charles was astonished and not pleased by this enthusiasm, though fair enough to admit that Jenny had reason to remember the boy kindly. Still, he wasn't a boy any longer. Wilson must be twenty-three, and hadn't Betty said he'd gone north with a small fortune?

"What has Wilson been doing of late?" Charles asked, still frowning.

"Working the keelboats," answered Errington with a shrug. " 'Twas either that or the pits, though he had money when he came back to Tyneside, big ideas too. Bought land near Gateshead, began to build himself a manor house. Then the South Sea Company did for him, as it has for plenty of others. You'll find out, Radcliffe! Times are bad. We had floods last year and a drought this one. Dilston tenants all cry 'poor mouth,' and won't pay their rents. As I wrote Lady Derwentwater in my last accounting, I can't get out near the revenue I did when I first became her agent."

"Oh, then," said Jenny, her face clouding, "Robbie's *not* got what he wanted after all. He hasn't got the land he craved." She looked at Charles with such innocent certainty of his sympathy that he smiled at her, and said, "Yes, it seems he's right back where he started. It *is* a pity."

Jenny said nothing more, but her lovely face was solemn for some time.

Her face wasn't solemn *now*, Charles thought, as he twisted around in the saddle to see how she was doing. "Come up here, dear," he called. "I think there's room for us to ride abreast."

She flicked Coquet and trotted up beside her father. "Are we nearly there?" she asked. "Not that I care. I could ride through the moors for ever and a day, and *never* weary of them."

"You're an odd child," said Charles smiling. "And would you like riding the moors for ever and a day as well, without *me?*"

"Oh no, sir," said Jenny earnestly. "You're part of it—the —" She searched for words, and couldn't find the exact ones to express this new feeling of being sustained and cherished. "Part of the belonging," she said. "I never had that before."

"I know," said Charles quietly. "Jenny, do you think you could begin to call me 'Father,' or 'Papa'—if you prefer?"

She gave a little chuckle, and looked up at him from under the green riding hood. "It comes hard," she said. "I've had no practice all my life, and you don't look much like a 'Papa.' "

Charles straightened himself, and said with mock severity, "Nonetheless, Miss Impudence, I'm sixteen years your senior;

in fact I've just turned thirty, so I demand proper filial respect."

"Yes, Papa," said Jenny, her eyes dancing, and she made him a formal bow, from the saddle. They both burst into laughter.

Alec, watching from behind, thought, aye they're happy those two, and ye can't begrudge it to them, since neither's had much of it, and God knows what the future'll bring. What a pair they were—so bonny, with their big gray eyes, their fair hair, cleft chins, the grace with which they both carried themselves; even their laughs had the same ring. You'd think they were brother and sister. But they weren't. The girl had other blood in her too, for all the master wanted to forget it. The blood of that strange grim Border woman. It was bound to show sometime, and when it did would likely mean sorrow for the master. Alec shivered. He, too, was approaching the county of his birth, but he was not enjoying the moors as Jenny did. With each mile they covered, he felt an increase of foreboding and reluctance. And he thought of the last time he had seen Dilston. Right after the shameful defeat at Preston, when he had had to break the news to Lady Derwentwater. Aye—her poor little ladyship—so fired with joy she'd been when from the tower she saw old Monarch coming through the gate, and had thought it was her lord a-riding home.

Alec thought somberly of that night; how they'd loaded the chests of Radcliffe papers into a wagon, which he had driven all the way to the Swinburnes at Capheaton. The chests were still there, hidden in a secret room in the attic. Her ladyship had done all she could, yet if there ever was a broken heart 'twas in her ladyship's breast.

Alec shivered again, and chided himself. Going all nervish and wambly he was, getting fey like his old granny used to be, the one that had "the sight" and was forever yammering about "presences." It was Granny who'd scared off Molly— canny wee Molly Robson years ago. "Alec's na the mon fur *thee*, lass," the crone had said, glowering. "Ye'll niver hould him, fur his weird's to follow Radcliffes, he mun iver follow alang wi' Radcliffes!" Wuns! The old woman spoke true enough, thought Alec, but I wish master an' me was somewhere else, even with those jibjabbering foreigners across the water.

Ahead of him the two riders drew up on the brow of a hill, and Jenny cried, "Why, there's mist down below in the valley!"

"Yes," said Charles. "There's often mist in Blanchland. There was thick fog the night hundreds of years ago that Scottish raiders destroyed the monastery, and murdered all the monks."

"Ah—those Scots again!" said Jenny. "The bloody false thieving Scots!"

"My dear child!" cried Charles. "Your language is a trifle strong, and have you ever really known a Scot?"

She shook her head, slightly startled. "Why no—but 'tis what—what the Snawdons used to say. What happened at Blanchland, Papa?"

"A fog like this one came down and hid the monastery from the marauding Scots, who lost themselves on the moors and could not find Blanchland. Then the wretched monks rejoiced too soon at their escape. They rang the monastery bells in Te Deums of thanksgiving, and thus guided their enemies through the fog. Pillage, fire, and murder was the result."

"An' yet ye wouldna ha' me hate the Scawts!" Jenny cried indignantly.

"No sense in kettle calling pot black," Charles laughed. "An' I wouldna ha' ye slipping back into a Nor-rthumbr-rian dialect either! Lady Betty's taken far too much pains with your education for that."

Again Jenny was startled, she had not been aware of the change in her speech. "*Je vous demande pardon, monsieur mon père*," said Jenny in passable French, and she gave him a sweet, half-mocking smile, very like his own.

What a darling she was, Charles thought. An April child of quick enchanting moods. With her he forgot that he was a condemned man in hiding. He forgot the sad little household in Brussels. He forgot his intended marriage. Almost he forgot the Cause to which he had dedicated his life. The Cause which Jenny must be made to share. That she should had become of great importance to Charles.

"Master!" called Alec, trotting up to them. "The mist's bad. We'll not safely make Dilston tonight. We best find shelter in Blanchland?"

"I suppose so," said Charles reluctantly. The clinging gray dampness now swirled around them, there was not even a sign of the village below, except orange blobs which came and went like witchfire and must be candle-lit windows. "If this place were still Tom Forster's," Charles added fiercely to Jenny, "I'd not stop here for all the gold of Indies—but Errington said Blanchland's now part of Lord Crewe's estate."

"Who's Tom Forster?" asked Jenny, pulling up Coquet as

they groped across the Derwent River's ancient stone bridge.

"Forster's the cowardly swine who betrayed us at Preston," said Charles through his teeth. "Ah, child, you don't *know!* I shall see that you do—see that you understand!"

Jenny was silent. This Jacobite pother was the chief thing about her new-found father which she did not understand. In fact she resented it. Because of that so-called "King" in Rome, her father was in constant danger—though she had so far seen no evidence of it. Because of the Pretender, she had not even known who her father *was* until last month, nor now could publicly acknowledge the relationship. And why wasn't one king as good as another anyway? Especially when one was Protestant, and the other a Papist who, according to Miss Crowe, was not even legitimate. Miss Crowe fully believed that the Pretender had been smuggled into his mother's bed in a warming pan. And even if that weren't true— Charles had violently denied that it was—still the "Cause" had been lost eight long years ago. Why not forget it? Jenny thought. Why not accept what all of England wanted, or so it seemed to Jenny, whose opinions had been formed by the Lees and the school, and also by unconscious memories of the talk she had heard amongst the Snowdons in her babyhood. And if Papa would only give up all this treasonable striving, Jenny thought, would go on to King George and say he was sorry, then surely he would be pardoned. Everyone knew that Lord Bolingbroke had just been pardoned and returned to England from exile. Why even that Mr. Errington they'd met at York had been pardoned, though *he* was a Catholic. Then if Papa were free, everyone could know she was his daughter, they could live together openly, here in England, and be always as happy as they had been these last days. Thus Jenny reasoned, nor did she know of Charles's commitment to Lady Newburgh, for he had not told her about it. I'll coax Papa to change his ideas, Jenny thought, well aware of her power over him, and of his love, which she was beginning to reciprocate.

As they entered the village of Blanchland the fog lifted and changed to drizzle. They saw the ghostly shapes of gray houses, with their mossy stone roofs, they saw the dim outline of the old gatehouse, and guided by Alec, whose memory of Blanchland was surer than Charles's, they stopped by a square crenelated tower which had once been the Abbot's lodging four hundred years ago. "This was Forsters' manor house, sir," said Alec. " 'Twould be the place to ask for lodging." He pulled the iron doorknocker, which gave out a hollow bang.

Presently the door opened a crack, and a stout woman in a white mob-cap and apron stood warily behind with a candlestick in her hand. "What d'you want?" she called in a clear incisive voice.

Charles had dismounted and he walked to the door. "We're benighted," he said. "Is there room in the village to lay our heads?"

The woman held the candle higher and peered out. "We might have room," she said uncertainly. "Though we don't take in strangers, and besides—" She turned towards Charles, the light fell on his face. "Good God!" cried the woman. The yellow light trembled violently. "It can't be," she whispered, and slumped against the doorpost.

Charles took the candlestick from her limp hand and examined her closely. "Saint Mary and the angels," he said with a rueful laugh. "I believe 'tis Dorothy Forster! I'm not best pleased to find *you* here, and that's the truth."

"Come in," she said. "Come in out of the rain, your man can take the horses to the stable."

Alec was already on the cobbles, holding the stallion. He twitched at Charles's sleeve. "Have a care, sir! Can ye trust her?"

"Needs must—" said Charles. "I'll not have Jenny soaked and chilled any longer." Besides, he added to himself, he could manage any woman, and Dorothy had always seemed trustworthy, whatever her despicable brother was.

Dorothy silently led the way down a long passage to a lofty whitewashed taproom where a coal fire was burning. A frowzy little barmaid was playing with some beer mugs. Dorothy dismissed her at once. "You may go, Mab. We won't need you."

When they were alone, Dorothy bolted the door. Then she turned to Charles. "What are you doing here?" she said sharply. "Where've you come from?"

"Do you run an inn now, Dolly?" said Charles, watching her narrowly. "If so, is't your custom to question all your guests?"

"This alehouse isn't mine," she said. "It belongs to Lord Crewe's estate, but, as was his dying wish, I live here for a while each summer. What are you doing here?" she repeated. "Have you turned Whig at last, that you dare travel about in England?"

Charles eyes glinted, he examined her warily. She had

grown much heavier, her cheeks were crimson with tiny broken veins; there was a drift of gray through her chestnut hair, yet there were still signs of her former beauty, and her gaze was direct and fearless as ever. Charles put his hand slowly in his pocket, and drew out a white cockade. He fastened it with a flourish to his hat. "Does this answer you?" he said. "And *you*, Dorothy Forster, there was one member of your family not noted for steadfastness, have you followed his example?"

She opened her mouth, then snapped it shut. Color surged up her full neck. "We'll not speak of that!" she said. "Tom has suffered for all his blunders. As for your question, though there's no occasion for it any more, well, I can sing this as heartily as I once did." And she hummed the Jacobite song, "When Jemmie Has His Own Again!"

"So—" said Charles with relief. He took Dorothy's hand and clasped it warmly.

She smiled, and released her hand. "Who is this lass?" she said indicating Jenny, who was warming her back at the fire, and watching in some bewilderment the interchange between the woman and her father. "You were ever a gallant, Charles, yet this one seems o'er young to me."

"She is my daughter," said Charles curtly. "Jenny, come here and make your curtsey to Miss Forster!"

The girl obeyed. "How do you do, ma'am."

"Aye," said Dorothy looking at the fair young face with a pang of envy. "I can see she's a Radcliffe. Pray take off your wet things, later we'll sup. Here's something to warm you." She poured them each a mug of October, and heating the poker at the fire plunged it into the ale.

Charles thanked her with a bow, then held his mug high. "Long life to James the Third of England, our rightful sovereign!"

"To our king-over-the-water!" Dorothy replied. "Ah, it's been long since I've toasted him." She sighed.

Jenny did not drink, though the others were unaware of this. It wasn't right, she thought unhappily. That toast was treason. And this Forster woman—to Jenny she did not look like a lady—how unfortunate that Papa should have found her here, to aid and abet his wrong views. How can I make him *see?* Jenny thought.

Charles and Dorothy were talking. He told her something of his life abroad, and she said sadly, "I suppose you never ran across Tom?"

"I took pains to avoid it," said Charles. "I believe he's

living at Boulogne. I needn't tell you he's not welcome at King James's court."

She shook her head. "My poor brother. He had never the wits for aught but hunting and drinking, you mustn't be too hard on him." She sighed again and turned away. "It was lonely when I no longer had him to care for. Charles—I've not told you—I'm not Miss Forster any more. I wed an Armstrong, one of the Bamburgh lot."

"Indeed!" said Charles, astonished. Except for Alec he had known nobody of that name. "I trust you're happy? Where is your husband now?"

"Sailing in his coble, I suppose," said Dorothy lifting her chin. "He's a fisherman. A good one," she added defiantly. "Aye, I know what you're thinking, Charles. But he wanted me, and I'd no mind to struggle on alone."

"Of course not," said Charles without conviction. He was shocked when he thought of the suitors who used to woo Dorothy Forster, the young Widdringtons, the Swinburnes, Collingwood and Ridley, even a Percy once—the great names of Northumberland. Yet most of these were dead! he realized with a start. Still a *mésalliance* like this, for a Forster, a niece of Lady Crewe's! As bad as his own mismating, worse—since Dorothy's had been voluntary.

"The day will come," she said watching him with a faint smile, "when *all* classes will be mingled in England, and remember that in the past noble veins have oft been strengthened by a yeoman's blood. I can see you don't agree. Radcliffes've always been prideful."

Courtesy forbade Charles's answer, though Jenny was impressed. High and low blood were in her too, she thought. Even Papa could not make her of one piece, dearly as she'd love to please him.

"Hark!" cried Dorothy suddenly, putting a finger to her lips. "Someone's outside!" They listened and heard a man's voice in the passage, then somebody tried to open the taproom door. "Who is't?" called Dorothy.

The answer came in the whining, ingratiating accents Charles remembered instantly though it had been eight years since he heard them. " 'Tis Mr. Patten of Allendale, come to taste your fine ale again. Mistress Dorothy—d'ye mean you're locked in!"

Dorothy turned white and looked at Charles, who mouthed soundlessly "Patten, the informer?" She nodded and taking his arm pushed him towards the fireplace. "Inside up to the right. Priest's hole," she whispered in his ear. Then she ran to the door. "In a minute, Mr. Patten," she called. "There's a young gentlewoman in here who's swooned, and all disrobed." She ran to Jenny who had been dazedly watching her father scramble over the coals, up into the fireplace and disappear, while a shower of soot nearly extinguished the fire.

"Swoon!" said Dorothy fiercely in the girl's ear, and she pushed her down on the floor. The girl gave a gasp and shut her eyes while Dorothy flung a cloak over her. Then Dorothy unbolted the door.

"Come in, Mr. Patten," she said suavely. "Sorry to keep you waiting, but you see—" she indicated Jenny's still body. "I had to open her dress and loosen her stays."

"Dear, dear," said the vicar, his long nose quivering. He bent with interest over Jenny, whose heart was beating in great frightened thuds. "Her color's not bad—perhaps if I bled her—I've a lancet in my pocket—" Patten groped beneath the cloak for Jenny's arm, and Dorothy said, "I wonder could it be the *smallpox* striking?"

Patten jumped back. "Take her away," he said shrilly. "Take her out of here, I've never had it!"

"I don't like to disturb her yet," said Dorothy. "Perhaps 'twould be better if you left? Where are you bound, by the bye?"

"From Stanhope to Hexham," he said hurriedly. "On Government business. I can't go on tonight, the weather's foul, and my horse weary. Get rid of that girl! I command it, as agent to the Crown!"

Dorothy's eyes snapped. "Aye, Mr. Patten," she cried. "You've been well rewarded by the Crown for turning your coat, haven't you! So 'tis commands you give now to the sister of him who was once your master!"

The vicar wriggled and tugged at his clerical bands, his eyes shifted. "Mebbe I was hasty, just now, but I—" He glanced at Jenny, who had gathered that the intruder was a Whig, and yet disliked him intensely. She uttered a long shuddering moan, and cried, "Oh, oh, I feel so ill . . ."

Patten gave her a horrified look and fled out the door. Dorothy followed him into the passage. "They'll take you in at Pennypie House," she said pleasantly. " 'Tis only a mile. Good luck." She waited while he shouted to the stable boy for his horse, then she came back to the taproom. "Lie there a bit longer, Jenny," she said, "until I'm sure he's off. And if he falls in a bog on the way to Pennypie, the world'll not be the loser."

"He changed sides in the Rebellion?" asked Jenny slowly.

"He saved his own neck by selling information. Without that creeping louse's evidence, the Earl of Derwentwater'd be alive today—my brother and your father'd likely be free men instead of fugitives under a death sentence."

Jenny knit her brows. "If he'd seen my father now, you think he'd turn him in?"

"Beyond the shadow of a 'doubt. For Patten'd be well rewarded—maybe with an even finer living than the one they saved for him at Allendale."

"Why were you civil to such a man, Mistress Dorothy?" asked Jenny.

"Ah, my dear," said Dorothy. "What's done is done. And as one gets older one gets cynical. There'd be no custom at this alehouse, no market for my husband's fish, if we were too nice in our acquaintance."

While Jenny pondered this, they heard a tapping in the plastered wall above and to the right of the fireplace. "What's that!" she cried.

"Not a ghost," said Dorothy with a twinkle, "though we've ghosts at Blanchland—plenty of 'em." She went out and came back quickly. "He's really gone. I saw him head for Pennypie. Here, Jenny, help me throw ale on those coals, so your father can get down."

"Do you mean he's up in the fireplace yet!" cried Jenny. "I thought there must be a passage to the roof."

Dorothy shook her head. "There's a good-sized chamber built in the thickness of the walls; many a man's been hid there in the old days."

They doused the fire, and Dorothy called "All clear, Charles" up the chimney.

He appeared feet-foremost, covered with soot, his boots badly singed. "Whoof!" he said coughing and sneezing. "That's a well-warmed lodging you gave me! Though I'm heartily grateful for it."

"Could you hear aught?" asked Dorothy.

"Yes. There's a pinhole behind that picture! So the estimable parson of Allendale's on the prowl is he! What games I could have with him!"

"Charles, don't!" cried Dorothy. "Don't go on to Dilston! You must see now how dangerous it is!"

He smiled and whisked soot off his sleeves. "Dolly, I think I've never shown any particular reluctance to face a bit of danger? A tame life bores me. And d'you think I'd give up Dilston when I'm ten miles away, and there's never been a time these years that I've not longed to see it again?"

She shook her head. "Dilston is not the place you once knew, Charles," she said sadly.

Jenny slept that night in a big bed with Dorothy. The bedroom had been the Abbot's lodging in the old monastery, her hostess explained, and Jenny had never seen anything like it. The ancient beams were black, there were deep stone cupboards and niches in the walls. The triple lancet windows were of stone too, and had fragments of stained glass in them. They looked out over a garden which had once been the cloister. Little humps marked the graves of the murdered monks.

That night at Blanchland, an eeriness began for Jenny and continued for as long as she remained in Northumberland. It was an awareness of something close and wishful of communicating, a feeling that the veil was here very thin—more awesome than frightening—yet there were times when Jenny was frightened. She was during that night at Blanchland. Unable to sleep beside the gently snoring Dorothy, she listened to the crackles in the old woodwork, the scurrying of mice overhead. Again and again her excited brain presented her with pictures of the day just past; of the heather moors, and the cries of curlews—"whaups" she had called them in Coquetdale; of her father, and the loving teasing way he spoke to her, of the laughter they had shared. These pictures were radiant, then they darkened, as the moorland mists had swallowed the sun. There were such disturbing things about her father. His Catholicism for one. Jenny was embarrassed when he crossed himself. And worse even was his obstinate undeviating belief in the Pretender. A belief she had childishly thought to change. Patten's visit had exposed her error. The panic, the concealment, and the lies were daunting. She had herself been plunged at once into the momentary whirlpool. To refuse to do so would have injured her father. But it shouldn't *be* so, Jenny thought. She looked up at the bed's shadowy canopy, and felt a great weight in her breast. At that moment she heard the frenzied tolling of a deep bell. It seemed to come from far away and yet resounded in her ears. She sat up with a muffled exclamation.

Dorothy stirred and murmured, "What'sa matter?"

"The bell," said Jenny with a kind of sob. "Who's ringing that bell?"

"Ah, so you hear it!" said Dorothy awakening. "I don't, but others have."

"Where does it come from?" Jenny cried. "You said the church was in ruins."

" 'Tis the monastery bell," said Dorothy softly. "An echo from the long long ago."

"They rang the bell for gladness they were saved—and it was that which killed them," Jenny whispered. "Oh, it's horrible."

Dorothy soothingly touched the girl's shoulder. "You might say rather that they were punished by their own witless folly. It is often so."

Jenny put her hands to her ears, then fell back on the pillow. "It's stopped. Thank God, it's stopped."

Dorothy pulled the blankets up, and tucked them around Jenny. Poor pretty child, she thought. She's a sensitive. The future for her will never be an easy one.

The next morning Charles, Jenny, and Alec quitted Blanchland. They avoided the main road through Slaley, and struck out across Blanchland's high moor. Even Charles, upon reflection, admitted that it would be unwise to court the risk of meeting Patten, or any other unsympathetic wayfarer.

By ten they reached the brink of the Devil Water, and turning north followed the bank of that cascading turbulent stream. Now every foot of the way was familiar to Charles, and every place poignant with memory. Here was Newbiggin Cottage, where James had hid when the bailiffs were after him in 1715, and here the clump of giant hollies where Jacobite messages had been secreted; here was the Linnels Bridge, which James crossed with Charles before joining Tom Forster on that brave October morning. Here was the Dipton Wood and Swallowship, where the brothers had so often hunted the red deer together. And all along the way the burn tumbled and foamed in tiny cataracts between the fringes of silver birch, or the darkness of pines against the mossy rocks. There were glimpses now and then of the rowan ash's flame-colored berries.

Charles pointed out the landmarks to Jenny; she acquiesced quietly when he asked her if she did not think the Devil Water charming, then she added a strange remark, " 'Tis a good thing the rowan grows here, Papa, for that's a charm against evil, as everyone knows."

"Oh, nonsense, child!" said Charles. "Don't be superstitious! And what evil could there be by this beautiful burn!"

"I know," she said, and added in half explanation, "yet it has such a peculiar name."

Charles set himself to explaining the name. Jenny listened politely and was silent, as she had been all morning. There was no accounting for the melancholy which gripped her as they came upon the burn and it deepened as they rode along—not like the fear she had felt last night upon hearing the ghostly bells, but an impression of anguish. It was as though the waters sobbed. She felt thus perhaps because she had slept so little, Jenny thought, and rallied herself with the hope that soon, *soon,* she would see Robbie.

They clung to the shelter of the woods, until through the trees there loomed the huge gray-white shape of Dilston Hall, with its rows of tall windows, its balustrade and square built-in pillars—the great Palladian mansion James had built onto the old castle of his ancestors.

" 'Tis very big," said Jenny softly. "I've never seen a house so big!" She looked up at her father and saw that his mouth was twisted, his eyes filled with moisture. She looked again at the mansion and discovered that many of the windows had no glass, that brown streaks ran down the marble facing, that what must have been the lawn was waist-high in weeds. The place had a forlorn air of neglect and desertion.

"Best stay here, sir," said Alec behind them. "Under cover. I'll go see how the land lies."

Charles nodded without speaking. They waited. Jenny let Coquet browse, Charles's horse stamped and twitched. Charles paid no attention, his fixed gaze never left Dilston Hall.

In twenty minutes Alec returned. "It's all right, sir. I saw old Busby, he's been expecting you—and Mr. Brown's here!"

Charles started. "Father Brown, the priest? Why, he was in France!"

"Well, he's here now, sir. Has been for a month. He says to come to his quarters in the gatehouse. Nobody'll see you, the villagers are all at work."

"Is Rob Wilson here too?" asked Jenny in a small voice.

"Why no, miss. Though I believe there's some message."

Jenny sighed and clenched the bridle tight. They hurried from the wood, across the abandoned pleasure gardens, past the dilapidated summerhouse and the chapel until they came to the gate. The priest's quarters were next, and Father Brown in a black cassock was waiting in the doorway, his hands outstretched, his thin furrowed face beaming welcome. "My son, my son," he said hoarsely. "*Benedicite,*" and he blessed Charles, who fell to his knees and kissed the Jesuit's hand, while they both thought of their last meeting—in the Newgate cell on the day of James's death.

The priest led them into his austere whitewashed parlor. There was no furniture but stools, a table, and a large ebony crucifix on the wall. "So this is your daughter?" said Father Brown, smiling at Jenny. "Sit down, my child. Have a singing-hinny. Mrs. Busby just made them." He handed her a platterful of cakes, and Jenny took one, trying not to stare at the priest. She had never seen a priest before, but according to Miss Crowe they were all wicked wily men with serpent eyes who worshiped heathenish statues and took their orders from a scarlet monster in Rome. This Mr. Brown didn't look wicked; he looked kind and tired as he explained himself to her father.

"I've been worrying about my little Dilston flock—bereft of any spiritual comfort. I got permission from the Society to return here, until I can find myself a replacement. I had thirty at Mass last Sunday," he added smiling.

"I'm glad," said Charles, "that *something* is as it used to be. Almost I regret coming back, but I wanted to see—" He gestured towards the chapel next door, where was James's tomb. "I've brought an offering from my Lady Derwentwater she wants put there—" He broke off, and turned away.

"I understand," said the priest gently. "It will lighten your heart to know that the chapel has become quite a shrine to Catholics for miles around. I've had to forbid actual worship of the tomb of course; they had canonized him on their own, not but what it may come someday."

Charles and the priest both crossed themselves. Then Charles said, "I expected Robert Wilson waiting here with a document of great importance to me. Did Errington explain?"

"Yes. Wilson hasn't come, but there's a letter from him. A Rothbury lad brought it yesterday."

Jenny, who had been puzzled, faintly dismayed by the men's earlier conversation, jumped from her stool. "Oh Papa! What does Robbie say?"

Charles looked at the piece of folded paper, which was addressed in a firm, quite literate hand, "C. R. Jones esq. c/o Mr. Busby, Dilston." He frowned as he broke the seal and read the four lines inside. Beneath the disappointment of the message, he was startled that the young lout wrote so well and annoyed at the references to Jenny without the deferential "Miss." "This is damnably awkward," said Charles. "Damnably."

Jenny put her hand on his arm. "*Please* Papa, let me see what Rob says!"

Charles made an impatient sound. "Take it then!"

Jenny grabbed the letter and devoured the message.

> Sir—They wilnot give me what you want.
> Only Jenny might get it. Send her here.
> Not you. They'd shoot you on sight.
> I'll wait for Jenny.
> Resptfly   R. WILSON.

Jenny drew a happy breath, and held the letter close between her palms. "So I shall go to Coquetdale," she said.

"Certainly not!" cried Charles. "I'll go myself, I'm not afraid of a pack of crazy ruffians, I'll force them to behave! This is ridiculous." He was not aware that his sudden fury came as much from the way Jenny looked at the letter as from the bad news it contained. "I'll not let you go back to that miserable hole!"

Father Brown cocked his head, and surveyed Charles's angry face, then he reached out his hand to Jenny. "Give me this disturbing letter, my child." She yielded it with reluctance. He read it and said, "I think you had better leave me alone with your father. Alec is outside, he'll show you around."

Jenny sent her father a beseeching look. She had never before seen him angry. She went out with dragging feet.

"Now, my son," said the priest, "we will discuss this matter dispassionately."

Father Brown, who had known Charles since boyhood, exerted the calm authority which had always subdued the lad. He congratulated Charles on the prospects of an excellent Catholic marriage, and emphasized the need for written proof of the first wife's death. To Charles's sullen response that he knew all that but Jenny should not be involved, the priest replied with incontestable logic that Jenny was apparently the only one likely to be successful with the mission. And that it was natural the child should wish to see her birthplace once again, seemly too that she should pay some respect to her mother's memory; while it would be not only reckless but stupid for Charles to antagonize the Snowdons— let alone run the risk of getting himself shot.

"You're in enough danger here, as it is," said the priest. "Busby and I've decided that you'll stay in the steward's room in the old tower, and go forth only at night. I trust most of my own flock, yet even amongst *them* the temptation of a large reward might be too much. You'll be safe in the tower, because nobody dares go near it. Do you remember Mrs.

Selby, the blacksmith's wife, mother of the simple-minded lad?"

Charles said grumpily that he did.

"I think she's gone a bit soft in the head herself," continued the priest. "She broods on the Earl's martyrdom—can't blame her for that, but she's taken to seeing things. Now it's a white shape on top of the tower, holding a torch. She saw it first last week on August thirtieth, then last night too, and has convinced the whole village."

"Hokery-pokery," said Charles in disgust. "So I'm to be protected by a ghost!"

"I pray that the Blessed Virgin will protect you," said the priest sternly. "But I insist you take certain wise temporal precautions as well."

Thus it was that Jenny set out next day at dawn for Coquetdale, with only Alec as escort. During the first part of her journey through Corbridge and across the Roman Wall and on through open fields and marshes near Bavington, Jenny worried about her father. He had seemed unhappy when she left, though no longer angry. He kissed her hard, and impressed on her rather pathetically the importance of her mission. She saw that he suffered at being mewed up in a small dark room in the tower, and that he suffered at the general state of Dilston Hall with its tiers of echoing empty apartments from which the furniture had long since been sold. She understood that inaction was itself a punishment for him and even vaguely understood why he dreaded her journey into a place so alien to him, and so bitter in memory.

Then when they reached the moors and the edge of Rothbury Forest, Jenny forgot her father. Her spirit began to expand, a half-guilty excitement possessed her. The crag up yonder—was that where she'd found an eagle's nest? And that tumulus of stones amongst the heather, was that the one Rob had taken her to, and told her was made by the "wee folk" before the dawn of time? Mile after mile Jenny and Alec plodded on, seeing nobody but an occasional shepherd. The black-faced sheep scuttled off into the moor as they went by. The road grew rougher; they climbed around the edges of the great Simonside Hills. They skirted bogs, and sloshed through burns as brown as the peat moss.

While the sun dipped behind the darkening crags, the air freshened, and smelled of mountain grasses and burning bracken. They came to a turn in the road, and Jenny pulled up Coquet. "There's Lordenshaw," she said, pointing to a small gray stone farmhouse, surrounded with beehives. "It's a shortcut to Tosson, we'll take it."

"Are you *sure*, miss?" Alec asked anxiously. The so-called highway they had been traveling seemed bad enough to him without braving the wildest of hilly moorland.

"Aye," said Jenny guiding Coquet up a cart track. "See down there the old peel tower at Great Tosson?"

Alec protested no more, and let the girl lead him. There were still several miles to go. From time to time they passed an isolated farm, all of which looked alike to Alec, though Jenny greeted each gray stone building with a murmur of satisfaction. "Allerdene," she said beneath her breath, "Bickerton." As they passed, faces appeared at windows, staring curiously. Nobody spoke to them, the dalesmen did not encourage strangers. "There's the pine dell," said Jenny pointing with her riding crop. "We turn there, t'other side, and climb again—"

Alec said, "Very good, miss," sighing. They entered the pine glade and a man came running towards them. In the gloaming Alec did not recognize him and felt for the pistol his master had provided, but Jenny had pulled up her mare and dismounted in a twinkling.

"Robbie!" she cried, and holding out her arms started to run with the same joyous welcome she had ever shown him. Yet Jenny was no longer a child, and Rob was not as she remembered him. He had grown so big—taller and broader than her father, and his square face with its heavy black eyebrows was that of a man. Her arms dropped, she blushed and drew back. "Rob—" she said hurriedly, "I would hardly have known you."

His discomfiture was as great as hers. He saw the new beauty that had come to her, he saw the small breasts and narrow waist in the fashionable gown beneath the riding cloak, he saw the expensively gloved hands, he heard the cultured London accent in her maturing voice. She's near grown, he though. The brotherly affection and half-patronizing camaraderie he used to feel for her received a shock.

"So ye're here," he said smiling. "I've been on the watch. Good even, Alec. There's been a deal o' water o'er the dam since we last met." Rob spoke awkwardly, shifting brawny shoulders under his old leather jacket. "I see Mr. Radcliffe took my warning and bided at Dilston. A good thing too. The ould man crouches by the door, day in, day out, wi' his Bible on his lap an' his musket primed. He sleeps wi' the Bible an' the gun."

"Wuns!" said Alec. "Is Miss Jenny quite safe then?"

"D'ye think I'd let her come here, else?" said Rob. "D'ye think I canna protect her?"

"I was never afraid of Grandfather," said the girl.

"Will ye mount again, Miss—Miss Jenny?" Rob laced his hands and held them for her to step on. She hesitated, then, accepting the aid, vaulted into the saddle. In the old days, she thought, he would have lifted me by the waist, and he never called me "Miss" before. The horses began to walk, stumbling a little as they climbed the rough track up the slopes of Tosson Hill towards the Snowdon burn.

"Rob," she said after a moment, "who's now at the peel? Is it as it was—except for my mother?"

Rob shook his head. "Your Uncle Roger's gone. He married and moved to Hepple. Will, he stayed on, not being minded to wed. And now Nanny's come to bide in Meg's stead. Ye never met your Aunt Nan?"

"No," she said, and added in a low voice, "Rob, what is the coil about my mother?"

He did not answer for a bit, while he thought of what Will had reluctantly told him. Meg had never complained, indeed during the last year she seldom spoke at all, yet through the planks of the loft Will had heard her groaning many nights, and by days she often held her hand to her breast as though it hurt. She wasted away until the yellowing flesh shriveled from the sharp bones. It was old Snowdon himself who found her dead on her pallet one morning, Will told Rob, shrugging, and no wonder, for Meg had had the look and smell of death for months. Will was not there at the end. He had been off to Jedburgh selling some wedders. When he came back there was no sign of Meg's body, and the old man would not say what he'd done with it, though he muttered once that her kind of death was a judgment on them for their sins—and must be hid from all the world. To which his son indifferently agreed.

Meg's death might never have been known, if it weren't for Nan, to whom Will wrote a laconic note, bidding her come and care for their father. It was Nan who had seen the decency of telling Charles Radcliffe about an event so important to him. The Snowdon men, as Rob soon discovered, were not only indifferent but actively hostile. The hatred they had felt for Radcliffe when they forced him into marriage had intensified when they heard of his part in the Rebellion.

"Your mother must've died some time the end of March," said Rob at length answering Jenny, "but there's no proof when. And the ould man, he won't speak of it, says only that she's gan awa'—lang lang awa'."

"Then what can I *do?*" Jenny cried, remembering with dismay her father's anxious face.

"I divven't knaw, lass," said Rob more naturally than he had spoken yet. "But Snawdon, he used to be fond o' ye. 'Twas the only way Nan an' I could see to get Mr. Radcliffe's due. *We* couldna."

"It's good of you to be so friendly to my father, Rob," she said softly. "It makes me happy."

Again he was silent. It was not so much friendliness for Radcliffe which had moved Rob to connive at his escape from Newgate and now made him try to help in the matter of Meg's death. It was the love of freedom and justice springing from his own passionate, often thwarted, desire for both. Yet now for the first time he apprehended a new element which had, perhaps, always been there.

Was it because of Jenny herself that he felt inclined to aid the father? He looked quickly up at her face. It was luminous in the twilight, tendrils of golden hair blew back over the green riding hood. Her surprisingly full red lips were slightly parted in a worried little smile. Rob thought of a lass on Tyneside, an alderman's buxom daughter. They had been betrothed, during the brief period when Rob had thought himself a man of means—and a landowner. Her father had broken it off when Rob found himself penniless again. Bitter and desolate, Rob went to work in the keelboats, but the girl had felt the same—willing to throw her cap over the windmill for him—and he was pleased, and had lusted for her.

Now he did not. She seemed coarse, brash and hugger-mugger.

"Ah, there it is . . ." whispered Jenny, letting the reins fall on Coquet's neck while she gazed at the oblong thatched shape of the peel, dark against white birches beyond at the burn. The peel was smaller than she had thought, lower. She sniffed the pungent smell of warm dung and peat smoke. An old sheepdog barked warning from the byre on the ground floor. The second-story door opened above the long flight of stone steps, and she saw a woman's form there holding a candle. Suddenly Jenny slid back through the years and waited for her mother's voice to call, "Bairnie, bairnie, haste thee hame—thy supper's cooling on the hob!"

Jenny's eyes stung with hot tears, she did not look again, or heed the actual greeting which Nan was giving. She dismounted so clumsily that Rob put his arm out to steady her.

Far beyond embarrassment now, she clung to him, and buried her face on his shoulder. "I thought I'd forgot her," she whispered, half sobbing. "I thought I'd forgot her, but I haven't."

He understood, and after a second in which he held himself stiff, his arms tightened around the girl, he bent his face to her soft hair and murmured, "Hush, hinny, hush. The sorrow'll pass—the sorrow'll pass."

Nan at the top of the steps and Alec on the ground both watched with astonished disapproval, while Rob was aware of nothing but the piercing sweetness of the feel of her body against him, and Jenny knew nothing except that there had been anguish and now there was comfort. For the next few minutes Jenny was in a daze. She greeted her Aunt Nan, a thin sallow sad-eyed woman, and was relieved to see that there seemed to be nobody else in the stone room, which shocked her by its chilly bareness and dinginess. She stood forlornly by the fire. The horses stamped and whickered in the byre below them. The cow mooed inquiringly.

"Where're the men?" asked Rob of his sister-in-law.

"Will's out i' the moor," said Nan. "Faither's dozing," she pointed to a still figure in a dark corner, half screened by the plank wall of the women's cubicle. Old John Snowdon sat in his wooden armchair, a musket resting in the slitted window which commanded the northwest, from whence the plundering Scots used to attack. His big leather Bible lay on his lap, where his white beard half concealed it. His gaunt grizzled head rested against the chair back, and he slept. "I put laudanum in his beer-r," said Nan. "Faither was wild earlier an' I was afleyed Mr. Radcliffe maught be wi' ye. Wey, set ye down, ye mun all be empty as a tyum."

Nan fed them heather ale, oatcakes, and a hare stew, while she chatted politely with Alec about Tyneside. Rob and Jenny were silent. The old man snored spasmodically. Jenny herself was half asleep, worn out by a forty-mile ride and a variety of emotions, which had all simmered down to dreamy contentment that Rob was near her. Through half-shut eyes she watched him, the straight black hair which fell below his ears, the bluish cast of his close-shaven cheeks, his big brown fingers, as they spooned or knifed up the food. She noted the black hairs on his chest where his homespun shirt fell open, and the thick muscles of his neck. Compared to her father, Rob might be thought ugly, the realization drifted in and out of her mind! To her he was just Rob, and she longed to be held close to him, as in the moment when he comforted her. She did not think of the mission Charles had sent her on.

Nan thought of the mission. She ceased talking to Alec, and was watching the girl, perturbed by the expression on the lovely innocent face. What's this? she thought. 'Tis but a callow lassie, though raised to be a lady as poor Meg sent her off to be. What is this way she looks at Robbie? And he who never raises his eyes from the table! Was it a blunder to summon the girl here? Rob had suffered miseries enough already from wanting to get above his class, without adding yet another heartsick muddle with Radcliffes. God blast them all! She'd send the lass back where she belonged tomorrow! And yet this was Meg's child, and it was not only for doing justice to Charles Radcliffe that Nan wanted Jenny to try to find out about her mother's death, it was so Meg's body might be found, and the poor tormented thing given a Christian burial. Now was the time to try! Now! While the old man was hazed with the drink she'd given him.

"Play the pipes, Rob!" she said sharply. He looked at her in surprise. "Aye, play 'On Cheviot Side' or 'When the Battle Is O'er'!" said Nan. "They'll awaken Faither, and Jenny do ye gan to him an' try your wiles."

Rob walked to a wall peg where his small-pipes hung. He placed the thongs around his arm and body, the bellows under his right elbow, the goatskin bag and its straight wooden drones at his waist. He fingered the chanter, pressed the bellows with his elbow, and the first sweet, plaintive flutelike notes came out. As Rob played his face altered, a subtle radiance imbued it. He played masterfully—though no one there was capable of judging how much he surpassed the playing of his teacher, Jem Bailey, the Faw; yet Jenny knew the the music was truly beautiful, and that this was a side of Rob she had not guessed. He did not play either of the tunes Nan had suggested. He improvised something which had in it the wild magic of the moors, the sighing of the wind, and the song of the lavrocks; underneath there was an urgency, almost a command. The old man felt it, and stirred restlessly, he jerked himself upright, and clutched the Bible to his chest.

Jenny felt it, and going to her grandfather, stood beside him. She put her hand on his shoulder, looking down into his blurred vacant eyes. John Snowdon blinked. The fair face and its nimbus of gold hair seemed unearthly, as the music of the pipes seemed unearthly. Is it deid I am? the old man wondered. Is't the promised land, at lang last? "Wha' manner o' body be ye?" he breathed, gazing at Jenny.

Rob played very soft. Nan and Alec watched intently from the other side of the room.

"I'm Meg's daughter, Grandfather," said Jenny, smiling into the bewildered old face. "I've come a long way to see you."

He waggled his head. "Ye speak lak' a Southron," he said sharply. Did angels speak like Southrons? he thought in dismay.

"I dinna ha' t'speak lak' a Southron, Granfaither," said Jenny, her voice taking on the lilt. "I was bor-rn in this peel, d'ye remember-r?"

"Ye wor?" he said slowly. "Mony's been bor-run i' this peel, lang-syners back an' back. Which be ye?"

She leaned closer, full of pity, trying to penetrate the mists. "I'm thy gran-datter," she said with emphasis. "I'm Meg's bairn."

The old man recoiled, his skinny arms clutched the Bible tighter, his eyes narrowed in a look of defensive cunning. "Meg's gan awa'—" he said. "Far awa'—an' she's washed i' the blood o' the lamb!"

"Where's she gan to?" said Jenny, her heart beating fast. "Ye mun *tell* me where Meg's gan to!" Her voice rang with sudden authority, strength came to her from Rob's music, and from unplumbed depths in her own nature. Rob ceased playing, Nan held her breath, while the cunning faded from the old man's eyes, which became puzzled, uncertain. Jenny had straightened, and the stern expression of her face beneath the glittering hair gave him a quiver of superstitious awe. He made a helpless gesture. "She's i' the lough," he said plaintively like a child. "I carried her in ma arms an' put her i' Darden Lough, sae the watters o' eternal life'll wash her sins awa'."

Nan gave a low keening cry. Rob shook his head violently at her, and hastily covered the sound with his music, for Snowdon turned, almost aware of the listeners. In a moment he went on speaking to Jenny in the same plaintive voice. "The Lord tould me to hide her shame—she'd a canker i' her breast—'twas the de'il gnawing her—ye'd no want *them*—" he pointed in the direction of Tosson and Rothbury, "the unsealed, the unhallowed—to see Meg's shame, wad ye?"

Jenny shut her eyes a moment. Her strength was ebbing. She heard Rob's urgent whisper, "Get the Book from him!"

The girl did not quite understand, but Nan heard and in an instant knew what Rob was thinking. She glided over to her father, and said as briskly as she could, "We mun ha' reading now from Holy Scripture—Jenny s'all read to thee!"

The old man's face darkened with quick fear, he crouched over the Bible as though he were protecting a baby. "Ye'll not touch the Book, woman!"

"Not *I*," said Nan drawing back. "Gi'e it to Jenny! She's the reet to it."

The old man hesitated. Jenny? Jane Snawdon had been his mother. Was this she? Or was there a bairn once called Jenny who nestled on his lap, prattling, in the sunny days long past? And this bairn, had he not taught her to read from this very Book? His arms went limp. "Weel—" he said with dignity. "Ye may tak' the Book, lang enow to read me a Psalm, for m'een graw dim, and' I canna m'sel."

Jenny picked the Bible from his lap, and carried it to the table where the candle stood. The old man watched her without moving. The great leather volume fell open between the Old and New Testaments. Here there were separate pages, many of them covered with hand-written entries. Nan bent over and hastily turning a page whispered, "Look!"

Rob came out of the shadows, Alec crowded near. John Snowdon, mad as he was at times, had yet never neglected the patriarchal record of life and death in his family. Jenny saw her own birth date and the name Radcliffe. They all saw the last entry, written in a wavering crabbed hand, "Margaret my daughter, died Mar. 30, 1723 God have mercy."

John Snowdon stared at the group. What were they looking at? There was something in the Book they should not see, something he'd kept hid these many months. And there was a strange man too gawping at the Book. A stranger! The old man glared at Alec, he reached out for his musket. Rob whirled and rushing forward grabbed the gun. "Nay, sir," he said quietly, putting the musket behind him. "Nay Mr. Snawdon. There's no need for this!"

The old man made a whimpering sound, his limbs went slack. "Meg's gan awa'," he said. "Far awa'—I tould ye so." His chin sank on his chest, and he gave the sharp dry sobs of the aged.

Jenny ran to her grandfather and, kneeling, put her arms around him. "Dinna greet, oh dinna greet," she said, her face against his beard. "Ye meant it weel, Grandfaither. I know ye meant my mother to be washed clean, and she is now at peace."

The old man listened, he put out his trembling hand and smoothed Jenny's hair.

TWELVE

The next morning, Nan let Jenny sleep until the sun was high over the Simonsides. All night on the straw pallet they shared in the cubicle, the girl had scarcely moved. Nan went to wake her several times, it was growing over late for the journey back to Dilston, and Nan was anxious to get her off—away from Rob. But she hadn't the heart to disturb one who lay so childish and defenseless in her exhausted sleep. Nan came back into the outer room, shaking her head.

"I doubt ye'll mak' Dilston today," she said gloomily. Alec was gloomy too, he had spent the night in the draughty loft, and was not anxious for another like it.

Rob, who was eating porridge, said, "Let her be, Nan! Let her ha' one day here, afore she goes back to her other life." And he sighed heavily.

His sister-in-law set her lips. She flung gravel into her iron stewpot and began to scour it with sharp motions. "Glad I am," she said, "that Radcliffes've got the proof they want, yet it gars me verra sad that Meg canna ha' decent burial— the daft ould beggor," she added angrily, casting a glance at the loft where her father still slept.

"Is it worse," said Rob, "to rest in the deep clean waters of a lough than to crumble in six feet o' clarty ground wi' worms to feed on ye?"

Nan did not answer. Rob had ever been thus from a boy, an irreligious man, a kind man too, though a deep proud ambitious man—and naught to show for it after all but a skill with the pipes. "Ye'll be sune off to Tyneside?" she suggested. "Back to the keels?"

"Nay," said Rob. Just that and nothing more.

It was Jenny who later found out what he had in mind. When the girl finally awoke she was heavy-eyed and pale. Rob after one look at her forbade all thought of the journey to Dilston; though how he somehow got the authority neither Nan nor Alec was quite sure. Certainly the old man had none. It was as though a lifespring had broken in him. He no longer wanted the Bible near him. He was feebly querulous, and would not leave his bed.

Rob ignored Nan's protests and asserted calmly that after porridge and milk Jenny needed a ramble on the moors. The girl brightened at once. "Oh, I'd like that, Robbie, and take your pipes, won't you? You often used to take your pipes."

He nodded. Nan lent Jenny her woolen shawl and looked glum while Rob slipped oatcakes and a piece of cheese in his pockets. "We'll be back by dark," he said.

Nan frowned. "Gan sae *lang?*" She grabbed her brother-in-law's arm, and made him face her. "Rob Wilson, d'ye knaw weel what ye're about?" she asked in a low fierce tone. "Are ye after heartache or wor-rse!"

Rob looked at her steadily. "Ye're a bubbleheaded fool, Nan," he said, "if ye think harm could ever come to yon lass—through me." He went out the door and down the steps with Jenny into a sparkling September morning.

"To the Wishing Well, first!" Jenny cried excitedly. "Do you remember how we used to go there, Rob? I used to wish for a pair of shoes to wear like the gentry. Wasn't it silly!"

He glanced down at her little feet, finely shod in Spanish leather. "It seems ye got your wish."

"Wey aye," she agreed. "And what did you wish for, Rob?"

"To better m'self," he said after a moment. "To have folk look to me wi' respect, to be beholden to none. And wasn't *that* silly!"

"Not at all. It's come true!"

"Kae-e—" said Rob making the local sound for derision. "Niver mind, off we go!"

They scrambled a mile towards the huge, romantic freestone precipice called Keyheugh, past a fantastic confusion of tumbled rocks at its base, towards a dell known as Midgy Ha. They found the Wishing Well with some difficulty, since the brink was overgrown with nettles. It was really a small spring-fed pool inside remnants of the bricks which once had lined it. A roughly carved and broken stone cross stood near; the well had been one of the hundreds dedicated to St. Cuthbert, though its rites were unchanged since the Stone Age people here propitiated the water gods.

"I've a pin," said Jenny, leaning over the well, while her long loosened hair fell forward, touching the peat-dark water and framing her profile in pale gold. She shut her eyes, and intoned with childish solemnity, "Halliwell, halliwell, tak' ma gift, an' cast a spell." She dropped the pin into the water. Then her eyes remained shut so long that Rob gave one of his rare chuckles, and said, "What'sa matter, hinny?"

She opened her eyes with a start. "I couldn't make up my mind," she said, and drew back from the well, looking troubled. Her first instinctive wish had been for Rob—Rob and her to be together like this always; yet hard on that wish had crowded another, for her father, that having found him she might never lose him. She recognized the essential conflict between these two wishes, and had ended by trying to do both, which she feared would not be efficacious. "*You* wish now, Rob!" she commanded.

He shook his head. " 'Twould be the same ould wish, an' I havena pin."

"Then here's a penny," she said, pulling one from her pocket. "Wish with that—I *want* you to, Robbie." Her limpid gray eyes were very earnest, her pink lips puckered in a mixture of pout and pleading which stirred Rob to another chuckle. "Ye're a hard lass to resist," he said, "but I'll not tak' yer penny, thank ye—at least I've still a farthing o' me *own*." He tossed one into the well. "Now come along, Jenny, 'tis a rare day when ould Simonside divven't wear his cloud cap. I want ye to see the view from up there."

They set off walking, "dandering" over the moors, not speaking much, though easily amused by tiny incidents—when Rob's shoe came off in a bog, when a brimstone butterfly settled on Jenny's nose, and when they stumbled over a stray donkey in the bracken. It followed them a while uttering mournful heehaws as Jenny called to it, "Come Cuddy, Cuddy, Cuddy!"

Jenny was aware of how young Rob became once they left the peel behind—almost as young as she. Again he was the teasing playmate of the old days. She was even aware of how startled anyone else would be to hear him laugh like that, or to see him make her a crown of tansy and heather-bells, but she did not think about it. She was completely happy in the moment, and Rob was careful that nothing should disturb her. He led their rambles towards the east, away from Darden lough or any reminder of the mournful scene last night. He took her to the windy top of Simonside where she could follow the winding bright pewter ribbon of the Coquet from the Cheviots on the west to the dark blue of the North Sea as it stretched away towards Denmark. They explored stone circles, made by the ancient people who had lived near these crags before the coming of the Romans. They jumped over tiny burns, and discovered caves, in one of which there was a whiskey still with the clear white liquid dripping merrily into a cask. "The bonny mountain dew!" said Rob, tasting a few drops. "Ugh! I'd not be risking the revenue officers for *this* muck!" And they both laughed.

"I'm hungry," said Jenny. "Where'll we find a pretty place to eat? Oh, I know—Whitton Dene. Isn't that where the elves and fairies dance?"

"Did I tell ye that?" asked Rob grinning. "I fear I tould ye a deal o' nonsense, hinny, but we'll go to Whitton Dene. Today ye shall do everything ye like."

"Today . . ." she repeated, with the first chill of realization.

Hand in hand they scrambled down the slopes and reached the little dene. If the fairies chose it for their revels they chose cannily, since there was magic in the glen. Here, watered by the Whitton burn, there grew tall ferns. Here the violet water-mint still bloomed, and the orange asphodel, beneath oak and ash and a graceful willow tree. An otter peeked at them, then dived into a pool. Rob found an ivy-covered log, where they sat side by side and consumed their food, then watched the amber water gurgling over mossy stones.

" 'Tis like the ballad," said Jenny. " 'The Oak and the Ash.' Do you know it, Rob? I love it. I've often sung it in London. 'Twas in a songbook Lady Betty has."

"I divven't remember it," he said adjusting his pipes. "You sing it and I'll follow ye."

She hummed the old tune, which had an enchanting minor cadence, and as he picked it up on the pipes she began to sing softly.

> *"A North Country lass up to London did pass*
> *Although with her nature it did not agree,*
> *Which made her repent, and so often lament*
> *Still wishing again in the North for to be.*
> *Oh the oak and the ash and the bonny ivy-tree*
> *Do they flourish at home in my own Countree!"*

She sang several more stanzas in the same nostalgic strain.
Rob did not stop her, though he was dismayed and moved.
She went on to the last verse:

> *"A maiden I am, and a maid I'll remain*
> *Until my own country again I do see,*
> *And I'll have a lad that is North Country bred*
> *Him that's allotted my love for to be.*
> *Oh the oak and the ash and the bonny ivy-tree . . ."*

She broke off short at Rob's expression. She had sung the
verse in all innocence but now she blushed. He let the bag
and pipes fall on his knee. "Ye mustna feel like that, Jenny,"
he said gravely.

"Like what?" She looked down at the soft green moss
beside her foot.

"Like any of it. Ye mustn't hanker for a place ye can niver
live in, nor could be content lang if ye did. And when ye
wed, it'll be no rough North Country lad your father'll find
for ye, nor my Lady Elizabeth neither. 'Twill be a lordling,
na doubt—and there'll be plenty'll want you," he added with
bitterness he could not control.

"I don't want *them*," she said staring at the moss. "I never
will."

"Niver's a big word, Jenny. You're full young now. Ye
don't know what the years'll bring."

She turned her head towards him, her eyes troubled as the
winter sea. "All this day, Rob, you've been helping me to say
farewell, haven't you? Farewell to Coquetdale and—" She
did not add the "you," though it trembled between them.

He shifted on the log. He toyed mechanically with the pipe-
drones. When he spoke it was to the glimpse of dark hills
through the trees. "This is m'own fareweel to the North," he
said gruffly. "Farewell," he emended. "I must conquer the
dialect."

"Why?" she cried. "Why, Robbie?"

"Because 'tis laughed at elsewhere, because 'tis not the
speech of an educated man, which I still mean to be."

"What are you going to do?"

"Try again to be m'own master. I failed before. I thought
I'd money and lands, but I'd neither. I'd nothing but a
bubble. Wuns! How they sniggered on Tyneside! Sniggered
and nickered at me for a credulous fool, and at the house I
started to build—brick it was to be—foursquare and staunch,
white cornices an' twenty windows glazed wi' crown glass,

standing i' the fair center o' my acres—fields and pastures I had—well watered, I'd planned the stables for my horses, the barns for my cattle, there were groves of oak, pine woods, and along my own bit o' burn there was a dell not unlike this one—" He shook his head and added in a different voice. "Well, it's gone. And my debts're gone too now. Two and a half years I've warked them off in the keels. I'm a free man again!"

"What will you do with freedom?" she asked timidly.

"Ah, I've thought much on that. I'll no' be the simpleton I was before in Lunnon at the beck an' call o' depraved culls like His Grace o' Wharton! I thought o' shipping to America." At her horrified gasp he shook his head. " 'Twouldna do, since I'd have to be bonded. Give up my liberty for five years. Nay, this time I'll learn a fine trade I can rise in. I'll not believe I'm good for naught but heaving coals and running races."

"You're going to London?" she cried, the joy clear in her voice.

"No, Jenny," he said slowly. "I'm going to Oxfordshire, to Ditchley Park, aye, I see how that amazes ye! I've been writing to my Lord Lichfield. He's torn down the ould castle, as maybe ye know, and is rebuilding from the ground up. He's offered me a chance to learn the building trade there under Mr. Gibbs, the architect. 'Tis rare luck and I'm grateful to his lordship."

"Yes," said Jenny. "It seems we must both be grateful to Lees. And I'm glad for you, Rob—glad you see a way of doing what you want, but—" She paused, then went on with a desperate rush, "Am I never to see you more? Surely, you can't mean that?"

He had meant exactly that, for now he knew that it was dangerous for him to be near Jenny too long, and he began to know, improbable as it was, that the girl's childish feelings for him had not altered.

Yet as she sat there looking at him so sweetly beseeching, her full mouth trembling, the foolish heather and tansy crown he had made her a trifle askew on her small beautiful head, he said the words he had never meant to admit, "An' if there's love between us, Jenny—if there is a kind o' love—"

"Yes . . . ?" she whispered.

He banged his hand on his knee. "Then we mun cut it from us!" he said violently. "Cut it from us, and fling it awa'!"

They sat silent several minutes, until Jenny stiffened. She gave him a level somber look. " 'Tis not so easy, I think, to

307

cut out love, and fling it away. Yet since you want it so—
I'll try."

She arose from the log and began to walk out of the dene,
her chin up, her shoulders proudly held under Nan's shawl.
He strangled the impulse to call her back, and then to rush
after her and cover with fierce kisses the soft white hands, the
primrose face. Instead he got up quietly and followed her,
several paces behind.

Soon they reached the road near Tosson. He came abreast
and walked beside her for a long time, while he struggled
against a weakness which he thought he had subdued. Yet
he had not, for as they passed by Bickerton he burst out,
"We might write each other—maybe—no real harm in that."

"*I* see none," she answered, without turning her head.

Now he was ashamed of his weakness, though he could not
gainsay it and by way of counterbalance, he spoke sternly.
"Tomorrow ye'll be wi' Mr. Radcliffe, as ye should be. Mind
that ye be a good, obedient daughter to him—in all things."

"Ah," she said. "I don't need *you* to tell me that, Rob. I
want to please him, though I cannot believe as he believes. I
can't bear to see him suffer for the Stuarts and for Papacy."

"Ye may come to understand," said Rob.

"Do *you* believe in them?" she asked quickly.

"I've no Stuart blood, as ye have, nor a Catholic father. I
believe in m'self, in hard toil an' in decency."

"More than that I think," she said, "or you'd not make
music as you do, nor ramble o'er the moors with me as you
did today."

" 'Tis the soft daft part o' me," he cried with anger. " 'Tis
flabbiness!"

"To be cut away—along with love?"

"Aye!" he barked out the monosyllable, stuck his hands in
his pockets, and, quickening his pace, pressed rudely ahead
of her and walked along the road as though he were alone.
She watched him as he spat suddenly at a stone.

Her sore heart seized with relief upon this vulgarity. Only
a coarse lad, after all, she thought, a pit lad—what shame that
I have yearned for him.

As they turned up the home burn, by the pine trees, Jenny
said with a childish tremble in her voice, "I shall be *glad* to
be with my father, and I shall take your advice, Rob. I'll
sing no more 'The Oak and the Ash and the Bonny Ivy-tree.' "

Rob's hands clenched convulsively in his pockets, but he
did not speak.

It was twilight of the following day before Jenny and Alec crossed the Tyne at Corbridge and entered Dilston's parklands. They had been delayed by rain, which ceased as they came in sight of the castle, perched on its high cliff. Jenny looked up, and exclaimed, "Why how strange—isn't there a torch burning on top of the old tower?"

Alec followed her pointing finger. "I don't see nothing, miss. The place looks mighty dark to me."

Jenny was uncertain herself, as a bend in the road hid the tower. It was certainly dark in the woods, and very quiet, except for the clop-clop of the two horses' hoofs. She put her hand nervously under her lace collar to feel again for the paper she was bringing her father. It was a "true copy" of the Bible entry on Meg's death, written by Rob, and signed by Nan Wilson and Alec. Now that Jenny was nearing her father, she began to rejoice in her mission's success. Of Rob she tried not to think at all. He had left the peel, during the night—set off, said Nan with obvious relief, to catch a carrier's wagon at Rothbury. They had had no more words together after reaching the peel last evening. Rob disappeared into the byre, Jenny shortly went to bed. And though there was a monstrous hurt, deep down, she was able to subdue it under both anger and reason.

"Yet there *is* a light!" she said suddenly to Alec as they came out of the copse. " 'Tis like a cresset burning. Surely you see it now?"

He peered this way and that, but saw nothing, and though a shiver went down his back, he said calmly, "Mebbe Busby's put it up to guide us. 'Twas what the family always used to do, when any o' its members was afield."

"It is a woman up there," said Jenny, puzzled. "A woman in white holding the torch high. I can see her arm. Now who could that be?"

As she spoke her mare jerked her head, gave a snort, laid her ears back, and balked, trembling. "What's the matter with Coquet?" cried Jenny, almost unseated, while Alec's hunter reared and neighed.

"The horses see her too!" said Jenny patting Coquet's neck. "Coquet raised her head and saw that woman on the tower!"

Alec wasted no time. He grabbed Jenny's bridle, yanked the mare, and mastering his own frightened horse led them both into a gallop. "Hold on tight, miss!" he cried. "We'll go around by the bridge!" In a moment the tower was out of sight. Coquet ceased trembling, both horses slowed at once to a weary plod.

"What *was* it?" said Jenny breathlessly, rearranging her cloak and skirts.

She was more startled than alarmed. At that distance she could hardly have seen the woman's face, and yet she had got an impression of terrible sadness.

"I dunno, miss," said Alec. "And I don't like it," he whispered to himself, "there's more trouble a-coming." They went the long way around by the mill, and across the Earl's Bridge up towards the front of Dilston, which obscured the tower. They drew up at Father Brown's quarters in the gatehouse, and the priest came out at once.

"I give thanks to Saint Christopher for your safe return!" he cried. "Mr. Radcliffe's been worried."

"Oh, poor Papa." Jenny dismounted and curtsied to the priest. "Where is he? I've got the paper with me."

"Good, my child. Very good, though I fear other news is bad."

"Not Papa, not to do with *him?*"

"No, no, he's well enough. He's in the chapel praying, we mustn't disturb him just yet. Come in—you too, Alec."

Father Brown led them into his bare parlor, poured a glassful of madeira for each of them. "Mr. Errington was here today," said the priest, sighing, "with a letter from Brussels—it's—it's tragic." The priest shut his eyes and murmured a prayer.

"My Lady Derwentwater," stated Alec with certainty.

The priest bowed his head. "She died on August thirtieth of virulent smallpox, and was buried immediately at Saint Monica's, Louvain. *Requiescat in pace.*" He made the sign of the cross. "Mr. Radcliffe is praying for her soul, as we all will. It must be at rest, so young as she was and has suffered so much in this life, purgatory for her can't be long."

Alec interrupted, unheeding. "It was on August thirtieth Mrs. Selby first saw the white woman in the tower holding a light!"

"I believe it was," said the priest frowning. "A coincidence."

"Miss Jenny saw her tonight!" said Alec hoarsely. "Waiting and watching as she always did for his lordship to come home. Oh, my poor, poor ladyship." He uttered a broken sound and covered his face with his hands.

"Is this true, my child?" Father Brown asked of Jenny, who was staring with round-eyed sympathy at Alec, who she had never thought possessed much feeling.

"I saw a lady, sir," she said very low, "just as Alec describes. He couldn't see it, yet the horses did."

The priest sat down abruptly on his stool. His weary thoughts ran together in confusion. He believed this girl, where he had not believed Mrs. Selby, and then the *date*— was it at the very moment of death the unquiet spirit had returned to the place of its greatest happiness, or was it for another reason? Ann had sent over to England with Charles a small silver box which she had asked him to put in the Earl's coffin, as earnest of the day when her own mortal remains would come to Dilston to join those of her lord. The box contained a lock of her hair and a private prayer, Charles thought, though he hadn't cared to ask. Anyway, it had meant a great deal to Ann, and she had seemed to regard it as a substitution for the martyred Earl's miracle-working heart. The latter Father Brown himself had conveyed to France, where it was now cherished by the Augustinian canonesses in Paris. The Earl had so willed it, during the last desperate days in the Tower, having developed great reverence for this particular convent during his childhood at St. Germain.

And now, because of the tragic news from Brussels, the disposition of the silver box had become a dying request, and was the only mortal part of the poor lady which could ever be united with her husband. We shall have to open the coffin, thought the priest with revulsion. He had been combatting this morbid wish of Charles's and had insisted that to place the box in the vault on the tomb was quite enough. It apparently was not. There might also have to be a form of exorcism. *"Pater Noster, libera nos a malo,"* he murmured, turning his anxious eyes towards the crucifix.

Jenny spent that night in a little room next her father's in the old part of the castle. From the moment she saw him— pale and haggard, his eyes red-rimmed, a hastily made black band around his left arm—she set herself to console him. And it was balm to her to see how well she succeeded, and how fervently he welcomed her. He called her his darling, and his pet. He praised her for having got the certificate, though he showed no interest in the actual events at Coquet-dale; nor did she try to tell them.

Charles, always volatile, and weary of sadness, reacted from the shock of Ann's death, and set himself to entertain his daughter and forget the dismal rites Father Brown had ordained for tomorrow. Charles did not know of what Jenny had seen on her ride home. She found herself exceedingly reluctant to mention it, partly because she knew he would chide her for being fanciful, partly because she hardly believed it herself.

When Mrs. Busby, the steward's wife, showed her to her room, Jenny made an excuse and ran up in the tower. There was nothing there at all except a small empty stone platform open to the night wind and mist.

Charles and Jenny had a gay little supper by the fireside. It was served by Mrs. Busby, who brought them brandy and a rare old claret from the cellar, then left them alone. Charles told amusing stories of his travels abroad; he even told her in a light and prankish way about some of his more respectable love affairs. Jenny listened fascinated, and was flattered that this evening he lost all paternal manner and treated her as an equal and a grown lady. He encouraged her to drink with him, he toasted her in gallant phrases, he sang the old French folk song "Auprès de Ma Blonde" and was highly amused when she admitted to understanding the words.

"Ah, sweetheart," he said, being half tipsy and much exhilarated, "what merry times we'll have together on the Continent! What pleasure 'twill be for me to dress you in the latest Parisian gowns, and to show you off to all the beau monde!"

"Am I going to the Continent?" asked Jenny, startled and excited. "But I thought we were poor!"

"Ah, well," said Charles airily, snapping his fingers. "We won't be when I marry—then everything'll be quite all right!"

"Marry?" she repeated, her jaw dropping.

"Of course, darling! Why'd you think I wanted the certificate so badly? Come, come, don't look like that! Silly one. 'Twon't change a thing between us! 'Twill only mean that you may 'sit on a cushion and gloriously dream, and feast all day long upon strawberries and cream'!"

Jenny frowned, trying to adjust to the thought of his marriage, though aware that she had been childish not to guess it before.

He leaned across the table and gently tickled the corners of her mouth. "Smile!" he commanded, giving her one of his most brilliantly tender mocking looks.

She resisted a moment, then burst out laughing. "Oh Papa! Anyway it isn't 'sit on a cushion and gloriously dream'—it's 'sew a fine seam' instead."

"Is it indeed?" said Charles, raising his eyebrows. "Yet I've noted in you a certain resistance to such labor, so you shall have a maid to do it for you—two, three maids, a whole gaggle of maids to serve my poppet!"

"Don't you think," said Jenny, "that I might get rather fat, just sitting on that cushion and feasting?"

"God forbid!" Charles cried. He cocked his head to one side, and examined her first critically, then admiringly. "I don't think you would, not the way you're made—like a willow wand—but I'll see to it you do a lot of dancing and riding just in case."

"Won't I have to go to school any more?" asked Jenny, dazzled.

"A pish to school!" said Charles. "I'll finish your education myself, and we'll travel, see the world—there's a lot of it outside this damnably dreary little island!"

Charles began to tell her about Venice, the shining water streets, the gondolas, the sunlit pink palaces where mandolins and romance eternally dwelt. He became so charmed with his visions and Jenny's rapturous reception of them that he totally forgot Lady Newburgh, or any of the other stringent realities of which his actual life was composed. His voice dropped to its most caressing note, he spoke to Jenny as though he were luring a desired woman to an assignation, as he passed from recounting the seductive pleasures of Venice to those of Paris and Rome. And when at last Jenny, being flushed with wine and very sleepy, said reluctantly that she had better retire, Charles burst out irrepressibly, "*Auprès de ma blonde, qu'il fait bon . . . fait bon dormir!*"

"*Oui*, Papa," said Jenny sweetly, a trifle puzzled. "It will be nice for us to sleep near each other tonight. It must have been lonely for you here by yourself."

Charles stiffened, his drunkenness cleared, an immense sorrowing awareness deluged him as with icy water. "Yes, child," he said slowly. "Go to bed, you must be very tired. I'll stay up and finish the bottle. And Jenny, I fear I've talked a lot of twaddle."

"Oh, I loved it, Papa," she said earnestly. "It was like going to the playhouse with Lady Betty, only better because I was partly in the play myself!"

She made him a smiling curtsey, went to her own little room and shut the door, Charles sank back in his chair, and stared into the dying fire.

While Jenny and Charles were supping, Father Brown and Busby were performing a mournful duty, informing the village of Lady Derwentwater's death, and that there would be a Requiem Mass for her tomorrow morning.

The news was received with varying degrees of lamentation, and in some cases downright apathy, while Abraham Bunting, the weaver, actually shrugged and said, "Good riddance, her ladyship wor a wicked fule."

"How dare you say that!" cried the priest. "She was good to you, and everyone at Dilston."

"She wor a Southron," said Bunting stubbornly. "Anyways she wor a false fulish woman, like i' the song Mrs. Selby sings."

The priest repressed his irritation. Mrs. Selby again! A mass of blind prejudices, fancies, and monomaniac hero-worship for the martyred Earl. Still—he thought, constrained by justice—some of her fancies, like the apparition in the tower, seemed to have foundation, and since she was a devout Catholic and also a leader in the village she had been helpful to him.

He crossed the village green and made for the blacksmith shop. Selby was still banging away at his forge; he greeted the priest respectfully and said his ould wife was i' the kitchen.

Father Brown knocked and walked in. Mrs. Selby was knitting. She was a little stick of a woman, with wispy hair, and a faraway glaze in her watery blue eyes. She jumped up as the priest came in, nearly falling over Jackie, her idiot son, who lolled on the floor playing with the ball of yarn. "Good even, sir," she cried. "Wot a honor!"

The priest replied suitably, inquired after Jackie, who gobbled something and dropped the ball of yarn, then he said, "Mrs. Selby, since I've come back here, I've heard often of a song you sing about Lord Derwentwater, will you sing it to me?"

"Ah," she said flushing importantly. " 'The Lament.' It come ter me in a dream, it did, like *he* was telling it to me, hisself." She gestured towards a picture on the wall, which the priest had never noticed. He got up and examined it. It was a crude daub, painted on wood and barely recognizable as a man, yet the Radcliffe coat of arms, and the golden crucifix the Earl had often worn, identified it. A candle burned below the portrait.

Father Brown returned to his seat without comment. "What is 'The Lament'?" he said.

Mrs. Selby put down her knitting, clasped her scrawny hands, and, looking worshipfully at the portrait, began to sing in a reedy voice that yet had a true folk quality of feeling and pathos.

314

"Fareweel to bonny Dilston Hall
  My father's ancient seat,
  None o' my own s'all bide there now
  Which gars my heart to greet.
  Fareweel each loving well-known face
  I always held so dear,
  My people now mun thole it alone
  'Tis more than I can bear.

"No more along the banks of Tyne
  I'll rove in autumn gray;
  No more I'll hear at early dawn
  The lavrocks wake the day.
  Wi' me the Radcliffe's name s'all end
  An seek the silent tomb,
  An' many a kinsman, many a friend
  Wi' me has met their doom.

"And fare thou weel, my lady wife,
  Ill, ill thou counselest me!
  I wish my ears had been stricken deaf
  Ere I heeded thy false folly.
  So when the head that wears the crown
  S'all be laid low like mine
  Some honest hearts may then lament
  Darntwatter's fallen line."

Mrs. Selby's voice quavered off, she wiped her eyes on a corner of her apron, and said, "Niver a day goes by I divven't sing it fur him, it gi'es me comfort."

The priest grunted. "It wouldn't give *him* comfort, Mrs. Selby. It's a very touching ballad, but I must request you never to sing it again."

"Whyiver not?" she snapped, disgruntled by this unexpected response. She was accustomed to praise from the village, praise and tears; indeed, her ballad was known and admired as far away as Hexham.

"Because it is partly untrue," said Father Brown sternly. " 'Tis most unfair to Lady Derwentwater, who was not responsible for urging his lordship to go out in the 'Fifteen. Also, you have no right to suggest that little John, the present Earl, will not come here to his own someday."

"I knaw he *won't*, then!" said Mrs. Selby, with spirit. "I ha' the sight, an' my dreams are niver wrong. As for her ladyship, I knaw how she wheedled an' cozzened him to—"

"You know nothing of the sort!" cried the priest, and clamped his mouth shut on anger. This was the way legends started, founded on half truths, twisted interpretations, and witless obstinacy. Yet there was no more use in scolding Mrs. Selby than there would be in scolding Jackie.

"Lady Derwentwater is dead," he said starkly. "I trust you may find some pity for her now."

The woman drew back and crossed herself, a momentary expression of shock gave way to triumph. " 'Tis what I thought," she said nodding. "I *tould* ye sir, I saw a presence i' the tower, an' ye wouldna—"

Father Brown held up his hand decisively. "We'll not discuss that. It is sufficient that you join us tomorrow morning at the Mass for the repose of her soul. Good night."

The priest went back to the gatehouse, heavyhearted. He dreaded the coming day, he dreaded the future and the increasing difficulties of guiding all the souls who were under his care, beginning with Charles Radcliffe. He spent most of the night in prayer.

It was nine o'clock of the following evening before Father Brown thought it safe for Jenny and Charles to come over to the chapel. By that time the villagers—having been given a holiday and two casks of ale by Busby—had drunk themselves into slumber.

Jenny had spent a dismal day wandering about the great deserted Hall, forbidden to go out lest someone see her. Charles had not awakened until noon, and then he had a splitting headache and no wish for company—even Jenny's. He had, however, told her what was planned for the evening, and that he insisted upon her presence. Jenny felt a thrill of horror when she understood what her father meant. They were going to open Lord Derwentwater's coffin. "Do I *have* to be there, Papa?" she pleaded. "I've never seen anyone dead."

"I'm sorry, my dear," he said inflexibly. "But you are a Radcliffe, and I can see no better way to impress on you the sacrifice one of us has made for the True Faith, and the True Cause, in neither of which you have apparently any belief."

This was Charles at his grimmest, and Jenny dared not protest. She escaped to sit on the window seat of the empty drawing room and watch rain leak through the rattling panes. In her heart there was a spark of mutiny all but smothered under apprehension. I'll not look at the horrid thing, Jenny thought. They can't *make* me open my eyes, and no dead body could convince me of *anything*. Nevertheless, she could not stop picturing what the corpse would be like, and by the time they gathered in the locked chapel she was much afraid.

"Sit down," said Charles, indicating a hassock. She obeyed. The altar candles were lit, they cast flickering shadows over the three men gathered in the chapel—her father, the priest, and Alec. The latter had a crowbar, and other tools in a basket. The priest murmured something to the altar, then turning, said to Alec, "Are you certain we're safe?"

"Aye, sir. Busby's keeping an eye on the village, yet they're all muzzy, an' wouldn't come near here at night anyhow." Alec spoke confidently though he was uneasy, not only from the gruesome task which awaited them, but from ponder whether anyone suspected the story he had told them to explain his appearance at Dilston. He said he'd left Mr. Radcliffe's employ, not being able to stick life in foreign parts, and had a fancy to see his homeland. After the first surprise, nobody had questioned him very much, except Bunting, the weaver, who had shown a stubborn hostile curiosity and disbelief.

"Well, we'd best begin," said Father Brown in a low voice. He stood aside while Charles and Alec began to prize up the flat stones which covered the Radcliffe vault. Jenny sat petrified on her hassock, while sweat beaded her forehead. The priest suddenly became aware of her fear and put his hand on her shoulder. " 'Tis hard, my child," he said softly. "Many a thing in life is hard . . ." His voice trailed off as he watched the two men, who worked in silence. The chapel floor gradually opened. Then the priest took a candle and peered down into the vault. " 'Tis that one," he said in a hushed tone to Charles, "between your father and grandfather. I'll help you raise it."

The three men hoisted the coffin up and laid it on the altar step. "Holy Blessed Virgin," whispered the priest. "It looks as fresh as the day I saw it lowered in here near eight years ago."

At this Jenny could not help a frightened glance at the great casket covered with crimson velvet. She saw the brass inscription plate and the gilt knobs twinkling.

Her fear increased as she noticed the expression of her father's face. "Open it," he said in a thick strange voice. "Let me see my brother!"

"Have you her ladyship's box ready?" asked the priest.

Charles made a sign of assent. Alec murmured a Pater Noster, gritted his teeth, and set to work with his tools. Except for the noises he made there was utter silence in the chapel while the rain spattered on the roof. Nobody saw the door handle turn softly, several times, as though someone pushed against the lock. Nobody saw a face appear and press itself against one of the south windows.

Jenny shrank tight into herself when Alec raised the coffin lid, her heart pounded, the image of the three men wavered and dimmed as she saw them lean over the coffin. She swayed and her mouth went dry as wool. Alec's trembling cry revived her.

"Blessed Mother!" cried Alec. " 'Tis a miracle!" He fell to his knees on the altar steps.

Charles and the priest stood motionless, gazing into the coffin, then the priest made the sign of the cross, and said to Jenny, "Come here, my child. Of *this* you need not be afraid!"

Jenny rose and slowly obeyed the command, she came to stand beside her father, whose hands were clenched on the casket's edge.

She looked down at what seemed to be a very pale young man, fast asleep. A young man in a full blond periwig, his small delicate hands crossed on his breast. Around his neck there was a broad linen band, faintly spotted with rusty blood. The lips were lifted in a gentle and yet enigmatic smile, the whole ivory-colored face with its closed eyes gave an impression of peace and exaltation. There was no sign of decay. On the contrary, it seemed to Jenny that she smelled a faint spicy scent like cloves, like gillyflowers.

She felt her father move beside her, saw him reach out and place a silver box on the shrouded chest above the quiet crossed hands. She heard her father whisper something about a sacred vow, and, "I swear it again by Almighty God and Our Lord Jesus Christ." Then he pulled himself upright and leaning over kissed his brother on the forehead.

The priest stood transfixed, tears running slowly down his cheeks. So bemused were they all, that a crash behind them of splintering glass seemed no more real than a distant clap of thunder. For a second even the shrill eruption of a man's voice could not rouse them from the other-worldly quiet.

Then the priest turned as a man came stamping down the aisle, shouting, "By God—Bunting was right when he sent for me! It *is* Charles Radcliffe! And the girl. You'll not diddle me again as you did at Blanchland!"

It was Patten, brandishing a pistol, his hand bleeding from the shattered window glass, through which he'd forced himself.

Alec jumped up and reached for the crowbar. Jenny could not move, while Charles stretched out his arms as though he would shield the coffin. The priest stepped forward. "What does this brawling mean?" he said. "Brawling in my church!"

The Allendale vicar gave him a furious look, then stopped dead as he reached the edge of the open vault. He recoiled, and recovered instantly. "Oh, I saw you—you Jesuit," he cried, "through the window, up to some tomfoolery. Was that to be your new hiding place, Radcliffe?" He pointed to the vault, and laughed. "There'll be no more hiding for you! I've six bailiffs outside, stout Hexham men, Bunting too, soon as I shoot this pistol, they'll be here—"

"No!" said the priest in a tone so commanding that the chapel rang with it. "Even you, I think, would not defile the House of God! Approach and see what lies before the altar!" He motioned the others to stand aside.

Patten blanched as he saw the crimson velvet coffin, he tried to turn away from the priest's steady, commanding gaze but he could not. He grasped his pistol tight, and warily came forward step by step. He mounted to the coffin and looked inside. He gave a gasp and turned violently as though to run. His legs would not obey. He looked again into the coffin, and his mean little face crumpled. The priest, scarcely breathing, thought he saw a light reflected upward onto it.

Patten stared down for a minute, then made a harsh noise in his throat. "Forgive me, my lord," he said to the corpse. "I loved you well, despite—" He threw his arm across his eyes, and backed off until he reached the chancel wall, where he stood shaking.

The priest closed the coffin lid. "Aye—" he said on a long drawn breath. "And now, Robert Patten, will you still fire your pistol?"

After a silent moment the man shook his head. "There shall be no more deaths through me," he whispered as the priest bent to hear. "Let him go! Let Charles Radcliffe go! Tell them, Mr. Brown, tell them out there that I made a mistake, that they may return to Hexham."

As the priest unlocked the door and went out to the waiting bailiffs, Patten sank onto the stone floor, and buried his head in his arms.

Charles, Jenny, and Alec left Dilston as soon as there was

light. They went back south the way they had come, along the Devil Water, where the same sorrow, the same sense of doom pervaded Jenny, though now she knew the reason. She had learned about suffering since she passed this way before, she had learned about fear and death. Her thoughts went again and again to the pathos and grandeur of that motionless figure she had seen in the coffin. She knew that Alec considered they had witnessed two miracles, the extraordinary preservation of the body and the complete change in Patten. It might be so, she had no means of judging. She knew too that her father had hoped for another miracle, that of her own conversion. This had not happened. She felt awe, pity, wonder. She now understood why her father felt as he did. But in her innermost heart something still resisted, and her heart was sad and tired.

They passed through Blanchland and did not stop, they crossed again the high Durham fells, and for Jenny the bliss was drained out of them. She sniffed the heather and the moors, she heard the curlews cry, while only pain gathered in answer—pain and the memory of a day on other moors near Tosson.

Mile after mile the subdued trio plodded on. It was not until the country changed completely, became gently green and rolling, that their spirits lifted.

On Saturday, September 28, Michaelmas Eve, they entered the village of Welwyn in Hertfordshire, and found a little fair in progress. The church porch was heaped with sheaves of grain, and apples; there were gaily painted booths set up beside the churchyard; in the lot across from it, a noisy cockfight was in progress; a troop of Morris dancers cavorted up and down the High Street, knee-bells tinkling, ribbons fluttering, and the clumsy hobbyhorse uttering realistic neighs. Best of all to Jenny, there was music—a fiddler, a guitarist, and a man with a triangle who bawled out a very ribald song about a lusty young smith "with a *jingle* bang, *jingle* bang, *jingle* hi-ho!"

The village was celebrating its harvest festival. From the Swan Inn opposite the church there floated a delectable odor of Michaelmas geese a-roasting.

Charles and Jenny, forced to pull up anyhow to let the dancers pass, looked at each other and nodded in agreement. "Very well, poppet," said Charles, as eager as she for a bit of gaiety, "we'll stay here tonight. 'Tis a goodish ride into London tomorrow, but no matter! I'll buy you a fairing," he added indicating the little booths. "What would you like?"

"A bunch of blue ribbons," she said laughing.

"To tie up your bonny gold hair? You shall have them—as token of the gewgaws I'll buy you when I can."

She sobered. They had not spoken of her future since the strange foolish night at Dilston, yet their imminent separation had begun to hang heavy over both of them. They found rooms at the Swan, left Alec to tend the horses, and sauntered out to the booths. Charles bought her sky-blue ribbons, which she tied in bows at her temples with such a distractingly pretty result tht Charles hurried her out of the crowd of leering, desirous yokels into the inn parlor.

"You can hear the music from here," he said opening the window. "Not that I consider it suitable for a maiden's ears!" He shrugged and laughed, as he recognized a raucous rendition of "The Jolly Tinker and the Landlady." He pulled the bell rope, ordered roast goose and claret. After supper he cracked walnuts for her. She took a nut, and toyed with it a moment.

"When will you leave London, Papa?" she asked carefully. "I can't bear to have you go, yet I've learned in how much danger you are!"

"I must leave at once, sweetheart," he said sighing. "Ann's death means that there's a lot I must do for the children—especially my nephew, the little Earl, who's not strong. As soon as—as all my affairs are settled, I'll send for you at once."

"Yes, Papa," she whispered. She bent her head over the nuts, knowing that he could always read her face and would see dismay there. She longed to be with him, longed to see some of the wonderful sights he had promised her, yet she did not want to leave England. Why not? she asked herself sternly. Nobody in England really loved her except Lady Betty. Yet—if there *should* be a letter, if someone *should* try to find her, and she were on the Continent . . . You idiot! cried Jenny to herself. That's finished. All finished—while underneath she heard the echo of her own voice saying, " 'Tis not so easy to cut love out, and throw it away." Not so easy to dislodge a long, long loyalty, even in favor of a new compelling one.

She glanced sideways at her father, wanting to tell him something of her doubts, hoping he might help her rid herself of them, and was startled to see an odd expression on his handsome face. He was leaning back in his chair, absently cracking nuts in his strong fingers, while he gazed through lowered lids, past her head towards the doorway. Jenny turned and saw a coarsely attractive young woman standing there. She was well, if garishly, dressed in orange taffeta and a green velvet mantle. Her black pomaded hair was piled up elaborately, her black eyes were returning Charles's stare with bold and obvious pleasure. "Is this the parlor?" asked the woman sweeping in. "I trust I don't intrude?" Her voice was rather mincing, it had a hint of cockney.

Charles got up and made her a low bow. "Indeed *not*, madam. My daughter and I were wishful of company, though dared not hope it would appear in so lovely a form!"

"La, sir!" said the woman, airily tossing her head. "How too kind you are! My coach has broken down, and forced me to stay in the midst of these rustic revelries." She waved a dirty hand loaded with cheap rings towards the street. "I presume your plight is somewhat similar?"

"Somewhat," said Charles. "We must console each other, madam!" Their eyes met in a long look, which made Jenny go hot and bewildered. When the woman quitted the parlor for a few minutes, Jenny said incredulously, "Papa, do you *like* this lady? I don't."

"She's not a lady," he said in a cold, tense voice. "She's a slut, and I believe an actress."

"Then why . . . do you . . ." She could not finish.

Why indeed? thought Charles. Why, because I haven't had a woman since London, that's why. "Go to bed, Jenny," he said. "You could not possibly understand."

She went upstairs, rebuffed and puzzled. Later she heard noises through the wall which divided her room from her father's. High-pitched giggles, the creaking of a bedstead, once an excited cry, "La, sir! You are so bold!" Then quiet.

Jenny still did not understand, though she nonetheless suffered a variety of miseries. There was jealousy and embarrassment, there was sharp disappointment that their last evening alone together should be marred like this; yet running through these dark feelings, like a silver streamlet, was a curiously maternal pity for her father.

Four days later, Jenny was back at the Hackney School, and found it nearly impossible to believe she had ever left it. Miss Crowe and her singing lessons were the same. The dancing master and the French master were the same. The sour smells, and draughts and tasteless food were the same. But Evelyn was not.

It was as well for Jenny, that she had Evelyn Byrd's heartache to distract her from her own, for she missed Charles desperately. She even missed Alec, and the journey to North-umberland now seemed a radiant dream, of which nothing remained except a kaleidoscope of poignant impressions—and Coquet. The school allowed her to keep Coquet, since most of the young ladies had their own horses; Jenny spent many an hour in the stables, stroking the mare and talking to her, and sometimes weeping into the glossy mane.

Evelyn did not weep. She had hardened since Jenny had seen her last in July; the beautiful dark eyes held a defensive, almost cynical look. Her voice had acquired an edge, but that she suffered deeply Jenny knew, though it was some days before the older girl would tell her what happened. When she did, it was one night in their bed, before they blew the candle out.

Evelyn suddenly sat bolt upright, clutching the blankets around her, and said sharply, "Would you like to see the letter my father wrote me about Wilfred?"

"Of course, Evie," said Jenny. "I've been longing to know."

Evelyn jumped from bed and unlocked her gilt jewelry box. She took out a letter and thrust it at Jenny; then she climbed back in bed and lay rigid, staring up at the tester.

Jenny held the letter near the candle and read, skipping some of the pompous phrases, as she grew more appalled at the content.

The letter was headed "To Amasia, July 20, 1723."

Considering ye solemn promise you made me, first by word of mouth, & afterwards by letter, that you wou'd not from thence forth have any Converse or Correspondence with the Baronet, I am astonisht that you have violated that protestation in a most notorious manner. The gracious audience you gave him the morning you left ye Towne, & the open conversations you have with him in the Country have been too unguarded, to be deny'd any longer. Tis therefore high time for me to reproach you with breech of duty & breach of faith, & once more to repeat to you, my strict and positive Commands, never more to meet, speak or write to that Gentleman, or give him an opportunity to see speak or write to You. I also forbid you to enter into any promise or engagement with him of marriage or Inclination.

I enjoin you this in the most positive terms upon the sacred duty you owe a Parent . . . And that neither he nor you may be deluded afterwards with Vain hopes of forgiveness, I have put it out of my power, by vowing that I Never will.   ..

Jenny made a shocked sound, and put her hand on Evelyn's arm. The girl did not move, she said through clenched teeth, "Have you finished it?"

Jenny shook her head and returned to the letter.

And as to any Expectation you may fondly entertain of a Fortune from me, you are not to look for one brass farthing, if you provoke me by this fatal instance of disobedience.

Nay, beside all that I will avoid the sight of you as of a creature detested.

Figure then to yourself my Dear Child how wretched you will be with a provokt father, & a disappointed Husband. To whome will you fly in your distress, when all the world will upbraid you with haveing acted like an Ideot? . . . For God's sake then my dear child, for my sake & for your own, survey the desperate Precipice you stand upon . . . The idle Promises this man makes you will all vanish into smoke, & instead of Love he will slight & abuse you, when he finds his hopes of Fortune disappointed. Then you & your children (if you shou'd be so miserable as to have any) must be Beggers, & then you may be assur'd all the world will deservedly dispise you, & you will hardly be pity'd so much as by Him who would faign continue—&c.

Jenny put the letter on the table, her cheeks blazing. "It's cruel!" she cried. "Cruel! I thought Mr. Byrd was fond of you!"

"He considers this a proof of fondness," said Eveyln in a toneless voice. "He can make himself believe anything he wants to."

"What are you going to do?" cried Jenny, flaming with sympathy.

"Nothing," said Evelyn. "There's nothing *to* do. He wrote an even worse letter to Wilfred, and made me read a copy. I've not heard since from Wilfred, and I believe he's gone to Cumberland."

"Oh Evelyn," Jenny said shocked, her eyes widening, "you mean Sir Wilfred gave you up? Oh, that isn't *worthy!*"

"And when does one love a man, because he's *worthy?*" said Evelyn.

Jenny was silenced, for she now knew that this was true.

"Wilfred loved me, he still does," Evelyn continued in the toneless voice. "But he's not a romantic fool, he has his career to think of, he's not well off either. The dowry and inheritance Father always promised me would have been sufficient, Wilfred and I talked about it. But to marry a penniless Colonial whose father's rage would be bruited all over a jeering London—that's another thing. And as for me —" she said suddenly turning and burying her face in the pillow, "perhaps I couldn't stand to have my father view me as 'a creature detested'—perhaps I couldn't!"

She gave a shudder and began to weep quietly into the pillow. Jenny hugged her close, searching in vain for words of comfort. After a few minutes Evelyn raised her head. "I'll love Wilfred 'til the day I die. Father may think he's won, but he hasn't. For he'll never be able to marry me off in accordance with his own stupid dreams, nor shall I ever in my deepest heart forgive him!"

THIRTEEN

On the morning of King George's official birthday, May 28, 1725, Jenny joined Lady Betty Lee at breakfast, and exhibited such a serious face that Betty put down her chocolate cup, and said, "What's the matter, dear? The doleful dumps?"

"I suppose so, my lady," said the girl trying to smile. "It's raining again," she added inadequately. She curtsied to Lady Betty and nodded to the children, then seated herself and toyed with a rasher of bacon. She knew that the depression she had awakened with was not caused by the rain; it arose from a dream she had had last night. A dream about Rob Wilson in which she was blissfully lying in his arms on a bank of heather, while the sky above them shimmered gold and violet, and from somewhere came the music of the pipes playing a love song. She had awakened crying out "Robbie—stay with me!" so vehemently that she frightened herself. What a stupid dream, when she seldom thought of Rob, and had received only one laconic note from him since their strained parting in Coquetdale nearly two years ago.

Betty had been studying the girl's face across the table, and said, "Well, cheer up, Jenny, you've treats in store. A holiday for one!"

Betty's little girls, Bess and Caroline, let out squeals of joy. They loved Jenny, who had now become their semi-governess, and toiled daily in the nursery to teach them reading, writing, and figuring, but on a holiday they could go to the kitchens, where Mrs. Prouty, the cook, let them mess about making sweets.

Harry, whose lessons with his Latin master were not affected by any maternally granted holiday, continued to eat stolidly.

"Jenny—" said Betty, "I've been thinking about you, how you have so few distractions, and that you're fifteen now. I'm going to take you to the King's Birthday Drawing Room today. You're old enough to be presented."

Jenny raised startled eyes. "Why, my lady," she said. "Do you mean it? Why, I didn't know *you* were going, you haven't been out in so long."

"I know," Betty interrupted. "I've grown to be a dull dog. 'Tis hard to be anything else without money. Yet it's only right we pay respects to the King, who has himself shown some interest in my poor husband—and the diversion will be good for both of us."

Jenny's spirits did rise, she gave Betty her singularly sweet smile, then she frowned. "But, my lady, I've nothing to wear that wouldn't disgrace you, and you—" She stopped for fear of being rude.

Lady Betty had not bought a single new gown during the past year since Jenny had left school and come to live on George Street. True, Colonel Lee had partially recovered and held a small honorary Court appointment; he could walk a little, he could speak in a halting way, but he had not recouped his fortunes. The Lees lived on Lord Lichfield's bounty, which had become smaller since the rebuilding of Ditchley Park, and the punctual production of heirs by the Catholic Lady Lichfield.

"I'll wear my old yellow tabby," said Betty, "and I've borrowed my Lady Palmerston's diamond necklace, since she is ill and can't attend, so I'll be quite fine enough—as for you, Jenny, I told you there were several treats in store!" Betty rose and opening a cupboard in the passageway reappeared with a rustling mass of rose over her arm. "Stand up," she said. "Let's see how it looks!"

It was some time before Jenny could believe that this beautiful gown was hers, a grown-up lady's dress of rose taffeta, with lace ruffles and sapphire velvet bows, the full skirts spread over enormous hoops disclosed a white satin petticoat, embroidered with forget-me-nots. There were brocaded slippers too. They had red heels and brilliant paste buckles.

Betty produced them with a conjurer's flourish from behind her back.

"But *how?*" Jenny cried, smoothing the shining taffeta

folds. "Lady Betty, you mustn't give me anything like this!"

"I couldn't, child," said Betty, sighing. "Can't you guess who sent it? It came from France," she added as Jenny shook her head.

"Father?" whispered Jenny incredulously. From Charles she had not heard in nearly a year, not since he had married Lady Newburgh, and sent a hurried though affectionate letter enclosing a draft for ten pounds. After that her own little letters brought forth no reply, and the last ones came back "unclaimed." Jenny had learned to live with this particular hurt, and was wise enough to know that Charles would always be immersed in whatever he was doing at the moment, and that for him it would be often a case of "out of sight, out of mind," though she had felt forsaken all the same.

"There's a letter," said Betty, handing it to her, "brought by the same messenger who brought the dress."

Jenny tore open the seal and saw her father's sprawling, almost illegible hand. "My dear Jenny—This gowne is to be fine in for your birthday I wish I c'ld see you in it, however [here a line was heavily crossed out] we are liveing near Paris, my lady expects a child soon, I do not wish to trouble her just now. If you write send to M. Jones, vis-à-vis La Fontaine de Carmelites, Rue et Fauxbourg St. Jacques—my homages etc. to Lady B. Your affct. C.R."

Jenny read it and handed it to Betty. "He hasn't quite forgotten me," she said with a rueful smile, "and I am so grateful for the beautiful gown and shoes—but—"

"Aye. There are many but's in life," said Betty shaking her head. "Never think he doesn't love you, and does all he dares. You're old enough now to understand that Lady Newburgh holds the pursestrings, and I rather think she has her own methods of trying to hold Charles's exclusive affections, too. I wish her luck," added Betty grimly.

Jenny's bright gaze rested on her benefactress, seeing Lady Betty, as for the first time. A pale woman with curly red hair, not handsome perhaps—the amber-brown eyes were smallish, the nose quite blunt, the big mouth curved for laughter was held too tight—yet Jenny knew the face had charm, the charm of courage, breeding, and innate goodness of heart. Jenny guessed now that Lady Betty loved her father, and saw clearly for the first time how intimately this love had affected her own life.

She went to Betty and, putting her arms around her neck, kissed her hard, then she gathered up her new dress and shoes, and hurried upstairs.

At St. James's Palace in the crowded anterooms Jenny caused a sensation, which both pleased and perturbed Betty. She heard the constant whispers of "Who *is* she?" saw the ogles and leers sent Jenny's way by the gentlemen, the envious stares of the ladies. Betty thought that Jenny handled herself well, with a subdued dignity, and only heightened color betrayed that she was aware of the attention she was causing.

There was no doubt that Charles's magnificent dress showed off Jenny's tiny waist and round breasts to perfection. The dress fitted, of course, even the shoes fitted passably; Charles was the kind of man able to make a guess at his daughter's probable size now. Betty herself had donated a wisp of Mechlin lace to perch on the brilliant golden hair, and Jenny had the beauty of Aurora—of the fresh and rosy dawn, or, as old Lord Peterborough said when he had made his way through the crush to greet Betty, "Botticelli's Venus to the life, that's your little Miss. You'll have small trouble finding her a husband in spite of well—certain drawbacks."

"You mean no money and no parentage?" asked Betty with her usual frankness. "She lacks the former, and the latter must be kept a secret, but I assure you she is true-born and of excellent lineage. As a matter of fact," Betty added, "if it came to question of a really good marriage, a fair jointure *might* be found for her!"

"Indeed," said the Earl thoughtfully. "Well, in that case you must take her about, show her off, play your cards cleverly. And beware," he added with a shrug, "of debauched married dukes . . ."

Betty followed Peterborough's glance and saw Philip, Duke of Wharton, staring at Jenny through his quizzing glass, and obviously trying to push his way over to them.

"Come, dear," said Betty to Jenny, "I think we can get into the Drawing Room now—see, the line is moving."

The King sat in a crimson velvet armchair, beneath a purple and gold canopy. He was short and very fat, his jowls hung down, his watery pop-eyes gleamed at the debutantes who were being presented to him. He rose occasionally and kissed the prettiest of them on the lips.

He kissed Jenny unctuously, murmuring, "*Schönes Mäd-chen*," while she tried not to flinch from the foul breath and shiny wet mouth. The King's German mistress, now the Duchess of Kendal, stood behind the throne. The King said something to her in German and laughed, while he still clutched Jenny's hand.

The German duchess leaned her big ungainly body forward. "His Majesty says you are to bring this *klein Backfisch* to Court more often, my lady," she said to Betty.

Betty curtsied again. "His Majesty does us honor, Your Grace." The audience was over.

They backed off and out into the farther anteroom. Here there was no way of avoiding Wharton, who was waiting for them with Dr. Edward Young in tow. "Good day, Cousin Betty," said the Duke bowing elegantly, "*and* Miss Lee, I believe. It's devilish stuffy in here, and since we've all done honor to his glorious Majesty's natal day, I propose that we take a walk in the park together."

"But it's raining," protested Betty, "and anyway I must get back to my husband."

"Not raining at all," said the Duke waving his scented white hand towards the window, where in truth there was a burst of sunlight. "And surely Colonel Lee can spare you a little longer, or I'll take charge of Miss Lee and see her safely home."

Betty gave in rather irritably. It was silly to make such a fuss about a casual invitation, and it was also rather cruel to drag Jenny home so soon, on this first outing in months. Moreover, Philip seemed on his best behavior, and not drunk. Besides, Peterborough's advice was good—if a husband were to be found for Jenny, she must be seen.

So among half the fashionable London world they strolled in St. James's Park, along the Pall-Mall promenade beneath the avenues of elm and lime trees.

Jenny, at first reluctant and embarrassed, soon began to think the Duke quite charming. He made no reference to their last unfortunate meeting when she had slapped him, he took no liberties of glance, touch, or speech. He was gravely courteous as he continuously responded to bows from passing acquaintances, and he pointed out many well-known figures to Jenny. Behind them Betty walked with Dr. Young and also enjoyed herself more than she had expected. The doctor had apparently given up writing tragedies in favor of satire. He recited some of his lines to Betty, who thought them witty, as clever as many a line of Alexander Pope's. She said so, and Young was delighted. He told her how pleasing it was to meet a charming intelligent lady, and that he hoped the pleasure might be soon renewed. Betty agreed they must meet again and really meant it, suddenly aware of how restricted her life was, and that really there was no law decreeing that she should wither away completely at the age of thirty-two.

The quarter continued to stroll for some time. They admired the ornamental ponds which were studded with geese and wild ducks, they fed the tame roe deer, and finally left the park enclosure, and were joined by the Duke's Italian factotum, Serpini. The Italian slithered along several paces behind in case the Duke should need him. The party ended up at a small tavern near Queen Anne's Gate, where they sat outside in complete democracy and the Duke ordered wine for the ladies and Young, fiery arrack punch for himself.

The May afternoon grew into one of London's finest, the sun glinted on cobblestones which the earlier rain had washed clean. A small southerly breeze blew away the smoke from nearby chimneys. There was music in the air, strips of bunting at the windows. The citizens were celebrating a gaudy day, and Jenny's heart celebrated too, not for the King's birthday, but because she was well dressed and admired, because Lady Betty was actually laughing with that queer-looking Dr. Young, and because there was a band of mountebanks coming down the street—a tumbler and a bearward leading a shambling bear, and a tiny monkey in a red cap who somersaulted, and gibbered and ran right up on the table behind them.

The Duke watched Jenny's delighted face, and beckoned languidly to the chief mountebank. "Make the bear dance," he said.

"Yes, sir—yes, your honor," said the man bowing, while the bearward jerked his chain and the old bear shuffled heavily through a few paces. Jenny had prepared to be amused; then she saw that the bear's hind paws were bleeding and that it gave a grunt of pain each time the bearward struck it with his stick. "Oh, poor beast," she cried. "Let it rest!"

The Duke did not heed her. Instead he got up and, taking the stick, himself, administered sharper jabs, delivered at the bear's most tender parts. When the bear growled and made a feeble lunge, which the chain cut short. the Duke threw back his head and gave a ringing laugh of utmost enjoyment.

"Now give me the monkey!" Wharton cried. One of the mountebanks handed the monkey over eagerly. The Duke swung it to and fro by the tail. "A wager!" he cried. "I'll wager any of you I can throw this ape as far as that house across the street! Who'll take me on?"

"Naow, naow, your lordship." whined the mounteback. "If ye kill it ye must pay for it!" The Duke shrugged and gestur-

331

ing towards the hovering Serpini said, "Give the fellow a guinea."

"Don't throw the monkey!" cried Jenny violently. "Don't you *dare* throw it!"

Betty, Dr. Young, and the Duke all turned and stared at her in astonishment. Betty had not cared for the Duke's behavior with the animals, but Londoners were accustomed to bear-baitings, cockfights, and the pelting of human beings in pillory. And she was distinctly startled at Jenny's tone. She felt it necessary to say, "That is hardly the way to speak to his grace, who is, I believe, merely trying to divert you."

"I don't want him to hurt the monkey!" said Jenny reddening. The Duke stood there, swinging the little beast by the tail, and considering her through narrowed eyes.

"Very well," said the Duke. "Then perhaps *this* will amuse you." He suddenly reached down and scooped the hat and wig from Dr. Young's head. He dumped the monkey on top of the shorn pate, where it clung for a ludicrous instant scrabbling furiously, while the outraged Young tried to smile at his patron, who let out another high peal of laughter. Serpini also cackled in the background. The monkey scuttled down Young's arm and fled, squeaking, back to its master.

"Philip, you're mad," said Betty with the ring of truth and exasperation. She helped Young adjust his wig and don his hat again.

Jenny said nothing at all, for as she turned to watch the monkey scamper away, she had caught sight of a man standing on the tavern's second-story gallery and looking steadfastly down in her direction. It *can't* be Rob, she thought, and yet she knew it was—despite the sober well-cut clothes, the cocked hat, and the dark tie-wig. Ever since the dream last night she had felt him near her, felt against all reason that she would see him. She made an instinctive beckoning gesture, then checked it, half rising from the table.

"What are you looking at, Miss Lee?" said the Duke quickly, turning around. But Rob had vanished.

"Nothing, your grace—at least I'm glad you let the monkey go—Pray forgive me, I must be excused for a moment." She turned blushing to Betty, who put the natural interpretation on this request and said, "I'll go with you."

"No, my lady," said Jenny. "No need." And she was out of her chair into the tavern before Betty could move.

Jenny ran blindly up the stairs and found Rob on the landing. "I knew I'd see you today," she cried, "though I don't know how—"

"I followed you," he said with difficulty. "Saw you in the park. *What* are you doing with the Duke of Wharton!" His heavy black eyebrows were drawn together, his intent hazel eyes held hers with a sudden intimacy which cut through all their estrangement.

"Oh, the Duke—" she said impatiently. "I can't talk now, Rob—but I beg of you to come and see me at the Lees'. Lady Betty won't mind. It's foolish that we can't have a chat. We're old friends. Come tomorrow!"

"Jenny—" he said beneath his breath, resisting as best he could. Assurance she had now, an imperiousness added to the dazzling clothes and the increased beauty. "Aye, Jenny," he said slowly. "I'll come just once—though I'm a muttonheaded booby to do it."

"I think not," she said, giving him a small sideways smile. She ran down the stairs again and out to the table where the others were waiting.

The Duke had finished his bowl of punch, and grew very quiet as he watched Jenny. He saw the heightened sparkle and glow about her and suspected that her sudden flight had something to do with a man. I must hasten, he thought, or someone else'll have the maidenhead. Erotic images flitted through his mind amid the powerful arrack fumes. The dark and secret rites—the voluptuous pleasures hidden in the rites —the forbidden, the wicked, the blasphemous, the redness of carnality which needed for its exquisite completion innocence, white and simple innocence—to be deflowered. The destruction and the mockery which produced the godlike fervor in its devotees. These delights he had not tasted for too long. These thrills might be again in store, since now there was an instrument at hand.

Betty was startled by the sudden glistening pallor of her cousin Philip's face, that smooth girlish face with its painted lips and air of delicate sophistication. She saw that the blue eyes were hard and expressionless as agate. She said low to Dr. Young, "I believe his grace has had too much punch, and in any case, sir, 'tis getting late and we must go." She rose, and Jenny with her.

The Duke did not move. His eyes rested on Jenny with the same hard blue blankness. The girl felt an instinctive creeping distaste, while she made her thank yous. The Duke did not reply. Serpini, however, bowed and smirked and showed his pointed teeth ingratiatingly. Dr. Young said he would see the ladies home. They walked off to find a hackney coach. The Duke continued to sit on at the tavern table, until at last he spoke to Serpini. "I'm going abroad soon," he said. "I've had enough of England, enough of this mingy Court. But before I go there is a matter to be accomplished—you know what I mean."

"*La bella signorina*," said the Italian with certainty. "Yet it will be difficult—if your grace is thinking of the Mass—*this* one is a lady, and well guarded, not like the last—"

"Nevertheless we will find a way—my excellent Serpini," said the Duke drawling out each word. "And quickly, before I lose the humor."

The next afternoon the Lees had several callers—an event so unusual that Briggs, the sole remaining manservant, was quite stunned and finally got the cook to polish the braid on his shabby livery. The first visitor to arrive was Edward Young. Briggs ushered him unceremoniously into the drawing room, where Betty was darning socks. Jenny was seated at the escritoire correcting little Bess's sums, and a beagle snuffled on the hearth by a small coal fire. Colonel Lee was also present, dozing in his great armchair, as he always did after dinner.

"A pleasant domestic scene," said Young in his rather stilted way. "I trust I don't intrude. I took the liberty of bringing you my latest poem, my lady."

"I'm delighted," said Betty warmly. "We were feeling rather dull, weren't we, Frank?"

Her husband roused himself, held out his good hand, indicated in halting speech that the visitor was welcome, then leaned his head back again and shut his eyes. Betty and Young sat down upon a sofa, and began to chat. Jenny returned to the interpretation of Bess's straggling figures, while she wondered when Rob would come. She had told Lady Betty of her encounter, and in her own most serious and reasonable way had elicited a reluctant permission for Rob to call. "He's altered, you know," said Jenny. "He's no longer a raw Tyneside lad, nor anybody's servant."

"I know," Betty had agreed. She had heard reports of Rob Wilson from her brother. The young man had done a good job at Ditchley Park. Mr. Gibbs, the architect, had been pleased with him and sent him to other building projects later. Rob had remarkably soon risen to the title of master-builder. When last heard of he had set up on his own in London. "Though I still don't consider him a suitable associate for you, dear," Betty had added. "Not of your class."

"He's the same class as half of me," said Jenny with a little chuckle. "And you need never fear Rob'd do aught untoward, and anyway he's probably wed by now."

Jenny had said this lightly, but as she frowned down at the sprawling columns she wondered if it could be true, and had a qualm of extreme dismay.

She rose nervously as there was another bustle at the door, and Briggs ushered in "The Earl of Peterborough and my Lord Mordaunt."

Betty was astonished by these callers. The old Earl seldom left Parson's Green and the company of his Mrs. Robinson, while young Mordaunt, his grandson and heir, Betty scarcely knew at all. Mordaunt was a big lumpish youth of sixteen, who had a habit of blinking, and who seemed to be stricken quite dumb after his mumbled courtesies, and stood miserably staring at the poker.

His grandfather frowned at him. "Awkward young puppy," said the Earl to Betty. "But I'll shape him up yet. Does Miss Lee play the instrument?"

"Why, yes," said Betty beginning to see light. "Jenny, take Lord Mordaunt to the harpsichord and play something. He's fond of music."

As Jenny obeyed with some reluctance, the Earl and Betty exchanged a look of humorous understanding, and Peterborough said, "Nothing serious in view, of course, they're both so young, yet I'd like to see if a beautiful girl like that couldn't strike a spark, don't you know!" He gave Betty a sprightly wink, and walking over to Frank Lee, sat down by the Colonel and began to entertain him with the latest coffee-house tidbits.

Jenny looked up from the harpsichord, and said, "What shall I play, my lord? I'm not very skilled."

Young Mordaunt blinked, he turned red under his spots, his adam's apple rose and fell. Finally he said, "S-something rousing like 'Lilliburlero'—would you know that, ma'am?"

"To be sure," Jenny laughed. "By heart." Under her dark lashes, her long eyes gave him their unconscious look of coquetry, and soon, as she played, the youth was bending over her and humming the words in evident enjoyment.

On the sofa Dr. Young, having shown Betty his poem and basked in her praise, motioned towards the harpsichord, where the youngsters were giving a spirited rendition of "Lilliburlero," the great Whig rallying song. "The Duke of Wharton's father wrote that," Young remarked. " 'Tis a pity his grace's *own* convictions are so unstable."

"Yes," Betty agreed shrugging. "Philip is certainly unstable. I wonder how you endure him as a patron."

"I've had to," said Young seriously. "And he was most generous at times. But he's different now, if I may be frank—there is a deterioration—also, he is going abroad. I very much fear," said Young lowering his voice, "that he's going over to the Jacks again. I am certain he's been corresponding with the Pretender."

"So you'll have to find another patron," said Betty sympathetically. " 'Tis shame so fine a poet cannot live by his works."

Young leaned forward. "I have hopes, my lady, that Sir Robert Walpole may speak a word in my favor for a Crown grant, and perhaps you or Colonel Lee . . ." He left the sentence dangling, while he looked at her with earnest, rather doggy eyes.

Betty was more amused than annoyed. "We've no influence at all any more," she said briskly. "I had rather hoped you sought my company from simple compatibility, nothing else."

"I did, I do," said Young flushing, "only—"

"Only there's no harm in trying!" said Betty laughing. "Come, Dr. Young, don't pull a long face. I like you very much. Recite to me again from your 'Love of Fame, the Universal Passion'—a cynical title with which I don't *quite* agree."

Young's eager acquiescence was interrupted by the arrival of more callers. William Byrd and Evelyn.

Jenny jumped up from the harpsichord and kissed her friend, whom she had not seen in some weeks. Evelyn was dressed in white with touches of gray and mauve, as though she were in second-year mourning. This was one of the many willful peculiarities she had imposed on her father, ever since his destruction of her affair with Sir Wilfred Lawson. Outwardly compliant, the dutiful affectionate daughter, she yet managed to do exactly as she pleased, and Byrd who was anxiously fond of her, often felt an unhappy bewilderment, and even—sometimes—fear.

He was embarrassed to find the Earl of Peterborough at the Lees'. Last year Sir Wilfred had married the well-dowered Elizabeth Lucy Mordaunt, Lord Peterborough's plain-featured niece. It was impossible not to reflect that a man considered good enough to marry a Mordaunt might certainly have been considered good enough to marry a Byrd. Byrd's own motives in violently breaking up Evelyn's love affair were no longer as clear to him as they had been. He was not one for regrets or introspection, and he felt entirely justified, since Sir Wilfred had indeed cooled off upon finding that Evelyn would not have a penny.

Evelyn now augmented her father's discomfort by greeting Lord Peterborough with extreme cordiality and saying at once in her low deliberate voice, "And *do* tell me, my lord, how is your new nephew Sir Wilfred and dear Lady Lawson?"

"Quite well, I believe. I see them seldom," answered Peterborough a trifle astonished. He knew nothing of the abortive love affair, and thought the intensity of Evelyn's question, the hint of malice in her handsome dark eyes rather odd.

"My wife, Mrs. Byrd," interjected Byrd loudly to Betty, "begs to send her respects, my lady—she has not entirely recovered from her lying-in or she would have come today."

"I'm sorry to hear she's ailing," said Betty politely. "You must bring her here soon." Though Maria Taylor Byrd was the most shadowy possible figure to her, and Mr. Byrd himself did not interest her. She was merely sympathetic towards the long friendship between Evelyn and Jenny.

"What do you hear from Virginia, sir?" asked Peterborough of Byrd. "I'm sure Colonel Lee will be interested." He turned to include the man huddled in the armchair who said, "Yes—indeed," while his dull eyes grew livelier, and he struggled to join hospitably in all this untoward gaiety by looking at Betty and forcing out the word "Refresh-ment."

"Oh, lud," she said beneath her breath, wondering what the condition of the larder was. "I'll ring at once!" and pulled the bell rope.

The two girls drifted together, and Jenny whispered, "Help me entertain Mordaunt." They glanced at the youth, who was moodily stabbing out notes on the harpsichord.

"Why not?" said Evelyn. "I'm most fascinated by the Mordaunt family I assure you. Is this a suitor for your hand?"

"Merciful heaven!" Jenny cried. "Really, Eve, the things you say. I can't imagine why we're still friends."

The mocking light died from Evelyn's face, she gave Jenny a look of pure affection. "You're the only one I have," she said, quietly.

Jenny was deeply touched, though she protested, "Yet you go out in the world a lot, you meet so *many* people with your father!"

"Ha!" said Evelyn. "I meet toadies and lick-spittles, or I meet those who expect *us* to toady and lick-spittle. None of these are friends."

Jenny was silent. She only partially understood Evelyn's

bitterness or at least the continuance of it, and she knew that there had been several tentative marriage offers which the girl had squashed in the most decisive manner, though it seemed to amuse her to provoke them, and raise her father's hopes.

"Evelyn," she said, "are you unhappy with your new stepmother? Is it hard to live with her?"

"Not in the least," said Evelyn calmly. "Mrs. Byrd is an amiable woman. She has to be to endure me—and my father —poor man—" she added with a faint enigmatic smile.

Jenny sighed and gave it up. She put her hand on her friend's arm, "Well—come and frizzelate at Lord Mordaunt, I pray you. I've done my share."

"And it is *you* he wants," said Evelyn laughing, "if those languishing calf looks mean anything. Still, I'll try." She walked to the harpsichord and addressed something to the youth, who jumped and turned scarlet. At that moment Briggs entered the room and walked towards Betty.

"There's a—a gentleman below, m'lady," he said nervously. " 'E asks for Miss Jenny, but 'e come to the *back* door. I didn't know where to put 'im."

Betty turned and gave Jenny a meaning look. The girl had heard, and stood tensely, twisting her fingers.

"You have a caller, Jenny," said Betty. "We'll ask him up here."

Jenny felt a wash of panic—not Rob in here with *these* people! Jenny had never imagined anything like that, she had thought they might meet for a while in the anteroom below. For the first time in her life she was angry at Lady Betty, who had already given Briggs the command, and on whose face was clearly marked a "cruel in order to be kind" expression. She *wants* me to be ashamed of him, Jenny thought. She wants him to look a fool. Jenny backed away until she stood apart from the rest, pressed against the window seat.

Rob came in slowly, unannounced by Briggs, who didn't know what to make of him. Jenny exhaled her breath, as he hesitated a moment at the door. His eyes grew puzzled, defensive, as he saw all the fashionable company, yet there was dignity about him. He looked very odd to Jenny, for his wig was powdered, his plain white cravat was correctly knotted, there were silver buttons on his long buff waistcoat— in short, he was dressed like gentry. When Betty, coming forward, said "Good day, Mr. Wilson," he bowed over her hand and answered "Good day, my lady—please to accept my compliments" with scarcely any awkwardness, and in a voice which held only a faint inflection of the North. And he was so big, Jenny thought, still watching from her corner. He towered half a head over them all, as he gravely bowed again in response to Betty's quick introductions.

"May I present Mr. Wilson, who was engaged in the rebuilding of Ditchley for my brother Lichfield—my Lord Peterborough—my Lord Mordaunt—Mr. Byrd and Miss Byrd, Dr. Young—Colonel Lee—oh, and I believe you've already met my ward—Miss Lee."

Rob and Jenny exchanged a look while she sketched a tiny curtesy. Jenny barely suppressed a wild desire to giggle. She did not suppress a glance of triumph at Lady Betty.

"Come seat yourself here with us, sir," said Betty quickly, patting the sofa. "I'm sure we're all vastly ignorant of housebuilding. Is it true that you work now in the new sites north of the Oxford Road?"

"Oh?" said Peterborough with interest. "Y'aren't by chance the architect fellow who's doing Bingley's house on Cavendish Square?"

Rob shook his head. "No, my lord, I'm only a builder in a small way as yet. I'm raising a house on Wigmore Row, and hope to find a buyer for it."

"Indeed," said Byrd. He intended to rebuild "Westover" when he finally returned to Virginia, and had studied several books of designs. "What sort of brick do you use, and where do you get your timber?"

"I get gray stocks from Camden, sir, and fir logs from the Baltic. I've a bit of mahogany from Jamaica on hand too," Rob added proudly. "I'll use it for the stair rails."

"Do you do the carpentry *yourself?*" asked Byrd, raising his eyebrows. Noblewomen like Lady Betty were entitled to their whims, but one did not expect to rub shoulders with a tradesman in her drawing room.

"Aye. 'Tis what I've learned best, sir, carpentry—I've let out contracts to the others—bricklayers, slaters, plumbers, and the rest."

"Ah—" said Byrd shrugging. "In Virginia we train the blacks to all those trades, and a bonded servant or two over 'em."

"Slavery is certainly a far less costly system," said Lord Peterborough smoothly, "since obviously nobody has to be paid at *all*."

"They have to be fed and housed and doctored," said Byrd with as much sharpness as he would permit himself to an earl. Byrd was annoyed by what he took to be criticism of Virginia, and disappointed in the company. He would have taken his leave at once, except that Evelyn was sitting beside Lord Mordaunt on the music bench, and also Briggs finally staggered in bearing a trayful of chocolate cups and cake.

Jenny helped dispense the food, and had a bad moment as she saw Rob balancing the delicate porcelain cup in his great brown hand. He gave her a long considering glance, as though he wondered if she were trying to make game of him. She shook her head slightly in denial, and his eyes smiled ruefully, though the rest of his square, dark face remained sober while he answered the old Earl's continuing questions. Peterborough had retained curiosity about almost everything, he found this young Wilson knowledgeable, and the Earl cared not a jot whether a man were technically a gentleman or not, if he were congenial.

Evelyn, while drinking chocolate, abruptly abandoned young Mordaunt and came over to join Jenny on the window seat. "Who is that very large young man?" she whispered, gesturing towards Rob.

"I—used to know him," said Jenny, blushing.

Evelyn's eyes narrowed; she cocked her head and examined her friend. "In your mysterious past?" she asked. "I believe you know far more about *that* than you've ever confided in me."

"I do, Eve," said Jenny after a pause. "I'd tell you, if I weren't bound not to. But you wouldn't like my past—or at least Mr. Byrd would so dislike it that he would *never* let me see you."

"Dear me," said Evelyn dryly. "What I like and what my father likes are not often similar, as must have occurred to you, nor does my father necessarily know what I know. Still, I'll not tease you, Jenny. Whatever your dark origin, you retain my affection! And," she added with a glance at Rob, "I rather approve of yon great bear of a man, though I'm quite sure Lady Betty and my father don't."

By six all the guests had left except Rob. He stayed on, not because he did not know how to take his leave, as Betty at first suspected, but because, having finally made up his mind to talk with Jenny, he would not permit any feminine maneuvers to circumvent him.

Betty looked at the girl she had raised and whom she dearly loved. She saw that the pretty face was clouded, and that Jenny—as she had so often done—was preparing herself to accept a disappointment. Betty had an impulsive change of heart. The young man was decent, he was respectable, and more harm than good might come from undue opposition.

"Would you like to show Mr. Wilson the garden, Jenny?" she asked suddenly. "It is a pleasant evening. Myself, I must see that Colonel Lee rests."

She almost regretted her impulse when she saw the leap of delight in the gray eyes, while Rob, bowing, said quietly, " 'Tis a kind thought, my lady. I should like to see the garden."

The Lee garden was an ordinary town garden; it had a vegetable patch, a few fruit trees, a rose arbor and a sundial. Jenny had been in it a thousand times, but she had never seen it look as it did tonight.

The roses and an apple tree were in bloom. The air smelled of them instead of the smoke and drains it usually did. The air was light and fresh, the slanting sun filtered through it to gild the peeling old wooden benches, the green-stained sundial. It beautified the dilapidated stable mews and the disused coach house. Jenny and Rob walked without a word as far as they could, to the mossy brick boundary wall, where there was a bench, concealed from the house by the rose arbor. Jenny sat down and he sat beside her. A cuckoo called repeatedly from the Marylebone fields; they could hear it above the rumble of traffic.

Rob suddenly turned, and looked down at the girl. "Did you mean to make a fool of me today, Jenny?"

"Oh, Rob!" she cried. "How *can* you ask that! Will you never understand me? And you weren't a fool. I was proud!"

He brushed this aside impatiently. "Why did you want to see me again? I thought we parted for aye in Coquetdale."

"Why did you follow me yesterday, from the park to Queen Anne's Gate?" she asked.

"Because you should not be with Wharton. The man is vile, you don't know him."

She tilted her head, her eyes were luminous, they looked up at him steadily. "Was that the only reason, Rob?"

He clenched his heavy jaw, a muscle worked in his cheek; then he made a harsh sound and said, "No, by God, it wasn't! I've seen and followed you before—these months I've been in London. At church and when you take the children walking. So now ye know!"

"And why, Rob hinny?" she said very softly, still looking up at him. "Why?"

"Don't ye go badgering me into saying what I shouldn't, as ye did in Whitton Dene," he said violently, averting his gaze. "Let me go, Jenny! I'm making my own way at last, and soon I'll get me a proper wife—a cozy little body wi' a nice jointure, and a Dad in trade who'll understand *my* trade."

"Do you want to hurt me, Rob?" she whispered. "Why must we always quarrel?"

"Why must ye keep questioning when ye know the answers?"

"Turn to me, Rob!" She put her hand on his cheek.

At her touch, he shivered. His head jerked around, he looked her full in the face. "Verra weel, lass—" he said through his teeth.

His arms shot out and lifted her from the bench onto his lap. He bent his head and kissed her with a furious hunger that cut her breath. She trembled and went limp, tears brimmed her eyes and rolled down her cheeks. His violence passed as he felt the tears. His bruising grip on her relaxed, he cradled her against his chest and began to kiss the wet cheeks. "So ye're greeting now," he whispered, resting his own cheek against her hair. "Hinny love, divven't greet."

" 'Tis for joy," she said. She raised her face and offered him her lips.

He kissed her this time, deep yet gently. "Feel joy then, my lass, if you can. I canna. 'Tis fear I feel. Foreboding. There's trouble coming nigh us, hinny. I knaw it—I tried to play me pipes yestere'en—they wilna work. The chanter's cracked."

"Robbie, Robbie," she whispered. "That's naught, it can be mended. 'Tis not like you to talk thus. And there can't be trouble and fear when there is love."

"Ah, there *can* be! Ye wouldn't knaw. Ye're but a bairnie yet."

"I'm not!" she cried. "Kiss me, and I'll show you if I am." She twined her arms around his neck.

They did not hear St. George's clock strike seven, they did not hear a call from the house. They did not hear the crunch of hurrying footsteps along the gravel path; for an instant more they did not notice Lady Betty, who stood transfixed, staring at them.

"Merciful heaven!" cried Betty in a voice shaking with anger. "I'd never have believed this! Jenny, you little slut!"

Rob rose with the girl still in his arms. He put her down carefully, then stood away from her. "Jenny's no slut, my lady," he said in a heavy flat tone. " 'Tis all my doing, and all I can say in defense is I didna mean to."

"We love each other, my lady," said Jenny pushing back her disordered hair.

"Nonsense!" Betty turned her angry eyes from one to the

other. "A chit of a girl like you knows nothing of love. And though I see you've hot blood, I should think your pride would control *that* when it comes to lolligagging in the shrubbery like a serving-wench."

"Harsh words, my lady," said Rob. "Jenny doesn't deserve them."

"As for *you!*" cried Betty, still too much outraged to listen. "You, Robert Wilson, since I can't control *your* behavior, I shall have to keep Jenny under constant watch, so as to prevent this disgusting sort of thing!"

"No need of that," said Rob quietly. "I give you my solemn word I'll never try to see Jenny again. I know she's not for me, and I ask you to believe me, my lady."

Betty swallowed. She encountered his direct level gaze, and did believe him. "Very well," she said in a more temperate tone.

"But what about *me?*" Jenny cried. "I love Rob, I always have."

"Ye'll get over it, hinny," said Rob with a wan smile.

"But I've tried and I didn't!"

Betty recognized the note of hysteria and spoke gently. "Be reasonable, my dear. I don't know what you have in mind. You couldn't possibly marry this man, and indeed he obviously recognizes this himself. Many things seem tragic at fifteen, I know, but Rob is right—and with determination you will get over it."

For an instant as Betty spoke, she had a qualm. There had been another young girl, once, who had fallen in love and been told to "get over it." Yet there was no resemblance at all. *That* love affair had been eminently suitable.

"I'll be going, my lady," said Rob, "and I'll never trouble you again. Farewell, Jenny." He took her hand and kissed it quickly. "God be with you."

He heard Jenny give one agonized sob, as he walked past the stable mews to the alley which led back to George Street. Rob felt Jenny's sob constricting his own chest. He walked aimlessly, dragging his feet, until he found himself in front of St. George's Church. He wandered inside, for no particular reason except that it was quiet and cool. He sat down in a pew and bowed his head.

A spineless fool he'd been once again. Why had he gone to the Lees' today? Why had he allowed his desire for the girl to get out of hand in the garden? "The woman tempted me," he thought wryly. Adam's ready excuse. But Adam was a weak man, and I am not. This hankering for what could never be his—a hankering far worse now since their kisses in the garden—this shameful weakness should be extirpated now, once and for all. I'll wed Peggy Miller, wed her as soon as they've called the banns, he thought. No, sooner—we can have a Fleet marriage—any parson'll do it there. He turned his mind resolutely to Peggy, her father was a well-to-do surveyor, Peggy was comely, even-tempered and well educated, she'd make a good wife for a rising young master-builder. She'd not disgrace him even when he got his own house and land as he meant soon to do. Wi' Peg in my bed I shall forget Jenny, he thought. Still, he was not comforted. Underneath ran the formless foreboding, and the anxious wonder as to why he had found his chanter broken when he went to play the pipes. The pipes had been made by Jem Bailey, the Faw. It was not so easy to make another chanter, the proper wood for it did not grow near London. He rose abruptly, cursing himself for sickly fancies. Action was needed and the first thing to do was go seek Peggy Miller.

Rob quitted the church, and had taken three steps on the sidewalk, when a man brushed past him, walking up George Street. There was something both furtive and familiar about the man. Rob turned and watched him for a moment. "Wuns!" he said to himself. " 'Tis that foreign rapscallion o' the Duke's."

Rob turned and followed the mincing, meager figure. It was after eight, yet still light. Rob stayed well behind, though Serpini doubtless wouldn't recognize him after all these years. I'm mad, Rob thought—I'm going daft as ould Snawdon. The slinking creature was on some harmless business for the Duke which would take him to Hanover Square, or even beyond. It was, however, no surprise to Rob when Serpini crossed the street and after another furtive look around stood staring across at the Lee mansion. Rob stopped too, while passersby jostled him, sedan chairs whisked past him, a coach and two great drays rumbled along beside him on the cobbles. The Italian disappeared down the alley for a bit, then he came back, and continued to lounge across the street from the Lees. He curled himself over the areaway fence of the house opposite, pulled out a pipe, lit it, and began to smoke. Rob watched frowning. Why didn't the fellow knock at the Lee door, if he bore a message from the Duke? What was he waiting for?

Rob's uneasiness grew. The Italian showed no sign of moving. Could it be he was waiting for darkness? But why?

A sickening suspicion gripped Rob. He turned and strode

a block down George Street until he reached Conduit. He looked to the right and saw the Duke of Wharton's unmistakable coach drawn up before a small dingy brick house which Rob well remembered. It was in this house's upper story that Wharton diverted himself with meetings of his Hell-Fire Club. The meetings had been the subject of much ribald comment in the Duke's servant hall while Rob was in service there.

The favorite footman—a pretty boy—had been taken along to the "club" by the Duke. The footman later reported a farrago of childish obscene nonsense, to which Rob had scarcely listened. There had been something about a dark room fixed up like a Catholic chapel, but with the crucifix hanging upside down—and a naked woman painted on the altar. There had been several cowled figures like monks, swathed in red. The Duke was dressed as a priest. The red monks used a skull full of brandy as a Communion cup. They had gabbled the Lord's Prayer backward, the footman said, and a shocking din it made. There had been more to it than that—something the footman hinted at with lewd winks and sniggers—a fair young virgin—a mock marriage to the priest —a couch brought on—the maiden tied to it—"Christ!" said Rob aloud, standing there on Conduit Street. "He wouldn't dare, filthy as he is—even he wouldn't *dare*—"

Rob walked slowly along past the Duke's coach. The coachman and footmen sat impassively, the horses stamped a little, the coach was empty.

"Is his grace in the house?" said Rob to the postillion, whom he had never seen before.

"Aye," said the lad. "Wot's it to yer?" As he spoke two chairmen ran up and rested their chair before the brown brick house. A man got out whom Rob recognized at once— Francis Charteris, the vilest rogue in England, and the Duke's chief crony at the Hell-Fire orgies.

Rob walked back to the corner of George Street, and standing there tried to think. Should he warn Jenny? Yet he had sworn never to try to see her again, and he didn't wish to frighten her either. Lady Betty then? Even if she let him in she'd never believe a fantastic tale such as this; she would think him demented, or, that he was inventing pretexts for breaking his word. Moreover, he did not really believe himself in the monstrous thing which half of him feared.

He glanced up George Street and saw that Serpini had disappeared. I *am* going daft, Rob thought. It's all a mare's nest.

Nevertheless, he suddenly hailed a hackney, and instead of giving Peggy Miller's address as he had meant to, he gave the address of his former lodgings in the City. In the old chest he'd left there were bits of the Duke's livery—the coat and badges, the wand he'd used as running footman. He was still undecided, unwilling to make a fool of himself; yet suddenly he urged the coachman to hurry, hurry towards the City. And he made a lightning plan. If his suspicions were unfounded there'd be no harm done.

At eleven o'clock that night, Jenny was deep in exhausted sleep, intensified by a draught Lady Betty had given her. Jenny slept alone in a tiny room off the nursery and back stairs. Stupefied by emotion and the drug, she had forgotten to lock her door, and Briggs walked in when she didn't rouse to his discreet knocks. He shook her hard by the shoulders.

"What is it?" she cried jumping, and gaping at the man-servant's stupid face.

"Ye're wanted below, miss," said Briggs. "Sh-h-h- 'tis, a secret."

"*Who* wants me?" she cried, still dazed. "Oh, is it Rob?"

"I wouldn't know, miss," said Briggs, who had been well bribed. "But 'ere's a note." He put it in her hand. It said, "Come quickly to the stable mews, for just a moment. One who loves you."

It must be Rob's writing, she thought. She had seen so little of it, she wasn't sure. It was strange of him to break his promise to Lady Betty—and yet—if he had been suffering as she had, what difference did a promise make? Her muddled thoughts went no further. She made Briggs wait outside, while she put on her pink dimity dressing gown and slippers. She went downstairs through the sleeping house, and out the garden door which Briggs opened for her. She walked along the path which she and Rob had trodden today and turned at the end towards the stables. Someone ran towards her from the dark musty stable entrance. Someone wound a woolen scarf tight around her face, someone else pinioned her arms, and bound her legs. Suffocating and struggling, she was carried through the mews and dumped in a sedan chair. The chairmen ran expertly through the darkness towards Conduit Street.

At half-past midnight, Lady Betty lay sleepless, mulling over the day's events and worrying about the best way to help Jenny recover from her foolish infatuation. Suddenly she was petrified by a high wailing scream, which seemed to come from outside and below her bedroom windows. She jumped up and ran to the window. The street below was deserted; she leaned farther out, and thought she saw a peculiar shapeless light mass at the bottom of the area, ten feet below the ground floor. There was no further sound.

Betty got up and summoned Briggs, who came staggering after her in his nightshirt, holding a candle. They clambered down to the area and found Jenny lying on the pacing stones near the coal-chute. There was blood running from the girl's nose, her right leg was twisted under her. She was unconscious though breathing.

"Gawd," whispered Briggs in horror. "Wot 'appened? I didn't think nothing like *this*'d 'appen!"

Betty subconsciously noted what he said, and she also noted that Jenny must have fallen from the entrance steps above, for a strip of torn dimity was caught on the rail. She proceeded with tight-lipped calm. She summoned the neighbors for help, their footmen came, they found a table top, and lifting the girl carefully on it, they got her upstairs and onto Betty's bed. Betty sent Briggs running for Sir Hans Sloane. Until the physician arrived, Betty sat by the bed bathing the girl's temples with vinegar, and praying in little formless sounds.

Sir Hans came, and looked very grave. Jenny's right tibia was fractured. He set the leg and splinted it with deft, tender hands. "I fear, Lady Betty," said the physician, "we have a skull fracture too to deal with. I'll bleed her, otherwise she must be kept absolutely quiet, and for weeks probably."

"But she *will* recover—" Betty whispered.

"I don't know, my lady. I've no way of telling the extent of the damage. She has youth on her side. I'll stay the night with you and watch. Whatever happened to the poor child?"

Betty shook her head. "She must have pitched over into the area while running on the steps. I heard her scream as she fell."

"What was she doing out there at such an hour? Or was she walking in her sleep? Somnambulists are frequently injured despite the popular belief to the contrary."

"That was perhaps it," said Betty, resting her head on her hand. And she tried to think so, though in her heart she did not. She knew that something more sinister than sleepwalking had happened to Jenny.

"I won't let Jenny die," said Betty in a low dragging voice.

"*God* wouldn't let her die like this—when she has not yet begun to live."

The physician looked at Lady Betty very kindly. He knew all that she'd had to bear with Colonel Lee's illness, and he suspected a great many other heartaches too. "Well," he said briskly. "I'll help all I can—and see, her color's a trifle better, that's a good sign. I really believe she may pull through."

It was the end of June before Jenny regained full consciousness. By that time, Betty—being assured by Sir Hans that the girl was well out of danger—dreaded the moment when returning health should bring memory and worse than that—questions. Up till now during these anxious weeks of nursing, Jenny had roused at times from her coma, once and again she had been quite lucid, but she never referred to any moment later than the arrival of Rob at the afternoon gathering, and she said in a small triumphant voice Betty found infinitely pathetic, "He astonished you, didn't he, my lady? You didn't think he'd look and talk so fine, *did* you?"

Betty always agreed, though she had to turn away to hide her face. Jenny seemed to think vaguely that she had hurt her head and leg that afternoon at the party, all memory after that had receded into some limbo, from which—said Sir Hans— it might or might not emerge. It was often thus with a head injury, he said, particularly one which had followed on such shattering emotional experiences as Jenny had suffered. Sir Hans now knew what these were. Betty knew, her brother Lord Lichfield knew, and the Earl of Peterborough. Evelyn Byrd, who had come nearly every day and helped with the nursing, knew a good deal. But the London world in general had no suspicion of the truth. Among Betty's small circle of friends, it was thought that Jenny had hurt herself while sleepwalking. As for the rest of the incredible, dreadful, tragic tale—the news-sheets never got wind of it. Influence saw to that. Influence and money. These two powerful factors had also saved Rob's life—just.

Yet Betty was not sure that he thought it worth saving, under the conditions imposed upon him.

On the balmy morning of June 30, Lord Peterborough came to inquire after Jenny, as he had frequently. Betty received him in the study from which she could keep an eye on her children, who were playing in the garden. One of the maids sat with Jenny, who had awakened without a headache at last, and had actually eaten three eggs for breakfast. Betty reported this, and the Earl's withered little cricket face brightened with a momentary smile, then he shook his head.

"Well, Wilson's gone, poor wretch. The ship sailed last night. I saw him loaded on, chained to the other convicts. I spoke to the Master. He'll be treated specially well. They'll unfetter him after they clear Gravesend, and I understand he'll get a good owner in Virginia—a man called Harrison, probably."

"Oh, dear—oh dear—" whispered Betty brokenly. She took out a handkerchief and wiped her eyes.

The Earl patted her knee. "Don't fret any more, Lady Betty. Suppose he'd been hanged at Tyburn, as he would've been if it hadn't been for you and Lichfield."

"And *you!*" she cried. "You've been so good!"

"Bah!" said Peterborough. "Simple justice! The whole shocking business makes me sick. No words can express what I think of Wharton—except that he's mad, and the Pretender's welcome to him. Has got him too, by now, I suppose. Our fine Duke scuttled away fast enough at the hint of trouble."

"I wish Rob Wilson *had* killed him as he meant to, instead of Serpini," said Betty violently.

"I know," said Peterborough, "but if he had we'd never've got him off with just transportation, poor devil."

Betty was silent, unable to stop her painful thoughts. Probably nobody would ever know just what had happened in the disgusting Hell-Fire Chapel. She herself had not been able to see Rob because until his trial at the Old Bailey he had lain in the Condemned Hold at Newgate. But her brother had seen him before the trial. Lord Lichfield had come up at once from Ditchley, at Betty's frantic summons. Betty had not taken long to find out through the terrified Briggs that it was Serpini who had brought the note which summoned Jenny on the fateful night. This led her at once to Wharton, whom she confronted herself.

She found him at his home, half drunk, a trifle ashamed yet full of a glossy bravado. He referred to Rob's shooting of Serpini as "a tipsy brawl between my servants." This also, fortunately, was the line he had taken with the bailiffs when they had arrested Rob.

The arrest had taken place downstairs in the Conduit Street house, no one had known anything about the Hell-Fire Club. What knowledge Betty had of that had come through Rob's private talk with Lord Lichfield before his trial. From this Betty knew that Rob, in the Duke's livery, had gained access to the rites in time to save Jenny. That he had held the red monks and the Duke at bay while he told Jenny to run—run for home only two blocks away. She had obeyed, and in her confused panic had pitched off the steps into the areaway.

Then Rob had somehow shot Serpini instead of the Duke.

No word about Jenny had come out in the trial. Rob would not permit it. The two earls thought his chivalry natural. Betty felt immense gratitude.

Fortunately Wharton had not bothered to prosecute. He said he had been bored by Serpini anyway. Then the Duke almost at once left London. May he burn in the hellfire he mocks, Betty thought.

"Stop brooding, my dear," said Peterborough. "What's done is done, and the girl's going to be well."

"It's Jenny I'm *thinking* of!" Betty cried. "How am I going to tell her about Rob Wilson. He saved her from—from—"

"Never mind!" said the Earl. "And why tell the girl? She may never remember any of it."

"She is beginning to already. She knows Rob rescued her from something terrible, she wants to see him. And oh, Peterborough—when I think of that poor young man, so proud, so ambitious—he'd found his independence, he was doing well. You know yourself, you were impressed by him, and again through no fault of his own, he's ruined—worse than ruined—a transported convict."

"Yes," said the Earl, "that's all very true, my dear. But at least he's not dancing on a length of rope 'neath Tyburn Tree. His sentence is not long, considering it was murder, only fourteen years. He'll be quite a young man yet. As for Jenny, she'll forget him in time."

"No," said Betty. "I thought that only a month ago. I don't now. Jenny was born loyal. She won't forget him. Nor do I think she should."

FOURTEEN

On a cold drizzly morning in December of 1725 six months after Jenny's injury, she first set foot on French soil, or rather she climbed down the ship's ladder and stood upon a chilly wharf at Calais.

Lady Newburgh had preceded Jenny down the ladder, so had Lady Newburgh's French maid, Marie, and her equerry, Mr. Clement McDermott—a bleak taciturn Scot. Jenny in the three days of their association had never seen McDermott smile. Nor for that matter had she seen Lady Newburgh smile, not really—nothing but mechanical response to the demand of courtesy. Marie did not count. She had been either coach-sick on the way to Dover, or seasick on the twelve-hour Channel crossing.

"We might as well prepare ourselves for tedium," said Lady Newburgh on the wharf as she pulled her fur-lined travelling cloak tighter around her. "McDermott—where's the hamper? Miss Radcliffe and I will eat, while you and Marie dicker with the customs men."

McDermott fetched a large hamper stocked with boiled fowl, jugged hare, mince tarts, orange brandy, and cinnamon water. Lady Newburgh was fond of food. The equerry installed his lady on a bench in the customs house. Jenny waited until her stepmother said, "Sit down, Jane, cut the chicken."

Jenny obeyed, thinking it a very odd thing that Jenny Lee had now become Jane Radcliffe, and an even odder thing that she should be in France with the clatter of sabots, and jabber of a strange language all around her. It was impossible not to be a bit excited by this, and by the prospect of seeing her father in a couple of days—whenever they could reach Vincennes. Yet there were a great many other circumstances which dampened excitement. The readiest to hand was Lady Newburgh. Jenny took a morsel of chicken, and while the Countess ate in single-minded concentration, Jenny thought about the events of the last days.

Lady Newburgh had spent the autumn with Sir John and Lady Webb at their town house in Poland Street, though she had not bothered to make this known to Lady Betty or Jenny until last week. Then she had come to visit them.

Charlotte Newburgh was a tall heavy woman in her thirties. She was dressed in maroon velvet, and wore several diamond rings; her face was swarthy, her hair shiny black. She was not entirely unhandsome, nor precisely discourteous, yet she was completely lacking in humor and both her speech and carriage showed awareness of her position—a countess, born so in her own right.

Jenny's strongest impression of the interview was that Lady Newburgh was reluctant to hold it at all. "I am in London," she said, after the first civilities, "primarily to look after my estate, and arrange certain family matters for Mr. Radcliffe. I've also investigated the possibilities of a pardon."

"Oh?" said Betty in astonishment. "Do you mean that Charles hopes to be *pardoned?* Has he then relinquished Jacobite sympathies?"

"Certainly not!" said the Countess sharply. "I'll not go into details with you, Lady Elizabeth, except to say that I've been unsuccessful. I'm returning to France on Saturday. Mr. Radcliffe desires that Miss Radcliffe shall accompany me."

"Miss Radcliffe?" Lady Betty repeated, her jaw dropping. "Oh, you mean *Jenny!* She's known always as Miss Lee here."

"I'm aware of that," said the Countess. She threw Jenny the sort of long-suffering glance one gives a clamorous puppy, though the girl had not spoken. "But I see no reason to maintain fictions where they aren't necessary. I also think nicknames foolish. Mr. Radcliffe has been anxious to see his daughter, quite—" added the lady thinly, "*insistent*, in fact. Especially after you wrote him of her accident."

"Jenny was in great danger for a while," said Betty. "I didn't tell him until she was recovering, since he could do nothing."

" 'Tis a pity you disturbed him at all," said the Countess. "I'll set off by coach for Dover, Saturday morning at eight. Jane and her boxes must be ready, I'll have her picked up here. I trust she hasn't much luggage?"

"She hasn't," said Betty in the voice which Jenny knew meant she was trying to keep her temper. "Am I to understand that Jenny will make her home with you? And in that case perhaps her own wishes should be consulted."

"I can't see why," said Lady Newburgh. "A minor child obeys its father's commands. And I believe that you are selling this house? And have—er—well, various embarrassments, and will be relieved to get rid of one of them."

Betty flushed. "It is true," she said slowly, "that through His Majesty's kindness we are going to move to a 'Grace and Favor' lodging in Somerset House, and lucky to get it. Wherever we go there'll always be room for Jenny."

"Most kind of you," said the Countess. "Mr. Radcliffe has frequently expressed his gratitude towards you, but he has quite decided on this procedure, and I've given my consent. There can be no argument about the matter. Jane will be treated as well as my Clifford daughters and my niece-at-law, little Anne Maria Radcliffe. Fortunately I have a large establishment at Vincennes."

That had been the tenor of the interview, during which Jenny had said nothing. Indeed she spoke little nowadays. All strong emotions seemed to have drained from her, after she had finally recovered enough to be told about Rob. Her leg healed, and her head healed; yet so often there seemed to be a veil between her and the world, a veil she was too listless to penetrate. She knew that this worried Lady Betty, and tried to rouse herself, though the dullness persisted. She had acquiesced later after the Countess left when Lady Betty with one of her impulsive changes of heart, had cried, "Perhaps this *is* the best thing for you, dear. New scenes often raise low spirits, and I can do so little for you any more. I can't say I fancy your stepmother—but you love your father."

"I did," said Jenny. "I suppose I do. Dear Lady Betty, forgive me, I don't much care where I am."

The trancelike state had lifted twice before she left London. At the end when she kissed Lady Betty goodbye, and they both wept. Also the time when she saw Evelyn.

Jenny shifted suddenly on the bench in the draughty Calais customs house. She didn't want to think about her farewell interview with Evelyn, pain had come too close, the protective veil had almost shredded because Evelyn mentioned Rob. Nobody else ever did. Evelyn had spoken of him tentatively and with sympathy, while watching Jenny's face and then she had stopped short, crying, "Jenny, don't look like that! He's all right, wherever he is. Virginia's not the African jungle, you know!"

Lady Newburgh, having finished half the chicken and two mince tarts, wiped her mouth on her handkerchief and said, "You've a bad habit of fidgeting, Jane. I trust you're not a nervous girl."

"I'm sorry, my lady," said Jenny, who had been twisting her fingers in and out around a fold of her mantle.

"And," continued the Countess, "I am surprised that Lady Elizabeth permitted you to wear beauty patches, you're far too young for such vanity."

"I—I *don't*, my lady," said Jenny in astonishment. She touched the little black mole on her left cheekbone. "This grew on me, I can't help it."

"Oh," said the Countess, slightly discomfited. She was extremely myopic, and between the general annoyance of travel and the annoyance of adding an unwanted member to the party, she had scarcely examined Jenny at all. She now perceived that the girl had a showy sort of looks, and also that there was a discreet ring of porters, vendors, and urchins all staring at Jenny and making complimentary remarks. *"Quelle est belle, la petite anglaise—eh la jolie blonde! Donne-moi un petit sourire—eh chérie?"*

Lady Newburgh frowned. "Pull your hood over your hair," she said, "and keep your head modestly bowed."

Lady Newburgh's exasperation grew during the night at a Calais inn, and during the three days of travel together in the post chaise the Countess had hired. Jenny caused attention everywhere; at every posting stop there would be a barrage of bold Gallic stares, lip-smackings, and occasional whistles. On their last night, at Beauvais, an infatuated French youth actually fell to his knees on the inn courtyard, and made a declaration of love before anybody could stop him.

Lady Newburgh was forced to admit that the girl never exactly did anything to incur these advances. In general she hardly seemed to notice them, but her appearance was provocative—the long brilliant eyes and the way she used them, the fullness of her red mouth above the cleft chin, the narrow waist and round high breasts, the startling abundance of her curly yellow hair.

And by now the Countess had discovered Jenny's close resemblance to Charles, which also displeased her. She loved her husband in her own forceful way, and had hoped that their baby—James Bartholomew, born last August—would resemble him. Instead it was a very plump and black-haired infant. It might not have been Charles's child at all—except for the unfortunate little defect, the Stuart fingers. The proof of Stuart blood. One had accepted this defect with Christian resignation, and one must accept the company of this girl with Christian resignation too, thought the Countess determinedly, though by the time they reached Vincennes her misgivings were frequent.

The Countess had rented an old château a mile outside the Paris walls on the edge of the Bois de Vincennes. The park had clipped formal gardens, now bare and covered with hoarfrost. The château was square, gray, and turreted; the surrounding leafless trees were carefully placed to form radiating avenues. It all looked very cold, and very neat to Jenny—not like a place to live in.

The great front doors swung open as the post chaise approached, rows of liveried flunkies in powdered wigs were disclosed drawn up inside a huge stone hall. There were children too, three small girls curtseying, a pale undersized boy of thirteen. Jenny saw them vaguely, then she saw her father coming towards them down the marble steps. He peered into the chaise and greeted her with a joyful flicker of the eyes, though he confined his exclusive attentions to Lady Newburgh, as he handed her out of the chaise, crying, "Welcome home, *ma bien-aimée!*" and kissed her ceremoniously on each cheek. Not until the Countess was inside the hall with her two daughters, and Anna Maria Radcliffe, and the little Earl of Derwentwater, did Charles reach his hand into the coach and extract Jenny. "Thank God you've come, darling," he said and kissed her full and long on the mouth.

She gave a gasp which was largely dismay. Nobody had kissed her lips since Rob had, in the garden. She had forgotten the feel of that, as she had forgotten so much afterwards. But her body had not forgotten the feel. It came back with an agony of longing as her father kissed her.

"My sweetheart," said Charles below his breath. "How lovely you are!"

"Radcliffe!" the Countess called sharply from the entrance. "Bring Jane inside. The open door is chilling us."

There was more of chill than the wintry air for Jenny in that château, she soon discovered. Lady Newburgh's influence pervaded it, as her money had provided it. There was much ceremonious grandeur and little comfort. The sparse furnishings were dark and medieval, the wood fires warmed only a section of the great rooms. There were dozens of servants, all of whom treated Jenny with subtle contempt, knowing well their mistress's inner attitude. The exception was Alec, who welcomed her enthusiastically. Yet he had changed. His hair was pomaded, his clothes were of satin like his master's. His sole duties were the valeting of Charles, between times he flirted with the maids and lorded it in the servants' hall.

The three little girls, Frances and Anne Clifford and Anna Maria Radcliffe, were quite indifferent to Jenny. She was too old to be one of them, not old enough to have authority. John, the Earl of Derwentwater, tried to be kind. He asked her questions about England, which he longed to see, he asked her about Dilston, which he referred to pathetically as "my own true home"; but he was a sickly, feeble boy, he coughed a great deal, and spent most of the time in his suite with his French tutor.

There was warmth near Charles—when they were allowed to be alone together. Then they both recaptured something of the intimacy they had enjoyed on the trip to Northumberland. These moments were few because Lady Newburgh always seemed to be there, and Charles treated his wife with a rather anxious deference. This hurt Jenny, who had never seen him deferential. It diminished him. There were other slight changes in him too. He was heavier, there were faint pouches under his eyes, he drank a lot of *eau de vie*, and did not ride out daily as he used to. Lady Newburgh did not care for riding, and, besides, in France gentlemen did not live on horseback as they did in England. A *grand seigneur* always used his coach.

Shortly after his arrival Charles took Jenny to the nursery to see his heir, while Lady Newburgh was engaged in giving orders to her maître d'hôtel.

The wet nurse stood up and curtsied as Charles and Jenny came in. "*N'est-ce-pas qu'il devient grand et fort, monsieur?*" she said proudly of her charge, who lay in a canopied cradle waving his arms and cooing.

"Behold your brother, Jenny," said Charles laughing. "Viscount Kinnaird!"

Jenny smiled and leaned over the cradle. "He seems rather young to be a lord," she said. "May I call him Jemmie?" Then before she could stop herself, she added, "Oh, what *is* it with his hand?"

She gazed horrified at the baby's left hand where the two middle fingers were fused into one, which was curled inward like a tiny hook.

"Oh," said Charles with a rueful shrug. "His title he derives from his mother, but the webbed fingers came through me. Our little Prince has them too. 'Tis the mark of a Stuart."

"Of *all* of them?" cried Jenny, staring. "But you haven't . . ."

"No, child. Not all of them, of course. It crops up from time to time. Ever since James the First, I believe. His Majesty was most interested when I wrote him about this baby's fingers. The King is James Bartholomew's godfather."

"And his godmother?" asked Jenny looking at the dark wriggling baby and trying to realize that this was actually her half brother.

"Lady Middleton," said Charles frowning. "Not Queen Clementina as we'd hoped, because she's been acting very strange since the birth of Prince Henry, and has retired to a convent. This greatly distresses His Majesty."

"Oh, I didn't think *he* would care!" said Jenny impulsively.

Charles glanced at her. He leaned over and patted his son, then he said, "Jenny, I want to talk to you. We'll go to the Salon de Tapisserie."

The Tapestry Room had a small fire burning, but it did little to mitigate the drafts which blew the dark old tapestries in ripples against the stone walls, yet the room was secluded and Charles wanted no interruption for the lecture he was about to give Jenny.

The lecture was delivered at Charlotte's request. After she and Charles had retired last night, she had made clear her stand in regard to Jenny.

"The girl has many stubborn Whiggish fancies. And I shall not criticize Lady Elizabeth, but I really can't see that Jane has had any religious education to speak of, even Protestant. Perhaps that's just as well. However, she has now entered a Catholic family, whose members are all dedicated to the restitution of England's rightful king. I've tried talking to her, and she simply doesn't attend. I sometimes wonder if she has *quite* all her faculties, Charles? After all, her mother was an ignorant peasant—or possibly that peculiar blow Jane somehow received on the head—pray don't scowl at me like that! I've already discovered that you dislike any comment on the girl. I make this one for her own good. She'll be very unhappy with us if she doesn't alter her wicked little prejudices. I beg you to talk to her—and I think—" she had added in a weaker voice, "that you might do that much for me since I've done what *you* wanted, Charles—"

Charlotte's dark skin flushed, her eyes suddenly grew wistful, much younger. "Didn't you miss me at all while I was in England? You haven't said so."

Charles had gallantly reassured her. He had also made love to her, while she astonished him as she often did by the abandon of her passion. And he had promised to lecture Jenny.

He began now by asking, "What did you mean by saying that you didn't think that King James would care whether the Queen had left him or not?"

"Why," said Jenny uncomfortably, " 'tis what I've always heard that the Pre—the Chevalier neglected her frightfully, and has many mistresses, with whom he openly insults his wife."

"Mother of God!" cried Charles. "These are *lies!* My dear girl, don't you realize that Walpole has set up a whole machine to discredit our King, that there are agents who spend their entire time forging letters and inventing rumors?"

"I didn't know, Papa," said Jenny.

"And don't you realize that now when there is hope that Austria and Spain will aid France at last in restoring our King, that filthy hog who usurps England's throne is quaking, and no slander is too foul for his use?"

"I—I didn't like King George much," said Jenny feebly, awed by her father's vehemence. "I know most folk don't, but they like the Prince of Wales—and Papa, please don't be angry. England just doesn't want a Catholic King. They're afraid."

"Bah!" said Charles. "The same old dead horse to flog! In the first place, King James would not impose his own faith on his subjects, and in the second place—though this I don't quite approve—little Prince Charlie is, I believe, to join the Church of England. So where is *that* argument?"

"I don't know, Papa. But I don't think war is right. I don't see how you can, after what happened in the 'Fifteen, after what happened to the Earl of Derwentwater."

"That's just *why!*" Charles shouted, turning on her in a fury. "You little idiot—Holy Mother, I wonder if Charlotte's right, and you've gone soft in the head!"

Jenny winced, she put her hands to her face and began to cry without sound. He stared at her a moment, while his anger melted. He walked over, and kneeling down put his arms around her. "There, there, darling," he whispered. I didn't mean it. You know I love you, there, there."

It was onto this scene that Lady Newburgh walked. She had been searching some time for Charles and finally thought of the Tapestry Room. For a moment she was stricken dumb at the sight of the two blond heads so close together, of Charles on his knees, embracing the weeping girl. Nor was she pleased by the guilty start Charles gave, though he recovered at once, and jumping to his feet said, "My lady, I've been scolding Jenny, as we agreed last night. I'm sure she's convinced now, and acknowledges King James as her true King."

"Do you, Jane?" asked the Countess coldly.

"Yes, my lady," whispered Jenny.

"You see!" cried Charles in triumph. "And now, Jenny, repeat after me the oath of allegiance." He drew the crucifix King James had given him from under his waistcoat. "Kneel down and touch the cross!"

Jenny obeyed, and she repeated after him in a faint toneless voice, "I swear by the Holy Trinity, and by this crucifix, that I will bear faith and true allegiance to my sovereign lord, King James the Third, and serve him unto death—so help me God."

"You may get up now," said Lady Newburgh.

Jenny rose slowly. What did all this matter? What did anything matter except peace. Let me alone, she thought. Oh, let me alone. It was not Charles and Lady Newburgh that she meant. It was to her misery that she spoke—the realization of it, which she had fought off so long and was still fighting.

A month passed, one of some outward gaiety. There were large family sightseeing parties, organized by the Countess, whenever the bitter weather permitted. In the great gilded coach they would set off from Versailles, where they caught a glimpse of the young French King, Louis Quinze, at his levee; or they went to St. Germain and saw the outside of the Palace which had used to be the Stuart court. Jenny and the little girls were also shown the improving sights of Paris, the King's library, the new façade of the Louvre, the Sainte Chapelle.

Jenny was much moved by Notre Dame, its Gothic statues, its dark mysterious aisles—a stone forest smelling of incense, the hundreds of shimmering taper-tips, the gorgeous jewel tones in the rose windows. She delighted Charles by her appreciation and when she said how much more beautiful Notre Dame was than St. George's bare new whiteness at home even Lady Newburgh was pleased.

"I hope you are beginning to see, Jane," she said, "the difference between the old True Faith and the empty travesties of Protestantism."

Jenny acquiesced. Why not turn Catholic as they all wished her to? Nothing seemed worth the trouble of combatting, and Lady Newburgh was kinder to her, when she began to have hopes of Jenny's conversion. And then Father Brown arrived from Pontoise on a visit.

The Jesuit had left Dilston many months ago, having found a monk to take charge there. He had resumed clerical duties in France.

After supper on the night of his arrival, he sat long at the table drinking port with Charles. They ceremoniously toasted King James and the royal family, then the priest said abruptly, "What's happened to Jenny, my son? She's like a blown-out candle."

"Why, I think she's well," said Charles startled. "Beginning to settle here—to be sure she had an accident last summer, but she's all over that—only her leg aches sometimes where it was broken."

Father Brown interrupted. "I don't mean body aches, I mean soul sickness. Something is wrong."

"I don't know *what*," said Charles frowning. "Of course, at first my lady was perhaps not as cordial as she might be, yet she's better pleased now that Jenny has become a Jacobite, and is showing interest in Catholicism. You'll help with that, Father. Give her instruction while you're here."

"Certainly," said the priest, "if she wants it. Yet I doubt she'll make a Catholic now. If conversion comes 'twill be in God's own time." He took a thoughtful sip of port. "Jenny isn't by any chance in love, is she?"

"In love!" repeated Charles finding the idea as repugnant as it was ridiculous. "Who with, I'd like to know! Oh, Lady Betty did write me that Peterborough's grandson, young Mordaunt, paid Jenny marked attentions, but Jenny's mentioned him herself, said he blinked and looked like a spotty pig— that doesn't sound like love!"

"No," said the priest smiling. "All the same, my son, I believe there's a great deal you don't know about your little girl. I don't mean that she's deceitful—far from it, yet the very circumstances and mysteries of her life have taught her an unchildlike reserve. Also, as she wishes to please you, she cannot help having two natures which get into conflict. In thirty years of trying to help distress, it's been my observation that most unhappiness springs from conflict or grief. I believe that Jenny is suffering from both. Though—" the priest continued in a musing voice, "the devil sends fear too, to afflict the human soul. As the old French saying has it, *L'eau bénite du diable c'est la peur!*—Fear, the devil's holy water. The devil is always alert to sprinkle it, one must wipe it off with Faith—Faith and the Love of God, as our blessed Saint Ignatius Loyola has said—"

"Yes, yes sir," interrupted Charles. "Quite true, and if you think Jenny is doleful, I'll give a ball to divert her." He spoke impatiently, thinking that the old priest had grown irrelevant and garrulous, and at the same time Charles wondered whether he could really persuade Charlotte to give a ball. It would be fun to show Jenny off to the neighboring seigneurs and the Parisian Jacobites. It would also be interesting to invite Madame de Montfort, to see her for once without the need of secrecy and intrigue. Charles's thoughts ran happily for a moment on the charms of the vivacious Marianne de Montfort and on tentative plans for their next amorous rendezvous at the secret little house in the Faubourg. Then he happened to glance at Father Brown and received a severe check. All this would have to be confessed on Saturday night, and there would certainly be a stern lecture and most arduous penance.

On the night in which the letter came which changed Jenny's life, there was a small party at the château. Lady Newburgh had not consented to giving a ball, and when she announced complacently that she was pregnant Charles could not insist. She did, however, invite a few people in for cards in honor of George Seton, the Earl of Winton, who had turned up unexpectedly on his way from Rome to the Netherlands.

Charles was delighted to see his old friend, who was now forty. Winton's lean otter's face was a trifle wizened, yet the small brown eyes were as bright as ever. The Earl appeared one afternoon at the château, riding a very jaded dirty nag, and with no luggage except saddlebags. When he had finally got past the scandalized Newburgh footmen, he cheerfully explained himself to Charles and the Countess.

"I'm off to Scotland, for a bit of a surreptitious visit, ye might say! I'll find me a ship at The Hague."

"But how imprudent!" cried Lady Newburgh. "You're under sentence of death in Britain!"

"So is your husband, my lady—and I believe he took a wee jaunt to England once, which is far *more* imprudent," said Winton laughing. "Scotland's a verra different matter. Most Scots're Jacks—'tis partly for that I'm going. His Majesty wants me to alert some of his good friends there, like the

361

Murrays, and Lords Balmerino, Tullibardine, the Cameron o' Lochiel, others."

"You mean there's really hope of an invasion!" cried Charles eagerly. "My instructions've made no mention of it —though to be sure I've not had any dispatches lately from Rome or Spain. The weather's been too bad."

"There's been hope ever since the Vienna treaty, as ye know," said Winton, "though I'm not saying it'll come tomorrow. When we strike 'twill be in Scotland. Spain'll send a fleet to help us. They want Gibraltar and Minorca back, Austria's with us, and France should be too, though I'm bound to admit this king is pretty much of a lukewarm fainéant!"

"Yes," said Charles shrugging. "Louis has time for little except making love to his young wife just now."

"What's wrong with that?" said the Earl with a faintly mocking bow towards Lady Newburgh. "I intend to see m'own wife in Scotland if she's still alive. I've missed that braw lassie from time to time."

"I didn't know you had a—well, a wife," said Charles grinning and remembering the tawdry fair-haired woman called Magdalen whom Winton had brought to Widdrington Castle and presented most unconvincingly as his "Countess."

"I wed her by Scottish law wi' an exchange of vows in the Tower, just before my escape," said Winton, "and I'll tell ye why. She was near term with my brat, which I heard later she was brought to bed of in your own Northumberland, Charles—at Bellingham, while she was fleeing north. The boy's still there, being raised by a saddler called Carr. He must be ten now."

"Good gracious," said Lady Newburgh. "I trust you can get him away from that sort of life!" She found the Earl rather crudely eccentric, but his name and title were impressive and he had been the richest of all the Scottish lords captured at Preston in the '15.

"Time enough for that, my lady—when King Jemmie 'hae his own again' and I my estates. 'Twon't hurt him at all, to learn a trade, didn't harm me any. He was named Charles, by the bye, Charles Seton. I feared you'd be hanged, y'know, man." He turned to Charles. "And 'ld leave nobody behind ye —a sentimental gesture!"

"For which I deeply thank you," said Charles, smiling. "But I had someone to leave behind me whom you didn't know about!" He indicated Jenny, who was sitting across the salon, playing at draughts with young Derwentwater. Lady Newburgh stiffened, as she saw the warmth in her husband's eyes duplicated in Lord Winton's.

"She's ravishing," Winton said. "What a lass to be proud of! I never saw such hair in m'life!"

"It's very untidy," said Lady Newburgh, peering across the room. "I've told her not to wear her hair so loose, she takes little trouble to obey me."

"O-ho," said Winton under his breath, "so that's the way the land lies." His bright gaze rested on Charles's doting face as he looked at his daughter, then passed to the dark discontented face of the Countess.

The following evening a half-dozen friends arrived at the château to play at ombre, piquet, and hazard. There were also musicians installed in the hall, a flutist and a violinist. These were Charles's idea. Lady Newburgh had thought that Jenny might as well spend the evening at the harpsichord, since it would save the expense of hiring anyone, and the girl didn't play cards anyhow. Charles had been adamant; he had in fact been so annoyed that his wife was a little frightened. She gave in, but her affection for Jenny was not increased, nor was it by the girl's appearance in the magnificently becoming rose taffeta dress her father had sent her.

Charles and Lord Winton had been drinking champagne for some time, and were both in high spirits. "Come here with me, darling!" Charles called to Jenny as she shyly appeared in the doorway. He put his arm around her waist and introduced her to the guests—Lord Middleton, Mr. and Mrs. Stuart, Colonel Greene and his wife, staunch Jacobites all of them. There were besides a French marquis and a count accompanied by their ladies. "Sit down with Winton and me, Jenny!" said Charles exuberantly. "We'll teach you to play hazard, and perhaps one of the ladies will join us?"

Mrs. Greene said that she would. The others, including Lady Newburgh, arranged themselves at various tables for ombre or piquet. Father Brown came in, bowed to the company, and sat down quietly by the fire to listen to the music. Charles provided Jenny with a louis d'or's worth of change, and soon had her rattling the dice box and assessing her throw as well as any of them.

The watching priest saw that the girl smiled a little when she won, that she turned affectionately to her father, who spoke to her in his most wooing voice, and kept his arm around her shoulders. Yet the priest saw plainly the muted, strangely frozen quality about her. As though her inner self were not really there.

At ten o'clock McDermott, the equerry, entered the salon carrying a small black leather bag. He went to Charles and stood waiting until Charles, after a lucky cast, triumphantly raked in a pile of coins, then looked up and said, "Well, what is it, McDermott?"

The tall Scot bowed. "I've picked up these letters for you in the Faubourg, sir. I thought they might be important, and you'd want them immediately."

"Quite right," said Charles. He turned to Lord Winton and Mrs. Greene. "You will forgive me a moment if I glance at these? There may be important news."

Charles fished two letters from the bag, they were both addressed to "Mr. Jones" at the accommodation address in the Rue St. Germain. He opened the larger one, looked through it quickly. "'Tis from the Duke of Ormond in Madrid," he said. "Nothing of great import, except that the Spanish court is increasingly warm towards giving us an expeditionary force. Oh, and that lunatic of a Wharton has turned up, is making a drunken nuisance of himself, babbling all manner of indiscretions to the English minister."

Jenny shrank back on her chair, her heart began to thump. Wharton. The Duke of Wharton. She hadn't seen him since the tavern table at Queen Anne's Gate on the King's birthday. Why then should his name bring a suffocating fear, why did she see his face like a leering mask of evil, floating amid red shrouded figures, why did she feel a scream rising now in her throat? She clenched the edge of the table and sat petrified, all her forces bearing down on the control of that scream.

Charles finished Ormond's letter, and looked at the other one. "This is from London," he said. "It's gratifying to think how many agents we have there, and how our cause is growing." He broke the seal. "Why, the letter's for you, Jenny! Lady Betty perhaps? Though it's not her writing. Would you like to read it now, dear? What ails you, dear? You look very pale."

"I feel a little faint," said Jenny with tremendous effort. She took the letter in her hand and recognized through giddy swirling waves Evelyn Byrd's writing on the direction "Miss Jane Radcliffe." "May I retire?" she whispered.

Charles nodded in concern. "Lie down for a bit. Her ladyship's maid shall bring you restoratives. I'll send her."

Jenny quitted the salon, but she did not go upstairs to her bedroom, where Marie would interrupt her with tisanes and cluckings. She took a candle from one of the gilded sconces and made her way through the passages to the Tapestry Room. A dying fire flickered on the hearth. She threw a log on, lit another candle, and sat down in the chair she had occupied when Charles had scolded her on the morning she had sworn allegiance to King James.

Jenny looked at the letter for several moments before she opened it. She skimmed through it fast once. Her heart ceased pounding. The veiling mists and the giddiness vanished. "Thank you," she said out loud to the empty air. *"Thank you!"* She smoothed the letter carefully on her lap, and reread it with calm deliberation, pausing on each word.

London, January 15, 1725/6

Dear Jenny—

Lady Betty and I have had a chat which is how I know your reale name and address, and all about you, though my Father does not. He thinks you in France to visit a kin of Lady B's—true in a way I suppose! Jenny, we are going back to Virginia. My father has to for necessities to see his affairs there. We will sayle about March the first. Will you come with me as companion gentlewoman? My father is agreeable to this. Perhaps your happy where you are, then never mind. But you should know, Lady B. thinks so too, that Rob Wilson was bought by Mr. Harrison, who owns Berkeley the plantation next ours. I don't know more, yet I think you may be interested. If you can come with us, you must hasten. Believe me Jenny, ever your devoted freind

EVELYN BYRD.

Jenny folded up the letter and sat with it in her hand. Dimly from far away she heard the music, also she heard the hiss of rain against the old leaded windows. The tapestries bellied out, the room grew very cold, and still she sat on. Until Charles burst in and shouted in the furious voice of one who has been needlessly alarmed, "My God! What are you doing here? I've searched all over. You naughty girl, I thought something had happened to you!"

"It has, dearest Papa," said Jenny. She stood up and gave him a look compounded of a mature gentleness and quiet inflexibility so unlike her that he was shocked.

"What do you mean?" he said. "I don't understand you—what's that letter, is it from a man? Give it to me!"

"Of course," she said. "You will have to read it. It's from Evelyn Byrd."

"That little Colonial school friend of yours? What can *she* say of any moment!"

Jenny silently handed him the letter, he held it near the candle and read it contemptuously. "What nonsense!" he said, throwing the letter on a table. "As though you'd go off to the wilderness, as a kind of upper servant! That woman must be mad!"

Jenny lifted her chin, and gave her father the same maternal composed look. "I am going, Papa," she said. "I regret very much to give you pain, but I am going to Virginia."

"You can't!" he cried. "I won't permit it! Holy Mother, what's got into you? It can't be that you're following that Wilson—a transported convict—it can't be that!" Charles suddenly collapsed upon the other chair, staring at her with something like fright.

"He's a transported convict because of me, Papa," said Jenny. "You don't know the story. I didn't really remember it until tonight. Hush," she added as Charles made a violent movement. "I'll tell you what happened." She put her hand on his shoulder, and in clear dispassionate sentences she told him of her abduction on last May 29, and of what Rob had rescued her from.

He sat for some moments silenced and appalled, then he said, "Aye, it's horrible, horrible. And I see we've cause to be grateful to the fellow. I'll send him a gift—write to his master recommending leniency. I'll even let you write to him, if you want."

Jenny shook her head. "It's no use, Papa. Nothing that you say can sway me. I am going to Virginia. And after a while you won't mind it. You have your wife, your child, and another one coming. There's no place for me here, you know that in your heart. I've been drifting, aimless, in the shadows—now I am awake. Look at me and you'll see that's true!"

He raised his head and looked at her swiftly. What he saw exploded his baffled dismay into anger. He jumped up from the chair and shouted, "I won't let you go! I won't! You cannot disobey me! I'm your father! Come with me, you wretched ungrateful child, come to Father Brown. He'll tell you what your duty is!" He grabbed her by the wrist, and pulled her after him. She made no protest. Her expression of pitying inflexibility did not alter.

Charles suffered much through the next day of bustle and hurried plans, during which Lord Winton departed on his nag after remarking that he would greatly enjoy an adventure to Virginia himself. There was nobody on Charles's side at all. Father Brown said sadly, "I believe you should let the child go, my son. It is better for everyone, and I have seen that for you both there's danger in your feelings for this girl. Each soul must choose its own path, and she has obviously chosen hers. I think that if you tried to keep her here by force you might kill her."

Lady Newburgh did not try to hide her relief. Her pleasure at Jenny's departure was so great that she furnished all the traveling expenses and offered McDermott as escort to London, also one of the undermaids as a chaperon. She even presented Jenny with a draft on her London agent for three hundred pounds, so that no one might think her niggardly or lacking in duty towards her stepdaughter.

On the next morning but one after the receipt of Evelyn's letter, Jenny set out with Charles in Lady Newburgh's coach, bound for the *auberge* in Paris where a post chaise could be hired for the journey to Calais.

Lady Newburgh had not begrudged Charles this last half hour alone with Jenny, she had been so much relieved that he had not insisted on going all the way to Calais with his daughter—a plan Jenny herself had vetoed as too painful for both of them. Jenny had consistently shown herself logical, calm, and efficient, yet as the coach drew away from the château steps—where the Countess, the young Earl of Derwentwater, the three little girls, and Father Brown all stood waving goodbye—she turned to her father, put her head on his shoulder, and began to cry.

Her traveling hood had fallen back and he stroked her soft bright hair. "Ah, darling, don't go," he said brokenly. "You see you don't want to leave me. And I've need of you. Great need."

"No, Papa," she said, wiping her eyes. "You have not. You'll be happier without me, because my lady will be, and you have many distractions."

"Perhaps you're right," he said reluctantly. " 'Tis too much to say I *need* you—but if there ever came a time when I did —" He put his hand under her chin and raised her face, looking deep into her eyes. "Jenny, promise that you'd come to me!"

"I don't know—" she faltered. "I don't know what the future'll hold for me, Papa—"

"I'd not summon you on a whim. I scarcely know what I mean, Jenny. I'd not insist upon your coming to me, even if—when—King James and all of us are re-established in England, but if I ever summon you in the name of my martyred brother—then will you promise to come?"

His gray eyes, so like her own, were brilliant with tears, and she felt a shiver of fear. Her arms raised to throw themselves around his neck, her tongue ached to promise whatever he wanted—yet she could not.

"I—I will promise to—to try," she whispered.

He turned away from her with a long sigh of disappointment. "There is a vow you have already taken," he said coldly. "Your oath of allegiance to King James, I trust you mean to respect *that!*"

"Yes," she said after a moment. "I'll respect my oath. In all the ways that I can, I wish to please you, dearest Papa."

"Then do not see that fellow, Wilson!" he burst out. "Don't let foolish stubborn fancy lead you into shame and disaster. For this I'll pray night and day. Since you've rendered me powerless, otherwise."

"I'll not let foolish fancy lead me," she said quietly. "Trust me, Papa—I'm no longer a child."

"No," he said with a kind of groan. "You're not. Jenny, you don't wear the Radcliffe ring I gave you in the cellar, the night of my flight from England. What's become of it?"

"Lady Betty has it, in safekeeping. She was afraid the crest would be recognized. I will wear it from now on, I promise."

"Good," he said, taking her hand. "I trust your word, darling. The ring will remind you of your pride of birth and lineage, it'll keep you from demeaning yourself, and you must retain the name of Radcliffe—that's *one* advantage of going to Virginia," he added bitterly.

"I'll do as you say, Papa. Oh, the coach is stopping—" They looked at each other in startled anguish.

McDermott threw open the coach door, and stiffened to dour silence as he saw the two locked in a close embrace like lovers, and both weeping. He waited beside the coach until Jenny stepped out. She turned once and waved, her tear-stained face as white as tallow. Then she walked with slow, resolute steps into the *auberge* to wait for the post chaise to be ready.

PART FOUR

1726

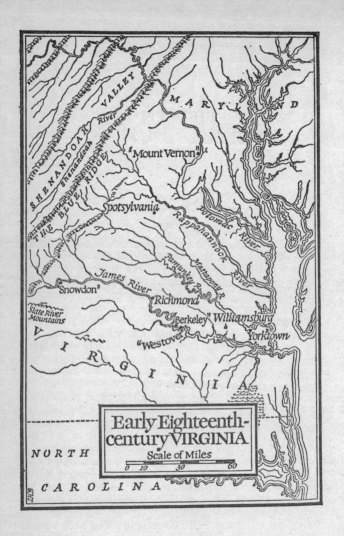

Early Eighteenth-century VIRGINIA

Scale of Miles

0   10   30   60

FIFTEEN

On April 20 the stout ship *Randolph* sailed swiftly up the James River, borne by the tide and a brisk southeasterly wind. It was warm and—except for the creaks of the rigging —very quiet. The newly risen sun already glared white off the broad waters.

The Byrd party were strung along the rail of the poop-deck watching the flat wooded shores flow by. Mr. and Mrs. Byrd stood close together, Byrd's ten-year-old Wilhelmina beside them. Evelyn and Jenny were across the deck, both silent with their thoughts.

William Byrd was as elegantly dressed in a powdered wig, brocaded waistcoat, and silver-gilt buckles as he had been in London. One must be careful not to let down standards upon return to the Colonies. He had impressed this on his family. Maria Byrd, his plump, docile young wife wore her wedding dress of green-sprigged buff taffeta, and her best lace cap on her mousy hair; she stood pressed against her husband, staring with affrighted eyes at the flat sandy banks fringed by the distant darkness of virgin forest. She watched in vain for roofs, for a church tower, a smoking chimney, any sign of a village. "Doesn't anyone *live* here, Will?" she whispered.

"Very few right here," he said smiling. "The back country to the south is largely unexplored, but upriver there are dwellings, and see ahead, there is Jamestown!"

"Where?" cried little Wilhelmina eagerly. Byrd had whiled away the eight-week voyage by improving his daughter's knowledge of Virginia. Wilhelmina knew the history of James-

371

town, and was disappointed to see nothing except trees and the stump of a church among half-burned ruins. "Is that all?" she aked.

"I *told* you the town was abandoned long ago," said Byrd. "And that the capital is inland at Williamsburg, which you won't see today." He looked north towards Burwell's Landing, where a brig and a sloop were unloading cargo for Williamsburg. "We'll proceed up the river to Westover," he added.

"Oh dear," said the child. "How *long?* I'm so weary of this old ship, I feel as if I'd been on her a year. I can't even seem to remember what England was like—it's *so* far away."

This remark affected her hearers painfully. Maria gave a stifled moan and gazed at the empty ruins of Jamestown. Byrd set his lips and gave way to gloom. A multitude of problems awaited him here.

The probable state of his long unseen plantation was one problem, and the condition of the precious tobacco, so precious that it was used for currency. Moreover, he had doubts as to the honesty of John Fell, his head overseer. The security of his absentee seat on the Council and its reception of himself were other problems. He knew that he had enemies among the Councilors—enemies who called him anglophiliac snob, and who thought that while enjoying the pleasures of London he had skimped his duties to his native Virginia. And in London not one of his early hopes had been realized, though he so dearly loved the city that he had put off from year to year this inevitable moment of return. He had never got his appointment as Governor of either Virginia or Maryland, neither had he settled all his debts nor found the high-born heiress whom he had wanted. Though Maria was a good wife, restful—after the turbulent Lucy, and then the debauched years of widowerhood.

He glanced fondly at Maria, saw that she was weeping, and knew that she was thinking of their baby girl, Anne, who had been left behind in the care of Maria's sister.

The ship neared Green Spring Plantation, where Byrd had so often visited the Ludwells. Byrd saw it through lackluster eyes, the entertainment he had once enjoyed there seemed sparse, dreary, provincial. It would not be so at Westover, he thought, trying to comfort himself. In the ship's hold there were amenities. He had brought over a thousand books packed in black walnut presses; also there was furniture, silver, damask—and the portraits. If he could no longer rejoice in the company of the great men he had known he could at least have visual reminders of them. There was Kneller's portrait of Sir Robert Southwell—dear old Sir Robert, who had first launched him in London, who had proposed him to the Royal Society. Then there was the portrait of Charles Boyle, the Earl of Orrery; a warm and merry man was Orrery, godfather to little Anne, and the friend Byrd knew that he would miss the most. There were also portraits of Lord Oxford, Lord Halifax, and the Duke of Argyle—these were not exactly friends, but they *were* acquaintances, and their elegant representations would grace Westover.

One portrait he had wished to leave behind. It was of Sir Wilfred Lawson, Sr., the dead father of the Wilfred Lawson Byrd detested. He had seen no reason for hauling a likeness of any member of the Lawson family across the Atlantic, but Evelyn had insisted. She said that she wished to have a reminder at hand of how much gratitude she owed to the good offices of her dear papa. A perfectly filial speech, yet it had a curious undertone and made Byrd uncomfortable.

Behind him, Byrd now heard Evelyn give a low mocking laugh, as she said something to Jenny Radcliffe. Radcliffe was apparently the girl's real name, though nobody had mentioned this until they were well out at sea. Then Evelyn in her detached imperious way had unfolded an extraordinary tale of a forced marriage in Northumberland, of a father's Jacobitism and death sentence, of escape from Newgate, and exile. Byrd's first indignation at having such a young woman foisted onto his household was, however, soon over. The Whig ministry had consistently ignored Byrd, in fact Sir Robert Walpole had pointedly passed him over in favor of Hugh Drysdale, who was no doubt at this moment lording it in the Governor's Palace at Williamsburg. Jacobitism did not seem as outrageous to Byrd as it had, particularly since Lord Orrery had Jacobite leanings. And then there was consolation in the thought that Jenny was granddaughter to an earl, great-granddaughter to a king. Besides, she was vastly pretty.

One night last week he had drunk too much wine with the Captain, and on finding Jenny alone had "tried to play the fool with her," as he later penitently noted in his secret diary. The girl had cooled him off with a blank astonishment which was humiliating. Her presence at Westover might lead to other embarrassments of all kinds. Still, if Evelyn wanted Jenny's company, there was nothing to do about it.

Byrd frowned abstractedly towards the north shore, as the ship veered to starboard and began the tortuous passage around the point on the narrowing river. There never seemed to be anything to do about Evelyn's whims. One of the greatest disappointments in London had been her disdainful treatment of two eligible suitors. Yet she was still only eighteen, and much as she troubled him at times, he would have greatly missed her had she stayed in England. I'll find her a worthy husband here, he thought—a Carter perhaps, or a Ludwell if there are any free and suitable ones. The choice was limited. Plantation society was limited in so many ways. It would be hard to adjust to a world without coffeehouse gossip, and daily gazettes, without balls, opera and masquerades, without the company of famous wits, and peers, and sophisticated ladies who appreciated his own sprightly literary efforts.

Byrd sighed deeply. He was fifty-two years old, and this morning, on his home river, he felt the weight of every year. "We should be there in another couple of hours, if the wind and tide hold with us," he said to Maria. "I wish to write a letter."

"To send home?" she asked, her anxious blue eyes clouded.

"To England," he said with a tinge of reproof. "To assure Lord Orrery of our safe arrival. There may be some ships in port that will take it."

"Yes, Will," said Maria. She dabbed at the perspiration on her upper lip, and said faintly, " 'Tis growing so warm, I believe I'll lie down."

The Byrds left the deck. Wilhelmina squatted on a step and began to play with her wax doll. The two young girls leaned their elbows on the rail and stared at the shore. "What's that house?" said Jenny pointing to a rooftop in the trees to their left.

"Brandon, I think," said Evelyn. "Remember, I haven't been here in nine years."

"Are you glad to be in Virginia?" asked Jenny after a moment. "Do you think you can forget England and—and the people there?"

"All but one," said Evelyn calmly. "I shall forget the others."

"You mean Sir Wilfred?" Jenny whispered. "Eve, you never mention him, I didn't think you could—" She stopped before adding "be in love with a married man."

Evelyn read her thoughts. "I told you I'd never change," she said. "Look, Jenny!" The older girl drew a pearl-studded locket from inside her bosom and opened it. "Have you wondered what's inside?"

Jenny nodded and gazed with astonishment at a tiny miniature of a smiling plain young man, in a white tie-wig. "Sir

Wilfred?" said Jenny. "How did you get this?"

"He gave it to me," said Evelyn, shutting the locket. "We still love each other."

"You've *seen* him!"

"Now and again." Evelyn's beautiful eyes grew somber. "But I found it too miserable. That's why I was willing to come home with poor old Father. I didn't wish to become Wilfred's mistress, which would certainly have happened if I'd stayed."

"Oh," said Jenny, having found nothing else to say. The girls were silent again. Jenny sniffed the salt air and smelled the intermingling scent of pine trees. The latter evoked something poignant and long ago—the grove of pines at the turn of the way to the peel tower; it evoked Rob's face as he had met her the day she came to Tosson with Alec.

The ship's great rudder creaked beneath them as the steersman veered his course again to follow the river around another bend. The monotony of the densely wooded shore to the north was broken by the shadow of a house and a lawn.

"Weyanoke," said Evelyn. "We're getting nearer."

Jenny inhaled sharply. "Evie, I'm frightened. I don't want to get there. I don't really want to find out what's happened to him. I'm afraid to."

"You've come an extremely long way to decide that," said Evelyn dryly. "Courage, my dear."

"But suppose something terrible's happened to Rob, I mean worse than slavery even, which is as terrible as could be. Eve, it's nearly five months since you had that letter from Mrs. Harrison! Suppose he never went to Berkeley!"

"Jenny dear, I'll suppose anything you like if it comforts you, though I shouldn't think it would. Oh, look yonder at that fishing boat! The Negroes have caught a shad; I trust it's a Westover boat and that we'll have shad for dinner. 'Tis a tasty fish."

Jenny refused to be distracted by the shad. "Evie," she said, "are you *sure* that Mr. Harrison actually did b-buy Rob, and not some other planter?"

Evelyn shook her head. "We've been through this a dozen times, my pet. You know that I wrote as strong a letter as I could about your Rob's virtues, and of the value he would have for any planter. And you know that Madam Harrison replied that her son, Ben, had sent an overseer to Yorktown to await the arrival of the convict ship, and had duly secured Rob when he landed. What more do you want?"

"Oh, I know—" said Jenny. "Eve, you've been so kind, but I'm fair distraught, and Mr. Byrd knows none of this?"

"Certainly not," said Evelyn. "I'll handle Father when there's need, nor have you reason to fear him. You are not bound, Jenny, even to me. You paid your own passage money."

"Aye—" said the younger girl on a long breath. She thought of the little strongbox which was hidden under her clothes at the bottom of her chest in their cabin. It held money: 360 golden guineas. There has been more, but she had paid 20 of them for her passage. It was Charles who had supplemented the £300 of dowery Lady Newburgh had given Jenny, by slipping a purseful of louis d'ors into her hand before they parted in Paris. Jenny had felt herself very rich. In London she had tried to buy presents for Lady Betty and the children, and been gently refused. " 'Tis little enough you have, my dear," had said Lady Betty. "No settlement at all for a girl of your birth, and you must spend it wisely— young as you are, again you must keep an old head on your shoulders. Ah—" she had added with vehemence, "that woman could easily have doubled your portion—and *should* have!"

Jenny did not think Lady Newburgh ungenerous; she tried not to think of her at all; or of the past which she had cut herself away from. Particularly in this moment, when she had begun to dread what was in store for her in Virginia. Jenny glanced down at the middle finger of her right hand, which bore the Radcliffe ring. It was of gold, with a tiny edging of chip diamonds around the bull's head crest and the motto *Sperare est timere*. The motto had never before seemed baleful, yet now it did. There was indeed fear in hoping.

Oh, why did I want to come, Jenny thought, leaning her head against the painted cabin wall. Why was I so sure? Suddenly she could not even remember Rob's face, except for a heavy frowning bar of black eyebrows above grim eyes as they were when she had parted from him after their day on the moors. All that had happened later seemed unreal, the kisses in the Lee graden were a fantasy, and the sacrifice he had made in rescuing her from the Duke of Wharton was no proof of love. Decency alone might have moved Rob—or even revenge. Jenny slumped down on a stool and stared at the ship's ruffled spreading wake.

In the saloon William Byrd, having finished a gay informative letter to Lord Orrery, made cipher entries in his secret diary to cover yesterday's activities. He noted that he had arisen at six, having slept ill, that he had said a prayer, and read Greek and Hebrew. That he had "danced his dance" as best he could on shipboard. This was a form of skipping exercise he had begun years ago in his London youth, at the suggestion of a physician. It prevented the gout. So did the one-dish meals he stubbornly adhered to. Lucy used to jeer at him for his eating habits, but Maria did not. Before they left England he had even converted her to his boiled-milk breakfasts. He added a few ciphered scribbles to indicate that he had lain with his wife yestereven and thereafter not neglected his prayers, when Captain Randolph entered the saloon and said heartily, "Well, Colonel! You'll be home now in a cat's wink! It's not been a bad voyage, has it?"

"A most pleasant one," said Byrd. It was agreeable to be called Colonel again, a title he had acquired here by mustering the Charles City County Militia. "I'll never sail with any captain but a Randolph. You're as able as your brother Isham." He smiled at Edward Randolph, who was the eighth-born of the Randolph brood from Turkey Island Plantation up the James. Byrd knew all the Randolphs well and had been an intimate friend of the Captain's father.

"It's been a memorable voyage for *me*, sir," said Randolph while the ruddiness deepened beneath his weather-tanned skin. "I've never before had the honor to carry two beautiful young ladies in my ship!"

"Oho!" said Byrd merrily. "I've noted a kindling in that sea-blue orb of yours. Towards which of the young ladies does Cupid aim his dart?"

Edward Randolph hesitated, and Byrd, who had scant doubt of the choice, thought that the Captain would make a satisfactory son-in-law. He was personable, despite some missing front teeth, and a rolling gait; both defects attributable to the seafaring life. Ned was of excellent family, and followed a profession of tremendous use to a planter; without the good-will and services of ship captains, the planters could not subsist. Moreover, thought Byrd, a husband who spent half his time at sea or abroad would probably leave his wife in her father's home. A gratifying arrangement.

Randolph, with some embarrassment, dashed this dream. "Miss Byrd is very handsome, sir, but—" He hesitated, being naturally unable to say that he found Evelyn too tall, also too cynical, almost masculine in her bluntness and self-command. "It is Miss Radcliffe," he said reddening further. "She is so—well—in a word, sir—I've come to love her immoderately. She—she troubles my sleep. I *must* have her."

"Indeed," said Byrd, raising his eyebrows, and recovering rapidly from what was, after all, no great disappointment. Evelyn would find a better match than this, and there was no hurry. "Have you acquainted Miss Radcliffe with your passion?" he added.

"No, sir—at least I've tried but she's so modest and delicate, I believe she doesn't understand me, and I admire her for it. Besides, isn't it true that you're in a way her guardian? I thought it best to speak to you first."

"I am not officially her guardian," said Byrd. "She seems to be a singularly rootless young woman, though well born, and is virtually penniless, I believe. You must remember that!"

"'Tis of no consequence," cried Randolph rashly, knowing that his eldest brother would not agree. "I want her. And shall woo her lustily in the months before I sail again!" His blue eyes snapped with fervor.

"Well then," said Byrd, laughing, "you have my blessing."

Randolph bowed and glanced through the porthole. "You'd best get on deck, sir," he said. "We're drawing nigh."

William Byrd stepped out on the poopdeck just as the lookout in the bow blew a shrill horn and the gunner fired off a cannon. Byrd went up to Evelyn and put his arm around her. "There is Westover, my dear," he said. "There is your birthplace."

Jenny roused herself and went to the starboard rail. They all looked towards the north bank and saw a dingy wooden clapboarded house of one story, and an attic which had dormer windows. Nearby clustered some small boxy brick huts. The home-house was set back from the river on a ragged lawn, beneath huge poplars. The house was in need of paint, and a pane of glass had been broken in one of its lower windows; someone had stuffed a blue shirt in the hole.

"I remember the house as much larger," said Evelyn without inflection.

She was thinking that this Westover, for which she had felt though never admitted homesickness, would hardly make a decent lodgekeeper's cottage on any of the great English estates she had visited with her father. Byrd's thoughts were much the same. He noted the broken window, the lawn full of dandelions, and that, alerted by the ship's horn and cannon, two Negroes in open shirts and rolled-up pants had come drifting out from behind the house. They waved languidly and pointed west up the river. Otherwise there was no sign of welcome. Byrd next perceived that his wharf had collapsed, and most of the planks had fallen into the water.

"Where's John Fell!" cried Byrd in a shaking voice. "Where are my overseers? What have the damn villains been *doing?*"

The Captain also stepped out on deck. "We shall have to go on to Harrison's Landing," he said shrugging. "I can't unload here."

"So I see," said Byrd furiously.

Evelyn gave Jenny an ironic smile, not devoid of sympathy. "You'll know what you came to find out sooner than we thought," she whispered, "since we are going directly to Berkeley."

The Captain shouted his orders, the ship proceeded the mile and a half upriver to Harrison's Landing, which was as bustling as Westover's had been deserted. A huge warehouse stood by the long wharf. It was filled with hogsheads of pickled beef, naval stores, and last year's leftover tobacco crop ready-packed for loading. Nearby there was a half-built sloop in its cradle; the Negroes swarmed over it hammering away under the direction of a white indentured shipwright. In the several little shops behind the warehouse, Negro coopers and blacksmiths plied their trade, while a burly overseer in a cocked hat and a silver-buttoned coat walked to and fro across the landing. He had a pistol stuck in his belt and he brandished a stout cane while bawling out oaths, admonitions, and threats. The overseer's bellowings grew louder after he hailed the *Randolph* and hurried all the available slaves to catch the towline and help maneuver the ship alongside the wharf.

The sailors put out a gangplank and the overseer came aboard, his purplish moon face glistening, his jaws working on a quid of tobacco. "Welcome, Cap'n Randolph, welcome!" he said officiously. "We wasn't expecting you, though Mr. Harrison'll be mighty glad to see you! What've ye brought us?"

"A flock of Byrds," said the Captain, with a chuckle. "Bound for Westover, but we couldn't land." He turned to William Byrd, who had been standing by in annoyed silence.

"I doubt that you know Matt Corby, sir? Mr. Harrison's chief overseer—has come here since you were last home."

"How d'e do, sir," said Corby, squinting at the elegant Mr. Byrd without much interest. A folderol English coxcomb, this long absent owner of Westover seemed to be, and 'd have plenty of trouble getting his plantation in order, by what that shiftless John Fell said.

Matthew Corby had contempt for badly run plantations.

Twenty years ago he had been 'prenticed to his father, a London butcher in Smithfield. But there were many other sons, and Matt hadn't cared for the butchering trade. So he bound himself for five years to go out to Virginia, and had long ago worked off his indenture. Gradually he had developed a talent for overseeing. By constant vigilance, the frequent use of the lash and other necessary punishments such as the branks and the salt rub, he got more work out of the Berkeley slaves and bond servants than any other overseer on the James. Or maybe in the whole of Tidewater. Corby was inclined to think so. He knew his worth, and Mr. Harrison greatly relied on him too, not being himself a gentleman for vigorous measures.

"Things seem lively at Berkeley," said the Captain, eying the busy landing. "I see you've another sloop a-building."

"Aye," said Corby, squirting a long stream of tobacco juice over the rail. "Can't complain. Good season so far. I keep the black buggers sweating away, and we've a fine stand o' 'bacca plants already. The manor house is finished since ye was last here, Cap'n."

"Indeed," said Byrd interrupting with a frown. He was not accustomed to being ignored, while it was impossible not to feel envy at all this evidence of his neighbor's prosperity. "So there is a new 'manor house'? Are we to be permitted to visit it, or shall we stand here in the sun indefinitely?"

"Oh, to be sure. To be sure," said Corby airily. "Just step up the hill to the manor. Mr. Harrison's always glad of company." He turned his back on Byrd to ask Captain Randolph whether he had any nails for sale in the cargo.

"Insolent dog," said Byrd beneath his breath, glaring at Corby, who was completely insensitive, and had never concerned himself with the fine points of Virginia hospitality.

Byrd collected his womenfolk—Evelyn, Maria, Wilhelmina, and Jenny. They silently stepped across the gangplank, traversed the landing, and trailed up the dusty road away from the river.

"My head feels so queer," said Wilhelmina, clinging to Mrs. Byrd's hand. "Wobbly, and the road goes up and down like the ship."

"Yes, dear," Maria murmured. She had a headache, and the sun had grown fiercely hot. She was, moreover, almost certain that she was with child.

Evelyn said, smiling at her little sister, "You had to find your sea-legs on the ship, Mina—remember? Now you must lose them again!"

William Byrd and Jenny said nothing.

They came to a low wooden house much like Westover; here the Harrisons had been living when Byrd was last home so briefly, five years ago. Beyond it, and set farther back from the river there was now a new mansion, an imposing three-story structure entirely made of rosy bricks. Above and on either side the central doorway there were nine tall windows across the front, with twenty-four glittering panes in each. Beneath a classical pedimented roof there ran an elaborately carved cornice, painted white. The cornice was unfinished on the east side, some fifty of the bracket-like modillions were missing. As the Byrd party drew nearer, Byrd saw that the great brick walls were laid in Flemish bond, each header glazed dark and sparkling like a sapphire.

" 'Tis vastly handsome," said Evelyn astonished, staring at the mansion.

"And how did Ben Harrison get it *done!*" muttered her father. " 'Tis a bit like the work of Gibbs himself. How'd that lad find such building here? That is what I want to know!"

"You'll soon find out," Evelyn answered. "Isn't that Mr. Harrison in the doorway?"

From then on there was no lack of hospitality. Jenny and Maria particularly, being unused to it, were overwhelmed by their welcome; by the Harrisons' eager cries of astonishment and delight, by the flood of questions, and the tumultuous scurryings of house-slaves bearing punch, tea, rolls, cake, dark red slices of ham, syllabubs; and dishes of thick yellow ice cream, as soon as the kitchen boy had finished churning the freezer.

Jenny had no appetite, yet she could not resist the ice cream, which was flavored with coffee and rum. She nibbled at it and sat quietly at the big polished mahogany table watching the Harrisons, whose speech she found rather hard to understand. It was not quite like any English she had heard. It was slower, thicker, and the ends of words trailed off. And the Negroes talked much the same way.

Benjamin Harrison the Fourth was a tall, heavy young man of twenty-six. He wore his own chestnut hair clubbed back, and a simple snuff-brown suit with a plain ruffled shirt. He also wore riding boots, since he was in and out of the saddle all day long, and detested walking. He was in fact languid by nature, though horse racing and cockfights could excite him. Otherwise he liked nothing better than to sprawl in the coolness of his beautiful new rooms playing cards and drinking punch with whatever company turned up at Berkeley. Yet he had many responsibilities as a planter, which he did not evade, and he was thoroughly aware of his position as owner of one of the largest plantations in Virginia—and of his position as husband to Anne Carter.

This young woman was short and would have been pretty except that her body was swollen, her face puffed by pregnancy, though she carried herself proudly with the elegant condescension of a princess, because she, and all of Virginia, so regarded her. She was the daughter of the redoubtable "King" Robert Carter of Corotoman on the Rappahannock; he who was President of the Council, owner of nearly a half-million acres of land and a thousand slaves, a potentate feared and respected by the entire Colony.

The third member of the Harrison family was Ben Harrison's mother. Betsy Harrison was cousin by marriage to William Byrd and they had known each other all their lives. She was tall, stout, and her hair was as white as her widow's cap, though she was only forty-nine. She had been widowed for sixteen years, and had made shift herself to run the plantation, send Ben, her only son, to the College of William and Mary, and at his majority turn over his inheritance undiminished. She had been gratified by his marriage to the heiress Anne Carter, but had refused to be awed by it. She herself had been a Burwell, a more aristocratic name than plain Carter. She adored her son, and found it galling to play second fiddle both in his affections and in the management of the household which had once been all her own.

The friction between mother and daughter-in-law was obvious to Evelyn, who was amused by it. Evelyn had relinquished for herself any further active emotional roles in life, but she had no intention of moping, and she remembered enough of Virginia to know that one must amuse one's self with the smallest of dramas. There *was* however a drama of considerable moment which concerned Jenny. It would be better not to broach the subject in front of her father, and Evelyn intended to wait until she could get Mrs. Harrison alone, though her plan failed.

When they had finished eating Mrs. Byrd craved permission to lie down. Wilhelmina trotted out to the kitchen-house, where the servants received her warmly. The others crossed the spacious hall to the Great South Parlor. This room was handsomely paneled, it had a marble fireplace, it had cornices and archways to the other parlor. The Turkey rug and walnut furniture had recently come from England on one of Harrison's own ships.

The company all sat down, and William Byrd said to Ben,

whom he had known since his birth, "I fear I haven't properly congratulated you on this very fine house you've built yourself. Has it been finished long?"

"It's not finished yet," Ben drawled, stretching his legs and unbuttoning his vest. "Oh, we moved in last month, but the capstones aren't on the chimneys—nor all the what-you-call'ems carved undah the outside cornice. By the way, sir—'twas that damned fellow you made me buy, that jailbird—he built a lot of the house. It was *his* idea to make a pedimented roof, and the carved cornice—seems he'd been a mastah-buildah once."

"My dear Ben!" cried Byrd, half laughing. "I haven't a notion what you're talking about. I vow, Cousin Betsy," he added with a ponderous wink at the elder lady, "your young sprig here has had a drop too much! *Me* make you buy a jailbird, indeed! Why, I wouldn't wish one of those convicts to my worst enemy."

Jenny sat frozen, her eyes fixed on Evelyn, whose poise fled for a moment. Evelyn flushed, then said quickly to Ben, "It wasn't Father who wrote to Madam Harrison. It was I. Don't you remember?"

"*You*, my dear?" said Byrd, turning to her in amazement. "What is this coil?"

"I'll explain later, Father," said Evelyn recovering her assurance. "It was for—for Lady Betty Lee, in a way."

"For Lady Betty?" asked Byrd, momentarily distracted. "Lady Betty Lee is sister to the Earl of Lichfield," he explained to the Harrisons. "She's a great friend of Evelyn's—and of Miss Radcliffe's, to whom she has been a mother."

The Virginia ladies were impressed, though not unduly. England and its peerage was an enchanting concept, like a fairy tale. It was the motherland, and one was proud of it. But except as the remote source of credit, luxuries, and fashions, England had no immediacy to these Tidewater aristocrats.

"I told Ben not to buy that villain," said Anne Harrison, reverting to the previous subject. "But Madam Harrison *insisted*. Now Ben's out fifty pounds!"

"*Why?*" cried Jenny suddenly jumping to her feet, and glaring from one Harrison to the other. "Why is Mr. Harrison out fifty pounds? It seems to me that Robert Wilson has done excellent work for you here!"

With the exception of Evelyn, who felt inclined to cheer, the entire company gaped at Jenny's flushed defiance. This angry outburst from the silent retiring girl was as startling as the appearance of a two-headed calf in the parlor.

"Well—damme—well-a-day . . ." said Ben uncrossing his legs, and taking his first real look at Jenny. "I'm not saying the rogue's not a good buildah, miss. Still he's done what they all do—that white trash—he's run off."

"Run off," she repeated, her face crumpling. "You mean run away . . . Rob wouldn't do that."

"He *has* done it." Ben spoke more gently than he would have had not Jenny been so remarkably pretty. " 'Twas a month ago. I'd made Corby give the fellow a lot of liberty, I admit. I had him take the fellow's chains off. I trusted the rogue, liked his face—the moah fool I. Then one day Corby gave him a floggin'—thirty lashes I believe—because he wouldn't hurry the cornice, get it done for Eastah. The next day he was gone."

"My husband's had the rogue posted at the Charles City Courthouse," Anne interjected plaintively. "And even in Williamsburg, offered a reward beyond the usual—but theah's no word of him. Most vexin'. We wished to hold a housewarmin', but I dislike to when the house isn't quite finished."

"So!" cried Jenny, her eyes gone hard. "Amongst all your other slaves is there none able to finish your house?" She stared directly at Ben, who was embarrassed.

"Not propahly," he said. "But we'll have to make do. Wilson trained one of my people as his 'prentice, a big buck Nigra named Nero, and—"

"You admit, sir," Jenny interrupted fiercely, "that this Wilson was invaluable to you. In the six months you had him you've plainly got more than his price out of him. Was it then wise to permit your overseer to give him a brutal flogging?" She confronted the discomfited planter, her chin lifted, and her arms akimbo, in the age-old posture of scornful challenge.

"Reahlly!" dawled Anne Harrison, lifting her eyebrows. "Is this a sample of English uppah class manners?"

Evelyn emitted an unmistakable giggle, while her father, who had been silenced by astonishment at Jenny's behavior, for which nothing had prepared him, said, "Miss Radcliffe! It is hardly meet that you should tell Mr. Harrison how to run his plantation, nor do I understand your need to champion an escaped convict."

"A murderah too, he was!" said Anne. "It said so on the bill of sale. 'Transported for murder.' I vow I'd not an easy moment while he was heah!"

"Nonsense!" said Madam Harrison tartly. "That's not the

way you acted—drawin' plans with him, consultin' with him at all hours, praisin' him to his face for his skill and strength —oh I heard you, my deah."

The two Harrison ladies exchanged an unamiable look, and Byrd said hastily, "I'm sorry, Ben, for any discomfort you've been put to, because of my daughter's recommendation, which I don't yet understand. I suppose the villain's made for Carolina or the northern neck—they all do. What did he steal to take with him?"

"Nothin'," said Ben grumpily. He was tired of the subject. "Only his clothes an' a knife. I reckon he'll starve."

"Oh no, he won't!" cried Jenny, tossing her head. "He can take care of himself, and I'm glad he got away from here. *Glad! Glad! Glad!*"

"Hush!" said Evelyn at last taking part. She put her hand over Jenny's mouth. "Miss Radcliffe's not quite herself. 'Tis the long voyage, change of climate, and perhaps a touch of fever. I think we should go home, Father. Mr. Harrison, would you be so kind as to order your coach? I fear some of us are not fit for walking."

The Byrd ladies all went by coach, around by the highway, and up and down the plantation drives. Byrd instantly forgot Jenny while he walked along the shorter river path, as he had done so often in the past. He passed the boundary oak between Berkeley and Westover, and entered his own estate, then presently came to the church, which served the entire parish. It was of brick, with a peaked roof, and no tower or spire. The little building was like all the dependencies on Byrd's own plantation, singularly plain and boxlike. It had no elegance. Byrd sighed deeply.

He wondered into the cemetery to the Byrd plot. It was shin-deep in grasses and weeds. He stood looking at the tombs of his father and mother. They had been dead a long time—and deserted here a long time, he thought with a prick of remorse. Well, he was back now, and would attend to the place they had left him. Beautify, enhance it. They would both have resented the magnificence achieved by young Harrison, who had no more notion of true culture than one of his own hound-dogs. I'll build *me* a manor house, Byrd thought, it'll be the finest one on the James. And a new library—Ben Harrison would never do that! It was unlikely that he'd opened a book since he was forced to at the College. *Plebeians*, that's what they were, these planters, Byrd thought contemptuously. Yet this was the society in which he must live, and take his place as leader—eminently suited for leadership.

The westering sun was still very hot, it glared off the shining river below, there was no air stirring. Under the gold-laced tricorne and the curled wig, Byrd's head was sweating, but he scarcely noted this as he thought of his accomplishments. Who else in the Colony read Hebrew and Greek as easily as Latin? Who else had been sponsored by a Sir Robert Southwell, and become a Fellow of the Royal Society? Who else had read law at the Middle Temple? Who else could write pungent, sophisticated "Characters" and satire quite in the manner of Addison? Who else had been accepted in Court circles, conversed with the King, and numbered peers amongst his closest friends?

Byrd glanced down at his father's tombstone, and the glow of superiority was dimmed. A forceful, shrewd, and energetic man had been William Byrd the First. It was he who had secured the Virginia lands and made them prosper, he who had attained the seat on the Council which his son had inherited—and that first William Byrd came of tradesman stock! *His* father had been a London goldsmith. This unpalatable fact Byrd had never mentioned in England, where he had vaguely let it be known that he sprang from the Cheshire Byrds, while taking every opportunity to emphasize his mother's Cavalier descent from Sir Warham St. Leger of Ulcombe.

In a rare moment of evaluation, as he stood by his parents' tombs, Byrd faced other uneasy truths. What had he ever done to justify his fellowship in the Royal Society, except read them one brief juvenile paper about a dappled Negro? And of what use had all the intimacies with noblemen actually been? Not one lucrative office had come his way, since he had been Agent for the Colony. The Earl of Orkney, titular Governor of Virginia, had concerned himself as little with Byrd's worthiness to be appointed Lieutenant-Governor as he had with Colony affairs. Orkney's only duty was to draw a fat salary, which was yet only a drop in the bucket of that Earl's enormous revenues.

Byrd stirred and laid his hand solemnly on his father's tomb, as though some strengthening, blunt voice had spoken from it. Forget England and its disappointments, for it was *here* that power lay! Here in this new land, where ambition had no limits, and where a member of the ruling class—a member of the Council—might still acquire land grants so vast that they would beggar by contrast any Duke's estate in England.

"A-hey, there!" called a man's voice from the river path, and Byrd turned to see Captain Randolph, newly shaven and dressed in his best shore clothes. Randolph glanced towards the tombstones and stopped. "Do I intrude, Colonel? Forgive me."

Byrd shook his head. "I've communed long enough with the dead. May God Almighty give them rest! Have you business with me?"

"Why, no, sir, but I left my ship in order, the crew's started to unload her, and I thought, perhaps—if 'tis not too soon—I might wait upon the ladies."

"Oh, you did, did you!" said Byrd, chuckling. "Sea-dogs are ever impetuous lovers. Still, I must warn you that the young damsel who's captured your affections has an astonishing side to her character!"

"What do you mean?" asked the Captain frowning. "I've observed her closely for better'n eight weeks. Shipboard brings out the worst in passengers, yet Miss Radcliffe never failed to show angelic patience, good humor, gentleness."

"Enough!" cried Byrd. "Save your rhapsodies for *her* ear! But, Ned, Ned, remember a man's heart can be well diddled by a pretty face! Miss Radcliffe seemed sadly lacking in the traits you mention a while ago at the Harrisons'. The girl has a temper, and if I mistake not, she has a vulgar taste in men, not, alas, uncommon to her sex."

"I don't believe it!" cried Randolph hotly. "How dare you speak of her so!"

Byrd checked an angry reply, for he now greatly favored the Captain's suit. If Jenny Radcliffe was beginning to show eccentricities, the sooner she was married off and away from Evelyn the better. So he contented himself by saying, "Tut! Tut! Spare me the quarterdeck voice—and it may be the girl has a touch of fever. I'll give her a purge."

The men proceeded across a little bridge and into the housegrounds of Westover. The Berkeley coach at the same time drew up at the north front door and debouched the ladies before a silent, neglected house.

By sundown the entire plantation was in an uproar. News spread from the house to the shops, to the stables, and finally to the Quarters that Master had come home and was in a fury at what he found. He had begun by discovering Johnny Fell, the overseer, fast asleep in the Master's own bed, with

Annie, the white bond servant, snoring naked beside him, and both of them drunk on wine pilfered from the Master's cellars. Colonel Byrd had caned them at once just as they lay. In the Quarters nobody minded that—the overseer and his whore were a no-good pair—but the Master's rage had not stopped there. He had whipped all the Negro house-servants—Eugene, Joe, Tom, Hampton, Dora, and Moll, even old Anaka, the cook, who practiced witchcraft and would doubtless work a conjure in revenge.

In the Quarters the hundred slaves drew together fearfully, murmuring or weeping, for they knew that punishment would soon come their way too. The tobacco seedlings had not been transplanted or thinned as they should be, the seed beds were run wild. The entire crop was threatened. Nor had they sown the hemp that the Master had written from England he wanted done. Jacko, the mulatto overseer of the field hands, he hadn't troubled himself much what they did. He liked to loll in the shade of his cabin and shoot the knucklebones, did Jacko, and he didn't fret himself if the hands lazed away with him. Now Jacko was as scared as any of them; he flung himself on his pallet and took to groaning so the Master'd think he was sick.

That was a smart notion of Jacko's, and the rest of the hands thought they'd try it too, though Cato, who'd been a king in Guinea thirty years ago, he said it wouldn't do any good. The Master wasn't easy-fooled. First thing he'd do is give them all a vomit which'd tear up their guts, then gag them with the iron branks.

So they waited, and some of them prayed to their own gods, like the Black Snake, Ibo Leli, while a few said prayers that Mr. Fontaine, the Westover minister, had taught them.

Retribution did not come that day. In the forms pictured by their terrified imaginations, it did not come at all. Byrd's rage exhausted itself on the overseer and house-servants, with whose punishment Captain Randolph had helped energetically.

In time, Anaka sullenly produced a meal of boiled bacon and corn pone, which the men washed down with a surviving bottle of madeira. The ladies did not join them, having pleaded extreme fatigue, so that Randolph had no chance to pay court to Jenny that evening.

Jenny and Evelyn waited silently until Moll, the sniffling cinnamon-hued chambermaid had righted Evelyn's bedroom, aired the sheets, and made the bed. Then Evelyn sent her to the kitchen for some gruel, and dropping into a chair said, "Mercy on us! Lord, what a day! Jenny, I'm so very grieved, dear. I've dragged you to Virginia for nothing."

Jenny walked slowly to the window. She pulled back the shutter and looked out at the broad glimmering river, and at the black ribbon of forest on the other bank. " 'Tis so silent out there," she said. "A vast and silent land. There's mystery in it. It holds itself away in secret—and yet I think I understand it."

Evelyn stared at the girl curiously. This was not the reaction she had expected. She decided that Jenny was dazed by disappointment, and had not realized the impossibility of finding Rob Wilson now.

Jenny, as she so often did, surprised her. "I can see him," she said in the same musing tone. "I can see Rob. He's far off. There are mountains. He kneels by a campfire near a stream, and a big river. There's a little hill behind him. It is something like Tosson, and the stream is like our burn. He is thinking of me. I *know* it, Evie! Nay," she said smiling as she saw her friend's expression, "I'm neither mad nor feverish. 'Tis just a certainty. He has heard me calling him. I've only to wait."

"But Jenny," Evelyn began, then stopped. She would not ruin the girl's quiet exaltation by scepticism, or by reminding her of the fearful plight Rob would be in if he did return. A runaway convict might even be executed. Tears sprang to Evelyn's eyes, her proud mocking mouth quivered. "I've known love," she murmured, "I know it now—yet yours, Jenny, is touched with something that I have never known." And to herself she added, Please God the something is not tragedy.

SIXTEEN

On April 27, a week after landing in Virginia, William Byrd rode out from Westover at five o'clock in dawn light, bound for Williamsburg. With him went Evelyn and Jenny. Also Eugene, a sleek young Negro born on the plantation, whose rearing had been personally supervised by Byrd with a view to his present status as body-servant. Not one of Eugene's peccadilloes had ever escaped instant punishment. He had been whipped routinely for any negligence. For wetting his bed in his early years, Byrd had made him—as he noted in his diary of 1709—"drink a pint of piss." The boy had run away once, and when brought back and beaten, had been muzzled for two days with the iron branks. Byrd considered that his methods had been successful; though Eugene, like the other servants, had backslid woefully in his master's absence, he was relearning his duties, and was obviously proud of his livery—a neat cocked hat, a suit with brass buttons, and a small black cape.

Byrd rode ahead down the old Indian road, which was sufficiently inland from the James to facilitate the crossing of many little creeks.

The Reverend Peter Fontaine, Westover parish's Huguenot minister, rode beside him. Mr. Fontaine would accompany the party as far as the Chickahominy Ferry, for he and Byrd had much to talk about—not only parish affairs but the state of the Colony.

Evelyn followed the two gentlemen, and Jenny lagged behind because she had naturally been given the worst of the family mounts, a barrel-shaped gelding who shuffled along at his own weary pace.

It was "Publick Times" again at Williamsburg. Twice a year, in fall and spring, the General Assembly gathered from all the counties to do the Colony's business. The Assembly, which sat in the handsome brick Capitol building, was as much like Parliament as the Virginians could make it. The Council, though it had only twelve members and those twelve all related in some way to each other, nonetheless represented the House of Lords. The Burgesses, two elected from each county, were equivalent to the Commons. Over all, as surrogate for King George, was the acting Governor. At present this was Hugh Drysdale, but Byrd, who had been extremely busy gathering information during the first week of his return, had discovered that Drysdale was ill, had—by report—some sort of distemper gnawing at his vitals, and was unlikely to survive. It was therefore imperative that Byrd should get to the Capitol and secure his absentee seat on the Council before the Assembly dispersed for the summer. It was imperative to find out which way the political wind was blowing.

Maria Byrd had not cared to make the trip. She was oppressed by the unaccustomed heat, and queasy in the stomach. Since the cause of this was pregnancy and Byrd passionately wanted a son, he had spared her the physics and purges with which he dosed himself and any of his dependents upon hearing of the smallest symptom. Byrd wanted to show Evelyn off to Williamsburg, and had wanted to leave Jenny home, where she would be further exposed to Captain Randolph's wooing. Randolph had appeared at Westover daily this week. But Evelyn would not go to Williamsburg without Jenny. So that was that.

The quintet jogged along the narrow monotonous winding road. On either side them was the forest—towering stands of virgin timber mile after mile. At length the sun came up, and the morning was filled with bird song. Eugene rode several respectful paces behind the others and crooned to himself a cheery sort of chant that sounded like "Ho-de-dow-dow, ro-de-dow-dow" to Jenny, whose quick ear was caught by the rhythm and melody. "What are you singing, Eugene?" she asked, turning in the saddle.

The Negro grinned, displaying a startling blaze of white teeth in the midst of ebony skin. "Ol' song my mammy teached me, mistiss," he said. "Dancin' song from Guinea. Mammy she say sing it to make happy things come, but I dunno what the words mean."

"I *hope* happy things come," said Jenny smiling. "Sing your song, Eugene!" A slave can sing and hope, she thought, even a slave who has been beaten twice this week. So why should I despond? The certainty that she had communicated with Rob on the night of their landing had never quite failed her. Though there were moments of discouragement, they passed, and her primary mood was one of unreasoning anticipation. She hammered her heels on her horse's ribs and slapped its neck, thinking with a pang of Coquet, who had been sold long ago when Jenny left school. The gelding snorted resentfully, then lumbered a bit faster until Jenny was abreast of Evelyn. "It's very lovely out here this morning," said Jenny.

Evelyn looked about her in astonishment, seeing nothing but the everlasting denseness of trees hemming them in. "What's so lovely?" she asked crossly. She disliked riding, and her father had given them time for no breakfast except his tiresome boiled milk.

"This—" said Jenny, waving her arm. "Oaks, beech, pines, holly, all bigger than I've ever seen, and then the flowering ones—in there looking like tulips," she pointed, "and those violet redbuds, and the wild pink crab, see it? The air's so sweetly fresh and scented. And look, what's *that?* That glorious red bird, like a flying ruby!"

"Like a cardinal's hat," said Evelyn. "For which it's named. Virginia's full of them. Lud, Jenny, you're daft about nature! I'm not. I find this countryside lonely and fearsome. There may be wolves in there. For all we know, there may even be Indians. Oh they say the hostile ones are fled to the West, but that's what the settlers thought right here, before they got massacred."

"That was a long time ago, wasn't it?" said Jenny.

Evelyn shrugged. "Why do you suppose we have an escape tunnel to the river at Westover? You saw it yourself."

"I didn't think it was for fear of *Indians*," said Jenny very low, glancing quickly over her shoulder to see that Eugene was out of earshot.

"Oh, that's a topic never to be mentioned!" Evelyn gave her ironic laugh. "I saw that you've been shocked by the way my father has had to deal with his people, but I assure you it's the only way they understand. At that Father is milder than he used to be, or than my mother was. Well do I remember when she branded her maid across the mouth with a curling-iron for lying."

"And did that cure her?" asked Jenny.

"She never spoke again, and was sent to the Quarters for a field hand, where I believe she was a good worker." Jenny made a sound, and Evelyn went on swiftly. "Oh, the system has grave faults, but you mustn't be mawkish. The Negroes don't toil as hard as many a cottager on his own plot in England, and every planter constantly tends to their health and well-being."

"Like any valuable livestock," said Jenny. "Why not?"

Evelyn laughed again. "I hold no brief for my father usually, yet one must be fair. He's not of those who think the Negro has no soul—is nothing but a talking beast. He prays with them nightly, and on the whole most of them respect or even love him."

"Just the same," said Jenny stubbornly, "there is the escape tunnel to the river."

"And so there is," said Evelyn. "Jenny, can you not find a more congenial subject for conversation, and *can* you make that nag of yours move faster? There's Father way ahead and beckoning to us."

Jenny ceased frowning and gave Evelyn her quick enchanting smile. "I'll try on both counts," she said.

At ten o'clock they reached the Chickahominy River, and the ferry, which awaited them. Here the minister, Mr. Fontaine, made his farewells. Peter Fontaine was a tall, thin widower in the thirties. He had been born in France of an ennobled Huguenot family who suffered bitter prosecution after the revocation of the Edict of Nantes. The Fontaines had fled to England, and then Ireland, where Peter had been educated at the university in Dublin. He had gone into orders and been ordained by the Bishop of London, then he and his family had emigrated to Virginia in 1716. Young Fontaine had been appointed to Westover parish in 1720, when Byrd met and approved him during the latter's brief visit to Virginia.

Byrd found Fontaine to be an intelligent godly man, sound in doctrine, observant of his duties, while tactful enough never to exceed them or to offer unwanted advice. A minister should know his place—which was in no way equal to the level of the plantation owners. Fontaine looked solemn enough in his black clerical suit, yet it was obvious to Jenny that the minister's mind was not at the moment on religion, or even politics, as he helped Evelyn dismount. There was the way he bent over Evelyn, after pressing her waist a little longer than was necessary, there was the look in his prominent brown eyes and his caressing tone as he said, "Ah—Miss

Byrd, I hope you have not fatigued yourself on this long ride." Though he had little accent, his inflections were French, which somehow enhanced his mellow voice.

Evelyn denied fatigue, while vouchsafing the minister a languishing look, and he cried, "Good! Pray take care of yourself amongst the fleshpots of Williamsburg!"

Evelyn laughed. "I'm *longing* for them! Do I dare hope I'll be subjected to temptations as wicked as in London?"

Fontaine shook his head. "You are pleased to jest with me," he lowered his voice, "but I assure you that I shall be so anxiously awaiting your return." He bowed over her hand, brushing it with his lips, bowed to Byrd who had not heard this speech, and then to Jenny. He mounted his horse and rode back towards his rectory.

Eugene tethered all the horses except his own to a hitching post to await the ferry's return with some of the servants Byrd had sent ahead yesterday. They were now on the other side of the river with Byrd's coach and pair, which was ready to continue the journey.

Everyone boarded the ferry. It was a large flat barge, poled and paddled by three men. The Chickahominy, though only a short tributary of the James, was a large river—as broad as the Thames, Jenny thought in astonishment. Everything over here seemed so big, except the houses. She was quiet for a time, enjoying the breeze and sparkling water; then she turned to Evelyn, who sat next her on a bench, and said, laughing, "I observe, Evie, that you've made a conquest of the minister!"

Evelyn tilted her head, her huge brown eyes held an answering twinkle. "I believe I have," she said. "Father'd have an apoplexy if he was aware of it—and you needn't be jealous, my pet. You've got our doughty Captain Randolph moaning and sighing like a grampus."

"I'm *sorry* for Mr. Fontaine," said Jenny with spirit. "You lead him on, Evie. You know you do."

"Why not?" asked Evelyn. "It's amusing, and though I shall never marry anyone but Wilfred, I've not gone into a nunnery. Life is dreary enough without refusing any diversions it does offer. I give you this sage advice also."

"Perhaps you're right," said Jenny. She turned farther and looked squarely at her friend. "Evie—you spoke as though you thought there was a chance that you and Sir Wilfred might still marry. How *can* you?"

Evelyn's face changed. It became for a second defenseless, while her hand went to touch the locket hidden in her bodice.

"I don't know," she said seriously. " 'Tis a feeling, a certainty, as you said about Rob—that Wilfred and I will be together somewhere—someday. It's not like me, I know, to have fancies, much more like my romantical Jenny. But I *have* it. It rather frightens me."

Jenny, who loved her friend, wanted to say something encouraging, but could not find appropriate words. Wishing for Evelyn to be together with Sir Wilfred meant wishing for the death of Elizabeth Mordaunt Lawson. What else? And this was the dark, strange part of Evelyn, which Jenny dared not explore. They were both silent, until the ferry's prow grazed the shore. Then Evelyn jumped up, crying gaily to her father, "I hope, sir, the servants have food for us in the coach! I'm hollow as a drum, and you wouldn't wish to exhibit a starving daughter to the big-wigs of Williamsburg!"

At noon they reached the capital. Byrd was pleased that they had slightly bettered the usual time for the forty-five miles' journey. He was also pleased to note as they entered town from the Jamestown road that several new houses had been built near the College of William and Mary. The little capital was expanding nicely, though now it was jammed with the visitors who had come here for the spring session of the Assembly. In the ordinaries they were sleeping three and four to a bed—if a bed could be found. Every lodging was pre-empted, and although he was not a bit fond of his brother-in-law, Byrd had already secured an invitation to visit John Custis in his town mansion on the Back Street, south of Palace Green.

As the coach turned down Duke of Gloucester Street the girls hung out of the windows to see what they could, and Byrd amiably gave them information. "Here you see the College," he said waving his hand towards a long brick building with a cupola. "Sir Christopher Wren made the design of it. To the left is Brafferton House, where Indians are educated, at least it was built for that purpose, though the savages take sadly to civilization. Halt!" he called to Job, the coachman, who pulled up his horses. "Look down the street, my dears," said Byrd. " 'Tis the nearest thing in this country to an elegant vista."

Evelyn and Jenny looked. Duke of Gloucester Street was a scant mile long and straight as an arrow. It was lined with shade trees and small white clapboard houses behind picket fences. At the further end loomed the imposing brick mass of the Capitol. It was topped by a tall cupola, where the British flag hung limp today below the weather vane. "I see, said Evelyn, nodding to her father. "College at one end, Capitol at the other. Very neat. But it's so odd never to see anything built of stone over here. I confess I expected a trifle more grandeur in Williamsburg."

"It has certainly no resemblance to London," said Byrd dryly as the coach began to move again. "Bruton church ahead on your left," he continued, "where that old tartar of a Commissary Blair no doubt still thunders away from the pulpit on Sundays. The rest of the time sticking his fat paws into every single piece of Colony business. I'll soon find out if he's got a stranglehold on *this* Governor the way he had on Spotswood and the rest." Byrd had so far kept on neutral terms with the formidable James Blair, who was not only Commissary—or Deputy—for the Bishop of London and Rector of Bruton parish, but President of the College and senior member of the Council as well. Blair was a tough old Scot, and in quarrels with past governors he had always won. It was he who had eventually ousted Nicholson and Spotswood; for the latter feat Byrd gave the old man uneasy credit. Governor Spotswood had been Byrd's enemy.

Just before they came to the Palace Green, the Byrd coach turned south a block then into a driveway which entered the Custis place, called "Six Chimneys."

"So this is where my uncle lives?" said Evelyn, looking past the large brick great house to the separate little shacks which served as kitchen, washhouse, necessaries, and slave quarters. " 'Tis a plantation in miniature!" The coach stopped, Eugene dismounted and went to apprise Major Custis of their arrival.

"My brother Custis has done very well for himself," said Byrd scowling. "Small wonder since he enjoys your mother's inheritance, as well as that of his poor wife."

This acid speech was not strictly true, and Evelyn knew it. "Why, Father," she said, "you made a *bargain* with Uncle Custis, didn't you? You got all my mother's lands in exchange for assuming Grandfather Parke's debts?"

"A foul bargain," cried Byrd. "They concealed the extent of the debts from me! Those debts which still crouch on my back like the Old Man of the Sea—and that usurer—that Shylock—Micajah Perry in London, I'll never be free from him, and 'tis all the fault of John Custis!"

"Oh, Father," said Evelyn shaking her head. "Don't shout! We shouldn't stay with Uncle Custis if you're going to be angry at him."

"I wouldn't stay," Byrd snapped, "except for you. Can't

lodge you in an ordinary! Besides you're blood kin to his children, and the least he can do is to expend some of his ill-got wealth on our entertainment!" Byrd drummed his fingers on his satin-clad knee, thinking of old wrongs.

"Father . . ." said Evelyn tilting her head, and looking up at Byrd through her lashes. "Is there any man you really *like?* I mean here in Virginia, of course."

"Naturally!" he shouted, glaring at her. "And, miss, you are impertinent!"

"Forgive me, sir," said Evelyn sweetly. "I only wondered."

Jenny had perforce been silent during this interchange, in which Evelyn as usual had managed to make her father look slightly ridiculous, without his being aware of it. Jenny was sometimes a trifle sorry for Mr. Byrd, and was relieved when Eugene opened the coach door to announce that Major Custis was in his garden—please to come in and he'd be with them directly.

John Custis received his relations in an abrupt way, with the air of a man who has been interrupted in an important task. He had been supervising the disposition of holly bushes and cedars just received in a cargo from England and, though the season was late for it, he was laying out a new rose bed. Gardening and his son, Dan, were his only vital interests. His dress was careless, his shorn head was covered with a stained old cap; at forty-seven he was bowed by rheumatism, his thin mouth twitched from the effects of chronic pain, sternly ignored. And he was a woman-hater. His marriage to Frances Parke had been a nightmare of quarrels which finally became shamefully public when they resulted in legal action. Frances had, however, been dead ten years, and Custis never scrupled to thank the Lord for his release.

"Well, so here you are!" he said to Byrd. "Had enough of your beloved England, eh? And this is Evelyn. Looks like her mother, and her not lamented aunt. A handsome lot, the Parkes, but that's all I can say for 'em. Evelyn's got a temper like all the Parkes too, I dare say?"

"My daughter has an excellent disposition," said Byrd stiffly. "This is her young gentlewoman, Miss Radcliffe."

Jenny curtsied, while her host gave her a sour stare. "Didn't know you were bringing another *female*," he said. "Pshaw!"

Jenny was so accustomed to a kindling in masculine eyes when they beheld her that she was dismayed and blushed scarlet. "I'm sorry, sir—" she faltered. "Perhaps I can find lodgings somewhere . . ."

"Nonsense!" said Evelyn, sinking into a chair and adjusting her skirts carefully. "We're here, Uncle Custis, and you'll have to put up with both Jenny and me, though I *assure* you we'll prefer to keep out of your way!"

"Hoity-toity!" said Custis with a snort of laughter. "You're a Parke sure enough! Brother Byrd, I commiserate you. Come take a look at the garden. I want to keep an eye on those black rascals. As for you, Evelyn, direct my servants as you please, for I'm quite sure you will anyhow."

The men went off into the passage towards the garden.

"Ha!" said Evelyn, shrugging. "The old goat, he made my aunt miserable, but he'll not gammon me!"

"I'm sure he won't," said Jenny sighing. Evelyn enjoyed these sparring matches. Jenny did not. And her own cool reception by Major Custis had awakened an unhappy question. Where on earth did she really belong? Had there ever been a home to which she had a clear right? Certainly not at the Vincennes château, nor at Westover, where she knew that Mr. Byrd thought her superfluous. Even at Lady Betty's she had not been on quite the same footing as the Lee children. Always and everywhere she went there was an element of being there on sufferance, because somebody had championed her. Forlorn, she thought, that's what I am.

Forlorn—a deathknell word. Had her mother not used it so once, long ago in Northumberland? Suddenly, between one instant and the next, Jenny lost her conviction that she would soon see Rob, or that their hearts had somehow communicated. She saw that conviction as childish folly. Virginia was as big, they said, as a hundred Englands, it stretched far beyond the knowledge of white men, west and west to another sea. Rob might be anywhere in all those myriad miles. She was glad that he had freed himself, as glad as she had been at the Harrisons'. She knew that there was no way he could have known of her coming, and waited for her, and yet she was suffused with bleakness, and a sense of betrayal.

Evelyn did not notice that Jenny stood stiffly near the door, her hands twisting on each other, and her face gone pale. Evelyn was thinking of the practical matters needed to make their stay in Williamsburg agreeable.

"I'm going to find the servants," she said. "See what they're doing with our luggage. I'm sure they're a shiftless lot with no mistress over them." She swept out, leaving Jenny to the chill and comfortless parlor, where any feminine touch was notably lacking. There was a closed harpsichord in a corner near the window. Jenny walked to it, hesitated, then, wiping off a layer of dust with her handkerchief, raised the lid and touched the yellowed keys. She sat down on the bench and began to play a succession of minor chords, formless snatches of tunes, which gradually resolved themselves into a song Lady Betty had taught her three years ago. Lady Betty had laughed very much as she taught her the song, saying, "If it weren't for this ditty, my dear, I dare say you'd not exist at all!"

Yet there was nothing to laugh at in the words or music. Jenny now sang the song slowly, her eyes fixed on the bare wall above the harpsichord.

> "My lodging it is on the cold ground,
> And oh! very hard is my fare,
> But that which grieves me more, love,
> Is the coldness of my dear.
> Yet still I cry; O turn, love,
> I prithee, love, turn to me
> For thou art the man that I long for,
> And alack, what remedy!"

She sang all the verses in the same quiet way, while tears began slipping down her cheeks.

She did not hear footsteps behind her, nor was conscious of anyone in the room, until she was interrupted by a kind of strangled gasp. She jumped and saw Edward Randolph standing in the middle of the floor, his hat crushed in his hands, his blue eyes staring at her in adoration. "Miss Radcliffe," he whispered. "Oh, Miss Radcliffe—don't stop—oh damme, you're weeping! Don't weep!" He stumbled across the floor, and flung himself down on his knees. He grabbed her hand and held it violently against his chest. "Miss Jenny—oh my angel," he gasped. "*Why* are you sad?"

Jenny repressed an impulse to snatch away her hand and shove him off with it. She knew it was unjust to feel a leap of fury because the intruder was the wrong man. She was angry nevertheless, and she said crisply, "Indeed, Captain Randolph, how should I be sad, when it is with this song that my great-grandmother captured the fancy of King Charles?"

"What?" stammered the Captain. "My sweet angel, I don't understand you."

"Why," said Jenny, " 'Tis simple. Moll Davis sang this song one night at the Duke's Playhouse, and thereby exchanged her hard lodging on the cold ground for the soft heat of the royal bed."

Randolph bit his lips and recoiled a trifle, while loosing her hand. His blue eyes were confused. "You—you speak very coarse," he said. "You are joking."

"Not at all," said Jenny. "I *am* coarse. Oh, Captain, *do* get up! Suppose someone saw you."

Randolph flushed, and rose to his feet. He stood looking down at her. Sunlight through the window shed a nimbus on her yellow hair, it glistened off the tears on the rose and white of her cheeks. Her head was averted from him, the line of her profile was so pure and he found her so beautiful that he instantly forgot his dismay; in fact he ascribed her remarks to some form of girlish mystery, and he cried, "Miss Radcliffe, I'm never alone with you, you seem to avoid me. But can you doubt my feelings? I love you. I wish you for my wife. I know I've not much to offer, but I should try to make you happy!"

Jenny turned and looked at him more kindly. A stocky young man was Ned Randolph. His sandy eyebrows twisted now in pleading above the vivid blue gaze. It was a pleasant face despite the roughened skin—and the missing teeth were not visible unless he smiled. "Ah, Captain," said Jenny. " 'Tis a great compliment you pay me, and would you indeed try to make me happy?" She sighed and touching one key softly let her hand fall on her lap.

"Aye," he cried. "Aye. I'm quite well off, there's my share in the family ships, and there's my plantation, 'Bremo'—it's not in order for a woman, but I can make it so. The house is trim, and you'd have plenty of servants, and if my—my person is—is not entirely pleasing to you—well you'll not be overtroubled with me, since my voyages are long—" She made a faint pitying gesture, and he went on quickly, "Yet— oh, Miss Jenny—if you come to love me, if you should wish it—then I'd find some other Master for my ship. I'd stay at home with you."

Jenny swallowed, and shook her head. "Don't," she said. "Please don't talk like that. For I could never make *you* happy. You don't know me, Captain, you don't know my people or beliefs or what I'm like inside. You don't even know why I came to Virginia!"

"It doesn't matter!" cried Randolph. "Nothing matters except that you give me leave to hope! You aren't pledged to another, are you?" he added in sudden fear. "You're not affianced?"

Jenny lifted her chin and stared past the imploring Captain. "No," she said flatly. "I'm neither pledged or affianced."

He did not hear the bitterness in her voice, he heard only the context, and he cried, "Then sweet, sweet Jenny, I may hope?"

"Why not?" she said with a half smile. "Everyone may hope. Hope and fear—see, 'tis the motto on my ring." She held it out to him, but the Captain was not interested in mottoes, nor could have read the Latin.

"Miss Jenny, may I kiss you?" he asked in a reverent whisper. This time Jenny smiled outright. No man whom she had ever known had been tentative or reverent in love-making, no man had acted as though she were a chalice made of fragile glass. She stood up and gracefully extended her cheek to him. She heard his indrawn breath, and saw him tremble as he kissed it, and to her the kiss was no more moving than had been those of the Lee children. Could I learn to love him enough? she thought. He deserves it, poor soul. And she thought too of what he had offered her—a home of her own, position, security—and all that without exacting on her part any return but the gift of her body. They were romantic, these Virginians, they treated women like flowers. No Englishman did.

"And now, Captain," said Jenny, seating herself at the harpsichord with a finality which precluded more kisses, "shall I sing you something cheerful? How about 'Begone dull care, I prithee, begone from me'—'twill suit us both." And she began at once on the rippling melody.

William Byrd, on his way to his chamber preparatory to dressing for a call on the Governor, was attracted by the music. He peered through the door and was pleased to see the enamored Captain draped over the harpsichord, and clearly on good terms with the fair singer. Byrd went on his way, feeling benevolent. John Custis had grudgingly admitted that the Council was eager for Byrd's return, that poor ailing Governor Drysdale himself had expressed a desire to see him at once, and be guided by his reports from England. The slanders and suspicions about Byrd's accountings as Receiver General some years ago—these were forgotten. They had all sprung from Spotswood's hostility, anyway, and Spotswood no longer had a shred of power in Virginia, or much in England, where he had returned to sulk, stabilize his Virginia land grants on the frontiers in Spotsylvania, and incidentally get himself a wife.

For the first time since his landing, Byrd was lighthearted.

He caught a glimpse of a pretty mulatto chambermaid in the passage, and felt instant resurgence of the old temptation, so often yielded to, so often repented of. Perhaps tonight, he thought, then quickly read a page of Greek in Lucian as antidote. He was jovial and forbearing with Eugene, even when the youth buttoned the brocaded vest awry and couldn't find the gold-banded Malacca stick which Byrd always carried on dress occasions. It was as though Jenny's determined song "Begone Dull Care" had permeated the whole dismal house.

Evelyn heard the singing and was glad for Jenny, though puzzled. John Custis heard it as he returned from the garden, and listening a moment in the hall to the fresh, young, and yet wistful voice, checked the angry comment he had been about to make on female frivolity in his parlor.

The next day continued to be pleasant for the visitors. The girls strolled around Williamsburg, escorted by Captain Randolph and young Daniel Parke Custis, Evelyn's cousin. He was a handsome tall lad of fifteen; he had flashing eyes like Evelyn's and wavy hair, lightly powdered and queued. He skipped his classes at the College that day, though his father, still immersed in the garden, did not know that. The young people amused themselves by eating syllabubs and drinking beer at Marot's Ordinary, and they bowled on the green behind Stagg's little theater near the Palace. Jenny flirted airily with Ned Randolph, allowing him to hold her hand when they walked, and even to snatch another kiss in the dusk, when they parted.

As for William Byrd, he had gone to the Capitol at ten, mounted to the Council Chamber—which was vastly more elegant than when he saw it last—and been cordially reinstated in his proper place at the great oval table with its Turkey rug covering. Senior to him there were only the doddering Edmund Jenings, "King" Carter, and the Commissary, James Blair. All older men who might be expected to die off soon, thereby making Byrd President of the Council—or even, Byrd thought (glancing at the Governor, who was so obviously ill), by the renewed exertion of influence in London—why not the *head of the table* in the great chair with the Royal Arms carved on it? Yes, I'll be Governor yet, he thought.

The Council business was routine: the appointment of excise officers, repairs to the Governor's Palace roof, examination of the currency and bills of exchange, and talk about westward expansion with a view to curbing the encroachments of the French along the Ohio. The latter interested

Byrd, who wanted more western lands; he was also interested in the need for surveying the dividing line between Virginia and Carolina. It was flattering that the Governor and fiery old Blair seemed to think Byrd fitted to be one of the Commissioners on what would certainly be an adventurous expedition. All in all, so agreeable was Byrd's reception that, on leaving the Capitol at two, he reflected that there were compensations for being a big frog in a little pond, and decided to put aside any further regrets for the hurly-burly of London.

The following day, on Saturday, April 29, the Governor and his lady entertained at the Palace. All morning liveried servants had been running up and down the Williamsburg streets, delivering invitations to members of the Assembly and the very few resident elite of the town.

John Custis refused to accept, but the rest of his household set off with enthusiasm. Though the distance was only three blocks, Byrd and the two girls were driven in the coach, as his importance required. Beside the coach, under the catalpa trees through the fine spring evening, walked Captain Randolph and young Daniel Custis.

In the coach the girls' best dresses, with their panoply of hoops and stiffened petticoats, took up so much room that Byrd had good-naturedly seated himself opposite on the other seat. They were a pair to be proud of, he thought. Jenny was exquisite in her Parisian rose taffeta gown, her wealth of golden hair falling in curls down her back and on her shoulders. Byrd reflected with satisfaction that she would soon be off his hands, judging from Randolph's ecstatic behavior. Then Byrd's eyes lingered on Evelyn—Amasia, the beloved one that she was and had always been, despite the anger she often roused in him. She looked very much as her mother had twenty years ago on their wedding day, the same huge dark eyes, the same lift of the head, even the same length of black curl falling on her right shoulder. Evelyn's gown was of rich gray brocade—he still remembered the exorbitant bill for it—and he wondered again why she insisted on dressing herself always in the hues of semimourning. He had remonstrated with her time and again to no avail. Then he noted that she was carrying the ivory and lace fan he had given her, and he said, "Ah, my dear, what a tale that little fan could tell! I remember how you dropped it when you curtsied to King George . . . and His Majesty himself retrieved it for you!"

"Yes," said Evelyn. She had dropped the fan because her Presentation occurred during her secret engagement to Wilfred Lawson, who was a Groom of the Bed Chamber and she had just caught sight of Wilfred standing behind the King and smiling at her. "I remember it well," she said. "And do *you* remember that the King asked my name, translated it as 'Vogel,' then made some German pun at which he roared with laughter?"

"I don't remember that," said Byrd stiffly, wondering why Evelyn was always deflating. He did not like puns on his name, since that lampoon of the despicable Lawson's, though once he had been complimented at being called the "Black Swan" and had even signed various love letters as "Inamorato L'Oiseau." Long ago, that was.

The coach stopped at the Palace gates, Negro flunkies opened the door, Byrd handed the ladies out, then drew Evelyn's arm through his. Randolph, rushing up, offered his arm to Jenny, who accepted with a demure smile. They crossed the court, where tall cressets were burning fragrant applewood. They mounted the steps and entered the great hall, a luxurious chamber of dark gleaming woods and flashing crystals beneath the lights of a dozen wax tapers.

At once they heard the tinkle of music from the ballroom. Jenny recognized a gavotte she had learned at school, and turned impulsively to her escort. "Oh, there'll be dancing!" she cried. "I do love it, don't you, Captain Randolph?"

He, who didn't know a jig from a minuet, murmured an untruthful assent, while squeezing her arm timidly and gazing at her in rapture. Others were looking at Jenny too. The hall was rapidly filling with guests, who had to wait there for their turn to mount the staircase and salute the Governor in his private parlor. The Governor's steward explained that His Excellency had not felt well enough to come down tonight, and that he had strength for only a few visitors at a time.

Byrd, and Captain Randolph, were constantly bowing to friends and kinfolk as they all waited. There were Beverleys, Stiths, and Ludwells, Nathaniel Harrison of "Wakefield"—uncle to Ben Harrison; Mann Page of "Rosewell," the Carters—a great many Carters, including the huge patriarch, "King" Robert Carter himself. Byrd proudly introduced Evelyn, who immediately presented Jenny to all these people. "My friend, Miss Radcliffe from London," she said to each one. Jenny was so busy curtseying and murmuring the proper howdye do ma'am's or sir's that all the curious admiring faces were a blur. Neither she nor anyone else noticed a small man in a baggy brown tradesman's suit who had squeezed himself near the door. He had a face like a puckered one-eyed monkey, mournful and a bit raffish because of the black patch which covered his right eye. His name was Willy Turner, and he was servant and Jack-of-all-trades to Dr. Archibald Blair, the Commissary's brother. Dr. Blair had sent Willy Turner to the Palace with some new pills for the Governor to try, and instructed him to deliver them personally to the Governor. So Willy waited, unobtrusively, until all the grand company should have been received. Very soon his eye lit on Jenny, and grew rounder. His keen ears had no difficulty in hearing her repeated introductions as "Miss Radcliffe" and he said "Holy Blessed Saints!" under his breath. He stared after Jenny, as the summons came and she mounted the broad mahogany staircase with the Byrds and Randolph. "I've *got* to know," he muttered to himself, and set his wits to working.

The interview with the Governor was brief. The old man was huddled in shawls and coughing. His skin was jaundiced. In a rasping wheeze he spoke a few gracious words, as befitted the King's representative.

Other guests were ushered in, and the Byrd party went downstairs into the great ballroom. Here Mrs. Drysdale greeted them. She was a plain, dumpy woman under her vice-regal coronet, and she could not quite hide her fears for her husband; yet she received her guests with practiced cordiality and begged them to enjoy themselves.

Both Jenny and Evelyn obeyed this request. They burst into Williamsburg society like a couple of sparkling Catherine-wheels. To their different styles of beauty they also brought the charm of novelty and the aura of London.

The men were dazzled. "King" Carter himself, after rather ponderously likening the girls to "Rose-red" and "Rose-white," led each one out for a dance.

The ladies were not as dazzled. A group of wallflowers on the gilt chairs beneath a portrait of King George decided that Evelyn was too tall, that the extraordinary gray dress (could that be the present fashion in London?) made her skin sallow, and that her manner was too bold. It was harder to find fault with Jenny, until someone said that a cleft chin was a sign of lewdness, and that surely the girl painted, such coloring couldn't be real; whereupon the ladies felt better as they watched their menfolk making fools of themselves.

Evelyn had her cluster of eager beaux, Jenny had hers,

though Captain Randolph, after several drinks of punch, grew jealous and so proprietorial of Jenny that one of his elder brothers, John, drew him aside and said, "Look here, Ned! You haven't made a serious offer to that lovely little creature, have you? Not without consulting the family!"

"Yes, I have!" said the Captain angrily. "And no pack of brothers'll stop me!"

"Now, now," said John Randolph. "You're a man of sense, Ned, or used to be. I've been talking to Colonel Byrd, who was evasive. There's something odd about that girl—something discreditable in her background, and she's practically penniless, nothing but a dependent of Miss Evelyn's. Believe me, Ned, she's not the sort that Randolphs *marry!* I fear she's trapped you into thinking so."

"God damn you for a blathering fool!" shouted the Captain, and turning on his heel he stalked to the supper room, where he found Jenny with one of the Ludwells, drinking punch.

"Come for a walk in the garden, Miss Jenny!" said the Captain, glaring at Ludwell, and in a voice of distinct command which Jenny quelled by lifted eyebrows and a questioning smile. "I mean," said the Captain, instantly humbled, "if you please, I—I wish to talk with you so much. The garden's pretty, there's a maze, and—flowers."

Jenny laughed. "Most gardens have flowers, and isn't it rather dark for the maze? But very well, I'll welcome a breath of air for a few minutes."

He took her arm and they stepped out to the garden. The evening air was balmy and smelled of boxwood and lavender. There was light from the Palace windows and light from a newly risen moon. Other couples were strolling along the graveled paths. Randolph's determination ebbed. Stung, in spite of himself, by his brother's remarks, he had meant to question Jenny, find out something of her early life, though now that she floated along beside him, so ethereal in the moonlight, he lost courage, knowing that he was afraid to find out much, and that also she had given him no real right to question her.

Jenny was both relieved and rather bored by this unexpected silence. She longed for more dancing, more merriment, and more adulation. In the ballroom she had thought of nothing except the gaudy moment, intoxicated with pleasure—to which some glasses of punch had materially contributed. "Well, Captain," she began gaily, "shall we go in?" and moved aside as a little man with a black patch on his eye darted down the path towards them. She expected the man to go by, but he did not. He stopped and peered at her.

"I was hoping ye'd coom out here, miss," he said in a rather squeaky voice. "I've been watchin' for ye, if ye'll forgive me presumption, sir," he added to Randolph, who stiffened and said, "What do you want of the lady?"

"Your honor," said Willy Turner meekly, "could I speak wi' her alone—just for a twinkling, just there—" He pointed to a spot a yard away. "I mean no harm."

"How silly," said Jenny, laughing and heedless. "Whatever you have to say can be said right here." And she laughed again, for the punch and the beauty of the garden and the general excitement of her first real ball made of the funny little man a ludicrous dream shape. She put her hand on Randolph's arm to quiet him. She could feel him chafing, and she said, "Speak out. What is it?"

Willy hesitated, and it was for her protection that he hesitated. Then he said, "I've no wish to be forward, miss, but ye look much like a mahn I once knew, and ye also bear his name."

Jenny ceased smiling. She drew herself tight and wary, for now she had heard in the little man's speech the accents of northern England.

"Where did you know this man?" she said.

"At Preston," replied Willy with a quick nervous glance at the scowling Captain. "An' he was the bravest, dearest man I've ever seen. He saved me life, though he wouldn't admit it, in the heat o' the skirmish. He saved me life, did Charles Radcliffe, though he was wounded himself."

"Oh-h—" said Jenny in a strangled voice.

"What is this farrago!" demanded the Captain. "Who's this little knave speaking of?"

"My father," said Jenny, and her voice trembled.

"But what's this about Preston?" pursued Randolph. "Wasn't that where the vile rebels were captured in the 'Fifteen?"

Willy shook his head, and made an involuntary motion to stop Jenny. She ignored him. "Preston," she said each word clipped, "is where a gallant band of men made their last stand for their rightful king—James the Third of England!"

Randolph's jaw dropped, he gaped at Jenny in dismay, while Willy shook his head and murmured, "Lass, lass, ye shouldna've said it. I didn't mean for you to say it."

Randolph, recovering from the shock of Jenny's treasonable speech and incapable of being angry with her, turned violently on Willy Turner. "You puny Jacobite scum—you traitor—aye, I see you don't deny it! And you'll suffer for it. I'll tell the sheriff and we'll see if jail'll change your views!"

"Oh no you don't, sir!" said Willy with a mournful chuckle. "Can't kill a dead dog twice. I've served me time. I was transported ten years agone. Ask Dr. Blair—who I work for. He knows."

"Get out then!" shouted the Captain. "How dared you come butting in here!"

"I don't wish him to go," said Jenny in a firm quiet voice. "I wish to talk to him, Captain Randolph, alone."

"You can't!" cried the baffled and unhappy Randolph. "Miss Jenny, you mustn't!"

"Oh, but I *can*," she said, beckoning to Willy, and pointing to a wooden bench beneath a huge box tree. He followed, and they sat down together while Randolph paced up and down the walk, his mind in turmoil.

Jenny and Willy Turner talked at length. He came from Lancashire, from Preston itself, and had been an orphaned youth of twenty, a starveling apprentice cobbler, when the Jacobite army marched into town. At first he had hesitated to join them, even though he was a Roman Catholic.

"And are *you* one, miss?" he whispered. "If so, hide it, like I do, until I earn enough to mebbe get me to Maryland."

"I'm not Catholic," she said. "My father is—go on about him, please."

Willy nodded eagerly. It was the Radcliffes who had brought him into the Rising. The Earl of Derwentwater and his brother Charles. Not personally, but the sight of them on their horses in the market square when they proclaimed the king. He couldn't explain how he had felt, though he made Jenny understand how gallantry and romance had seemed to flow from those two proud figures. The little Earl, "No bigger'n me, yet he *seemed* big," said Willy. And Charles, who had looked like all the heroes Willy had ever heard of—Robin Hood and King Arthur rolled into one. So Willy had joined the Rising. He had been fighting at the church barricade just behind Charles when the dragoons came pouring over. One of them had run at Willy, his bayonet fixed, and Charles interposed himself between the two and spitted the dragoon on his sword. "The bayonet grazed me eye," said Willy. "That's how I lost it, but I'd've had that bit o' steel clean through me brain-pan wi'out Mr. Radcliffe's being there. Later, I saw him just once more before the surrender, an' I tried to thank him and he laughed; he'd the merriest laugh I ever heard, and he hugged me around the shoulders, like we was old friends. Ah, I loved the man."

"Yes," said Jenny. All her gaiety had gone. With every word that the little man spoke she could see Charles more clearly, and she began to feel anguished longing for him. Why had she not stayed with him as he had implored her to, why had she not ignored Lady Newburgh's attitude? What was the demented purpose which had seized upon her when she read Evelyn's letter in Vincennes, a purpose which had made her desert the only person who really loved her, to go on a senseless quest after a man who had doubtless forgotten her existence, or to whom she could be nothing except a miserable reminder of his ignominy and suffering.

I could go back, Jenny thought. I could go back to Papa. I don't have to stay here. Captain Randolph was now of no importance, nor the transient considerations she had given to accepting his offer. I was fooling myself *again*, she thought wretchedly.

Willy Turner was still speaking of Charles. "It does me heart good to meet his daughter, miss. You're the spit an' image o' him. I knew it when I saw ye, an' heard ye laugh. Would ye tell me why ye aren't wi' him, if I don't offend in asking?"

"Aye," said Jenny rising, for she could bear no more. "I will, sometime—William—is that your name? Willy. Would you like to go back—to see him again?"

The monkey-face looked up startled. "I can't go back to England, miss. I was transported for life—most of us Jacks was—those that wasn't hanged."

"I know. But Mr. Radcliffe is in France. No, don't answer now. I'm not sure of what I'm saying, yet if *I* went—" She broke off with a sharp indrawn breath, twisting her hands together. "Oh, I wish I *were* with him!"

Willy looked at her in consternation. "I didn't mean to upset ye so, miss. And I'd do anything for ye, for his sake, not to speak o' your being a mighty sweet lass yoursel'."

Captain Randolph had had his fill of pacing the path and he now stalked up to them. "Miss Jenny, aren't you finished *yet?*"

"Yes," she said. "I am." She gave Willy Turner a distracted nod. "I'm glad you spoke to me. We'll speak again."

She turned to the Captain. "I fear I must go home to Major Custis's. I'm unwell. Please escort me, then return

409

and tell Evelyn." She began to hurry towards the garden gate.

"My dear Miss Jenny," protested the Captain, "there's no need to run away, or feel shame. I'll forget what you said. Nobody shall know. You're so young, and can't help what bad influences've shaped your early life, and the female mind is easily swayed."

"You make excuses for me, Captain," said Jenny. " 'Tis good of you. Yet you know nothing of my early life, nor have I the wish to tell it." She hurried on along the Palace Green, so fast that Randolph had to exert himself to keep up with her, and had no breath for talking. As they entered the Custis gates he made a last despairing attempt. "Miss Jenny, oh Jenny, you're not running from *me*, are you? I've told you I'll condone your foolish words. I love you, so help me, and I fear would condone anything you did."

She stopped then, and sighing looked up at him. "You're a good man, Captain Randolph. Please don't say anything more. I'm tired—no, I'm bewildered and heartsick. And I must be alone. Forgive me."

She turned and ran into the Custis house, leaving him to stand desolate on the walk.

Evelyn returned from the Palace two hours later. She entered the room the girls shared, and found the candle guttering. Jenny, still fully dressed, was lying across the bed in an exhausted doze, her head buried in her arms. She was murmuring in her sleep.

Evelyn bent over her to push the tangle of hair back from the flushed face. Jenny stirred and said "Papa, Papa" in a childishly pathetic voice.

Evelyn gave Jenny's shoulder a gentle nudge. "Wake up, dear," she said. "Wake up!"

At last Jenny opened her eyes. "Is it morning?" she asked. "I was dreaming of my father—I was with him—there was a ship—there must be a ship sailing soon—"

"Wake up!" said Evelyn again. She went to the washstand, poured water onto a towel, which she brought to Jenny. "Here, sit up and wash your face."

Jenny slowly obeyed. She gave herself a little shake, and glanced at the mantel clock. "Oh heaven!" she said. "It's only midnight. I didn't want to wake up. Why did you wake me, Evie?"

"You could hardly spend the night in your ball dress," said Evelyn lightly, but she tilted her head and examined

410

her friend thoughtfully. "I woke you because there's news I *think* you want to hear. I'm sure you do, though these last days I've not quite understood you, my dear."

"I've not understood me, either," said Jenny.

Evelyn sat down on the bed. "I was chatting with Mr. Nathaniel Harrison, after the dancing ended. One of his servants came in today from Wakefield and brought news too of Berkeley. To Mr. Nat Harrison there was one item of very slight importance, though he told me of it. Can you guess what it was?"

Jenny's eyes widened; she made no sound. She waited.

"Well," continued Evelyn, "Rob Wilson has returned to Berkeley. He limped in on foot two days ago. He gave himself up to Ben Harrison. Said he had come back to finish his bondage."

Jenny sat quiet, her eyes dark and still as mountain tarns.

"Did you hear me, Jen?" said Evelyn, somewhat frightened. "Rob Wilson's come back of his own accord. You can see him now at last. Isn't that what you wanted?"

"It was," said Jenny. She moistened her lips and repeated, "It was—oh, it *is* what I want. To see my Robbie . . . Yet I don't know what *he* wants. Have they hurt him d'you think? That beastly overseer?"

"I hope not," said Evelyn. "I fear they'll not be very gentle."

Jenny got off the bed and began to unhook the bodice of her taffeta gown. "Where'd they put my riding habit?" she said. "Major Custis must have a horse to lend me, or I'll take Eugene's."

Evelyn jumped up and shook her head. "You can't leave *now*, dear." She spoke with authority. "We'll go in the morning. I promise you. Be sensible, child!" she added more sharply, as Jenny stood uncertainly in her long white shift above a fallen ring of rose taffeta. "Come to bed!"

"Sensible!" said Jenny. "Waiting and wondering. Waiting and wondering. Is that the way to make a body sensible?"

"Maybe not," said Evelyn. "But it is unfortunately the way life is."

SEVENTEEN

Jenny and Evelyn did not reach Westover until dusk of the next day, because their precipitate return caused many difficulties. It had taken all Evelyn's guile, storming, and finally tears to persuade Byrd of the necessity, without giving him a convincing reason. He did not yet wish to leave Williamsburg himself. He still had much business to transact, including the finding of a new overseer, and even for Evelyn, Byrd would not relinquish his coach. So the girls ended up on hired horses with Eugene as escort.

When they at last turned off the highway onto the Westover Plantation road, Evelyn was casting anxious glances at the silent forest on either side of them and straining ahead to see the lights of the home-house. Dauntless as she was in many ways, she was afraid of the dark wilderness.

"You can't see Rob tonight, dear," she said to Jenny. "It's so late."

"But I must," said Jenny. A flat statement of fact.

Evelyn peered at her friend's face, which glimmered through the dusk; it was pale, set, and somehow looked much older than usual.

They did not speak again until they had passed the tobacco fields and the Quarters, from which came a medley of sounds —singing, barking dogs, the whine of jew's-harps, and the high wail of a baby.

Evelyn waited until they were near the house, then she checked her horse, and said, "Eugene!"

"Yessuh, mistiss," answered the young Negro, coming up to them.

"You know the way to Berkeley's Quarters, I suppose?"

"Sho do, mistiss. Is a yaller wench there, I goes to see— Sundays only o' course," he added hastily, that being the one day the slaves were sometimes allowed off the plantation.

"Yes—well—" said Evelyn. "How would you like a lace handkerchief for your wench, and chewing tobacco for you?"

"I'd like it fine, mistiss." Eugene smacked his lips.

"Do you know where at Berkeley Robert Wilson used to live—the convict who was building the manor house?"

"The one who run off?" asked Eugene.

"Yes, but he came back."

Eugene gave an incredulous and pitying grunt. "He used to live this side the Quarters, a li'l way off in a cabin he made hisself."

"I want you to guide Miss Jenny there tonight, whenever she's ready. And, Eugene, you'll say no word of this now or at any time to anyone. Is that clear?"

"Yus, *ma'am*," said Eugene heartily.

An hour after their return to Westover, Jenny set off on foot with Eugene. She had dressed herself in a plain brown wool dress which dated from her schooldays, and wore over it a hooded brown cloak. She carried an awkwardly shaped black plush bag, over two feet long, which was tied with a silken cord. Evelyn had protested when she saw the bag, and asked what it was. Jenny did not answer. In fact she scarcely heard Evelyn, though she drank a little wine when Evelyn gave it to her. She had passed into a kind of suspended animation, where will power alone sustained her.

Eugene led Jenny down the plantation drive for a quarter of a mile, then turned left over the fields on a nearly invisible path which many secret feet had trod. He carried a dark lantern, and would have carried Jenny's plush bag, but she would not let him. They splashed through the bottom of a little creek, clambered over a zig-zag rail fence, then entered Berkeley's fields, picking their way among the young, sweet-scented tobacco plants. The night grew brighter as the moon rose, and presently Eugene spotted in the distance the village of whitewashed cabins which were Berkeley's slave quarters.

There was no sound from them; Matt Corby, the overseer, had long since made his Sunday night round to be sure each slave was in the proper cabin, and presumably asleep, so as to be ready for field work at dawn.

"Ovah there, mistiss," said Eugene pointing with his lantern towards a small isolated hut near a giant hickory. "I see smoke from the chimbley—must be cookin' hisself supper. If it is Wilson sho' nuff."

"I—I'll go and see," said Jenny. "Wait here, Eugene." She crossed the edge of a cornfield, skirted a bramble patch, and approached the cabin. Her heart was pounding in heavy thuds, her palms were wet as they gripped the plush bag, but she was unaware of this. Next to the closed door there was one small window, and behind it the flicker of firelight. She stole up to the window and looked in.

It *was* Rob who knelt inside by the flames, turning a corn pone in the ashes. His black hair was matted and grown far below his ears. He was naked except for a pair of rolled-up canvas pants. On one of his feet was a cracked and shapeless boot; the other was wrapped in a dirty cloth. She saw the ribs standing out sharply either side of his great hairy chest. He moved a little and she saw the old welts on his back, livid purple lumps and ridges, also three fresh stripes, black with caked blood. He got up from the fire, holding the cooled pone and limping, turned to face the window. Then she saw what his hair had concealed—an iron collar around his neck and some writing scratched on it.

Jenny drew back from the window. She backed away as far as the brambles; she stood still, while her stomach heaved. She retched, and sour fluid came into her mouth. She swayed, and clutched at the brambles. Pain from a dozen sharp scratches revived her. Her sick giddiness ceased. "God—dear God—" she whispered. The moon swam up from behind a passing cloud and shimmered on the cornfield, the hickory tree, and the little cabin beneath. Jenny loosed the bramble and lifted her head high. Strength flowed into her. Strength and a peculiar kind of almost gay assurance. She walked rapidly back to the cabin, and knocked on the door.

Inside Rob jumped, almost he cowered. Then he straightened himself and said, "Who's there?" in a hoarse angry voice. There were no locks on cabin doors in the Quarters, and nobody ever knocked.

Jenny lifted the latch and walked in. "It's me, Rob," she said smiling, and as casual as though she had seen him yesterday. "It's Jenny."

Rob recoiled. He flattened his mangled back against the log wall, staring at the slender figure, the yellow hair under a brown hood, at the long gray eyes which looked at him steadily and sweetly.

414

"I was afeard of this," he muttered. He had seen her before—her fetch, her phantom—once when he had fever on the convict ship, and again many days ago when he had been camping in the far western wilderness by a little stream. Yet never had she seemed so real; and what could that mean but madness at last, the fantasies of a broken spirit and mind. "Gan awa', woman," he whispered. "Leave me be!"

"No, my hinny," she said, putting her plush bag carefully on the dirt floor, since there was no furniture except a straw pallet. "I'll not leave you again, or ever. What a way to receive me who has come so far to find you!" She threw her cloak off, walked up to him, and took one of his great calloused hands between hers. "It *is* Jenny," she said, looking into his astounded face. "Kiss me—and you'll know. Nay—R-Robbie," she added, lapsing into the broadest of Northumbrian accents, "I canna kiss ye, laddie, if ye'll not bow down your-r head a bit, for ye knaw weel ye're a gr-reat tall gawk!"

She put her hands around his neck, perfectly concealing a wince as they touched the cold iron collar, and she pressed her body close against him. "D'ye knaw me now, laddie? D'ye feel that I'm war-rm and a live woman?"

He felt her breasts against his chest, and the beating of her heart; still he could not believe. He ran his hands slowly down her back, from the delicate shoulder blades over the narrow waist and the swelling of her hips. Suddenly he shuddered, and gave a low gasp like a sob. He caught her desperately in his arms and kissed her tremulous, bravely smiling mouth. They kissed without moving, both drenched by a wine-red rapture in which thought had no part. Then a log fell to pieces on the hearth, sending out a shower of sparks. His arms dropped, and though she still clung to him, he turned from her.

"They put the collar on me," he said dully. "And d'you see what it says? 'Property of Benj. Harrison—Berkeley,' that's what it says. 'Tis riveted on. I expected the flogging, but I'd not have come back if I'd known that swine Corby'd put the collar on me."

"Why did you come back, Rob?" she asked after a moment.

"It was *not* because I couldn't make my way," he said sharply, thinking of the weeks of walking, following the river to the west, and eating far better than he had here, on fish and wild honey, and once a small bear he had trapped. "Fool that I am, I wanted to finish the house, no one could

415

finish that cornice but me, and then I've never run off before from anything, and then too—"

"What?" she whispered. "Rob, did you hear me calling you?"

"Aye. Aye. I thought so once, yet I didn't believe it. I don't believe it now. Jenny, if it *is* you, I'm dazed. Can't get my wits together. What are you doing here?"

She stooped and picked up the plush bag. "I brought these to you, Robbie. These'll best answer why I'm here."

He took the black bag in continuing bewilderment. Fumbling a little, he undid the cord. The bag opened and he saw what was inside. "The pipes," he whispered. "The Northumbrian pipes. You brought them to me . . ."

At the expression on his face her eyes filled, but she answered steadily. "They're not as good as the ones you used to have. I bought these in London. Will you play, Robbie?"

Still fumbling, still dazed, he buckled the strap around his waist and the bellows to his arm. The bag was of red velvet fringed with gold. He fingered the chanter and the drones tentatively.

"Play 'The Oak and the Ash and the Bonny Ivy-tree,'" Jenny said quietly.

After a false start or two, he began the tune and she began to sing.

"'Oh, a North Country lass, 'cross the ocean did pass . . .'"

"That's not right," Rob said with the ghost of a smile. "'Tis not ''cross the ocean' in the real song."

"No, but it is now in mine. Let me go on, Robbie—

> *"Oh, a maiden I am, and a maid will remain*
> *'Till my North Country lad asks to wed me,*
> *And now in this place, I at last see the face*
> *Of him that's allotted my love for to be!*
> *Oh, the oak and the ash and the bonny ivy-tree*
> *They do flourish at home in our own countree."*

She sang in an infinitely sweet and wooing voice. He did not look at her as she sang. His fingers stumbled at times on the chanter, his swarthy face paled, and then flushed. When she stopped his hands fell down from the pipes. She waited, a tender half smile on her lips.

"Shall I sing the verse *again*, Rob?" she said. "Did you perhaps not quite understand it?"

"Jenny—" he said. "Jenny, I can't wed thee. A convict cannot wed during his bondage, and I've thirteen years more of it. A just sentence it was. I killed a man."

"My father killed several at Preston," she said briskly. "*They* may have been good men. The one you killed was evil, and you did it to save me."

"You know *that!*" he cried. "Then you've come to me out of gratitude and pity, and this I cannot stand."

Jenny stiffened, she tossed her head and cried with anger that was nearly genuine. "Robert Wilson, you're a pigheaded dolt! A blind mawthering fool! You know well that I've always loved you, and you love me, whatever you pretend, for you've proven it. And we'll not mention again what you did for me in London if you wish, but I'm quite sure nobody kisses a woman as you did me—without there's true love."

He did not speak. He looked at her quickly with pleading. She stamped her foot. "Am I wrong, Rob Wilson? Am I wrong?"

"No, hinny," he said very low. "I love thee. But *you* must not love a slave in an iron collar."

"Well, I do," she said. "And we won't waste breath on what I must or must not do—there's been plenty of that in the past. As for your bondage, there's a way out." She spoke with far more conviction than she felt, for now that her doubts were resolved certainties outside herself seemed to direct everything she said.

"What way out?" he asked in a dead voice. "Except escape again. And I couldna take you with me—to the wilds with a hunted fugitive!"

"I've brought some money," she said, and at once retrieved her mistake as she saw his head lift proudly, and his hazel eyes harden. "Your *own* money, Rob! Three hundred and near sixty pounds of it!"

"What!" he cried. "You're daft, lass, I have no money! They stripped me of all in Newgate!"

She thought rapidly, and found an answer. " 'Twas for your house, the one you'd built on Wigmore Row. The Earl of Lichfield sold it for you after you left England. Naturally he couldn't get much—in the circumstances." Jenny stopped, afraid to go on, afraid that the transaction might sound too implausible; but Rob did not question. His face was transfigured, he grabbed her hands and held them between his own.

"Three hundred sixty pounds," he whispered. "Oh, Jenny is it true?" She nodded, and he said hoarsely, "Is't enough to buy my freedom, d'ye think?"

"Of course," she said, refusing to consider the difficulties ahead, and knowing herself completely ignorant of the legal aspects. "It'll buy that and a lot left over to give you a start."

In his gaunt square face the lines vanished, his eyes glowed.

"To the west," he said, "a hundred miles, nay more, along the river there's a canny bit o' land—a stream nearby tumbling down a hill, mountains to the north—"

"Like Tosson and the Cheviots?" she interrupted softly.

"Nay," he answered surprised. "These are high blue mountains, higher than the Cheviots, and there's no moors. *This* land will grow crops, and too, there's a stand o' timber— oak and walnut, and a slate quarry, that'd make any builder shout for joy, and clay pits too for bricks, and I found iron ore in a spot about a half mile off."

"Off from what?" she asked very softly.

"Why, from the house site. The bonniest house site I ever saw. It's on top a hill, yet sheltered by oaks. The days I was there I paced off and measured as best I could how it would go. If I'd had a hatchet I'd 've started it."

"Did you picture a woman in that house?"

"How could I dare?" he said. Suddenly he smiled down at her. "Yet I do now, hinny. I'll build you the finest house in Virginia—not at first, that'll have to be a cabin, but in time."

"Ah-h—" she breathed, resting her cheek on his chest.

"Yet," he said holding her close, "if I'm free, we wouldn't have to go so far—'tis way beyond white man's ken, 'tis the wilds. Nay, Jenny, it wouldna be right to take a soft dainty lass like you into such a rough way o' life, and we maybe shouldn't go so far."

She heard the hidden disappointment in his voice and she said quickly, "I was born to a rough way o' life, remember, Robbie? Besides, land out there can be had for the asking, I know that much, and you'll need your every penny to get started."

"And to buy Nero," he said unexpectedly. "He's a huge, able Negro here. Strong as an ox. I've trained him to carpentry and he does well. We've become friends, I know he'd go wi' me, 'specially if I freed him."

Jenny gulped, and drew away from Rob with a worried frown. She knew that it would be hard enough to arrange one freedom, without endeavoring to deprive Corby and Mr. Harrison of still another of their best workers. Yet she had not the heart to dampen Rob's dream. It was rare enough that she had seen his face like this—hopeful, boyish, eager. Nor was it surprising that, after so much degradation and suffering, his normal common sense should be a trifle blunted.

He shifted unconsciously to ease his injured foot, and she said, "What's happened to your foot, Robbie? Sit down, and let me take that filthy rag off it."

" 'Tis nothing. It's healing. My shoe wore out and I stepped on a jagged rock." Yet he obeyed her, and sank down on the pallet with a grunt of relief.

The sole of his foot was heavily calloused from the weeks of walking, but on the heel there was a puffy wound. She silently bathed it from the bucket of water which stood near a peck of cornmeal, the usual daily slave rations. There being nothing else in the cabin, she lifted her skirt and held out to him a corner of white linen petticoat.

"Tear, Robbie," she said. "I've not quite the strength. Not yet," she added with a smile, "though I'll learn."

He tore a strip from the petticoat, and as she bound his foot the homely, wifely little action struck to his heart. She had always seemed so far from him, separated by her youth at first and then her class and rearing, separated too by his own repeated determinations to forget her, and his stubborn pride. He realized, as he watched the blond head bent over his foot, how little he had ever thought *with* her, or listened when she tried to tell him. He was appalled to think of the journey she had made for his sake, and of which he hadn't even asked, so overwhelmed had he been by thoughts of freedom.

"My darling," he whispered.

She looked around startled. That endearment sounded strange from Rob. The ordinary folk of the North did not use it. Her father did, and the word gave her a faraway muffled pang.

"My darling," said Rob again, looking deep and steadily into her widened eyes. "If God lets us be wed, I'll try to be worthy of ye."

She shook her head in protest, but he went on solemnly, "You may wonder that I speak of God—I never thought much about Him, yet out there, alone—in the wilderness—there was a night, when—" He stopped, unable to express the feelings he had had that night, and he added only, "I believe there *is* one."

"Aye," she whispered. "Perhaps I've felt Him too."

He smiled at the childish earnestness in her voice, and thought how very young she was, despite the moments when she was all woman. "You must go, dear," he said. "I've been the mawthering fool ye called me earlier to let you stay so long. Suppose someone saw you! And besides, Jenny," he

419

added with violence, "if you sit beside me like this, and keep looking at me like that, I shall have to kiss you again. And I fear I'll not stop wi' kisses, lass, for I want ye very badly. I've even forgot that I'm a slave!"

"I don't wish to go," she said. "So it's best I should. I'll bring your money tomorrow, after I've talked with Evelyn. We must have her help. It—it won't be an easy matter, Rob."

"I know." The light died out of his eyes. "I know."

Jenny stumbled over Eugene curled up in the cornfield, where he was snoring peacefully. They went back to Westover. Evelyn was waiting in the hall. "Heaven, Jenny, what a time you've been! I was worried." She held her candle high and examined the girl's face. "I see matters've taken an upturn. You've seen him, and there're no more doubts?"

"None," said Jenny. "Come well or ill, Rob is my own true love and I am his, and he knows it at last."

"Ah—" said Evelyn softly. "I'm glad of that." She kissed Jenny, a rare gesture from Evelyn. "But, my dear—"

Jenny interrupted her with a sigh and a motion of her hand. "You needn't say it. And I can't think tonight. Tomorrow, Evie—you will help me think, won't you?"

By breakfast time next morning, Evelyn was in possession of all the facts of Jenny's interview with Rob the night before, and she saw the obstacles ahead even more clearly than Jenny did. "The faster we move the better," she said. "Not only for poor Rob's sake but before Father gets home, we should at least get an agreement from Ben Harrison."

"What difference would Mr. Byrd make?" asked Jenny, frowning.

"Father knows the law. Ben doesn't. And I don't believe a convict *can* buy his freedom, or own money. Everything he has belongs to his master. No, the more I think of it, we'll have to tell Ben the truth—that it's *your* money, you wish to buy Rob yourself."

"Oh, I couldn't!" Jenny cried, aghast. "You don't know Rob's pride. And what man could stand being bought by his wife! Besides, now he has self-respect again. You should have seen his face when I told him he'd earned the money by the London house he'd worked so hard on."

After a moment Evelyn nodded. "Yes, he's had enough humiliation, poor man." She thought hard, rather enjoying the pitting of her wits against all these problems. "You'll have to lie again to Rob," she said at last. "It's the only way. Tell him that he and you must pretend it's *your* money, until he's freed. I'm sure he'll see the sense of that, for otherwise he'll neither be free nor able to wed you."

Jenny considered this for some time, then she agreed. "I believe you're right. I'll go now to Berkeley Quarters and tell him."

"He won't be there, my dear," said Evelyn ruefully. "At this hour Corby'll have him at work somewhere. Come, we'd better go to Berkeley and try our luck!"

The girls set off along the river path between the two plantations, having told Mrs. Byrd that they were going to call on the Harrisons and with difficulty discouraged little Mina from accompanying them. The morning was still fresh, a western breeze made ripples on the James as it flowed below the bluff. Mockingbirds trilled and fluted from the woods on either side of them, the copses were spangled with blooming dogwood, white and shell-pink. As they neared the church, Jenny saw a drift of bluebells underneath some birches. She stopped and stood gazing at them. "It's May Day, Evie," she said. "I've just remembered that it's May Day." She ran to the bluebells and knelt down.

"What *are* you doing, Jenny!" Evelyn cried with some impatience, as she watched Jenny bury her face in the flowers.

"There's still a bit of dew on them," said Jenny. "So maybe I'll get my wish. 'Tis lucky to find blue flowers on a May morn. At home I never found them. I had to make do with buttercups."

"At home?" asked Evelyn, smiling a little.

"In Northumberland."

"Strange you still call that home," said Evelyn beginning to walk.

"It is, perhaps," said Jenny, discomfited. "But where else have I? As yet."

They fell silent. They passed the church and its attendant burying ground. They both glanced at the church, Jenny with a yearning hope; but Evelyn turned from it and stared somberly at her grandparents' tombs.

A scarlet streak flew over the tombs—a nesting cardinal. Evelyn shivered suddenly. "I hate those birds," she said. "They're like blood, and I hate graves!"

Jenny was astonished at her friend's vehemence, and dismayed by a flash of fear in the great dark eyes. Such reasonless fear was upsetting at this particular moment when she so needed Evelyn's coolness and self-command. However, Evelyn recovered at once. "You and your superstitions, Jenny!" she said in her ironic tone. "You've infected *me!*"

They continued walking along the river path, past the boundary tree and into Berkeley. There was the usual bustle at the landing. Captain Randolph's ship had gone upriver to Turkey Island, since he had discharged his cargo for Westover, but the new sloop was being launched amid a turmoil of shouts and scurryings. They saw by the wharf the stout gesticulating figure of the overseer.

"He'll know where Rob is, won't he?" Jenny asked anxiously.

Evelyn nodded. "Best let me do the talking."

Matt Corby was busy cursing at his men for having tangled the lines, and he scowled harder as he saw the girls approach. Women had no business on the wharf; but Evelyn had drawn herself up to her full height, and used a tone which could not be ignored as she said, "Mr. Corby, I wish to see Robert Wilson, the convict, for a moment."

"Whatever for?" demanded the overseer. "The blackguard's behind enough wi' his work as it is—them months he run off."

"That's just it," said Evelyn smoothly. "I've a curiosity to see the man, I've heard so much about him."

"Ha! He's naught to look at, miss, an' 'ld be less so if I'd had *my* way! Branded with *R* on the cheek he'd be, same as all runaways. I'll talk Mr. Harrison inter it yet."

Evelyn heard Jenny's quick breath, and squeezed her arm to stop her from speaking. "Well, Mr. Corby," she said lightly, "now I'm more than ever curious. Where *is* Wilson?"

"Carpentry shop," he said pointing with his whip, and was fortunately distracted—since he meant to go with them—by a splash, and the sight of a terrified slave who had carelessly rolled a tobacco hogshead into the water. Corby started off to discipline the offender and the girls escaped.

They found Rob working intently with a fret saw and chisel, carving the beading and modillions on a length of pine destined for the unfinished cornice.

Evelyn threw one shocked glance at the iron collar, and said "Hurry, dear" beneath her breath to Jenny, then stood guard outside.

Rob looked up and saw Jenny standing by the door, seeming to bring in all the sunshine of the May morning. "Wuns!" he whispered. "Hinny, I'd begun to think you were a dream!"

"Listen," she said smiling, yet anxious, "I've something to tell you, but what about—" She pointed to a gigantic Negro who was planing a board in the back of the little shop. He was a Senegalese, six and a half feet high, his skin the golden brown of polished walnut. He had a red sweatband around his head, and a bit of sheepbone stuck through each of his ear lobes.

"Oh, he's all right," said Rob. "That's Nero."

The slave heard his name, and raising his head made Jenny a dignified, unsmiling bow. He showed no surprise at her appearance. Nero never showed surprise.

"Then listen, Rob," said Jenny. "Evelyn thinks, and I'm sure you'll agree, this is the best way to proceed."

She told him of the plan, while he went on working—his big blunt fingers handling the fret saw as deftly as a woman does a needle. When she had finished he swallowed. "Aye. I can see the sense to it. Yet I'd like to've bought my *own* freedom."

"You *will* be," she said quickly. " 'Tis only pretense. And, Rob, pray—you said you believed in God—pray for the result of this interview with the Harrisons."

"Oh, Jenny, it galls me that you should have to do all this, while I stand by helpless! It galls me like this hellish collar does!"

"Hist!" whispered Evelyn from the door. "Come out, Jen!"

Corby was pounding up the slope from the wharf, Jenny got out of the shop just in time, and the overseer's suspicious glare inside showed him nothing except the two slaves silently carpentering.

The girls walked up the road and arrived at the great brick mansion. To their dismay the Harrisons had other visitors, the John Carters from Shirley Plantation next door on the north of Berkeley. John was Anne Harrison's brother, eldest son of the "King" and a man of consequence himself, being permanent Secretary to the Colony as well as Councilor. He had married Elizabeth Hill of Shirley and come to live at that oldest and most elegant of plantations.

The Harrisons were delighted to see Evelyn, and in the interest of diversion willing to overlook Jenny's odd behavior or her last appearance. Refreshments were pressed on them. Everyone settled down in the north parlor for a nice long family visit. The Carters asked one or two questions about London, though nobody was really interested. The ladies were interested in the visit to Williamsburg. Evelyn, chafing, reported on whom they had seen, the health of the Governor, the guest list at the ball, and any pregnancies, engagements, or scandals she had got wind of.

While she talked she observed that the relationship between Anne Harrison and her mother-in-law had not improved. The ladies contradicted each other; it might be said that they snapped. There was a contretemps over the coffee pot. Anne seated herself to pour, as became the hostess. Madam Harrison then asked acidly, "Do you think you should lift that heavy pot in youah condition, my deah? Besides, *I've* always dispensed the coffee for our guests." Anne pretended not to hear.

The morning wore away. Once Jenny found herself being teased about Captain Randolph. It took all her self-control to answer civilly. Presently they were asked to stay for dinner, since it was nearly two o'clock. The Carters accepted promptly, while Evelyn and Jenny exchanged a look of desperation. Evelyn did not want anyone except Ben Harrison to hear Jenny's request, and certainly not John Carter, who had even better legal training than Byrd, and was moreover endowed with much of his own father's authoritarian intolerance.

There was nothing to do but sit it out, especially as Carter and Ben Harrison drifted off to the stables to inspect a mare Ben had just bought—or at least intended to pay for when this year's tobacco crop was sold in London.

For two hours Jenny waded through the interminable dinner: scalloped oysters, saddle of mutton, cold ham, hominy, scrambled eggs, spoonbread, a few new peas from the garden. And then the second course, ice cream, custards, and brandied peaches, after which the tablecloth came off and the company were served figs, raisins, and almonds, while Ben circulated bottles of madeira, port and cherry cordial. Jenny thought of Rob's rations in the Quarters—the peck of cornmeal. In fact she thought of him all the time, and her frustration produced a dull headache.

The Carters left at last, returning to Shirley in their chariot. Ben yawned and said he reckoned he'd take a nap. The Harrison ladies, both stupefied by food and longing for their own rooms, looked expectantly at Evelyn, who would certainly make her adieus now. But she did not, instead she took a deep breath and said, "Cousin Ben, just a moment, please. We—Miss Radcliffe and I—have a matter of great importance to ask you."

"Well—" said Ben, reluctantly, "if it won't wait." And he led the way to the south parlor. His wife and mother followed, since neither was willing to leave the field to the other, if there were any matter of importance to be talked of with Ben.

They all sat down, Ben sprawling in his armchair, Madam

424

Harrison at once securing the other armchair next her son and lowering her bulk into it. She picked up a peacock fan and waved it languidly. "What do you want of son Beñ, Evelyn?" she asked, wheezing slightly.

"It's to do with Robert Wilson, the convict who returned," said Evelyn plunging in. "Miss Radcliffe wants to buy him."

"What!" cried Ben, sitting up and gaping at Jenny, who drew herself tight and lifted her chin.

"I do," she said. "I'll pay you very well for him."

Ben gaped harder, having as yet no reaction except astonishment.

His mother however, suffering from indigestion and a longing to loosen her stays, snapped out, "How uttahly ridiculous! Ben wouldn't sell the fellah, now he's got him back, and I wouldn't *dream* of lettin' him!"

"Oh? Indeed, Mother Harrison," Anne drawled from the ignominious corner seat. "I believe Ben is of full age and able to make his own decisions! Personally I think it a *good* ideah to get rid of that fellah." And she sent her mother-in-law a look of open battle, while Evelyn relaxed a trifle, perceiving that such are the inscrutabilities of fate that Madam Harrison's ill-judged remark had greatly bettered Rob's chances.

"But Miss Radcliffe?" said Ben, still groping. "What would you do with the man? Damme, why do you want him?"

"I want him for a husband," said Jenny, her color deepening, her eyes very bright.

There was a startled silence, then Ben Harrison burst into a loud guffaw, he slapped his thighs, and roared again. "Damme!" he cried still laughing. "You want to buy youahself a stud, eh? Oh, this is rich! But, my deah gel, such a pretty creature as you are, don't need to waste money like that. What about Ned Randolph?"

"Ben!" cried his mother sharply. "I pray you be seemly. And, Evelyn, I'm shocked that you should be pahty to such an indecent transaction!"

"Not indecent at all," said Anne loudly and firmly. "I think it sweetly romantical!"

Her husband stared at her. He was so accustomed to the tussles between his womenfolk that he scarcely noted them, yet in the rare occasions when he was forced to take sides, he naturally tended towards his wife, who was, moreover, quick with child and should be pampered.

"I want the fellah to finish the house," he said plaintively.

"And he's valuable to me. Most useful. I paid fifty pounds for him."

"That's why I'm offering you more than that," Jenny said. "Moreover he *will* finish the house for you. There's only a few days' work left, and I warrant he'll do it."

"What *are* you offerin'?" asked Ben slowly.

Jenny drew a heavy pouch from her pocket. "Fifty guineas," she said, taking a coin from the pouch. "Fifty golden English guineas. And I've brought ten of them which you may have now as earnest of the rest, which are at West-over."

All three Harrisons drew in their breaths and leaned forward staring at the gold. In Virginia actual money was very scarce. Most payments were made by bills of exchange, by clipped Spanish silver or by tobacco. The two Harrison women had never laid eyes on English gold before. Even Madam Harrison was silenced, for they all realized that in purchasing power this gold would go much further than its face value.

"You shuah must want him real bad, ma'am," said Ben to Jenny, as he hefted one of the coins in his palm. I can buy me three able young Nigras, he thought—or that Arab stallion I looked at.

Anne had her own thoughts, which had to do with a pearl necklace she coveted. "Take it, husband," she said softly. "I want you to."

He nodded. "I reckon I will."

Evelyn sprang up at once. "Where's paper and a pen?" she cried. "We must write a bill of sale."

Anne went to the secretary and produced writing materials, then they paused. None of the young people had ever sold a slave, nor knew what form should be used. Madam Harrison did know something about the procedure, but she had no intention of helping. She folded her arms and sat in affronted silence, while Evelyn, with tentative suggestions from Anne and Ben, wrote out something she trusted was legal. Jenny stood by, her heart beating hard, not daring to rejoice until Ben had signed his name.

Just as he was about to do so his mother, goaded by the sight of Anne's triumphant face, remarked suddenly, "Much good all that nonsense'll do anybody. Miss Radcliffe's not of age. She can't buy property unless her guardian vouches foah her."

They all looked around in dismay, and Jenny began twisting her hands, her eyes darkening.

426

"I reckon that's true, Mothah," said Ben, disappointed now that he had made up his mind. "We'll have to wait for Colonel Byrd, perhaps."

This was the last thing Evelyn wanted; not only was she sure that her father would make many objections, but there was danger that Madam Harrison might yet sway Ben if she got him alone.

"Father's not Jenny's guardian," said Evelyn. "She hasn't any. At least, except in France," she added abstractedly, and the last word gave her an idea. "I'm quite sure," said Evelyn, who wasn't at all, but managed to sound it, "that *any* responsible gentleman may second this purchase for Miss Radcliffe. Mr. Fontaine, for instance. And I guarantee that he will do so."

"The ministah?" asked Ben. "He'll put his name to this thing?"

"Yes," said Evelyn. "And there's room at the bottom for his affidavit. So you sign here, Cousin Ben!" She pointed, and after a moment he complied. "Witnesses?" cried Evelyn breathlessly, remembering all she'd heard of wills. "Cousin Anne, you, please. And then me!" When they had signed, Evelyn took the paper and thrust it into Jenny's hand. "Here!" she cried. "It's yours!"

Jenny hugged the paper against her breast; her knees shook.

"Now will you take the collar off him?" she said angrily to Ben. "It was vile to put the collar on him when he came back of his own will!"

"Why," said Ben, honestly bewildered, "you *have* to punish runaways, but I wouldn't let Corby brand him, and he only got three lashes!"

"Aye—well—" said Jenny suddenly collapsing. "He's mine now, and you must take your collar off him."

"Not yet!" said Madam Harrison, making a last stand. "Not until the ministah has signed that papah, and I doubt very much that he does."

"We'll soon see," said Evelyn coolly. "Cousin Ben, you may expect us back tonight, with the paper signed and the rest of the money. Will you be so good as to tell Robert Wilson of this transaction, so that he may be ready?"

It was on the night of Monday, May first, that Rob became Jenny's property, and he remained so. She could not free him at once as she had thought, because it developed that the Governor himself must sign a pardon for a convict.

Peter Fontaine told Evelyn this when she rode to his Glebe House and cajoled him into sponsoring Jenny on the bill of sale. The minister was easily persuaded, not only because he had a real attachment to Evelyn and dim hopes of marrying her, but because the whole slave system, for white or black, revolted his conscience, though he was well aware that the great plantations could not flourish as they did without slave labor.

Evelyn told him Jenny and Rob's story, suppressing nothing except the Catholic and Jacobite angle, which she knew would be repugnant to this Huguenot. When she had finished the minister was much moved, his prominent brown eyes were moist. "It is a veritable romance—this tale," he said with his French inflection. "The murder committed by this young man was justified, and he has paid also in much suffering. Decidedly he should now be freed. 'Blessed are the merciful' our dear Lord has said. I will go myself to the Governor. I will go at once."

"You're very kind, sir," said Evelyn, her eyes glowing. "And, Mr. Fontaine, if you should run across Colonel Byrd in Williamsburg, I pray you not to tell your errand."

The minister showed dismay. "Your father would not approve?"

"I fear not," said Evelyn. "My father detests haste and unconventionality. He would be shocked at the alliance of *any* member of his household with a convict slave—no matter the reasons. It will save agonizing delays if we can confront Colonel Byrd with an established fact."

"I comprehend," said Fontaine after a moment in which he examined the consequences to himself of incurring Byrd's displeasure, then staunchly ignored the prospect. He shut his eyes, his lips moved in prayer, while Evelyn waited anxiously.

He opened his eyes and spoke with decision. "So be it. It is not only that *you* ask this of me, Miss Byrd, also God puts it in my heart to feel our course is meet and just, and I believe I shall succeed in my mission."

Peter Fontaine left for Williamsburg on the Tuesday morning after having consulted his friend, Francis Hardyman, the sheriff of Charles City County. Consequently, he was armed with the correct papers, including Jenny's plea for pardon and then manumission of her property—one Robert Wilson. She had sealed the petition with her Radcliffe ring, which gave her a painful sensation. She could not help remembering the beseeching words her father had spoken when he asked her to wear the ring. During those days of yet more uncertainty and waiting she scarcely saw Rob.

True, he had moved to Westover, to a room in the overseer's house, and the collar had been removed. Yet there was a constraint between them. She knew that Westover's ineffectual overseer had sniggered and made lewd jokes much like Harrison's about Rob's ownership by a fine London miss. And too, Rob spent all his waking hours finishing Berkeley manor house. He labored in the carpentry shop by candle-light or by day on scaffolding, fitting up the last of the cornices under the roof. Corby, who no longer had rights over him, ignored him but found many ways to heckle and even punish Rob's co-worker, Nero—until a trivial incident when Corby, for no special reason except a need to show mastery, tweaked one of the bone ornaments from Nero's ear. The overseer surprised a look of such malignant hatred in the huge Negro's yellowish eyes that he felt a chill run down his back. Thereafter he avoided both men.

On Thursday at dusk Rob was still at Berkeley when Peter Fontaine rode up to Westover. Jenny, who was constantly on watch, saw him first and ran to open the north front door. Then she stood mute on the step, afraid to ask, while the minister dismounted. She saw his tall lank figure silhouetted against Westover's beautiful wrought-iron gates, with their entwined *WB* ciphers picked out in gold. There were stone eagles too, poised on the gateposts. Jenny stared at the eagles. Eagles were strong free birds, but these were not. They were forever frozen here, enslaved. An omen—a horrible omen! The minister did not greet her. He seemed to look disconsolate. He's not got the pardon, I know he hasn't, Jenny thought. The Governor wouldn't grant it—or perhaps is dead.

The minister had not seen her huddled near the door in her dark dress. He came up the steps and bumped against her, uttering an exclamation and apology.

"You needn't tell me," she said in a harsh high voice, so unlike her own that he was alarmed. "You haven't got the pardon."

"But I have, my poor child," he said gently. "I *have* got the pardon, right here in my pocket."

"You mean Rob is free?" she asked in the same queer voice.

"Robert Wilson is a free man, as of eight o'clock this morning."

Jenny made a little mewing noise, she pushed her hands feebly out in front of her, and fainted on the doorstep.

When Jenny opened her eyes again, she was lying on the sofa in the parlor and Rob was kissing her, whispering "Jenny, Jenny" over and over in a frightened imploring way. Mrs. Byrd and Evelyn were hovering beside her with sal volatile. Mina had crowded in between and was staring pop-eyed at the spectacle of Miss Jenny being kissed by a big, strange, dark man in the canvas pants and loose shirt that the slaves wore. The minister was there too, his long face twisted in concern.

Jenny sighed and rested her cheek against Rob's. He smelled of earth and sweat and new-sawn wood. She nestled against him. "I'm all right," she said. "Oh, Robbie, are you indeed free?"

"I am, hinny," he said in a choked voice. "But you needna take it so hard, you've scared the wits out of me!" He gave a shaky laugh, while the minister blew his nose violently. Mrs. Byrd and Evelyn both drew back from the sofa, their eyes misting.

"Can ye sit up, lass?" Rob asked in the rough-tender voice she had loved since she was five. "A couple must be dignified in front o' the minister that's to marry them!"

Jenny sat up, leaning against Rob's arm, pushing back her disordered hair. " 'Tis true," she said. "We must be dignified."

"Shall we wed tonight, Jenny?" asked Rob eagerly. "I believe Mr. Fontaine will waive the banns, and now I've the twenty shillings to pay for special license." He added this very proudly.

"Certainly I'll waive the banns," said the minister, "but we can't get the license, the clerk's office is closed, and to-morrow—"

"Tomorrow is Friday," cut in Jenny. "Oh, Robbie. You know how it was always thought at home to be terribly bad luck to wed on a Friday! Saturday morning we'll be wed, and in church, I beg you—" she cried turning to the minister, and then to Evelyn. "May we be married in Westover church?"

They both nodded. The minister was pleased because it was seldom that the Virginians used church for a wedding, and Evelyn was startled because she had not expected religious formality from Jenny. Then she remembered what the girl had once said about her own parents' hole-in-corner marriage in the depths of Northumberland, a marriage that was a failure from the start, and she understood that Jenny wished hers to be in all things different.

As for Rob, he said, "We'll be married on the moon, or in the middle of the James, if you wish it, hinny. I'll abide by what you say, *until* we're wed!" And he gave the rare transforming chuckle which had startled and charmed the few who had ever heard it—as it did now.

William Byrd returned the next day from Williamsburg, and his anger when he discovered the outrageous goings-on in his absence was very much what Evelyn had expected. She kept Jenny out of the way, and protected the bewildered and innocent Maria Byrd from her husband's wrath. Then as the storm abated a little, she meekly obeyed Byrd's stern summons to the library. In this small detached building which housed his precious books, where he kept his diary and other writings and where he felt most at home, Byrd turned on his daughter and said, "Sit down!"

Evelyn sat. Her father took the chair behind his desk, and in a voice he strove to keep calm, he said, "I begin to understand that *you* are behind this extraordinary, this monstrous huggermuggery!"

"In a way, Father," said Evelyn mildly. "I've helped all I can."

"I think you must be mad! It appalls me to find that you've been a party to this buying of runaway slaves, this freeing of convicted murderers, and even arranging marriage in *my* church for that poor deluded little fool of a Jenny—I think you're all mad! Fontaine too, I can't conceive of how you dragged *him* into it!"

"I didn't, Father. At least he saw the rights of the matter—the justice, more clearly than you do." She added with quiet precision, "And so did Governor Drysdale."

Byrd frowned and bit his lips. "The old man's so ill he didn't know what he was doing!"

"Oh yes, he did, Father! Mr. Fontaine talked with him for quite a while. They went over all the aspects of the case. The Governor said he was grateful for a chance to do some good in this world before he left it, and that he signed the pardon without hesitation."

Byrd gave an exasperated grunt. "Well, they can't be married in my church, it's—it's iniquitous. The girl, for all her idiocies, has noble blood, even royal blood. And such a shameful misalliance is degrading to everyone concerned."

"It's not your church, Father," said Evelyn still mildly. "It's the parish church, if anything it's Mr. Fontaine's. And I should think you'd be pleased to give happiness, as the Governor was. Besides it would make *me* happy to have this wedding at Westover."

"That's just it!" Byrd cried. "What possible interest have *you* in this imbroglio? Evelyn, I never understand you. You say you're fond of the girl, yet you do all you can to help her leave you. And for this you clandestinely brave my disapproval, my extreme displeasure!"

Evelyn tilted her head, her dark unfathomable eyes looked straight at her father. "Perhaps," she said, "it is because there was once a time when I did *not* dare brave your disapproval, when I *could* not! A time when I cared very much whether I became to you 'a creature detested' or not."

He started. "Who said *that*? Who used such words to you?"

"You did, Father. In a letter you wrote me on July twentieth of seventeen hundred and twenty-three."

Byrd recoiled. He moved his hand aimlessly back and forth on the desk. For an instant he saw Evelyn clear, and he saw himself too. "Evie, my dear child," he whispered. "You know I love you. I acted for the best. And so it was. The—man proved worthless, you admitted it yourself."

"He would not have been, if you had given me even the two thousand pounds you'd promised from my share of my mother's estate!"

"You can have it any time—for marriage to the *right* husband!" Byrd cried rashly. He no longer had any such sum about him; fashionable London life, and gambling debts, had melted it away. But he was much upset, and he yearned to remove this scornful look from the beautiful accusing face.

"My dear father," Evelyn said with frigid patience, "there is only *one* right husband for me. And only one for Jenny. Some women are like that—not many, I admit. But that's another reason I've helped her."

"I—I see," he said almost humbly. And he did see momentarily into the depths of his daughter's passionate, thwarted, and adamantine character. He understood at last that she had suffered greatly. And he was sorry for the vindictive role he had played three years ago, aware for a painful instant that his hatred of Sir Wilfred as a son-in-law had sprung not from the profligacy he had so eloquently insisted on to Evelyn, but from bruised pride at the young man's negligent mockeries of himself.

He could not tell her he was sorry, nor was he, for more than an instant. Yet he loved her, and that flash of insight made his voice hesitant and tender as he said, "Well, my dear—what's done is done. And no matter what you say I don't believe that you will become an antique virgin! As for Jenny Radcliffe, arrange her marriage as you like, but," he added more sternly, "I will not have that ill-matched couple living here!"

"There's no question of it, Father," said Evelyn sighing. She had exposed to him more of her inner feelings than she meant to, and regretted the weakness which had made her allude to the beloved man who was the cause of the rift between herself and her father. A rift which she perceived he would now again forget. "Rob and Jenny are going to the western part of Virginia," she said dully. "During his escape, Rob found some land where he wishes to settle."

"Indeed," Byrd said, pleased that she seemed submissive, and relieved at the introduction of a neutral topic. "I'm glad of that! Virginia needs settlers on the frontier. Where is the place?"

"It hasn't any name. I gather it's near a river, over a hundred miles west of here. There's some hills, and then beyond you can see blue mountains."

"The Blue Ridge!" said Byrd with interest. "That knave Spotswood crossed those mountains ten years ago, on his 'Golden Horseshoe' junket. I was in London of course, but I heard that all they did was carouse, and bury a wine bottle somewhere with King George's name in it—hardly an impressive claim to the lands!"

"Can Rob Wilson settle where he wants to out there?" she asked.

Byrd nodded, anxious now to be agreeable. "If he goes into the wilderness, he can choose a thousand acres where he likes and take his time about surveying, then travel to Williamsburg for a grant, which won't cost him anything, since I'm on the Council. We *must* settle the West, it's our best protection here against the French and Indians. I want to have a talk with Wilson, see what sort of spot he has in mind."

Evelyn gave a sad, secret smile. So the rage and unhappy allusions of the last hour were all forgotten now, effaced by her father's relief at getting rid of Jenny and Rob, and by his enthusiasm for a pet hobby—the development of western lands. This result was a fortunate one for Jenny. What about *me?* Evelyn thought, realizing how cruelly she would miss the girl, and how dreary life at Westover would be. Yet Evelyn would not harbor such weak sentiments as self-pity and loneliness, and she attacked herself with irony. As for me, she thought, I can reread Dr. Swift and Mr. Pope, who will help me enjoy the foibles of those around me. She arose and said, "If you'll excuse me, Father, I'll go consult Mother Byrd about arrangements for the wedding."

Jenny and Rob were married in Westover church at noon the following day. There was quite a gathering for the ceremony. Byrd, who enjoyed dispensing hospitality and had been agreeably surprised by his interview with Rob, sent an invitation to the Harrisons. Ben and Anne accepted at once. Mrs. Harrison curtly refused, then thought better of it. There was really no point in sitting home alone, when there was any diversion in the neighborhood.

Accordingly, the Harrisons came in their best clothes. Ben had even donned a white bag-wig for the occasion. The Byrd family sat in the other front pew across the aisle. Maria Byrd's eyes were full of sentimental tears. Wilhelmina, stiff in her London party dress and very much awed, was squeezed in beside her father, who had amiably offered to give the bride away—and very glad he was to do it.

During the night it had occurred to Byrd that all Evelyn's peculiarities might be attributable to Jenny's influence, and that with the girl's departure his daughter would immediately forget her silly notions, and become meek, gentle, and obedient to his every wish. This comforting theory had produced in Byrd a mood of indulgence and gaiety. He had given all the field hands a holiday, and permitted the house-servants to view the wedding from the gallery in the church, where they were now shuffling and whispering excitedly. He even permitted his delinquent overseer to sit in the last pew, though Fell was under notice of dismissal.

Mr. Fontaine began in his mellow voice, "Dearly beloved, we are gathered together here . . ." and they all stood up.

It must be admitted, Byrd thought, that the pair at the altar rail made a striking couple. The girl wore a white muslin dress of Evelyn's, her corn-colored hair flowed over it loose to her waist; a wreath of magnolia blossoms and syringa on her head, her cheeks like the magnolias tinged with pink, her gray eyes wide and brilliant. She seemed far too ornamental a creature for the life she was about to lead—but no matter, she was going to. And Wilson, for all his awkward bulk and his shock of unruly black hair tied in a queue, looked very nearly a gentleman. Not quite, of course. The only suit to be found at Westover which came near fitting him was a brown velveteen which had belonged to the overseer. It was too short, and strained to bursting across the back, yet it had silver buttons and a striped satin waistcoat which Byrd was certain Fell had stolen from a wardrobe during his master's absence.

Again no matter, now. Wilson had insisted on paying Fell for the suit. He showed indeed a commendable desire not to accept anything as a favor. Not a bad fellow after all. And it appeared that he had a little money, which made the match more respectable.

Evelyn watched the ceremony with thoughts far different. Sadness overpowered her, sadness and misgiving. Had she indeed done right to facilitate this marriage? Would Jenny ever bitterly regret relinquishing the side of her which she derived from her father? Would she tire of catering to Rob Wilson's thirst for independence and his fierce pride? For after all, the money which he now controlled was really Jenny's—though he did not know it. And there was the business of the rings.

Jenny had taken off her Radcliffe ring this morning. It seemed that Rob had asked her to. He had bought her a wedding ring, unearthed one through the county clerk. It was of alloyed gold, two thin wires twisted together, a poor shabby little thing compared to the Radcliffe ring, which Jenny had wrapped in a piece of silk and stuffed in the toe of one of her scarlet-heeled French dancing slippers. "I'll leave this here with the ball dress, Evie," Jenny said. "Such finery'll be of no use to me now! Can you put it in some chest in the attic?" The girl had spoken lightly, but Evelyn had seen the expression in her eyes as she drew off the ring, and seen the secret caress she gave the rose taffeta ball dress.

Evelyn had wanted to protest, and then checked herself. It was natural that a wedding day should mean a fresh start and no reminders of the past, and yet—could the past ever be forgotten, did it not always lie buried somewhere like a sleeping beast, ready to spring up and sink its fangs in the defenseless heart?

Evelyn stiffened and looked up. The minister's voice had taken on a louder tone, and he held up his hand.

"Forasmuch as Robert Wilson and Jane Radcliffe have consented together in holy wedlock, and have witnessed the same . . ."

'Tis the last time she'll bear the name of Radcliffe, Evelyn thought.

"I pronounce that they are Man and Wife in the name of the Father, and of the Son, and of the Holy Ghost, Amen," said Mr. Fontaine.

"Amen," Evelyn whispered. For a few moments after the blessing she could not rouse herself to rush forward with the others, who crowded up to the altar rail, smiling and congratulating the couple. Byrd benevolently shook Rob's hand, then said archly, "I claim the usual privilege, my dear," and kissed Jenny with relish. Ben Harrison followed suit, so did his wife; and even his mother, carried away by the universal good-will, said, "I hope you'll be very happy."

Jenny smiled mechanically and curtsied. All these laughing faces weren't real, the giggling, waving Negroes in the gallery weren't real, nor the bare little church and its white box pews. Even Rob, when she looked sideways at him, didn't seem real. A stranger, he was—a big, dark stranger in an ill-fitting brown velveteen suit. They all left the church, and began to walk along the path towards Westover. "What splendid weather for the wedding, Mrs. Wilson!" said Anne Harrison, gaily.

Mrs. Wilson—who was that? Jenny looked around to see who might have joined the company, and Rob gave a brief, constrained laugh. " 'Tis *you*, Jenny. I find it hard to believe it myself."

"How silly of me," she said, but it was as though someone else spoke for her. Rob touched her arm, and without knowing it she drew away.

They reached the house, and at once Jenny took off her bridal wreath and, having pinned up her hair, replaced the wreath with the fashionable square of Mechlin lace Lady Betty had given her.

In the dining room the wedding feast was spread out. Rob and Jenny were seated together at the head of the table. The bride-cake was iced in white curlicues. Anaka had stayed up all night making it, and grumbling constantly. Hurry, hurry, hurry—that was Miss Evelyn for you, and you couldn't hurry a bride-cake, which should age at least three months.

Yet the cake was good, or so the guests said—after Jenny had cut it with a silver knife. She ate some when Rob did, though she couldn't taste it. Besides the cake there were great silver platters heaped with food, and there was a special punch which Byrd concocted ceremoniously in front of them, pouring from odd-shaped bottles, squeezing lemons, and stirring carefully in the great china punch bowl. Then Byrd got up to propose a toast to the bride.

As they all rose, Jenny felt Rob looking down at her. She would not meet his eyes, and knew then how much she was afraid. Afraid of the moment when she would be alone with this stranger, afraid of what would then happen between the two of them, and of the surrender for which she had so often yearned. In that moment of fear she shrank inside, far off from Rob, who had become not only a stranger but an enemy. And when Byrd next proposed a toast to the King, she jumped up and cried wildly, "May *I* propose it, Mr. Byrd? May I drink to the King as *I* would like to?"

"Certainly," said Byrd smiling. "On this day your wish is law!"

"Then here's my toast!" Jenny cried, lifting her glass.

> *"God bless the King, the Church's true Defender,*
> *God bless—no harm in blessing—the Pretender,*
> *But who is that Pretender—who that King,*
> *God bless us all, is quite another thing!"*

There was a small startled silence, which Ben Harrison broke by saying, "Damme, that's an odd toast, it don't make much sense to me. Howevah—" and he drained his glass. The others rather dubiously followed suit. Byrd, who knew this for a famous Jacobite toast, hesitated and then shrugged. Let the girl enjoy herself today, if this were how she wanted to. She'd soon get over her nonsense in the wilderness, and by the look of him her new husband would soon change her views too. He was frowning and he hadn't touched his glass.

Jenny sat down, very flushed, and Rob said to her gravely from the corner of his mouth, "Jenny, why did you do that?"

"No reason," she said. "I felt like it. Oh, Mr. Byrd, did you say that we'd have dancing? Is there someone to play? Oh, I so dearly love to dance!"

"Why, yes," said Byrd, who liked dancing himself. "We can make up a set, and Job shall play his fiddle if he's not too drunk in the Quarters. I sent them all some rum."

"*I* don't know how to dance, sir," said Rob, "but I could play the pipes for you. The Northumbrian pipes. I've played for many a wedding in the North Country."

"Oh, no—" Jenny whispered involuntarily. "Not the pipes."

"Why not?" said Rob loud enough for all to hear. "You used to like the pipes, and it would please me to play for my host," he bowed slightly to Byrd, "and my late master." He bowed to Harrison.

"Oh, *do* play!" cried Anne Harrison, who could not bring herself to call him either "Sir" or "Mr. Wilson" and made up for it by excessive enthusiasm. "I'm suah we'd all *vastly* like to heah the pipes whatevah they are!"

Rob bowed again and walked out of the dining room in quest of his pipes. The others trooped into the parlor, where Mr. Fontaine edged near Evelyn, while the servants rolled up the rug and shifted chairs. "What ails the little bride?" he said low in her ear. "She's acting rather frantic."

"She's frightened," said Evelyn. "It may be that if one longs for a thing very hard, and despairs, and then suddenly gets it—one is frightened. I've never had the chance to find out."

The minister bent closer. "Ah, Miss Evelyn, is there something *you* want very much?"

"Yes," she said.

"Is it also a man?"

"Yes."

"And you cannot have him?"

"No. At least not yet. Someday, I think—I don't know." Her hand went to the locket in her bosom, he noticed the gesture and understood. He sighed deeply, and said, "We can at least be friends, you and I."

"Oh yes," she said fervently. "I need a friend." She turned as Rob came in, the small-pipes strapped around his waist and arm.

Anne Harrison and Mrs. Byrd went up to him curiously, exclaiming and questioning. Rob barely answered them; he walked straight to Jenny, who had gone as white as her dress.

"Shall I play 'The Oak and the Ash and the Bonny Ivytree'?" he said to her.

She would not meet his stern, sad gaze. "No, no," she cried. "*No!* I want to *dance!*"

Evelyn interposed quickly to Rob, "Do you know 'Sir Roger de Coverley'? Here they call it the 'Virginia Reel.' "

"I believe I do," said Rob. He set the drones and lifted the chanter.

At first all except Jenny were so startled by the strange sounds which came out that they could not help laughing. Rob took no notice and played on, accenting the rhythm, until Byrd bowed to Jenny, saying, "*Now*, I recognize the tune—" and led her to the head of the set. The young Harrisons followed; then Evelyn and the minister, and little Mina, who was jumping up and down in her desire to join, was good-naturedly partnered by Mrs. Byrd.

Rob played several reels for them, and presently a minuet, which Byrd and Jenny executed with graceful precision. Jenny glanced once at Rob when he started the minuet. Where could he have learned it? Anywhere, she thought—in all those years when they had not seen each other. The fear she was covering grew sharper. What madness was it that had made her feel she knew this man at all? Dear God— she thought while her body moved of itself through the stately measures. And Rob loomed there by the mantelpiece, as impassive and impersonal as the portraits on the parlor wall of Lord Orrery and the Duke of Argyle.

Jenny would have danced on all night, if possible. But Byrd stopped them, and mopped his forehead with his handkerchief. "Enough," he said. "I'm not as young as I was, and you, Cousin Anne, are somewhat imprudent in your condition. My wife also."

The set broke up. Ben, with a view to being agreeable and thanking the player, said to Rob, "Damme, man—if I'd known you'd a talent like this, I'd nevah have sold you!" And he laughed, nudging Rob in the ribs. "But as it is we can all guess you've had your fill of pipin', eh? There's bettah things to do on a weddin' night!"

Anne Harrison giggled, while Byrd said indulgently, "Quite so, Cousin Ben, quite so. Another glass of punch all around, and then we'll escort the bridal pair upstairs!"

"Undress 'em!" agreed Ben exuberantly. "And put 'em to bed. D'you remembah, Anne, the teasin' *we* took on our weddin' night—that knavish brothah of yours!"

"I think," said Evelyn sharply, "we could dispense with these bawdy old customs. I assure you they're no longer kept up amongst the quality in England." She had seen the terror in Jenny's eyes and the dark withheld angry look in Rob's.

Evelyn's rather scornful voice dampened Ben. He shrugged and ladled himself some more punch. "Then we might as well go home," he said. "You ready, Mothah?"

Madam Harrison asserted that she had been ready for some time. The three Harrisons departed in their coach. Mr. Fontaine took his leave, Mina was sent to bed, Mrs. Byrd retired, and Evelyn, greatly troubled, said a hurried good night to the bridal pair and escaped from them to lock herself in her room and try to calm her apprehensions.

Byrd, however, was determined to do the hospitable thing. Guests were always escorted to their rooms, and tonight, whatever his merits, Wilson had become a guest. The small spare room had been readied. The four-poster bed had this morning been draped with white ruffled muslin. New fresh pink dimity curtains were hung over the little dormer window.

Byrd ushered the two upstairs, and as he waved them through the spare-room door, he began a sly and sprightly remark which seemed appropriate to the occasion, but the utter silence of the two disconcerted him. So he merely wished them good night, and received no answer.

As the door shut Jenny retreated to the window wall, and stood pressed with her back against it, her fingers twisting together.

Rob remained by the door, his heavy eyebrows drawn together above his hazel eyes, his mouth set into another bar below them.

"I have no wish at all to touch you," he said in a cold dry voice. "So you needn't look like that."

She swallowed, and moistened her lips. This was not what she had expected to hear. Her heart pounded in such shaking beats that it tore at her chest. Without her knowledge her twisting fingers paused on the new ring, the unaccustomed little ring, and she glanced down at it.

"Aye," said Rob, deadly quiet. "Already you miss the ring you wore before, don't you! Mr. Radcliffe would think this a vile match, to be sure, and who's to blame him!"

Jenny's hands fell abruptly apart; she pressed her palms behind her, flat against the wall. She looked at Rob at last. His head near touched the ceiling, the space between them in this little room was not ten feet, yet it might have been the width of the Atlantic—of the world.

"You can get an annulment," said Rob. "It will be quite easy, under all the circumstances. I'll leave you now and inform Mr. Byrd, so there'll be no chance of misunderstanding later." He put his hand on the doorknob.

Jenny gasped. Her fear of him dissolved, and in its place rushed in a different kind of panic. "Wait!" she whispered. "Robbie, ye canna leave me *again!* Robbie, we're wed now."

She spoke in the lilt of her childhood, and despite himself he paused. "We're wed for the nonce," he said. "And ye knew it for a mistake, e'en i' the church—d'ye think me such a dolt I didna feel it?"

"It was the strangeness—" she said in a strangled voice. "I couldna help the feel o' strangeness. Rob, I *wish* to be your wife—you know well I ever wished it." As he continued to stand hesitant yet unbending by the door with his hand on the knob, she added, almost inaudibly, "You don't want me, then? Yet there've been times when you wanted me."

He made a fierce impatient sound. "Any man may want to bed a pretty lass!"

"You're cruel," she whispered. "Cruel!"

His hand dropped from the knob, and he turned on her

440

violently. "D'ye think my lust so strong that I'd take you like this, when you've been shrinking from me like a lamb that sees the butcher knife at its throat! For the matter o' that d'ye think I'd take you for the first time in another man's house, in a stifling cubbyhole filled wi' gewgaws and fripperies someone else provided!" He reached out and tore one of the white ruffles off the bed's canopy.

There was a silence filled only by their rapid breathing.

"Let us go outdoors then," said Jenny.

"What!" he cried, staring at her incredulously. "What did you say?"

"Let us go outdoors," she repeated. "I find this room as stifling as you do."

She glided past him, and opened the door. "Come, my dear love," she said quietly. "We'll go down the river. There's a bank of moss I know of underneath pine trees, and near a burn that ripples softly like the one in Whitton Dene."

"Jenny—" he whispered, catching her by the shoulder, and turning her so that he might see her face. "Jenny, are you *sure?*"

"Aye, Robbie," she said.

Five days later in the early morning, Jenny and Evelyn stood upon the riverbank in front of Westover, watching Rob and Nero loading a capacious bateau with all the Wilsons' worldly goods. The sun was shining after a night of gentle rain. A southerly breeze ruffled the river, and would combine with a flowing tide to help the adventurers on the first lap of their long journey to the far-off western lands.

The bateau was an amorphous sort of broad shallop with a slight keel, a tiller, and a large sail; it was also furnished with poles and oars. Evelyn had persuaded her father to give the young couple this useful craft as a wedding present. She herself had added a smoked ham, and delicacies such as wine, preserves, and spices. Also a bolt of homespun for when their clothes wore out.

Everything else Rob had bought himself, either from the plantation or from neighboring farms; the sacks of corn and tobacco seed, the hoes and shovels and plow, the axes, the saws and carpentry tools, two old but serviceable guns with extra flints and a keg of powder. And he had bought the animals—a sturdy, docile farm horse, and a pregnant sow who it was to be hoped would not farrow until journey's end.

He had also bought Nero. There had been none of the expected difficulties over this purchase. Ben Harrison had even knocked the price down to thirty pounds, partly from good nature, but mostly because Corby urged him to get rid of the Negro. "He's a bad un, sir. Since that Wilson left here, Nero he won't work. An' the looks that devil gives me! Not to put too fine a p'int on it—he makes me uneasy—and he's unsettling the other black bastards. Ye know we daren't risk that."

Ben did know very well the unmentionable and terrifying threat of revolt which hung over all the plantations.

So Rob got Nero, and freed him that same day at the courthouse.

"You'll regret it," said Byrd, most disapproving of this precedent. "You'll get no use of him at all. He'll never stay with you!"

"I think he will," said Rob calmly. "We understand each other."

And even Byrd had to admit that the huge Negro had been toiling prodigiously in the preparations for departure. The departure which was imminent. As the two girls watched, Rob and Nero were even now coaxing the sow into the bateau and tethering her tight in the center by means of ropes.

"Oh, Jenny," said Evelyn trying to disguise by a laugh the wrench she was feeling, "I hope that pig doesn't founder your Noah's Ark!"

"It won't with *Rob* in charge," said Jenny proudly. "He thinks of everything. And how clever he was to think of his marvelous invention."

Evelyn smiled. She knew all about the invention, since nothing else had been talked of at supper last night, and even Byrd was impressed by it. The horse had already started upriver by road. Rob had hired a farmer's lad to ride it on the journey. When the bateau had progressed up the James as far as the falls, where it could go no farther, Rob proposed to haul the boat to the riverbank and fit it with wheels; then the horse, and men also, could haul it along until the river became navigable again.

"Your Rob is most ingenious," said Evelyn, "and I can't imagine how he's accomplished all he has in so short a time."

"Aye," said Jenny with a pleased chuckle. "My Robbie's a very canny lad, and 'tis easy to work well when you're happy."

Evelyn sighed unconsciously. "Yes, he's happy," she stated, "and so, thank God, are you. Jenny, I had grave doubts on the wedding day."

"So did I—" said Jenny, knitting her brows. "It's odd I

can't remember them now. Oh, Evie, 'tis so—so wonderful to be part of a man and he of you." She stopped, blushing a little. "I hope you'll know this yourself, soon." She spoke to Evelyn, but her eyes were on Rob, a brawny, confident young figure, who was laughing as he finished tethering the squealing sow. He turned and beckoned. "Come, hinny—" he called in the tender-teasing voice she adored. "Make your farewells! I'm ready to ship my most precious bit o' livestock now!"

" 'Tis my summons!" said Jenny laughing. She turned and threw her arms around her friend's neck. "I don't know how to thank you, Evie—and oh, how I shall miss you! We'll write, won't we! Rob says there'll be Indian traders to carry letters someday."

"To be sure," said Evelyn as lightly as she could. "It's not quite another world you're going to. Only a matter of a fortnight's journey, Rob says." And then what? she thought— the wilderness, and peril of bear, snakes, wolves, and Indians, not to speak of the hardships of actual existence when all was still to be wrested from the sinister wilds.

William Byrd, his wife, and Mina came hurrying up to say goodbye. They all went down to the rebuilt pier at the river's edge, and Byrd, running his eye with approval over the laden bateau, called to Rob. "Well, you're off, are you? Good luck, and pray send back one of my people from Falling Creek to tell me of conditions there."

Rob nodded. "Yes, sir. I'll do that, and thank you again for your kindness." Byrd had a small plantation thirty miles by water up the James. It was run by an overseer to whom Byrd had written a note for Rob to deliver so that the boatload might be cared for one night at the last outpost of civilization.

"Hop in, wife!" said Rob smiling at Jenny. "Your ship's about to sail."

Mrs. Byrd and Mina kissed Jenny goodbye. Evelyn kissed her once quickly. Jenny shook hands with Byrd, and dropped him a curtsey. Could it be the last curtsey she would ever make? she thought in wondering amusement. She had no qualms at all as she jumped down from the pier into Rob's waiting arms. He stowed her on a sack of corn, well away from the pig in case it got restive. Rob cast off, he and Nero picked up the oars, and hoisted the sail. The bateau moved sluggishly away into midstream, where the south breeze and the incoming tide both propelled it fast. Jenny waved until the figures on the pier grew blurred. Then she settled contentedly upon her sack, turning a bit so that she might see

Rob, the rhythmic power of his arm and shoulder muscles while he rowed, the assurance of his watchful eyes as they scanned the river.

At Westover the Byrds climbed the bank towards the house. Byrd was filled with satisfaction at a good deed well done, and calculating how soon a report would get back from Falling Creek, when he was struck with concern by a glimpse of Evelyn's face. It had a white, shut look, her forehead glistened, and she seemed to be shivering. The ague! he thought. It was almost time for the fevers to start and none of his unacclimated family had had "the seasoning" yet.

"My dear!" he said. "You don't look well. I must give you the bark instantly."

"Very well, Father," she said in a muffled voice. "In a minute, I'll come in. I wish to stay outside for a minute."

She wandered away from him towards a little point of land where she could see up and down the river. She stood there gazing after the bateau, which had become a sliver on the distant water. Then she looked to the left—downstream. Not even Jenny had known how often she stood here, waiting to see a ship from England sailing up the James. A ship bearing news. Someday there would be a letter, of that she was certain. He had promised it. And was it not also possible that someday there might be a passenger in quest of her?

Always as she stood there gazing at the empty river, one part of Evelyn jeered at herself for a fool; but stronger than that was the hope that miracles might happen, if one were staunch and could wait, and was it not a sort of miracle which had finally happened to Jenny?

PART FIVE

1737

EIGHTEEN

On Michaelmas, September 29 of 1737, Jenny sat in her little
garden, on a rustic bench Rob had made for her the second
year after they had come to the West. She sat dressed in a
black homespun she had dyed herself, sadly pensive, holding
an open letter on her lap. The letter was from Lady Betty in
England, and had taken eight months to reach this frontier
plantation in a Virginia country, which had as yet only the
vaguest boundaries, and was now called Goochland after
William Gooch, the Governor who had replaced poor old
Drysdale.

Letters were extraordinary events for Jenny. Often she did
not even hear from Evelyn in months. Mail delivery depended upon the kindness of a passing fur trader, or of one
of the rangers whom the Governor had appointed to patrol
the frontier.

A ranger had brought the letter this afternoon. He had
picked it up some days ago from the Shocco tobacco store-
house at the Falls of the James, on William Byrd's property.
There was a new town called Richmond being planned there
by Colonel Byrd, the ranger said. Otherwise he had no news
of Westover.

Jenny was unused to sitting idle. These had been years of
constant struggle, with everything to learn—cooking, cleaning, mending, doctoring, gardening, and at this moment she
should be in the kitchen to see that Peg was roasting the
piglet properly, the Michaelmas treat which should of course
have been a goose. They had no geese, but they had quantities

of hogs. She could hear them grunting as they rooted for mash in the woods behind Nero's cabin. And there was no really pressing task until Rob came home for supper.

He had gone to the south end of their property, where there was good iron ore; he hoped to build there someday an ironworks and forge. He would probably do so. One by one Rob had realized nearly all his dreams. Jenny leaned her blond head against the bench back and thought how much Rob had accomplished in these eleven years at Snowdon, though to be sure he had had help from the motley household gathered around them. No slaves, however, at Snowdon. Rob wouldn't have them, and he scrupulously meted out a share of the profits to Nero and to Willy.

"Snowdon," Jenny thought with a faint smile. That was the name of their plantation, and once again she could recapture the excitement of that sixteen-year-old bride on the June day when they tied their battered craft on the south riverbank and Rob, jumping out onto a pebbly shore, waved his hand exultantly and cried, "This is *ours*, hinny. This is our very own land!"

She exulted too, and was delighted when Rob told her that nothing yet was really named, not the river, which had been their highway, nor the little hills to the south, nor the mountains to the northwest, nor the creek near which they stood. He had been startled when she began to name the landmarks after fancied resemblances to that faraway North Country where she had first learned to love Rob. That hill up there should be Tosson, the bluff could be Ravensheugh. The river should be the Tyne, since it was too wide to be the Coquet. Here Rob laughingly protested. "I think this river *has* a name. Mr. Byrd believed it to be called Fluvanna, after Queen Anne. Yet now *I* think, having come up it, 'tis but a continuation of the James. In any case, both good Stuart names, which should please you."

"Aye, indeed," said Jenny happy that they could laugh about a subject which had once been a sore one. "Then we'll call this little burn for King George," she gestured towards the creek. " 'Tis only fair. And, Rob, might we call our whole plantation 'Snowdon' in memory of my mother and the peel?"

"Why not?" said Rob, after a moment in which she knew that he was reluctant to live with any reminder of the past. "Snawdon it is, and Geordie's Creek, an' ould Tosson an' anything else ye like, m'lass, for 'tis m'weesh ter gi'e ye pleasure!"

Jenny stirred on her bench as she thought of that day. Rob

447

never now used their old vernacular, and except for "Snowdon" and "George's Creek," the other names she gave had lapsed. Like the traders and rangers, Rob spoke of the Green Mountains to the north, while the distant western ones were simply the "Ridge." Rob had neither the time nor the nature for sentiment, though she never doubted his love. And she rejoiced in his success.

Snowdon was now a flourishing little plantation. It grew wheat, corn, and the coarse Orinoco tobacco. There was a mill on George's Creek; there were fences, and tobacco sheds, and pastures; there were cabins—widely separated— for Nero's family, and for the Turners. There was also the beautiful new house.

Jenny glanced behind her at the house, which had been finished only two months ago and was a source of wonder to everyone. The house was built of clapboard above a brick foundation and was shaped somewhat like a miniature Berkeley. The bricks had been made and fired at their own clay-pits. The roof was blue slate, quarried on their property. There was a chimney at each end of the house, and four large rooms inside: a kitchen and a dining parlor below, two commodious bedrooms upstairs. The house was glazed with crown glass from England. Rob had bought the glass on one of his spring trips to Williamsburg to pay the quit-rents.

Jenny had never accompanied him on these expeditions— because of little Robin. She sighed deeply and looked down towards a glimpse of river, and to a small gray stone almost hidden in the shadows of a magnificent live-oak. Anguish stabbed up through the constant dull ache.

In this letter Lady Betty had asked about Robin:

Your little son must be ten now, and I am sure is a great joy to you in that wilderness home which I can*not* picture try as I will. Your description of your household amazes us, Negroes, and Indians, and Papist gaolbirds— what a bedlam it sounds! It quite makes me shiver, here in my placid Hertfordshire parsonage. My own small Frederick is well. It must seem odd to you to think of this ancient dame with a child of five, I thank God that we have him—he is balm for the loss we suffered last October. It was my Betsy, newly married to Henry Temple, Lord Palmerston's heir, she died at Lyons— poor poor child. She was very fond of you.

Jenny put down her letter again. She had already read it twice, and would reread it many times, though the news Lady Betty gave her about the people she had known in that other life seemed remote and mournful. There had been so many deaths, so many changes. And it was still difficult to realize that Lady Betty was married to Dr. Edward Young, the poetic parson, and living at Welwyn in Hertfordshire. Welwyn, of all places! Jenny thought of another Michaelmas, so many years ago, when she and her father had stopped at Welwyn after their Northumbrian trip. The fair, the music, and the smell of roasting geese. So Lady Betty's husband, Dr. Young, was now the vicar there, while then he had been living with his patron, the Duke of Wharton.

Lady Betty had married Young a year after Colonel Lee's death. Wharton was dead too; he died at thirty-three in Spain of drink and debauchery. Jenny thought how extraordinary it was to realize the chain of circumstances Wharton's debauchery had caused in her own life. Had it not been for the vile rites of the Hell-Fire Club, Rob would not have been transported, nor would she then have come to Virginia. I suppose I might have stayed with my father, she thought. She picked up the letter and searched for another paragraph Lady Betty had written.

Your father is living in a Roman palazzo, very near to the Pretender. I suppose you know your father is now the "Earl of Derwentwater." Poor young John died from a cutting for the stone. Dr. Young doesn't like me to write to C.R., and I *obey* better than I did with Colonel Lee! But I believe your father and Lady N. have several children now, though I know he'll never love them as he does you, Jenny. He was in London two years ago, on Jack business I fear, disguised as Mr. Jones again. I saw him briefly. He was terribly upset at the news of your marriage, I never saw him so moved. He said he had never heard from you since the day you left him in Paris. I said perhaps it was better that way. He is still a most handsome man.

Jenny let the letter fall to her lap. Her sad gaze went again to the little tombstone under the live-oak. Her father thought she had forgotten him, and she had tried to do so. It had not been possible because of Robin. Jenny got up slowly, and walked down the hill to the slate tombstone. It was carved by Rob, and it memorialized so short and so blighted a life.

Three months ago Robin had caught a fever from one of Nero's children. In two days he was gone, despite her anguished nursing. And in their hearts, they knew—she and Rob—that for his own sake the little boy's death was a mercy. Jenny slid down on the grass beside the tombstone, she put her arms around it, and rested her cheek on the cold hard edge.

The agony of Robin's actual birth she had forgotten. It had happened in the little log cabin they first built here. Nero's squaw, Shena, had helped. Rob too had helped, she could just remember his frightened face. The shock which came later when he silently brought her the baby—that could never be hazed. The baby was a pretty infant with a fuzz of silvery hair. She held him proudly against her breast, wondering that Rob did not rejoice, since he had longed for a son. And then she saw the baby's right hand. There were six tiny fingers on it, and one of his feet was webbed between the toes like a little hoof. She knew that she screamed, and cried out again and again that it was her fault, that this came of her Stuart blood. Rob had been very gentle; he held her and soothed her, but he also questioned as to what she meant.

She told him of the deformity on the hand of her half brother, Lord Kinnaird, and that one of the Pretender's sons had also such a thing. Rob said nothing more, and they never but once mentioned the Stuart blood again.

Robin grew slowly. He was a delicate serious child, subject to colds and fevers, yet he never seemed unhappy. He played with Nero's sons, and with Peg and Willy Turner's little girl, Bridey, nor ever seemed to notice that his hand looked different from theirs, or that his limp was a handicap. Rob carried his son a great deal, off on trips to the woods, and early taught him to ride a horse. And always Jenny dreaded the day when Robin would meet strangers, and the cruelty of strange children. For there were a few other settlers now, not so very far away. Year by year the good lands along the rivers were being taken up. One heard that there were even settlers in the wild Indian valley, the other side of the high mountains.

But Robin had not had to face strangers. He lay here in peace, his gray eyes shut, his pale golden curls falling back against the sweet-smelling pine pillow he had always loved.

Jenny turned and pressed her lips against the tombstone. She rose slowly to her feet as Peg came skittering towards her down the hill.

Peg was a tiny mouselike thing, a slatternly mouse, with her stringy brown hair always falling about her ears, and her apron ripped and stained. But she had been good to Robin. "Now, now, mum," she said, in the unmistakable tongue of Ireland. "Don't ye be a-brooding here—and Oi've come to tell ye that the applesass is burnt."

"Oh, Peg!" said Jenny. "Not again! You know Mr. Wilson always wants it with his pork!"

"Faith, he'll not be getting it," said Peg putting on the look of mournful penitence which had stood her well in Bridewell prison. " 'Twas the end o' the sugar."

"I'll have to open the last jar of blueberry jam then," said Jenny, beginning to walk towards the house.

"I wonder will ye be finding it, mum," said Peg in a small voice.

Jenny stopped and stared at the elfin ugly face. "Do you mean to say you *took* it? *Really*, Peg. You might have asked me!"

"It looked so good, mum. And Bridey, she wanted some too. The jam kinda got et."

"No doubt," said Jenny, exasperated. Peg was sometimes a help, more often a trial. Particularly in the childish impulses which made her lax with other people's property. It was this trait seven years ago which had landed her in Bridewell, and led to transportation. I'll have to speak to Willy again about her, Jenny thought. Willy Turner had his own methods of disciplining his wife. At least one called Peg his wife, though since there was no Catholic priest nearer than Maryland there had never been any ceremony.

It must be five years since Willy Turner and Peg knocked on the Wilson door one day—a small, weary, footsore pair; the sacks slung over their backs contained their sole possessions.

At first Jenny had not recognized Willy despite the black patch on one eye, so far behind her had she put all her life before her marriage. And when she did remember this little Jacobite who adored her father she was not best pleased to find Rob inviting the couple to stay, which was what Willy had hoped.

Peg had skipped her bond to a planter on the northern shore. In plain words, she was a runaway, and it was wise to take her to the wilderness where no questions would be asked. Willy was tired of working for Dr. Blair anyway, and he bethought him of Miss Radcliffe—his hero's daughter. Inquiry at Westover (during which visit he hid Peg) disclosed that Miss Radcliffe had become Mrs. Wilson and gone to the wilds past the frontier. Miss Byrd had told Willy to follow the James, and they had, trudging through the forests for weeks.

At first after his arrival at Snowdon, Willy had wanted to talk about Charles Radcliffe and the Battle of Preston. He soon learned better, since Rob went into one of his black frowning moods when this happened. Willy was clever, and he wanted to stay at Snowdon, so nothing disquieting had been mentioned in years.

On the whole Jenny thought the acquisition of the Turners had worked well—or rather Willy had, and Peg was at least an extra pair of hands, and a woman to talk to. You couldn't talk to Shena. Her English consisted of about four words. How she ever communicated with Nero nobody knew; nor probably did he care if she didn't communicate.

One day shortly after they came to Snowdon, Nero disappeared and was gone for a week. When he returned he brought with him a stout, beady-eyed young squaw, wearing three necklaces of roanoke shell beads and very little else. Her mahogany skin was oiled with bear grease, she gave forth a pungent smell.

"My woman," Nero announced to Rob. He seldom spoke to Jenny. He shoved Shena towards the Wilsons and gave the only grin Jenny had ever seen. "I buyed her in the valley over yonder past the Ridge! She'll wuk hard foh us."

Shena giggled and stared in amazement at Jenny's yellow hair.

That was practically all they ever knew about Shena, except that Nero had found a tribe of Catawbas hunting buffalo in the valley the Indians called Shenandoah, and had bought Shena with his old gun and a round of powder. Nero didn't understand her name and called her Shena after "Shenandoah." The squaw turned out to be as prodigious a worker as her enormous mate. She planted corn, and tended crops; she hauled wood and water from the spring, and punctually every two years she bore Nero another boy.

There were five little reddish-brown "mustees" now tumbling around Nero's cabin, or working in the fields, and Shena was hugely pregnant with the sixth. A good breeder, Jenny thought, while suffering a bitter pang of jealousy. How desperately she and Rob hoped for another child—hoped and feared, in case the Stuart taint should appear again. But Rob thought not, the once he had mentioned it. He knew much of cattle breeding, and did not believe a hereditary defect would be constant. At any rate they'd chance it. Yet in all these years her womb had not quickened again.

Jenny's eyes stung, and she hastily basted the pig to conceal her face from Peg. She turned quickly as she heard Rob outside calling her.

"Here I am!" she cried running to him in some surprise, for his voice had an edge of excitement.

He was standing near the spring washing something in a bucket. Her heart gave its usual leap of gladness when she saw him safe-returned of an evening. Twice he had not come back on time. Once when he had been mauled by a bear he had shot, and the horrible day when he had been bitten by a rattlesnake in the mountains. Nero had been with him, and saved his life by cutting deep into the wound and sucking out the poison.

"You're early, Robbie," said Jenny, coming up to him. "I'm so glad, I've been a bit dreary. What *are* you washing?"

"I wish I knew," he said, smiling at her. "Look!" He held out his hand and disclosed a lump of dark stone in which were tiny yellow specks.

"Is it iron ore?" she asked, puzzled.

"It's ore—but not iron. I know that, and I know coal when I see it—of *that* you may be sure! And I've a curiosity about this bit o' stone."

"Rob!" she said wide-eyed. "You don't think it might be gold, do you? Where did you find it?"

"By the north branch of the Slate River, just beyond my boundary line. I'm not sure what the mineral is, though I've a fancy anyway to take up another five hundred acres to the west, whatever this stone may mean."

"Aye," she said softly. "You've not yet had your fill of the land, have you?"

"No," said Rob. "And when I think of the miserable days on Tyneside when to own twenty acres free and clear seemed to me the top o' glory!" His voice trailed off, as he glanced involuntarily towards the little tombstone. Land he had now in plenty, but there was no one to leave it to, no one to carry on.

Jenny read his thoughts and took a sharp breath. He looked at her. At twenty-seven she was as fair as she had been when he wed her, her hair as thick and golden, her body as slender and firm; yet her sparkle was dimmed and the hot Virginia summers had paled the English rosiness of her cheeks, while the beautiful eyes were somber.

"Hinny—" he said suddenly, "we're going to take a trip to Williamsburg! You and I."

"Oh!" she said startled. "I think I'd like that! Though you went in the spring before—before Robin—"

"I know," he interrupted quickly, "but I can take the tobacco down instead of Nero, and I want to get the new land grant. Besides you need a change."

She considered this, and found that she was eager to go, eager to see new people and new styles, eager to be in a bustle—even of so tame a little place as Williamsburg. At least it had seemed very dull when she was fresh from London; now it was a gay metropolis to her.

Her face lit up, she smiled her sudden lovely smile. "And I could see Evelyn, couldn't I? We'll call at Westover?"

"To be sure," said Rob heartily. "I wish to consult with Colonel Byrd too." He stooped and gave her a kiss. "Wey, hinny! We'll spend a whole month or so and have ourselves some gaudy-days! I warrant we've both earned them."

Their preparations for departure took time, and the journey down the river lasted a week, so that it was October 12 before Jenny and Rob quitted their bateau at the Falls. Then they waited until their hogsheads of tobacco had been inspected at the Shocco warehouse. Rob was jubilant. The tobacco price was high this year, nine pence a pound, and he received far more than he had dared hope in tobacco notes, which were legal currency. He had also brought gold in his purse, part-remainder of the original three hundred and sixty pounds which had bought his freedom and Nero's. Rob had been very saving of the gold, after the initial expenses, and only in the first years had he been forced to use some of it for his annual quit-rent of a pound.

Since then the plantation paid for itself.

"We'll do some shopping in Williamsburg, Jenny!" he said happily as they left the wharf. "You'll want some gewgaws, and I could do with a decent suit myself."

"You certainly could," she said laughing. Rob was still wearing the deerskin jacket and coarse Osnaburg pants which he wore at home and in which he'd poled down the river. His only "good" suit was the brown velveteen he had worn when they married. It fitted no worse than it did then. Rob had not gained an ounce in his years of outdoor toil, but it certainly was not appropriate to a successful planter.

They hired saddlehorses at the village which William Byrd had christened Richmond and referred to as his "city in the air." It was located on the property where Byrd had been born, and seemed an agreeable site with its little hills, and its position by the Falls at the head of navigation from the sea. Yet Jenny was sceptical. "I shouldn't think this could ever be a city," she said looking at the three ramshackle wooden buildings—livery stable, general store, and a cabin someone had built on a small plot outlined by stakes.

"I wonder," said Rob, as they mounted their horses. "I heard in the spring that Colonel Byrd's had no luck populating all those lands he took up to the southwest, near the Carolina border. Yet he's a shrewd man when it comes to business."

"Perhaps," said Jenny thinking of the bad bargain Byrd had made when he had assumed his father-in-law's debts. "I've never quite understood Mr. Byrd."

They rode away down the road on the James's north bank. This October day was not too warm. The blue air felt fresh even here in Tidewater. A flock of wild geese flew honking above, the squirrels bounded in the dappled woods searching for nuts. Rob felt buoyant. Thirty-six I am, he thought, and that's not old. I've got more strength than I ever had, and I've accomplished much of what I wanted.

By afternoon they came to the fence and driveway which marked the entrance to Berkeley. "Ugh," said Rob grinning. "I've no wish to go in *there*. Do you suppose any of the slaves've murdered Corby yet?"

"Oh, Robbie!" she said. "I'm glad you can laugh about it." She thought of his back, the long welts and lumps which he would carry to the grave from Corby's vicious floggings, and the scar on his neck where the iron collar had chafed.

"Laughter's a healing thing," said Rob as they headed on to Westover. "I've come to see that. I was ever too serious; and you, hinny, have grown so. Aye, we've had heartache and disappointment, and so has every mortal. 'A merry heart maketh a cheerful countenance; but by sorrow of the heart the spirit is broken.' "

She twisted in the saddle to stare at him. "Is that the Bible, Rob? Since when do you quote Scriptures?"

"Well," he said a trifle embarrassed. "I've been reading them o' nights at times, when you're asleep. There's meat in them to mull over when a man's working."

She gave the soft little chuckle which he hadn't heard in years. "Long as I've known you, you can still surprise me, Rob Wilson," she said.

They went up Westover driveway. The fields and the Quarters looked the same, but there was no house in the place it had been. Perplexed, they rode on, almost to the river, then pulled up their horses in astonishment. There was a new brick house at Westover. It was long and low and graceful, flanked on either side by brick dependencies. It nestled like a jewel beneath the towering poplars, and seemed as much part of its setting as the lawn and the new gardens and the bright river flowing nearby.

"Wuns!" said Rob in awe. "What a beauty! Four chimneys—and look at that doorway! Mr. Gibbs himself might have done it; *I* never could!"

"You *could*," she said staunchly.

He shook his head. "I'm a master-builder, not an artist. There's art in this house—and maybe a bit o' luck too. Look at the fenestration. It's perfect."

Jenny did not know what fenestration was, and as Rob seemed lost in professional admiration, she dismounted, and banged the handsome brass knocker. The door was opened by Eugene, who greeted her with beaming smiles and cries of welcome. "Lawd above, Miss Jenny—yo' shuah is a sight for sore eyes. Step in, step in! They's all in the music room!"

Evelyn drifted out into the hall to see whom Eugene was welcoming, and gave a joyful cry when she saw Jenny. They rushed into each other's arms, then stood back, both tearful, to look at each other. "You've not changed," said Evelyn, tilting her head in the old way. "The wilderness suits you."

Jenny tried to reply that Evelyn had not changed either, but the words stuck in her throat. Evelyn had altered woefully. Her great dark eyes, glowing like coals, were sunk back in her head. She had grown so thin that the cords stood out in her neck, and the bones of her face showed sharply through the tautened skin. On each cheekbone there was a patch of red, not the fresh color of her early years, but a hectic crimson. Even while she questioned Jenny eagerly, she coughed a little, a dry hacking of which she seemed unconscious, and Evelyn was possessed of a feverish gaiety, an excitement which Jenny did not understand.

The Byrd family were all at tea in the music room, and they also greeted the Wilsons cordially. Wilhelmina was not there, she had gone off on a visit to her Ludwell cousins, but Maria Byrd's quartet were clustered around the tea table— three little girls, Anne, Maria, and Jane. One boy, William Byrd the Third, who was nine, and the obvious darling of his father's heart.

"Here is my son," said Byrd presenting him proudly to

the Wilsons. "He supports me against the gaggle of women at Westover! You have a son too, did not Evelyn tell me?"

"Not any more," said Jenny briefly. They all looked at her rusty black dress, and there was a moment's sympathetic silence.

"God's Will be done!" said Byrd shaking his head. "I know what sorrow it is to lose them, and I feel deeply for you. 'Tis best not to think about it." He turned to Rob. "How do you like my house, eh? I don't wish to offend you, but Ben Harrison doesn't lord it over me about *his* house nowadays!"

"Your house is magnificent, sir," said Rob. "May I look about?"

Byrd was delighted, and nodded complacently while Rob admired the stuccoed ceilings, the carved, pedimented doorways, the paneling, the huge embrasured windows. He minutely inspected the monumental black marble fireplace in the parlor saying that the only thing he'd ever seen to touch it was the one Gibbs made for Lord Lichfield at Ditchley. In the hall Rob ran his hands down the gleaming mahogany balustrade and its carved spindles. He turned to Byrd. "How *did* you get such work done here, sir?"

"Oh, we didn't, not most of it!" said Evelyn, who was also watching. She laughed in a rather strident way. "We sent to England for the doorways and the balustrade and mantels. We weren't niggardly with money, *were* we, Father!"

"We spent no more than suitable," said Byrd stiffly who had gone further into debt over the house. "We built from drawings in Salmon's *Palladio* and Gibbs's book. Evelyn was invaluable, she directed the builders we got from Williamsburg, and selected those of my people here who had the most aptitude for this kind of work."

"I congratulate you, Miss Byrd," said Rob heartily. "You make a splendid architect."

"Oh, it gave me an interest," said Evelyn in her mocking tone. "What else could an old maid do!" She was seized by a spasm of coughing and her father frowned.

"I can't see why that summer cold of yours hangs on so long," he said. "You should be purged again, and I'll give you ginseng root—a sovereign remedy."

"My cold is *nothing!*" said Evelyn with an angry fierceness Jenny did not understand. There seemed something here beyond the usual sparring with her father. Evelyn acted highkeyed, exhilarated, as though she had cause for secret elation. It was a little disturbing, and when Jenny later found out the reason she was not entirely relieved.

Byrd took Rob off to show him all the new outbuildings, which included two sumptuous necessary houses, each with a fireplace and five holes of differing sizes, to accommodate all ages.

Evelyn and Jenny drifted towards the garden. Byrd had planted it with box and imported shrubs of every kind, including mulberries and wisteria. They sat down in the summerhouse, beneath a mass of honeysuckle. Evelyn leaned forward and began to speak in a breathless, excited manner. "Jenny, I've so longed to see you, there's nobody else I can tell. He's coming! Wilfred's coming here at last!"

"Oh, Evie," Jenny whispered. "Eve, darling, can it be true . . . You've heard from him?"

"Yes. I've heard from him three times since you left. The last letter was a year ago, he always says he loves me, and in that letter he said he too felt it wouldn't be long before we met again."

"Is his wife—"

"I don't know, he never mentions her. But he said he wasn't happy, and if there's a divorce it wouldn't matter here, nobody'd know, or even if there's *not* a divorce," added Evelyn sternly.

"Mr. Byrd," Jenny said, floundering, and still much startled.

Evelyn raised her chin, the flush deepened on her cheekbones.

"Father cannot stop me this time. I'm thirty years old, and I have my own property—'Evelynton,' which he finally gave me. Besides, he's tired of having a spinster daughter around. He's absorbed in his new family, especially little Will."

This sounded reasonable, and Jenny said after a moment, "I'm so glad for you, Eve," she put her hand over her friend's dry, thin, hot one. "When did you hear that Sir Wilfred was on his way?"

"In a dream," said Evelyn, with a tender reminiscent smile, her burning gaze looking into space.

"A dream—" Jenny repeated, trying not to show dismay. "You usen't to believe in dreams."

"I believe this one," said Evelyn. "It was on the night of July thirteenth. I wasn't quite asleep when I saw Wilfred standing beside my bed looking down at me. I saw him clear as I do you. He had on a green suit, and a cream waistcoat brocaded in a leaf pattern. Under his chin, pinned to the stock was a small dark tie—such as we've never seen over here. He wore a white bag-wig with two rolls on either side his face, and his eyes held the rueful beckoning smile he so often gave me. He spoke to me and called me Lilith—it was a joke we had." Evelyn paused for breath, she coughed twice, yet she was smiling as she went on. "He called me Lilith because she was Adam's first wife, and he found her far more fascinating than humdrum Eve."

"I see," said Jenny, and now in maturity she did see many pathetic aspects of Evelyn's strange love, which she had never glimpsed before. "What did he say in the dream?" she asked gently.

Evelyn clasped her hands, still staring into space. "He said, 'You've had a long vigil, my poor girl, haven't you! You've been faithful a long time to this laggard lover. 'Tis over now, I sail today. I'm coming for you!'"

Jenny was silent. She did not know whether she believed or not—yet there was a night when she had dreamed of Rob, and seen him the next day. There was also the time here in the old house at Westover, when she had had a vision of Rob in the wilderness and seen the very stream now called Fluvanna, and the hill she had named Tosson.

"So you see," Evelyn went on quite matter-of-factly, "if he sailed July thirteenth, he will be here any day, indeed I've been looking for a ship on the river this past month."

Against Evelyn's certainty and exaltation Jenny had nothing to offer. Three months was a long passage, but by no means unheard of, if the winds were contrary, if there were storms, or if the vessel encountered pirates. Evelyn had always had a secret and uncanny sureness. She was imbued with it now. Though again she was coughing, the short dry hackings which she covered with a handkerchief.

"Evelyn," said Jenny, "you cough a good deal, dear, and you don't seem well."

Her friend turned on her, showing the same fierce anger she had shown her father. "It's nothing!" she cried. "A stupid cold! Why do you all harp so!"

"It's only that you want to be strong and at your very best when Sir Wilfred comes. Take the ginseng Mr. Byrd recommends, and eat a lot, won't you, Evie?"

"Oh I do!" Evelyn said, her anger gone. "I choke down all the eggnogs they give me, and—you haven't commented on my gown. Wilfred likes green. Do you think it becoming?"

Of course! Jenny thought. *That's* why she looks so different. Evelyn was no longer wearing the grays and whites of half mourning, her gown was a leaf-green velvet, over a hooped brocade petticoat of bottle-green.

"It's most becoming!" said Jenny. "It vastly suits you. Only you need a flower in your hair." She jumped up and picked two marigolds.

"There," she said fastening them high to the left in Evelyn's soft dark waves. She pulled a curl over one shoulder. "Now!" she said. "You look very like the portrait of you—and as you did when Sir Wilfred last saw you!"

Evelyn smiled, then frowned. "I hate that portrait because of the cardinal above my shoulder. The horrid bloody thing. I made Father put the portrait in the attic."

"How very silly," said Jenny briskly. "You know, I believe you need diversion. Come with us to Williamsburg!"

Evelyn stared. There was a touch of her old impatient scorn as she said, "Didn't you understand what I've been telling you? I must be here when the ship comes, which it will do very soon."

Jenny thought of using reasonable arguments, that the ship might dock at Yorktown, and that wherever it docked Sir Wilfred would have no trouble finding Evelyn, yet she did not speak, for her friend went on in a happy voice, "You know it's just occurred to me, Father's going down to the Assembly next week. That's probably when Wilfred will arrive, so that we may be alone together here for a while. I'm not in the least afraid of Father. But he does fuss so!"

Down Jenny's back there went a quick shiver. Evelyn's speech was perfectly lucid, granted that it was based on a premonition, her tone in speaking of William Byrd was quite as it used to be, and yet— Then Jenny realized another change in Evelyn. For the first time in their long friendship Jenny felt herself much the older of the two. How strange and disturbing to feel maternal towards Evelyn.

During the two-day visit at Westover, Rob and William Byrd were unexpectedly congenial. Rob was impressed by Byrd's new library, which contained nearly 4000 books in several languages, and he was impressed also to find that Byrd actually had read most of the books. Byrd warmed to Rob's admiration and finally rather shyly asked if he would like to hear excerpts from some "English writing" he had toyed with. This writing proved to be a humorous, rather bawdy, and very informative "History of the Dividing Line" —the boundary which Byrd and a large party had run between Virginia and North Carolina in 1728.

Rob was highly entertained by it, and said so. He asked why Byrd did not publish the account, and was surprised to have his question shrugged off with a smile. "I take a lesson from the mother bear," Byrd said, "who never permits her cubs to be viewed by the world until they are quite licked into shape."

Rob was startled by this modesty. Jenny was also, when Rob told her of it as they rode away from Westover. "How little we really know our fellow beings," Rob said, and Jenny, thinking of Evelyn, agreed with a sigh.

The Wilsons arrived in Williamsburg just before the opening of the autumn Assembly and consequent "Publick Times." Nor would they have found lodging in that crowded little town except that Byrd gave them a letter to Mrs. Sullivan, owner of Marot's Ordinary. Jean Marot had been a servant of William Byrd the First's; and his widow, the inn's landlady, now Mrs. Sullivan, was much indebted to the Byrd family. She finally produced a tiny room, which at least was private, and clean.

Jenny was delighted. She hung out of the one window, watching the colorful traffic on Gloucester Street, as the Burgesses and Councilors streamed into town. Chariots and chaises rolled by, here and there a coach. There were many horsemen, and a few carts laden with produce for the market square. Presently a sedan chair appeared on the cobble sidewalk opposite Jenny's window. It was carried by two Negroes in scarlet and gold livery, and obviously contained the Governor's lady, since the royal arms were painted on the door and passersby all curtsied or bowed. The sedan chair stopped at the apothecary shop and Jenny watched, fascinated, as Mrs. Gooch emerged.

"Hoops are evidently smaller," Jenny announced to Rob, who was shaving himself at a cracked mirror. "And she's wearing a broad leghorn hat over her own hair. Lots of ruching, but no lace. That striped gown is pretty. Red and white."

Rob grunted amiably, scraping away at his stubborn beard. "We'll get you something to wear, besides that black. Something blue, I hope. I've a fancy for blue!"

Jenny drew her head in and smiled. "There's a milliner just down the street. I see the sign. Rob, have we money enough for new outfits for both of us?"

"Aye, love. If we don't go hog-wild. We're going to enjoy ourselves on this trip!"

At the sudden radiance in her face, and the grateful seductive look she gave him, he threw his razor onto the stand. He took a quick step and grabbed her against him. "So, my lass—" he said half laughing. "And have you *that* in mind?

I'm more than willing. 'Tis the best way I know to start off our junket!"

He lifted her in his arms and put her down on the bed. She made a token resistance, for the pleasure of being wooed. And Rob did woo her; he kissed the tip of her nose, and her ears, he whispered love words, as he undressed her; until the wish for teasing play left both of them, and they stared into each other's eyes with the grim, intent look of passion. Their bodies had always responded to each other, but this time they achieved a depth of response and a height of joy neither had known before. While afterwards they lay quiet—floating in a blissful contentment. "Happy," whispered Jenny in wonder, turning on his shoulder to kiss his half-shaven chin. "Happy. What a silly little word to express *this* feeling."

"Aye," said Rob, and rested his cheek against the soft golden hair.

The happiness lasted, with one exception, throughout their stay in Williamsburg. Jenny found a blue muslin gown at the mantuamaker's, it was secondhand and consequently cheap, even after alteration. She embellished it around the neck and at the elbows with white ruffles. She bought a flat straw hat which tied with ribbons under her chin like Mrs. Gooch's. She bought a small hoop petticoat, and cream-colored gloves and a pair of fashionable black kid slippers. Thus attired and having been told how pretty she looked by Rob, she felt herself suitably dressed, though not as elegant of course as the *rich* planters' wives who rode by in silks and satins. Rob had the tailor make him a maroon broad-cloth suit of a conservative style, then added a small brown tie-wig from the wigmaker's, and a cocked hat discreetly edged with silver braid.

No longer feeling like back-country yokels, the Wilsons took in all the sights. There were horse races outside town, and they often went to see them. Rob would not bet. Jenny was a bit disappointed and thought briefly of her father—of the York races and the lucky bets which had resulted in the purchase of Coquet.

The Wilsons twice watched the mustering of militia on the market square. And Rob, who had not touched his pipes in months, was moved by the fife and drum corps to wish he'd brought them along. They ate sometimes in their own inn, but often they sampled the other taverns—Blue Bell, Red Lion, and Wetherburn's. The latter's real name was the "Raleigh," but the landlord, Harry Wetherburn, was so genial and influential a man that his personality pervaded the

Raleigh, which was always crowded with Assemblymen. It was too expensive for Rob and Jenny to do more than drink a glass of small beer there.

One evening they went to the theater to see *The Beggar's Opera*. Rob had great difficulty in securing seats for this most popular production which had opened in London nine years ago, and made Polly Peachum, Macheath, and their songs, famous even here in Williamsburg. Eventually Jenny and Rob found themselves squeezed into a narrow space on a bench in the pit.

From the moment that the curtains parted Jenny was enchanted. Doubtless the actors in this touring company were not exceptional. They did not have to be. The comedy carried itself, so did the songs and their familiar tunes and fresh, apposite words. Polly was pretty and appealing, her husband, the highwayman Macheath, was a swaggering gallant. As did the rest of the audience, Jenny followed their turbulent love story with breathless interest. She laughed and applauded when the rival wives Polly and Lucy sang in duet, "I'm bubbled."—"I'm bubbled."—"Oh, how I'm troubled!"— "Bamboozled and bit!"

So absorbed was she that when the curtains parted for the last scene in Newgate prison's Condemned Hold and the highwayman began his farewell song, "Oh cruel, cruel, cruel, case! Must I suffer this disgrace?" Jenny thought only of the two girls who fought to claim Macheath, and she waited in suspense until she could be sure that Polly would win.

It was during Macheath's song that Jenny suddenly noted Rob's unnatural quiet, and that he held himself stiff as a ramrod, while staring at the stage, his eyebrows drawn into the frown she dreaded.

"What's the matter?" she whispered.

Rob jerked his chin towards the stage. "Yon's nothing like Newgate's 'deathhole'! They're making a mock of it!"

Startled, Jenny gazed at the flimsy canvas walls painted to look like stone, with a barred window and a few fetters inked in. "It's only a play," she said dismayed. "I never thought, Rob—I mean—it's supposed to be *funny*."

"It's not so funny when you've been there," he said.

"Papa too," she said, speaking more from astonishment than anything else.

"Aye," he agreed, so loud that the woman in front shushed him angrily. "Your father too. And I don't like reminders o' the past."

"Shall we go?" she faltered, upset by his vehemence.

He shook his head. "I paid plenty for these seats."

There was very little more to the play, though what there was Jenny neither saw nor heard, aware that Rob had gone into a black mood of the kind he had shown her but once or twice since their marriage. The play ended to the spirited tune, "Lumps of Pudding," and the Wilsons silently filed out with the rest.

This sad interruption to their gaiety was fortunately ended by the sudden appearance of William Byrd outside the theater. He had been with old Commissary Blair watching the play from a stage box, and he had noticed Jenny and Rob in the audience, also noticed their greatly improved appearance. He came up to them and bowed to Jenny. "How d'ye do?" he said smiling. "Having a good time in the capital? Wilson, I've not forgot your land grant. The Council sits again tomorrow, and I expect to put it through then—there's been so many."

"Thank you, sir," said Rob, his face clearing. He had found a lawyer, and sent in his application to the Council the day of their arrival in Williamsburg, then heard nothing further, and caution had kept him from showing his lump of mineral to anyone until the land was patented.

"Come take a glass of punch at the Raleigh with me," said Byrd, who had already had madeira served him in the box, and felt mellow.

The Wilsons accepted gratefully, and Byrd, pleased at the admiring glances Jenny attracted, gave them supper at a table in the Apollo Room among the fashionable crowd of Councilors and Burgesses. Jenny was relieved to find that Evelyn had seemed well when Byrd left her, coughing less and eating better.

It was also through Byrd's kindness that the Wilsons went to the King's Birthday Ball, which was held at the Capitol on Monday, October 30. The festivities had already lasted two days. The town was most beautifully illuminated—a candle in each window. Cannon had been discharged and the colors displayed on every public building.

The ball itself was very lavish. Governor Gooch might and did complain bitterly of the expense to himself, yet he knew the worth of such festivities in cementing the Colony's loyalty.

The Capitol was accordingly lit up in a dazzle, and garnished with greenery, and the throng—which included Rob and Jenny—made obeisance to the Royal Surrogates and were mightily impressed.

This was a far more public ball than the one Jenny had

gone to at the Governor's Palace. The rooms were mobbed with guests of all degree, except of course pretty tradesmen and servants. Jenny enjoyed herself thoroughly, for there were fiddlers and French horns playing in an anteroom, the myriad bayberry candles gave forth fragrance, and the tables in the cleared committee rooms were loaded with punch and wine and elaborate sweetmeats.

It was only when they started drinking toasts to King George and the royal family that Jenny thought of the purpose of the ball. She stole a quick look at Rob. He was in high spirits, having this morning received his grant of five hundred acres near the Slate River. And now he had just encountered a Mr. Holman who was one of the Burgesses from Goochland. Rob and Holman were talking frontier conditions animatedly, though they paused and drank the toast as the Governor proposed it. "To our Glorious Sovereign, King George the Second of Great Britain! Long may he reign!" cried Governor Gooch.

I can't drink to that, Jenny thought, feeling both embarrassed and a trifle foolish. What difference did a long past and childish oath of allegiance to King James really make? And yet it did. King James still lived, and near him in Rome—as Lady Betty wrote—lived her father.

Under cover of the cheer and huzzahs which greeted the toast, Jenny slipped behind the curtains of an embrasured window. There she could see Capitol Square and the Governor's guard, who marched to and fro behind the cannon which boomed out a salvo after each toast. There were a great many toasts. To Her Majesty Queen Caroline. To Frederick, the Prince of Wales. To Augusta, the Princess of Wales. To William, the Duke of Cumberland, and so on down through several princesses. The Hanoverians seemed very well established, a most prolific lot, Jenny thought in a detached way, while the cannon boomed and the people cheered. She knew that her behavior would seem silly to Rob, that it would in fact annoy him, as did any reference, no matter how oblique, to her father.

Rob, however, did not notice her disappearance until the toasts were well over, so interested was he in discussing with Mr. Holman methods of improving navigation on the upper James. Then Jenny beckoned to him, and he joined her in the window to watch the fireworks.

On the morning of November 4, Rob and Jenny, still in bed, were talking of their departure. Besides their clothes they had bought sundries in Williamsburg, mostly drugs, the Peruvian bark which controlled fever, laudanum for toothache, a few spices and unguents—all things they could cram into their saddlebags. The main supplies Rob would get at Shocco before they boarded their boat. Also, he would have to hire a stout lad to help him row and sail up the river against the current. Rob was eager to get home, and remarkably cheerful considering that he had finally had his lump of ore assayed, and found that it was copper pyrites. "Fool's Gold," he said ruefully. "But never mind. I'd not of known what to do wi' a gold mine, and I *do* see how to develop an ironworks, if I can ever get some labor in for that new tract. Mr. Holman said he knew of several families we might persuade to settle near us. I'm to talk it over with him this afternoon."

"Good," said Jenny absently. She was depressed this morning—not at the prospect of being back at Snowdon, for she had had enough frivoling, and was as eager as Rob to be sure that all was well at their plantation. Her depression came from the discovery that she was not with child. Two days late, and she had so hoped—though had not mentioned this to Rob.

From the distance, Bruton church clock clanged out seven times.

"Well—" Rob yawned, "we'd better get up! I've grown lazy as a lizard. Can't get ahead *that* way—now what!" he interrupted himself as there was a pounding on their door and the landlady's urgent voice.

"Mrs. Wilson! Mrs. Wilson! You're wanted!"

While she was bundling on a dressing gown and hurrying downstairs, Jenny had an intuition. It was no surprise to see Eugene standing on the landing, his eyeballs rolling anxiously, his underlip thrust out. "Oh, Miss Jenny!" he cried. "Please to hasten to the Marster's. Theah's trouble at Westovah!"

"Miss Evelyn?" said Jenny.

"Ah reckon so. She'm took bad—or leastways that's what Cap'n Randolph come to tell Marster. They's waiting foh you."

Jenny and Rob dressed fast. In ten minutes they had followed Eugene down the street to the house where Byrd kept permanent chambers. William Byrd was in his parlor, wearing a flowered dressing-gown, a nightcap on his shaven head, writing last-minute notes with violent stabs at the paper. Captain Edward Randolph was pacing a strip of Turkey carpet in his restless, rolling sea-gait.

"What's *happened?*" cried Jenny as they entered the sitting room.

Byrd gestured to the Captain. "You explain, Ned. I must finish this letter to the Governor."

Randolph bowed to Jenny, nodded coldly towards Rob, and said, "I've got the *Gooch* anchored by Westover—sailed in night before last. I've brought furniture Colonel Byrd ordered from London. It's been a long voyage, since I ran foul of the edge of a hurricane in September and was blown—"

"Yes, yes," said Jenny. "What about Evelyn?"

"Why, Miss Evelyn seems to be ill. Mrs. Byrd is so much concerned she begged me to summon the Colonel—and *you,* ma'am, at once. She says Miss Evelyn particularly asked for you."

"How ill?" said Jenny.

"I didn't see her again before I left, but Mrs. Byrd said she'd had a kind of swoon, and then spat up a cupful of blood."

"Which signifies nothing!" said Byrd sharply. " 'Twill do her good like any blood-letting."

Even Randolph could distinguish fear under this remark, and he shook his head. "I hope you're right, sir."

"Did you bring over any passenger from England?" asked Jenny, with a nervous glance at Byrd and speaking as casually as she could.

"Passenger?" repeated the Captain, his weather-beaten face puzzled. "Why, I had a few, but they'd all shipped for Norfolk, and I landed them there."

"Any letters?" said Jenny, very low.

"A sackful of letters directed all up and down the James, and some for here which I'll leave at the Raleigh to be distributed."

"I mean letters for Evelyn."

"There might've been," said the Captain. "There was a packet for Mrs. Byrd and the Colonel—my quartermaster sorted them." He was puzzled by her questions, and dismayed to find that she had all her former attraction for him. He had been angry at the way she had treated him eleven years ago—leading him on then leaving him flat for this great lunkheaded jail-bait, and he'd relieved his hurt by marrying an English girl, Miss Grosvenor of Bristol, on the very next voyage back. A good wife, and no body, face, or hair of the kind to upset a man and make him jealous.

As for Jenny, she hardly saw Randolph at all, except to

467

note vaguely that a full set of china teeth made him look quite old, as did the deep crow's-feet around his blue eyes. All her thoughts were of Evelyn, which Rob—awkward as this delay might be—quite understood. Nor was he ever a man to neglect the payment of a debt, and he knew how much he owed to Evelyn's friendship.

"You'll be leaving at once, sir?" he asked Byrd, who nodded.

"Yes. The coach must be at the door. Ned, will you deliver this to the Governor? It explains my absence at his supper tonight."

It was four o'clock and drizzling, when Jenny and William Byrd arrived at Westover in Byrd's coach. Rob had stayed to finish up his business and would follow in a day or two. During the long drive up the James the occupants of the coach found little to say. They chatted a while about the King's Birthday Ball; Byrd asked a few questions pertaining to life in Goochland, then he pulled a volume of Tillotson's sermons from the door pocket, put on a pair of spectacles, and began to read.

Only once did he break the silence. It was after the troublesome ferry passage across the Chickahominy, when Byrd said abruptly, "I *don't* believe there's cause for anxiety about Evelyn. You know how strong and brisk she's always been. The instant I get home I'll consult *Radcliffe's Dispensatory*. Are you perchance any relation of Dr. John Radcliffe's?"

"I think he was a cousin of my father's," said Jenny politely. "Was he a good doctor?"

"The best. I sent him a Negro boy once as a present, Juba. He gave the lad to the Duchess of Bolton—Evie was two at the time. She used to play with Juba before he left here. It doesn't seem like twenty-eight years." Byrd picked up the book of sermons again, opened them with some violence, and began to read doggedly, while his hands trembled on the cover.

Maria Byrd received them at Westover's doorway. Her lace cap was awry, her mild eyes peaked with worry. "Evelyn's no worse," she announced. "At least I don't think so. Yet she won't eat and she just lies on her bed with such a strange expression, as though she were listening for something. Mr. Fontaine's with her, though she didn't seem to want him."

"I'll go right up!" said Byrd. "Have you sent for a doctor? Not that there's one of them worth a farthing in Virginia."

"I sent Tom for Dr. Tschiffeley, but he hasn't come yet."

"Bah! That Swisser. I'll soon find what's the matter myself!"

"Will—" said Maria putting a timid hand on her husband's arm. "Evelyn wants to see Jenny at once. It's the only thing she's said."

"Very well," said Byrd impatiently, "though I should think she'd be *more* eager to see her father. Come along, Jenny."

They mounted the mahogany staircase and turned right into Evelyn's luxurious white-paneled bedroom. Evelyn lay on her four-poster, propped up with pillows, her head tilted towards the river windows. The minister sat beside her, reading from the Bible, in his mellow voice. He had now been married many years, there were two children in the rectory, and he had long since transmuted his love for Evelyn into the friendship he had desired. It was as a friend that he now stroked her hand while he read, an action under which she lay entirely passive.

Since she did not seem to notice the entrance of her father and Jenny, they came around to the other side of the bed, and her hollow dark eyes slowly focused on them. Her pale lips parted in a faint faraway smile. "I'm sorry to tear you from the fleshpots of Williamsburg," she said in a voice like the rustle of dry leaves. "Father, did you best old Commissary Blair as usual, and have you got the Governor in your pocket?"

"My dear child!" said Byrd, relieved by this echo of her normal self. In the fortnight of his absence, she had wasted alarmingly. His eye lit on a mugful of milk by her bedside. "You haven't drunk this!" he said. "I must supervise your diet, Evelyn!"

She shrugged slightly, and gave him the remote little smile, tinged this time by pity. "I can't drink it," she said, "for then I cough and it comes up—colored pink."

"There are remedies!" he cried. "Dr. Tschiffeley's coming, and I myself will consult the *Dispensatory*. A clyster—that's it! A clysterful of camomile, and cream, and poppy oil. That'll nourish you!"

Evelyn shook her head. "Dear Father," she said in the hoarse rustling voice, "I wish to be alone with Jenny. Please—please go now."

Byrd frowned, the minister silently took him by the arm, and the two men went out shutting the door.

Evelyn's eyes closed, for a few minutes she lay drowsing while Jenny stood by the bed, quiet tears running down her cheeks. Then Evelyn stirred, she opened her eyes and spoke with more energy. "Under my pillow, Jenny. The letter. Read it!"

Jenny drew out a heavy sheet of paper which had been sealed with black wax. It was addressed to "Mistress Evelyn Byrd, Westover-on-the-James, Virginia." Inside was a woman's handwriting.

London, July 1737.

Dear Madam:

My husband, Sir Wilfred Lawson, died of smallpox on July 13th. A private letter attached to his will requested that you be notified of his death whenever it might occur. This sad duty I have now accomplished.

Faithfully yours,

ELIZABETH LUCY LAWSON.

"You needn't cry, Jenny," Evelyn said. "You should laugh as I do, that I didn't think of this after my dream. How silly I was. But you see he *did* set sail on July thirteenth on a long, long voyage, and he is coming for me as he promised. I've simply to wait some more."

Through Jenny's anguished mind ran all the things that she should say. The bracing, reasonable ones. That this was a morbid coincidence, that Evelyn could get well if she tried. That she was still young, and that now that hope of marriage to Sir Wilfred was for ever ended she might find happiness with someone else. Jenny could say none of them.

"Burn the letter, please," Evelyn whispered.

Jenny took the letter to the fire and threw it in. Evelyn lifted herself on her elbow to watch, and was seized by a paroxysm of coughing. When she dropped back exhausted on the pillows, her handkerchief was flecked with blood.

Jenny went and knelt down beside the bed, she took Evelyn's hand and laid her cheek against it. "Evie, darling—" she murmured.

A tremor ran through Evelyn's hand; she turned it so the hot dry palm caressed Jenny's cheek. "You'll stay with me, won't you, until the end?" Evelyn whispered. "I'm a bit afraid sometimes."

"I'll be here," said Jenny.

The days blurred after that, days and nights of nursing shared with Mrs. Byrd and the frightened servants. The Harrisons came every day: Ben, Anne—who had grown

470

softer since her mother-in-law had died—and little Benjamin the Fourth, who was of an age to play with Byrd's son.

Dr. Tschiffeley came and went, having examined Evelyn and pronounced it "galloping consumption," for which there was nothing to do. Byrd would not believe him. He continued to try new drugs and clysters, until Jenny went to him in his library one day and said, "Mr. Byrd, I beg of you not to torment Evelyn any more with remedies which won't save her. I know you're frantic—but, you see, she wants to die."

"*Why?*" cried Byrd, raising an old and haggard face to Jenny. "Why should she? She has every luxury to make her happy, she was pleased with the new house, she's devoted to me, my wife, and the children—and as for marriage, there still are suitors."

Jenny hesitated, then made up her mind. "Evelyn wants to die, because Sir Wilfred Lawson is dead."

Byrd started. "That's ridiculous! A sickbed fancy! How dare you make an outrageous conjecture like that!"

"I'm sorry," said Jenny softly. She looked at him with genuine sympathy, and left the room.

On some days Evelyn seemed better. She awoke without a drenching sweat, she coughed less, and everyone except Jenny was hopeful. On one of these days, she was alone with Evelyn, when the latter said, "I've been thinking of our past together, of our schooldays, and what a strange life you've led." She paused and rested before going on. "Jenny, I want you to get your Radcliffe ring. It's in the oak chest in the attic. Get it and keep it with you. It shouldn't be left here when I'm gone, and surely Rob won't mind if you wear it now."

I'm afraid he would, Jenny thought. She went to the attic and found the ring in the toe of her red-heeled slipper, which lay with its mate beside the rose taffeta gown. The gown was cracked open along the folds, there was mildew on it. Jenny put the ring in her bosom, because Rob had arrived at Westover, and was waiting as patiently as possible for the inevitable—which Jenny had convinced him of.

It came at three o'clock in the morning, when Jenny and William Byrd were both in the sickroom. Jenny had summoned him an hour earlier. There was a change in Evelyn's breathing, a change in her face. Her fingers plucked constantly at the counterpane and she was unconscious. They sat silent on either side of the four-poster bed, while the fire died low, and the candles guttered.

Suddenly Evelyn sat bolt upright in bed. She opened her mouth and blood gushed out, running down the front of her white nightgown. Jenny and Byrd were both frozen, as Evelyn stared down at the bloodstains. "Why see!" she said in a strong voice which seemed to hold both wonder and amusement. "A whole flight of cardinals. They're such beautiful birds."

Jenny ran for a towel, and Evelyn turned to look at her terrified father. "Poor Papa!" she said. "You're a beautiful Byrd too, though you don't like name puns. I forgot. I don't mean to tease you, I really do love you, but you see Wilfred has come."

Jenny stood transfixed with the towel, while Evelyn slowly moved her head and gazed at the wall between the river windows. Jenny followed the direction of the huge exalted eyes, and thought that she saw against the strip of paneling a shimmer of green and a dim face beneath a white wig.

Evelyn made a small, contented sound. She dropped back on the pillows, sighed once, and was still.

PART SIX

1746

NINETEEN

All the sultry July afternoon there had been distant rumblings of thunder in the mountains. They made Jenny restless, apprehensive in a way thunderstorms never used to, for they could be so fearful in Virginia. Lightning had once killed three of their hogs, and far worse than that was the news last year of Ben Harrison's incredible death. He had been watching a storm from a window at Berkeley, two of his little daughters beside him, when a bolt of lightning felled them all.

So young Ben was master at Berkeley, as young Will was master at Westover. Jenny couldn't picture Westover without William Byrd—or Evelyn—and she had never gone back there since the day they stood beside Evelyn's grave in the little churchyard while Mr. Fontaine read the burial service in a shaking voice.

William Byrd had moved the church after Evelyn died, moved it downriver onto Herring Creek. Hers was the last burial in the old Westover churchyard by the river. Her father, who died in August of 1744, had not cared to join her there. Mr. Fontaine had written to the Wilsons in a slightly disapproving tone, that Byrd desired to be buried in his own garden with an obelisk and a copious epitaph to cover him. In fact, wrote the minister, Colonel Byrd had never mentioned Evelyn's name again after her burial, though, on the other hand, he kept her portrait in his library. " 'Every way of a man is right in his own eyes; but the Lord pondereth the heart,' " Mr. Fontaine wrote. "So *I* cannot presume to. The Colonel was a good man according to his lights, & most certainly a cultured, and at times a witty one. He has left some writings about his western journeys which are delightful, and his vast & well-thumbed library indicates a quality of intellect I fear we shall not soon see again."

A just enough summation, Jenny thought, and glanced nervously towards the mountains, where there was another growl of thunder. Her brown beagle, Spot, came streaking out from the woods, his tail flattened to his behind, his eyes beseeching.

"You don't like storms much either, do you?" said Jenny, lifting the dog and kissing his muzzle. "Well, stay with me, and we'll shut the house windows."

Spot returned the kiss and wagged his tail. Rob had procured him as a puppy from Spotsylvania, where he had traveled one summer to inspect the ironworks and furnace established near Germanna by former Governor Spotswood. Hence the dog's name. And there were other substitutes for the baby which had never come to replace Robin. Jenny kept school in the winter; she had taught all of Nero's seven children to read and write—also there was Bridey Turner, now twelve and a quick lovable child who adored Jenny.

Jenny toured her house, shutting windows and feeling as always a small glow of satisfaction. The windows were curtained in soft blues and reds which she had dyed and made herself. There was a Turkey rug in the dining parlor, Evelyn had left her that, and a mammoth silver punchbowl from London, and an elaborate walnut highboy which glorified the simpler pine pieces Rob had made.

We must give a party, Jenny thought, trying to lift her mood of apprehension. As the oldest settlers in these parts it was high time they asked the new neighbors. There was Dr. William Cabell, who had established himself across and up the James, not twenty miles away, and Peter Jefferson, whose wife had been a Randolph—they lived farther off; yet, with trails so much improved and actually a few roads built, distances had shortened greatly. There was even a courthouse now, across the river, and their county, carved last year from Goochland, was christened "Albemarle." Rob said it would probably have another new name someday, so fast was the western tide progressing, and she knew this did not altogether please him. He wanted more land, and the best was already taken up. Nor did Rob like to feel crowded.

However, they should give a party, and she would coax Rob to play his pipes. He was always so busy that he seldom found time for them; while at night, after doing accounts or worrying about the crops, Rob tumbled into bed and fell into a heavy sleep, often seeming to forget that she was there beside him and waiting for at least a goodnight kiss.

On impulse, in their bedroom Jenny changed from her workaday calico to the blue muslin dress they'd bought in Williamsburg. She combed the twisted-up plaits which kept her hair out of the way in hot weather. The hair was still very thick and fell to her waist, but wasn't it of a duller gold than it used to be? She pinned it up in a more becoming style and peered into the wavy greenish mirror.

"I'm thirty-six, Spot," she said to the dog. "Do you think I'm still pretty?"

Spot bounded towards her, wagging himself frantically.

"Thank you," she said. "No one else ever tells me. Come, we'll go find Willy. I want him to kill me a chicken for supper. 'Tis too hot for ham."

Jenny and the dog went outside, and she cast a practiced eye over the various departments of her realm. In the flower garden, some of the roses should be picked and the hollyhocks staked against the coming storm. In the vegetable garden the runner beans were ready. She looked beyond the paddock and tobacco sheds, and the cabins and the barnyard to the north tobacco field, where Nero and three of his sons were pinching suckers from the young tobacco plants. Black clouds hung heavy over the Green Mountains beyond, but perhaps the storm would not come here after all, the air seemed lighter.

She found Willy in the workshop, which housed all the skilled activities needed on the plantation—blacksmithery, carpentry, hidetannery. Willy was squatting on a cobbler's bench sewing on the sole to one of Rob's boots. He greeted Jenny with pleasure. "I've been wanting to ask ye something, ma'am, private-like."

"Oh?" said Jenny. "By the way, how's Peg? Is she taking the bark I gave her?"

He nodded. "She had a fit this morning, though she soon stopped shivering, and'll be all right tomorrow, always is the third day."

Peg never seemed to get "seasoned" as the others had, and developed fever every summer.

"Where's Mr. Wilson, d'you know?" asked Jenny.

"Gone to the mill, where they'd broke the wheel; he's mending it. Ma'am—" Willy put down the heavy cobbler's needle, and fixed his one bleary eye intently on Jenny, "have ye heard any more news about the Rising in Scotland? I keep a-thinking of it."

Jenny took a quick breath and shook her head. She too kept thinking of the rumors brought three months ago by an Indian trader. The trader said that the Young Pretender, Prince Charles Stuart, had landed in Scotland last summer with a force of six thousand men, that he had been victorious everywhere, and when last heard of in November was marching into England. Jenny had listened to this with poignant emotions. There had been an unconsidered leap of joy for her father. Was his passionate dream to be realized at last? Was it possible that there would be another Stuart restoration, and the king to whom she had sworn allegiance sit on his rightful throne?

Not possible at all, said Rob angrily. The English had more sense, as they'd already proved, and anyway he didn't believe the rumors. There were always Jacobite rumors of one kind or another, and they invariably turned out to be as wispy as the feckless lot which caused them. "And moreover," Rob added, frowning at Jenny, "what interest is all of this blather to you? I thought you'd forgot that Jack nonsense long ago."

"It's not surprising," she replied coldly, "that I should be interested in what might so concern my father."

"Whom you've not even heard from in twenty years," said Rob with brutality that was a measure of his annoyance. They had not referred to the subject again, but there was a constraint.

"I wish it could be true," said Willy sighing and picking up his needle. "I picture him in my head—Mr. Radcliffe that is—no, he's the Earl now, to be sure—I picture him riding next to the Prince, on a great white horse charging at the head o' the army, so gallant an' so bold like he was at Preston. He's waited long enough for his revenge."

Jenny too could picture this, and felt again the spurt of joy, followed by guilt, then anger, because of Rob's unreason. "Willy," she said, "do you understand why Mr. Wilson dislikes it so when the Jacobites are mentioned, or my father? It didn't used to be that way, at least, he helped my father to escape from Newgate."

Willy's wise eye turned sympathetically to her brooding face. "That was a long time ago, ma'am, and afore he loved you. And can ye not see reasons why he might mislike your Stuart blood?"

"Aye," she said looking away. Robin of course. There was that,

Willy had not been thinking of Robin. He was thinking of the strange jealousies which lurked in a man's breast, and of

477

how fair and winsome a lady Mrs. Wilson was.

"Then too," said Willy puckering his monkey-face, "he might dread what King Jemmie'd do to these Virginia lands. And I needna tell you how hard Mr. Wilson's worked to gain his lands."

"I never thought of that!" she said, startled. "Do you think King James *could* take back the land that King George has granted?' '

"I believe he *could*," said Willy. "I do not think he *would*. Yet Mr. Wilson has prospered here under Hanover, and so he might reason like that."

"I see," said Jenny slowly, relieved and contrite. Willy was doubtless right, and she would put away the hurt resentment she sometimes felt. She would also put away any thought of what was happening in that far-distant England, she would forget once more the father who had certainly forgotten her, and think only of the pleasant enough duties she had here, and of her husband. She asked Willy to kill the chicken—one task she abhorred—and went back to her kitchen to make an arrowroot pudding, of which Rob was extremely fond.

As though Rob had shared her resolution to patch the tenuous rift between them he came home for supper in a very good mood. He brought her a trout he'd caught above the mill and cleaned it for her. He noticed her gown and said that blue became her, and it was about time for another jaunt to Williamsburg. He praised the arrowroot pudding and agreed that they might invite the neighbors for a party. He said he must practice the pipes and got them out from a cupboard, while she sat down with her knitting. There were always stockings to make. Spot curled up at her feet.

The rumbles of thunder began again, and Jenny said, "I wish the thing would break. I was on edge earlier, though I'm never afraid when you're with me."

"Wey—hinny," said Rob, smiling and drawing a few notes from his chanter. "That's a canny speech. Will ye sing, love?"

He hadn't spoken quite like that in ages, and she was delighted. No premonition stirred in her, no impulse to touch wood, none of the usual superstitious fear that when matters go well fate is waiting to pounce. Even when the dog barked and Rob turned quickly to listen, saying "I hear horses outside, we must have visitors," she felt only pleasurable anticipation, put aside her knitting and rose as Rob went to open the front door. She held back a little as was proper, waiting for him to greet the callers whoever they were, and saw Rob clutching the knob of the open door in utter silence. She saw too that he had hardened into what she called his black look.

A voice outside spoke—a Northumbrian voice. It said, "Rob Wilson? Is it indeed you? I've had a de'il o' a time finding ye in this bloody wilderness where ye've buried yourself."

"And why have you wished to find me?" said Rob scowling and unmoving.

Jenny walked forward, and peered at the man on the doorstep.

A middle-aged dapper man, dressed in a smart black grosgain suit, a cocked hat, edged with a gold line, on top of a neat brown bag-wig. He had a sharp mottled face, which she did not recognize. But the eyes which looked beyond Rob to meet hers were cocky, humorous, deferential, and piercing. She knew those, and gave a cry of unbelief. "Alec! Alec Armstrong! It can't be!"

"It *is*, m'lady," said Alec, taking off his hat and bowing. "May I come in? And is there some place to stow the lad who's guided me here?" He ignored Rob and asked his questions of Jenny.

"Yes," she said. She put her hand against the wall to steady herself. "I don't understand. I feel giddy."

"Come into the parlor. You can sit down," said Rob to her in a toneless voice. "You too, Alec. The lad may go to the kitchen. We'll feed him presently. Here Jenny, drink!" He poured out some apple brandy and gave it to her. "Now, Alec, what means this! What are you doing here?"

"I've come for her ladyship," said Alec. "Her father has sent for her."

Jenny clenched her hands on a fold of the blue muslin. The brandy warmed her stomach but the giddiness continued.

"Why do you call my wife a 'ladyship'?" said Rob in the same flat voice.

"Because her father is now the Earl of Derwentwater."

"Is the Pretender, then, on England's throne?"

Alec hesitated. He looked away from the grim hazel eyes beneath the formidable eyebrows. "Nay," he said finally. "Not yet. There's been a miscarriage of the plans." There had in fact been the Battle of Culloden, a defeat so crushing that his lordship had not seemed to credit the news. Yet it was next day that he sent Alec off on the long search for Miss Jenny.

"Ah," said Rob. "Then Charles Radcliffe is attainted for treason, as he ever was, and his title but a heap of straw, and I'll thank you to address my wife as 'Mrs. Wilson,' which is all the title I am able to provide her with."

"Fakins!" Alec cried jerking his head. "Don't ye come the master over *me*, Robert Wilson, my Tyneside pit laddie! Ye may remember that I knew ye as a stable boy at Dilston, and I watched ye muck i' the cow-byre at the Snawdon peel, no matter what a piddling position ye've made for yoursel' in the wilds o' nowhere!"

Rob's eyes glinted, a white line showed around his mouth. "You can have supper, and a bed in the barn," he said hoarsely. "Tomorrow you'll go back as you came!"

"Not wi'out her ladyship," said Alec. "I come to fetch her at her father's wish—and I will." He was much shorter and ten years older than Rob, yet the men stood poised glaring at each other as though ready for equal combat. Jenny stood up and walked between them.

"Where is my father?" she said to Alec.

"In the Tower."

"*The Tower!* You mean he's a prisoner?"

"We was captured," said Alec flushing. "On a ship bound for Scotland to join the Prince—last November. Eighty of us was captured, besides his lordship and his son, Lord Kinnaird."

Rob exhaled his breath slowly, and sat down in his armchair. "So—" he said, "Radcliffe's not even seen the fighting, has he! I presume there *has* been some? And he's been caught again, as he was t'other time. And he has the insolence to think my wife would mix herself into his degraded affairs."

Jenny twisted her fingers together, yet she gave her husband a level cold look, and said, "Rob, I don't like your tone, and I don't like your words. Courtesy alone should make you hear a man out who's traveled all these thousands of miles to find us, but—"

"Aye," he said. "But I'm *not* courteous or gently bred! You knew that when you married me!"

She turned to Alec, whose face had gone impassive, as a well-trained servant's should, and she said, "Since my husband so dislikes the news you bring, I think you'd better tell it to me elsewhere."

She gestured towards the door and preceded Alec from the parlor. Rob poured himself a mugful of brandy and downed it in three gulps; then he sank back in his chair and sat scowling at the andirons.

Jenny led Alec around the gardens and outbuildings to Willy's cabin, which had a trim wooden porch on which he sat smoking a clay pipe and watching a murky purple sunset over the distant hazy mountains. "Willy," said Jenny, "I've brought you a most unexpected visitor. You will want to hear what he has to say as much as I do."

Alec talked for some time, while Willy asked excited questions, which gradually subsided into discouraged grunts. Jenny was silent. Alec told them of the Jacobite rejoicings of the last summer when it was known that Prince Charlie had finally sailed for Scotland. That he had landed safely, that Scotland had risen to join him. Prince Charlie had been treated as a king in Edinburgh, at Holyrood Palace—the home of his ancestors. There'd been an easy victory at Prestonpans, and no opposition to speak of, when the Prince's army marched into England and took Carlisle. Then they marched down the Western Road as they had in the '15, through Cumberland, Westmoreland, Lancashire, and into Derby.

Here the Prince had been forced to heed shocking bad advice, Alec thought. All his councilors were for retreat. They were afraid of the Duke of Cumberland's army only nine miles away and they were discouraged by the English lethargy. So few had risen to join them. They waited in vain for a French invasion to help them; besides that, the Highlanders were uneasy, as they always were on English soil. At length the Prince had turned and started the dreary march back to Scotland.

"But we didn't know *that* when *we* sailed o'course," said Alec with a heavy sigh. "All we'd heard of was victories."

Alec went on to tell his silent listeners that four years ago Charles Radcliffe and his family had moved back to France, to St. Germain, where Charles could be more active as agent for the Cause, and that he then took a commission as a colonel in the French army.

All the summer of Prince Charlie's successes in Scotland, Charles Radcliffe had been mustering arms, money, and men to follow the Prince on a privateer called *L'Espérance*. There had been delays, and they were held up by weather, but they finally sailed from Dunkirk in November, bound for Montrose. "His lordship," said Alec, "was happy as a lark, gay like I hadn't seen him in years. He'd been fretting in Rome and St. Germain—waiting, waiting while our Cause never seemed to ripen. The day we sailed he laughed that hearty rippling laugh o' his, like when he was young."

"I know well," said Willy quietly. "Then what went wrong?"

Alec hurried over the account of what had brought them to such misery and humiliation. They'd been sailing off the

Dogger Bank almost to their goal when King George's man-o'-war *Sheerness* had caught them and fired a cannon across their bow. The privateer's little French captain was a coward; he wouldn't fight, though in truth they were not equipped to battle a man-o'-war. All the passengers had been transferred to the *Sheerness* and carried down the coast and landed at Deal in Admiral Vernon's custody. Charles Radcliffe and his son, Lord Kinnaird, were treated very roughly, kept in fetters all the way to London, and pelted by the mobs. That was because, Alec explained, a rumor'd got about that young Kinnaird was really Prince Henry Stuart, King James's younger son. "On account o' his fingers growing together," said Alec. "The Stuart sign. They both have it."

Jenny pulled herself in tight and glanced towards the live-oak and the little tombstone beneath.

So Charles was imprisoned in the Tower, Alec went on—a concession to his rank. Lord Kinnaird too, but he had later been released and shipped back to France, on parole, since he had been born abroad and was technically an alien. Clement McDermott, Charles's equerry—"that mingy long-faced Scot," said Alec—he had been jailed in Newgate and then released, as had Alec himself and others captured on the *L'Espérance.*

"Ye see—" Alec said, "we wasn't caught fighting, and they couldna prove we weren't bound for Ostend or The Hague on private business. So 'tis only his lordship that bears the brunt."

"On what charge then?" asked Willy.

"The old one of thirty years agone. High Treason, and the death sentence already passed."

"Could he not profit from the Act of Pardon?"

"It seems not, because he escaped. His lawyer, Mr. Garvan, says the best plea would be to make them *prove* he's the same man as that Charles Radcliffe who was condemned, and the lawyer's done his best to confuse the matter by calling his lordship 'le Comte de Derwent' and claiming he's a French citizen, and colonel in the French army, which is true."

"There's been no trial yet?" said Willy.

"No, and there won't be yet awhile because the bloody bastards are so busy wi' the Scottish lords they captured at Culloden. The Duke of Cumberland, God rot his soul, he's the butcher who cut Prince Charlie's Highlanders to ribbons, and he was still at it when I left."

"Is my father defeated too?" said Jenny speaking for the first time.

"He wilna admit it," answered Alec with another sigh.

"Yet there's a sad change in him, he's not like himself—'tis all these months imprisoned—and nobody nigh to help or comfort him. Her ladyship's at Saint Germain wi' the children."

"What about Lady Betty?" asked Jenny. "She helped him before."

Alec leaned forward in astonishment to peer through the gathering dusk at Jenny, who sat on the step, her head leaning back against the porch pillar. "Lady Betty's dead!" said Alec. "She has been this five years or so. Didn't you *know*, m'lady?"

There was a silence before Jenny said, "No. Nobody writes to me from England any more."

There was another silence, then Alec burst out with vehemence, "Oh, my lady! He longs bitterly to see you again! It's become an obsession o' late. He talks of the time we went to Dilston, the time i' the chapel when we opened the blessed Earl's coffin—" Alec crossed himself quickly, "and of how you were wi' him then, and he said, 'If I'm to follow my martyred brother, I want to see Jenny again, for she's the only person except my brother that I've loved—and she promised me that if I wanted her, she'd come!' "

"I didn't—quite—promise," Jenny said very slowly. Still she leaned her head against the post, and her eyes rested on the dim outline of the hills across the river. "I will lift up mine eyes unto the hills, from whence cometh my strength. My strength is from the Lord." But there was no strength as yet—and no certainty.

"He doesn't think that you might help him," went on Alec in some desperation. So accustomed was he to obeying Radcliffe orders that it had never occurred to him she might refuse. "No, he doesn't think o' that, but *I* do. No one need know you're his daughter. As Mrs. Wilson ye could slip unnoticed about London, ye can maybe gain influence in high places if need be. Ye're a beautiful woman, Miss Jenny, there's a lot such a one can do."

She turned then, and asked in a low, steady voice, "In how much danger do you think my father is, Alec?"

He hesitated; he put his hand over the little wooden crucifix which was hidden beneath his shirt. "Blessed Virgin, we must have faith!" he said thickly. "Aye, one must have faith. Yet I fear—fear that he is in the greatest danger o' being hanged, drawn, and quartered at Tyburn on his original sentence." Alec's voice broke, he bowed his head.

Jenny turned her somber gaze back toward the hills. One

star trembled above them. The storm was not coming, she thought. Not the thunderstorm.

Willy blew his nose violently on his shirtsleeve. "Ma'am?" he whispered into the darkness. "Ma'am? Ye've *got* to go, he needs ye and ye must go."

Jenny got up off the step, she looked towards the two men who were the only beings in Virginia who would understand.

"Yes . . ." she said. "Yes, I've got to go."

"Thank God, my lady!" Alec cried. "And I've passage for both of us on the *Elizabeth* for London. She leaves next week."

Jenny went back to her house, she saw Rob through the door, sunk in his chair in the parlor holding a mug, and Spot was with him, curled up against his boots. This was the first time the dog had not followed her when she left the house, and though Spot raised his head at her return and wagged his tail, he did not rush to greet her, nor did Rob move. Jenny tightened her lips and went upstairs, where she pulled her old saddlebag from a cupboard and began to pack.

In ten minutes she heard Rob's unsteady footsteps coming up the stairs. He stumbled into their bedroom and shut the door against the dog, which whined and pattered away.

"What are you doing?" said Rob. He stood in the center of the drugget rug, a great lowering man who reeked of apple brandy.

She made a helpless gesture towards the saddlebag. "You see what I'm doing, Rob. But 'tis not for aye. It need only be a while. I beg of you, try to understand."

He folded his arms across his chest, his eyes narrowed to tigerish slits of yellow, yet he spoke with some control. "I ever knew 'twould come to this. I knew that naught I could ever do would satisfy ye long. And so, your ladyship, y're going back to the fine lords and ladies ye were reared with. Ye'd leave me for that mawking sprig o' royal bastardy—for a man who ne'er earned a penny in his life—whose very bread is paid for by his wife!"

She shoved aside the bag and her eyes flashed. "That last's a very odd taunt for *you* to hurl at my father!"

"What do ye mean by that?" he cried. He swayed and caught himself. "What d'ye *mean?*"

Jenny's throat constricted as she saw the sudden dilation of his pupils, and she saw too the long scar left by the iron collar on his neck.

"I mean nothing," she said. "I don't know what I said. But

you're so bitterly unfair, Rob. And you make a god of your pride. I think it no worse to make a god of loyalty as my father has. Rob, my dear husband, we're both fair distraught. Please don't let's quarrel now. I couldn't bear to go like this."

He scarcely heard her, red mists swirled in his head, he forgot what they had said as his blurred eyes focused on something else.

"You're wearing the Radcliffe ring, I see! Forbye, no doubt ye always wear it when m'back is turned!"

"No, Rob, you know better than that. Yet I should have worn the ring as I had promised. There's no hurt to you in that!"

"Ye can tak' mine off, then! 'Twas never grand enow for ye!"

"Robbie, Robbie," she said, trembling and afraid of the look in his face. "You're somewhat drunk, dear—you can't throw twenty years of marriage off like that—of good and loving marriage . . ."

"A sham!" he shouted. "*You* can throw it off in a trice, if Charles Radcliffe lifts his little finger towards ye! Bah! Ours is a barren marriage!"

She stiffened and stepped back. "That's true." Her gray eyes had gone hard. "You wish to hurt and you're succeeding."

He threw back his head and gave a furious, hollow laugh. "Aye, I wish to hurt, and, your ladyship, afore ye go I'll gi' ye something to remember me by!" Quick as a cat he lowered his hand, and struck her across the mouth and cheek. Even while she staggered and cried out, he grabbed her around the waist, lifted and threw her onto the bed.

He tore her blue dress off in one vicious motion. Still stunned from his blow, she struggled and screamed, while he pinioned her with frenzied strength.

He raped her violently.

When he had finished, he tossed her aside, got off the bed, stamped to the door, and went out banging it behind him.

She moaned and lay as he had left her, her whole body bruised, blackness in her heart.

She did not see Rob again. He did not come back to the house that night, nor had he come when she left with Alec in the morning.

Willy said that he'd still been up, talking to Alec on his porch, when Mr. Wilson streaked by him like a whirlwind. He'd gone to the stable and must've saddled a horse, for they heard the thuds of galloping later until the sounds disappeared down towards the Slate Mountains.

With horrified sympathy Willy stared at her swollen lips and the red marks which disfigured her cheek. And Peg spoke up, "Oh mum, did he hit ye? I niver thought Mr. Wilson'd do that!"

Jenny did not answer. She looked towards the little tombstone, and then towards the tobacco fields, where Nero, Shena, and their entire family were already at work. "Say goodbye to them for me," she said to the Turners. "You need tell them only that I've been summoned to my father."

Bridey, who had been standing awed and frightened beside her parents, gave a gasp and cried, "Oh, ma'am, ye're coming back, aren't ye?"

Jenny tried to smile at the child, but her lips were swollen stiff. And Rob's blow had loosened a front tooth which ached.

"I'm afraid not," she said with difficulty. "I had meant to, but it seems I'd not be welcome. Bridey, take care of Spot." She reached down to pat the dog, which she had found whinning outside the bedroom door at dawn. "You'll be all right," she whispered to the dog. "You're fond of him, and he has no cause to hate *you*." Spot thumped his tail and looked up at her mournfully.

She hugged Bridey, and Peg quickly, shook hands with Willy. All three were in tears. Jenny was not. Her eyes were fixed, stony. She mounted the other horse Alec had brought. The lad who had been his guide would go down the river again on some flatboat, and Jenny knew the landway, which simply followed the James.

The horses started off; at a turn in the road Jenny looked behind. She waved to the Turners, and saw that Bridey was on her knees holding Spot and sobbing. She looked beyond the child to the house standing foursquare and solid beneath the great oaks. The morning sunlight glinted off the windowpanes, the rosy bricks, the white clapboards. Her heart was steeled against it. Farewell, Snowdon, she thought. Farewell to all the side of her Snowdon represented, back and back to that early childhood in a crumbling peel tower in Northumberland. She twisted around in her saddle, and flicked the horse, which broke into a trot and carried her past the bend into the forest beside Alec.

Jenny and Alec made a fast trip down to Yorktown, where they arrived on the fourth night, having covered some fifty miles a day. Along the way there were settlers now, who were invariably hospitable and eager to provide food and a night's lodging, for which some of them even refused payment. Charles had furnished Alec with a hundred guineas for the journey, though to do this he had had to make sacrifices. "A day or two afore I left," said Alec, "his lordship requested from that blackguard Williamson who governs the Tower, that he might live wi'out suppers, and save two guineas a week board there."

"Oh, poor Father!" Jenny cried, encouraging every mention of Charles, casting her mind constantly forward into what awaited her, so as to preclude other thoughts. "Is he then so short of money?"

Alec shrugged sadly. "He had to pay seven guineas a week i' the Tower, wine, tea, and warder's fees extra. An' he's been there months. And there's the lawyers. We didna expect expenses o' this sort when we started out. Her ladyship'll send him funds from St. Germain when she can and mebbe his niece, my Lady Petre'll help, though she hadn't when I left. 'Tis risky for the Petres—being Catholics—in times like these. Besides, there's spies all o'er the Tower, and if his lordship's relation to the Petres was known, that's the end o' pretending he's not Charles Radcliffe."

"I see," said Jenny, trying not to be disheartened about her father's situation. *There* at least she was needed, and she talked incessantly with Alec as to what they'd do when they got to London. Both of them always ignored the fact that it might be too late.

There was much else to dishearten them both, Everyplace they stopped along the James, at Richmond, at Williamsburg, and in the ordinary at Yorktown before they boarded the *Elizabeth*, Virginians were exulting over the victory at Culloden. The news had actually been brought on the *Elizabeth* along with Alec, and Jenny found the *Virginia Gazette* full of the "glorious battle" and the ignominious flight of the Young Pretender, who was skulking somewhere in the wilds of Scotland.

At Yorktown the night before they sailed, Jenny and Alec had to endure the racket of a parade along the waterfront, in which the effigy of Prince Charlie dressed as a Highlander was dragged in a cart and then hanged, while a band played and the crowd cheered. There was also comic relief: a huge drunken man dressed as a nurse, waving a warming pan with a doll in it, while the mob, stamping and laughing, roared rhythmically "No Pretender! No Pretender! No Pretender!"

Jenny kept to her room, and Alec sat morosely by the bar, drinking ale.

It was a relief to sail, and a relief to sail from Yorktown, which she had never seen before and which held no memories. She leaned on the poop taffrail and watched the Virginia shores recede. Her lips were no longer swollen, the front tooth had ceased aching, she felt well. Beside her stood a plump middle-aged English lady, Mrs. Clarke, who would share Jenny's cabin. Mrs. Clarke was returning home after a visit to her distant kin, Governor and Mrs. Gooch in Williamsburg. She had earlier visited a younger son of hers who had settled as a planter on the Northern Neck. She disliked Virginia. "My dear, the *heat*, the mosquitoes, and all those blacks underfoot, I shall be so glad to be home!"

Jenny found this comforting. Mrs. Clarke had little curiosity and assumed from her speech that Jenny was also an English lady returning from a visit. She asked only one question—as to where Jenny resided at home—and was perfectly satisfied by the hesitant reply, "London." She forthwith chatted happily about her own affairs, her house in Kent, her grandchildren, and Jenny in one corner of her mind congratulated herself on the lack of drama or poignancy in this moment which she had dreaded.

The wind was fairly from the west, the ship sailed fast and steadily from the York's mouth into Chesapeake Bay. A fiddler played lively tunes on the deck below. There were few passengers to applaud him, but such as there were, Jenny thought, looking down, were *free*.

There were no slaves, white or black, on the eastbound passage. Each one was traveling at his own will and desire. There was comfort in that too. Then in a second Jenny's armor was shattered by a blast of pain, nor for a moment did she know why. She stood bewildered, clutching at the taffrail.

"Why, what ails you, Mrs. Wilson?" cried Mrs. Clarke, interrupting herself in a thrilling description of her eldest grandson, who had won an exhibition at Eton. "Are you seasick?"

"No, no," said Jenny hardly knowing that she answered. " 'Tis the tune he's playing."

Mrs. Clarke looked astonished, and listened. "An old dance, 'Sir Roger de Coverley,' I believe," she said.

Against the flowing blue waters of the bay, Jenny saw her wedding day etched sharp, the scene in the old parlor at Westover, Rob playing the pipes at Evelyn's request, and herself dancing, dancing frantically with William Byrd.

Jenny spoke again without volition. "Here we—" She checked herself. "Here they call it the 'Virginia Reel.'"

"Indeed," said Mrs. Clarke, hoping that her cabinmate was not a trifle odd. "There's no accounting for *what* they do in my opinion. Now as I was saying, Basil's an extraordinary child and—"

The fiddler changed his tune. Jenny's pain receded. She looked down at her wedding ring, the little twisted gold wires. She had not left it on the pillow in their bedroom, as she had meant to. Though she slid it up and down her finger now, she could not quite fling it into the heaving waters of the Chesapeake. Why not? The Radcliffe ring was on her other hand, its massive gold, encrusted with diamonds at the sides, its bull's head crest, its peculiar motto, "To hope is to fear."

"My dearest Jenny, you can't have it both ways. A house divided 'gainst itself must ever fall." That was Lady Betty's voice, years ago about some childish choice, no longer remembered.

Jenny pulled off her wedding ring, and put it into her pocket. Later on, no doubt, she would get rid of it.

The nine-week voyage pursued a normal course. There were calms, there were squalls, there was a pirate scare. Once they were a day from shore, the passengers forgot Virginia and could not envision England. They were locked in a separate world of their own, where shipboard incidents alone had meaning. Jenny grew very tired of Mrs. Clarke, and through the kindness of their Captain—Judson Coolidge—escaped into reading. The Captain owned several entertaining books, among them *Gulliver's Travels, Pamela,* and *Robinson Crusoe.* There was also a volume of Edward Young's, *Night Thoughts,* but Jenny let it alone, after discovering that Lady Betty's husband had produced the gloomiest of poesy, dealing mostly with death.

Though on some mornings Jenny felt queasy and their breakfast porridge revolted her, she thought little of that; even the dauntless Mrs. Clarke had seasick moments. It did occur to Jenny one day that the time for her monthly courses must be past, yet she did not allow this thought to disturb her protective insulation. Shock and sea voyages often produced untoward effects on the female; or perhaps it was the beginning of "the change." She had scant knowledge of feminine physiology, nor means of acquiring it; but Peg Turner, her only informant, had already had the change, and Shena had ceased breeding. Jenny plunged into a volume of the *Spectator* she had unearthed at the bottom of the Captain's book locker.

Captain Coolidge found Jenny very attractive. He made her sit next to him at meals, he paid her compliments, and tried to squeeze her hand after he had had a round of grog. Jenny smiled at him, listened to his yarns, and took an interest in the cargo, which was mainly hardwood, furs, and a few belated hogsheads of tobacco from last year's crop

One morning they passed the Scilly Islands, and presently saw Land's End to the north. "Land ho!" the lookout called. "Land ho—!" The passengers rushed to the rails. The fiddler came running and struck up "A song, a song for England, her woods and valleys green, Huzzah for good old England, and England's King and Queen!"

The passengers sang, the crew joined in—unchecked by Captain Coolidge. Jenny sang too, though her voice faltered, and her eyes were full of tears. She descended the ladder to the main deck, where she had spied Alec sitting on a hatch and smoking a clay pipe. He arose instantly and bowed, as she approached, putting down the pipe. "We're almost there, Alec!" she cried.

"Aye, madam," he replied solemnly. She had persuaded him to drop her title, since anonymity was essential. "An' I've a creeping up me spine," he added with a twisted smile, "for only God and His holy angels know what awaits us."

She nodded, and from then on during the days the *Elizabeth* sailed along the southern coast, then around the Foreland and into the Thames estuary, Jenny was no longer easy, nor could lose herself in reading.

On October fourth at Gravesend they picked up a pilot. Jenny, gazing at the cluttered little seaport, thought of Pocahontas, the homesick Indian princess who was buried here. And that was the last time for many weeks that Jenny had any conscious thoughts of Virginia.

Captain Coolidge stepped back as the pilot took charge, and Jenny, moistening her lips, put her head through the wheelhouse door and said to the Captain, "Could you—I mean would it be possible to ask him, sir, what's the news of the Rebellion?" Jenny gestured towards the pilot.

"Why o' course!" said Coolidge heartily. "Ask him yourself, ma'am. Ye won't disturb him. Jeb Sykes can sail the Thames blindfold, can't ye, Jeb?"

"Ar-r—" the pilot agreed ."Wot's the lydy wanter know?"

"The Jacobite Rebellion," said Jenny, "what's happening?"

"Ain't nuffink 'appening." The pilot took his eyes from the

490

river for an instant, and stared astonished at his questioner. " 'Tis all deader'n mackerel. The young Pretender 'e skulked abaht fer a w'ile in Scotland, but 'e's safe in France naow. We been 'anging and be'eading most of the other rebels ter wind up the business tidy, ye might sye."

"Rebel prisoners in the Tower?" Jenny asked faintly.

"Them Scotch lords!" said the pilot, shrugging. "They be'eaded two of 'em in August—Lords Balmerino and Kilmarnock. They died beautiful—I saw 'em—'twas a fair treat."

"It seems to me—" said Jenny. She stopped and started again. "Did I hear in Virginia that there was a French earl—count, I mean, in the Tower, a name like Derwent?"

The pilot nodded. "Oh 'e's still there. Some question abaht 'im, abaht 'oo 'e is. Lord Lovat's in the Tower too—they finally got 'im, the old villain—I 'ope 'e 'angs."

Jenny dared ask no more. She thanked the pilot and went in search of Alec, to whom she gave the information. Now and then on the voyage they had each had moments of great hope. The news of Culloden might have been exaggerated, or the French might have landed to reinforce the Prince, who might yet have been victorious.

"*Thank God*, Father's still all right," Jenny whispered, "but the Prince is gone, he went back to France."

Alec sighed, he creased his thin mottled face. "A failure," he said. "Like his father afore him, yet I didn't think this bonny young prince'ld fail. And I *canna* see why he turned back at Derby. London was in a panic, they was scurrving and hiding and fleeing. I was there, an' I know. And the Usurper's armies was *behind* the Prince. 'Butcher' Cumberland to one side, General Wade far away. The Prince could've took London, and even if he couldna've held it, my master'd 've been released."

"I know," she said, and added in a whisper. "The Stuart Doom."

"Don't ye say that, madam!" cried Alec fiercely. "Don't ye even think it! That's no way to help him!"

"You're right," said Jenny. She looked at the riverboats gliding by, saw that the cottages grew closer together, recognized ahead the Palace at Greenwich. London was very near.

Jenny's heart gave a frightened thump, but she spoke with determined briskness. "Have you decided what's the best way to present me at the Tower?"

Alec shook his head. "I'll not be sure till I've been there m'self—see who his warders are now—and, Blessed Mary, I hope he's got hold of some money, we've only nine guineas left."

"I've been thinking," said Jenny slowly, "that instead of me going to those costly lodgings in Piccadilly, I'll find me a job in a tavern as barmaid, and I can sing a bit. Aren't there music taverns in London?"

Alec was shocked. "Madam, ye could not demean yourself like that! Fancy *you* serving in a tavern!"

She smiled at him. "Oh, I'm not made of delicate stuff. And I'm very used to work, besides what difference does it make, since no one in London knows me anyhow?"

Alec, though reluctant, could not deny the practicality of her plan. And she was no helpless girl now. She was, Alec thought, a real "ladyship," with an air of quiet authority which should handle any rough men who'd try liberties. And they'd try for sure. She was still a beauty, her yellow hair curling under her hood, her lashes dark and thick around the long eyes, her wide mouth red above the cleft chin, and the graceful way she moved her slender body, which seemed tall but wasn't. Ingrained loyalty prevented him from ever criticizing a Radcliffe, even privately; yet he did wonder what madness had possessed her to lower herself to that brute of a Wilson.

The *Elizabeth* docked in the Pool beyond the Tower. Jenny glanced once at the forbidding gray fortress as they passed it. She made no comment, nor did Alec.

After they had landed, Alec hired a hackney, stowed their skimpy luggage in the boot, and started off with Jenny to find her lodging and a job. The coachman, when consulted, proved sympathetic, and suggested a couple of nearby inns which might prove likely. While they drove to the first inn, Jenny had much ado to keep up her courage. The smells, the noises, the bustle and confusion of London appalled her. Had it used to be like this? There was stench from the open sewage gutters, from pigs rooting in garbage, and the all-pervasive coal smoke. She hadn't smelled coal smoke in twenty years. And then the racket, the rumbling of drays on cobbles, the constant clop of horses, the creaking of signs, the screaming street cries—"Who'll buy my oranges?" "Milk below!" "Old shoes to mend!" "Cockles and oysters alive, alive oh!"—interwoven with the jangling bell of the muffin man and the whine of beggars—"A penny for the love o' Gawd, a penny, kind masters!"

There were so many people, crowding, shoving, shouting on the sidewalks, as the coaches and hackneys and drays went by spattering mud. "It's bedlam," said Jenny, putting her hands to her ears.

Alec, who was pleased to be back in London's bustle, and heartily sick of wilderness and shipboard, said grimly, "Well, 'tis quiet enough i' the Tower."

"Aye—" she said. She let Alec go and inquire at the first two inns whether anyone wanted a barmaid. They did not. The coachman had no other suggestions, and Alec, who was anxious to get her settled so that he could see his master, said they'd better go to Piccadilly after all, when Jenny was seized with an idea.

"Wait!" she cried. "There used to be an inn where they had music, and splendid pork pies. Mr. Byrd took Miss Evelyn and me there once when we were at school in Hackney. It was at Spitalfields—the King's Arms, something like that. Tell the coachman!"

They went back through the City and up Bishopsgate, where they turned right for the Spitalfields district, which was the center of London's silk industry. The narrow streets were lined with weavers' cottages, here and there were studded the more pretentious houses of silk merchants. The weavers had a second trade, they caught and sold singing birds. Little cages containing thrushes and linnets hung before the cottages. In the center of the district was a market square, nearby it a long half-timbered building with Michaelmas daisies growing by the door. This was an inn, the King's Head, the one for which Jenny was searching.

She left Alec in the hackney this time and went inside herself, spurred by memory and intuition. The inn was very old and built around a courtyard. She went past the taproom, where two men were drinking. She heard from another room upstairs the tinkle of a harpsichord, the squeak of a fiddle. She had some trouble finding the landlord and his wife, until, directed by a chambermaid, she knocked upon the door of their private parlor.

The landlord was called John Potts. He was stout, ruddy, and had a wary eye. The landlady was also stout and ruddy and decisive. She had iron-gray hair under a mob-cap trimmed with mauve bows; her eyes were black, and shrewd like her husband's. They were both in their mid-fifties. He had his feet on the hob and was smoking a pipe and reading the *Gazette* Mrs. Potts was knitting, having finished a pint of bitters, and the hour being a slack one in the King's Head.

They both turned in some annoyance as Jenny entered and dropped a curtsey.

"Well, wot d'ye want?" said Potts, who didn't like his privacy disturbed. He took another look at Jenny, and sketching a rise to his feet, added "madam" uncertainly.

"Please to forgi'e me, sir," said Jenny softly. "I'm looking fur wark, and wondered would ye have some? I can sairve bar or tables, I can sing a bit."

Both Pottses contemplated her suspiciously. The landlady noted the good stuff, though worn, in the out-of-date clothes, and she noted in the voice a fluctuating and familiar accent. The landlord saw a pretty woman, with an air about her which might please his Friday night musical customers, who were mostly quality.

"Wot can ye sing?" he said. "Let's 'ear!"

Jenny cleared her throat, and after a quavering start sang a verse of "Begone Dull Care." As neither of her listeners said anything, she sang "My Lodging's on the Cold Ground" with a plaintive charm which would not have disgraced her great-grandmother, Moll Davis.

"Not so bad," said Potts grudgingly. "Though very old-fashioned!"

"I could ler-rn new ones," said Jenny eagerly. She turned and looked pleadingly at the silent landlady. "I beg ye, ma'am, ter gi'e me a chance. I'm in gr-reat need o' board and keep."

The landlady pursed her lips, a faint twinkle appeared in the small black eyes. "I'm a-wonder-ring," said Mrs. Potts meditatively, "why ye *speak* a bit like a Northumbr-rian, and *sing* like Southron gentry."

At the lilt in the questioning voice, Jenny was sure. Her dim memory had been correct. It was during the last month of her school days that Byrd had taken the girls here, and said, "The landlady comes from the uncivilized North somewhere near the Border, and I've heard is even a Jack, but we'll overlook that in favor of a pork pie, and a ballad or two."

"I've ler-r-ned m'speech in different places," said Jenny, giving a brilliant smile to Mrs. Potts.

"She sounds like a Scot ter me!" interposed Potts with renewed suspicion. "I don't want no Scots 'ere!"

"John, you booby," said his wife impatiently. "Can't ye *iver-r* tell the difference? Whate'er she may be, she's na Scotch."

The landlord grunted. Mrs. Potts continued to knit. Jenny decided on a bold move.

"Isna that dried heather, ma'am?" said Jenny pointing to a jug which stood on the mantel. "I'm a lover-r o' heather-r, especially white, though I've found none masel', an' I'm a

494

lover-r o' white roses—though 'tis too late i' the season for them."

"Faw!" said Potts, knocking his pipe out against his boot, and lumbering up from his chair. "Wot crazy talk. Belike the woman's drunk. Get rid o' 'er, Bella. I'm off to the cellars, to fetch up the port." The door slammed behind him.

Mrs. Potts continued to contemplate Jenny steadily. "Would ye knaw a *song* about white r-roses?" she asked quietly.

"I could hum one," said Jenny, and she hummed the tune of "When the King Shall Enjoy His Own Again."

Mrs. Potts's eyelids flickered, the color deepened in her apple-red cheeks. "Are ye truly Northumbr-rian?" she said.

"Aye," said Jenny with a sigh. "And so are you, ma'am. I beg o' you to help me."

"What is it?" said Bella Potts after a moment. "You're no sairving maid, an' shouldna want to be."

Jenny bit her lips, then spoke in a desperate rush. "I've come to London to—to be near someone who's in prison. He was captured in the Rising. I fear greatly for him. I've no money, and must find work."

"Your husband?" said Mrs. Potts.

Jenny shook her head, afraid to say too much, uncertain what clues might lead to the identification of her father.

"Your sweetheart then?"

Jenny implied assent, she put her right hand to her hair, and pushed a lock back nervously.

Mrs. Potts started. She got up and came towards Jenny so quickly that Jenny had no time to move. Mrs. Potts grabbed Jenny's hand in a vicelike grip, and peered down at the ring. "What're ye doing wi' *this!*" she cried. "Did ye steal it?"

"No," Jenny cried turning white. " 'Twas given to me! And, and what's it to *you!*" She snatched her hand away and put it defiantly behind her back.

Mrs. Potts gave a small bitter laugh. "D'ye think a body bor-rn in Cor-rbridge wouldna knaw the Radcliffe crest?"

Jenny did not move, there was a roaring in her ears, her heart beat in sickening thumps. What a fool to come here! What a wicked fool to forget to turn the ring under as she had meant to!

The landlady suddenly sat down, and motioned Jenny to the chair Potts had vacated. "Divven't gawp at me like that!" she said in a softer tone. "But ye better speak the truth, lass. Ye needna fear me. M'first husband was out i' the 'Fifteen wi' the Erringtons under James, the Earl o' Darntwatter.

495

M'man was hanged at Lancaster. I've had no traffic wi' the rebels since, an' I *want* none, yet I'll not betray one neither, especial if they're from the North."

Jenny collapsed in the landlord's chair. Different possible stories sped through her mind, denials—some lord had given her the ring, she hadn't known what it was—she was going to sell it for benefit of the sweetheart in—in Newgate. Careful! she thought. Already she had made a bad mistake.

Mrs. Potts put down her knitting. "Lyeuk here, lass," she said briskly. "Ye needna tr-rouble yoursel' fadging up a tale fur me. Time an' time agyen I've seen Charles Radcliffe i' the Angel's taproom at Cor-rbridge, thirty years agone it was, yet a blind mole c'ld see ye're his kin. An if ye want a job here, ye'll be honest!"

"Oh-h," Jenny whispered. She bowed her head a moment, then lifted it and said, "Very well."

In hesitant, broken sentences she told Mrs. Potts most of the truth. She did not mention her marriage, she said only that she'd been out of the country, and her father had sent for her.

"But, ma'am," she cried, "they can't prove that the man in the Tower is Charles Radcliffe, for he denies it. Do you understand me, ma'am?"

"Aye," said Mrs. Potts after a moment. "And I want naught ter do wi' the situation, one way or t'other. I've suffered enow through Radcliffes in me day, an' Potts he hates the rebels. But I'll help a fellow Northman this far. I'll gi'e ye board'n lodging wi' four shilling a week, sae lang as ye' wark well, hours from six 'til we shut o' nights. Days ye may ha' to yourself—fur any skulduggery ye've a mind to. But *mark ye*," said Mrs. Potts sternly, "ye'll not go about prattling o' white roses, nor mentioning this subject ter me, or anybody agyen."

"Thank you, Mrs. Potts," said Jenny faintly. "I'll remember." Here was not the ally she had hoped for, and yet one must be grateful that the first problem of her return to London was solved.

TWENTY

Several days passed after Jenny landed in London before, on October 9, she was able to get into the Tower and see her father.

On each of those intervening days Alec reported to Jenny, though not at the King's Head. Jenny scrupulously observed her promise to Mrs. Potts that no private business should be transacted there. In the market square adjacent, among stalls and bins of vegetables—mostly potatoes—and amid the twitters of singing birds for sale in cages, Jenny had no trouble meeting Alec casually. He was cautiously laying the groundwork for her introduction to the Tower.

In August, Charles had been moved from his suite in the Lieutenant's Lodging to make room for Lord Traquair, another captured Scot. The Lieutenant-Governor of the Tower was General Adam Williamson, a small-minded and vindictive old man, who disliked all his Jacobite prisoners and treated them as badly as he dared. In fact Lord Balmerino just before his execution announced that had he not just taken the sacrament he would be glad "to knock down the Lieutenant of the Tower for his ill-usage."

Williamson particularly detested Charles, who was a Papist, who drank King James's health openly, and who wrote justifiable letters of complaint to the Secretary of State, the Duke of Newcastle—thus going over Williamson's head. On the theory that it might cause Charles the maximum mental anguish, and also induce the admission of his identity, Williamson, in August, transferred his prisoner to the Beauchamp tower, to the very chamber where James, the Earl of Derwentwater, had spent his last days. The chamber, long disused, was dank and bare, inhabited by spiders and rats. Charles disappointed Williamson by complete silence when the latter took pains to inform him who had been imprisoned there.

As it happened, said Alec, in explaining all this to Jenny, his poor lordship had had a bit of luck in the move, by acquiring new warders. There were two yeoman warders, or Beefeaters, responsible for Charles's security. One of them, called Cox, was the Governor's tool, sly, greedy, and insolent. However, Hobson, the other warder, was a brawny middle-aged man who happened by great good fortune to have been one of James's guards here thirty years ago. He had conceived an admiration for the Earl, and was inclined to be sympathetic towards his brother.

"But Alec!" Jenny protested. "Nobody *knows* that!"

"They suspect, madam. It's clear Hobson does, yet so far they can't prove it unless his lordship's trapped into admitting it. 'Tis a legal quibble, yet may save him when he comes to trial."

"When will that be?" she asked steadily.

"Next month, his lordship thinks. That brute Williamson won't tell him much, and what he does—my master don't always remember." Alec flushed and looked down at the miry marketplace.

Alec had been grieved by his first sight of Charles, after the valet had had his credentials reattested and been allowed the privilege of daily attendance in the Beauchamp tower. State prisoners of rank, before they came to trial, were always permitted a personal servant to come in and shave them, take away their laundry, and bring sundries to augment the prison fare. The prisoners were also allowed certain other visitors, at the discretion of the Governor, and an airing on the battlements if a warder were in charge.

Williamson constantly tried to curtail these privileges, even to excluding Charles's lawyer, and flatly refusing to admit a priest. Charles therefore wrote angry and pleading letters to the Duke of Newcastle, scrawling them in pencil since he was not permitted pen and ink. The Duke usually ignored these pleas, if indeed he received them. And that the letters might not always be coherent Alec was now unhappily aware.

Charles had been like a trapped, snarling old badger when Alec finally saw him on the morning after the return to London. It was several moments before his master recognized him, once the warder had let Alec into the dark bare dingy cell which was only furnished with a table, chair, and rickety wooden bedstead. Wind whistled down the great, old fireplace, for which a porter furnished coals, if he were well enough paid.

"Where've you been, you faithless villain!" Charles cried furiously, after Alec succeeded in rousing him from a semi-drunken stupor. "You've been skulking off to France to save your hide like all the rest of 'em, I suppose!"

"My lord—my lord—" said Alec. "I've been a journey, 'tis true—but ye sent me on it—and 'twas not to France, don't ye remember?"

Charles's bloodshot eyes focused slowly, some light came into them. "You went for Jenny," he said. "I had forgot you went for Jenny. There's been no one of my own to see me since you left, and I live with beasts in shadow. Beasts in shadow—" he repeated thickly. He picked up a mug from the table and took a long draught. The mug contained gin which the warders could supply much cheaper than wine.

"My lord," said Alec, with a glance at Hobson, who stood impassively by the door, in his flat Tudor hat, his starched white ruff and embroidered flaring crimson tunic, his halbred held out at arm's length. "My lord, I've brought—uh—the young woman you sent for. She—she loves you dear."

"Ah—my Jenny," said Charles in a dreaming voice. "Has she indeed come to me? When can I see her? She'll fight the beasts in shadow, won't she? Like a sunbeam is my Jenny. *'Auprès de ma blonde, qu'il fait bon, fait bon, fait bon, Auprès de ma blonde, qu'il fait bon dormir!'* "

Charles's chin sank forward on his chest, his breathing grew sterterous. Alec looked sadly at the warder. "Is he often like this now?"

"Often enough," said Hobson. "Ye know I feel sorry for 'im. Don't 'e 'ave a wife, nor friends nor nobody? 'Is brother when 'e was 'ere, in this very cell, I mind 'ow 'is poor wife used ter come often, an' they took comfort in each other. Touching it was."

"The Count had no brother in the Tower!" said Alec sharply.

The warder shrugged. " 'Ave it *your* way, mate! 'Oo's this Jenny—some light o' love?"

That gave Alec an idea. He explained Jenny as an actress who had been on an extended tour, and who was devoted to the prisoner. "A matter o' many years," said Alec with truth. He mentioned her present work as a singing barmaid in a tavern, and the heartbreak she felt at learning of her lover's capture.

He made a moving story of that, and Hobson, who had sensibilities despite his grim job, said, "She might come Thursday at three, when I'm on duty. I'll tell the warder below to let her in—needn't bother the Gov'nor abaht a visitor of no himportance, an' I must admit 'is Excellency's a tough one, makes it 'ard for the rebel lords. 'E don't want no escapes like there was after the 'Fifteen. Lords Winton and Nithsdale, they both got outa 'ere. Lax we was then, I suppose. But we ain't *now*, mate!" Hobson grinned at Alec, who had not been able to hide a thoughtful widening of the eyes. "So no use getting notions in your 'ead."

Alec did not report much of his master's condition to Jenny, and he devoutly hoped that it might be one of the good days when she saw him. The only hint he gave her was to suggest that Charles had aged. And when she was worrying for fear the warders might note her resemblance to her father, Alec shook his head.

"No fear, madam," he said sighing. "Ye don't look alike no more."

On the Thursday at two-thirty Jenny met Alec in the market square. Beneath her cloak she was dressed in her working costume, one concocted by Mrs. Potts with an eye to business. The material was therefore of a cheerful red sprigged calico, the skirts very full, the black bodice laced, and the neck so low that it showed the rounded tops of her breasts. A fichu today, however, gave more modesty. Her white muslin cap, banded with fine green ribbon, was tied under her chin, and her hair fell in curls on her shoulders, an effect both youthful and alluring. In sort, Jenny was dressed as a barmaid, a rather theatrical one, and she pleased the King's Head customers, as even Potts had come to agree. Her duties were to carry drinks, to encourage the consumption of punch, which was expensive, and to sing one song at each table. Mrs. Potts had a collection of songbooks from which Jenny refreshed her memory and learned new ones. She went through her duties mechanically, smiled at everyone, and took care to speak very little. She was a successful novelty, and something of a mystery to the upper-class customers, who recognized the quality of her speech and singing.

When questioned, Mrs. Potts replied that the inn's new attraction had been a Colonial actress. This satisfied the King's Head patrons, none of whom knew anything about the Colonies.

As Alec had foreseen, her dignity and genuine aloofness discouraged most amorous overtures, and when as last night a silk merchant had got out of hand, and started fumbling for her breasts, there was always Potts to rescue her. He kept a respectable house, and wouldn't have hesitated to evict a duke if one should prove offensive.

Thursday was a dull, chilly day. Jenny shivered inside her old brown cloak and hood. It was about a mile from Spitalfields to the Tower. As Alec and Jenny hurried through the crowded lanes and alleys, she was struck again by the filth and noise of London, by the pallid ragged children swarming in the slums they traversed, and by the gin shops, one in every block, many sporting a sign tacked on the door: "Drunk for a penny, dead drunk for 2d." The proofs of this claim were to be seen vomiting into the gutters, or snoring on the sidewalk where passersby stepped over, or on them, indifferently.

"How ugly London is," Jenny said, shivering again. "I never used to think so."

"Ye didn't know *this* part," said Alec. "And I wish ye didna have to now." They were silent the rest of the way, as they went down the Minories, then past Tower Hill, where the scaffolds were sometimes erected. It was now an ordinary square filled with rumbling drays. They skirted the moat and crossed the first drawbridge to the Lion tower, which was named for the most popular inmates of the King's menagerie nearby. At the Lion tower Jenny presented the pass Alec had procured for her through Hobson. They crossed the drawbridge over the stinking, slimy moat which was used for sewage. They paused at the Byward tower, where each visitor must give the password—which changed daily, and enabled one to enter the Tower after three, and leave it again when the bell clanged for the night's key ceremony and lockup. Alec had learned today's password in the morning. It was "Daf-'fodil," which startled Jenny, and calmed her mounting panic. Such a word *must* be a good omen, especially as Alec said the words were picked at random from a dictionary. Fate then was perhaps sending encouragement with this reminder of spring, and the joy spring brought.

Having left the Byward tower, they entered the gloomy stone alley which was the outer yard, and walked as far as Traitor's Watergate to the Thames. The actual entrance to the stronghold was opposite the watergate, a narrow passage through the Bloody tower beneath an iron portcullis where a sentry stood on guard. At last they were inside the great fortress, with its thirteen prison towers strung along the

501

curtain wall. Ahead loomed the great whitish turreted stone keep, the original castle built by William the Conqueror. They turned left onto Tower Green, where there was some withered grass and a flock of agitated cawing ravens. Jenny did not like ravens; in the North they were considered harbingers of death. She held fast to the thought of daffodils. They reached the high semicircular Beauchamp tower, and Alec took his leave. The valet had already shaved and dressed his master in the morning, and was not permitted to see him again that day.

The downstairs warder expected Jenny and unlocked the door, staring at her curiously. She slowly mounted the winding stone stairs and found Hobson standing at the top, a burly figure in his Beefeater uniform.

"So there ye are, m'dear!" he greeted her pleasantly. " 'Is lordship's dithering to see ye." He unlocked the heavy barred door, and accompanied her into the chamber. Then he locked the door again and stood against it, as were his orders. Charles must see no visitor alone any more, not since his move to Beauchamp tower.

It was dim in the large vaulted stone room. The solitary window was heavily barred and set back deep in an embrasure; little of the gray October daylight penetrated. The cheap coals in the grate smoldered, a wall candle in an iron sconce flickered impotently over the damp stone walls and the dozens of inscriptions carved by other prisoners long ago.

Charles had been hunched over his table near the window. He turned when Jenny and Hobson entered. He struggled a moment, leaning heavily on the table before he could rise; it was the pains in his knees that hampered him. He was quite sober, had taken nothing but a little wine at dinner. He and Jenny confronted each other.

"Well, darling," he said in the caressing, slightly mocking voice she so well remembered, "this is scarcely the way I expected us to meet again!"

For an instant Jenny could not move. His voice had not altered, but the rest! Alec had seen to it that he was bravely dressed in an embroidered yellow velvet suit, a gray French peruke on his head, an elegant lace handkerchief in his sleeve. Yet the suit could not disguise the bowing of his back, the paunchy thickness of his middle, nor could the lace jabot and stylish peruke conceal the down-dragging lines of his face—like an old mastiff's—nor the puffiness around his eyes and the broken purplish veins in his cheeks; while his hands, which had been so slender—like her own—were swollen at

502

the joints and mottled like an old man's.

"Won't you give me a kiss, Jenny?" he said, attempting to laugh. "Do you find me so distasteful?"

"No, no—" she whispered, and she ran to him throwing her arms around his neck as she had used to do, her heart brimming with pity. He hugged her convulsively and kissed her on the cheeks, the forehead and the lips. "Thank God, you've come to me," he murmured. "Thank God."

At that she began to weep, as she had not wept in years.

The warder made a choked sound, and turning his back began to scrape at a fleck of rust on the padlock. True love, that's what it was, he thought, and mighty rare in this miserable world. The prisoner, for all his woes, was lucky to have so pretty and faithful a mistress. Hobson wanted to leave them alone awhile, and he didn't want to spy on them, but orders were orders. In thirty-two years of service at the Tower he'd never disobeyed an order.

Charles led Jenny to the bed, there was no other place where they could sit together, he pulled her head against his shoulder, while she sobbed uncontrollably, covering his yellow velvet coat with tearstains.

"Come, come, sweetheart," Charles implored. "Do hush! You've no cause to weep like this!" Though his own eyes were wet.

He held her tight, he smoothed her shoulder and her hair, so silken-soft and clinging to his hand. *Capello d'or e capello d'amor*, he thought—hair of gold is the hair of love. That was an Italian proverb, and when he had first heard it he had thought of her. It seemed to him now that through these many years he had always thought of her; that the dozens of other women had been phantasms, mistlike bodies which had never touched him and in whom he never found completion.

At last she quietened. She lifted her head and, groping, took his lace handkerchief from his cuff, blew her nose, and wiped her eyes. "I'm sorry, Pa—" she began, and checked herself with a glance at the warder. "My lord," she covered the break.

"You're a silly child," said Charles tenderly. "Once my trial's over, I'll be out of here, a free man. They can't hold me."

"I'm sure they can't," she said. "To be sure they can't."

"Let's have a look at you," said Charles, pulling away and examining her. "Lovely as ever, but what *possessed* you to dress up like a serving-wench!"

She widened her eyes in warning, indicating Hobson,

knowing that Alec, while shaving Charles, had been able to whisper to his master the role in which she was to be presented here.

"I *am* a serving-wench," said Jenny. "At the King's Head in Spitalfields. 'Tis a good situation."

Charles gave an angry grunt. "Well, you won't be there long. Once I'm free we'll go abroad, to the south of France where there's sunshine. There's a villa near Marseilles you'd love, orange trees and jasmine and the deep blue water outside the windows, you'd like that, wouldn't you, darling?" He spoke with buoyancy, believing it himself, yet a memory stirred, memory of a different cell in Newgate thirty years ago and of a redheaded woman to whom he had said much the same thing. Betty Lee, who had loved him, and was dead. No, of death one must never think. Not now, not with Jenny here, Jenny and the bright comfort that she brought.

"We must have some wine," he said. "Drink a toast together! A toast to the future!" He rose from the bed and winced. "A touch of gout—'tis the infernal dampness here, and then I'm not young any more."

You're only fifty-three, she wanted to say, and stopped herself in time. Charles Radcliffe's age was known. Alec had told her that the fact that her father looked ten years older than he should was one of the points which hampered the identification.

Hobson fetched a bottle of claret from a stone alcove, and poured out two glasses for them, then resumed his place by the door.

"To King James!" cried Charles lifting his glass. "May he enjoy his own again!" He drank, and she did too.

"He will, you know," said Charles exuberantly. "Either King James or Prince Charlie'll be on the throne of England yet!" He turned to the warder. "And you can report *that* to Williamson, if you like!"

Hobson shrugged and said without rancor, "Your sentiments're well known, m'lord. Ye've not scrupled to 'ide 'em."

"And as a Frenchman why should I!" said Charles, with a quirk of his eyebrow. "To our happy future, Jenny!" He lifted his glass again. "We'll have good times together—soon. You'll see!"

"Yes," she said smiling at him as she drank. Deep within her something twisted and throbbed painfully, yet she wouldn't heed it. The sagging heaviness had lifted in her father's face, he bore himself straighter. The shock of meeting over, she saw him more as he had been, jaunty, hopeful, touched with gallantry.

"And until then," said Charles pouring himself another glass, "you'll come every day, darling—won't you? Take dinners with me! I've some funds again. Garvan, he's my lawyer, forwarded them yesterday. Madame la Comtesse has bestirred herself to send them over from France."

The warder listened more carefully, as he had been told to do, when the prisoner made any family allusions.

"How is she?" asked Jenny politely. She had earlier wondered why Lady Newburgh was not here in London helping her husband, as had the wives of all the Scottish lords, but now she understood that the lady would be recognized, and the whole defense depended on there being no proven link with Charles Radcliffe.

"She's well, I believe," said Charles. "Much occupied with the children." He thought briefly of Charlotte and their five children: Jemmie, now safe again in France, the twins Clement and Barbara, little Charlotte and Maria. Frances Clifford too—his spinster stepdaughter, a useful woman. They were a good, solid, devout brood, and Charlotte was absorbed in them, so much so that, to his relief, she had long ago lost her vehement passion for himself. They had settled into a formal, friendly relationship, far pleasanter than the stresses and jealousies of their earlier years. He would be glad to see his family again when this embarrassment was over. Yet the prospect had none of the poignancy and charm that was offered by the hope of a villa in the south of France with Jenny.

It never occurred to him to ask about her life in Virginia. The whole subject of her ignominious marriage was distasteful to him, and he assumed it was to her—since she was here. And he noted with satisfaction that she wore no wedding ring, only *his* ring on her right hand, with the crested seal prudently turned under.

"My love," he said, putting his arm again around her. He was somewhat elated by the wine, and amused that the endearments he felt like giving her would seem quite natural—not excessive—to Hobson.

"My darling, I'd forgot you had that black mole on your cheek. A wicked little mole that would make any gallant's heart throb to kiss it." He leaned over and did so.

She hid a slight recoil, and answered in a bantering tone, "Fie, m'lord, you are most bold, and kisses should be stolen more discreetly."

The warder was much entertained. A very pretty scene, he thought. And a treat to see a bit o' love-making in this dismal place. Then he heard footsteps mounting the stairs and stiffened to attention. There was a sharp knock on the door, followed to his dismay, by Governor Williamson's unmistakable rasp outside, "Open up there, Hobson!"

Charles and Jenny both arose, he stumbled and she put her hand instinctively under his arm, as the warder unlocked the door and opened it.

The Lieutenant-Governor of the Tower was disclosed in all his majesty of scarlet and blue uniform, medals, sword in jewel-encrusted scabbard, gold-laced hat, and his private guard of honor behind him—two officers in full regimentals. Without them Williamson never visited prisoners.

"What's this! What's this!" said the Governor staring at Jenny. He was a spare, elderly, catlike man, a gray-faced man whose eyes were a pale stony blue. "What's *she* doing here?" he asked angrily of Hobson, pointing at Jenny.

"I thought no 'arm, sir," answered the warder staunchly. "She's some actress 'oo used to know 'im hintimate, ye might sye."

"Oh, a trollop," said Williamson with a curt laugh. "You forget, Hobson, I'm not the easygoing Governor that Colonel D'Oyley was. You'd no business letting her in!"

"No, sir. I'm sorry, sir," said Hobson.

Williamson, outraged by this flouting of his authority, nevertheless reflected that he had given no positive orders excluding chance females since the prisoner in eleven months had seemed to have no friends. Also, Hobson had a very long record of faithful service, and had obviously remained on guard in the cell, as he should. The Governor therefore fixed his hard blue eyes on the warder and said, "Well, did you hear anything useful to us pass between them?"

"No sir," said Hobson truthfully.

Williamson gave a snort and turned back towards Charles. "I came to do you a favor," he said in a voice he strove to make pleasant. "A letter's come for you, the messenger said it was of great importance. I thought you'd want it at once." He held out a folded and sealed white square; he even walked with it to Charles and put the letter in his hand.

Charles took the letter, and moving stiffly towards the candle. squinted at the superscription. "This letter's not for me." he cried. " 'Tis for a Mr. Charles Radcliffe."

Williamson stopped smiling. His sharp nose quivered. "Oh, for God's sake, fellow. When will you stop this farce!"

"I'll thank you not to call me 'fellow,'" said Charles. "You'll give me my title, as I know His Grace of Newcastle has enjoined you to. And I find it interesting that you should mention God, in Whom, I understand you've no belief."

Williamson saw red. From the beginning, the insolence of this man had infuriated him. "You bloody Papist traitor, God or the devil's all the same to me!" he shouted. "So long as justice is done and I get you hanged as you should be! In the old days we had the rack for such as you, there's *still* a gentle 'questioner' or two in the dungeons," he stopped, knowing that he had gone too far. Torture was no longer permitted in the Tower, and even threats were frowned upon in these namby-pamby times. He glanced back quickly at the warder, and his two officers in the passage beyond. All three stood at attention, erect, expressionless, their eyes fixed straight ahead on space.

Williamson took a breath and achived control. "You don't want your letter, Mr. Radcliffe?" he said smiling again. He had thought of another plan.

"I'm not a Mr. Radcliffe," said Charles. "It is not addressed to me!" And he flung the letter at the Governor's feet. Instantly Hobson stepped out, picked up the letter and handed it to one of the officers, then returned to his stance.

"Well, well," said Williamson, pleasantly. "There's been a mistake made, I suppose. I see you've been having a glass of wine with your young woman. An excellent idea. I believe I'll sample some, if I may, your lordship. Hobson, get a chair from the upper cell. Dear, dear—you do have rather scanty furnishing in here, don't you, my lord! We must rectify that."

Charles was wary, though nonplused. The Governor had never been civil to him before. It might be that on seeing his trick had failed he had given up the effort. Or it might be because of Jenny, Charles thought, looking at his beloved, who stood there silent and pale in her barmaid's gaudy dress, her golden curls falling on her shoulders.

This must be so, for the Governor turned to her most courteously.

"My dear," he said, "I'm sure your company is very charming, and I quite see why his lordship enjoys it, yet I must regretfully ask you to leave. The Tower soon will close for the day. Outside it's quite dark, and I think it unwise for so handsome a woman to brave the streets when it's getting late."

" 'Tis true, darling," cried Charles, instantly alarmed. "You must go! I hadn't thought of that; but I'll see you tomorrow."

She hesitated, uncertain, mistrustful. She knew that her father had had enough wine to fuddle him in his present state of health, she remembered that when one of his quick tempers was over he quickly forgot the cause. She went to him and kissed him on the cheek, whispering "Be careful" in his ear. He nodded and hugged her.

She put on her cloak, then curtsied to the Governor and Charles. "Good night," she said, her eyes downcast. Hobson stood back from the door, and she went through past the officers, one of whom gave her a quick approving pinch on the buttock. She went downstairs and out towards the Bloody tower, where Alec was patiently waiting, as they had agreed. They left the Tower together.

In the Beauchamp cell, Williamson and Charles sat down. "A tasty jade," said Williamson of Jenny. "I too always like the fair-haired ones myself. Have you known her long?"

"For some years," said Charles, with a tender reminiscent smile.

"Does my Lady Newburgh object to these—ah, little affairs of the heart?" asked the Governor casually.

Charles laughed. Silly old man, he thought, to think of catching me like that. "Who is my Lady Newburgh?" he said.

"I'm inclined to think that you know," said the Governor, also laughing, though the hard eyes examined Charles intently. "I see the bottle's empty," Williamson continued, "and it's just occurred to me that we might broach some fine old brandy I have in my cellar. Hobson, go fetch it!" The warder bowed and disappeared.

"To what do I owe this honor?" asked Charles, who was enjoying himself. He could hold his own at this game or any game the Governor wanted to play. "You've not, so far, shown a desire for my company!"

"I believe I've misjudged you, my lord," answered the Governor apologetically. "I find the rigors of my office make me irritable at times. As a matter of fact this is my birthday, which induces a certain mellowness. I trust that past disagreements won't prevent you from joining me in a toast to my birthday?"

"Not at all," said Charles. "I'm very fond of brandy, and the leanness of my purse makes indulgence in it difficult."

"Unfortunate," said the Governor sympathetically. He filled in the time before Hobson's return with tidbits of Tower gossip. Lord Traquair had suffered an attack of bloody flux and was confined to bed. There was a probability that Flora MacDonald, the Highland lass who had sheltered the young

Pretender, would soon be imprisoned at the Tower. Lord Lovat, despite his great age, and the virtual certainty of his execution, constantly brawled and played indecent tricks on his warders. "But what could you expect of the Scots?" said Williamson shrugging. "And now I realize that as you are the only Englishman of rank imprisoned here, I *should* show you special favor!"

Charles almost let that pass, so gratified was he by the change in the Governor's tone, which seemed to augur better things; as had the happy meeting with Jenny. He caught himself, however, and said with mocking reproof, "My dear Governor, you forget that I'm a French subject, and a Colonel in the French army."

"But you were *born* here, weren't you?"

"Why, that's an event I don't remember," said Charles grinning. "And one mustn't rely on hearsay."

Williamson gave a dry cackle. "*Touché.* You've a pretty wit. Ah—here's our brandy!" He gestured for the bottle which Hobson put on the table. The Governor poured some into each glass.

"Stay a moment," said Charles. "If you'd really do me a favor, will you for once dismiss those men?" He pointed towards Hobson and the two officers. "At least let us be alone awhile, I'm weary of watching eyes, I'd like to feel for a few minutes that I am as other men, simply drinking with a friend."

The Governor hesitated. This did not suit his plan, since he wanted witnesses for what he hoped to accomplish. On the other hand if he refused, he knew that Radcliffe might suddenly go surly and even decline to drink at all. "Very well," he said. "Hobson, you may wait in the passage with the others, and shut the door."

"Now we'll toast your birthday!" said Charles, much pleased. He could make the old boy do *anything*. He wasn't such a bad fellow, it seemed. The brandy was delightful, smooth as cream. So smooth it had no effect, Charles thought, except that the pains vanished from his knees, and he found himself telling ribald stories at which the Governor laughed and slapped his lean shanks. Charles's glass stayed full, he did not particularly notice why, nor notice that the Governor's stayed full for the opposite reason—because it was never emptied.

The Governor waited until he judged the time was ripe, when Charles's speech had thickened and he started tales which rambled, then forgot what he had been saying.

Williamson introduced the topic of escapes, escapes from the Tower like Lord Winton's and Lord Nithsdale's, thirty years ago.

"O-ho!" said Charles, conspiratorially, now regarding the Governor as his bosom friend. "They were sly ones, those two! Musht've been a bit o' cash changed hands too, don't you think, old boy?"

"Possibly," said Williamson. "That was before my time, of course."

"And a bit o' cash might help now? Eh?" said Charles winking. "Thash what you mean, old boy?"

"Don't be a fool!" Williamson spoke loudly, distinctly and with just enough calculated anger to touch off Charles. "You wouldn't have the brains to carry out an escape, not *you!*"

"Oh, I wouldn't, would I!" Charles cried. "Thash where you're wrong—you old simpleton. I had the brains to get out of Newgate!"

"Did you indeed," said Williamson softly. "Then I've misjudged you again. Was it on December tenth that you escaped?"

"Dechember eleventh," said Charles. "An' a raw, cold day it was."

"Thank you, *Charles Radcliffe*," said Williamson.

"What're you thanking *me* for?" asked Charles, bewildered.

"For your diverting company, Mr. Radcliffe," Williamson rose and picking up the half-empty brandy bottle, tucked it under his arm.

Charles quivered. He stared at the Governor, whose image shimmered and wavered. What had he said, what had they been saying? Charles wasn't sure, but there had been mention of Radcliffe, and tears came to his eyes. "Why do you keep saying 'Radcliffe'?" he asked in a hurt, reproachful voice. "I thought we wash friendsh. I'm Comte Derwent, you know that, ol' boy."

Williamson walked to the door, and opened it. "Come in, Hobson," he said. "You can put him to bed. I'm well satisfied."

Six weeks passed before Charles's arraignment on November 21. During that period Lieutenant-Governor Williamson inflicted on his prisoner every tyranny that was legal. There were no more visitors of any kind, not even Alec. There were no more airings on the battlement, except one in mid-November, during which Charles was marched back and forth on the narrow walk by two warders, while hostile eyes—brought here by the Government—peered and spied at him from the adjacent Bell tower. An extra warder was assigned to guard him inside his cell, so that he was never left alone an instant. His diet was restricted to the coarsest prison fare, and all wine, beer, and spirits were forbidden him completely. The latter prohibition was partly because Williamson knew it would cause Charles suffering, which it did for a while, but was chiefly from fear that drinking would kill him and thus rob the hangman and the London populace of a well-merited pleasure.

Charles spent his time in misery and in writing letters—to Jenny, to the Duke of Newcastle. The letters were discreet, there was no liquor now to fuddle his mind, and they bored Williamson, to whom they were immediately carried, and who tossed all except a couple to the Duke into the fire. Naturally there were no answers.

Still, Charles did not give up hope. He knew he must have said something foolish to the Governor, whose subsequent behavior showed how false the show of congeniality and favor had been, but he thought himself a match for Williamson. Also, Hobson, his only friendly contact with the outer world, said that he believed the Government's bloodthirstiness was sated, that in some quarters "Sweet William," the Duke of Cumberland, was not quite the hero that he had been. Many people, no longer panicked by fear of invasion, were tired of executing the captured rebels. So said Hobson, partly out of pity, for he thought the Governor's behavior shocking, though as usual Hobson obeyed orders.

The days crawled by, and Charles's health improved. His joints ached less, his paunch dwindled. He had appetite, even for the gruels and boiled salt beef the porter brought him. One day, after pacing his cell for some time, he took to examining the inscriptions on the walls. It was a crudely carved little word "Jane" that first awakened his interest. Jane was Jenny's real name, and Charles lovingly darkened the letters with his pencil. Hobson said the name probably referred to Lady Jane Grey, that most unhappy nine-day Queen, but Charles continued to view it as a link with Jenny.

Then he discovered, as James once had, that someone called "Eagremond Radcliffe 1576" had been imprisoned here, though that memento Charles thereafter avoided. There were two inscriptions made by Arundel, the sixteenth-century Duke of Norfolk who had died a prisoner in this cell. Hobson told Charles about it and added that the Duke had been a Papist; whereupon Charles mustered his feeble memories of Latin, and finally deciphered the writing: "The more suffering

511

with Christ in this world the more glory with Christ in the next. Thou hast crowned him with honor and glory, O Lord! In memory everlasting He will be just." And the other said, "It is reproach to be bound in the cause of sin; but to sustain the bonds of prison for the sake of Christ is the greatest glory."

Charles pondered these words, which were the only spiritual comfort he had. They had taken away his crucifix and rosary when they captured him and thought him the Pretender. He had been allowed to see no priest, nor, to be honest, had he much wanted one.

He read Arundel's inscriptions again, and began to think about James. The brother who had suffered here before him, the brother he had sworn to avenge. Heretofore the thought of James had brought such pain that he had kept it at bay with bravado—with drink. Now he began to question Hobson, though never admitting the relationship. The warder understood, and reminisced freely. "'Is lordship 'ad a big crucifix 'anging there on the wall. 'E used to pray to it somethink beautiful. The Gov'nor then 'e wasn't so strict abaht Papacy as this 'un."

And also, James had Father Brown, Charles thought sighing. The Jesuit priest had died eleven years ago at Pontoise. Charles missed him more than he expected to.

"'Er ladyship, the Countess," Hobson continued, "she was a little bit o' a dark lydy, sweet an' gentle an' brave, wi' child too she was. I allus wondered wot 'appened to the byby."

Ah yes, Charles thought. That posthumous child was Anna Maria, now the widowed Lady Petre, who lived at Ingatestone in Essex. She would certainly come to him after the trial, when he was freed and it was safe.

"If I'm not making too bold, m'lord," said Hobson, "that Jenny 'oo was 'ere, she puts me in mind o' 'er lydyship—not in looks o'course, nor rank, but 'er pretty manners, an' the love she bears you, m'lord—it put me in mind o' 'er lydyship."

Charles shut his eyes a second, and slumped down on his chair. "I miss her," he said fiercely. "I miss her terribly. Why'd that vicious devil have to shut her out!"

Hobson, though in agreement, was discreetly silent, and whenever he was on duty he did all he could to bolster Charles's spirits.

On Friday, November 21, when Charles had been a year less one day in the Tower, Williamson received a habeas corpus for the prisoner, and forthwith set out gleefully with

Charles for the King's Bench in Westminster Hall. They rode together in the Tower coach, and the Governor had neglected no safety precautions. Two armed officers rode in the coach, four warders, two sergeants, two corporals, and thirty-two men walked beside the coach. Everyone was armed except Charles, who had been deprived of his sword but wore his scarlet and black French colonel's uniform, a gold-laced waistcoat, a gray tie-wig, and a dashing broad-brimmed Spanish hat with a white plume.

Their procession through the City, and along the Fleet, Strand, and Whitehall, was perforce slow with such an escort. Williamson had ample time to taunt his victim, nor did he neglect to show him the row of fresh heads stuck up on Temple Bar. "There's room though for one more," said Williamson, with his dry cackle.

Charles bore it all in silence. His wits were clear, and he was trying to formulate the points that he would make at the King's Bench. The crowds along the way merely stared at the procession, unsure as to which rebel lord was now being carried to trial in the Tower coach.

In Westminster Hall Charles stood with dignity before the King's Bench and listened to a repetition of the conviction for High Treason, which he had heard here thirty years ago. He replied in a steady voice that he was not the Charles Radcliffe mentioned in the indictment, that he was the French Count of Derwent, subject to the King of France, and then he produced his commission as Lieutenant Colonel in the French army. He also said that he was astonished at English justice which had lately denied him all access to a lawyer. Here there was some consternation on the Bench, and looks of disapproval directed at Governor Williamson.

The court at once assigned the counsel Charles had asked for, the firm of Ford and Jodrell, of which Mr. Garvan was a member. After some delay, Charles's counsel requested time to consult with the prisoner and bring defense witnesses from abroad. The court ignored the latter request, but postponed trial until Monday.

Williamson did not return to the Tower in the coach with Charles, and he had to endure rebuke from Mr. Justice Foster on his treatment of the prisoner.

During the weekend Charles was accordingly permitted private interviews with his lawyers, Alec was summoned back by Hobson, the dietary restrictions were lifted, and Charles at last got a note through to Jenny at the King's Head. It was an optimistic note, telling her of his trial on Monday, and that

513

she must not worry, his lawyers were certain of success. "Only three more dayes, sweethart, then we'll feast at King's Head if you like, & you shall sing me a merrie tune but not as a serving-wench."

Jenny was immeasurably relieved. These weeks of no communication had been a fearful strain. She and Alec had supported each other as best they could; she had worked diligently and for longer hours in the inn, to occupy herself.

On the Sunday after receiving her note, she decided to go to church. To St. Paul's, which she had never visited. She started to dress in her best gown, the fine green wool in which she'd twice crossed the Atlantic, and which she had freshened by means of elbow ruffles, and ruchings. The gown was too tight across the bust and at the waist. She was getting fat, Jenny thought impatiently. Too much of the King's Head's excellent cooking. She left a hook or two undone, and covered deficiencies with her best green wool hooded cloak.

In St. Paul's, that great dim Renaissance cathedral, Jenny was awed by the grandeur of marble and the painted dome. She found a seat midway down the nave, settled back, and listened dreamily to the pure high voices of the choir. When the others knelt or rose she did. She listened also to the Collect for the day, which was the Sunday before Advent, and the Epistle which had to do with a righteous king, when suddenly two words struck her into sharp awareness, "out of the *north country*." Had that formless voice up in the shadows by the choir really said that? She had no prayerbook, yet so urgent was her need to find out that she borrowed from the woman beside her, and looked it up. Yes, it was there. "The Lord liveth, which brought up and which led the seed of the House of Israel out of the north country, and from all countries whither I had driven them; and they shall dwell in their own land." What did it mean?

Why should those enigmatic words penetrate the barrier which she had so successfully erected, and make her think with an almost frightened compulsion of Rob? She had been praying for her father, praying in awkward desperate little petitions, unaccustomed to calling on the Deity, yet having felt the need for higher help. Now, as the service continued and the lovely music swelled out and floated through the vast cathedral, she became more and more uneasy.

She could no longer follow the service, she could no longer pray for her father. She felt giddy, there was a weakness in her legs. The thought of Rob overpowered her. Suddenly without volition she turned. Three pews back and to the left of her, she thought she saw him. At least she saw his intent eyes gazing sadly in her direction.

Jenny caught her breath and veered back towards the choir, her heart pounding. "You're mad!" she said aloud. The woman who owned the prayerbook gave her a startled look. Jenny clutched the pew ahead until her knuckles whitened. At last she calmed a little, and turned again. That pew behind was empty. Nobody in it at all. I *am* mad, she thought. The minister had mounted the pulpit, and was eloquently launched into the sermon, of which Jenny heard not a word. She sat rigid, trying to marshal her common sense. Rob was more than three thousand miles away on a plantation in Virginia, and he had cut her from his life, as she had him from hers. But what if it *was* a vision, she thought with a stab of fear. Like Evelyn's, and something had happened to him. Yet, in a moment, she rallied again. That glimpse had not seemed like either vision or dream. It had looked like Rob himself sitting there, even to the black hat with its thin silver edge, the maroon suit he had bought in Williamsburg—or did she imagine these details? Surely at the time she had been aware only of the intent, sad gaze. Jenny looked back once again. The pew behind was still unoccupied.

She was far more disturbed when she left St. Paul's than when she entered it, though some of her agitation wore off during the long walk back to Spitalfields under fitful November sunshine.

Mrs. Potts was in the kitchen supervising the cooking of the family dinner, which Jenny now shared with her employers. The other servants ate earlier, but Bella Potts had become fond of Jenny, and Potts himself grew indulgent, for she had increased his business. At the Friday musical club she not only sang but played the harpsichord acceptably, and new customers were coming from the City, and even the West End.

"Sit ye down," said Mrs. Potts in greeting. "Tak' a dish o' tea, and a bite o' jam tart I've been making." She thought Jenny looked pale and strained.

"No thanks, ma'am," said Jenny smiling in a distraught way. "I'll go to my room a while, besides I eat too much, I'm getting fat."

She went up the twisting back stairs to the tiny garret room she had been given. Bella Potts, the mother of eight grown children, stared after Jenny, an odd expression on her face. "It divven't seem reasonable she wouldna *knaw*—" she remarked in the general direction of the kitchen cat and the old deaf cook. "Poor lass, in some ways she's but a green girl yet."

The next day, Monday November 24, the procession started out again from the Tower, as Charles was conveyed to his trial. Williamson rode in another coach, so Charles was spared unwelcome company. An unknown officer and two warders, including Hobson, rode with Charles, who was in high spirits. "Here we go again!" he remarked chuckling to Hobson. "And on the way back we'll stop at the Mitre and have a bowl of their punch to celebrate! All of us."

"Thankee, m'lord," said Hobson solemnly. The others said nothing. Charles had had some wine with his breakfast, enough to increase his confidence and induce well-being. He was dashingly clothed as he had been Friday in his scarlet and black regimentals, and the broad Spanish hat garnished by a white plume. His cheeks were ruddy, his eyes bright, and he was further heartened by the cheering crowds which lined the streets. By now they knew who was riding in the coach. At least they knew that it was not one of the Scottish lords. An Englishman, some said it was, and had been kept a whole year at the Tower, which was no way to treat an Englishman, especially one who hadn't actually been in the rebellion at all. Besides, they liked his looks, so they cheered and wished him luck. Charles bowed and smiled and waved his hand as the coach rolled by. To cap his elation, as they went along Ludgate he saw Jenny standing at the curb, watching anxiously.

"Put the window down!" said Charles to Hobson, who obeyed.

"Hullo there, darling!" Charles called. "I'll see you later! I'll send Alec!" He blew her a kiss, and she nodded and smiled.

Charles arrived again at Westminster Hall. He bowed familiarly to everyone, including the Lord Chief Justice on the Bench—the formidable Earl of Hardwicke, who had tried the Scottish lords and executed them. Charles did not know it, but Lord Hardwicke was a self-made man, the son of a petty lawyer in Dover, and though he had himself achieved an earldom by ability and assiduous attention to King George the Second, he despised the aristocracy—especially Stuarts, not to speak of Papists.

The trial began by Charles's counsel asserting that there was no proof that this prisoner was the same Charles Radcliffe as the one mentioned in the Record. The Attorney-General replied that the Crown considered this the same man and was prepared to prove it. Defense Counsel again asked for adjournment, which was denied. They then began to empanel a jury. Charles's exuberance gave way to astonishment and then outrage as he saw the type of talesmen they had called to form his jury. A butcher, a haberdasher, and even a scavenger. Charles jumped to his feet, crying that he had expected to be tried by a jury of his peers.

Lord Hardwicke replied in a silken voice that this was not a trial of any importance, merely one to establish identity, and averted his cold eyes from Charles as more jurors were sworn in.

Charles was dazed for a moment, then recognized the next talesman to appear. It was one of the guards who had man-handled and spat at him when he and his son had been hustled up from Deal to London. Charles made a peremptory challenge. Lord Hardwicke ruled at once that no challenges were permissible in a trial of this sort. The jury was rapidly empaneled.

Charles was directed to stand, and the prosecution brought on a string of witnesses. The first ones were most disappointing to the Crown. There was a barber who had once shaved Charles in Newgate. He hemmed and hawed, squinting at the prisoner, and finally said he wasn't sure if this was the same man. He was told sharply to stand down, and the Crown produced the next witness, a shabby whining knave, who immediately swore that this was indeed Charles Radcliffe, since he'd seen him at the Earl of Derwentwater's funeral.

At that Charles laughed immoderately, and said, "Is the Crown suggesting that the Earl of Derwentwater's funeral was held in Newgate? For I understand that's where Charles Radcliffe was at the time."

There were snickers in the courtroom. Lord Hardwicke angrily rapped for order, the Attorney-General colored and dismissed the witness.

"If they can't do better than *that!*" Charles whispered to Mr. Ford, his senior counsel.

"Hush," whispered Ford, who was growing less sanguine. He didn't like the look in Hardwicke's eye.

And then to Charles's dismay they brought on Northumbrian witnesses. He hadn't thought they'd send North, he hadn't really believed that the case would be handled quite so seriously. The first Northumbrian was Thomas Reed of Aydon, a playmate of long ago at Dilston. Mr. Reed testified that he had watched this prisoner as he walked the battlement at the Tower, and that he saw him now, but if it were the same Charles Radcliffe then the alteration was such that he didn't care to commit himself.

Mr. Reed was ordered to stand down, and later suffered for his honesty, since the enraged Government refused to pay his expenses home again.

Sir William Middleton was next called, and flatly refused to testify.

"So far, so good," Ford whispered with relief.

The Crown's next Northern witness was a different matter. Charles was much dismayed to see Abraham Bunting, the Dilston weaver, who had never felt loyalty to Radcliffes, who had refused to follow James in the '15, and who had undoubtedly been responsible for summoning the informer Patten on the night the latter had broken into Dilston chapel bent on arresting Charles.

Bunting took the stand, said he came from Hexham now, though had formerly been employed at Dilston. "Where," said Bunting pointing at Charles, "I seen *him* graw up, an' seen him ride out i' the 'Fifteen, too. He's Charles Radcliffe reet enough, an' I'd swear it to Gawd himself!"

"Tell us, Mr. Bunting," said the Attorney-General smiling, "how can you be so sure?"

"By that scar on his cheek—aye, leuk har-rd masters, an' ye'll see it plain! I can from her-re! I mind the verra day he come back to Dilston wi' the wound, arter some scrimmage he'd been in."

Again the ripple through the courtroom was shushed. Mr. Ford leaped up and protested that anyone might have a scar, that this wasn't evidence. Lord Hardwicke ruled that it was.

There was a pause, a consultation, then another stir and craning of necks as General Adam Williamson, Deputy Lieutenant-Governor of the Tower, was called up as a witness.

Williamson did not glance towards Charles, who stared at him with fury, yet not much apprehension, so fast had all this gone, and so obviously flimsy was the evidence.

After taking his oath, Williamson testified in a soft regretful voice, giving the impression that this was to him a painful duty. "The unfortunate prisoner," he said sighing, "after some glasses of wine on October ninth the last, boasted to me of how he had escaped from Newgate prison, and when I addressed him as Charles Radcliffe he answered to the name. That is all, my lord."

"And quite sufficient, General Williamson!" said the Earl of Hardwicke with a thin triumphant smile. "We have now established—"

"Stop!" Charles cried wildly, staring forward. "Why should you take this man's word? Has he a witness to what he alleges? And what value is an oath to a man who himself has told me he believes in neither God nor devil!"

"Mr. Radcliffe," said the Lord Chief Justice, "your insolence has tried my patience severely. If you persist in these outbursts, I shall have to put you under restraint."

"I'm *not* Mr. Radcliffe," Charles cried. "I'm the Count of Derwent."

Again there was a stir throughout the crowded courtroom —a stir of sympathy, Hardwicke knew. The justice near him, Mr. Foster, had even made a deprecating sound, as though he disapproved the proceedings.

"Prisoner," said Hardwicke leaning forward, "Papist or not, you certainly represent yourself as a Christian. Will you tell the court something?"

Charles signified assent.

"Will you put your hand on this Bible, and swear by Almighty God and the future disposition of your own soul that you are not and never were Charles Radcliffe?"

Hardwicke waited in considerable anxiety during the startled hush which followed, knowing that if the prisoner *did* so swear, there was every chance he would get off, since the proofs against him were dubious.

Charles was silent. Dear Lord Jesus Christ, sustain me, he thought, for Thou knowest I *am* the man. He put his hand to his forehead in a groping way, then he lifted his chin high, squared his shoulders, and walked slowly back to his seat. Mr. Ford gripped Charles's arm hard for a moment. "You're a brave man, an honest gentleman," he murmured. "But I fear we're lost now."

The Lord Chief Justice's direction to the jury was so plain that even the scavenger understood it. They returned in ten minutes with their verdict. Then Mr. Justice Foster made an attempt to save the prisoner, he invoked the Act of Pardon which had been passed in 1717, by which all the condemned rebels in the 'Fifteen were released. Why should not Mr. Radcliffe profit by that too?

Hardwicke definitely, and with annoyance, said that this prisoner could not so profit, since he had already escaped and was in France when the Act was passed.

"It is therefore, Mr. Radcliffe," said Hardwicke hurriedly forestalling more interruptions, "incumbent upon me to pronounce the original sentence of death for High Treason, which was passed on you May 18, 1716. 'That you, Charles Radcliffe, return to the prison from which you came, from thence you must be drawn to the place of execution; when you come there you must be hanged by the neck, but not till you are dead, for you must be cut down alive, then your bowels must be taken out and burned before your face, and your body divided into four quarters, and these must be at the King's disposal.' And God have mercy on your soul."

Charles did not move. It was his lawyers who were affected, and Ford got up to plead brokenly, "My lord, this is the harshest of the commoners' sentences. My client has noble blood, can we not commute some part of—"

"The prisoner is not a peer," Hardwicke snapped. "And by his treasonable actions he has twice put the Government to a great deal of expense and annoyance. The execution will take place this day fortnight on December eighth." He turned to Williamson, who stood near the courtroom door. "Lieutenant of the Tower, take the prisoner from the bar!"

Since noon on that day, Jenny had been waiting for Alec to come with news. Every half hour she slipped out to the market square and looked for him. The singing birds twittered in their cages, housewives, stewards, and innkeepers haggled for vegetables as usual, but there was never a sign of Alec.

At five Mrs. Potts sought her out, and for the first time broke the rule she had made and which Jenny had never transgressed. Anyone who took in a morning paper as the Pottses did, would have known that the Radcliffe trial had taken place today; Mrs. Potts knew, and despite her stern endeavors, she discovered that she shared some of Jenny's anxiety about the outcome. "M'lass," she said to Jenny, "I knaw weel, why ye've been running to the square. Ye've heard naught?"

Jenny, flushing, shook her head.

"Ye may run out agyen," said Mrs. Potts, "arter ye serve some new customers. Quality they are, and they want ye to sing 'Cease Your Funning' fur them."

"I'll do so, ma'am. Thank you." said Jenny faintly.

She found the customers at the best table in the taproom—three elegant beaux in satins, periwigs, and ruffles, all taking delicate pinches of snuff from a gold filigree snuffbox they were passing around.

"Ecod, 'tis a comely wench," said the smallest and oldest of the three, surveying Jenny as she dropped a curtsey. "I'll wager she knows better sports than *singing!*" And he ran his hand down her neck onto the top of her breasts.

Jenny eluded him with practiced ease, and said coldly, "What will you drink, gentlemen?"

They ordered various complicated and remunerative drinks, a sherry-flip, porter cup, rum booze, which took Potts and his drawer some time to prepare. When Jenny started back bearing the tray, Bella Potts came along behind her to inquire from these lavish customers if all was to their liking. Both women paused instinctively at the door as they heard the small man cry with relish, "So that's the end of the jape that Radcliffe tried to foist upon us!"

The other two leaned forward, questioning.

"You haven't heard then?" said the small man. "Radcliffe was condemned again today. It'll be a special fine hanging, what with the drawing and the quartering. You don't get many of those now!"

"I've never seen one myself," said the youngest man. "Have you, sir?"

The small elderly gentleman smiled. "To be sure. It gives you an exquisite thrill that one doesn't get from bear-baiting or an ordinary hanging—they choke the fellow just a little, then they slit his belly most carefully, it's an art to keep them alive as long as possible, then they draw out yards and yards of those blue guts to burn, and they start lopping off a leg here, an arm there—what the devil!" he cried jumping and turning around.

Jenny's tray had clattered to the floor, which ran with different shades of liquor amid a welter of jugs and broken glass. Jenny herself was clinging to the doorpost, her face white as the plaster wall.

"Go to your room, lass," said Mrs. Potts quietly. To the customers she said, "My apologies, kind sirs, the wench slipped. We'll soon fetch ye a new round." She stooped to pick up the broken glass; the drawer came running with a mop.

In a few minutes, Bella Potts mounted to Jenny's room and found her lying on the cot in the darkness and panting as though she had been running miles. The landlady had brought a candle and she set it on the chest. "Sit up, my dear," she said briskly. "Here's some hartshorn to drink. 'Twill calm ye better'n any o' the stuff Potts sells."

Jenny's unwinking, dilated eyes remained fixed on the ceiling beams.

"Did you hear?" she panted. "Oh, my God, ma'am, did you *hear!*"

"I did," said Mrs. Potts. "And if it is any comfort to ye, that's precisely how m'first husband died. Come now, drink this!" She pulled Jenny up and forced her to drink.

Jenny choked down the fuming hartshorn and water, gasped, and buried her face in her hands. "I can't stand it," she whispered. "Can't stand it . . ."

"Oh, aye, but ye can, lass. 'Tis wondrous what a body can thole. Forbye, I'm a-thinking the time's come for ye to help him."

"How?" cried Jenny raising her head. "How can I?"

Mrs. Potts hesitated. Though she had said nothing to Jenny, nor even wished to think of it herself, she was as avid a reader of the news-sheet as her husband, and she had foreseen this tragic outcome. Moreover, she was shrewd and knowledgeable—a successful innkeeper must be—and she had kept her ears open.

"I divven't mean to raise your hopes," she said at last. "And there's none at all to get your father free, why should there be? He's guilty o' treason. But I divven't think it reet for him to suffer quite so cruel. Ye might go to the Earl o' Chesterfield. He's in power now and from what I hear he *might* use influence for mercy."

"Oh ma'am—oh dear Mrs. Potts!" Jenny cried, transported by a wild hope. "Do you think Father can yet be saved, kept in the Tower until there's another Act of Pardon, as maybe there will be?"

Mrs. Potts did not think so, yet she gave Jenny an encouraging maternal smile. "Ye can try," she said.

TWENTY-ONE

The following morning, Mrs. Potts finally met Alec, who came to the kitchen door sadly inquiring for Jenny. Potts had gone off to Smithfield to buy meat for the inn, and his wife, having committed herself to Radcliffes once more, was not a woman for half measures. So she welcomed Alec, fetched Jenny, and took them both into the private parlor.

Alec had aged very much during the sleepless night. His eyes were sunken, his hands trembled. When he saw Jenny, he broke down and choked into his handkerchief. "I feared it—I told ye, madam, I feared this in Virginia—yet I didna believe it—an' o' late there seemed to be such hopes!"

"How is he taking it?" asked Bella Potts in her matter-of-fact way.

"I don't know! That blackguard Williamson, God blast him, he's moved his lordship to the Byward tower, to an upper dungeon where he put Lord Balmerino, an' they won't let me in again. Holy Blessed Mother, that there should be no one nigh him, for him to face alone what's coming—the degradation and the agony—Tyburn and the tortures. Sweet Christ, they're treating him worse than the basest murderer what ever slunk outa the brothels o' Dockside!"

"Aye," said Mrs. Potts quietly. "Matters do seem bad. There may be a way t' r-rectify them a bit."

She picked up her knitting, and explained to Alec the plan she had conceived. He listened dully at first. He knew nothing of the great London lords any more; he had never heard of Chesterfield. The mighty noblemen who had tried to save

James, Earl of Derwentwater, they were dead. Lady Betty, the Earl of Lichfield, and Queen Caroline, who had actually saved Charles thirty years ago—they were dead too. Yet Alec had seen enough of the world to know that influence was the only hope left, and as he listened to Mrs. Potts, his grief-numbed wits began to clear, and he grasped the points which she was making.

The Earl of Chesterfield after a long career of diplomacy had recently returned from a brilliant administration in Ireland as Lord-Lieutenant. There he had made himself beloved, even by the Catholics, whom he treated with extraordinary leniency. During the Rebellion he had not even closed their churches, as had been done in the '15. Chesterfield was a man famous for his wit, his moderation and urbanity. He was a dedicated aristocrat, believer in the privileges and superiority of birth. And he had the reputation of a gallant. A lovely face would not cozzen him, though it might certainly facilitate a hearing. Chesterfield had been out of favor with the King, but was in high favor now. On October 28 he had been appointed Secretary of State for the Northern counties, while the Duke of Newcastle administered the Southern ones.

He was therefore, said Mrs. Potts, along with the Duke of Newcastle, the most powerful minister in the country at present.

"Why, then," asked Alec slowly, "wouldn't Miss Jenny try appealing to the *Duke*, which is what his lordship's kept doing?"

"Because," said Bella Potts briskly, "the Duke is a timid shilly-shally fusspot. They call him 'hubble-bubble' behind his back—an' he niver did aught to help Mr. Radcliffe, did he?"

Alec shook his head. "Not to speak of. I see you're right, ma'am, and I know a deal about the means needed to approach a great lordship. It'll take money."

"I have some," said Jenny, who had been following all this intently. "I've not spent a penny of my wages. Though surely you don't mean Lord Chesterfield could be bribed!"

"Not by any pound or so *you've* saved, lass!" said Mrs. Potts with a faint smile. "What's the money for, Mr. Armstrong?"

"She must be dressed proper, like a ladyship," said Alec. "She must be carried in a chair, wi' me alongside as her steward. She must have several guineas for fees to the porter and footman, or she'll never pass the front door."

"Aye," Mrs. Potts nodded in complete agreement. She had

respected Alec on sight, aside from her own natural pre-disposition towards a fellow Northumbrian. "I've a guinea or two put by," she added and forestalled gratitude by snapping, "No more palavering, we s'ould all get to wark."

It was Thursday morning before Jenny started out for Lord Chesterfield's mansion in Grosvenor Square, since it had been impossible to get ready sooner. First there were the clothes to be hired from a mantua-maker who specialized in secret aid to needy peeresses. The gown was of sapphire taffeta and had a Watteau panel in back, all embroidered with golden vines. The lemon satin petticoat was brocaded, the wide hoops were enormous, as was now fashionable in London. This elegant gown, when tried on in Jenny's room, needed letting out. "I *am* getting fat," said Jenny frowning, as she stood in her shift and Mrs. Potts deftly began to rip the bodice seams open.

"My dear lass," said Mrs. Potts, biting off a thread. "Ye've plenty o' woes, so I've not spoke, yet sur-rely ye know ye're breeding?"

"Breeding?" Jenny repeated blankly, she put her hand to her slightly rounded belly. "Oh no, it's *impossible!*"

"Have ye had your courses regular?"

"N-no. It's the 'change,' I suppose. I'm old enough."

"I tak' leave to doubt that," said Mrs. Potts tartly. "And if anyone knaws breeding signs, 'tis Bella Potts. Ye're not expecting me to think ye a virgin, I trust!"

Jenny flushed scarlet. "No," she said. "I'm married, and was for twenty years." She sat down abruptly on the bed.

"Weel—" said Mrs. Potts, considering, and believing Jenny as she would not one of the other maids, who were often caught in trouble, "if ye've a husband, when did ye last lie wi' him?"

Jenny stared at her landlady. The painful color burned brighter in her cheeks. Years ago in another world she had been with Rob. What need to remember it now? What right had Mrs. Potts to force an intrusion, to be sitting there with her practical penetrating gaze.

"I hate him," Jenny cried. "And he hates me. I want never to think of him again!"

"Wey aye, na doubt," said Mrs. Potts calmly, squinting at her needleful of thread. "But when did ye last lie wi' him?"

"I didn't!" Jenny cried. "He forced me and hit me. And he let me go without even a farewell."

"He roughed ye up a bit, when ye were leaving him fur

525

your faither, I presume," said Mrs. Potts shrewdly. "And when was that?"

"Late July."

Mrs. Potts nodded. Four months was about what she had figured it to be. With all the rest she had to bear, it was a pity the lass couldn't have her husband at this time, but obviously she couldn't. And many another woman had gone through it alone. It happened every day. What didn't happen every day was to have a father in the Tower, sentenced to the vilest death man could devise.

"Ye can stay here, Jenny," said Mrs. Potts, taking another quick stitch on the loosened seam. "Ye can have your babby here. I don't care what Potts says. I'll handle him."

Jenny murmured thanks from inbred politeness, yet she did not, would not, believe in the child.

The church bells rang eight o'clock in the morning when Jenny started off through the London streets towards Grosvenor Square in the sedan chair which Alec had hired. He had taken great pains to find a smart chair and two liveried chairmen. He had also, by the simple expedient of standing drinks in the ordinary nearest Lord Chesterfield's house, struck up acquaintance with one of the Earl's footmen. From this encounter he learned something of the Earl's habits. At nine, after breakfast, his lordship was always alone writing letters, before he dressed to go to Whitehall, or St. James. After that no telling when he'd come home.

Alec was gratified, as anyone in his state of apprehension could be, by the elegance of their turnout and of his lady. A lady she was today, and no mistaking it. He glanced through the chair window. She sat erect and dignified, her face in profile, her gloved hands hidden in a muff.

They had hired a crimson velvet mantle edged with black-flecked white rabbit, which only an expert might tell from ermine. The pearls too, earrings and necklace, no casual eye could distinguish from the real. And at six this morning Mrs. Potts had summoned a *coiffeur* to do up Jenny's hair in all the puffs and rolls and curls fashion demanded. The elaborate result was then powdered, topped by a small ostrich plume and a flat blue bow. The *coiffeur* finished by applying touches of rouge to her cheeks and lips, darkened her eyebrows with burnt cork, then, carried away by his achievement, vowed that for beauty and elegance even the famous Duchess of Queensborough in her prime would have had to yield the palm.

Alec quite agreed, and it made him sick to think how brief

a time this transformation could last, while his heart swelled with hatred against the pitiless fate which was forcing degradation on all Radcliffes.

The chairmen bearing Jenny went the quickest way to the West End, along Holborn, and then on to what was beginning to be called Oxford Street and was amazingly built up, since the old days when there were open fields everywhere. It was still, however, a famous road for highwaymen and pickpockets. Alec kept a sharp lookout.

There was little danger in daytime, yet you could hardly call "daylight" this murky dark November morning. There were wisps of fog to mingle with the pall of coal smoke, and it was hard to see a block ahead.

When they left Spitalfields and again on Oxford Street, Alec had the impression that they were being followed. He turned quickly each time, to catch a distant glimpse through the mist of a tall male figure walking behind them, keeping at an even pace. Alec fingered his pistol, and said a quick Hail Mary for protection. When he looked around again the figure had disappeared.

They hurried on, the chairmen loping along, crowding what pedestrians there were, against the wall, and shouting, "Way there! Give way to her ladyship!" They had agreed on this. For the last time, Jenny was to be a "ladyship." Alec knew how much a title bettered chances of running the gantlet of servants who protected a great nobleman.

Jenny had been very nervous earlier, now she was calm. The fine clothes gave her assurance. She put away from her the gestures and slips of speech which sometimes conflicted with Lady Betty's teachings and example. She thought poignantly of Lady Betty, who had once gone on an errand of this kind to the then Princess, Caroline. Wherever you are, dear foster mother, she thought, help me now!

The chairmen deposited their chair before the steps of the Earl's mansion. Jenny waited until the bowing Alec had handed her out. She settled her hoops, and lifted her chin while Alec dealt with the porter, feeing him ten shillings and whispering that her ladyship had come on a most important errand. The porter shrugged and stepped aside, leaving Jenny free to mount the steps, where the second footman opened the door. She must now fend for herself. Alec had to remain by the chair.

"I wish to see my Lord Chesterfield," Jenny said haughtily to the second footman. "I am Lady Jane Wilson, and have urgent business with him."

"He don't see nobody at this hour, m'lady," said the footman, eying her with respectful admiration.

"I trust he will," said Jenny smiling. She put her white gloved hand into her purse, then nonchalantly proffered a guina. The footman pocketed it. "Please to step into the reception room, m'lady," he said. "I'll fetch Mr. Portman."

Jenny's appearance and her bribe had procured her direct access to the house steward instead of the next ranking footman.

The house steward presently appeared, bowing deeply, but said it was as much as his place was worth to disturb his lordship at this hour.

Jenny gave him her enchanting wistful smile, and tendered two guineas. "I *pray* you," she said, "to arrange an interview. I can see you are the sort of man in whom his lordship would have confidence. If you succeed in having me admitted, I shall prove my gratitude again when I leave."

Portman bowed, and went in some trepidation through the stately halls and drawing rooms to his master's French morning room. Once inside, he waited some time before Lord Chesterfield noticed him. "What is it, Portman?"

"A young ladyship, m'lord, to see you. She's *very* urgent."

Chesterfield frowned. His small froglike body was clothed in a brocaded dressing gown, a red silk turban was perched on his big shaven head. At a Louis Quatorze porphyry table he was writing his daily letter of precept and guidance to his illegitimate, though beloved son, and his orderly mind disliked surprises.

"Did you not tell the lady, that I *never* receive at this hour? She can come back some other time, if she must!" Chesterfield picked up his pen, and returned to his letter.

"My lord," said Portman, hanging on to his courage. "I believe this lady's really in distress, and she's—uh—beautiful, m'lord, and her face so proud and yet so pleading, if she could see you but a moment, m'lord!"

The Earl put down his pen; from his dark, slightly malicious eyes he gave his steward a look of amused exasperation.

"This mysterious female certainly must have a generous purse. I've never knew you to be lyrical, Portman! What's her name?"

"Lady Jane Wilson, m'lord."

"Never heard of her," said the Earl. "For that matter I never heard of a Wilson in the peerage. Must be an imposter."

"I—I don't think so, m'lord—she has quality," said Portman nervously.

The Earl snorted. "Merciful heaven! One way or another she's bewitched *you*. You end by intriguing me. Let her in, and if she isn't the paragon you say, you'll suffer for it."

After depositing her mantle and gloves with the footman, Jenny was ushered into the morning room, where a huge fire sparkled off brass, gilt, and the many *objets d'art* which the Earl collected. He rose and gave her a courtly graceful bow despite his dumpiness and the dressing gown and turban.

Jenny executed a slow, stylized curtsey in return. "This is very good of you, my Lord Chesterfield," she said, low and quiet, in the unmistakable accent of breeding.

Chesterfield noted this at once and sent her a smile which had charm even though some of his teeth were brown or missing. "Pray sit down, Lady Jane," he said indicating a gilt armchair upholstered in rose velvet. "You will forgive my deshabille. I am not accustomed to entertaining pretty ladies at this hour, and I confess to slight curiosity as to why you were so—shall we say, importunate?"

She sat down. He continued to stand, his back to the fire, watching her narrowly. He had a vast experience of women, and had enjoyed many amours, though never among the lower classes. The Earl was fastidious and would brook no vulgarity. He was accustomed to place-seekers, which he assumed this lady to be, yet he was puzzled. Her clothes, bearing and voice were excellent; nor had Portman exaggerated her beauty; but he did not fail to note the quivering of a pulse in her long white throat, the desperation, not quite hidden, in the gray eyes she finally turned up to him. It was one of his maxims that when people sought favors, one should let them speak first and declare themselves. So he waited, and amused himself with interior speculation.

She wanted a Court position for her lover? The lack of wedding ring precluded husband. Or one of the political blocs now out of favor had sent her to wheedle a promise of influence? No, neither would explain her tension. She was in trouble herself, more likely. A gaming loss? Or even pilfering, at which she'd been caught? Women often committed follies when their silly heads were turned by finery and jewels.

"I don't know how to begin, my lord," said Jenny abruptly. "I find that I'm very afraid."

"My dear lady," said the Earl kindly. "You needn't be. I'm no ogre, and I assure you *nothing* shocks me. You've come here to ask a favor, and I suggest that you do so promptly."

"A *favor!*" she repeated with such sad bitterness that the Earl was startled. "Aye—" she said. "I suppose it is by *favor* that a man might be saved from torture and infamous death!"

The Earl was too skilled a diplomat and courtier to show surprise, and reluctantly discarded his former theories.

"What man do you refer to?" he asked.

Jenny breathed hard, she twisted her fingers tight together and said, "Charles Radcliffe, the titular Earl of Derwentwater."

"Ah . . ." said Chesterfield. So that was it. An unsavory case from every angle, and one which he had been very glad had not concerned him. "Why do you trouble yourself about this traitor?" he asked sternly.

"Because he is my father, and I love him."

Chesterfield raised his eyebrows. He was almost certain that Charles Radcliffe had no mature daughter by Lady Newburgh. "Forgive plain speaking, my dear. But are you legitimate?"

"Yes. 'Twas long ago when my father was sixteen, a forced marriage in Northumberland to a Border lass, a farmer's daughter."

"I see," said the Earl. A *mésalliance,* naturally concealed. He thought of his own son, and wished that he, who also was the product of a mismating, might achieve the elegance and charm that this lady had. "You were not reared by your own mother, I judge?"

"No, my lord," said Jenny. "By Lady Betty Lee, my father's cousin." And what difference did it make? she thought, biting her lips against agonized impatience.

"Ah, yes," said the Earl. "To be sure. I remember her. A delightful woman. You are well connected on one side, but my dear madam, you must be aware that you have no legal right to a courtesy title?"

"Oh, I am, my lord," said Jenny. "It was only to get in here."

The Earl surveyed her with approval. Such candor was refreshing, and he was diverted at the way she had got past his usually impregnable servants. By fees, of course, and they must have been large, yet there was more than that, a winsomeness, a naïveté, mixed with poise, a curious mixture of the voluptuous, and yet the childish. Beauty too—fine bones. If I hadn't been ill so recently, he thought, if I were a trifle younger—

"My Lord Chesterfield," said Jenny in desperation. "I came here to beg of you to help my father!"

The Earl's heavy eyelids hooded his brilliant dark eyes. "Why should I do aught for Charles Radcliffe?" he said judicially. "I detest the Jacobites, I detest traitors, and here is a man who had twice been justly condemned. What reason can you bring forth?" He sat down in the chair opposite, and waited with an air of quizzical patience.

Jenny immediately stood up. She threw her head back. Strength flowed into her, and, gazing directly at her questioner, she spoke in a controlled voice. "The first reason is that you, my lord, are now minister for the Northern counties, and Charles Radcliffe comes from them."

"That is scarcely pertinent," said the Earl, waving his hand in dismissal.

"And the second is that common Christianity demands—" She stopped as the Earl shook his head sharply.

"That line won't do, madam," he said. "I think that I'm tolerant enough. People may believe any folderol they like for all of me, but it's no use your sentimentalizing about Christianity, nor any form of mawkish piety—leave that to the preachers."

"Then there is this!" She went on swiftly, having accepted his rebuttal. "Charles Radcliffe's father and brother were English earls. The latter the Hanoverians murdered. It is not forgotten, either. You may think the counties of Northumberland and Durham unimportant to your own administration; *I* think they are not, and they have made a hero out of Derwentwater."

"Indeed," said the Earl with a slight smile. "Go on." She was now showing a subtlety which amused him.

"Charles Radcliffe is of noble blood," said Jenny vehemently. "He is of *royal* blood. The people know it. He is by birth a member of your aristocracy, and his wife, Lady Newburgh, is a countess in her own right. Are you then not degrading all your class, and weakening it, if you allow one of your body to be—" She paused and swallowed, went on steadily, "To be hanged, drawn, and quartered?"

"*Now*, you argue shrewdly!" said the Earl. He lifted a jeweled snuffbox from the marble table next to him, took a pinch, and inhaled thoughtfully. There was truth in what she said. There had been rumblings lately, criticism in many quarters at the harshness of the sentence. Criticisms also of Hardwicke's handling of the trial. There had not been sufficient legal proof of identity, even though there was no doubt of the fact. The Duke of Richmond had protested to New-castle, and been met by the usual waverings and timidity. Newcastle was afraid of Hardwicke, afraid of the King. But I am not, thought the Earl, and I can manage the King.

"Oh—" cried Jenny, her voice breaking. "This is an *Englishman*, your countryman, and you persecute him worse than you ever did the Scottish lords. They were not given such a sentence, they are not tormented in the Tower the way *he* is!"

"What do you mean?" said the Earl sharply. He had scant use for the Scots, and it displeased him to think that they might have been favored.

"The two Scottish lords already executed were not kept in solitary confinement as my father is," she cried. "They saw their friends, relatives, and servants. My father's faithful valet is not even permitted to tend him."

"He isn't?" cried the Earl deeply shocked. "That is out-rageous! Surely not Newcastle's orders," he added frowning.

"His grace doesn't seem to concern himself about the Tower Governor's restrictions," said Jenny.

"Then I will!" cried the Earl, rising. "My dear madam, you have brought to my attention a state of affairs which I confess I would willingly have ignored. Yet I am not inhuman, and you are quite correct in saying that a man of noble birth—whatever his crime—should *not* be treated like a commoner. That has ever been our English precedent. No," he said as he saw her face transfigured, and the flare of hope in her eyes. "He will not be pardoned. You must not expect that. But his few remaining days in the Tower will be somewhat eased, and I believe that I may promise you that he will be beheaded like a peer—not hanged."

"Oh, my lord—" She sank to her knees and took his hand. She kissed it and held it against her cheek. "Thank you," she whispered. "I had not really dared hope for pardon, but I prayed for this—that he should die with dignity, and that I might see him again."

He felt her tears on his hand, and his cynical heart was touched. "When you see him, madam," he said, "tell him that, miserable as he is, he is fortunate in that he has for advocate so devoted and so persuasive a daughter."

Governor Williamson did not receive the Duke's orders con-cerning the lifting of restrictions on Charles Radcliffe until Monday. These orders said that the prisoner was to be per-mitted the daily attendance of his valet, he might receive relatives alone, he might even have a priest. It was understood that the Lieutenant-Governor had moved the prisoner to the Byward tower dungeon for greater security, and this move was approved. It was requested, however, that all the comforts possible should be provided in that dungeon, and the prisoner, in general, should be treated like a peer.

Williamson was infuriated, he cursed the ever-wavering Duke of Newcastle, but he did not dare disobey. There was no accompanying hint that the death sentence might be commuted, and there was no precedent whatsoever for treating a man like a lord when he was to be killed as a commoner. One more week, Williamson thought angrily, and I'll be rid of this nuisance—a more troublesome prisoner I never had! He stamped off to rescind some of his commands in regard to Radcliffe, but no more of them than he could help.

Thus Jenny was still forbidden to see her father, though she was the only person Charles asked for. She was *not* a relative, said Williamson. Charles said that she was, she was his daughter. The Governor snorted and said, "A likely story! Mr. Radcliffe, your inventiveness continues to amaze me!"

Until Saturday, Jenny had again to rely on Alec for news of Charles, though she walked every day to the Tower, and stood across the moat and waved to the grated slit of window in the Byward tower, sometimes waiting a long while before a white handkerchief waved there in response.

Charles's new cell was a horrible place, even with the improvements Williamson had reluctantly ordered—a cot, a chair, and table, a fire, candles, and rushes on the dank stone pavement. The cell was so small that three people could hardly squeeze in at once, and the slit in the window wasn't big enough to get one's hand through. There was stench from the moat beneath, and a peculiarly noxious odor which seemed to come from the ancient stones, doubtless from the excrement of all the condemned prisoners who had been confined here since the fourteenth century.

During the week in this dungeon, in cold and virtual darkness, Charles had spent much of the time lying on a straw pallet in stupor, not from drink—he was allowed only water—but from a willful drugging of the mind to blot out the fate in store for him. Sometimes in this stupor he whimpered like a child, sometimes cried out as nightmares seized him. The warders came and went, though now they usually stood outside the door; there was no possibility of escape from *this* cell. They forced him to eat; Governor Williamson wanted his prisoner kept alive. Charles was scarcely aware of them —even Hobson.

Then on the Monday when his conditions improved and he saw Alec again, he roused himself a little, he drank some wine and ate of the fowl Alec brought him. Yet his apathy continued. Even when Alec told him of Jenny's visit to Lord Chesterfield and the promise that the Earl had made.

"Promises from statesmen," Charles muttered. "Would you have me count on *them?*"

"To be sure, my lord," said Alec heartily. "See how much better you're treated now!"

Charles glanced indifferently around the gloomy cell. "The order's not come to commute my sentence. I'm still off to Tyburn on Monday."

Alec was silent, and grew each day more apprehensive, since no further word came from the authorities. And he had trouble rousing Charles even to wave to Jenny through the window. "I am sure 'tis better she forgets me," Charles said. "She must never let anyone know it is her father who dies so shamefully."

On Thursday afternoon Charles at last had visitors. The head warder ushered them into Charles's cell, and remained outside with Hobson. Charles gazed blankly at a small dark lady in mourning and a chubby man also dressed in black.

"Oh, my poor uncle," cried the lady, staring around the cell and at Charles in horror. "Don't you know me? Anna Maria Petre! Your brother James's daughter."

"Why yes, niece—" said Charles after a silence. " 'Tis kind of you to visit me. I see you are affrighted. 'Tis too bad you are affrighted." He gave her a dim vague smile, returned to contemplation of a flea which was hopping zigzag up the damp stone wall.

Lady Petre shook her head dolefully. She had rushed to London when she heard of the sentence. Since then she had been staying in Essex Street with Viscountess Primrose, who was an open and influential Jacobite. The two ladies had brought to bear all the pressure that they could on Charles's behalf. Lady Petre had even gone to the Duke of Newcastle. The Duke hemmed and hawed, he was excessively polite, he apologized, he regretted, his hands were tied, he understood the pain the prisoner's family must suffer, but the King was adamant. The subject could not be reopened. Lady Petre knew that she had failed, and from bitter experience she knew that her religion, and Charles's, contributed to the failure. As

534

it had also been a factor in her father's execution, here from this very Tower.

It had cost Anna Maria a great deal of misery to come and say farewell to her uncle, and now that she saw him—hopeless, dreary, not quite clear in his wits—she wanted to get away as fast as possible. But first she must discharge her duty. "I've brought you my chaplain, Uncle Charles," she said. "He'll lodge nearby, and has permission to visit you. At this dreadful time you must turn for comfort to the only Source of comfort. Go to your Saviour, Uncle, ask Him to forgive your sins. Think on the agonies that He endured for our sakes. Shut your heart up in His, and pronounce with Him the great words, 'Father, Thy Will be done!' "

Charles looked around at her earnest frightened face, her solemn brown eyes like her mother's. "The Saviour," he said, "did not suffer such a dreadful death as I will. They left *His* body in one piece, so that there was something to rise at the Resurrection."

Anna Maria recoiled. She looked helplessly towards the priest, waiting for him to rebuke this blasphemy. He was a well-fed portly little Frenchman whom she had brought along when she returned to England and married Lord Petre. To the few Catholics at the Petre seat in Essex he was known as Mr. Dupont, not his own name, but one they could pronounce. He had always led a comfortable chaplain's life in great houses. Nothing had prepared him for the ordeal he saw here awaiting him. He cleared his throat and said, "*Ecoutez, mon fils*, there must be penitence, there must be humility. We shall pray together that the Blessed Virgin may bring you by Her grace to a better state of mind."

"*You* pray, Father, if it amuses you," said Charles. "Leave *me* alone!" He returned to the contemplation of the flea, which had got stuck in a tiny crevice and was struggling.

Anna Maria and the priest exchanged despairing looks. She stooped and kissed her uncle on the cheek. He did not move. They went out, Anna Maria weeping, the priest's cherubic face very grave.

The next day, Friday, December 5, the priest came again and found Alec in the cell, about to leave. Charles was sitting as before, staring at the wall.

"Any news?" Father Dupont whispered to Alec, who shook his head, not trusting himself to speak.

The little priest sighed. He went to Charles and gripped his shoulder, shaking it slightly. "*Mon fils*," he said with all the sternness that his squeaky voice could muster, "bestir yourself. You were born and raised a Catholic. You know that you are steeped in sin, for which you must repent, and ask forgiveness before it is too late."

Charles gave an angry shrug which displaced the priest's hand.

Father Dupont bit his lips, his pink cheeks grew redder. "*Doux Jesu et Sainte-Vierge, aidez-moi!*" he prayed. He had never seen a Catholic who was not devoutly penitent, nor ever seen anyone approach death without a holy resignation. He tried again.

"I understand they've deprived you of the symbols of our Faith. I've brought you them." He tendered a silver rosary and crucifix, put them on Charles's knee, when he didn't move. "And here is something else," said the priest, more sharply. He held out towards Charles a porcelain statuette of the Virgin, an exquisite French piece; the sky-blue robe and gilt hair were translucent, every detail of the tiny face under a starry crown was clearly modeled, the downcast eyes, the slightly smiling mouth, the expression of serenity and pity.

Charles did look at the statuette, he looked for some moments. " 'Tis a bit like Jenny," he said.

The priest was shocked. He snatched away the figure and put it carefully on the table. "I do not know who Jenny may be," he cried, "and I assure you that irreverence will only compound your sins! Has it not occurred to you that you are to die on *Her* feast day, the Feast of Her Conception? That She might therefore hold you in especial tenderness, that Her ears might open to your prayers, if you will only say them."

Charles made a furious gesture, he turned at last towards the priest. "No prayer of mine has ever been answered. And I've lost the habit. Father Dupont, damn it—will you *go!* Leave me be! I've enough to bear without your pesterings!"

The little priest flushed again, feeling helpless and incompetent, trying to subdue dislike for this rude, obdurate man he was trying to help. "*Bien*," he said in a trembling voice. "I will go, though not until I ask you what your noble brother must think of you, as he looks down from heaven! What despair he must feel!"

The priest whirled and banged on the door for the warder to unlock it.

Charles bowed his head when the door clanged shut and he was alone again. Despair. The word reverberated in his ears, like the toll of a passing bell. Des-pair. Des-pair. Des-pair. Beneath the tolling of the bell, and louder than the bell could ever be, he heard another sound that was like the rush of water. Devil water flowing, flowing, rising ever higher, swirling now inside the cell. The swirl of inky fetid waters, waters that would drown, yet not *quite* drown, only suffocate a little, so that through the waters one could see and smell one's own burning flesh, could feel the wrenching agony of the disjointing knife on arms and legs, while the jeering, evil faces watched and laughed and cheered for the Devil water which flowed around, yet did not touch them.

"Stop it! For God's sake, stop it!" Charles shouted to the waters which were roaring through the cell. He got up, the rosary and crucifix fell to the rushes, he did not heed them. He strode back and forth from wall to window, back and forth, the ice-sweat dripping from his forehead.

At six Hobson was due for the evening guard duty. He was several minutes late, which Cox, whom he was replacing, commented on acidly. "I've been delayed at the Lodgings," said Hobson referring to the Governor's quarters. He said nothing else to Cox, but his broad honest face was beaming. He quivered with excitement.

"He's wild today," Cox said jerking a shoulder towards the cell. "Been shouting out and pacing like one o' them lions, ever since that bloody little priest left. Watch it, mate, he don't do ye harm." Cox departed, and Hobson unlocked the cell door.

Charles shouted, "Go away! Leave me alone!"

"Not yet, m'lord," said Hobson softly.

Charles was startled by the title which he had not heard from the warders since the trial. He turned his haunted eyes on Hobson. "Why do you call me that?"

"Because, m'lord," said Hobson with a deep breath, "you are to die like a lord. The sentence 'as been commuted. Naow, naow—" he said as Charles staggered, putting his hands to his face. " 'Old up! Or mebbe ye'd better sit down."

Charles sat down. His knees were too weak to support him. "I don't believe you—" he whispered. " 'Tis a trick."

" 'Tis true, m'lord," said Hobson. "I was there, reporting to the Gov'nor wen the messenger come with the horder. 'Is Excellency was fit to be tied. 'Opping mad 'e was." Hobson paused in reminiscent relish. Williamson had actually let loose a spat of barrack room oaths, and when his first rage died he had been indignant at the lack of consideration for himself in this chuckleheaded new directive. There was no time to build the proper scaffolding on Tower Hill. He'd have to hire carpenters who'd work on Sundays. He himself would have to work on Sunday, to insure the requisite ceremonial procedure for the beheading of a peer. He had still been expressing his views on the unparalleled trouble Radcliffe had caused from the beginning when Hobson left to report at the Byward tower. " 'Tis true, m'lord," Hobson repeated gently. "Ye're to be spared the 'anging—and the rest."

For another moment Charles did not stir. Then his wondering gaze traveled slowly to the little statue of the Virgin, which the priest had left on the table. She stood there so quietly, clothed in her translucent blue and gilt, the serene yet pitying smile on her tiny mouth.

"Forgive me, Blessed Lady—" Charles whispered. He pushed the chair aside and fell to his knees on the rushes, his hands clasped. "I am unworthy of this great gift," he whispered to Her, "unworthy of the Grace Thou showest me, *mea culpa, mea culpa, mea maxima culpa.*" He knocked his breast three times, and bowed his head on his clasped hands.

Jenny had spent the agonizing days in work. Mrs. Potts kept her busy every instant, cooking, cleaning, laundering, and serving in the taproom. She did not require that Jenny sing. She explained to disappointed customers that the wench had temporarily lost her voice.

On Saturday morning Jenny set out again for the walk to the Tower. When she got to Tower Hill, she stopped, clutching at one of the guard posts along the sidewalk. There was no traffic on the Hill, and in the center a dozen carpenters were hauling timber, hammering away on planks.

So it has come! Jenny thought. Thank God! And yet she could not be entirely sure—there were other prisoners in the Tower. She crept up to one of the carpenters. "Who is the scaffold for?" she asked faintly.

"Earl o' Darntwater," said the carpenter, grinning at her. "And an 'ell of a rush we're in ter be ready for Monday. Ye comin' to watch, miss? We expect a big crowd."

Jenny murmured something and continued walking down the hill, towards the Lion tower. Her request for permission to enter was at last granted. "Radcliffe" or "Derwentwater," the warder really did not know what to call him now; it was confusing. At any rate, that prisoner might see anyone he chose—today and tomorrow.

Charles was writing letters when Cox let Jenny into the cell. Charles had been given a larger table and several candles, which stood grouped on either side of the little statue of the Virgin. The silver rosary and crucifix were arranged at Her feet.

"Welcome, my darling!" cried Charles, rising and smiling at her as though they had a happy meeting yesterday. "I knew you'd come this morning!" He kissed her warmly on the mouth. "This is a cramped and stinking place in which to receive you, but no matter. I won't be here long!" And he laughed, with genuine amusement.

Jenny swallowed. She did not know what to say. Rejoice that he was so buoyant, that his voice had the old hearty ring, that he looked well—dressed by Alec in the yellow velvet suit, his gray bag-wig freshly curled, immaculate ruffles at his throat and wrists. Yet how to rejoice, when plain to be heard through the slit of window were the hammerings and shoutings of the carpenters who were building the scaffold.

Charles followed her involuntary glance towards the window. "Oh, I don't mind them," he said. "I think of the excellent company who've preceded me on Tower Hill." He ceased smiling and crossed himself, though his voice remained strong and calm as he added, "I think of James. I dreamed of James last night, and you know, darling, in the dream he told me I *had* kept my vow to avenge him, and he said he was pleased with me now. He even laughed, I think."

Jenny tried to smile, she sat down upon the cot. She looked at the statuette of the Virgin.

"Yes," said Charles resuming his own chair. "You resemble Her a little, Jenny. The face. And She worked a miracle for me, through you."

"And through Lord Chesterfield," said Jenny earnestly.

He nodded. "I'm grateful to you, sweetheart—yet I believe the human agencies were directed by Those Merciful Ones above us, and that He Who marks it even when a sparrow falls, was moved despite my grievous sins to accord me the Gift of Grace."

"I'm so glad for you," she murmured. She could not share his exaltation; the Catholic symbols and the Catholic way of reaching towards the Spirit were still alien to her. Yet her heart was convinced that a Spirit existed, that there was Something outside one's self which could be called upon for help, and which did help, in no matter what Name it was invoked.

"I'm writing to my King," Charles announced, matter-of-factly. "To King James and the Prince, for whose cause I'm going to die. You know," he added in a musing voice, "I think I have a sort of right to believe that I understand loyalty, and to teach it to others. I am saying so to His Majesty—do you think me presumptuous?"

"No," said Jenny. "It is true. And you are fortunate, Papa,

that your loyalties have never been divided," she paused, "as mine have been."

He startled a little, looking at her with attention. "You mean your husband, Jenny?"

"Yes . . ." she said, looking away. "Rob, and the other life. The moors, the peel tower, and all that from which Meg Snowdon came." Even as she spoke she felt a feeble fluttering in her belly, like a bird imprisoned there. It had happened last night too, but she had given herself some other reason for the sensation.

Charles noted that her lovely voice dragged, he noted too that there were dark hollows beneath the fearing eyes, that she was very pale. She had been suffering for him, he knew. Now for the first time in their relationship he realized his selfishness. He had despised and resented all that part of her she called "the other life." He had repeatedly tried to pretend that it did not exist, and thereby added to her suffering.

"Jenny," he said, "do you still love your husband? When I'm gone you will go back to him?"

She did not answer for a moment, then she spoke very low. "He doesn't want me."

The blackguard! Charles thought, his ready anger roused. That yokel, that peasant, who had dared to sully his treasure, and then repudiate it. "Alec will take care of you!" Charles cried. "He'll take you to Anna Maria. Unless you'd rather return to my wife?"

"Dearest Papa," she said sadly, "I wish to live neither with Lady Petre nor Lady Newburgh. I couldn't."

Charles drew back, seeing something else he had never seen before. Not in features, nor in voice; yet, subtly hidden in the brooding eyes, the set of the full mouth, there was a resemblance to her mother. To Meg Snowdon. And on seeing this an image rose in Charles's mind. The town moor at Newcastle, the little brown girl behind him on the horse, the clinging of her arms about his waist. And then the Faws—the gypsy tinkler's camp. The old crone saying that she saw the white rose wither and turn black, and that in his palm she saw an axe—a bloody axe. What else had the Faw woman said? Something at which he'd laughed impatiently, but Meg had gotten frightened. What was it the Faw woman said? That the royal blood in his veins was accursed. "True love cannot flow in it. No sweetheart need hope for true love from thee."

And no sweetheart had ever got it—only Jenny. And what

had he ever really done for Jenny except entangle her in doom?

"I couldn't help it, darling," he said aloud. "I believe I could not help it. A Faw woman saw the future coming long ago, and yet my sins are none the lighter for all that. I shall pray now, Jenny, for your conversion, and I shall pray for your happiness. If prayers are permitted me, wherever I am going, I'll pray for you there."

"Oh, my dearest Father," she whispered. She went to him and knelt beside him. He put his arm around her, and they stayed so in silence until the priest arrived bearing the objects necessary for the celebration of the Mass, which Charles had asked for.

TWENTY-TWO

The following evening, Charles finished his last letter. It was to his wife in France, and it said:

> From the Tower, 7th Decr. 1746,
> The best of friends takes leave of you. He has made his will. He is Resyned, to morrow is the Day. Love his memory. Let his friends join with you in prayer: 'tis no Misfortune to die prepared. Lets love our Ennemys and pray for them. Let my sons be men like me. Let my daughters be virtuous women like you; my blessing to them all; my kind love to Fanny that other tender mother of my Dr Children.
>
> Adieu! dear frien,
> DARWENTWATER.

Charles folded and sealed the letter. There was nothing more to be done, until the priest came again at dawn to celebrate the Mass.

Jenny had supped with Charles earlier. Her farewell visit, though this neither of them stressed. They had drunk from a bottle of excellent madeira, they had eaten a portion of the rabbit pie and boiled capon the Governor sent in. Charles told her that he had not made provision for her in his will, because there was nothing to leave beyond what Lady Newburgh had given him, and she would be justifiably upset if he left anything outside of her family. But Charles had insisted that Jenny take fourteen guineas, the only cash he had on hand, except what must be saved to pay his executioner—

as was the custom. Jenny at first refused. Then she gave in, her shimmering eyes strained, saying that she took the money not for herself, she knew well how to fend for herself, but for someone else, someone weak and helpless who might be in need.

Charles did not question her. There was so little time for questions, and he had no wish to probe the secret places of her life, if they did not concern himself.

He spoke once quietly about his funeral. He would be buried at St. Giles-in-the-Field, but he wished his heart conveyed to Dilston to be put with James. At her expression, he shook his head. "You do not see, Jenny, what joy this prospect gives me? How in a way it is the sealing of the vow I took? No more of this. Drink your wine and let us be gay for a while!"

He had meant to let her go tonight—forever. To free her, as he would himself be freed. To protect her from more anguish, to leave her with the memory of a merry and gallant father who had no slightest apprehension of what would happen on the morrow. Yet just before she left him, when the bell clanged for the shutting of the Tower, he faltered in his resolution.

That was when she took his hand and said "Papa?" in the old sweet childish way. "Papa?" she said, her eyes fixed on him steadily. "Would it comfort you if I were there—tomorrow?"

His hands had trembled as he thought how much he did want her near him at the end. The heavenly consolation, in which he confidently believed, was as yet only a pale thing beside the love he felt for her. And there would be no one else there of his own flesh. True, his niece had remained in London. She and Lady Primrose and the lawyers had arranged the details of what must be done with the senseless carcase when all was over. But Anna Maria would not be on Tower Hill, nor did he wish her to be.

"I'd not ask it of you, darling," he said, and Jenny instantly took his real meaning as she always had.

"I'll be there," she said. "Standing where you can see me." They parted silently, clinging to each other for a long moment, while Hobson stood waiting to usher her out, blowing his nose, and more overcome than either of them. "She's a brave 'un—your little love, m'lord," he said, shakily, when Jenny had gone. "Ye don't see many sweet'earts, nor yet wives like that!"

Charles realized then that Hobson had never known that

Jenny was his daughter, nor did Charles tell him now. It did not seem important.

The following morning at eleven o'clock, the Middlesex sheriffs came to demand of Governor Williamson that Charles Radcliffe be delivered to them for the execution of his sentence. Charles left the Tower and was transferred to a mourning coach drawn by four black horses. Hobson and Cox walked on either side. There was a further escort of sixty men, a company of Foot Guards who marched solemnly, their bayonets fixed, their heavy footfalls thudding through the muffled rolling of a drum.

The crowd waiting behind the surrounding ring of Horse Guards was not as large as had been expected, though it was a clear sunny day. On the tiered stage erected for the comfort of officials and any lords and ladies who had tickets, there were many empty benches. The rooftops and windows disclosed few spectators. A surprising number of the London populace, eager as it was for gory spectacles, signalized its disapproval by staying away. This was an unpopular execution.

Ever since the trial sympathy had been building up for Charles, who was an Englishman, who had once so cleverly escaped from Newgate, and was to be killed on a charge made thirty years ago in a different reign. When Charles emerged in a stately way from the mourning coach those hundreds who *had* come to view his ordeal let out a sympathetic cheer. He was dressed in his scarlet and black regimentals trimmed with flashing gold buttons and lace; his quilted waistcoat was lavishly embroidered; he wore white silk stockings, diamond buckles on his shoes, and the dashing black Spanish hat was topped by the jaunty white ostrich plume. He held the silver rosary in his hand.

Charles, smiling slightly, bowed to the officials and graciously acknowledged the cheers. He took a polite indifferent leave of Governor Williamson, who delivered him to the sheriffs and then immediately drove back to the Tower.

Charles looked up at the high scaffold, which was draped with black serge. It was not yet time to mount it. They had built a small, black-lined booth at the foot of the steps. Here Father Dupont waited. Charles went inside with the priest to receive the last rites. Alec stood outside the booth, tears streaming down his face. He had arranged a spot for Jenny to stand, where her father would surely see her. She stood on a doorstep of a house near the corner of Catherine Court. Her green cloak showed up vivid against the oaken door.

Alec had accepted without question her desire to be here, as he was. He did not think of her at all. He thought of his master—and so it had always been.

The crowd was silent while Charles and the priest were in the black booth. There was no movement except the occasional stamping of the guards' horses. They waited.

At eleven o'clock as Charles left the Tower, Bella Potts was sitting in the empty taproom of the King's Head polishing already spotless pewter tankards. Potts was ensconced in their snuggery, and she did not want his company just now. She polished and sighed, and sighed again, her florid face set into doleful lines.

She looked up angrily as a great dark hulking man walked in. "We're closed," she snapped, then added "sir" because the intruder was dressed like a prosperous merchant.

" 'Tis not that," said the man, in a heavy voice. "Are you the landlady?"

"Aye, I'm Mrs. Potts. What d'ye want?"

"I'm Robert Wilson," he said. "Jenny Wilson is my wife."

Bella Potts set the pewter tankard down with a clatter. "Wuns and begock!" she whispered, her black eyes popping. "Ye don't mean it! What're ye doing in London?"

"I've been here a month," he said. "I took the first ship I could from Virginia."

"Then why, i' the name o' Gawd, ha' ye not come to see her?"

"I was ashamed," he said, clenching his hands, then letting them fall open. "Ashamed o' the way I treated her, and yet more 'shamed when I got here and found out—"

"Found out what?" asked Mrs. Potts sharply, since he seemed to have forgotten she was there.

"The money," he said. "The three hundred and sixty pounds that bought my freedom and started me afresh. 'Twas never mine. 'Twas hers. Lord Lichfield never sold the house on Wigmore Row for me."

"Good Lord, man!" she cried impatiently. "I divven't knaw what ye're speaking of, but if 'tis hur-rt pride ye're nursing, I'd remind ye that at times in life we mun all accept help fra' others and that nobody stands by himsel'."

" 'Tis true," he said. "I know that now."

"How did ye find Jenny?" asked Mrs. Potts. "How did ye knaw she was here?"

"A man told me where Alec Armstrong lodged. I had but

to follow Alec to your market square, and then see where Jenny went."

Rob stared at the sanded floor. It was Willy Turner who had told him where Alec lodged, told him that and much more on the miserable day when Rob had returned from the mountains sober yet still crazy with resentment, certain that Jenny had left him for a glittering life of ease and aristocracy which her father would provide. Certain too that the Jacobites had won. Willy corrected him. He told Rob of Culloden, and he told him of the real danger Charles Radcliffe was in. Willy Turner lost his temper; he became a furious gadfly, he buzzed at Rob continually, until at last Rob saw that, far from having deserted him for a pampered life, Jenny herself might be in want and danger. Jenny whom he loved and whom he had tried to injure.

And he had sailed. Uncertain, suffering, often calling himself a fool. When he landed, he soon found how fearsome, how sternly tragic Charles Radcliffe's predicament really was. That, and the discovery of what he himself owed to Jenny, had prevented him from approaching her. Particularly as the first sight of her in the market square had stricken him. Her proud little head, her drawn, anxious face, the way she walked, the shabby old brown cloak, all these hurt him. He longed to rush towards her, to ask forgiveness, to protect and guard her from the lewd looks he saw men giving her. He did not dare. They had parted in hatred; and once, when she raised her left hand towards Alec, Rob saw that she did not wear her wedding ring.

Bella Potts broke the silence. She too had been thinking. "Ye're afeared to come nigh Jenny, it seems, Mr. Wilson. An' wi' some reason I believe. Like most men ye thought only o' yourself, and not o' her. I'd like to knaw why ye've finally come terday?"

"Because her father is to be executed this morning and I thought that I must find out at last—if as a friend—as a friend, I could help her. She may not want to see me, but would you ask her?"

"I canna ask her," said Mrs. Potts grimly. "She ha' gone to Tower Hill."

"What?" He stared at her. He moistened his lips. "What did you say?"

"That Jenny's gone to Tower Hill to be near her father when they—they do it. He wanted her there, and naught I could say 'ld stop her. 'Tis wicked—wicked. Forbye, Rob Wilson, here's another-r thing ye divven't knaw! Jenny is quick wi' *your* bairn, the poor lassie!"

"She is quick with child?" He gaped at Mrs. Potts.

"Aye. Pull your wits about ye, man! And gan to Jenny! Ye may be sur-re she needs ye!"

Rob ran from the King's Head. He sped through the London streets as he had not raced since he was a running footman. In the alleys and lanes through which he ran, he attracted scant attention. One sight was like another to the apathetic gin-soaked dwellers in the East End.

He ran down the Minories, and turned west for Tower Hill. On the black scaffold there was no one as yet, except the masked executioner, who stood waiting by the block and leaning on his longhandled axe. Rob pushed and shoved through the silent crowd behind the ring of Horse Guards. Still he could not find Jenny.

Rob shouldered his way through half the circle towards the far buildings on the square, when the crowd stirred. They made a strange collective sound, part groan and part exultance. Charles Radcliffe had walked out from the booth and started to mount the scaffold, the priest following behind.

Rob paused. The brilliant scarlet figure climbed up on the scaffold. Rob's keen farsighted eyes could see the features plain, the slight smile on the lips, the look of youth and swagger.

Charles saluted the executioner and said something to him, then turned and surveyed the crowd. Rob saw the smile broaden into one of relief and recognition. He followed the direction of Charles's gaze and at last saw Jenny, her face, white and glistening like a candle, outlined against a house door.

Again Rob pushed and shoved, heedless of the curses and angry looks he produced. Still he did not quite reach Jenny.

Charles paid the executioner ten guineas, saying that he was a poor man, regretted there wasn't more, and trusted that the axe was sharp. The coffin, covered with black velvet, stood open and ready on the scaffold. The sheriffs stood beside it.

Charles held up his hand almost as though in blessing, and he called out in ringing tones, "I'll not weary you all by a harangue. I've but one thing to say—I die a true, obedient, and humble son of the Catholic Apostolic Church, in perfect charity with all mankind, and a true well wisher to my dear country that can never be happy without doing justice to the best and most injured of kings—James the Third. I die with sentiments of gratitude, respect, and love also for the King of France—Louis the well-beloved . . . I recommend to His Majesty my dear family. I heartily repent of all my sins, and have a firm confidence to obtain pardon from Almighty God, through the merits of His blessed Son, Christ Jesus our Lord, to whom I recommend my soul."

Charles kneeled down beside the block in prayer; all those on the scaffold, including the executioner, kneeled too. It was while Charles rose and the two warders started to divest him of his hat, wig, coat, and waistcoat that Rob finally reached Jenny.

She did not see him. Her face was a silver mask. Her breathing was like the tearing of silk. Her two hands were clamped tight around her throat, her unwinking eyes stared at the scaffold while the executioner rolled down the collar of Charles's shirt.

Rob jumped to the step beside her. He grasped her head in his arm, his hand on her cheek, he forced her face against his shoulder.

"You shall *not* look!" he cried fiercely, and held her face pressed downward on his shoulder.

She made no sound. She went limp against him, nor tried to move.

It was Rob who watched the execution of Charles Radcliffe. He saw Charles cross himself and kneel down with composure, stretching his bare neck across the block. He saw Charles's hand move in the signal. He saw the flashing of the axe under the sunlight as it descended. He saw the fountain spurt of crimson blood, the undertakers running with a red baize cloth to catch the head. He saw the still-quivering trunk stowed in the waiting coffin, the head also carried to the coffin. He saw the hearse draw up beside the scaffold and receive the coffin. The Horse Guards parted to let the hearse through, and it drove away towards Great Tower Street.

" 'Twas well done," said a man who stood smoking a clay pipe near Rob. "A good death. I've seen 'em falter, whimper, and shake like leaves on the scaffold."

"Much better sport when they do," said his companion in a fretful voice. "This is too soon over." The men sauntered off. The square was rapidly clearing.

"Can you walk, Jenny?" said Rob bending down. "Just until I find a hackney."

She raised her face from his shoulder. "I think so," she said. She showed no astonishment at seeing the anxious, tender hazel eyes peering into hers. She felt no astonishment. She felt nothing.

They walked a block and Rob hailed a hackney. Soon they arrived at the King's Head. Bella Potts was waiting. She took one look at Jenny and said, "We'll get her to bed!"

Limp-jointed as a puppet, Jenny let them undress her. She swallowed the dose of laudanum Mrs. Potts gave her. Rob put her in the bed, and she shut her eyes when he told her to. She went at once to sleep.

"I'll stay nigh her till she wakes," said Rob.

"It may be hours," said Mrs. Potts. "I hope it is."

Rob nodded. "I'll stay nigh her." He sat down beside the bed.

All that afternoon and all of the night Rob kept vigil. Mrs. Potts brought him food and beer. Several times she examined Jenny, and each time sighed in relief. "She'll do," whispered Mrs. Potts. "She and the babby, as well. There's na sign o' tr-rouble. Ye've the sturdy North Country stock to thank for that. What Jenny's been through'd kill any o' your finicking, wambly fine ladies."

"Aye," said Rob. "My North Country lass." He looked down at her as she slept, her golden hair spread out on the pillow, her face so young and fair—a rose flush on the cheeks. "She's the oak and the ash and the bonny ivy-tree all together," he said.

Mrs. Potts grunted in some astonishment, and left the room. Rob bent over and kissed Jenny on the forehead.

The sun was struggling through the December murk when Jenny finally awoke. She lay still for some moments, idly watching a flickering ray of sunlight on the plaster wall. It was warm and snug in the bed. Peaceful. Delicious to be awake after the bad dream she'd had, to awaken and find that one need not fear the ghastly phantasms of nightmare. She yawned, and turning a little saw that someone was sitting by the bed. A man. *Rob!*

She struggled up. "What are you doing here!" she cried.

"I'm here to take care of you, Jenny." He spoke calmly, without emphasis. "You're my wife and I love you. You once loved me and shall again."

"It's true then, what happened today—" she cried in horror, clutching at the quilt. "I thought I'd dreamed it. I thought it was nightmare!"

"It happened yesterday," he said with gentle firmness. "It is over. I wish you not to talk about it yet. Right now you must eat." He gave her a bowl of bread and milk Mrs. Potts had left on the table.

"I don't want it," she said piteously. "I can't eat."

"Aye, but you can. Start in and see."

She obeyed him as she always had when he used that quiet assured tone. And he was right. She found that she was ravenous. She finished all and leaned back on the pillow. "Rob, did I see you behind me in Saint Paul's?"

"You did, hinny. I've followed you often."

"Why did you come to London?" She added with sudden realization, "How could you leave the plantation! What'll happen to it!"

"It must take its chances," he said smiling. "Willy can run Snowdon very well. As to *why* I came, I've told you. For love, I followed you across the ocean, as you once did me."

"Oh Rob—" she whispered. She hid her face in her hands, and gave a convulsive sob.

"Weep then, my lass," he said tenderly. " 'Twill do you good."

She cried then, though not hard. He waited silently until she had done.

"When you're able," he said, "you should get up and make ready whatever is needful for departure."

"Departure," she repeated, her eyes gone frightened. "What do you mean, Rob?"

"I've passage for us both on the *Carteret*, which sails from London tomorrow. I took it last week. I had little hope that you'd be with me, but now I think you will."

"Rob—I can't go—not now!" she cried. "I must go north. To Northumberland, to Dilston!"

"And why for, Jenny?" he asked. "There's naught there for you any more. Your folk are gone from Coquetdale, and Dilston is deserted. You must face this."

"The heart," she cried wildly. "He said he wanted it put with his brother—at Dilston. I must take it."

"No, dear," he said. "Alec will carry the heart to Dilston. For you, all that is *finished*." He took her hand, and gazed solemnly into her distraught, protesting face. "There is nothing more that you can do for your father, Jenny. You've *done* what was needed."

"He's dead," she whispered. "They're all dead, Evelyn— Lady Betty—"

"*I'm* not dead," said Rob. "And—" He pulled down the bedclothes, put his hand softly on her belly. "What have you in here, Jenny?" he asked with a half smile. "What have you here, Wife?"

She stared down at the big brown calloused hand lying so softly on the white shift which covered her belly.

"It is our babe," she said.

"Our son," said Rob, with certainty. "It'll be a son, nor maimed in any way as Robin was. I feel it. For you, Jenny, there is no more shadow of the Stuart doom. You've come out into the light. I was never a religious man—and yet, I have heard answers from a higher place than I can reach. This is one o' them. You're out o' the shadow. And I must tell you of something else I have thought on all the night while you lay sleeping." He paused, his face darkened a little. He spoke again more hesitantly.

"I've been a stubborn, stiff-necked beggor—over and over. I've made you suffer, I've been jealous o' the very half o' you which made it possible to buy my freedom, and the land. Aye, Jenny, I found that out here. 'Twas your own money, and so shamed was I for a while that I near—well, never mind." He took a deep breath and went on.

"Yesterday I saw a brave man die. He died as a man should, wi' a smile on his lips and a prayer in his heart. When our son is born, Jenny, I should like him to take the name o' Radcliffe wi' my own.

"This is for *you*, Jenny, and for a gallant man whom I have often wronged, in thought and deed. Our son needna take the first name o' 'Charles,' that'll be as you like; but he shall bear in the new world, in the place where we now belong, the name o' Radcliffe Wilson."

"You'd do *this*?" she whispered. "You'd let him take a name you've so detested!"

"I would. And when he's old enough we'll tell him of his grandfather. It cannot but help a lad to hear about courage, and of deathless loyalty to convictions whatever they may be. Now Jenny, will you rise, dear. We've much to do this day. Moreover," he said with a faint twinkle, "I long to get you out from this wee stuffy garret room. 'Tis no palace that I built for you at Snowdon, yet you must admit 'tis considerably better than this!"

"Aye, Robbie," she said quietly, and held out her arms to him.

AFTERWORD

Radcliffe, unhappy in his crimes of youth
Steady in what he still mistook for truth
Beheld his death so decently unmoved
The soft lamented, and the brave approved.

(Part of a verse frequently recited by
Samuel Johnson, and possibly written by him.)

Charles Radcliffe was the last Englishman to be executed for
the Stuart cause. He was the next-to-last human being to be
decapitated in England. In 1747 Simon Fraser, Lord Lovat,
the old Scottish renegade, closed for ever the long chapter
of executions on Tower Hill. It has startled me to find that
Charles is not mentioned in the commemorative plaque near
the site of the scaffold, only the Scottish lords executed after
the '45 are listed. This seems to me a sad oversight.

At various periods, Charles Radcliffe's life is fairly well
documented, though no two accounts—particularly of his
last days in the Tower—quite agree. The contemporary accounts were all written by his enemies. The most illuminating
of these is probably *The Official Diary of Lieutenant-General
Adam Williamson of the Tower of London* (Camden Third
Ser., 1912, Vol. V, p. xxii).

References in the newspapers and the *Gentlemen's Magazine* I have carefully combed.

*A Genuine and Impartial ACCOUNT of the Remarkable
Life and vicissitudes of FORTUNE, of Charles Radcliffe, ESQ.*

by "Gerald Penrice" (London, 1717) is anything but "impartial" and actually contains little about Charles. It deals more with the two rebellions and with Charles's brother James.

There are three valuable Derwentwater biographies, which also emphasize James, though they treat of Charles too: *Dilston Hall* by William Sidney Gibson (London, 1850); *The Life of . . . James Radcliffe, Third Earl of Derwentwater . . . and . . . of his Brother, Charles Radcliffe, de jure Fifth Earl of Derwentwater*, by Major Francis John Angus Skeet (London, 1929) (this biography is written by a Roman Catholic Jacobite); *Northern Lights: The Story of Lord Derwentwater* by Ralph Arnold (London, 1959). This last title, the most modern, is also the most valuable. My warmest thanks to Ralph Arnold for his personal help and his gift to me of several documents he had used.

The farewell letters and speeches of James and Charles Radcliffe I have quoted verbatim in the text.

It may be interesting to note that I have followed Charles's trial exactly, including the identification of the scar by Abraham Bunting and Lieutenant-Governor Williamson's evidence.

The Earl of Chesterfield's role in securing the commutation of Charles's sentence is attested by a note among the Stuart Papers in the Windsor Castle Archives.

Nobody can write about the 1715 Rebellion without constant reference to the account given by the turncoat curate who participated in it. *The History of the Late Rebellion* by the Reverend Robert Patten (London, 1717) enabled me to disentangle the Battle of Preston.

Lady Betty Lee's life is extremely difficult to trace. I have done my best, and am particularly indebted for suggestions to Professor Henry Pettit of the University of Colorado, who is an authority on Edward Young, Lady Betty's second husband.

The Stuart syndactylism (webbed digits often associated with extra ones) is mentioned in three contemporary references, including the *Gentleman's Magazine* for November, 1745, and a Whig lampoon. I have consulted historians and biographers and members of the Radcliffe family, who have all "heard of it," but to my amazement I have not, so far, found mention of this anomaly in any Stuart biography. Dr. William J. Schull of the University of Michigan Medical School is an authority on genetics, and has kindly answered my questions about this fairly common defect.

It would be tedious to enumerate the dozens of other source books I have used in trying to present the historical characters accurately. For the constant checking of dates, I have long since had to buy the *Dictionary of National Biography*, and all the Peerages, especially the exhaustive fourteen-volume *The Complete Peerage*, also known as the *G.E.C.*

I have naturally consulted pertinent biographies and histories. Perhaps I should mention *London in the Jacobite Times* by John Doran, F.S.A. (London, 1877) as particularly entertaining. A biography of the Duke of Wharton by Lewis Melville (*The Life and Writings of Philip, Duke of Wharton*. London, 1918), as well as various books on the Hell-Fire Clubs were obviously necessary to my story.

I also wish to thank Robert Halsband of New York for his advice and the use of his fine eighteenth-century library.

I have read all the Northumbrian histories and guides, including the invaluable David Dippie Dixon's books on Coquetdale. Of the general guides, *Northumberland* by Herbert L. Honeyman (London, 1949) seems particularly useful, and I am most indebted to *North Country Life in the Eighteenth Century* by Edward Hughes (London, 1952).

My affectionate thanks for their Northern hospitality throughout the years, and for their interest in my work, to Lord and Lady Tankerville in Northumberland, and to Lord and Lady Downe in Yorkshire.

Also my gratitude to all the Northumbrian clergymen who helped me search records, particularly to the Reverend and Mrs. Bernard Garman of Bellingham and the Reverend and Mrs. William Hinkley of Riding Mill.

The Northumbrian portions of this book were a true labor of love which began on the day when I first saw the tragic, beautiful ruins of Dilston Castle and developed my first interest in the Radcliffes—especially Charles. And then, on a visit to my Snowdon cousins in Felton, Northumberland, I heard the outline of Jenny's story. My grandmother was a Snowdon, and "family tradition" has always provided hints and allusions to that Border branch of the family which had such an unexpected connection with the Radcliffes.

The documentation of Jenny's story, and Rob Wilson's, has been frustrating. Those who have just read *Devil Water* will see why her existence never became generally known.

I did a lot of research in Coquetdale, and wish to thank Dr. Annie Forster of Burradon (Thropton) for help with the Rothbury Parrish Registers. There were hundreds of "Snawdons" living along the Coquet River in the early eighteenth century. I believe that I found the right family, and the death date of Jenny's grandmother, "Jane, ux. John Snawdon, Great Tosson, Jan. 14 1709." But since these Snowdons were a Nonconformist branch, most of their vital statistics are not in Rothbury—or anywhere that I can find.

I did approximately locate the Snowdon peel, one of the many ruins in that district which is marked on the one-inch ordnance map for Alnwick.

My thanks to Mr. William Pigg, the gifted Northumbrian piper who gave me a rare history of that county, who explained to me the small-pipes, and played for me "Derwentwater's Farewell" and many other North Country tunes.

Jenny's life history, her rearing by her father's cousin, Lady Betty Lee, her love for Rob Wilson, her meeting with Evelyn Byrd at the Hackney School, her marriage in Virginia to a transported convict, her life in the Piedmont, her return in 1746 to try and aid her father, and the birth of a son in Virginia, all these are embodied in the family tradition. Scholarly proof has been hard to find. Great was my disappointment when I discovered that William Byrd's diary is missing for the very years 1726 and 1737 when I most needed it. And I spent many a long day guessing and speculating as to *where* in Virginia Rob and Jenny went. My pleasure was then considerable when I discovered "Snawdon" marked on the Fry-Jefferson maps of both 1751 and 1775. "Snowdon," now in Buckingham County, was bought by Peter Jefferson, Thomas Jefferson's father, and during the late eighteenth century belonged to the latter's almost unknown brother, Randolph. I visited the site, and am grateful to informants in nearby Scottsville.

I have not tried to trace the Radcliffe-Wilsons down the years, but I think the last name was dropped in the next generation, and I found Ratliffs (the spelling was always variable) in the North Carolina mountains who were quite sure that they were descended from English royalty— "Granny" always said so. Nor did this ancestry particularly interest them. In the Revolution a James Ratcliffe from North Carolina was fighting the British. I suspect that this was Jenny and Rob's son.

There remains the subject of William Byrd and Evelyn. And here first, I wish to emphasize my thanks for personal help to Louis B. Wright, Director of the Folger Shakespeare Library and co-editor with Marion Tinling of two of Byrd's diaries. Mrs. Tinling is the percipient lady who "broke" Byrd's secret cipher, or shorthand. They are currently editing

Byrd's letters. Mrs. Tinling and I have worked closely on many facets of Byrd's life, and Evelyn's. I hope that Virginians will at last relinquish the persistent legend that Evelyn's forbidden suitor was the Third, or Fourth, Earl of Peterborough. When Evelyn left England for ever in 1726, the third Earl was sixty-eight and married to Anastasia Robinson. The subsequent fourth Earl was seventeen, and had not yet matriculated at Oxford. Moreover, the letter forbidding the marriage which Byrd wrote to Evelyn specifically refers to a "Baronet." The letter is given verbatim in my text in Chapter Twelve.

The editors of the Byrd diaries and I think that Evelyn's lover was Sir Wilfred Lawson—whose life I have studied carefully. That Sir Wilfred actually married the Earl of Peterborough's niece is probably how the Peterborough name got into the legend.

The late Maude H. Woodfin, co-editor of *Another Secret Diary . . . 1739–1741*, was convinced that William Byrd had been in love with Lady Betty Lee, addressed her as "Charmante," and proposed marriage to her. Tempting as this identification is, the dates don't seem to fit.

Aside from the unpublished letters to which I have had access, and several Victorian magazine articles on Byrd, the prime biography is *The Writings of "Colonel William Byrd,"* edited by John Spencer Bassett (New York, 1901), and the three "Secret Diaries" themselves: *The Secret Diary of William Byrd of Westover, 1709–1712*, edited by Louis B. Wright and Marion Tinling (Richmond, Va., 1941); *The London Diary, 1717–1721, and Other Writings*, edited by Louis B. Wright and Marion Tinling (New York, 1958); *Another Secret Diary of William Byrd of Westover, 1739–1741, with Letters & Literary Exercises*, edited by Maude H. Woodfin, translated and collated by Marion Tinling (Richmond, Va., 1942). My special thanks are due to all of the departments at Colonial Williamsburg, where I have spent many happy weeks of research. Mrs. Rutherfoord Goodwin and Professor Thad Tate of the Colonial Williamsburg Research Department have been particularly helpful.

And my thanks to the Library and many of the faculty at the College of William and Mary. Dr. E. G. Swem gave me personal encouragement and so did Dr. Richard L. Morton, and the source books written by both these gentlemen have been invaluable. Professor Carl R. Dolmetsch and his wife, Joan, have heartened me with alert interest too.

I am indebted to so many friends in Williamsburg that I

scarcely know how to thank them properly, except by hoping that I have been accurate in re-creating the town in print which *they* have all helped to re-create into historical tangibility. In Richmond, at the Virginia Historical Society, John Jennings and Virginius Hall were most helpful.

To the gracious present-day owners of Westover and Berkeley plantations, Mrs. Bruce Fisher and Mr. Malcolm Jamieson, respectively, my thanks for putting up with my frequent appearances there, and for answering my innumerable questions. My thanks to Clifford Dowdey for his book on Berkeley, *The Great Plantation* (New York, 1957), and for his personal interest.

I have been particularly careful in checking every genealogical detail pertaining to the Virginia families who appear in this book—the Byrds, of course, the Harrisons, Randolphs, Carters, Peter Fontaine, and others. Occasionally there are the most extraordinary mysteries. For instance, the dates on Evelyn Byrd's actual tombstone are wrong, according to her birth as given in her father's diary, and to the day of her death as given in the *Virginia Gazette* for December, 1737. Perhaps the tombstone was erected much later.

My greatest debt of all is to Miss Amy C. Flagg of Westoe, South Shields, Durham, in England. She is my dear friend and kinswoman; she is above all an indefatigable sleuth. For her researches through the years, for the masses of specialized material which she has patiently copied for me, for her constant encouragement when I've been with her, and by letter when I haven't—for all this my fervent gratitude is but sparse return.

Dorothy Eden

Ms. Eden's novels have enthralled millions of readers for many years. Here is your chance to order any or all of her bestselling titles direct by mail.

☐	AN AFTERNOON WALK	23072-4	1.75
☐	DARKWATER	23153-4	1.75
☐	THE HOUSE ON HAY HILL	X2839	1.75
☐	LADY OF MALLOW	23167-4	1.75
☐	THE MARRIAGE CHEST	23032-5	1.50
☐	MELBURY SQUARE	22973-4	1.75
☐	THE MILLIONAIRE'S DAUGHTER	23186-0	1.95
☐	NEVER CALL IT LOVING	23143-7	1.95
☐	RAVENSCROFT	22998-X	1.50
☐	THE SHADOW WIFE	23699-4	1.75
☐	SIEGE IN THE SUN	Q2736	1.50
☐	SLEEP IN THE WOODS	23706-0	1.95
☐	SPEAK TO ME OF LOVE	22735-9	1.75
☐	THE TIME OF THE DRAGON	23059-7	1.95
☐	THE VINES OF YARRABEE	23184-4	1.95
☐	WAITING FOR WILLA	23187-9	1.50
☐	WINTERWOOD	23185-2	1.75

Buy them at your local bookstores or use this handy coupon for ordering:

FAWCETT BOOKS GROUP, P.O. Box C730, 524 Myrtle Avenue, Pratt Station Brooklyn, N.Y. 11205

Please send me the books I have checked above. Orders for less than 5 books must include 60¢ for the first book and 25¢ for each additional book to cover mailing and handling. Postage is FREE for orders of 5 books or more. Check or money order only. Please include sales tax.

Name_____

Address_____

City_____State/Zip_____

Books $_____
Postage _____
Sales Tax _____
Total $_____

Please allow 4 to 5 weeks for delivery

Anya Seton

Tempestuous Novels of Passion and Violence

☐	AVALON	23308-1	1.95
☐	DEVIL WATER	23633-1	2.25
☐	FOXFIRE	X2916	1.75
☐	GREEN DARKNESS	C2728	1.95
☐	KATHERINE	23497-5	2.25
☐	MY THEODOSIA	23034-1	1.95
☐	THE TURQUOISE	23088-0	1.95

Buy them at your local bookstores or use this handy coupon for ordering: